A Part of Me: A Love Story
An American Novel

By Carl L. Jones, Sr.

© Carl L. Jones, Sr., 2012—Grampa Jones Publishing

Printed in the United States of America by Grampa Jones Publishing

All Rights Reserved. Excerpt as permitted under the United States Copyright Act of 1976, no part of this publication may be reproduced or distributed in any form, or by any means, or stored in a database retrieval system, without the prior written permission of the copyright holder, except by a reviewer, who may quote brief passages in review. The scanning, uploading, and distribution of this book via the Internet or via any other means without the permission of the publisher is illegal and punishable by law. Purchase only authorized electronic editions, and do not participate in or encourage electronic piracy of copyrighted materials.

This story is fiction, any resemblance to anyone living or dead is coincidental.

ISBN 978-1-4507-9764-1

To Angle, the light of my life.

And thanks to everyone who helped ... no person is an island.

The more things change, the more they stay the same—the end is sometimes the beginning.

The sayings and poetry in this work were either written by the author or are folk art recalled from his youth.

Preface

Imagine music in the background and a pleasant fragrance invading your senses, as I step forward into the spotlight. I smile into the camera, or rather from the first page of this novel. You might smile back as you begin to read and imagine me saying ...

My name is Flash. Well, it's not really Flash; it's Dr. Gordon Adam Lamont, PhD, ABPP. Those last initials stand for American Board of Professional Psychology, credentials that I think in themselves make a pretty compelling case that I know what I'm talking about in telling the story of my cousin, William Robert Jones III, or Bill, the arrogant ass. His father and my mother were siblings, which is the reason for our different last names. I've learned to live with the nickname he gave me, Flash—in fact, I have learned to love it, like Winston learned to love Big Brother in George Orwell's *1984*. But I feel a little like I've betrayed myself, as Winston betrayed Julia. Well, maybe not that dramatically, with the rats and such, although my cousin wasn't adverse to using night crawlers, pocket knives, or anything else to get his way. Bill was being sarcastic when he nicknamed me Flash, but what led to his choice of the name was a dangerous and exciting experience, which I'll describe later. I've always wanted to beat up that bastard to get even with him; not just for the nickname, but for everything he did to me when we were growing up. I have quite a few scars, both physically and emotionally, from all the beatings and bullying. Most of them, at least physical, were legal, because we wore boxing gloves, but he put metal in them, and he always broke his promises that he would take it easy on me. The main reason I wanted to grow up at all was to beat the shit out of him; but fate intervened, and he finally got what he deserved without any help from me. He was always too big, anyway. He thought I should thank him for the permanent part in my hair. Hell, he almost killed me the time I got that injury—and I should thank him?

His end was such a horrible way to go that I almost feel sorry for him. He loved his princess and queen, Victoria, more than life itself. He lost her when her father took her away to Scotland, but Bill found a very unusual way to get her back and for them to be happy together. All in all, that period without her did irreparable damage to his mind, which already was damaged by rheumatic fever, and it contributed to his demise. He was crazy and delusional, especially at the end.

Let me tell you what happened. It's a sad, bittersweet love story, which could break a person's heart, and in the long run, I think I might miss him. I've decided to write this story in Bill's voice, by the way, to add realism and drama, but I'll also show up as a character in the story. Don't let the Flash from the past and the Flash from the present confuse you. Just remember, I'll be telling the story as if I'm Bill, but I'll also appear in it as Gordon or Flash. Most of this story takes place in the past. Bill, with me talking for him, gets more delusional as we wind our way through the complex maze he made of his life. One thing about Bill is that he was exciting to be around, even if he was crazy and undisciplined. You never knew what he was going to do, and I don't think he did, either.

I can see why he was adored by the girls; he was a good-looking guy, with thick, blond hair and beautiful blue eyes, and always tall for his age and tanned, as if he spent a lot of time without a shirt or under a sunlamp, although there were no sunlamps then, of course. He had his dad's olive-colored skin. He kept everyone laughing, even if he was a bit crude and didn't believe in God. He was one hell of a storyteller and always had admirers around, even as he lied to them. He had a cruel nature, which made me wonder about his humanity, and ... he had a huge proboscis—and I don't mean a nose.

He thought himself special, and, following a session with his church patriarch, whom he had decided was a fortuneteller of sorts, he assumed that he was of royal blood. This was a big part of his delusional nature, and I think it stemmed from him being molested by a church clergyman when he was in the boys' Hallelujah Choir. These problems may have contributed to his fall.

He read a lot, everything he could get his hands on: funny books, the Bible, most of the classics; he especially liked King Arthur and his valiant knights, and Einstein. And he wrote profusely. He carried a notebook pushed down his pants in the back, and when it was full, he stored it in what he called his "Me box," and started a new notebook. He took that Me box virtually everywhere he went, especially after his dad put wheels on it. I'll say more about the Me box later.

Most people called him William, but his friends—if he had any real friends—and I called him Bill. His dad, William Robert Jones II, was a chemist of some sort who had worked his way up to a good position in a chemical company without getting a formal education. He was just pretty damned smart. When the war arrived in 1941 and, with it, a surge in good jobs, he quit the chemical company and started working as an electrician at the Gardenia Steel Plant near Springtown, Utah. On the Orem Tram, as he went to apply for that job and to be qualified, he read a thin book called *The Basics of Electricity*. Bill inherited a lot of his father's intelligence, but he didn't have much of his mother's niceness.

Shortly after Bill's dad got the electrician job, he was suspended indefinably without pay for stealing from the plant. This made prospects much dimmer of getting his family out of Aunt Helen's "dungeon," as they called it. His aunt was planning to provide better lodging as soon as her own kids could find jobs and she could get them out of her house and on their own, but they were lazy bustards!

I've heard a lot of stories about Bill from my little brother, Dale, who was Bill's favorite—the little brownnoser. In places where I couldn't be sure exactly what happened, I sort of made it up. The truth is, I hated Bill; but even so, I've tried to make him look a little better than he really was, if only to lighten this sad tale a little. I ended up with the notebooks Bill wrote throughout his life and during his final days in a furnace room in the rear of the partially condemned Camelot-Avalon Apartments in Salt Lake City, a dungeon of sorts, where he lived only because of the charity of the manager, a woman named Mary Katherine Merlin, whom he called Aunt Mary.

In some ways, this dungeon was not much different from the one in which William began his life during the Great Depression, in the basement of his real Aunt Helen's washhouse. Living in that first dungeon was supposed to have been temporary, until Bill's father, who was the town drunk, could find a suitable job, or until his suspension at the steel plant was lifted. But circumstances were slow to change, and the family was forced to remain there for quite a while.

Bill's Aunt Helen was a saint, who never would have allowed her niece to abide in such a hovel, if she could have avoided it. She had a little money, but not enough to move her grown kids and grandkids out of the place to make room—and consider this: she was old and feeble. Her children and grandkids had come back to her because of the depression. I think she might have found a way to move Bill and his family into accommodation that was at least a little better than the washhouse basement, which she saw as a day-to-day situation, but as it turned into week-to-week and then month-to-month and then year-to-year, everyone became accustomed to it, except for Bill's mother, Caroline.

After Bill tried to get rid of me, in Butte, Montana, during what I'll call the "train incident" (actually, he tried to get rid of me in Winnemucca, Nevada, too, which was another adventure I need to write about someday), and after I recovered enough from the ordeal to travel, I made my way back home to Eden, Montana. I met Martha there, who later became my wife and who inspired me—well, coerced me—to go into the field of psychology. It was mostly for the money, and it was a big mistake. I never stopped working toward becoming a writer. Bill had an interest in writing, too; more than an interest. It was almost an obsession, and maybe this is why he was such a daydreamer. I hate to admit it, but Bill probably was my inspiration to become a writer. One thing that made me want to write was Bill's expression, "There is no one as close to being a god as a writer is. Who else is able to create, order, and end life as they can?"

I'm not going to worry about how bad his writing makes me look—I just want to write a best-selling novel, or at least something good. And remember, Bill was a god-damned liar! I've even taken a few courses in journalism and creative writing. Now that Martha has passed on, a victim of cancer, I can do as I please. I loved her, but hell, was she bossy.

As I near retirement, I have been studying the writings of Bill, who wrote everything down, volumes of it. He wanted to write a Western and a science fiction story, and for some odd reason, something to "bring religion into reality," which doesn't surprise me, because he saw religion as a sort of mythical fiction.

Bill's story began a long time ago, when an old adversary, Alex, subdued him and imprisoned him in a furnace room. In order to reason with Alex for his release, Bill relived his life in his mind, to discover why Alex hated him to the extent of wanting to murder him. Bill's quest for these elusive answers started with an examination of his life several years after he was born, in a shanty a good distance down a shady, dirt alley in Springtown, Utah.

I've designed his story to go back and forth in time and tense. As I've mentioned, Alex will appear in the past as a character, but also in the present from time to time, to taunt and question Bill. Remember, I'm narrating the story as Flash, but I'm also a character in it. If you wonder how I can feel comfortable about writing in William's voice, when he is so humiliating toward me as Flash, I refer you again to my credentials in psychology. Hang on tight—I don't want to lose you.

The story begins at the partially condemned Camelot-Avalon Apartments located on the south side of the street between Second and Third East on Broadway in Salt Lake City, Utah, about 50 miles from Springtown. It's the late 1970s, and Bill is in his late thirties. He is sitting on the steps of the washhouse behind the Camelot-Avalon Apartments, which has become his imaginary version of King Arthur's Camelot. The apartment building is a horseshoe-shaped complex. The Avalon side is in terrible disrepair and has been condemned by the city. He writes in his notebook as he imagines, hallucinates, and contemplates life, trying to fit the pieces together. It's evening, becoming dark. And then, in William's complex imagination ...

Chapter 1

A sudden breath of air moves the evening mist from the symbols of royalty, which, to the unbeliever, are simply refuse and stench. This tepid breeze carries with it the assurance that winter's relentless bluster is nearly exhausted. I sit amazed at this splendor, as I so often do, here at the rear of the Camelot-Avalon apartments on the washhouse steps; it's my favorite place to ponder life and its difficult questions. The fleeting winter bluster has turned the concrete steps frigid—they feel bitterly cold against my butt. Nonetheless, it's a good and almost comfortable feeling. It makes me realize I am alive and I have Victoria by my side— maybe forever this time.

Well, Victoria, my queen-to-be, is not really here with me now, but she is "with" me nonetheless, in wish and intent. We will soon no longer need to use pretense or illusion. Our new abode, Castle III, will dwarf Castle I and Castle II. High above the rugged Elk River in Eden, Montana, Castle III will make the other castles appear to be hovels by contrast. There, we will rule side-by-side in our rightful kingdom, with little, if any, need for pretense!

A movement from below catches my eye. I look down ... a pill bug. The creature seems to float across the concrete step below me—strange how they are able to move their brush-like legs with so little effort. I reach down to touch it, but before I can, it curls up to envelop itself, as does an armadillo, although instead of a large, silver ball it becomes a tiny, charcoal-colored one. I watch it patiently for a moment, and then carefully pick it up and allow the tiny, innocent sphere to roll slowly and carefully around the confines of my concave palm.

"This must be how God feels as he taunts and teases his subjects," I muse.

As a god might do in his or her supremacy, I will wait for the pitiful creature to unwind, and then deal with it at my whim. It is such a magnificent feeling to hold this sort of power over another living creature! Maybe I'm even more powerful than humanity's God: my victim's god is at least more than an illusion ... or at least I think I am. The tiny armadillo clone has unrolled now and crawls slowly across my open hand. I can see and even feel its rows of tiny legs moving it along as if by magical, mysterious brush strokes. It is most definitely a magnificent feeling. The bug is like a young boy in nature, innocent and vulnerable—it makes me want to do it harm.

I hold the innocent, oblivious creature low, to allow it to move onto the concrete step from which I had taken it. I watch its pitiful strokes for a moment; it's not even conscious of its mammoth surroundings or of me; simply and with routine nonchalance, it brushes itself slowly along, as if inviting disaster, as we humans do, in our ignorant indifference. Quickly and ruthlessly, I do what it seems to be pleading for, and without even standing, I squash it under my shoe. Such a feeling of power and righteousness, to squash something so innocent and meaningless! Only a small, wet spot remains on the concrete, and a few tiny, charcoal fragments scattered about.

"It's still there, just in a different form," I ponder with a cruel smile, maybe like humanity's image of how a god might act. "It will be a bitch to resurrect." I almost laugh, and look about, and then turn back to my writing about Victoria and castles.

It's not a real castle, nor is it King Arthur's Camelot, but I can imagine it as such if I choose. Even if it's not in the setting of jolly England, it is at least in a building bearing that name and with an actual Merlin living there. If I had been so lucky—and they, as well—to have been born in the time of King Arthur and his enchanted knights, there is little doubt I would have been in that select and noble clan. Even in this age, I have my own isle of Avalon, with its old, knurled, and twisted apple trees galore, as well as a North Cromwell nearby, although it's actually an East North Cromwell. My Avalon just happens to be a condemned, crumbling building with dead and dying apple trees, and not an exotic island reaching toward heaven. Nonetheless, it's the same in name and spirit and, at least to me, surely as magical as Arthur's own. His god was more tolerant and forgiving than mine is. But I am, as they were, only a pawn in life, with its twists and turns made by both God and fate that are useless to contest.

Suddenly, a loud, raspy whisper breaks my guarded pleasure.

"You bastard!"

In the shadows at the foot of the steps stands a figure. Its face seems to be trying to smile, but even in this dim light, I can see it is a pitiful, grotesque grimace. The right arm, crooked and nearly worthless, hangs to its side, but with some sort of rope held dangling from the hand. He, or it, struggles to maintain its balance. In the left hand there is a shiny, chrome pistol; the pistol is pointing at me.

The "creature" stands glaring. "You did this to me, William," the raspy whisper says. "You crippled me! You tried to blame those murders on Oscar and me!"

I taste what I assume sulfur would taste like; it fills my mouth. I stand frozen and terrified. "Alex?" I utter in bewilderment as I drop the pencil I've been writing with. "I thought you were dead."

"Do I look dead?"

I allow the question to pass. "It *was* you, Alex. You or Oscar. One of you killed those boys."

Alex tries to make his crippled face smile again. "You're so sick, William."

"How did you find me?"

"Mrs. Larsen, the postmistress in Eden, told me where you'd be."

"That busybody," I say under my breath, but I can't be too mad at her, after all she did for Victoria and me when we were together in Montana.

"Say something in your own defense," Alex struggles to say.

I don't know what to say, what to do. "I thought you were dead, I thought you and your brothers were dead," I hear my voice say again, but it doesn't sound like my voice. It sounds distant and hollow, as if someone else is talking—like when reality becomes too ghastly or wonderful to be real and I pass through a kind of window, becoming a voyeur to an event rather than a participant in it. Whenever that happens, it's like I'm viewing events from above.

"When your brother Oscar took you and Craig with him over the high cliffs at Castle III, I was sure you were all dead," I say.

My eyes have become more accustomed to the dimness now. Alex tries to smile again. Through my fear, I feel a sudden pity for his horrible appearance. I can now distinguish the scar below his left eye from where I kicked him when he was trying to kill me on the high ledges of Castle III.

"I fell on top of Oscar," he says. "He saved my life; he protected us both, William—but he protected me even in his death, because I fell onto his dead body. I was severely injured but floated out into the river and managed to crawl onto a timber and float into the reservoir. I was picked up by the river patrol just before I went over the spillway at the dam."

I stand stunned, unable to speak. I don't want to die—especially not now that Victoria and I are finally together, maybe forever this time.

Alex's face and voice are filled with hatred and revenge. "I didn't report what happened, because I wanted to get even with you myself. My fall must have dislodged my brothers' bodies from the rocks after they saved me from being killed. Their bodies were never found; maybe they floated down and went through the turbines at the dam. I just told the constable that I'd lost my footing and fell from the high cliffs." He smiles cruelly.

"What are you going to do now?" I ask, afraid to know the answer.

I've been watching you for days ... now I'm getting even."

"Getting even? Even for what? I don't even know what you're talking about."

"Get up!" Alex hisses.

My legs refuse to obey; I can't stand.

"Go to your room," he demands. "I want you to suffer like you made us suffer."

"What the hell? Go to your room? Am I a child? You're treating me like a child," I say as I try to force my shaky voice to be calm; but it won't be calm—I'm terrified.

"Just go to your room!"

"Don't kill me Alex, I don't want to die," I plead.

"I'm not going to kill you, unless I have to. I'm just going to watch you die an agonizing death."

Finally, my legs obey, and I stand clutching my notebook to my breast, but still watching him suspiciously from the corner of my eye. I begin walking toward my room—the furnace room at the rear of the Camelot-Avalon Apartments. He follows limping, struggling to walk, as we make our way down the dank, dark stairs to the huge, ancient, wooden, ironclad door of the old furnace room. I hear a bumping along the steps behind Alex, and realize something is attached to the rope he still holds in his crippled hand. "This is where you belong," he laboriously whispers, "in this hell. You belong in a dungeon. You shouldn't have ever gotten out of your old dungeon in Springtown where the Depression had put you and your family when you were young."

"It's just for a while, just until Victoria and I rule Eden," my quaking voice says.

He tries to laugh; it is a pitiful, almost comical grimace that emits a strange, hoarse whisper: "You're getting closer to ruling, I'm sure, but it will be in hell." He prods me into the dark furnace room with the barrel of the pistol.

"Here, Bill," he snarls, as best his damaged face will allow, and he hands me the rope he's been holding.

I stifle a laugh; on the end of the rope is my Me box! I take the rope, pull the box inside and open the lid. "It's all here," I smile, but my pleasure is short-lived, as Alex pushes the door shut. I hear him locking it. Then there is only quiet. It is too quiet––and then, banging!

"He's nailing the door shut," I whisper, and then I scream, "HELP! HELP!"

Frantically I try to open the door; it won't budge. I run to the window, but bars and heavy screen cover the glass. My breath is coming in short, anxious bursts; lightning shoots up my spine and bounces around in my skull, and the tastes of fear and sulfur coat the roof of my mouth.

"You bastard!" Alex tries to scream in his pitiful, raspy whisper from the other side of the door. "Now you've graduated to a larger and a little nicer dungeon than you had in Springtown."

I can imagine him trying to make his crippled face smile. "Maybe you'll see those poor little boys in hell," his broken voice whispers.

There is only thick silence, and then his hateful whisper again. "I'll hang around for a while." It comes out as a strange, muffled laugh that has an eerie softness, but also a certain piercing cruelty to it.

"I'll be looking in on you. I found those old notebooks you always wrote in. I went to Springtown and found Victoria. She is living there in a little house near your old place with her new husband, Fredric something or other—a Frenchman. She had all of your old notebooks and your Me box. She said the writing rambled so much, she couldn't get the gist—so she gave it all to me. She asked me to give it to you—I don't know why I did, but I try to keep my promises."

Then, only quiet. He is gone and I am alone. But he will be back––I am sure of that. At least my Me box is here with me. Without thinking, I pull it over by the commode and the sink, where my tin drinking cup hangs.

That wasn't Victoria he saw, that was an imposter—the one I mistakenly gave my Me box to, at the reception after her marriage to the Frenchman. My mind is swimming; I am shocked and filled with questions. I have to remember how all this had come about! What the hell is Alex even talking about? I couldn't kill anyone; at least I can't remember that I did. Maybe I can reason with Alex, if I can just remember. I have to go back to my youth. I also have to find Victoria and warn her. I need to pass through the window of time and reality––back to when I was young and pure. I have done it many times—I have to go back in time.

When I first began going back, it came spontaneously, either when something horrible happened or when an event occurred that I didn't believe I was worthy of. But now I've come to the point that in certain anxious moments, I can do it by sheer will. Einstein enhanced this ability of mine when we were together in his laboratory.

I wait patiently, and finally, I sense the moment coming ... and then, somehow softly but also suddenly, it embraces me like an intimate old friend.

The years begin to whisk past. I seem to be getting younger and younger. I recognize my past life as events race by, finally arriving at the earliest ones I can remember. It is that certain winter's day when America is teetering on the brink of economic disaster in the 1930s, but the country is now beginning to gain strength and is recovering from the deep depression. To me, everything is foggy. I need to be patient; I need to wait for it to completely develop. This is where I need to begin. This will be the way, the key, to dealing with Alex—poor, dumb Alex. I have to relive this part of my life—and it has to be done in a certain way, as if I am actually there again, exactly as it had been in the past, if I am ever to understand what's going on. Why Alex is so angry with me? Why does he hate me so much that he wants me to die? I have to figure it all out; I have to find a way and a reason to deal with him and his unwarranted vengeance. And most of all, I need to warn my REAL Victoria. If this method doesn't work, maybe I will find the answer in my notebooks in the Me box.

Ever so slowly, as I'd always been told and believed happens to a person faced with immediate death, life flashes before me in vivid detail. Even if death isn't immediate for me now, it seems to at least be imminent. In a similar fashion, I pass further through the window in an effort to begin reliving my earlier life in a vivid, albeit virtual way.

At first, everything seems as if I am looking through an illusory fog, but it is strangely familiar and also somewhat comforting. I go deeper and deeper within my earlier life to begin living it over, as if I'm passing through a window. And then, finally, I see a flash—a glimpse of it. I am almost there, I am actually almost there. I try to be patient—and then another glimpse.

There had been a long cold-air inversion, bringing with it an unusual cold that blanketed the earth with a deep snow that seemed to suck every piece of warmth out of everything. The surging, frigid wind turned small snowflakes into ice crystals and drove them, as darts, into uncovered flesh. It penetrated with its fierce cold even bodies wrapped in layers of winter garb. This driven, icy, cold stuck to and enveloped everything in its path with a frosty white.

The few cars traveling precariously along the slick, snow-covered main street of Springtown stir cascades of small snow fluffs that mix as they pass with the ones falling and blowing, to make it seem even colder. I shiver in spite of myself, as I immerse myself into this charade. The small, dreary town—always solemn and isolated even during the warm summer months—is now cloaked in winter with this bitter cold and bluster, causing few people to venture out at all. Even then, they leave their homes only for pressing or dire reasons, bundled in layers of winter attire, the steam billowing from their mouths and nostrils. Gradually, these phantoms of that time and my family begin to take shape and become very real. I wait patiently as everything continues to materialize, until it's all here, now and real, every bit as much as I am here, now and real. And then, as I enter and begin to virtually relive my past, it is as if I'm doing it for the first time, but as if I'm watching from above like God might do, from a vantage of knowledge and the experience I have gained throughout my life.

Chapter 2

To find warmth and comfort during those cold winter days, Mom took my sisters, Ellen, Martha, and me to the library in the basement of the Boyer Building on Main Street. Then on Sunday, when the library was closed, we found our warmth and comfort in the long, boring meetings at church until mid-afternoon, when we went to Aunt Helen's for dinner. We assembled around the huge, wooden Zenith console radio in her stylish living room to listen, to be enchanted, and to dream.

Entering the library brought with it a definite rush, from the stark contrast between the luxury and elegance of the library and the misery of the dungeon, mixed with Mom's requirement for reverence and quiet, the smell of old paper and books, the warmth and the almost hallowed atmosphere. For me, it was a holy feeling that would be relived and relished anytime I visited a library or any place where a large store of paper or books re-created that ambience. We each had our own library card, because they were free, and Mom had taught Ellen and me how to find books with the Dewey Decimal System.

Martha, seemingly astonished at the vastness and hallowed feeling of it all, wandered aimlessly on chubby, unsure legs among the shelves of books or sat straddle-legged on the floor, staring vacantly into space. Her dishwater-colored hair was in chronic disarray. She was very quick to befriend anyone and smiled continually; even her hazel eyes smiled and seemed to emit dancing sunlight that covered her entire chubby face. Her countenance suggested she didn't understand anything. She would have been a perfect target for a pedophile.

Ellen entertained herself with the books that Mom helped her to find, as she sat with a look of dreaming and distance in her pale blue eyes, a little bit like Martha did, but with her lips pursed as if with a thought she was about to reveal as a profound prophecy. I sat with a book opened to the same page for hours, not even conscious of it or of anything else, as I dreamed about adventure, mystery, and about someday being rich and famous and not being the son of a poor town drunk. Mom had her own trance, but because she was an adult, she could pretend it was thinking or planning. But we were all dreamers, to be sure.

In spite of myself, I had become quite a good reader for my age, which was partly because both Mom and Ellen worked on me, but mostly it was because we spent so much time under these bright, unforgiving lights at the library with not much else to do. Mom told us to read whatever we could. "Anything learned is never wasted," she echoed endlessly. We sat in the quiet warmth of the library, slowly dissolving its comfortable illusions indelibly into our psyches; silently reading or daydreaming, experimenting with origami, or trying to keep the coloring from the library's fruit jar full of broken and mismatched Crayola crayons inside the lines of the interesting and primitive pictures that Mom drew for us.

When the long, boring, but comfortable day had finally drawn to an end, when the evening dimness had drawn the color from the dust-covered windows high on the library's basement walls, when they had become completely overcome by the dismal shades of evening and when the perpetual swinging of the clock's pendulum finally caused the closing-time chime; then, with an armful of books checked out by the old, grumpy-looking, white-haired librarian and with bodies warm and happy, we stepped out into the patiently waiting winter elements to walk the cold, dark, and dreary several blocks to the one-room, unheated basement of Aunt Helen's washhouse, "the dungeon," as Mom called it, for a quick meal of stale bread and milk or a peanut butter sandwich. We huddled together, still within our winter garb against the chill, to wait for bedtime, when each of us wrapped up into a ball in the reclaimed-from-the-trash lace curtains and velvet drapes that had become our royal bedding. We lay within this magical protection without removing our shoes, coats, or hats, to shiver and wait for the morrow, when we would again return to the warmth and comfort of the library, or go to church on Sundays, and then to Aunt Helen's.

One day, while exploring at the library, I discovered—out of the way and seemingly hidden—some dusty, neglected old books. One was about a scientist, Albert Einstein. Others were about the atrocities of medieval England and early America, and one was about King Arthur and his knights. Still others were about healing, casting spells, Voodoo, witchcraft, how to commit the perfect murder, how horrible and awful hell is, and how a person might go about getting there. These books really caught my interest!

Mom had always checked the books out for us, but the process looked easy. I gathered my newfound treasures into a bundle and silently carried this exciting, but probably prohibited reading, to the grumpy lady to check them out. The nameplate on her desk said, "Miss Phelps." She looked older and sterner, now that I was on my own. It was like I had never really noticed her before. Her hands and head shook as if palsy had gained total control of her frail body. Her hair was gray, but impeccably groomed into place; it had the look of molded Plaster of Paris, as had her pale, stoic face. Horns, projecting from her narrow forehead, might have made a reasonable devil of her. She was a molded and frightful mechanical figurine, who did the library's bidding in a kind of somber retreat.

She looked at my reading choices and tried to assume a smile of approval that instead took on the look of a patronizing sneer. Maybe the handwritten poster on the wall behind her, "Support the new library bill of rights movement," with her signature handwritten at the bottom, curbed her impulse to criticize and censor my selections. With that same forced smile, Miss Phelps opened each book, stamped it, and slammed it shut. "Hope you enjoy your reading, William," she said in a voice that seemed filled with sarcasm.

"Thanks," I whispered. I could feel my face turn red, like it always did when I was embarrassed or the center of attention. I carefully placed the books together so the titles wouldn't show and tried to ignore Miss Phelps's icy stare, which surely assaulted my back until the oak door filled with little windows closed between us. Then I hurried home to the dungeon to hide my ill-gotten goods.

I hid the forbidden reading under the mattress in my cubbyhole and hurried back to the library, hopefully before Mom missed me.

I made it!

It was rare indeed for me to ever be clever enough to get away with much of anything, and this time was no exception. Mom found the books that evening while she was placing a warm iron wrapped in a cloth by my ankles, to warm them enough for me to sleep. She told me in terms that left no doubt: the consequences would be dire, indeed, if I ever brought anything so sanctioned by the devil and so obviously evil into our home again!

"What about learning and reading whatever you can?" I asked.

"You know it is wrong to read things that are written by the Devil ... and that Einstein fellow is an atheist. William, why are you reading about the perfect murder? Are you thinking about killing someone?"

"Hell, I'm just reading, I'm not doing anything. And, people wrote these books, not the Devil," I continued to argue. "And Einstein isn't an atheist; he just has a different view about God."

"The books go back tomorrow, William. When your dad gets

home, I'll let him explain it to you a little better," she said in a loud, forced whisper, to add emphasis, but also with that certain prejudice in her voice. But when Dad got home he didn't explain; he just yelled and threatened my life and soul, as he sprayed alcohol-saturated saliva scented with smoking tobacco into my face.

"God will casteth yer soul into hell and then the Devil hi'self willest deal with you. Yer a horse's ass William; you should use yer head for somethin' 'sides a hat rack!"

I placed the proper shameful expression on my face in order to cut the torturous and demeaning lecture short. He soon tired of insulting me, found his way to bed and fell into it, in his typical late-night, drunken stupor, filling the small enclosure with snorts, snores, and disgusting farts that kept the rest of us annoyed and awake.

I hated him; maybe I would use one of the things in the books to get even with the old fart, I thought. None of us would miss him—he wasn't good for anything, anyway.

Chapter 3

Mom, Ellen, Martha, and I should have been grateful to have the dungeon to survive in. It was all because of Aunt Helen's charity and because that's all we could afford ... well, it was free. And Mom told us Aunt Helen would help us more if she could, and she planned to as soon as circumstances in her life changed.

The dungeon was small and crowded even with our few belongings: a rickety old card table and four chairs, each held together with baling wire; an old foot-pedal White sewing machine; Dad's shoe last, which he sometimes placed our worn-out shoes on, to repair them; Mom and Dad's narrow bed; and an old wooden box, with the name "Grand Rapids" in fancy cursive writing on the sides.

And below that in large block letters was "Brewing Company," and other writing of some sort below that. The box was filled with Mom's True Love magazines; Dad's science, chemistry, and math books; a couple of classic novels, Robinson Crusoe, Moby Dick; and a tattered old Holy Bible.

Everything sat up off the ground, on pieces of wood or flat rocks away from dry rot. Two small windows high up—almost to the ceiling—let some light in, and a single light bulb that dangled precariously from the ceiling by a frayed electric cord struggled futilely to help the little windows illuminate our dreary cell. There was the permanent and chronic odor of rot and mold.

Martha slept in between Mom and Dad. Ellen had a couple of blankets made up on a piece of plywood by their bed, because she was afraid of the dark. My room was a huge cardboard box that sat in the corner of the room, to give me a little privacy, with a door cut out and an old pee-stained, small baby mattress that pretty much covered the entire floor of the enclosure; we called it my "cubbyhole." Mom had placed a lace curtain on a stick and hung it over the opening "for a little more privacy," she said. I had to bend my legs and sort of scrunch up to lie down.

"That's called the fetal position; that's how a baby is in its mother's belly before it's born," she smiled.

I pretended I hadn't been born yet. I lay cuddled in my sheets and blankets dreaming and imagining what I would do after my birth; what kind of king I would be. I wanted to be wise and noble enough to be remembered as good, but instead I waxed wicked, like the kings in the Bible and Sunday school always do, lusting after my harem. I had anyone who threatened them put to death for their evilness. I pampered my chosen princess and groomed her to finally be my queen, fortunate enough to rule by my side. She understood my needs and forgave my iniquity and then, like the kings in Sunday school always do, I saw the wickedness of my ways.

I repented and asked God to forgive me, promising not to do it any more—even though I knew I would.

"Looks like a vision, William–God is happy, he's talking to us," Mom said when the morning light streamed through the dirt-streaked window.

"No, he's not; it's just the sun, Mom."

"Doubting William," she smiled.

The night turned everything to frightening monsters. "Looks like we're being invaded, William. God is sad; we need to repent," Mom said.

"No, he's not. It's just the night, Mom."

She smiled; she seemed to understand.

Mom had found some old velvet drapes and lace curtains in the trash pile behind the thrift store. She washed them in Aunt Helen's washing machine and we used them for sheets and blankets. "This is the kind of bedding kings and queens use," she smiled. It made me feel like royalty as I snuggled secure in their warmth and magical protection.

Mom said, "The dungeon's a good place to escape the heat of summer, but not so good for winter." We huddled together inside our coats and tried to escape the cold as we burrowed into the magical royal bedding to await the luxury of sleep.

We used the same outhouse as Aunt Helen but we also had a white porcelain "thunder mug," as Mom called it, which sat in an out-of-the-way corner. A lid hid the disgusting contents and somewhat suppressed the odor. It was used at night in bad weather, or when we were lazy. When it was full, it was emptied into the big hole in the outhouse in turns by Ellen or me, but emptying it was also punishment for being bad.

Mom swept the dirt floor down to the hard-packed bottom, and then pushed the loose stuff onto a piece of cardboard and carried it carefully up the stairs and outside to mix it with the wind, or with the weeds at the edge of the yard, if the day was still. She climbed the rickety wooden stairs carefully now, ever since she had fallen while trying to bring down some of her delicious, homemade root beer. She used the galvanized washtub that we bathed in to mix the root beer, but only after she had carefully cleaned it out.

She had sprained her left shoulder and leg in the fall on the stairs, so my big sister Ellen and I waited on her and Martha. Dad searched for a job, and then went to the Dirty Shame Saloon to drown his disappointment about not finding one. But Mom was better now—not really better, but getting better. Ellen sat with me for hours on the concrete steps of the washhouse but on dreary days and dark evenings we retreated to the dark, damp quarters or to the upstairs of the washhouse, where Aunt Helen kept her gas-operated washing machine and where she stored a menagerie of things she thought were too good to just throw away. The gas washing machine was the main reason we took over the basement—because of the deadly fumes when it was running. Hoses were connected to take the exhaust outside, but they leaked profusely. But we still used the space in between Aunt Helen's treasures for other purposes, like when Ellen read, or pretended to read to me or to store certain things. Aunt Helen had strategically placed a large fan to blow away the poisonous fumes when the gas-operated washing machine was running.

Ellen pretended to read magazines or books from the old Grand Rapids box that had gotten me excited about reading and writing.

She pointed to pictures, making up stories that fit. I watched and listed as she guided my imagination to create images and impressions in my own mind. This box was, for all practical purposes, my little library—for safekeeping, I put in it my drawings and stories and books I'd borrowed, found, or stolen.

There was a certain pleasure about her reading to me that was relaxing and enjoyable. It was probably her fault that I wanted to be a writer or a scientist; I liked her a lot when she wasn't in one of her holy or vicious moods

Sometimes I indulged in illusory episodes, during which I pretended I was someone else—maybe an author—and tried to write like they do; it was fun. Here, I'll show you what I mean:

> My mother's name is Caroline. She is thin and frail but is able to do about anything with just grim persistence and determination. Her ashen face and pale blue eyes, framed by pure white hair, make her appear delicate. Even her soft, genuine smile isn't able to entirely remove the grief that years of substituting creativity and courage

for money have indelibly painted there, but in spite of it all, she retains just a hint of her mischievous, joyful youth.

Her hands are small and dainty, stained from years of housework, picking fruit, working in the garden, canning, and raising a family during the Depression. The ruby engagement ring and the silver wedding band that time has imbedded into her finger make her hands seem even more fragile and tarnished. The ruby had belonged to her mother and was supposed to have been just a temporary arrangement until Dad could get enough money to buy a special one. He had somehow found money for the thin silver wedding band in time for the wedding and Grandma had died shortly after, so there was no need to give the ruby back.

Mom usually wears a cotton housecoat and comfortable slippers, but when outside, even in warm weather, she wears a sweater and a hanky on her head—not fastened on the top of her forehead like the glamour girls do—just tied under her chin. For church on Sunday, she wears her best dress and shoes and a small woven hat, held in place with a long fancy pin.

Chapter 4

Our meals mostly consisted of cereal, cooked on a hotplate connected by a black extension cord that ran above it. Mom baked her homemade bread in Aunt Helen's fancy wood-burning stove, when she didn't get bread from the "bread line," or from the Bishop's warehouse. Mom made creative sandwiches out of anything we happened to have. Sometimes we just had potatoes she carefully sliced into just the right thickness, which we cooked ourselves on the coiled surface of the hotplate—sometimes, just bread broken into bits with milk poured over it. We ate corn flakes and cheese when we could get them along with any fruit that could be picked from neighbors' trees or off the ground at orchards. When we had leftover cooked cereal, Mom fried it into patties and we ate it as meat or on a sandwich. Dad poached a deer once in a while, when he could stay sober, and milked the neighbor's cow every morning and night for a quart. Dad was conscientious about the milking; he was good for something, at least. I think deep down he was a pretty good person. We used what milk we needed for cereal and to drink; from the rest, Mom made cream, cottage cheese, and used the whey in place of water to make bread.

Our food supply got low. None of us was going to church and the bishop had cut off our church welfare, trying to entice us to become more active. Mom was somehow able to keep Dad away from the Shame for a few days, and the two of them got jobs picking peaches. Ellen and I played under the peach trees; Mom had just had one of her blind-stagger spells and was still getting over the fall down the dungeon's stairs, so she couldn't really do much except watch Martha and scoot along on her butt picking up fruit that had fallen to the ground. I was always eager to help.

"Can I climb up and help, Dad?" I asked earnestly.

Dad looked at me with a certain amount of contempt, as usual. "Yer more hep if ya just keep out'a the way."

After a long day, the pay was what we had eaten and the bruised fruit that Mom had managed to pick up off the ground for Dad to carry home in a gunny bag. Of course when we thought no one was looking, Dad added some of the fruit picked from the tree to the bruised peaches.

After a few days we all suffered from "the Rocky Mountain quick step," as Dad called it. The overused chamber pot and the methane gas in our damp and musty basement quarters made some remarkable odors.

I fell in love with a battered little wooden wagon in the orchard. It had nice large, rubber wheels and said on the side in fancy, fading red lettering, "Piggly Wiggly Coaster." It had a handle for pulling or to fold back and guide while sitting in it to go downhill. I filled it with just about anything and pulled it around pretending I was a truck driver. The orchard owner thought it cute that I liked the wagon so much. "Hell, just keep it, let your son have it, it's getting old and we were thinking of getting our son a new one anyway."

Dad was against me having anything nice or having any money. "Hell, he don't need no wagon. If he needs one, I'll get it fer him," he scowled.

But Mom, Ellen, and I pleaded, telling him how it would be nice to take the peaches home and to bring home flour and heavy stuff from the store and the Bishop's warehouse, and he finally gave in and let me have it. For years I took the battered old piece of decrepit machinery with me about everywhere I went. I only wished it had pedals like a tricycle.

I craved excitement and adventure and took any excuse to explore or experience anything new or different. Mom, Dad, and Ellen were always finding me and bringing me back. One time I took the wagon with a few peaches in it and started down the sidewalk, eating the peaches as I went. When Ellen found me, I was in front of a church sitting in the wagon and talking to the priest, sharing my peaches with him. Seems I always had a compelling and unusual interest in religion.

"That boy knows his Bible," the priest said.

"I know, I taught him," Ellen returned.

When we got back to the orchard, Dad said, "Them damned Catholics brainwash their kids so much it's most impossible to get em ta see the truth. Best ta stay away from 'em."

"All religions do that, Dad."

"Ya horses ass, William, our'n don't!"

I raised my eyebrows in contradiction; he slapped me on the back of my head.

When the peaches ran out, we made a sincere promise to go to church and pay our tithing, which once again opened the Bishop's warehouse to us to supplement our meager provisions. A small amount of cash was also offered, like the classic dangling of the carrot before a stubborn donkey, as incentive for us to return as earnest members of the flock.

It was my job to gather the kindling for Dad to build Aunt Helen's fire both in the summer and the winter, and it was Dad's job to get in the coal. He was pretty conscientious about doing this, too, but not so conscientious about providing wood for me to make into kindling. Once, after I'd cut up every possible piece of wood I could find—even any loose wood on the houses and any unguarded neighbors' toys—I resorted to chopping up the handles on all of Dad's and Aunt Helen's yard tools. I caught hell for that, but it did inspire Dad to get some pieces of wood for kindling. And

I was always amazed at how Dad could half-carry, half-drag me out into the yard for my thrashing, and at the same time kick my ass with both feet as he was pounding the back of my head with both hands.

Mom sat late into the night in the dimly lit basement, her frail-looking arms resting on the old tattered card table as she darned socks stretched over a burned-out light bulb. She magically created coats and clothing that looked store-bought, by carefully picking the stitches from worn-out or discarded items to use as material. She used flowered chicken feed sacks, cleaned on a washboard in the galvanized root beer tub, for shirts and dresses that looked like they were ordered from Sears. She repaired shoes with fishing line and covered the holes in the soles with heavy cardboard placed inside the shoes until Dad got time, between drinking, to tack on a piece of rubber cut from an old worn-out tire.

Dad said, "Yer lucky ya got shoes at all. Most kids don't; they just go barefoot in the summer and wear rubber boots in the winter." If we complained, say, about the meat being too tough, he would respond, "Hell, that ain't tough. When ya don't have none at all, then that's tough."

He always wore Levis that were too large and immediately found their way down around his hips, the belt holding them precariously there. He wore a flannel shirt, a ball cap, and engineer boots with hard toes that he had somehow obtained from the plant where he used to work. It was never clear how he had come to own ten pairs of them; as they became too worn to be respectable, he dug out a new pair and gave the old ones to me. I got his old hats, too. In cold weather he wore a coat or jacket, fuzzy cloth gloves, a fluffy cap with earflaps, and a blue handkerchief in his back pocket with the end sticking out so he could easily grab it to wipe away the watery snot that continually ran from his crooked, humped nose.

He was short like his Welch ancestors and I was taller like Mom's Danish folks, and this contributed to his frustrations. "How did I sire such a tall, for your age, different and difficult-to-handle offspring? Or did I, after all?"

He farted, it seemed, almost at will. "Whoops!" he would exclaim while he looked around, as if he were surprised and disgusted, as if it had been somebody else. He had chronic hemorrhoids and had decided that the Mullen Leaf plant—because of its softness as well as its magical healing effects—would be his tissue of choice. In milder weather, we frequently saw him searching out back for his "medication" on the way to the john.

I never completely understood him and was never sure when he was kidding and when he wasn't. Take the time he told me he had gone to the doctor for medicine for his hemorrhoids and the doctor gave him suppositories. He said, "The pills are so damned big, it's dammed near impossible to swallow them, and for all the good they did my hemorrhoids, I might just as well have shoved them up my ass."

On Sunday, when he went to church, he wore a dark rumpled suit with scuffed black shoes and silk dress socks with brightly colored, embroidered designs on them. "God likes us to look our best when we visit him," he advised.

Chapter 5

Injuries were home-remedied, for the most part. To see a doctor, something had to be torn completely off or broken and dangling. Appendicitis and tonsillitis were questionable candidates that had to be approved by the churches' welfare program. The catch was the entire family had to go to church and pay tithing to be eligible for these benefits.

Mom and Dad were staunch advocates of the school that taught the principle, "The body will heal itself. We need only to repair broken items." That translated to, "If there is a choice between being injured yourself or doing damage to an inanimate object, for hell's sake, select the former."

Everything else was treated from Dad's medicine supplies, which included a large, partially filled bottle of turpentine stored on a shelf in the outhouse for dousing and killing the germs in open, bleeding wounds. A tin of Bag Balm, applied to chapped lips, scrapes, and crotch rot, was kept in the shed with the cow. To use it, flies and cow manure had to be pushed out of the way with a stick or finger and a little of the magical and disgusting healing substance pasted onto the ailing region. There was a bottle of Bayer Aspirin, up high in the dungeon, away from inquisitive delinquents.

Also, a vast collection of remedies that had been passed down through generations was stored in Mom's or Dad's heads, or treatments were made up on the spot at chaotic and critical times. Over all of this, the local health agency kept a watchful eye and tried to keep up with the ailments of the populace by tacking up cardboard signs on the fronts of houses, announcing that the household was infected with a particular contagious disease. To create a more urgent warning for serious ailments such as diphtheria, typhoid, and scarlet fever, a red sign was used. But beyond the red sign, no other, more stringent restrictions, were ever enforced.

In Dad's opinion, the more something hurt and the more torture it inflicted, the better were its healing effects. Similarly, he thought the worse or more terrible something tasted, the better it was for your health. Fevers were controlled with aspirin or by bathing with a cool wet cloth or just ignoring the fever until it went away. I was treated in such a manner one time when I lay in bed for more than a week with fever. I lay tossing and turning in Mom and Dad's bed, trying to get away from hallucinations. Mom sat close, trying to restrain and reassure me. Between cooling me with a damp cloth and administering aspirins, she catnapped.

Dad yelled obscenities that mixed with my delusions, making them impossible to discern.

"Lazy horse's ass, I got ta git some sleep. I won't be able ta look fer work if I don't," he complained.

"Are they hiring at The Dirty Shame?" Mom asked sarcastically.

Dad's face swelled and turned red, as if it would burst. He turned, climbed the stairs, and disappeared.

For quite a while, I didn't get any better. My legs and neck ached, and I had difficulty even getting to the chamber pot. Aunt Trudy, Dad's youngest sister, dropped by one day and the moment she saw me she screeched, "You better get William to a doctor. He's got rheumatic fever!"

"What causes that?" Mom asked.

"Living in this damp, dark dungeon don't help nothin'," she said.

God only knows how she knew, but she was right. Dr. Orton confirmed it. "Lucky you kept him as cool as you did and gave him aspirin. It didn't harm his heart too bad; he just has a murmur and will probably outgrow that," Orton said. "Take it easy for a few weeks. Rheumatic fever sometimes damages the brain, but William seems to be all right."

"He daydreams a lot, but seems to be smart enough," Mom said.

The doctor gave an all-knowing look and nodded his agreement as we left the office and went back out into the chill.

"I told you we should take him in," Mom told Dad as we walked home.

"Them doctors er just after yer money. They ain't nothin' wrong with the boy."

Mom rolled her eyes. "What's the use?" she said.

Dad left us in an angry huff, heading for town. Mom held her hanky to her eyes and nose, sobbing softly as she walked toward the dungeon and I walked behind her, trying to go slowly, as Dr. Orton had told me to do.

Chapter 6

Aunt Trudy Lamont was a large woman; so large, in fact, that her pregnancies were obscured. One day she wouldn't have a new baby and the next day, without looking any different, she would. She knew when the time was right and called Mom to be midwife. If not for her weight she would have been nice-looking. She had thick, naturally curly, long brown hair, accented with gray or rather white. It swept forward like the olive boughs of the Emperor of Rome, Julius Caesar, but rather than aggrandizing her, it served to define her as a peasant.

A round nose, the roundest ever, sat evenly in the center of her round face. Round nodules sat beside each round nostril, with a round, pursed mouth below. And above this, round gray eyes, with long eyelashes and thick dark eyebrows, which arched into a surprised half-circle.

She wobbled when she walked and squeaked when she talked. She and Uncle Arthur lived about three blocks away in a nice frame house that he built for her. He was a carpenter by trade and worshipped the very ground Aunt Trudy walked on.

He was slight in build but wiry and usually wore a cap to hide his prematurely bald head. He was ultra-friendly and accommodating, especially to Aunt Trudy. He had almost fatal halitosis—not fatal to himself but nearly fatal to anyone he was talking to. He dressed like Dad did, although almost all the men dressed similarly.

Uncle Arthur had not only built their house by hand but had dug the basement in the same way. Industrious as an ant, he worked every morning before his regular job at the foundry and on both sides of supper until early into the morning. With a shovel and wheelbarrow, he had slowly removed dirt to make the basement, and then slowly but steadily built the forms for the footings and foundation.

He then recruited a battalion of charitable neighbors and orchestrated their mixing of the cement, sand, gravel and water into concrete, directing where and how it should be poured and into which forms. For days, the ant-like procession shoveled sand, gravel, cement, and poured water into the three cement mixers and emptied the wet concrete into wheelbarrows. Then they pushed the wet, sloppy, heavy loads up ramps and dumped them into Uncle Arthur's forms from the catwalks above. Moving now a little quicker than ants, they turned the wheelbarrows backwards and pulled them as they ran to the mixers for another load.

Finally, the piles of sand, gravel, and beige sacks filled with cement were reduced and transformed into white walls of concrete, waiting to dry. Then they were topped with lumber walls and covered with a siding that defined the new abode. After that, Uncle Arthur did most of the work himself, covering the structure with a shingle roof to complete Aunt Trudy's house.

The couple had two sons. Gordon was the oldest, two years younger than I; and Dale was five years my junior. Gordon had been held back in school twice. He had a great memory but seemed dull when it came to common sense.

One day, when I had important business at their place, I found Aunt Trudy standing on her front porch, mixing something in a large aluminum bowl. It was probably candy; she made the best melt-in-your-mouth, drop-dead creamy fudge in the world.

The large aluminum bowl was cradled in her left arm, as if she were a wrestler using a headlock on an opponent. Her face was red from the effort of stirring the contents with a large wooden spoon.

She would give anyone just a taste of her fudge, and then she would fake a migraine, and place custom-made blinders over her eyes. She would command whoever was there to take her to her bedroom, as she clutched the almost-full aluminum bowl filled with fudge defiantly in her arms. When she reached her room and closed the door, the lock would click. If you peeked through the window, she would be reading from her stash of funny books and eating spoonfuls from the aluminum bowl, with the blinders pulled up around her forehead. God, she looked content.

The day I found Aunt Trudy on the porch mixing something, Gordon was playing "cars" in front of her on the ground. He was a sight to see! When he stood up straight, he seemed to be leaning a little backward. When he walked, he bounced along, keeping both elbows behind his body and almost touching behind him. A portion of his hair on the right side had been removed in an unusual accident when he was very young and he happened to be in my care. He was often injured, it seemed, while in my care.

He had large, fat lips, just like Dad's family and I did, and his nose was too large for his head. His ears were sort of pointed at the top; they weren't really pointed, but they seemed to be, if you looked at him from the front. If he had been dressed in a green suit and stocking cap, he might have passed for one of Santa's elves. His eyes bugged out; he looked a little like a bloated sunfish. He had a winning smile that was more effective with adults than with his peers, siblings, or cousins.

His brown, unkempt hair was permanently parted with a scar that ran almost where a real part should have been. He had caused that injury himself by being directly under me as I tried to drag a large piece of metal up into our tree house a few years earlier. I lost my grip and the metal fell on his head, making a pretty impressive wound. I could have repaired it myself with one of Mom's needles and thread, but he went bawling to Aunt Trudy and blamed the whole thing on me. The injury probably should have had stitches, but his parents thought it might heal all right; and it had, except for the quite noticeable scar, but he never had to part his hair again. He should have thanked me. This was one of many times Gordon was forbidden to play with me, but like a lot of other things, the warning wore off with the passing of time and the relief, comfort, and need of babysitting.

I wasn't flattered when Aunt Trudy said Gordon looked like me. I thought his parents were jealous of me because I could entice the girls to go out with me and he couldn't; at least not the good-looking and nice ones.

His little brother Dale almost worshipped me. Well, Gordon did too, underneath it all. They followed me around as if they were faithful puppies when I allowed it, and they tried to imitate me in almost every way. Dale was pleasant and easy to get along with and to control, unlike Gordon, who tried to challenge me at every turn. Dale's appearance was normal, with light brown hair, brown eyes, and an easy laugh that made people like him. He was agreeable, smart, and good-looking, except for his huge ears; all the kids kidded him that if his ears had muscles, he could fly.

"Where's Dale?"

"With his paw," Aunt Trudy yelled back, "They went to town for me. How's your heart?"

"Still beating," I yelled and placed my hand on my chest and bent forward as if I were falling. "Can I talk to Gordon?"

"Ask him yerself."

Gordon trotted over, almost wagging his tail like a good dog.

The reason for my visit was that I wanted to trade him, sight-unseen, a very large, in fact huge, and very sharp, two-bladed pocketknife with the smallest blade broken off, for a wooden bow and three arrows that his dad, my Uncle Arthur, had acquired from his father when he was a young boy. My dad was always against me making good trades, especially with younger kids, and the fact that it had been Uncle Arthur's boyhood treasure, as well as a fond memory from his father—and a lethal weapon, to boot—wouldn't improve my chances of keeping it, if Dad found out.

"Bring it over tonight; I'll meet you in Aunt Helen's barn," I told him after I revealed the "great" knife to him, trying to seem mysterious and clandestine. I'd have to hide the bow and arrows in the barn, I knew.

"I'll keep the knife until then; it belonged to Daniel Boone," I said with an expansive smile. "It's worth a hell of a lot of money and it's very sharp." He always believed just about anything I told him.

The next day, after the trade, I set up a target on the fence that separated Aunt Helen's place from her neighbors, the Richards, and I began practicing. The target was a magazine cover with a picture of Adolph Hitler, his hand raised in the Nazi salute as he talked to the German people. With practice, I became quite a good archer, and the Fuhrer's face began to look like a man with smallpox. But I had lost a couple of arrows and decide to conserve the remaining one, so I began shooting it into the air, where I could keep an eye on it. Unfortunately, the arrow would go so high that it would disappear from sight; and as it re-entered the atmosphere, it became a dangerous missile. I cowered under the apple tree for protection. The sparse branches offered little protection, but made me feel a little more secure, just the same.

I imagined the arrow as one of the buzz bombs Germany sent to England. It was just a target arrow with a pointed metal tip, not the kind for killing animals or people, and each time I sent it back up, I tried to get it higher and higher.

One launch made its re-entry a bit off-course, and I watched aghast as it approached Mr. Richards, who was bent over weeding in his garden. With a dull thud, the out-of-control arrow hit him in the back. Lightning shot up my spine and bounced around in my shoulders and skull, as the taste of sulfur covered the roof of my mouth.

"He's dead, I killed him; I know I killed him," I mumbled and fell to the ground, hiding beneath the apple tree. I lay quiet for a long moment, imagining the blood gushing out of Mr. Richards as he lay on the ground, shaking in a horrible death ritual.

"This is the way my life always goes. I'm always lucky with bad things but never with good ones. Things always go bad even when I try to be good. How in the hell could I hit Mr. Richards with the arrow at that distance? It must be over a million feet."

I couldn't help but marvel at both my good shot and my bad luck. Finding at last the courage to crawl to the fence and part the weeds, I looked over the riddled face of Hitler, but Mr. Richards wasn't in his death throes; the blood wasn't squirting out of an open wound. He just stood there with the arrow in one hand, rubbing his back with the other, looking into the heavens and saying over and over, "I'll be god-damned. I'll be god-damned."

Since I didn't know what else to do, and since that was my last arrow, I stood and walked over and took the arrow out of his hand.

"Thanks," I said, and quickly walked to the washhouse.

I turned to look back. He was still rubbing his back and looking up, his lips forming words; he looked completely bewildered. I climbed the concrete steps of the washhouse and quickly went inside and down into the dungeon, happy to have escaped free and clear, and with my bow and last arrow safe and sound.

I decided to hide the not-very-effective lethal weapon in Aunt Helen's barn for more practical use later, should the need ever arise. After Aunt Trudy told Dad what had happened, he impressed pretty indelibly on me what a "horse's ass" I was, found the bow and the surviving arrow, and took them back to Gordon. I ended up again with Daniel Boone's very big, sharp, two-bladed pocketknife that had only one blade.

Then, to make things worse, Mr. Richards informed my parents that I had "tried to kill" him.

"Jesus," I stormed, "talk about exaggeration. If I had wanted to kill him, I could have used the Daniel Boone knife to cut his head off. This is so dumb."

I was happy I had the knife back—it would come in handy, I was sure.

To impress upon me how inhuman and awful my actions had been, my punishment was to weed Aunt Helen's Victory Garden. In addition to everything else she did for us, she had given us a small portion of her Victory Garden, where we grew some of our food, but I would now be weeding the entire plot that had been allocated to us. Actually, it was quite small, and yet this task, designed for my penance, loomed larger than almost anything I had ever encountered. I sat and looked at the garden. And then I sat and looked at it some more. I even lay down and looked at it. I always got a sick feeling when confronted with physical labor. It was a trait I developed when very young, almost assuredly an instinct and not something learned.

I was sick indeed, sick unto death, as Edgar Allen Poe wrote in *The Pit and the Pendulum.* I was easily as sick about this gigantic amount of labor as the unnamed narrator of the *Pit* was about being condemned to death during the Spanish Inquisition.

The garden looked big indeed.

"Mom," I complained, "I don't know if I can do it. It's so big."

Mom smiled. "You can do it. I'll give you a bottle of root beer to keep your mind off it."

The root beer tasted delicious, as always. Mom was about as stingy with it as Aunt Trudy was with her candy.

"The root beer didn't do any good, Mom, and I'm getting sick," I said, almost crying.

"You haven't even done anything yet, William," she said when she inspected the area.

"It's too big and I'm sick," I complained.

Mom thought for a moment. "I'm going to rope off a small portion so it won't be so intimidating to you."

"Okay."

"And I'll get another bottle of root beer for you, too."

The root beer tasted divine but the weeding was still

intimidating even after I had consumed the drink and had looked at the weeding from all angles.

"William," Mom said again, "you haven't done anything."

"It's too big, and I'm sick."

Mom gave me a glance that meant she was exasperated and at a loss for words. "I'll let your dad have a talk with you." She made her way back to the dungeon, and then turned and said over her shoulder, "You just sit there and think about what's going to become of you if you don't get some ambition. We love you, William, and want you to amount to something."

It was good to have some of the threat of weeding erased, temporarily, at least. It kept my pride intact and made me feel pretty damned healthy, but then the sky suddenly turned dark and it began to rain. The downpour became torrential, as if God were punishing Job, who struck me as a dumb bastard to take all that abuse from anyone, but especially from a god that he looked up to and worshiped.

Mom had told me to stay in the garden, so to make myself a martyr, I sat and allowed the raindrops to pelt me, as Job had endured numerous hardships from God. Grimacing, I imagined myself being wounded behind enemy lines. Bravely, I lay quietly in my pain, so as not to reveal the location of our battalion and my buddies. I was so brave and dedicated that even in this downpour I lay strong and true, like a toy tin soldier left on a windowsill by his owner, who will never return. The red brick house that belonged to Aunt Helen was a blurred image through the downpour; and beside it, sheltered by a box elder tree that spread like a huge umbrella, was Aunt Helen's little frame washhouse, its faded white paint peeling off. And in its bowels, as if it were being digested, was our pitiful abode—the dungeon.

Chapter 7

One Sunday afternoon after dinner at Aunt Helen's, Ellen and I were lying on our stomachs on the thick, fragrant, flowered maroon carpet, with our chins cradled on our hands, listening. Our empty eyes gazed up at the big console Zenith radio as we enjoyed our favorite weekly radio serial, *The Lone Ranger*, its *William Tell Overture* booming out with an excitement intensified by the smell of the carpet, the odor of Aunt Helen's plentiful food, and the rhythmic hoof beats and hearty, "Hi, Ho, Silver, away." It was our favorite program. Aunt Helen and Mom took turns holding Martha and talking about sewing and other old lady stuff.

It was shortly before Christmas. We lay cheering for the masked lawman and his sidekick, Tonto, who responded unquestioning and perhaps sarcastically, "Yes, Kimosabe," to his lord and master's commands. An announcement broke into the program that the Empire of Japan had attacked our navel fleet in Hawaii and had inflicted severe damage. It was a brief, matter-of-fact statement that ended as suddenly as it had begun, with a promise of more news after the regular programming was completed. For an instant, it cut painfully into our Christmas spirit, and I looked at Mom for reassurance. She rolled her eyes and muttered, "Remember *The War of the Worlds*?"

Well, no, I didn't remember the Halloween prank narrated by Orson Welles that had broken into the Mercury Theatre's regular programming with Edward R. Murrow's voice, steeped in artificial panic, as he described the Martians advancing almost uncontested against our most modern defenses, just as the Japs were now seemingly doing in Hawaii. Mom and Aunt Helen stopped talking for a moment and listened, as if they weren't really sure, but then Mom winked and smiled and returned to chatting with Martha, more annoyed than alarmed. Ellen and I went back to our program.

When the Masked Crusader episode finally ended, the news came back on, the announcer insisting that the attack was real. The Empire of Japan had bombed our navel fleet in Hawaii and a large number of our ships had been either sunk or severely damaged. The announcer said the attack was still in progress. I looked again at Mom, and as the color slowly drained from her face, a look filled the emptiness that seemed like an alien possessing her body.

"My, God," she said––it was unusual for her to swear––"the news of war was preempted by the *Lone Ranger!*"

My body filled with a fairly new and startling feeling that was to become an integral part of my psyche. This was the feeling I've described earlier, as if lightning were traveling up my spine to fill my mouth with a taste that I assumed was like sulfur, based on the smell of sulfur. As this sensation overtook me, I realized that the broadcast was not fake; we were really at war.

America was shocked, bewildered, and frightened, held at bay from the old, now almost-forgotten, comfortable holiday passion of Christmas by the knowledge of war. Nobody knew what to do or what would happen next. It was a feeling Americans didn't want to acknowledge; they wanted to forget the heartache and worry of the old war two decades earlier, rather than become accustomed to a new one. But that feeling was quickly diminished by the confident, strong, steady voice and the encouraging words of Roosevelt over the crackling radio. He was desperate and angry, to be sure, but still confident and reassuring. "A date which will live in infamy," the voice said. "The United States of America was suddenly and deliberately attacked by naval and air forces of the Empire of Japan." As that awful truth sank into the depths of our souls, a different feeling arose with it; a certain calm fell all about us, which, simply by being there, warmed and comforted us in some elusive way. That feeling became a part of us all, of our psyche. It clung persistently to every pore, covering everything with a blanket of foreboding and dread mixed with a vague and perhaps counterfeit heroism. It could be felt and seen in the eyes and actions, and heard in the voices, of everyone.

Behind it all, the Commander-in-Chief stood as the backbone of the nation, although in effigy, because in reality he could keep his backbone straight only with the aid of his desk or the funny-looking metal crutches with which he struggled to stand or walk, as he tried desperately to disguise his own physical weakness in order to give the nation strength and confidence to endure. He encouraged Americans to regard fear itself as our greatest enemy. He declared Japan the aggressor and Germany as our other enemy as it continued to devour Europe. And then, as Italy joined in at the insistence of Mussolini, Americans realized they would be fighting all three countries.

This new feeling became even more than a feeling; it became central to the nation's psyche. It was deep-seated and continuous, more obvious and more enduring than anything most of us had ever known before! Strangely, it bore a striking resemblance, in flavor and character, to the odd and imposing sensation that I felt when startled or when it suddenly struck me that my soul would most certainly be cast unmercifully into the depths of hell, as Dad continually warned me would be the case when I refused to repent. It was that awful and all-encompassing, sulfurous taste and feeling.

And now that America being at war caused me to become more aware of this feeling, in order to cope and endure, I began to spend more time in one of my secret, illusory places.

Chapter 8

Over time, the war became less all-consuming to us at home. But in an effort to control hoarding and to distribute scarce items more fairly, stamped-out fiber ration tokens as well as paper documents were issued, to be used with money to purchase rationed items. In Utah, different colored tokens—green, gray, and orange—represented different portions of a penny, for precise currency exchange. There was more money available now because of the new defense jobs, and fewer people were going without.

Some opportunists realized they could appear patriotic and still use this rationing to their advantage. Merchants were most certainly among the ones who took advantage of this, but they weren't the only ones. Rationed items quickly became desirable commodities and suddenly just about everything had some sort of restriction. It was easy to tell bogus rations from real ones, which required a ration stamp or token. The others simply used a façade of some kind, such as a sign in the window saying, "Bananas, only two pounds to a family."

Even though we seldom had bananas, Mom thought we should get our share. She carefully selected the gorgeous yellow fingers for my sisters and me, and then, with explicit instructions to act as if we were all alone, she followed us through checkout with her own "two pounds" and the rest of the groceries. It was exciting. I liked to do it. I pretended I was a secret agent gone behind the front lines to rout out Hitler and his henchmen. It was my mission, I told myself, to go behind enemy lines and assassinate those evil henchmen, to gain essential war material. I stood stoically and straight, hugging the contraband in my arms as the delightful aroma filled my nostrils. I didn't even look back at the less adept and obviously fraudulent agents clustered behind me, obviously joined in clandestine activities, and just as obviously with Mom.

After this, in a secret rendezvous just outside the front doors, we unceremoniously gave Mom the change from the dollar and loaded the groceries into my battered little Piggly Wiggly wagon. Along with the praise for being so aloof, Mom always promised to someday give me all the bananas I could eat. My mouth watered as I imagined that, but at the same time, I was a little afraid this might be one of the promises of Mom and Dad that would never actually occur. Well, it turned out to be just that, just a hollow promise, but I wasn't going to forget, not ever. Even so, the more I pushed, the more she resisted. Each time we got bananas, I would painfully watch them on the shelf, turning brown-tinged and then completely black, and I would persist, "Mom, can I have my bananas now? I don't care if they're rotten."

"There's not enough to go around, I'm going to bake banana bread in Aunt Helen's stove and then just throw the rest away. Those rotten bananas will make you sick. I love you too much to make you sick."

Mom was usually giving and charitable, but I was handling it wrong. I know now I should have used reverse psychology.

"You're never going to give me the bananas, are you?" I would complain, to bring the issue to a head.

"I'm not dead yet," she would reply with light anger; she always said that whenever we argued about bananas, but this time with a smile. I smiled, too, because I knew then that the only way I would ever get all the bananas I could eat was if I bought them myself.

By this time the phrase, "I'm not dead yet," had been used so often that it had become locally famous; the whole family, even the neighbors and our friends, used it, sometimes for assurance that something that had been promised would be carried out, and sometimes for encouragement, or just as a matter of circumstance.

Chapter 9

As time passed and the war raged and grew, the war feeling became combined with resentment and controlled hatred. Strangely, this served to create yet another feeling, which rallied all Americans behind the legendary leader with the cigarette holder and crutches who warned about the fear of fear. That new feeling quickly took over and began to control the passion in all our lives. Children were first to adapt to the new feeling by mimicking the war with war-based games as they ran silently on tiptoe, killing the imaginary enemy with crude mouth made muffled shots. Dogs chased behind barking softly, as if they understood the need for restraint and reverence. Houses and inanimate objects even seemed to sit quietly, as if not knowing what to expect or do; even they seemed to exhibit the respect and bewilderment demanded by the new feeling.

Grown-ups realized the gravity of the dangers and the threat, but tried to keep the awful truth from the youngsters, and, strangely, away from their own consciousness. They remained secluded inside their houses, finding courage only with the setting sun to venture out with drinks and cigarettes to sit under the protection of porches, or in the recesses of the lawn, or the shadow of the houses, to talk softly and worry and fret, with tear-reddened eyes and color-drained faces, staring vacantly. Silence and doubt were everywhere; they were part of the new feeling, as real and as tangible as life itself. These attitudes might have been adopted just to emphasize the dangers we all faced and to help everyone to continue saving and giving as we rehearsed what to do in the event of an attack. In class, we students practiced hiding as best we could under our desks. If we were in the hallway during such a drill, the first student in line would fall down with their head and knees on the floor. The others would also be on their knees but with their heads on the rear of the student in front of them.

The American Japanese were rounded up and placed in internment camps. The German and Italian families found another type of confinement, as the American citizens restricted them to their houses with shunning gestures and sinister advances that kept them confined almost as effectively as if they were interned. The Chinese families wore signs around their necks saying, "I'm Chinese," and Mexican and other nationalities that were considered suspect tried not to be what they were. We were all filled with a strange mixture of patriotism, fear, controlled terror, prejudice, and anger. It wasn't a desire for justice, but a mixture of emotions for which there was no basis. Buying war bonds, war stamps to stick in books until there were enough to buy a bond, conservation, and the chronic and desperate rationalization that brought God to our side against the enemy became the hallmarks of this mixture. And salvaging to support our troops became the status-builder, maybe more in illusion than in practicality for the citizens.

Everyone began cutting both ends out of tin cans; we washed them out, smashed them flat, and then stacked and tied them into bundles. Tinfoil from gum and candy bar wrappers were carefully peeled off the paper and rolled into balls; pots and pans and any scrap metal was collected by community organizers and individuals. Then, in exchange for a few cents payment, it was all thrown onto the "Victory Truck" that came around. Everybody willingly gave up a portion of their tires, gasoline, sugar, and we gathered the duck-like tops from milkweed for a few pennies a sackful. We were told the milkweed would be made into life jackets, sleeping bags, and coat linings for the armed forces. Special trucks delivered different-colored gas to farmers and contractors in an effort to keep them from selling or using it for cars or other non-essential things. But it always found its way into cars, anyway. Everybody raised Victory Gardens, to produce food that could be sent to the front. As the war lost its urgency and we all became more accustomed to it, most people went against this ideology to hoard commodities, whenever such opposition could go undetected.

We all still wanted to help, for a number of reasons, but especially to keep the boys at the front fed and supplied with bullets, and yet, underneath all the seemingly good intentions was our real reason: to keep the fighting over there, across the ocean, where it could be an uncomfortable fantasy, and away from us, where it would become a horrifying reality. And then our good intentions were sabotaged when we were fed what everyone considered to be war surplus. It began with milk and concentrated orange juice. More surplus items were added, until at school, surplus eventually filled the entire lunch menu. The food tasted awful, especially the concentrated orange juice, I thought. Strangely, it caught on, until everybody seemed to favor it.

To keep us all updated about the war, newsreels at the movie theatre followed the previews and the cartoon. Weeks-old war news jerked across the screen, showing soldiers on both sides being killed and prisoners being captured. The soldiers sat smoking cigarettes. Everybody smoked; the cigarette companies supplied the solders without charge but then gouged the government for shipping and free advertising. And in the background, armored vehicles, their wheels turning backwards, carried troops and supplies to the frontlines, and tanks and large guns barraged away at the enemy. A little less dramatically, jeeps and half-tracks carried tactical officers and soldiers close enough to manage and fight the war firsthand.

The news was sensationalized and it seemed the war would sooner or later find its way over here, into out towns and homes, maybe to give us all incentive to keep conserving and giving. Fear was tangible, as tastable as sulfur on the roof of the mouth. It was a terrible time, especially for the parents of the soldiers who could only phone or receive phone calls from the few scattered homes that were affluent enough to own one. The few people who had phones were tolerant about letting anyone use them. The rural areas depended on news by word of mouth when their kids came home on the school bus or when they visited their friends in town.

The first draft accepted almost anybody with a heartbeat or pulse but then was quickly revised to pass over the 4-Fer's (who were the documented unfit to serve because of health or related reasons), the married with children, college students, and the essential workers. The latter usually included the children of the wealthy, big business leaders, and politicians, as well as factory workers, the last being the intended reason for this category.

Dad missed the first draft by luck and then the second one because of being married with children, and then as more fighters were needed, he missed it again because he had procured a job at the steel plant as an essential worker. His friends said Dad liked to spell it "steal" plant, because he took some lead home in his lunch box to sell at the salvage yard to augment his already-lucrative income and was caught and suspended without pay. And then he missed the draft again by being classified 4-F because of his addiction to alcohol, which, in a vicious circle, could have been brought about by losing his job and his fear of being drafted. The church helped him get the 4-F deferment status, and then helped him and us to keep food on the "card" table and clothes on our backs. But Dad still managed to end his "seeking employment quests" at The Dirty Shame Saloon, trying to drown his sorrow and guilt. Eventually, getting to the Shame and talking to his friends about religion and science and the way the country treats the little man took complete priority over looking for a job.

The rest of us were left to survive in the dungeon. We were there even when Dad had a job, and it looked like we would stay there, even though Aunt Helen was still trying to find a way to get us into a better place. I thought she would achieve that just as soon as her own kids found jobs and got out on their own—the lazy bastards!

Chapter 10

To cope with the war and my impoverished life, I usually found myself on the bridge that spanned the narrow ditch between Mrs. MacLean's Tudor-style mansion and Aunt Helen's modern redbrick house. The bridge was a fancy structure, out of place there and better suited for a fairy tale, with its carvings and a high, fancy handrail that I could sit under to kick my feet in the water or reach down and find any assortment of water creatures and bugs. My favorites were the bloodsuckers, or suckers for short. It was so fun to sprinkle salt and watch them squirm and roll as the salt broke their skin and made them bleed. A magnificent feeling.

The bridge was long and wide enough to allow me to stretch out to daydream, nap, or sleep. The roof was made of copper that the elements and time had turned a deep brown color. I had tacked up pieces of cardboard to cover the sides to keep out the wind and rain; it could be folded up when the weather was nice. As the old cardboard became weathered or torn, I tacked up new pieces.

After I finally got those forbidden books home from the library, I excitedly read and dreamed about them. It was easier to hide them during the better weather; I knew I had to get a better place to keep them before they got wet and ruined. They were exciting and unbelievable, a lot like my comic books. The Einstein guy made a lot of sense, even if he was an atheist. I was beginning to understand that there are atheists and there are atheists, just like almost everything else.

The stream under the bridge was usually just a trickle, and the ditch wasn't wide enough by any means to even need a bridge, but it had been built there by one of Aunt Helen's boys, Tyler, who was an artist, for his high school industrial arts project. The bridge had been used by everyone for foot travel between the two places until I began spending a large part of my days and nights there with my thin blanket, using my clothes as pajamas, until I finally more or less took it over. I guess I'd homesteaded it. It was a lot better than my cubbyhole in the damp, dark dungeon. I was glad it was finally spring.

When it was Aunt Helen's or Mrs. MacLean's turn to irrigate, the thin stream of clean, clear water rich with bloodsuckers and other water bugs that normally ran was overpowered by a rush of strawberry-colored, thin mud, as it made its way to the Victory Gardens at the back of the lots.

Chapter 11

The morning sun peeked over the distant mountains and fluttered pleasant beams about me as it shot frost-filled streaks of light through the aspen trees and into my half-opened eyes. But that pitiful effort at warming was useless against the early morning cold. I had spent the night on my bridge again; I guess Dad had been too drunk or tired to bother about getting me inside when he came home. I blinked and studied the threatening cumulous sky and the glittering slits of brightness and pulled my legs up under me to find some warmth in the thin, ragged blanket. Then I closed my eyes to glean the final minutes of sleep from the vanishing night.

Suddenly, a machine gun rattled; the Germans were attacking again! I sat up startled, sure that the enemy was here, but it was only the rain. Giant raindrops rattled the roof of the bridge with the sharpness and repetition of military drummers. A smile wiped the fright from my face. "Just the rain," I mumbled, much relieved.

I stretched, and then cowered from the torrent as I lay inside the protection of the brown copper-roofed, elegant wooden structure of my bridge with the decrepit cardboard façade. I peeked through the cracks in the cardboard at the dawn. It was a dingy morning, designed to spawn memories more than ambition. There were things to do; I hated to procrastinate, but my hatred would have to wait for another moment of delight, to reflect and plan my day.

Thank God I had brought my box full of books out here to the bridge. I opened it and looked at the contents. I felt the urge to write, so I took out my current notebook and began to write about what was happening now and how I felt; stuff like that. I thought about putting wheels on the box. Maybe Dad would help me if I could get him sober and in a charitable state—he did have a nice, gentle side to him underneath all that harshness and hate.

I had never noticed it before, but right below the block letters "Brewing Company" on the box, in smaller block letters was, "Best Beer in Michigan, since 1892." And below that, "A part of M..." It looked like what had most likely been "ichigan" had somehow worn off on both sides. I picked up my pencil and put an "e" right after the "M" to make it read "A part of Me." I smiled. "I will call it my Me box."

The rain always made my legs ache; Dr. Orton had told me the rheumatic fever that had weakened my heart would make my arms and legs ache when it rained or when the weather turned cold. Even so, I knew I'd rather be out here on the bridge than in the damp darkness of the dungeon, where I could invent and dream, even if it did hurt.

There were lots of suckers today, and the water in the ditch was low. It was easy to reach down to get them. It turned my mind away from my own desperation to sprinkle salt on their little black bodies and watch them squirm. I only wished they would scream; it would be nice to know that something else suffered as I did— that I wasn't alone.

Dad always said, "Trolls live under bridges. Why don't ya climb down under? Ya cain't even do a troll right!" And then he would laugh. "A troll and a horse's ass. Hell, God's been good ta me; he gave me everything."

He made me sleep inside the dungeon when he wasn't at the Shame. But he was the horse's ass, the drunken bastard.

As suddenly as it had began, the rain stopped and the clouds parted to let the sunshine through, in streaks at first, like God bestowing a blessing onto a prophet or to reveal some profound holy truth. And then the clouds fled as if in fearful desperation, which would be noticed and understood only by those who had known that sort of cruel dominance.

Dad walked past. "God-damned troll!" He spat the words at me. I just looked at him.

"Tell yer ma I'm goin' ta look fer work."

I sat still, stoic and silent.

"Hear me, boy? Tell yer ma I's a-lookin' fer work."

"Yeah, I hear ya," I tied to mimic his coarse English—but cautiously.

"Okay then ..." He turned to walk toward town, hissing from the corner of his mouth, "Horse's ass."

A fly whizzed past my head and landed on the rail of the bridge. "Why are you alive? You should be dead." I slapped it with my palm; it hadn't even tried to fly. "Too cold, huh?" It gave me a good feeling to do some good. Why did God even make flies?

I waited until Dad had taken a couple of steps, and then I flipped him off to his back. "Goin' ta look fer work, huh?" I mimicked him again, still very much under my breath. We both knew better; he wasn't looking for work, he was going to the Shame to drink with his friends.

Chapter 12

The floor of the furnace room is getting cold; but they should come soon to fill the furnace stoker and start a fire. If they do, they'll see me, and I'll get out. I have no idea when Alex will be back, or if he will be back, but I intend to have some answers for him, when and if he returns. I want to get the hell out of here; I am getting bored, the floor is getting hard, and it is getting bitterly cold. I know I am going to have to move along a lot faster than I have been, or skip a few phases of my past life, if I'm going to find enough information to deal with Alex before I freeze or starve to death. I look toward the huge, ironclad door, imagining Alex looking through the cracks. But to no avail—I will have to return to my quest to discover anything to use as ammunition for my release.

And then, as I have become so accustomed to do, I wait for that exotic, wonderful moment that will take me away from all, or at least most, of my pain, and allow me to be free. Finally, it comes, and I begin to dissolve ... until I have completely dissolved into the wonder and beauty of the illusion.

Chapter 13

The Orem Tram was a government-subsidized, electric mass transit vehicle that made it possible to travel from city to city in the area. Aunt Helen gave Mom some tokens and she took the girls to Aunt Ardith's in Salt Lake City for a few days; but for one reason or another, I was to stay home and "think about what you've done," whatever the hell that meant. Dad was tending me. I stood at the front, double-swinging doors of the Shame, looking in, waiting for him to be done.

The stench of stale beer, liquor, and cigarette smoke funneled into my lungs as I stood on tiptoes in my wagon, peering over the doors. He sat with other men on the high, padded chrome stools—slouched over at the huge, polished bar in the din and haze, laughing and telling nasty stories. I could barely hear what they said. "…Casey Jones said before he died, there were three more things that he would like to ride, a steam bicycle and an automobile and a bow-legged nigger on a Ferris wheel…"

I wished I could hear it all. The barkeep—in a dirty apron with a mostly-ash cigarette hanging precariously from his lips, polished the glasses and tabletops with a grungy, white towel. He joined in the conversation, patronizingly, as he encouraged the men to drink more.

One man said, "I got so drunk, I didn't know whether to shit or go blind."

The man sitting next to him said drunkenly, "Why didn't you just close one eye and fart?"

Maybe you have to be drunk to appreciate it, I thought as I stood on one foot and then the other, trying to remember what the Sunday school teacher had said about getting into hell or heaven and about walking on water—anything to elude the boredom. I fiddled with the sign on the front door: "Hours of operation 7:30 am until 1:00 am, closed on Christmas and Thanksgiving."

I wondered why I was standing here. I had my wagon and as usual now, my Me box in it—I hadn't gotten Dad to put wheels on it yet, because I hadn't found him in a sober or charitable mood. I stepped down, opened the box and took out the book about Einstein. I sat in the wagon in front of my Me box, straddling the handle, and began reading and imagining myself working with the famous physicist. After Dad had a few more drinks and was slouching even more, I decided to do some exploring. "He'll be amused for hours," I thought. The place next door, Buck and Edna's Diner, was impossible to resist, with its flashing neon lights spelling out the name in exciting colors. Aunt Mazy worked there. They served greasy cheeseburgers and thick, gravy-covered food. I wasn't supposed to go in there because they served beer, which maybe was why it was exciting.

Aunt Mazy was Mom's oldest brother's wife before he died; well, he blew his brains out with his military service .45 caliber pistol. It looked sickening, with all the blood and brains scattered about. All the good, upstanding citizenry had tagged Aunt Mazy as no good and of low standing, but I liked her.

I pushed the door open and pulled my wagon inside, and then just stood for a few minutes, waiting for my eyes to adjust to the gloom. Aunt Mazy was rushing around taking plates filled with food to customers, and then quickly taking empty ones back through the swinging doors to be washed. Her amber, graying hair was wound into a bun in back and covered with an almost invisible net. She leaned forward, as if running. I imagined the bun a malignant, supernatural growth that was chasing her, trying to push her to the ground. She always had a cigarette dangling from the corner of her mouth, squinting, trying to avoid smoke in her eyes, as she waited on customers or sat in front of her cup of coffee at the counter. There was always a long ash that should have fallen off into the food but never did; she always caught it just in time and dropped it into an ashtray. All this amazed me. Finally, she saw me, and showing her rotting, crooked teeth in a friendly smile, she rushed toward me.

"Where's yer Mom and Dad?"

"Mom's gone to visit Aunt Ardith and Dad's in the other side."

"He's always there. Just leave yer wagon over there against the wall—I'll keep an eye on it." She showed her unsightly teeth again, this time in a wicked smile, almost like she was winning at something, as if she and the rest of the world were in some sort of quarrel. Her rotting teeth and sallow face give the appearance of what you might imagine death to be like. From her mouth came the entwined odors of rotting meat, liquor, and tobacco smoke. Even so, I liked her a lot.

There were unsavory stories whispered about her and some of the more developed and mature young boys, as well as unscrupulous married men around town. She had been "knocked-up," as my friends called it, before she and Uncle Donald were married. Everybody treated the baby with disdain and contempt. They called it "a little bastard." I didn't make sense to me; it wasn't the baby's fault. Hell, I didn't think anyone should be blamed, especially not a baby. She didn't keep it. "Too much shame," she said. It was sent away to live in another town; the rumors were to an orphanage. She should have just told everybody about it—everybody knew, anyway.

"Want a piece of pie, William?" Without waiting for an answer, she turned on her heel and returned in a few moments with a large, heated wedge of apple pie with vanilla ice cream melting on top, and a steaming cup of coffee. I will never forget that enticing aroma or those tastes; especially the first time she served them to me. She was a great aunt, no matter what anybody says.

"Want it in the back booth so yer dad and the bishop of your church don't see ya?"

"Yeah!" It was against our religion to drink coffee.

"Crazy hypocrites," she whispered.

I didn't argue; I had my pie and coffee to take care of.

She continued, "Yer family's crazy, believin' God's blessin' them. Hell, they's poorer than church mice. That religion stuff's all a fantasy, and makes people prejudiced. It's more evil than evil; I hate it all."

I just shrugged my shoulders and kept stuffing the pie and melting ice cream into my mouth and pouring cream and sugar into the coffee until it resembled a milkshake, as I sipped it between bites of my exotic dessert.

It sounded like the people in the next booth had had too much to drink. "The sign says they use extra virgin olive oil," the woman said. "Where do the get extra virgin?"

The man said, "It's from olives that haven't even had a finger in them."

Whatever the hell that meant, I thought.

The door that connected the two establishments suddenly burst open and Dad staggered in to get a bag of Bull Durham smoking tobacco. I pushed the partially empty cup and pie plate to the other side of the table, as if it belonged to someone else. Aunt Mazy smiled and shook her head.

Dad saw me and came over, rolling his new cigarette as he talked through the Bull Durham label and string he held in his mouth. "Ya shouldn't be a-wastin' yer time here, William. God's got great things in store fer ya."

As much as he seemed to like God, he seemed to like science and singing almost as much, and now, it seemed he wanted to talk about science. "Ya kin go forward in time, William; ya jist can't never come back." He slurred the words.

I looked at him in a way that showed my disbelief in his time theory.

"If ya don't believe me, just think: since I said that, you've already gone forward in time a few minutes. Every second, you travel forward in time."

I had to smile. He was right; we all move forward in time as time passes, but I had never thought of it in that way before.

"I'm taken ya home, son."After he lit up and took a few puffs, he pushed me through the door.

"Hey, Dad, I need to get my wagon."

"Hurry. I ain't got all day."

"Will you help me put wheels on my Me box?"

"Why the hell ya need wheels on that box? Ya got a wagon."

"I don't know. I just want wheels."

He held my neck as we walked along the broken sidewalk, as if he were guiding me, but holding me was more to keep him from falling. We staggered on, maybe because pulling my wagon made me a little unsteady, but it was mostly because Dad was out-of-his-mind drunk.

As we walked along I thought, Dad's best friend was Lou Crandall; an anti-religious nut who had been some sort of scientist or chemist at the steel plant. He had taken an entire metal lathe from the machine shop. Maybe he also spelled it "steal" plant, like Dad did. He took it piece-by-piece and had it all home and assembled in his basement workshop. He only needed the electric cord, which he could have easily and inexpensively purchased from any hardware store, but he wanted to have the authentic one with the model number of the lathe on it. Well, they caught him with it concealed in his lunchbox, and that was clue enough to track down the missing lathe. He wasn't as lucky as Dad; instead of probation, Lou was outright fired. The word about his theft got around, and he was blackballed; couldn't get a job anywhere. He spent his time at the Shame arguing with Dad and others as he filled his stomach with draught beer and the heads of the other drunks with all sorts of scientific and anti-religious propaganda.

Lou caught me one day while I was visiting Aunt Mazy; I was the only audience available. "William," he slurred, "when I was your age, I read a book about the founding fathers. You know, the ones who wrote up the Constitution." The words came out with a fine spray that carried the odor of alcohol and Uncle Arthur's halitosis mixed together, and it stuck, seemingly indelibly, to my face and nostrils. Lou said the founding fathers weren't so fond of religion. They mostly believed in some sort of a God, but they thought religion was a fantasy.

Then he seemed to wander. "Ask your dad about DNA, William, everything's made of it, the building blocks of life. They're…" He stopped short as an old man came in for a drink, and Lou left me in mid-sentence for a more receptive audience, and one who could sit at the bar and maybe buy him a drink.

As Dad and I walked home, he lectured me, beginning with religion and getting into the "highest glory." As we made our way precariously along the cracked and broken blocks of the sidewalk, he ended with, "I'm hungry; I need a sandwich. You hungry, William?"

"A little." Shit, what else was I to say?

"Ya should be hungry—hungry for knowledge; you ain't gonna 'mount ta a hill a beans."

"I read books, Dad."

"Yeah, funny books." He forced a croaking, condescending laugh through his lips.

I was going to get a serious lecture; I could see it coming. I just hoped it wasn't about playing nasty with girls and going to hell.

"William," he went on, "I been readin' and they's a new discovery; it's called atoms, the building blocks of life. All things are made from them."

"I thought that was DNA? That's what Lou said."

"Shut up, ya horse's ass, an' listen'. Ya might learn somethin."

I shut my mouth and listened.

Dad had picked up the "horse's ass" thing when his boss, Mr. Holley, at the filling station—— one of his long ago, part-time jobs——called him that name for leaving the engine oil drain bolt out after he changed the oil, which ruined the car. A dollar had been held back from his pay each week to someday finally pay for the new motor. I had made the mistake of laughing, and ever since then, to conceal his embarrassment and get revenge, he had almost replaced my name with "horse's ass." He found the opportunity to begin this addition to his vocabulary right away. A couple of rowdies at the station were teasing me about my long hair and worn-out shoes; Dad just watched and smiled. I got shy, backed up and sat on a stack of eggs that was piled up between blue cardboard egg-holders designed to keep them from being broken.

The egg-holders had failed to protect the eggs, as they were supposed to do, and many of them were cracked or broken. We ate a lot of eggs for a while and my name to Dad became "horse's ass," as another 25 cents per week was deducted from his check to pay for the broken eggs. This also increased the wait until I could begin getting my elusive allowance, and it pushed back the time when I would be able to pay Flash a silver dollar I once promised him for eating a night crawler.

"Atoms is small particles, so small ya can't even see em, not even with a microscope," Dad went on. "They's made up of protons, neutrons, and electrons and in some ways they's lots like our own solar system."

"That's my theory, too. Lou told me all about it."

"Ya horse's ass; just listen! The atom," he continued, "ain't encapsulated an' is held intact 'bout the same way as our solar system is. The relative distance between the elements that make up the atom and the relative distance between the atoms themselves is greater than the distance between the planets in our own solar system. If the atoms was all lined up right and modulated correctly, solid matter could pass through each other without causing any damage, just like ghosts and angels does."

My hell, Dad talked like a scientist! He had lost most of his usual kill-the-English-language accent; to say the least, I was impressed.

"Ya know, William, ya might not be such a horse's ass if ya contacted some scientist and tried ta learn somethin'. Wouldn't hurt ya a bit."

"I talked to Lou ..."

Dad just rolled his eyes, like in defeat. "Shut up." He was bent on revealing something Lou hadn't told me. "Erwin Chargaff, an American scientist from Austria, took samples of DNA of different cells and found that the amount of adenine was almost equal to the amount of thymine, and that the amount of guanine was almost equal to the amount of cytosine. DNA is a string of microscopic material that's like a road map to life––it determines what a person will be the moment the egg is fertilized in the womb."

Dad's English was still scientific, in spite of everything.

"Lou told me all about DNA, Dad."

His face turned a bright red. "Ya know's what a womb is, William?"

His feelings were hurt. Lou had beaten him to the punch. I became afraid to not let him go on. "No," I lied.

And he began telling me how a baby is born, how it gets in there in the first place, and then after nine months, how it gets out. It was a lot more descriptive and more in depth than was necessary, especially from my dad. I was glad when we were finally home.

"Now stay here. The Dirty Shame is no place fer youngin's, and you needs ta rest yer heart. It's up to me ta see that ya do."

"But Dad, I can't sleep––I feel too lonely." I didn't want to be alone.

His face softened as he came close. He knelt outside my cubbyhole and leaned over near me. "Just relax and say your prayers. God will give you peace. You will be able to sleep. I need to see about a job."

And then he led me through a simple prayer, trying to bless almost everyone, like our religion taught. After "amen," he showed me how to position my body to go to sleep. "Place your right arm under your head, and look to your left, and place your left arm down to your side; and then think about pleasant thoughts, and before you know it, you will fall asleep."

He sat with me for a long time, and when he probably thought I had fallen asleep, he softly ruffled my hair and whispered. "I love you—I'll be home soon." Through the slits of my eyes, I saw him stagger to his feet, almost falling, and with some effort, slowly ascend the stairs and disappear.

Hell, it was no use; I still couldn't sleep. I went out to the bridge, where I felt better and finally fell asleep next to my Me box. Later, I half-woke, enough to recognize Dad taking me inside. It had to be him—his breath reeked of sour mash whiskey and his clothes almost dripped the smell of cigarette smoke. He removed all doubt as he whispered and sort of snorted softly, "Good thing we got the protection an' comfort a' the church."

He must have had a tinge of guilt, because he shook me awake and by the light of his flashlight, he gave me two thin, battered books, one about mathematics, one about electricity, and a handwritten, one-page letter. It looked like he copied a bunch of stuff from the Bible or at least some religious book. He frequently gave me some sort of gift after he had abused or neglected me; often, it was just a hollow promise or some questionable advice. It was clear that he wanted to be a good dad and that he had at least a certain amount of love for me; he just didn't know how to deal with all that mushy stuff and the guilt of being a worthless drunk.

He said, "Will, as soon as I get time, I'll put them wheels on yer box."

The following morning, I found myself on the bridge, reading Dad's books and letter and trying to understand his intent with this letter effort. Shit, it was no use. It didn't make any sense––he must have been drunk when he wrote it, and I didn't understand the stuff about mathematics. Dad hadn't even put his own thoughts into the letter; he had just copied it from that old history book, the Bible. I put the math and electricity books with my treasured books in my Me box for later reference, alongside books I had been collecting with nude women in them, and the women's underwear section that I had torn out of the Sears catalogue in the outdoor toilet. I folded Dad's amateur, canonized writings to secure them in my back pocket. The letter from him didn't seem to fit anywhere, so I crumpled it up and dropped it into the ditch, and watched as the red-tinted, muddy water carried it away to the Victory Garden—our way, real or fictitious, of saving America.

"Maybe the carrots and beans will get some inspiration from it," I thought sardonically.

Chapter 14

A few days later, my cousin Gordon and I were on Aunt Helen's lawn, watching Mr. Richards as he trimmed his grown-out-of-control shade tree—it was a weeping willow. The sweat ran off him in small rivulets that continually dripped from his chin and nose. It soaked his shirt under his arms and his hat around the band as he chopped and sawed. Finally, he reduced the flowing, spreading weeping willow to a gigantic pile of limbs and leaves. Then he began to soak it with liquid from one of several large, red cans. The cans looked heavy, and he used both hands to hold them—one by one, he emptied the cans to drench the huge pile. The liquid spilled and covered his hands and arms and saturated his shirtfront and pant legs. Gordon and I stepped closer for a better look.

"Get back! This is gasoline, I'm going to light a fire," Mr. Richards warned, and waited for us to move back. We took a few steps back to presumed safety, and then Gordon inched forward to about where we had been in the first place.

"Get up closer, so you can see better," I encouraged him.

Mr. Richards held one of the empty gas cans cautiously away from the pile of limbs and leaves, as a person might hold a skunk or polecat, with his head turned, to avoid the stench. He struck a match with his thumbnail, and reached to touch the flame to the gasoline-saturated pile. It caught fire immediately, but it also caught fire to Mr. Richards' hand, shirtfront, and pants. Almost immediately, there was a loud PUFFT, and then a soft explosion, and then a second PUFFT, much more impressive than the first, and Gordon and Mr. Richards were engulfed in a soft, yellow-edged, crimson-blue flame. It didn't look real; it had to be a dream. Suddenly, I passed through the window of my illusory life, and was watching William as he watched the two flaming humans.

Mr. Richards' eyes and face were filled with terror; his body jerked and moved as if it wanted to flee but couldn't decide where to go. It was like his feet were riveted in place. The explosion had turned him toward Gordon, and they now stood facing each other––Mr. Richards completely engulfed in the raging blaze and Gordon, singed hairless and black, but not burning, just watching as our neighbor stood in pain and silent panic, being devoured by the inferno.

William had witnessed this odor before when hair and flesh were burning. The local farmers burned carcasses of diseased animals in a blazing open fire, to keep them from infecting other animals. Also, after hogs were killed, they were immediately hung from a tripod above a large barrel of water boiling over a fire. The hogs were dipped into the water to soften their hair, making it easier to scrape off. The large pigs would scream and squeal and thrash about, threatening to tip over the barrel, and the water would splash over the top into the fire to create stench and odor. Then the pig would be taken out and hung up, so one of the women could cut its throat and catch the blood in a large pan as it ran down over the snout and mouth like a bleeding nose, to use for blood pudding. Then the head would be cut completely off and boiled in a large pan inside the house to emit even more vile odors. Then the overcooked skull would be stripped of eatable parts and pressed into a large block as Head Cheese to be used for sandwiches and meal condiments. William was used to horrible sights, stenches and smells, but Mr. Richards' was much more intense and penetrating, maybe because he was a human. His head thrashed back and forth and belched out froth and phlegm as he fought for air and life. William felt like the same thing was occurring in his own mind, even though his life wasn't at risk.

Gordon stepped back farther. People streamed out of the surrounding houses; someone sprayed the flaming human torch, Mr. Richards, with water from a garden hose. Someone wrapped him in a blanket and rolled him along the ground. Mr. Richard's face and arms were burned to a black crust with cracks of crimson showing through. Most of his clothing had been burned off his body; all of his hair was gone, and his rubber boots were melted onto his feet and legs. Small, gentle fires burned almost casually on the rubber boots.

The window effect faded, and reality came rushing in.

My hair had been singed a little, but the hair on Gordon's head, his eyebrows, his eyelashes, his arm hair, and even the fine hair inside his nose were all gone. Mr. Richards' accident was tragic, but Gordon looked funny as hell; I couldn't help laughing. I laughed so hard, I fell to the ground holding my sides.

"Bill did it!" Gordon screamed as Dad came rushing from the dungeon, breathless from the exertion.

"Why the hell are you laughing?" Dad screamed. "Can't you see Mr. Richards is hurt really bad?"

I just kept laughing; I couldn't help it.

"How the hell could you do this, William?" Dad yelled as he held me at arm's length and shook me.

As my head flapped back and forth I shouted, "L-look, l-look a-at G-Gordon!"

Dad stopped shaking me for a moment and looked; and for just an instant, there was just a hint of a smile on his face. Then he dropped me and went to mingle with the crowd that surrounded Mr. Richards. None of them did anything—they just milled around watching him pitifully with looks of indecision and wonder on their faces. Finally, they wrapped the burned-beyond-recognition body that used to be Mr. Richards in a blanket––more to hold the overcooked morsel together than for any other reason––and loaded the bundle into the back of a pickup, which was driven away.

Gordon wasn't hurt badly. More than anything, he was embarrassed; and he looked really funny.

"You're such a horse's ass, William," Dad said, and slapped me on the back of my head. The blow sent me tumbling and made me see stars. Anger brought the lightning and the sulfur taste, which, by now, along with my conditioned hatred for Dad, had become a part of my psyche.

"Get to your room," he said in a stern voice.

I hated the arrogant, drunken ass.

The fireman said the fire had been caused by what they call a "flash" from the gasoline.

"A flash?" I thought. A flash burned all the little bastard's hair? Maybe that'd be a good name for Gordon. Yeah ... Flash. At that moment, Gordon's name changed in my mind to Flash Gordon, like the comic book space explorer, and, as time passed, it became just plain Flash.

His hair grew back, all except his right eyebrow, his right eyelash, and a little patch just above that. The doctor said he had received follicle damage there. But it fit nicely with the artificial part in his hair that had been caused when I was trying to drag the sheet of metal up into the tree house and it fell on his head.

Once again Gordon, or rather Flash now, was prohibited for his own safety from playing with me.

Chapter 15

Pat Condie lived right across the street from Aunt Helen's. He lived in a gray, asbestos-shingle-sided, two-story house. His father was, among other things, an airplane pilot—they had a lot of money and their house and garaged cars showed it. Pat was a few years my junior. He was born in a hospital, or I should say "she" was born in a hospital, because until she was around three years old, her name was Patricia and then it "popped out" and he began wearing boy's clothing and was called Patrick. We kids still called him Pat. He was a good kid, we all liked him, but the grown-ups stabbed him with sage looks, snickered, and made wisecracks. Hell, he couldn't help it; it wasn't his fault. It seemed unfair to give him hell for something he couldn't help.

Pat sort of idolized me, like my cousins Flash and Dale did. He stood across the street watching me as I salted suckers on the bridge—as if I was supposed to give him a clue how to act. Maybe he thought I'd want him to come over or something like that. He was the new singer in the Boy's Hallelujah Choir—a tenor, I think, if that's the one that sounds sort of squeaky and high-pitched. His parents are very proud about him being the youngest in the group.

Dad resented it. "The little morph ain't no better singer'n you, William, and he ain't as old neither——it's his dad's money that's got him in. I wish you would try to get in there but now with that kid there, you'll need to wait for a openin."

I just shrugged my shoulders and rationalized, why does anybody want to be in the choir, anyway? I'd about as soon go to church or to jail. But I had to admit, it would be sort of nice; still, what chance did I have as long as he was there? Anyway, I had better things to do. I was practicing to be the best spitter in the world. Aunt Helen had put a new driveway in front of her garage. I didn't know why she had a garage, since she didn't have a car, but it was there, and full of all her kids' junk.

I had marked off a starting place with crayons and, with my toe on the mark, I hocked up a sizable logy from deep in my throat and blew it out as far as I could. I stood watching as it twirled around, flying through the air and finally hitting the driveway with a splatter. I smiled. "A record!" I grabbed Dad's old measuring tape and pulled out the blade with the numbers on it.

"My god, it's 21-1/2 feet!" I yelled. It WAS a new record. "This one is farther than any other!"

It wasn't anything like Rodney Bird's 50 foot pissing distance when he stretched his foreskin over the end and blew it up like a balloon and then let it go, but 21-1/2 is pretty good for a spitter. I was always careful to be more than 50 feet away from Rodney when I pissed him off.

"What's all the noise?" Dad came out of the dungeon; my jubilation had awakened him.

After he saw what I had been doing and after I had cleaned it all up with the promise not to do it anymore, I went to my bridge. I had to sit on one side of my butt, because Dad had tried to convince me not to do this spitting stuff anymore by repeatedly kicking the other side of it.

The water was high today. It was the turn of Aunt Helen and Mrs. MacLean to water their Victory Gardens. The red stream surged and boiled as it made its way under my bridge to the gardens at the end of the lots.

My mind began to churn. "It might be sort of funny if I could get Pat to get his head down low enough so the water caught it." I smiled as I pondered this prank.

"Hey, Pat, come see the alligator," I yelled.

He came running like a trained puppy. "Where is it, Bill?"

"You have to get your head down really low to see it."

The dumb little shit did it.

"I can't see anything."

"You need to get way down; here, I'll hold your feet."

His head finally got low enough, and as I pushed him forward, the water caught it and pulled his upper body under the bridge. It's like catching a very large fish; it became hard to hold him. I became frightened; the sulfur and lighting shot around my body and filled my mouth. I didn't want him to be swept away and get lodged under one of the culverts and drown. I did have enough humanity to watch out for the younger kids, but my main concern was that if anything bad happened to him, the culprit would obviously be me. As Pat kicked and squirmed, my grip got weaker; he wasn't helping, and he yelled at the top of his lungs every time his head came up.

"What the…?" Dad shouted as he ran toward us. He pulled Pat out and laid him on the lawn on his stomach and started to rhythmically push on his midsection. He began sort of singing, as if he were saying a poem, "Out goes the water, in comes the air." Pat gasped and coughed out water, and then he began to breathe better.

"Someday yer goin to kill somebody and go ta jail, ya horse's ass!" Dad yelled.

"I didn't do nothin." I tried to look repentant, like I'd learned to do in church.

"Go to your room, William. And stay there until you learn not to be such a horse's ass," Dad demanded as he kicked my already-sore butt, but with the side of his foot this time. The solid kick lifted me off the ground; but mostly, it just hurt my pride.

Dad carried Pat across the street to his house; he always wanted to impress the neighbors. He didn't even let me tell him my side of the story.

I sat in my cubbyhole, silently cursing Dad and Pat through the lace curtain. "You're the horse's ass," I whispered.

Later, my sentence was amended without apology, and with a stern warning to stay out of trouble. I was released on my own recognizance to go out and play with Ellen, Pat, Flash, and Dale.

Chapter 16

The larger stream, the creek that fed the Victory Garden irrigation ditches, was Hell Fire Creek. There was some argument about how that creek had acquired its ungodly name. Some said it had religious roots, and some said the reason was anything but that. Hell Fire Creek was fed and controlled by an Army Corps of Engineers-built earthen dam, one of Roosevelt's New Deal projects. The Civilian Conservation Corps, or CCC boys mostly did it with hand labor and workhorses. The water was let out as needed to irrigate the Victory Gardens; a concept passed to us from England. The Victory Gardens concept was supported strongly by the first lady, Eleanor Roosevelt, but her first love and passion was for human rights. She was a niece of President Theodore Roosevelt.

Dad always said, "She's so dammed ugly, ya can't tell her face from her ass—and she married her cousin." She wasn't a beauty by any means, but I think Dad did exaggerate some. And she and Franklin were pretty distant relatives, for hell's sake. She was a closer relative of Teddy, the Rough Rider.

When the water came out of the spillway to be used for irrigation, it came as a torrential rush. It ran red, almost as red as blood. Everybody called it strawberry water. But there always was a trickle of clear water in Aunt Helen's and Mrs. MacLean's Victory Garden ditch. Trees and bushes grew along the banks of Hell Fire Creek and had a nice way of concealing the garbage and trash that floated in it and lined the banks of the stream. City crews cleaned it occasionally, but usually it was more or less left to fend for itself. It was a good place for children or young adolescents to spend time carrying out all sorts of marginal, and sometimes immoral, activities. Through the years, several children had drowned in the turbulent, churning water, usually during the spring run-off.

Tonight, a familiar form walked along the trash-laden banks; the same form that often walked the streets of the small, sleepy town at dusk and after dark. But tonight it had a shape draped over its shoulders, wrapped in a cloth covering. The ominous form struggled under the weight, and then moved on. It seemed to know where it was going. The shape across its shoulders seemingly had no will of its own; it wiggled and waggled with the steps of the struggling urchin. In its right hand, the form carried a bag of some sort; it seemed to be a fragile bag, similar to a heavy grocery bag with a bowling ball inside. The form swung the bag to and fro, as if it were playing a game. It obviously was in no hurry and stopped to rest frequently, leaning against anything available.

Suddenly, the stream began to run faster as the irrigation waters were released. The water rose and ran red as blood. The form rushed to escape the deluge, but it was too late. The swirling red water caught the rogue and pulled him under. The form surfaced in a moment, splashing and floundering about, and tried desperately to retrieve the two bundles, but seeing the futility, it struggled to the bank to cling to a tree branch. It clung momentarily, watching the lifeless shape and the bowling ball as they were carried out of sight by the raging torrent.

The form sat for a long while, looking at the rushing, red water and then slowly stood and cautiously made its way back toward the west side of town, and then, as if rethinking, turned and walked in a different direction.

Chapter 17

Some weeks later, Dad came home one evening uncharacteristically early and said, "That little boy you tried to drown is missing. They ain't seen him for days." He looked at me. "What the hell did you do?"

"Nothin'," I said.

To deal with the incident with Pat on the bridge and for other reasons Mom and Dad had made up, they thought I should do some work. To them, work seemed to be the best way to combat any sort of evil. My cross to bear was to be hired out as slave labor, weeding and thinning sugar beets in the big fields around Utah Lake, just west of Springtown. We kids would go there on occasion to catch the large carp that gorged on the human feces. All the towns upstream dumped their sewage into the lake, which had become a large septic tank over the years. It wasn't a great place to swim but there were huge carp, in the river and the lake. It was said there was a great risk of contracting polio by swimming in the contaminated water, but it was worth it to catch the carp, which could be used for things, such as missiles when they were thrown from a moving vehicle.

We were driven to the weeding job at the lake in the back of a large Chevrolet truck. Ellen was sent along to try to make some money but mostly, I thought, to keep an eye on me. This punishment was much worse than that little garden Mom had insisted that I weed in Aunt Helen's Victory Garden plot. I had tried to hide my shoes to keep from doing the thinning work, but Dad found some old rubber boots and said they would do—the ass.

I was becoming ill just thinking about the drudgery of thinning, during which I was to be a slave for the Johnson brothers. The fields were huge by any standards. Once we arrived, in no time at all Ellen was far down her row, well ahead of us other slaves. If she had been sent to keep an eye on me, she wasn't doing a very good job. I tried for a while to find a place to begin, but I was getting pretty ill, and just sat and watched the others. I could see Ellen and the other thinners almost out of sight down their long rows, their backs bent as they subjected themselves embarrassingly to the will of the Johnsons. Ellen was still well in front. This brought to mind what Lou Crandall, Dad's friend, had said one time about someone bent over in labor: "All I could see was elbows and assholes."

Finally, Mr. Johnson, the boss, fulfilled my desires and fired me for being lazy and unmotivated, because I had just sat on my ass watching the others, or wrote nasty poems in the dirt. If he was so damned smart, he should have called it insubordination, like they do in the army. Anyway, it was much nicer there in the shade while I waited for them to be done, and my lunch tasted good. I would have gone home, but it was a long way to walk in the heat. Despite all this, Mr. Johnson gave me twenty-five cents for thinning part of one row. That was eight cents more than the other kids got for an entire row. Dad had told me if a person works for a part of a day or hour, the boss is compelled to give them the entire hour or day's pay. Maybe that's what the extra pay was for, or maybe he just wanted to be rid of me. Well, the feeling was mutual.

After I ate most of my lunch, I noticed a small log across the ditch. I thought I might be able to practice some tightrope work, but before I could go to try it, the Orem Tram came along. It was pretty full of passengers. To give them a thrill, I unzipped my pants and took out my proboscis and waved it in their direction. I don't know if they saw, but it was fun to imagine—I knew I was big for my age.

I went to do my tightrope work, but about halfway across, I lost my balance and fell into the dry ditch below. It wasn't a long fall, but I landed right on my royal left arm. I knew it was broken; I turned over and tried to push myself up with my good hand. I touched something smooth and round––it felt like a bowling ball, a small bowling ball, so I held it up and looked. It was a skull. A human skull!

It looked just like the bleached-out skull and crossbones on a bottle of poison, or one of those mummies in the museum up in Salt Lake City. My fingers went inside the eyeholes and my thumb into the nose. I opened my mouth to scream but nothing came out––fear had stolen my voice. I dropped the white skull, and finally the scream made its way out of my mouth. I scrambled up the steep bank to run and tell Mr. Johnson and the thinners.

Dr. Orton examined my arm and said, "It's a green willow break. That's usually what royalty get." He laughed and winked at his nurse. He wrapped my arm clumsily with wet plaster- -of-Paris-coated gauze, getting more on the floor and table than he did on my arm. He said it wasn't very serious and that I just needed to keep the cast on for a few weeks and take it easy. I asked him to put on a couple of extra layers to make it look more broken. He laughed and did as I asked. I couldn't help but wonder if he had created Mrs. Phelps, the library's custodian, out of plaster of Paris. I imagined him molding her stoic face and expression, which made me smile.

Mom was waiting in the room outside and when we got home, she fixed bread and milk in a tall glass and sat with that all-knowing smile, sewing silently as I ate.

"I talked to Dr. Orton while you were in the room with his nurse getting ready to go home. He asked some questions about you. He said you were raving about being of royal blood—I guess you passed out after Mr. Johnson brought you in. And I found your shoes. They were pushed way back under your mattress. They sure were wet and muddy; I have no idea how they got so muddy or how they got there." She winked.

I held up my cast in response.

"And I found your funny books, too." She paused. "And your other unwholesome reading. Sort of nice how you keep it all in that little box that we used to keep under the card table. It was out on the bridge—you keep it so neat and tidy."

She seemed to have given up about the books. Maybe I was getting older, or maybe I had finally just worn her down.

Dad stumbled down the stairs, a smell of whiskey on his breath, and reeking of tobacco smoke. He stood for a long moment, reeling and blinking. "The little boy across the street's still missing. Seems like they should a found him by now," and he glared at me.

"I didn't do nothin'," I repeated, holding up my new cast to add drama.

"Probably find him drowned in the ditch somewhere. Rule's a-lookin' fer 'im."

Sulfur filled my mouth; lightning shot up my spine. If something happened to him, they would suspect me because of the bridge-alligator incident. I knew that's what Dad was thinking. And he would be no help. I didn't want to go to jail for life. I wished I hadn't tried to drown him. I knew I would be blamed. I wondered if the human skull I had found could be his.

Chapter 18

Rule Everett, Springtown's constable, had learned that most things have a way of curing or solving themselves if given a chance. He was prone to wait as long as possible to see if they would do just that before he acted. In addition to being the town constable, he was also the notary, and had verified death certificates when a doctor wasn't available. He had even performed marriages after learning that a ceremony wasn't necessary—you just had to get the marriage recorded at the Hall of Records. He'd conducted funerals, and even said opening or closing prayers at church in a pinch, even though he wasn't a very religious guy. He was an all-around good guy, although a bit of a stooge.

He moved about slowly and deliberately, as he tried to force his blank but friendly, steel-gray eyes to take on the look of law enforcement authority. His right hand sat almost continually on the butt of his holstered .38 caliber revolver, as if he were about to draw. Maybe it gave him confidence, or maybe it was just a nervous habit. He wore an official police cap even when indoors, possibly to hide the widow's peak that the years and heredity had placed there, but whenever he pushed back the cap, his vain pretence was revealed.

He had been the constable forever, it seemed. Lately, no one even ran in opposition to him. He had more or less inherited the job from his father, Mathew, who was a strong and respected guardian of the townspeople. It was more for that reason than for any other that Rule had secured and retained the job.

A few unfortunate incidents had blemished Mathew's career, but they weren't enough to remove his aura of heroic grandeur. For instance, there was the time James Henderson parked Mathew's police car on the tracks when he caught the idolized police chief inside his house and in bed with his wife. A train came along and totaled the vehicle. Mathew filed a stolen car report to hide his misbehaving. Another time, he took a black inmate who was being held as a witness in a plea bargain case to his home for sex, and his wife caught him. Somehow, he twisted it all to his advantage, and even his wife fell for the story. These incidents and others were all but forgotten, replaced by a sort of worship. It would not be an overstatement to say Mathew was held in the highest esteem, and after his death he became even more a saint than a scoundrel.

But Mathew was dead now and Rule was in charge, and he was probably all the law enforcement needed for Springtown, anyway.

The skull was identified by dental records as belonging to Pat, but because Rule was stumped, he filed the case away in the "unsolved murder" file.

Chapter 19

Fredric's Music Store in Springtown decided to sponsor free dancing for the kids, probably hoping that the parents would remember this "unselfish" gesture and buy all of their musical wares from them, which was not a bad idea. Ellen and I were enrolled, mostly because it was free and would give us shelter, as well as some relief from the library. Along with the dancing, there were also free metal taps; all we needed to do was have Dad slip our shoes onto his shoe last and tack them into place. It wasn't easy to get him away from his buddies at the Shame, but one way or another we got him to do the job.

The troupe met once a week in the back of the store on Main Street, right next to the Boyer Building, which had our library in the basement. A worn, hardwood floor lent itself perfectly to the taps battering it. An elevated stage at one end was for dance revues. I had high expectations for myself.

I was an exceptionally good tapper, obviously the best in the class with my right foot, which was how we learned the technique. Ellen and the other tappers were jealous. With Mom and the other mothers proudly watching, I tried unsuccessfully to hide my gleeful smile and sense of self-importance as I tapped. As we all moved along, with me in front, I bent at the waist, folded my arms or held them out, and clapped my hands during strategic steps to accent my obvious gift. Mom sat with Martha on her lap, both of them smiling with delight and encouraging me with soft polite claps and head nods. Ellen stared jealous daggers at me for being so good. That's what caught Gay's eye: the great dancing, and especially my right foot, flapping as if it had a right to do so. And the way she was watching me attracted me to her. Gay was beautiful. For both of us, it was love at first sight.

And then we switched to tapping with the left foot. Mine wouldn't do anything; it just lay on the floor like a fat lump, flipping a little bit, but nothing like the right one had done. Dancing lost its luster for me, as I had to just stand, watching, while the others danced with their left feet. They moved far away from me as the music played, "Swim little fishy all over the dam." Mom and Martha weren't looking at me or smiling anymore.

The teacher said, "William, just stand and clap in time when it's your left foot's turn," and everyone laughed.

I practiced alone on the dirt floor in the dungeon to try to get my left foot to behave, but it was no use––old lefty just wasn't the dancing type. I dropped out of dancing class, and Mom didn't object. My dancing career was over, but I still went to sit with Mom to watch Martha and Gay. She could tap great with either foot. When I wasn't with her, I was thinking about her. I was positive it was love, and it was a lot better than sitting on my bridge, salting suckers.

Mom said, "You're too young to know about real love; this is just puppy love. True love will come when you're older. It can withstand anything; you're just in love with being in love."

It was more than just puppy love, I was sure of it; but it turned out Mom was right. One day, while playing hopscotch on the sidewalk in front of Aunt Helen's, Gay coaxed her taw into the proper square and began hopping. Every time her foot hit the cement sidewalk, she farted. Instead of just stopping and losing her turn, she kept on hopping and farting. She didn't say, "Whoops" or act like it was somebody else, like Dad did; that might have been funny, and I might have admired that, but she just tried to act like nothing had happened at all. Well, she was no longer an angel. When I looked at her, I just saw her hopping and blowing off gas and worse than that, trying to ignore it. Our romance was over.

Shortly after this, I met Sharon, who lured me into a closet at Sunday school by exposing her bare crotch. We hit it off from the start. For our second date, if you want to call being together so young a date, we visited young Gayland Cook, to witness his pain and suffering. He had stepped on a rusty nail, and his dad hadn't taken the precaution of washing the wound generously with turpentine like Dad always did. Blood poisoning had infected his foot and leg.

I well knew the pain of a rusty nail in a board, because I had stepped on one behind Sheriff Rule Everett's house, and try as I would, it just wouldn't come off. Gingerly, I had walked home with the nail and board attached to my foot.

"My God, William, don't be such a horse's ass. I stepped on lots a nails, and I never made no fuss," Dad had said as I lay on the floor while he twisted and pulled above me. Finally, the nail came out, and he doused the bleeding wound generously with turpentine.

"It's important ta kill them damned germs," he said, smiling gleefully.

Gayland lay writhing in obvious pain as the dangerous red line made its way up his leg toward his heart. A heavy rawhide shoestring was tightly tied around the leg just above the red line in an attempt to stop its advance. His face, pale and drawn, told of his torment, as his purplish-red, swollen foot lay soaking in a deep pan of too-hot water that had turned a reddish-brown from tobacco leaves and drainage from the infection.

"If that red line gets to his heart, he's dead," I whispered to Sharon.

Gayland turned his head back and forth, trying desperately to find some comfort in the soft stroking of his mother's hands on his ruffled, auburn hair. Mr. Cook, beside himself with worry, poured more hot water into the already too-hot, steaming vessel.

Sharon thought it was a great date. "Nice to do something different," she said. She seemed to be my sort of person; she liked unusual things.

Several days later, the Cook boy died. The funeral was held in their house. The whole neighborhood turned out, everyone dressed in their Sunday best. Even Mom and Dad came, and after a short, religious service, the homemade, pine-box coffin was lifted onto the back of Mr. Cook's old Model A pickup and taken to the cemetery. After a few words were said about what a great kid he was, the casket was lowered into the hole and filled with the freshly dug, sandy soil. Mr. Cook cried hysterically. He stood at a distance, so his howling wouldn't interrupt the services, but we could still hear him. As we left, we could see him standing over the mound of dirt that covered the coffin, looking up into the sky as if he were directing obscenities toward God and heaven for their ruthlessness.

He was never the same after that. He blamed God; but he blamed himself even more. He thought he should have found a way to save his son, maybe tied the shoelace sooner or tighter or maybe hotter water or more tobacco? He walked the streets alone at night. Everyone was afraid of him; he was usually drunk, and then he began to open his long overcoat and expose himself when he walked past anyone, even children.

Sometimes he stood naked in front of the large picture window in his living room. Sharon and I often walked past to witness his disgusting, obscene actions.

Mrs. Cook just sat in her rocker, with a shawl around her shoulders and a blanket over her legs, staring blankly through the window. Everybody in town knew about the Cooks and accepted them; anyone else would have been arrested for indecent exposure, but Mr. Cook got away with it, I guess because everybody understood that his son's death had driven him over the edge. I decided to always have a shoelace with me, to react quickly in case that terrible and fatal red line began making its way to my heart.

Sharon was a wonderful companion, but Mom was right again; our love ended late one afternoon when her father caught us in an awkward position in their basement, and set his big German shepherd on me. I was lucky to reach the safety of the dungeon, with the big dog growling and pulling at my pant leg as I ascended the concrete steps, pulled the door shut between us, and cowered in the basement below. Sharon was never as appealing to me after that, especially when I remembered what her father had promised to do to my privates if he ever caught me with her like that again. We were about to break up anyway; she wore her brother's shorts as underwear.

Then, partly to drown my sorrow about loves lost, I had a short affair with one of Rule Everett's daughters, Ruby. When I say "affair," it was just being naked and feeling each other's privates and rubbing our body parts together. Dad discovered us in the tall weeds along the ditch bank on his way to the Shame one day, and he physically, ruthlessly, and convincingly informed me that it was perverted and obscene to have a romance before marriage, especially with a blood relative or a neighbor.

He yelled, "Ya horse's ass, get yer ass into yer room and ask God fer forgiveness and stay in there and think about what you've done. Don't come out 'til you kin act like a adult!"

And then, as if it were an afterthought, he turned when he was walking away and growled, "And go wash yer hands and face."

A few days later, I was paroled and sat on my bridge trying to forgive Dad for being such an ass. I was holding a homemade boat by a long string; it skipped from side to side in the swift, turbulent strawberry water. A girl walked past on the sidewalk out front. I straightened up and reached for a sucker to scare her with. Even at that distance, our eyes met and held for a long time. I couldn't look away. I couldn't say anything. I couldn't even make my feet run over to scare her with the sucker in hand.

She was beautiful. She smiled and waved. I sat paralyzed. I couldn't move. I couldn't wave; I couldn't even find a smile. She stood smiling at me for a long time, as if she wanted me to speak, and then she just shrugged, turned and walked past, and out of my life. I felt a loss; it was a feeling that I had never known, like my heart was breaking. I ran to the sidewalk, but she was gone—vanished like a dream on waking.

"Maybe I will never see her again. I should have done something," I told myself. I tried to think about something else, but it was no use––I just couldn't get the picture out of my mind's eye of her looking at me and smiling.

After that she was always in my thoughts, almost like she had become a part of me.

Chapter 20

Seeing that girl caused me to begin thinking about certain things. I knew I needed to please God if I wanted to see her again—I had to muster up some good faith. I knew I wanted to be with her forever, like in Dad's church. It would be like a miracle—a wonderful miracle. Deciding to change my life for the better, I began searching for the truth that Dad talked about. I began going to Sunday school and listened carefully while the teacher read from the lesson books. Religion was indeed a mystery.

I sat there almost bored to tears. Thankfully, some relief was provided when we were allowed to stand and perform a little exercise. "Heads, shoulders, knees and toes," we robots proclaimed in monotonous unison as we touched those parts of our bodies. We concluded with, "Jesus sees, Jesus knows," and then sang a song about being sunbeams for Jesus.

Jesus? Sunbeams? What the hell? It seemed to me that the teacher was bent on filling our minds with as much useless garbage as we would accept, including the secrets of recognizing a true or false angel by touch or by willingness to shake hands. What a bunch of crap. In an effort to draw us even deeper into this fantasy, the teacher, Mrs. Crenshaw, promised to give something really, really nice to anyone with perfect attendance who completed all the assignments. Not just a book or some worthless thing, but something really, really nice.

And then I was transformed. Faith and righteousness began welling up inside me. I could feel it; it was wonderful to be so powerful, so all-knowing. I had little doubt now that believing anything was possible. The talk about moving mountains or walking on water with enough unyielding faith was exciting and made sense. Now I had faith––a lot of faith. But the mountains just sat there stubbornly in place; they didn't budge.

"Maybe it just takes a little time to work, or maybe they need to check with God?" I thought.

I was excited and didn't want to waste time while waiting for the mountains to get their answer. I decided to walk on water, and had no doubt that I could do it. As I stepped off the pier onto the calm canal surface, I was a mountain of faith. My faith held me there about as long as it took for my head to follow my feet into the rapture of the deep. I sank like a rock. Thanks to the saintly Mr. Bradley, who happened to be walking right behind me, I was pulled out like a drowning rat and, like the Good Samaritan helping the Jew, or whomever he helped, he carried me home to Mom and Dad, who wanted to know what the hell I was doing.

"I was trying to walk on water, like Jesus." I tried to make my expression the holiest I could muster.

"My God, William, get real," Dad said, and Mom rolled her eyes.

"Oh ye of little faith," I whispered.

The promise of a great surprise from Mrs. Crenshaw for being good and attentive in Sunday school turned out to be nothing. She probably just forgot about it, but I didn't forget. I prayed to God for a way to get even––the proper punishment for someone so evil, so corrupt. In books and documents, I searched for an array of powerful and mystical rituals, for a proper curse and punishment. I finally asked God to kill her and put her in hell. And then, for even more vengeance, I made a little doll, following my Voodoo book's instructions, and stuck pins into its stomach to inflict pain and suffering.

That night she was rushed to the hospital: her appendix had ruptured. My power was amazing! I couldn't believe the power of God and me! But at the same time, it scared the hell out of me; it must mean I was indeed of royal blood. I decided I had to be more careful and use my power only for good and righteous purposes. My faith had been strengthened to the point that I knew beyond any doubt I was special. I was able to do amazing things, like Jesus and Moses had done. Through their model and example, I felt the need to forgive the misguided, evil teacher, and I did. I also asked God to forgive her and spare her life. He answered my prayers, and she was spared, and came home in a few days to recuperate. In a few weeks, she was back teaching Sunday school, telling us about moving mountains, walking on water, how to identify true angels and such.

"All you need is faith," she said. "You can do anything—move anything—if you have enough faith." But she was more sincere now; she had learned her lesson. We had both learned our lessons.

Nevertheless, as I thought about all this, I realized my newfound faith had been damaged. I had wanted to believe, but I had seen that the mountains didn't move, and I couldn't walk on water, not even with my massive faith. What's more, I was sure that Mrs. Crenshaw's ruptured appendix had come from black magic, Voodoo, not from anything God did. I hated God for being so cruel and dishonest, but I did have some respect for him and for myself for allowing Miss Crenshaw to live. And I guess I could forgive him, too—he at least probably helped to save her.

I wondered about the other things Mom and Dad talked about, all the religious stuff. I wondered if those were just hollow promises, too, as this had been. Was it even possible to find the answers to life's questions in scriptures supposedly written by God and the prophets? "Maybe, instead of saying, 'Written by the prophets for the people,' it should be, 'Written by the prophets, for profit from the people,'" I thought. That made me laugh, and I felt a little better.

Chapter 21

A few months later, Ellen had me all excited about going to school––kindergarten seemed like it might be fun. She had brainwashed me, as she always did whenever I let my guard down. She had been going to school for about a year and had taken to it like a duck takes to water. She was smart and could remember things, too. I would have a lot to live up to. I felt ready––even anxious––to begin my "scholastic quest" as Lou Crandall, Dad's friend at the Dirty Shame Saloon, called it. And with September just around the corner, the school thing was going to happen, and soon. Maybe that would give my life some purpose and direction; I could only hope. Hell, it would be better to sit in class than to sit here on my bridge, day after day, with no one to talk to. Maybe Mom was right—we all have the right to feel sorry for ourselves once in a while, so long as it doesn't last too long or get into us too deeply. But I did intend to let my self-pity last, at least for a while. I shook my head, from both relief and boredom, and then bent my body to salt a sucker and watch the little black bugger squirm and roll in obvious pain. I smiled. It was indeed a magnificent feeling.

When I got so bored I was ready to scream, I went to look at my bug and butterfly collection, a large piece of cardboard with all sorts of butterflies and bugs on it. My favorite was the Monarch, because of its beautifully designed, black-and-yellow wings. A straight pin was stuck through its head into the cardboard.

It wasn't as inhumane as it might seem; I always put ether or chloroform on them to knock them out before the pin went in. Mom put me onto using that stuff, when she warned me about being on guard in the movie theatres, because she had heard about some guy who had come in and held a cloth soaked in chloroform over the mouth and nose of a little girl and had then carried her out unnoticed. I remember asking, does chloroform kill you? Mom had answered, no; it's what they do to you after they get you to their den.

Anyway, gathering these worthless insects caused me to learn some stuff. For example, I discovered that Monarchs migrate to Mexico every year, but the butterflies don't live long enough to make the whole trip, so they lay eggs that hatch and the offspring continue the journey. They piggyback in this way for several generations—in other words, the great-great-grandchild of the butterfly that begins the trip is the butterfly that finishes it.

And then there was the conifer seed bug, the bug that ...

"Whatchadoin'?"

I looked up, and couldn't believe my eyes; it was the girl, the one I had seen standing on the sidewalk looking at me and smiling. My voice caught in my throat again, just like before; words wouldn't come out. I had to say something; I simply couldn't let her go again.

At that moment, I passed through a window; I was watching William and the girl.

> "Saltin' sucker," William finally stuttered, not timidly, but as if he were unconcerned and macho.
> "What does that do?" the girl asked.
> William couldn't believe it; she wasn't just a dream. She wasn't just in his imagination.
> "Watch," he said, as reached for a new sucker, which he dropped onto the wooden surface of the bridge, sprinkling

it with salt.

"Eww, that looks sickening," *she squealed as she peeked through her fingers at the small, black eel squirming and twisting in its death ritual.*

William smiled in the way boys smile when they're trying to gross out a girl.

"Do it again," *she said.*

The window effect faded.

"What's your name?" I asked, my words coming easier now.

"Victoria—Victoria Leigh MacLean, but Daddy calls me his little princess or sometimes Victoria Leigh. What's yours?"

I paused for effect. "William—William Robert Jones III, but my dad calls me a horse's ass or sometime a troll," and we laughed. I gave her a friendly tug on her elbow. Immediately, we were best friends.

"Where da ya live?" I asked, still trying to be macho.

"Next door with Gramma. You know, Mrs. MacLean."

"Yeah. How come ya live with yer Gramma?"

"Just do," she says. "Daddy goes to Scotland a lot, and Mom just sends me here when he's gone. Sometimes she comes too—it just depends."

"Is he gone now?"

"No, we usually come here for the summer. We live in Santa Cruz, California, but we like it better in Utah––not so many people, not so busy."

"I never saw you before."

"They keep a pretty tight rope on me. I'm watched pretty close."

"Got a boyfriend?"

"Daddy won't let me. He says I'm too young. Besides, he wants me to marry a prince."

"Mom thinks I'm a prince," I said, with a mischievous smile.

"Your name sounds like you are of royal blood."

"Yeah," I replied. "There is some evidence that I am."

"Where do you live?" she asked.

"Right there." I pointed to Aunt Helen's large red brick house with its well-cared-for lawn and gardens with the weather-beaten, old wood-lapped washhouse to the side, under the large, spreading box elder tree.

"That's a nice house," she said. "I like brick. I don't think you're a horse's ... she stopped and said, "behind. I think you're nice." She smiled shyly for almost saying "ass."

"I think you're nice, too," I said, and felt my face turning red.

Anyway, we did live at Aunt Helen's place; I just didn't tell her it was in the basement of the washhouse. And I didn't tell about me actually being a kind of troll or that Dad was a drunk, either.

Chapter 22

Victoria's father, James H. MacLean, Jr., was a tall man. He was thin, with beautifully groomed black hair and a thin black moustache. He had a firm and determined--almost foreboding-- look, and was proper in every sense. He was very worried about what people might think. He was always talking about being of noble lineage that could be traced in origin to Scotland. An only child, he was used to being the center of attention. Because he was full of nervous energy, he couldn't stay still for long and usually made up little meaningless things to do. He had a slight stutter whenever he got anxious or excited.

He didn't seem to be crazy about me, or the fact that Victoria liked me, but she assured me, "He just doesn't like new people, William." She squeezed my hand and smiled to reassure me. I squeezed back. She made me melt. I guessed I was wrapped around her little finger.

Sophie, Victoria's mother, was a real lady; but that attribute had been acquired after she married James H. She had been born and raised on the other side of the tracks, the poorer part of Springtown, by her aunt, a career welfare waif who had since passed on.

Now Mrs. MacLean (James H.'s mother) was her family, and

they were almost as close as mother and daughter. In fact, Sophie was more a daughter to Mrs. MacLean than James H. was a son, even if biology didn't bear that out. Sophie gave her husband his way on just about everything, but she wanted her daughter to see the value in people––not just in their status or wealth, but rather in who and what they really were. Because of this, she insisted that Victoria be allowed to visit Mrs. MacLean in our little rundown corner of the world. James was almost forced to submit, if he wanted to keep peace in the family; and with this small concession he was able to get his way on almost everything else. Sophie seemed to truly like me, almost as much as her husband decidedly did not.

James H.'s business took him to Scotland often, and when he went, Sophie and Victoria would get into their new Cadillac and drive to Mrs. MacLean's to visit until he returned. They also had an understanding that Victoria would be allowed to spend summer in Springtown during school vacation. But James H. didn't like this new development. He and Sophie sometimes drove Victoria to Springtown, stayed a few days, and then left to do whatever they did when they were alone. On occasion, they went to Scotland together; Victoria had never gone there. She said she would rather be with her grandmother; and now, since we met, with me.

When Victoria was here without her father, I spent most of my time with her, sometimes at Mrs. MacLean's place, doing all sorts of things. Whenever James H. was here, we had to be more discreet. Mrs. MacLean had fine china and real silverware like Aunt Helen did; it seemed to make the food taste better. They even had indoor toilets that flushed when you pulled a chain. Their house smelled clean and was scented with all sorts of pleasant fragrances, like Aunt Helen's. Our dungeon was filled with the odor of mold and Dad's farts. The rest of us, I suspect, blamed Dad for our disgusting expulsions of methane. A continuous presence was the chamber pot.

As for Victoria, I didn't need to look any further; this certainly wasn't puppy love, it was the real thing. My entire body tingled whenever I was around her——hell, it tingled whenever I thought about her. Victoria's long, golden hair flowed casually down in back over her slim body. Her long legs were always slightly olive-tanned and her nails were always painted and clean, even her toenails. Only things of wonder and happiness marked the soft shape of her beautiful face and accented her sparking green eyes. She wasn't capable of any vengeance or malicious anger. She always accepted the world, and me, without reserve.

She was perfect; she didn't stink, and if she occasionally had any odor, it was wonderful. She didn't talk to other boys. When we played hopscotch, she didn't fart, and she wore girl's underwear. And when I farted and looked around and said whoops, she blushed and giggled. She was feminine and sophisticated in every sense. Little wonder that I quickly forgot about the heartbreak and sorrow of my other romances and my dismal life in general and fell deeply in love with her. My life had become a wonder of delights.

We searched for four-leaf clovers along the banks of the irrigation ditch. I showed her how to make a chain from the stems of dandelions, and she showed me how to tell if someone likes butter by holding a buttercup up close to the person's face and looking for a yellow reflection. We walked hand-in-hand to Boyer's Grocery Store and shared a bottle of Royal Crown Cola, unconcerned about the backwash, or maybe even relishing it. Slowly, we made our way back across Wheeler's vacant lot, stopping often to encourage each other with gentle words and loving actions and to explore our newfound friendship, as we lay concealed from view in the tall, fragrant grass.

We languished nude and unashamed in the old swimming hole in Hell Fire Creek by the power plant, mostly hidden under the drooping branches of a weeping willow tree, amid garbage lining the banks and floating past; our fresh new love transformed it all into a tropical paradise. We touched and giggled as young friends, not as lovers. We enjoyed the sweet perfume of summer and of each other, and in the bitter cold of winter, we found enjoyment wherever we were. When we weren't together, those pleasant things reminded me of her. It seemed that even when we were apart, we were together. She was becoming a part of me.

Victoria and I often met in the old sheds at the end of Aunt Helen's gardens when James H. was there. Of course, we met other places as well——it was exciting and fun. We found ways to delight in our rendezvous and escapades.

"Daddy doesn't know that your name is William Robert Jones III," she said one day, giggling.

"Yeah, I know."

"Tell him, William; maybe he'll realize you're royalty."

"Okay, I'll tell him next time I see him. Maybe I'll bow and curtsy, too, like I learned at dance class. That ought to prove it," I smiled.

"You're so funny!"

"Yeah, like a chapped ass."

"Be nice, William. This is our castle, this shed."

"Yes, our first castle," I repeated sarcastically. But secretly I was pleased that she knew I was of royal blood.

What hurt was that her father disliked me so intensely. It wasn't fair.

"Tell me a story," she said.

"I don't know, I'm not very good." But really, I knew I was pretty good.

"Please, at least try," she pleaded, her green eyes almost in tears.

"Hell, who could say no to those beautiful green eyes? Victoria, I'm going to call the story, 'Vomit and Diarrhea.'"

"Oh, William, those are naughty words."

"What makes them naughty?"

"They just are. Everybody knows that."

"Well, make believe you've never heard them before."

"That's hard to do."

"Think about it: vomit seems manly and has a nice ring to it, while diarrhea is really a beautiful name, a name for a princess, if you don't associate it with anything else. Just pretend they're new words and aren't naughty. Hell, they're just words; how can a word be naughty?"

She laughed. "Okay, but the names of body functions are disgusting. I'll try, but don't blame me if I have to laugh."

"Just remember, in my story they're simply names of people."

I began ...

"Vomit and Diarrhea—A Love Story."

"He-he," she laughed. "It's too funny."

"Victoria, I can't tell you if you keep laughing. Wait until it's all done, and then laugh."

"Okay, I'll try." She held her hand over her mouth to try to hide that impish grin.

I went on ...

> *A poor woodcutter and his wife moved to the enchanted forest, hoping that life would be better for themselves and their five children, but to their dismay they became even poorer than before. The woodcutter finally found a job working for a wealthy landlord, building a large dam. When he wasn't cutting wood he worked at the dam, but even though he worked day and night he was unable to earn enough to properly care for his family. With a heavy heart, he finally hired out his eldest son, Vomit, to the village tavern for a few pennies a night, to serve drinks and clean the floors after the drunks had been dismissed and the tavern closed. Vomit was the eldest son but hardly old enough to be subjected to the obscene and violent things that went on in the tavern late at night.*
>
> *Vomit had placed an old blanket on the ground at one side of the family home so he wouldn't disturb the others in the tiny cabin when he returned from the tavern early in the morning. His makeshift bed was made up of lace curtains and velvet drapes that had been discarded by the*

wealthy landlord. His mother had told him, "Vomit, this is the kind of luxury royalty sleep in. You are indeed of royal blood."

Sleep was slow in coming to Vomit, because of exhaustion and the unaccustomed bulkiness of his clothing and shoes that he wore against the bitter cold of the night. He twisted and turned, but finally slumber erased his discomfort and he fell into a deep sleep. It was a profound sleep, filled with dreams of a beautiful princess who someday would kiss him and take him away in her magical carriage from this dingy life, but the dreams were marred by the presence of evil villains.

The insistent crowing of a rooster awakened him. The princess, coach, and villains vanished and he arose to milk the cows and to complete his daily chores. He finished and entered the house, being careful not to awaken his family. Only then did he feel worthy of a crust of his mother's homemade bread.

His older sister, who was certainly his parents' favorite, sometimes saved some of her food for him to eat. She regularly did thoughtful things for him, but Vomit knew it was only to reinforce their parents' love of her, not because she cared for him. The unselfish peasant boy decided to travel to a distant city in search of a better life for his family and himself. His mother was ailing, and he promised her that he would soon return with a beautiful magic carriage, which would carry them all away from this dismal forest and to the kingdom that he was convinced was his birthright.

After bringing in a supply of wood for his mother to use for cooking and to take the chill out of the crisp morning air, he set out on his quest. He had saved three pence to use in pursuit of the enchanted carriage. The road was long and dusty. He plodded on with only the welfare of his family in *mind. Vomit was wearing his best clothes, as he was intent on impressing whoever his benefactor was to be.*

He received many attractive offers from would-be employers to abandon his valiant quest, but he resisted them all. One day, a handsome coach rumbled toward him and stopped, the dust caught up by its wheels settling a thin film on everything. The coachman offered the boy a ride for one pence. The boy accepted without hesitation. He got in the coach and seated himself beside a beautiful young woman. They greeted each other briefly, and then the coach lurched ahead, carrying Vomit and his newfound princess, Diarrhea, toward an uncertain destiny.

"That's really good, William," said Victoria, her voice taking on a kind of squeal of excitement, "except for their names." She always squealed when she was excited or really happy.

"Ya think so?"

"Yes, I do." She moved close. "But I think you should change their names to William and Victoria."

I placed my arm around her shoulders. She moved closer still, and I could feel her breathing. I felt her heart beating so close, as if it belonged to me, as if it were in my own chest.

"Our hearts are beating as one," I said, smiling.

"Let's promise to always be together."

"Honest Injun." We locked little fingers to seal the bargain.

My life had become wonderful beyond belief. But she was leaving, and I couldn't bear to think about it. Her father was coming to take her back to California, and I would be going to school.

"I'll wait for you, even if it takes forever," we said as one.

We made a pact that it was all right to have other friends, but we weren't allowed to love them. I knew I would miss her sorely, but I had to admit that I was excited about kindergarten. If nothing else, it would get me out of the dungeon and off my bridge for a while.

Chapter 23

After a little time and my best efforts to make this kindergarten stuff work out, I began to think it was maybe not my bailiwick. The first day, I got embarrassingly spanked for misbehaving during naptime. I ripped Harold Philip's shirt off over a misunderstanding, and ruined Beth Anne's dress trying to force her to dance with me.

The teacher had said, "Dance with whomever you choose." She should have been the one who got chewed out.

And I guess the sword incident didn't help, either. We had a bully, Bruce Singleton. I hated that bastard; we all did. One thing almost every boy had was a miniature sword. They were easy to make; just get one of your mother's large darning needles and wrap copper wire around it to make a handle. Then show it off to other guys and gals. It looked like a deadly weapon, sort of like King Arthur and his knights. But no one ever got hurt, until Bruce began to bully me. The bell had already rung and class was in session, but some kids always had trouble getting to class on time. Bruce had just finished bullying and humiliating me and had turned around. "Okay," I thought, "you son of a bitch," and I shoved the sword into the cheek of his ass, clear up to the handle—maybe two and a half inches. When he turned around, the expression on his face was about murder; painful murder. I quickly turned and ran into the far corner of Mrs. Witting's class, where I stood looking at Bruce as all of Mrs. Witting's class looked at me. It was quiet as hell; nobody knew what was going on. Finally, Bruce left and I meekly slinked out of the class.

Bruce caught me after school and promised to beat the shit out of me as he held my collar and most of my shirt in his oversized hand. Then he laughed. "That was pretty brave to do," he said. After that, he never bullied me again and he became as good a friend as I was able to acquire.

As time went by, I began to catch on to the ways of school. "You just have to stick up for yourself and kiss ass," I thought. But I wasn't very good at the latter. Given this poor start to my scholastic career, it seemed nip-and-tuck if I was cut out for school. When I was forced to stay after school, I found that I could just sit and outwait the teacher, who was always ready to go home before I was. Hell, it was a lot nicer in school than in the dungeon or the library.

One year, not for the first time Mom and Dad sat facing a teacher—well, at least Mom; it was the first time for Dad—with me as the center of attention, my head hung low as I tried to assume an "I'm sorry as hell" pose. Mrs. Kauffman's long speech began with, "William is so smart. His IQ is in the superior range—high in the superior range, but that's his potential IQ. His functional IQ is barely measurable; and he's incorrigible!"

I looked up. "They're encouraged. The teacher said they're encouraged." The words spilled out of my mouth against my will. My eyes opened wide was my face glowed in expectation of a look of approval not only from Mrs. Kauffman but also from Mom and Dad, as they all showered me with praise. But there was no look of approval; my dad's look was one of semi-controlled rage.

"I've tried to give William extra attention, Mrs. Kaufman continued, "but he just doesn't seem to have any interest in learning." Her eyes were directed down, as if she were searching the floor for answers.

I wasn't listening anymore. I was used to my parents not

supporting me, but now Mrs. Kauffman, whom I had thought was my buddy, was betraying me. I tried to look inside myself, to get away from it all. I began watching Mom and Dad talking to Mrs. Kauffman, with William in the middle, being ridiculed unmercifully. It was unbearable; I went even further away—I seemed to pass through and inside the comfort of the window. It seemed so rude and crude to belittle me so. And this meeting wasn't even necessary; it had all been because of a stupid misunderstanding.

> The problem had begun on May Day, which was a big event until we got into that Cold War thing with Russia. May Day was their biggest event, about like our Christmas. To get even with them for all of the imaginary stuff we disagreed about, we stopped recognizing May Day. Funny, we had taken their concept of Christmas and enhanced that—and now we demonized their May Day. But back before this rift, one of the best-looking girls in town would be elected May Queen and would circle the May Pole with her subjects in tow, each holding a long ribbon attached to the tip of the Maypole. The queen and her subjects would weave in and out, wrapping the pretty ribbons onto the pole as they carefully braided them into place. Then we would all stand around the braided pole and recite the Pledge of Allegiance (this was before the "under God" thing was added) and salute with one arm held out. This was the way it was done until Adolf Hitler and Germany adopted that very salute, and then our salute was changed to the hand over the heart.
>
> William didn't think it was fair. "They always have a girl for queen," he thought. "What about equal rights? Why can't we have a boy for queen this year? Women are gaining in all aspects of civil rights. Why can't men and boys also benefit from this new open-mindedness?"
>
> There was great excitement as they began their

campaign. They decided that Harvey Wendell would be their nominee. Harvey was bigger than William but had about the same color hair and blue eyes as he did, and Harvey was tall, a little taller than William; quite large for a boy of his age. Through the years, William had always been the biggest, or at least the second biggest in any of his classes, and the strongest—always really strong for his age. Harvey was thought to be a little slow mentally but a good guy and most important, he would accept the nomination. William suspected he wasn't as slow as he acted and knew he had a great deal of initiative and that he was clever. In fact, he had made William look a little slow in Mrs. Kauffman's English class a few months earlier.

William never got too overexcited about anything and in keeping with this attitude he had again failed to prepare for the class assignment of coming up with some sort of story. They were supposed to write a paper and then read it in class. It was also permissible to memorize their work and in this way not even be required to hand a paper in. Harvey sat right in front of William, who sat on the last seat in the row. As they took their seats that day, Harvey turned to ask William what he was going to say when it was his turn.

"The title of my story is, The Golden Watch," he said.

His dad told the story of how his great-grandfather had somehow acquired a valuable gold watch. It had been passed down to the oldest boy for generations." Someday it will be yours, William," his dad said. He kept it in his sock drawer. William had discovered it while trying to find a suitable pair of socks to wear, and longed for the day that the watch would be his. He told Harvey about the watch and that he might just make up some stuff to add some interest and then told him briefly about those things, to show off his intellect.

The class stood, one by one, to read or recite their

stories. When it was Harvey's turn, he turned to William and smiled. He smiled back as he silently rehearsed his golden watch story to tell the class next. Harvey began, "I have decided to talk about something my father will give me in a few years. I've entitled my story, The Golden Watch. It's a story that began with my great-grandfather."

Then he told the story about William's watch, the same way William had told it to him. William sat and glared at him for being so clever and made himself a promise. "I will get even, you lump of lard."

"I'm unprepared," he told the teacher after Harvey finished.

"Stay after school, William."

When Harvey sat down he let out a loud fart. Everyone turned; Harvey turned, too, and shook his head as disgust almost dripped from his face.

"William, go out into the hall for a few minutes," the teacher said.

"That retarded ass," William thought.

Now he was about to get even with him with the queen thing, but Harvey seemed to be delighted about it. After a hard-fought campaign, he won by a landslide. The girls had two candidates; their vote had been split.

"What a great example of the democratic system in action," William thought. The fact that the election had given us an impressive queen couldn't be argued. He imagined bathing in his revenge as Harvey, the new queen, frolicked around the Maypole in some sort of a toga as he and his subjects wove the ribbons. It made him snicker; it was delightful. Harvey would be so embarrassed. His revenge would be sweet. Plus, there would most certainly be a monetary or at least an academic reward for the students, mostly William, who had been so involved and set such an example of the democratic process in action.

"Two birds with one stone," he smiled. "Mom was right; you can get two birds with one stone. Life is great. Things are starting to turn around. Mom and Dad will be proud."

He was about to forgive Harvey for everything and congratulate him for his landslide win when the teachers called a special assembly. Then, just like the communists they were supposed to hate, they impeached the students' queen and, in a very un-democratic way, illegally installed their own.

William did have some satisfaction; Harvey seemed to be crushed that he didn't get to be queen.

"How does it feel, Harvey, to be disappointed?"

He just smiled and said, "Great! I loved it."

"That bastard," William muttered. "I'd like to kill him."

Marlene Bills and Joan Fillmore were the other two candidates, and because Marlene had been in second place, although far behind Harvey, she was unfairly declared the Queen of May.

The moving of chairs and the louder talking made the window effect fade and I was back with Mom, Dad, and Mrs. Kauffman. Mom was apologizing to Mrs. Kauffman and promised her that I wouldn't misbehave again. Dad had an appointment for a job interview and had gone. Mom and I walked home, her face getting paler; she always seemed so sad and forlorn. She was talking as we walked but it was almost as if I wasn't there, like she was just talking to herself. She seemed to be pleading rather than relating, "I have to get out of the dungeon. I'm not happy living like a rat."

"Me either, Mom," I said, but she didn't hear me.

And now because of my actions, I was only allowed to lie in my cubbyhole, do my chores, go to school, the library, church, and for only necessary meals and toilet needs. "Hell, is that the best they can do?" I thought, as I usually did whenever this lame rehabilitation strategy was administered. "Nothing changes. This is all I'm ever allowed to do, even if I'm good."

Chapter 24

The floor of the furnace room is getting cold; I wish they would start the fire. "If they do, they will see me and I will be able to get out," I whisper to myself again. My mind involuntarily goes back over what got me here in the first place and I begin reliving events that seem long ago, but in reality occurred only days or even hours earlier.

It's as if I am going back in time on my mission of discovery, but strangely, it's almost like I am riding in a car with one foot hanging out, just in case I need to make a quick getaway. I still have the maturity, intelligence, and experience gained as an adult, even if I am living my past.

I think about making these impressions into a poem or prose. "Hell, Mrs. Kauffman said you can get away with murder in poetry, so why not try to get away with murder?" I smile.

I have no idea when Alex will be back, or if he will be back. But I intend to have some answers for him when and if and when he does. Suddenly, I know what I have to do. I'm going to skip forward to my later years in grammar school. I can't imagine anything during my earlier school years that will impress Alex.

Maybe if I skip a few years of uneventful school, something spectacular will surface to reinforce my belief that it was indeed either Alex or Oscar who was the killer. If I can't find anything, I can always come back and look again.

"Yeah," I think, "unless I freeze or starve to death first."

I wait for the moment that will allow me to be free, and I dissolve into the wonder and beauty of the window.

Chapter 25

Near the end of elementary school, things hadn't gotten much better. I was still being picked on. It seemed to always be harder for me than for anyone else. On the first day of my time-traveling sabbatical from the furnace room, I found myself still struggling with the school curriculum. I would need to make some gigantic leaps and bounds if I intended to graduate and move along to the next grade. I needed help.

It didn't help my quest for learning very much that I was still seeing Victoria and we were going through life as we had been for years now. She was planning to be in Springtown soon—I couldn't wait. I was planning a new place for us to hang out so we wouldn't become bored and disenchanted with our relationship. My affair with Victoria had continued whenever she came to Springtown and from afar, we were still extraordinarily good friends. We had "played nasty" a little bit but had never had sex. But my hormones were running wild.

"William," my teacher, Mrs. Sutton, seemed to coo, "Is there anything I can do that will help you with school?"

I shrugged.

"I could tutor you, if you want."

I didn't exactly know what tutor meant. I shrugged again.

"I know. My lawn needs to be mowed; I'll pay you twenty-five cents. Do you have a lawn mower?"

"A customer is a customer," I thought, " because now mowing law had become my means of existence, the way of making my livelihood.

I did have a mower but I would need to bring it over here, "No."

"I have one you can use."

"I smiled. "Okay—but what about tutoring?"

"You can mow, and then I'll tutor you."

"Why not? I can use the money."

"Come over Saturday and we'll work it all out."

On Saturday, after the lawn was mowed and the trimming was all done, Mrs. Sutton handed me fifty cents. She said, "You did such a good job, I'm giving you a tip. You look hot; come in and I'll give you a glass of lemonade, too."

I was thirsty and the drink tasted good.

"Do you want to take a shower?"

"I don't know. I'm going to have a bath tonight; it's Saturday. I just wash in the old root beer washtub."

She smiled. "It will cool you off. Have you ever had a shower?"

"No," I admitted with a shy, sort of crooked smile, like I'd seen movie stars and celebrities do.

"Come here, take a look."

I followed her into the bathroom.

"Stand right here," she said as she guided me next to her.

I obeyed. She put her hand on my back, leaned over from the waist, and turned on the water. Her robe came open a little bit. I could see the edges of her breasts; they looked firm and soft; I was becoming excited.

"It's a nice shower, isn't it?" She smiled softly but kept leaning over for just a moment longer. Or maybe I imagined that she did.

"Yes," I stammered. My eyes refused to leave her open robe, and the edges of her breast.

"I'm going to the living room to correct papers," she said. "Have a nice shower. Come and tell me goodbye when you're done. We can go over some of your back homework if you want me to tutor you."

As the water pelted me, I fondled myself from habit. And then I seemed to pass through a window, to a time when Mrs. Sutton was with me, and I was dressed. I watched William and Mrs. Sutton...

> William begins unbuttoning his shirt, and lets it fall to the floor; then he pulls off his shoes and socks. He gets the water just right, as he unbuttons his pants. He doesn't wear shorts, his family can't afford them—his pants fall to the floor. The shower stall is great. It's made of pink tile. "Feminine, but nice," he muses. The water softly massages his body. He begins washing with the bar of soap. His family doesn't have soap—they can't afford it.
>
> "I could stay in here all day!" he yells to Mrs. Sutton.
>
> The shower curtain opens. "What did you say, William?" Mrs. Sutton has taken off all of her clothes and is standing beside the shower. He is speechless. Her body is void of the telltale signs of age that show in her face. There are no wrinkles or sags. She bounces slightly as she moves her firm body lightly into the shower stall next to him. She pushes her body close and begins washing him. He stands as if hypnotized and allows her to do as she wishes.
>
> "Looks like nature was good to you; you're big," she says.
>
> "Yeah, I guess," he agrees. "My dad said it's the Jones curse."
>
> "Let's dry off, William," she says. "I have something to show you."
>
> "Yeah? I hope it's not homework."
>
> She winks, and then dries him and takes him to the bed.
>
> "Want to suck this?" she asks, but moves her breast

away when he tries. "You're too eager," she laughs. "Okay, you can have it now."

"Yeah!"

After a while, she says, "Okay, you've had enough; get on top of me."

He obeys. She moans and rocks the bed, like she has gone crazy. He does his best to stay on.

"Okay," she finally says. "I'm finished with you. You can go now." And she pushes him off.

"That felt good."

"I like young men," she says. "I always get it my way with them."

"Anytime."

The window effect faded.

I dried on the large soft white towel and dressed. I felt awful and guilty. I didn't think Victoria would like this. I'm sure she wouldn't do anything like this. "I better not tell her."

Mrs. Sutton went over most of my old school work and told me a lot of useful stuff. It looked pretty easy if you just thought about it. After a little while, she began putting the papers and books away.

"I think you're just lazy, William. You really catch on quickly."

I had to smile. "It looks like we're done."

"Goodbye," Mrs. Sutton said. "Thanks for mowing the lawn; spend the fifty-cents wisely. I'll see you at school."

"Goodbye, Mrs. Sutton." I smiled somewhat sheepishly. I knew why I felt so embarrassed. I thought "tutoring," especially in the shower, was a lot more exciting than mowing a lawn.

Chapter 26

It was a dark and stormy night––the lightning flashed and the wind molded the rain into bullets that painfully pelted the bodies of the nearly indistinguishable figures slinking and stumbling along the underbrush close to the road. The indistinct forms walked in the opposite direction of the duplex at the west end of town—one of them was the same form that had often walked along this abandoned stretch late at night. It seemed to be in no hurry, as it used a long stick to tease and prod a mummy-like figure walking before it. A rope tied around the neck of the "gimp" also bound its hands. The "master" held the rope tight, to have total control as it cruelly pulled the rope and nudged the gimp with the stick. The gimp moaned and whimpered its anguish, which was lost in the violence of the stormy night.

It was late, and there was no traffic on the streets, but suddenly, headlights loomed and flooded the area. The master looked nervously here and there, and then quickly but cautiously guided his quarry off the road and onto a darker, more concealed trail. He stopped frequently to inspect the captive. Finally the trail turned to meet and follow another trail along the bank of Hell Fire Creek, and then detoured along one of the Victory Garden irrigation ditches. Silently now, the duo continued followed this path. A lightning flash revealed in its flickering light a vague and dismal image—a large structure. Everything seemed to scream doom and foreboding. It was the decrepit and disintegrating barn of the Cook family.

The master stood, breathing hard for a moment, and looked nervously around. Then, clumsily and cautiously, as it struggled to retain its footing in the slurry, it prodded the captive toward the silhouetted asylum. The walking was unsteady and treacherous, and several times the gimp lost footing and fell. The master stopped and impatiently poked it with the stick until it rose and floundered on. Any sounds or cries were lost in the noise of the angry storm. The large weeping willow tree waved its limbs violently to and fro, as if in protest of this inhuman act. The duo stopped for a moment, as if to heed nature's warning, but then moved on. They stopped again as they stood before the entrance of the sanctuary .

The door made an unnatural creak, as old doors do, when it was forced partially open from the bottom. The slave crouched, moaned and then went inside. The master followed. The wind howled through the trees, seemingly in protest, and the raindrops joined in a melody of protest that seemed insufficient to erase a feeling of indecency that penetrated the night.

Hours later, a solitary form appeared in the darkened doorway. With some difficulty, it made its way under the damaged door, looking this way and that. Satisfied that it was alone and unobserved, it retraced its earlier steps along the smaller stream to Hell Fire Creek, and then vanished into the night, headed toward the west side of Springtown along the banks of the creek. The storm slowly began to lose its fury, and as a prelude to the coming dawn, the first sliver of morning light crested the eastern sky above the mountaintops. Then, as if having satisfactorily demonstrated its dominance, the storm suddenly stopped, the storm clouds fled, and the sky was filled with soft clouds, from which fluffy flakes of white began to fall.

Chapter 27

There had been an early and unexpected snowfall a few days before, and a fresh white cover still lay on the ground. Everything looked pure and fresh. Victoria and her mother had finally come to visit Mrs. MacLean; her father was in Scotland. They had asked me to have Thanksgiving dinner with them, but Dad said, "Stay home, ya horse's ass. Ya's s'posed ta eat with yer family on special days."

"We havin' venison and potatoes again?" I asked defiantly.

"Better'n nothing," Dad said, trying to disguise his glee with a thick, patronizing tone.

The venison and potatoes weren't so bad––what bothered me was listening to that long, boring blessing; and then having to get up and say what you were thankful for. Hell, I had a difficult time being thankful for anything, unless I would have been brave enough to tell them about Victoria.

The Shame was closed on Thanksgiving and Christmas, but Dad had taken precautions about certain things. He had plenty of spirits stored out in Aunt Helen's barn.

He kept going out and coming back in. His eyes were getting glazed, and his nose redder and redder, as always happened when he binged.

"William," Victoria said when we met after dinner, "I know you don't live in the red brick house; I know you live in the washhouse."

I was stunned. I didn't think she would like me if she knew; and she was probably hurt that I'd sort of lied to her all these years.

"Well, what of it?" I said.

She gave a soft smile. "Nothing of it. It's okay––I don't love you because you're rich. I just love you because you're you."

Suddenly, tears filled my eyes; I hugged her so she wouldn't see me cry.

We had planned to use Aunt Helen's barn, but now, with Dad coming and going for his booze, that was out of the question. But there were no animals in the Cooks' barn anymore. It seemed to sit mournfully, in silence, with its back toward Hell Fire Creek. It was decaying, just like Gayland and the Cooks were doing. The seasons had baked the old building with sunshine, pelted it with rain, and covered it with snow. If used at all, it was just for occasional rendezvous of friends or lovers, as we were planning to do. Large cottonwood trees and small bushes surrounded the barn and encased it, so nobody could see who came or went.

We stopped, mostly hidden by the tall grass and brush, and waited, to make sure that the coast was clear. Someone was coming out—it was Mr. Cook. He forced the broken door open then stopped to look around, as if he were nervous, or doing something that he shouldn't be doing. Then he turned to fasten the hasp that secured the door. He stopped again to look around, then checked the zipper on his bib overalls, zipped it up, and shuffled through the skiff of snow toward his house.

We watched him go out of sight, and then we walked past the door a couple of steps, in Mr. Cook's snowy footprints. That way, if someone was following us, they wouldn't see our tracks go directly into the barn. The footprints were melting fast; it was warming up quickly. I held the bottom of the door out far enough to allow Victoria to squeeze inside, and then she did the same for me. It was dark and we stood close together in the shelter of each other's arms and waited for our eyes to become accustomed to the din. Then we began climbing the old ladder into the loft above.

Victoria stopped. "What's that?" she whispered.

I could smell it, too. "Something's dead."

There was something in the far corner of the loft. We walked closer, trying to see. "I'm afraid."

"M-me t-too," I stammered.

"I'm not going to touch it."

"Me neither."

There was a small door at the far end of the loft, where the hay used to be brought in when the barn was healthy. I walked over, unlocked it and pushed. Light flooded in. We blinked against the contrast.

Victoria screamed, "IT'S SOMEBODY IN A BAG! SOMEBODY'S DEAD!" And she screamed again.

It *was* a dead body. It was horrible. I couldn't look at it––it seemed distant and unreal; I felt myself begin passing through a window. I stood watching William and Victoria.

> *The face was black and puffed. The eyes opened and bulged almost out of the sockets. Bloody phlegm ran out of its mouth and nose. The tongue was swollen too large for the mouth, and grotesquely hung out. A black string of some kind, maybe a shoelace, was tied around its neck. The body was bloated and pushed against the buttons of the blood-soiled white shirt, like a wild animal trying to escape captivity. The pants were down, with one leg completely out. An old duffel bag, stained with blood, lay on the floor next to it.*

The window effect faded ... we stood as if frozen in time. Then, suddenly and together, we turned and ran. I led the way down the ladder and out the door, and Victoria was right on my heels. We ran to tell the sheriff, Rule Everett.

Chapter 28

The black, puffy, unrecognizable body turned out to be that of Harvey Wendell, our unfairly impeached May Queen in Mrs. Kauffman's class. He was older now, as we all were, but it was still Harvey. Well, it wasn't really Harvey in this condition, if you know what I mean, but you could still see that it was Harvey. He was one of the Hallelujah Choir singers, a neighbor from down the street, just past Rule's place. And now he was dead. I couldn't believe it––he was too young to be dead. I felt guilty about having wished him dead––or threatening to kill him over the watch story. I was so sorry.

"He had the voice of an angel, William," Dad said with his alcohol-induced slur. "You'd be smart ta get in the choir. Ya have a good voice, a gift of God––ya should share it with others and not be so damned selfish by hiding it under a bushel."

I was pretty sure "hiding it under a bushel" was some sort of Bible or church talk.

"Hey Dad, will you help me put wheels on my Me box?"

"My God, son, I put taps on yer shoes and I tends ya; what the hell more kin I do?"

"Please, Dad."

He stood looking at me for a while. "Got the wheels?"

"Yeah. Mr. Holley over where you used to work gave me some."

"He's a big ass—a horse's ass!"

"Yeah, I know," I agreed, trying to get more flies with sugar than vinegar.

"Why do you call it your Me box?"

I showed him where it said, "A part of Me" on the sides.

"Looks like somebody just gypped that 'e' in."

Dad put the wheels on and then I could pull it and didn't even need the wagon, but I still used it sometimes, nonetheless. The Me box was pretty light, even with the books and wheels, so I could easily carry it for short distances by holding onto the little slots in the ends, if I had to. It was about as long as from a man's knee to the bottom of his foot, as wide as from a man's hip to his knee, and as high as from a man's nipple to his hip. It was made from thin but very strong wood, reinforced at all of the corners, of course these are just SWAG measurements-- or Scientific Wild-Ass Guesses. The four wheels, which were from an old Radio Flier wagon that was mostly junk, made the Me box look and pull just like a real wagon, but without the handle in front to pull it with. I could sit on it and even ride to coast downhill if I chose to. If I wanted to pull it, I had to tie a rope through one of the cutout holes designed to put your hand in to lift it. I had always taken the Me box with me a lot, but now with the wheels, I took it virtually everywhere.

Chapter 29

Dad insisted that I sit with our family at Harvey's funeral. The only good thing was we were right in front of Victoria and her grandmother. I kept turning around to smile at my girl, and Dad kept flipping my head with his middle finger. When he clasped his hands together, in prayer or such, I could see four tiny red marks on the back of the right hand, which were the signs of my revenge when I stabbed my dinner fork into it after the old fart flipped my head on a long-ago Thanksgiving day. His hand bled profusely, and of course I was the proverbial horse's ass. I was surprised that he had the courage or the lapse of memory to flip me again.

The casket lid was kept closed. The mortician said, with that phony, sad demeanor of his trade, "Sorry, I couldn't do too much with him." It was a nice casket, all wood and brass. It looked like it had cost a pretty penny. I think his parents were rich––Harvey's paternal uncle was a famous artist who made bronze sculptures and exotic paintings. He was fat, like Harvey. The service lasted a long time, with lots of singing and people crying and saying what a great kid Harvey had been. Well, he had been a great kid––except for the cheating and always getting the best of me. But I had about forgiven him, and was pretty sure he was heaven-bound.

Harvey's Mom was distraught. Her eyes were red from crying

and her rubbing them. She had tried to cover it all up with makeup, but it hadn't worked very well. She looked ridiculous; not as bad as Harvey when he was in the sack in the barn, but maybe a distant relative of that look. Harvey's Dad had red eyes, too, but he seemed more intent on keeping Mrs. Wendell from going off the deep end than on worrying much about himself. Who could blame either of them? To lose a child is probably about the worst thing ever.

After the ceremony, and after we had Harvey planted—even before the grave was all filled in—Rule collected the usual suspects inside the chapel. We filled only one side of the front pew. Our brave and stoic protector solemnly took his place at the pulpit, where the mortician and the speaking mourners had stood only minutes before, and as he turned his head back and forth slowly, he surveyed his captive audience and then, as menacingly as he was able, began his inquest.

"Looks like young Harvey was strangled either before or after he was abused—strangled with this shoelace," he said, trying to fill his voice with as much feeling and authority as he could muster.

He stood less-than-magnificently before us, trying unsuccessfully to emulate his father's natural sheriff-like countenance. He held a long, heavy, black string clumsily in one hand and a duffel bag, also clumsily, in the other, as he attempted to pause for effect.

"I'll bet," he paused again for effect, almost comically, "he was carried here alive in this duffel bag and then molested both before and after he was killed by some sick son of a bitch. Some sick son of a bitch done this, is my bet."

And then, in his feudal, theatrical way, he slowly and purposefully moved his head from side-to-side in feigned and clumsy disgust.

"Some sick son of a bitch?" I thought. "Great deductive reasoning, Rule."

When he continued, it sounded like he was campaigning in earnest. "I wrapped up the Stanze case almost single-handed, a few years ago, and you can bet yer butt I'll wrap this one up, too."

His father, Matthew, used to say "butt," and curse mildly when he was solving a case, and now Rule was trying to emulate another of his father's attributes. He *had* wrapped up the Stanze case, but what the hell, anybody could have solved that one. A kid had fallen through the ice and drowned. His big brother, Oscar, had tried to save him––and when he couldn't, he just went crazy. Hell, what was there to solve? Rule hadn't had an actual case before or since that one. But election time was just around the corner, and he was trying to make the most of anything he could get his hands on, to use as campaign material. But this was not even necessary, because nobody ever ran against him.

Victoria and I repeated what we had told Rule when we ran to report Harvey's death. We talked about seeing Mr. Cook leaving the barn, zipping up his pants, and about him exposing himself through his front window. Victoria and I had walked past his window on occasion to see his disgusting actions, just as Sharon and I used to do—a lot of people did.

"That son of a bitch has finally cracked." Rule smiled like he thought a good cop would smile.

"He's pretty sick," I agreed.

Then he began talking to me, as if I were an adult. "The only tracks going in were his, yern, and Victoria's. I don't think you or Victoria did it, did you?"

"No sir, we didn't," we said in unison. This eruption of sincerity was enough to convince Rule.

Mostly, because it happened in Mr. Cook's barn, and because Mr. Cook acted so weird, and because Victoria and I had seen him coming out just before we discovered the body, Mr. Cook was picked up, questioned again, and then charged with the heinous murder and put in jail. That happened more because there was no one else to blame than for any reason to do with logic or discovery.

"Jesus, what a sleuth," I thought of Rule.

It looked like Mr. Cook was going to either fry or take a bullet to atone for shedding innocent blood. According to Dad, these were the ways executions were arranged in Utah. It was some sort of a religious repenting or forgiving sort of thing that would give the perpetrator a shot at getting into at least the lowest glory of heaven. Well—that and praying, and pumping in a lot of money, paid in a combination of different tithes.

Chapter 30

Oscar Stanze, the conductor for both the Hallelujah and regular church choirs, lived with his younger brother, Alex, on the other side of Springtown in a duplex. His mother had left it to them when she passed on. It was on the west side of the tracks, in the poorer section of town. It was in the same area where Victoria's "other" grandmother had lived. The dwelling and yard of the duplex were well-maintained.

Oscar's hulking frame could be seen often during the night, walking aimlessly along the streets and the banks of Hell Fire Creek, somewhat like a lost soul. Quite often Alex accompanied him. There were rumors that Oscar and Alex were homosexual, but nobody really understood much about what that was. That theory, at least concerning Oscar, was mostly discounted because he physically seemed so heterosexual; he looked and acted like a construction worker or football player.

The word "homosexual," just like "seduce," "pregnant," and "lesbian," and lots of others simply weren't used to describe anybody. Hell, I thought lesbians were people from Lesbos or Lesvos Greece that mystic island in the Aegean Sea. You weren't even supposed to think those words, let alone say them. Such suspicions about people were conveyed instead by a look––how do you say it––a sage look? Anyway, that was how you let others know what you were thinking.

Oscar was a large, robust man with rusty brown hair receding and thinning on top. He wore wire-rimmed glasses that didn't fit and slid down on his wide, pock-covered nose. He was always pushing them back into place. Sallow, piercing, deep-set eyes sat behind pink-tinted bifocal glasses. His bold gaze was cause for most people to look away. Overly nice, he was able to charm most adults and children alike. His teeth were a dingy color with gold wires that held an assortment of bridges in place. He stood close when he talked, belching out vile fumes and fine spray as he tried to impress listeners with his mechanical efforts to form unusual and exotic words, while stressing proper syllables and adding body language for emphasis. He was for the most part self-centered and as phony as a three-dollar bill. He had a quick temper, and when it surfaced, he usually caught himself and laughed it off in a joking manner—he obviously struggled to defuse the anger.

The middle finger of his left hand was missing, caused by a farm accident when he was young, he said. It had been pulled off so close to his hand that the index and ring finger had moved over to take up the room where the middle finger had been, until now it looked like there had always been only three fingers there. He had a joke, or I guess it was a joke: "It's easy for me to order three fingers of whiskey now." He laughed and held up the damaged hand. But he didn't drink––at least not in public.

Dad was the only one who thought the joke was funny––I guess because of his frequent acquaintance with ordering whiskey.

Oscar didn't have a wife or any kids, which tended to support the rumors of him being a homo. He spent all his free time in church work and the Boys' Hallelujah Choir. He was generous with his money and often took all of the singers with him in his Chevrolet Suburban for ice cream and other treats.

Alex lived in the other side of the duplex. He was shy and reclusive, extremely self-centered, and looked to his big brother as a buffer against the world. Everything about him seemed to point to the fact that he was homosexual. He looked, acted, and dressed like a girl. He even wore his dark, black hair long and curled. And to top it all off, he had the "limp-wrist syndrome" that homosexuals are supposed to all have. He was nice-looking and meticulous in his dress and style. All of this added to the suspicion of him being gay and also took some of the suspicion away from Oscar.

Others, especially the ultra-religious, shunned Alex on the grounds that God hates homosexuals. They thought homosexuality was a disease that could be cured with prayer and rituals––and then forgiven, again, through ritual and repentance. In Utah, a law prohibited homosexuality. "Jesus," I thought. "How can it be illegal to just be something? That's like having it illegal to be born black, or with a cleft palate, or to be ugly, or wear a green shirt. Well, not exactly with the green shirt; you usually have a choice of shirt color, unless your mother is overly imposing—which some people think is the very cause of homosexuality."

Even though Alex played the piano and organ in church, it was obvious he was an outcast. He was shunned not only by the religious but also by society in general. If he had friends at all, it was just for an occasional, late-night rendezvous.

Another brother was almost forgotten by everyone. His name was Craig, and he was a no-good drunkard who had seldom been home. In his young manhood, he spent most of his time, and the money he was able to steal from his mother's welfare checks, at the Dirty Shame Saloon. But some time ago he had taken his share of the inheritance from his mother's death and left Springtown. He did come back on occasion for quick visits, during which he stayed with his brothers, coming and going during the darkness of evening or early morning.

Dad's opinion of Craig was that he was "a drunken, stupid, ungrateful horse's ass. I wou'ent let my kids be around that ass; he'd kill 'em."

Rule had tried to include Craig as a suspect in the Stanze

drowning, but it was so obviously an accident that he finally gave up. But Rule continued to milk the case for all it was worth, keeping it open for months longer than it should have been.

The drowning incident had happened when Oscar took the fourth and youngest brother, Andrew, ice-skating on the pond behind their duplex. His mother was alive then and was watching them through the picture window, enjoying her sons at play on the newly frozen ice. Andrew's brain had been damaged at birth by cerebral palsy, but physically he had grown straight and strong. He just needed to be watched and guided as an adolescent might. He had never mastered the art of proper bathroom protocol and still wore diapers but was usually able to change them himself.

Oscar had gone inside, for one reason or another, and left young Andy for just a few moments. While he was gone, Andrew had gone to the middle where the ice was thin and had broken through. When Oscar came back out, Andrew was splashing and flailing wildly, trying to pull himself out of that wet, black hole. Oscar grabbed a rope, tied one end to a walnut tree and the other end around his waist, and raced to the rescue. As he neared the hole, the ice gave way under his weight and as he fell, he hit the struggling Andrew with an elbow and knocked him out. Oscar tried to dive deeper to rescue him, but the rope held him back.

The fire department finally arrived and pulled Oscar out by the rope. It took four of them to hold him from diving back into the freezing water after Andrew. But finally, as they watched, Andrew's pale lifeless body floated to the surface. Hours of respiration attempts and warming failed to revive him.

Oscar's mother tried to help, too. Coatless, she flailed about as she ran here and there, getting in the way more than helping. The overexertion and excitement were too much for her heart, and she grabbed her chest and fell into the snow—something else for the firemen to contend with. They failed to revive her, too.

It was too much for Oscar, and he sort of flipped out. Well, he didn't just flip out; he went crazier than a bedbug. He had to be hauled away in a padded wagon by four men in white coats. His eyes looked wild and crazy. For a long time they kept him in the big white asylum on the hill. Only recently had he returned from a year of counseling over the drowning incident; he looked weak and pale. He hadn't lost much if any weight but now had a sickly look about him, an almost incandescent, dull-yellowish appearance. But he was getting out more now, doing more and more each day, and getting more and more color in his face.

Oscar's main job was court bailiff, and Alex was his assistant. Their responsibilities were to keep order in the court sessions, transport prisoners from one place to another, lock prisoners in their cells and bring food and water to them. They also performed suicide watch and just about anything else the judge or Rule asked them to do. Alex had worked hard to keep Oscar's job at the courthouse open for him, but the jail had suffered immensely with only Alex there.

The two choirs, the Hallelujah Choir and the church choir (of which Dad was a part, when he wasn't looking for work,) had suffered as well. A less proficient brother of the church, Brother Tasker, had filled in with the church choir as well as the Hallelujah Choir. And now, with Oscar back, Alex was anxious to go back to just playing the organ and Brother Tasker to just sitting in first chair in the church choir and singing, and letting someone else run the choirs.

Brother Tasker made me sick; he was a jerk who cared nothing for anyone but himself. He loved and hated little boys; I could attest to that. He was always rubbing up against the young choir members and feeling them in inappropriate places. He didn't look gay, but he was a pedophile. I didn't like thinking back about Brother Tasker—I wanted to forget. My experience with him was embarrassing and demeaning. But it happened a while ago, and now it really just seemed like a dream—a very bad dream.

It began one day after choir practice, when Mr. Tasker was filling in for Oscar with the choir. With Dad and Oscar pushing to get me into the choir, I filled in on occasion when one of the members was sick or unable to make it. We had all stayed late, trying to get all the alleluias right while holding our heads in the proper way.

Mr. Tasker asked me if I wanted a ride home. It was late and pretty cold—I said okay. He had a wife—a pudgy, cheerful little thing—and they had about six kids. After we got into the car, he asked if I wanted an ice cream cone.

"Hell, yes." I said.

"William—God doesn't like us to cuss."

"Yeah, I know. I'll try to remember."

Dairy Queen was just closing, and after we got our cones and were driving away, the lights went out. We sat behind Fredric's Music Store eating our ice-cream cones. The music store was closed, too, and it was pretty dark.

"William, you're a good singer. You could be great with a little help," he said. "I would be happy to help you. He put his hand on my leg in a casual, friendly manner as we talked. "I could meet you at the church and give you some private lessons if you wanted."

His hand moved up to my crotch. At the time it felt good—I became aroused.

"I always like to help people—God likes us to do that," and his hand slowly and deliberately moved to my erect penis. I didn't want to let him do it, I felt so sick. But it also felt good, and I was afraid not to, because of his position in the choir. But it was more than that—it just felt too dammed good too stop.

"Do you know you are a good-looking young boy, William?" he said as he unzipped my fly.

As he held me in his hand, he began moving it up and down slowly. My face felt hot. His hand felt soft and warm. He leaned over toward me a little bit. "You have a tremendous penis for a young man—God has blessed you. And then he leaned even farther and allowed my erection to go into his mouth. My cone fell to the floorboards as he moved up and down. We were both groaning and moving. I guess I didn't think about what he was doing—or what I was doing either. And then, suddenly, I was finished—and immediately, I felt sick and dirty.

"You are really wet, William. Here, let me clean you with my handkerchief." He ran his tongue over his lips, like he was getting the ice cream off. "Then maybe you will return the favor?" He had his pants unzipped and his erection was sticking out. It was disgusting.

The lightning shot up my spine and deposited sulfur on the roof of my mouth.

"Shit! I'm not going to do anything like that, you creepy old fart." I felt so dirty and useless. I didn't think I would ever feel good about anything again.

I pushed open the door and zipped up my pants as I ran all the way home, past Grant Elementary, past the Fourth Ward Church, and past the old ball field where the horses and cows grazed during off season. I could feel the wetness inside my pants—it was disconcerting. I didn't talk to anyone as I descended the stairs to the dungeon—I went directly to my cubbyhole and climbed inside my bed with my clothes on.

I knew I would never be free from this self-loathing—why did that old fart even do that? I felt so dirty that I had enjoyed it and hadn't stopped him. He didn't care what he did to kids.

But for one reason or the other, which had much to do with coercion, it happened a few more times after that. That and the time I spent with Alex and Oscar not really knowing what they might do to me, was almost too much for me to comprehend or handle. I knew the two brothers, Alex and Oscar were gay, and I also suspected that Oscar tries to be my big brother, but rather than having my feelings or welfare paramount, he sought to pacify himself to deal with the persistent guilt for the death of his brother Andrew, which makes me nervous.

William isn't conscience of it, but he both likes and fears Oscar, but he mostly just fears Alex, which further complicates his views of religion, morality, and tolerance."

Chapter 31

Oscar was almost better now, but still needed counseling twice a week. Color was returning to his flabby cheeks, and he was beginning to look better, but not totally well. The pale, yellow translucent quality hadn't completely gone away. With the inheritance that his brother, Craig, had taken, he had purchased a bar and grill establishment in rural Montana. It was just northwest of Missoula along Highway 93 and just outside the somewhat rowdy little town of Rowdy. Craig seemed to be turning over a new leaf. He had gone into rehab for alcoholism and was doing pretty well. But owning a bar in rugged Montana might not have been his wisest choice—this would really test his resolve.

The bar was rundown, but in both the town and the bar, Craig could see something appealing. When he asked the lady who owned the bar how much she wanted for it, she said, "...a hundert bucks and you take over the mortgages." Craig didn't even ask how much the mortgage was, he just declared, "Done." They shook hands and drove into Missoula to legalize their deal at the courthouse on Broadway Street.

With a lot of elbow grease and quite a few dollars, the place took on a certain crusty glow, which was attractive to the local cowboy and logger types thereabouts. And because the previous owner had told him how a black bear had broken in and caused a great deal of damage and that this had been the main reason for her being willing to sell for such a low price, Craig had a professional-looking sign painted that boasted, "The Black Bear Inn."

He featured salted peanuts in the shell in miniature milking buckets sitting on the bar for customers to munch, hoping it would make them thirsty and buy more drinks. And he put signs up telling the patrons to throw the shells on the floor—it looked rustic and made the dancing easier. He hired the toughest bartenders and cooks he could find to add to that atmosphere. He began compiling a small fortune, and bought a new Ford pickup and a nice house on the outskirts of Missoula, and always dressed himself in the finest Western attire.

Chapter 32

Dad loved to sing, and would sometimes even miss the Shame to practice or sing in the Church Choir. His high-pitched, shrill, eardrum-shattering tenor voice, which could have passed for a woman's voice, could be heard distinctly above all the others. He had petitioned Oscar for years to be in the choral group and had finally been accepted on the condition that he would attend practice and repent of his wicked transgressions (namely the Dirty Shame), stop drinking coffee, and stop smoking. Since that day, Dad began to seriously encourage me to join the Hallelujah Choir, more vigorously than he ever had. It was as if he wanted me to follow in his footsteps. So I guess way down deep, he had some feelings for me. Hell, he didn't need to prod me; I would have killed to get into the Hallelujah Choir. I figured I would maybe have a serious chance to get in if I got to know Oscar better, even in spite of the personal danger of doing that, because of the homosexual thing.

Dad sat in the choir section, in the back row, at the right-hand side and just behind the organ, where Alex customarily showed off his musical talent. Dad wore his usual attire: scuffed shoes, wrinkled and too-small, dark choir suit, so stained it could seemingly be boiled in a soup kettle to make a tasty Irish stew. He sat in First Seat, which he had refused to relinquish to Mr. Tasker. Dad held his head high and his neck in a sort of arch as his eyes followed the hymnal that he held high, reading a song he already knew by heart, trying to impress God with his humility and the congregation with his shrill tenor voice—and his ability to hold a note that rang out solo after all the other singers had stopped. He smiled proudly, as if to tell the congregation, "I have enjoyed delivering this beautiful, short stanza as much as you undoubtedly have enjoyed hearing it."

I bowed my head––not in reverence, but in embarrassment.

Mom sat with the other choir widows on the front row, all of them wearing their Sunday best and appearing almost like young girls in love for the first time, admiring their harmonic husbands who were unselfishly performing so gallantly in the name of religion, God, and salvation. Following the closing prayer, and after Mom and Dad had said goodbye to and blessed almost all the other members and had found each other, they went to "offer me up" to Oscar and his exclusive singing group, the Hallelujah Choir.

I was excited and pleased beyond words.

Afterwards, Dad didn't say anything right away. He waited until we were back in the dungeon, and then maybe to add some drama, he let me go to bed and almost get to sleep. Then he opened the curtain of my cubbyhole. "William, yer in! Oscar had a openin'," he said to me through the darkness. I could tell he was smiling. He held my foot in a tight grip, like it would reflect his good character and God would be pleased by the father-son contact. His hand trembled, and he struck a match and held it quickly to the end of his homemade cigarette. In the flash of light, his face looked ashen-white; it made him look evil and sick. But it made me feel proud and even gave me a warm feeling that he had gone to bat for me.

"Just one won't do no harm." His voice trembled. He wanted to get to the Shame for his accustomed medication. He was fighting that, as well as the cigarette habit, and I guess I was also proud of him for this feeble effort. He was going to go to the Shame, all right, but first he wanted to savor the moment that I had joined him in his music career. He was paying homage to his beloved music and how this was reflected in his religion and by his new closeness to God. He wanted to pass that on to me, his oldest son; something Abraham might have been inclined to do as he passed on the Commandments or pleased God with the willing sacrifice of a living son, Isaac.

"Good things happen when we live under the protection and comfort o' the church," Dad mumbled. He was being holy again. He was beginning to tremble now quite severely. "Son, playing nasty with a girl is a unforgivable sin, and playing nasty by yourself is bad too, but not as bad." He was raving.

"Why are you telling me this, Dad?"

He disregarded my question as if it were so insignificant that it didn't even warrant a response. When he talked like this it usually meant that he was going to further entwine me in the mysteries of his baffling religion, without apology, as if his babbling were a gift through him from God.

After Dad had gone, Mom came in with a hot potato wrapped in a cloth to put at my feet for warmth. "I'm proud that you got the part in the choir."

I smiled at her in the darkness. "Dad acted like he really wanted me to do well, huh?"

I imagined her smiling in the way she did when she told me new and revealing things. "William, women always have to be able to guide men and still be crafty enough to make them think they thought of it and that they are the boss."

Chapter 33

The Hallelujah Choir met in the church auditorium two nights a week. At my first meeting, I stood and said my name and age and then, "Hello. Everybody echoed, "Hello." It was a little bit like when a new member came to church or an AA meeting. Well, I guess it was a church meeting. The church owned the Hallelujah Choir, and maybe, us too. I was the youngest now that Pat and Harvey had unceremoniously "dropped out."

There were several screenings to get the cream of the crop of us young singers. Mom and Dad were delighted when I brought home the news that I had made the first cut. But in reality, there weren't many voices from which to choose. In fact, I was the only one.

"It might be a good way to get rid of some of that excess energy," Mom said. "And also a way to keep ya away from unwholesome readin'." Dad nodded agreement.

"If you want unwholesome reading Mom, read the Bible," I told them.

They acted like I hadn't said anything at all. They did that a lot when they didn't agree with me.

Oscar assured Mom and Dad that he would be able to help me in my singing quest, and they all agreed that it would be spiritually healthy to have me with righteous people––safe and sound and also in a position to be learning something worthwhile, something about the gospel.

"Yeah, like old man Tasker," I thought.

The next screening required me to stand before the group and sing the scale. Hell, I didn't even know what the scale was. And even if I had, I was too insecure to sing alone in front of someone else, let alone a group. Oscar understood and assured me he could help. He said he had taken singing lessons and would be able to give me a lot of help developing my voice. Mr. Tasker was the First Counselor in the church and said he would as well, but I didn't want that asshole to get near me. Oscar began sitting next to me in Sunday school and leaned close to listen as we sang from the hymnal. He decided that I did, indeed, have a great voice. In fact, he told me I had "a reed tone" and that was very desirable, according to him. He described all of this to Mom and Dad as a "wonderful gift from God" that should be developed for the enjoyment of others.

Dad said, "I told ya, ya horse's ass."

The only thing I knew about singing or music was what I had picked up watching Dad embarrass us with his too-long-held solos and singing and strumming his potato-bug, a sort of old-fashioned mandolin. I decided, at least for now, I was just going to wiggle my lips and face in concert with the other singers, without letting any sound come out. But Oscar paved the way for me to actually begin singing. "When you sing words like hallelujah," he counseled, "drop off the 'H.' Just sing alleluia; that gives it a softer sound with the entire choir singing." Then he demonstrated in his strong, vibrating baritone. I wasn't ready to contribute yet, but I was getting closer.

Following practice, Oscar usually took the choir for treats of ice cream and candy. Sometimes he took us to fun and exciting places, like swimming pools and a theme park in the next town. I was enjoying my new life, but was careful about what I said and did. I didn't want to do anything negative that might cause me to get kicked off the choir and go back to the humdrum way things used to be.

Oscar obviously liked to have me around. He took me with him just about everywhere. "You remind me of my little brother, Andrew," he said.

"Where is your little brother?" I asked, but hell, I already knew. I don't know why I asked.

Tears formed in his eyes. "He died. I should have saved him, but I didn't. I guess I'll always be sorry for that, but I can help others." He smiled sadly. "You remind me of him, William," he repeated.

"Oh, that's nice. I would have liked to meet him," I said, filled with understanding and servitude, as a good Christian is supposed to be. And I guess I *was* a Christian––after all, I sang in a Christian choir, and Mom and Dad, who were Christians, of sorts, owned me.

Oscar looked at me for a long moment. "William, will you come with me to the counselor for one of my sessions?"

Hell, I didn't want to, but he looked so pathetic that I nodded.

"What kind of counselor is he?" I asked.

"You'll just have to wait and see; it's a surprise."

Chapter 34

Victoria was finally in Springtown for a few days; it had been months since we were together. We sat on the bridge, dangling our feet in the rushing strawberry water and talking about the murders and planning our future. She looked different; older, wiser.

"Tell me about your sister, Ellen," she asked.

It took me a few minutes to find a beginning. "Well, you've seen her. I'm pretty sure she has royal blood like me. She's tall and graceful with light brown, well-kept hair. She always keeps herself clean and neat. She looks like a princess, but in some ways she's like Flash; she always gets God or religion on her side and always tells on me if I do anything adverse or disgusting. She spends most of her time in her bedroom."

"Do you get along with her?"

"Sometimes when we're alone we make each other laugh, but if Mom and Dad are around, she gets me in trouble."

"Like how?"

"She tells them everything. She's the one who told Dad about the butter trick," I told her.

"What's the butter trick?"

I smiled. "Dad wouldn't let me have very much butter on my

bread and I loved butter, so I came up with a way to get my share; well, maybe more than my share. I would spread a very thin layer on one side of the bread and then put it very thick on the other. The trick was to always keep the thinly buttered side pointed toward Dad and Ellen."

"Tell me some more," she laughed.

"Okay, this one's about the bean battle. At our house, if there's anything left over from meals, it always shows up on the menu later. Mom would not waste anything. She has a gentle way to encourage a clean plate. But Dad tries to use force to make sure we waste nothing. 'God damn it, the people in Europe is starvin' and yer a wastin yer food.' His face always turns red and the large veins in his neck bulge as he tries to think of a demeaning, threatening way to drive home his point. What the hell does eating all my food have to do with feeding the people in Europe? I have no idea.

"'It takes a real horse's ass to take something and then not eat it!' he always tells me.

"'Hell,' I say, 'you dipped it all onto my plate—you should eat it!'

"'Ya horse's ass,' he'd yell.

"One time, we sat at the table locked in mortal combat over my plate full of cooked but dry beans.

"'Eat them damned beans, William, or I'll rub yer nose in 'em.'

"My tactic was to try to outwait him, like I do with teachers at school. It always works with the teachers, but sometimes it doesn't work with Dad.

"This time, he finally grabbed me and pushed my face into the plate, like he was trying to drown me. I don't think he really cared whether I ate or not; he just wanted to win. He was pushing my face around in the plate with one hand and trying to hold my mouth open with the other, like he was trying to force the beans into my mouth. If I'd thought about it, I would have bitten his finger off. I began to cry uncontrollably, and he let me go.

"'Go ta yer room.'

"Shit, I was glad to go.

"'Stay there til ya learn ta eat right; takes a real horse's ass ta treat food like that,' he yelled.

"I made obscene gestures and cursed him softly behind the safety of the cubbyhole curtain. Later, after he had cooled off, he came to the cubbyhole and gave me his old split bamboo fly rod with a promise that he would try to control his temper."

Victoria was laughing loudly now. "William, that is so funny—but so sad, too."

"I remember the first time I saw you," I said.

"I remember too. It was years ago, and right here. I walked past. You were sailing a boat."

"Yeah, you do remember." She looked down; she looked pale.

"Are you all right?" I asked.

"Of course I'm all right," she whispered.

"You look different."

"I'm not different," she whispered again and looked at me with half-closed eyes. "I'm just older; I'm getting older."

I smiled and looked down at the water rushing past our feet. I felt uncomfortable.

"I'll show you mine if you'll show me yours," she taunted.

Hell, we had already seen about everything each other had, but this was different––it felt different, because we had only touched and caressed each other. The blood rushed to my face. I felt my heart pounding. I knew what she meant, and I knew we shouldn't do it. I knew we could go to hell; but I guessed we could always repent.

Without saying anything more, we stood and went to the tall weeds at the water's edge. We touched and caressed. I had a wonderful, sick feeling, like we were doing something wrong, but right too; as if God didn't like it, but it was what we were supposed to do. It was like we were being tested as Adam and Eve had been tested. The desire to do it was more vital than anything I had ever done before; I felt hot. My face burned, but I felt more alive than I ever had in my entire life. The mild feeling of evil was wonderful.

"This must be like the highest glory," I whispered. She moaned. She lay in the soft fresh grass looking up at me; the edges of her lips were raised in a mysterious, pleasant smile. She seemed to be waiting for me to do just as I pleased. It excited me. I thought my heart would pound out of my chest and then stop altogether. I drew close. The fragrance mixed with the mood was like nothing I had ever known before. The boldness of doing such a forbidden thing almost took my breath away. She held my head between her hands and arched her body to meet me.

"Ohhhh, William."

I held my weight above her.

Her breaths came in short, rapid gasps.

I sighed.

"I love you, William."

"I love you, too."

"I guess it has been our faith that has made us strong," Victoria whispered. "Our faith and our willingness to live right."

"Yes, it most certainly has been. Most certainly." It was as if we were in a trance, our soft, whispered words were simply words; they had no real meaning.

"Oh William …"

Our breath was rapid and came in short sequence as we lay expressing our love.

"I want to always be with you." Her face was flushed.

"We will always be together," I gasped.

"Yes, my prince, you are a part of me."

"Whatchadoin', William?"

I looked up. It was Ellen, standing on the other side of the ditch, smiling.

The weeds had been trampled down, and she could see us.

Victoria pulled away. I rolled over, and as we pulled apart, we tried to cover ourselves.

"Nothin'," I said.

"Looks like nothing," Ellen grinned.

Victoria and I just sat embarrassed, trying to conceal our nakedness.

"That's called fucking, William. I'm telling Dad. I'm telling him that you and Victoria have been fucking," she said, and her smile got even more sinister. "Dad says fucking is like murder in the eyes of God, and we go to hell if we do it," she said, and then she went to tell him.

We quickly dressed. Victoria fled to Mrs. MacLean's, and I went inside to face the music. I felt bad, more for Victoria than for myself; it made me mad to see her so embarrassed. I promised myself that she wouldn't ever be embarrassed that way again

"William," Dad yelled, expelling a fine spray of alcohol, tobacco particles, and saliva into my face. "What the hell we gonna do with you?" I stood with my head bowed, trying to look like I was sorry; but I wasn't sorry. I was glad it had happened. I would do it again, even if I did go to hell.

"Go to your room, William," Dad scolded, "and don't come out until you can act like a grown-up."

Ellen rubbed one index finger over the other to shame me, and after that, whenever she saw either Victoria or me, she offered the same gesture.

Later, Dad came to my cubbyhole and stood quietly for a few moments before he spoke. "It's fer yer own good," he said when he told me that they––meaning Victoria's parents and he and Mom––had decided that, to protect us from the fires of hell and damnation and from ourselves, Victoria and I would be separated. "They took Victoria home, ta Cal," Dad said. "She's not ever coming back."

It seemed like the worse day of my life. I couldn't believe it. I asked Mrs. MacLean to tell Victoria I'd be waiting for her.

"I'll help you write a letter," Mrs. MacLean offered. I found three cents in Mom's purse for a stamp, mailed the letter, and then began waiting for her to answer.

In addition to not seeing Victoria, I wasn't supposed to leave the property except to go to guitar lessons. The old Spanish guitar that had belonged to Grandpa had been added for even more punishment, because it was the kind with the metal bar, the kind that you didn't need to press with your fingers, the sissy kind. It was a sort of double-edged sword thing––Mom loved to hear the music, and it was a fitting sentence for me.

I decided to pray. I hadn't prayed for a long time, but it was time. This was something I had to have; nothing I had ever known seemed more important. I went to the sheds in back and asked God to let me die if I couldn't be with Victoria. I didn't want to live without her. I waited and––nothing. I wanted lightning to fry me to a cinder. I decided to curse God. Everybody said God would strike you with lightning for cursing him. Still nothing. I used more obscene curses, the worse ones I could think of, and I even emphasized them with movements of my body and arms. Still nothing.

Finally, I gave up and went to lie on my bridge. "Just like the walking on water or moving mountains. It's all a lie," I said, appalled by all this God stuff as I glared with contempt into the star-riddled heavens and at God Himself.

Chapter 35

I haven't found anything concrete to tell Alex yet to change his mind about killing me. It all seems a blur, with no clear-cut edges. I get so caught up in my past that I wonder if I'm even looking. I am more than a little bit sure that either Alex or Oscar was the killer. I expected Alex to pay me a visit before now to torment me, as is his nature. I'm still hungry and cold, but I have to say, this dungeon has a familiar feeling, because of the old dungeon in Aunt Helen's washroom in Springtown. Sometimes, in a kind of delusion, I think I'm there and not here at the Camelot-Avalon Apartments.

I know the way to convince Alex not to kill me is near. I just need to keep looking and find something, anything to convince him. It shouldn't be long now. I will feel better when I have some information for Alex—that bastard.

I must keep looking ...

Chapter 36

Aunt Helen and Uncle Archibald were mismatched to be sure. She was soft and sweet, with snow-white hair always in place and rolled into a bun in back. She had a sort of sad but friendly smile that caused everyone to immediately love her. Pale blue eyes seemed to smile along with the rest of her somewhat wrinkled but handsome face. Her frail-looking body was bent slightly forward from hard work and time, and from living with Uncle Archibald and raising nine boys and a girl, who had now, for the most part, abandoned them.

She tolerated Uncle Archibald's loud and gruff ways and overweight, bear-like body, probably because of the illusory hope of rewards woven within the mystery of their church prophesies. He never seemed content with her or anyone else. He grumbled his displeasure continually. His brown eyes, heavy with bushy eyebrows, seemed to lash out hatred. His face had wrinkled permanently through the years into a hateful mold. Maybe he was the reason the kids left and now rarely visited.

When I was about the age to be a Teacher in Dad's church, Uncle Archibald received a large inheritance from somewhere, and Aunt Helen talked him into spending some of it on a new Buick with an air conditioner on the side that looked like a mailbox. They were going to go to "Cal," as they called California. Uncle Archibald was from there, and hadn't been back to see his folks since leaving on a freight train many years before. And now he was going back. Some of the kids lived there too, and they were going to try to rekindle the affections that had eroded over time.

Aunt Helen asked, in her generous way, if Mom and Dad would move into the house to tend it until they got back. "Of course," Dad said, "we'll hep ya out." He could always tell a good thing when it hit him in the face. Aunt Helen had decided to pay Mom and Dad for house-sitting, which meant we now would have enough money for food and maybe some clothes, if Dad didn't spend it all at the Shame.

We could hear the loud voices in argument at the house. Archibald protested, "They'll have the place in shreds when we get back!"

"Now, now, dear. She is my niece," Aunt Helen patiently insisted.

Finally he was appeased, and all was silent. We were getting out of the dungeon.

"We'll be back in a few months," Aunt Helen yelled through the open window of the Buick as it pulled away. Uncle Archibald didn't look; he just frowned at the windshield, straight ahead, as he drove away.

It was sad to see her go, but it would be nice to live in the luxury of a real house. As the words "Dyna Flow" on the red taillight in the middle of the trunk lid made their way out of sight, I was happy that they had got the Buick Dyna Flow because now I realized that wasn't the personalized name of the owner; it was the name of the hydraulic transmission mechanism of the car. Uncle Archibald had snarled that information at me when I asked him about it.

Now I had my own, real room; not a cubbyhole. We all had our own rooms. I just stayed inside, enjoying the luxury of it all. I felt a lot better, but the newness gradually began to wear off, and I began to miss Victoria. It had been so long— she was beginning to seem like a dream, a wonderful dream. But I knew she was more than that. I had no doubt that she was now, and would always be, a part of me.

Mom's cheerful nature was beginning to return, and her color looked better, too. But their good fortune hadn't gotten me off the hook as far as the guitar lessons were concerned. Once a week, holding the horrible yellow monstrosity under my arm, I walked the mile into town, caught the Orem Tram. I really liked the Orem––I could sit and think and plan as it clicked along. I could see the long rods through the window high above, bending and moving as they engaged the electrical wires, seemingly knowing just how and when to get more electric power, as it was needed. It was six miles to the neighboring town where I studied the horrible instrument. It happened be the same town that hosted the nuthouse in which Oscar had been confined.

Seven of us tried to drag some sort of music out of our embarrassing instruments. Mrs. Gibson sat facing us at the front of the room as she demonstrated the proper technique of tuning a guitar. We read the glossary of little scribbles and dots, with wings held in place by long arms or legs, and lines in neat rows, like a fence that went across the pages of the music sheet. She showed us how to touch the steel bar to the strings to produce different sounds.

And then, patronizingly and with not much tact, she handed us a flat, featureless piece of steel called "beginner's steel." We didn't even get to use the round piece of steel she used. I really hated it, but I had to serve my penance.

Victoria came to Mrs. MacLean's while I was learning my new art. Her father had gone to Scotland again, and her mother had decided to let her come to Utah. I was so excited. "Thank God," I said, and faced the heavens with my arms out as a gesture of gratitude and love. "I forgive you, God," I said–and I really had forgiven Him.

"William," Victoria squealed when she found out about the

lessons, "I'm so excited about you learning to play music–it's wonderful."

"Yeah ... want to go with me?"

"I'd love to."

So after that, in addition to spending about every waking moment together, every lesson day we met a short distance from our houses to walk the mile into town and then to ride the tram together.

"Maybe God does answer prayers," I smiled. "Mom says he answers them sometimes in a way that's better than you ask."

In class, Victoria sat in one of the seats along the wall. We smiled at each other as I strummed and slid the "beginner's steel" up and down.

"William, watch your fingers," Mrs. Gibson repeated over and over.

Before long, Victoria and I decided to skip the lessons and play in the park or walk around until the hour had gone by. Her father had decided to stay in Scotland for a while; he was fixing up a castle or something over there, he said.

"God, that's a hard one to swallow," I said. "Fixing up a castle? He's probably got a mistress over there," I kidded.

"Oh, stop it. He wouldn't do that. Just be happy I'm here and can stay for a while."

"More than a while, young lady–you're staying forever. I'm planning to take you to my castle in the sky on my white stallion."

She placed her hand on my chest—my heart pounded away—she excited me still, just being nearby, let alone when she touched me.

One day, while we were skipping the guitar lessons, we stumbled onto a railroad yard at the edge of town. There were tracks everywhere–hundreds of them–and quite a few trains, some just sitting idle, some with white smoke billowing out from underneath, and some seemed to feverishly blow out black smoke, as if angry and urgently straining to pull an assortment of cars behind them–some full, some empty, some with hobos lounging on or inside them. It was an exciting scene.

We discovered an old Mexican-looking building surrounded by trees with its back toward the yard, facing what might have been a small ethnic settlement of some sort. Everything was partially burned, abandoned and in the process of decay, but we were attracted to an old hacienda with a tattered, red tile roof and broken stucco on the walls. Most of the windows had been shattered and the doors set ajar. There was the smell of filth from years of transients and animals.

We found broken chairs and a box to put our feet on as we watched the rail yard through streaked and dusty or completely broken windows. Bums came into the yard and left on boxcars and we imagined we were them.

"Let's make this our castle," Victoria squealed. "Castle II."

"Now who's silly?" I laughed. "You like this better than our castle in the sky?"

She laughed, too. "But it *is* a real castle, not a dream castle. This is our castle, William, our second castle," she cajoled. "Let's fix it up––it wouldn't be so bad if it was fixed up––and clean," she said seriously.

"Let's do this room first." I began picking up and setting things in order.

She seemed to float across the room, her feet not even touching the floor, as she quickly moved about, arranging this and that, here and there. She was so graceful. It was wonderful; she was wonderful. "This is our second castle," I said excitedly.

Over the following weeks and months, it became just that, as well as my refuge from my other life and the torment of the dreadful guitar lessons, which I now attended only on occasion, if Victoria couldn't get away with me. But I began experiencing a new feeling, a mixture of guilt from lying to Mom about the lessons and delight that Victoria and I were together in our castle. I had much to be guilty about, for sure. I tried to imagine what I could possibly demonstrate to Mom about the new lessons I was learning, but those worries usually gave way to more pleasant thoughts about Victoria. We planned our future together, either in our Castle I or in our delightful new Castle II, when she could get away to the tram that carried us there, my guitar on one side of me and Victoria on the other. When it was time to head home again, my conscience always bathed me in guilt. I felt that my deceit was securely hidden within the splendors of our castle, but it was nonetheless there.

Chapter 37

"I think you're ready, William."

I opened my eyes and looked up, startled. Dad was standing over me, with that strange, holy look on his face. I remembered hearing him recite from the Bible the previous night, giving his rendition of Abraham and Isaac and how the father, I think it was Abraham, had taken God to mean that he was to sacrifice his son—I think that was Isaac. I cowered to the edge of my bed, as far away from him as possible.

"Jesus," I whispered, "Dad has heard from God, and I'm going to be sacrificed." I trembled.

Dad laughed. "No, this is for your blessing, son."

He began filling me in on a ritual that seemed to be like a séance sanctioned by the church. He said God would reveal quite a lot about me. The ritual would tell me if I was of royal blood and what the future might hold for me.

"This is great," I said. "A fortuneteller sanctioned by the church, God, and Dad."

"He is the patriarch of the church and you will be going this Sunday."

"I thought that was the day of rest?"

"You will be going this Sunday," Dad stoically repeated.

The patriarch was a thin, frail-looking man with white hair, dressed all in white. He did have a sort of holy look about him, like the geezers in pictures. His hands shook from palsy, like those of Miss Phelps did, but he had a more real look about him—he looked less like plaster of Paris.

He greeted me very warmly. He had the dreaded cold-fish handshake Dad had warned me about. "The same kind that bad people, bums, and niggers always use," he had cautioned me.

"What is your name?" The patriarch's voice trembled.

"Hell of a fortune teller," I thought. "Doesn't even know my name."

"It's William Robert Jones III," I patiently told him.

"What's in the box?"

"All my church stuff. I don't like to be without it; I call it my Me box."

He seemed to be pleased about all my church stuff. "Sit over there, William." Trying to make his decrepit face smile, he pointed to a large. overstuffed chair.

When he placed his hands on my head, I had to smile. "This is the way Oral Roberts cures his flock," I said.

He scowled and shook his head. "Hush." He began talking very softly, reading from a sheet of paper, almost as if he were in a trace, then he began talking louder in a monotone voice almost as if he were singing with no changes of scale. "You come from the very loins of David, who was sold into slavery," he said.

"Who the hell is David?"

Instead of answering, he flipped me on the head with his middle finger, as Dad always did, and then he went on. "You are of royal blood."

"Mom was right," I said softly. "I am of royal blood."

The patriarch's words became distant and indistinguishable as I slowly dissolved into being a king in a distant land ... I passed through a window.

As King William III, my subjects loved me mostly because of my humility, kindness, and wisdom. My curses were that my hands would bleed when they touched dirt, I got dizzy when confronted with physical labor, and—you could call it a curse—I had an unusually large penis. "Small price to pay for being royalty," King William chuckled.

Still in a daze, I mumbled a little bit too loudly, "Victoria's father will approve of me now."

The patriarch's voice became louder and he tightened his hands on my shoulders; he was glaring at me.

"Maybe he can tell what I'm thinking," I considered, and began listening again.

"Choice spirits will be sent to you and because of your superior knowledge and understanding you shall bring comfort to them and many others. You shall take part in many of the things that will occur in history." Already, I was not even listening again ... my mind wandered; through the window I could see a long line of children following an older person along the sidewalk. "Probably a Sunday school teacher taking the class on a field trip," I said to myself. "It is Sunday—anything to get out of those boring classes."

I well knew the boredom of sitting in a class of any kind, but I couldn't remember a single field trip any of my teachers had taken me on, either in school or church. I always had to stay in class with the dunce cap weighing down my head and my face in the corner or standing before the blackboard writing that I wouldn't do this or that anymore. I watched the procession move along the sidewalk, the students exchanging shoves and smiles, seeming glad to have left the drudgery of the classroom. "I can understand that; any kind of school is boring," I mumbled.

"What did you say?" the patriarch asked.

"Just clearing my throat," I lied.

He went on in his monotone voice and I escaped again through my window of illusion ...

During one of the long winter days in an arts and crafts class that all grades could attend, Flash, Dale, and I had decided it was so boring that something had to be done to relieve our suffering. We decided I would ask the teacher a question that would take some time to answer and hopefully would require her to turn her back to us as she used the blackboard to explain it. While she was distracted, Flash would place a shotgun shell that happened to be in his pocket on top of the large wood-burning stove. After the shell exploded, Flash would escape by jumping out of the second-story window into the deep snow below. Hopefully, as everyone watched Flash's escape out of the window, in the confusion Dale and I would be able to make our getaway downstairs and out through the front door.

I don't remember the question I asked, but it was something about how the planets circle around the earth or sun or that type of thing and how that related to atoms. It had nothing to do with the lesson, but to illustrate her vast knowledge, the teacher had turned to use the blackboard and chalk. Flash set the shotgun shell on the stovetop as the teacher concentrated on her boring lesson. It seemed to take forever for the shell to heat up, but finally there was a loud, deafening explosion and the schoolroom filled with smoke. A large hole in the ceiling above the stove was surrounded by buckshot holes and patches of black powder.

Flash opened the window and jumped out into the deep snow below. The teacher ran to the window yelling at him as Dale and I made our own escape. Not as dramatic as Flash's, to be sure, but just as effective. We pushed our way down the stairs against the crowd of students and teachers coming up to see what had happened. We grabbed our coats and hats, and Flash's, and ran to help him out of the snow. Then we set off along the snow-packed road, heading into the woods.

Hours passed as we floundered along. Finally, we realized we were lost and it was getting dark and we were hungry. Our feet were cold, our faces were cold, our bodies we cold; we were freezing. We sat on a fallen tree and tried to decide what to do. Then Dale saw in the distance a faint glow of light and we began struggling toward it. As we moved closer, we realized that the house belonged to an old bachelor, John Lockwood, who was famous for his homemade "raisin jack," a sort of alcoholic beverage. It was a concoction he had invented through years of practice. It was said that this strong beer could be used in place of coal oil for lamps or for gasoline in cars and that if touched with a match it would ignite into a blue flame. It was also said that he was an ornery, evil man who was best left alone. We had been warned many times to stay away from him. "He cooks little boys in his big stove and eats them." But we were not little boys; we were in our early and mid-teens.

The door was opened in response to our timid knock and around the frail body of the white-haired old man in the doorway came the delicious smells of cooking food. His evil reputation quickly melted as he served us each a bottle of his infamous brew and a bowl of ham hock and barley soup that had been cooking on the wood-burning kitchen stove; then another brew and still another. The wooden spoons were large, but we found a way to get the delicious meal into our mouths. A few thick slices of homemade bread were thrown in for good measure.

As usual, Flash ate too much. He went outside to empty his stomach of his three helpings of barley soup, five or six slices of bread, and three bottles of brew. Then he came back and had another bowl of soup and a slice of bread *and two more bottles of brew. The old man shook his head in delight as he shuffled around the room serving our food. Warmed by the food, the hospitality of the old man, and medicated by the beverage, we bade him farewell. With his shoulders hunched forward from age and a smile on his face, he told us to please come back.*

We headed for home to meet the consequences of our ill-spent day, during which the evil image of "Old John Lockwood" had been shattered and replaced by that of a gracious and humble host. The memory of a wonderful meal and the tonic that he had served would be treasured by us forever.

The window effect faded as the patriarch nudged me—he was glaring again. "And when you get married, take the girl of your choice to the temple of the Lord to be blessed by sacred ordinances. Then, after a long and successful life, you will be a candidate for the celestial kingdom." He paused.

"What is the celestial kingdom?" I asked.

"That's the highest glory," he said.

"Oh," I said. "You mean the highest kingdom?"

"Yes, the highest glory," he said again.

"I just want to go to the middle one," I said.

He looked stunned. "Nobody ever wants to go to the middle glory. You're supposed to want to go to the highest glory." He went on talking, as if he wasn't too concerned about what I wanted.

The fortuneteller concluded our session, like he was happy to have it over with; sort of like my teachers in school when I was promoted to the next grade. He anxiously glanced at the other robots waiting their turns in the lobby.

"You shall never want for worldly possessions and success shall crown your efforts."

He said a little prayer and gave me some instructions, a bit like when Uncle Arthur or Dad talked about not playing nasty with myself or with girls and stuff like that, but in this case, about how to live right and obey the bishop if I ever wanted to be called on a church mission.

"Okay, you can go now," he said, and handed me a rolled-up paper with a thin, blue ribbon tied around it. Then he pointed toward the door.

I nodded my approval and took the cylinder of paper with about the same amount of enthusiasm and sincerity that railroad conductors display when they help passengers on or off a train. He watched until the door closed between us and then, through the little windows in the door, I could see him turn to service one of the other waiting, frightened, and wary urchins.

"Thanks for nothing," I said when I was out of range of his hearing. I headed toward town, stopping briefly to unroll the paper and read it. It said about the same thing that he had told me. I dropped the blue ribbon on the ground and folded the paper into a small square and put it in my back pocket, intending to show Mom and Dad when I got home.

The Three Stooges was the feature at the Rialto Movie Theatre, two buildings up from the Shame and Buck and Edna's. There were short subjects, cartoons, and the jerky (and scary) war news, and also another feature that softened the frightfulness of the war. It was like a whole different world in there, very much different from the painful and frightening outside world. In fact, it was almost impossible to bring the real world in, unless the movie was a real dog.

When I got home, I unfolded the blessing and tried to get somebody excited about reading it, but it was like I wasn't even there. Mom was asleep, and Martha and Ellen were lying beside her, just staring at the ceiling.

"I should have stopped in to the Shame to show Dad—but it's too late now."

I retired to my new room in Aunt Helen's house and tried to be content, but it was no use. After a while, I went to sit on the comfort of my bridge. I tore the record of my séance into fourths, dropping one piece at a time into the strawberry water. As I watched them float along I thought, "Maybe they will indoctrinate some other poor vegetable into this strange cult instead of me."

Then, uncharacteristically, I had a change of heart and ran to retrieve the scraps of paper with a silent promise to resurrect the document by taping it back together.

Chapter 38

"William, do you have anything to tell me?" It's that bastard Alex. "Hell, no, I don't—yet. How about something to eat?"

I can imagine him smiling gleefully on the other side of the ironclad door. I really don't think he has intentions of letting me out—he just wants me to suffer, and for what? Even he doesn't know for sure who the killer really is, I'll bet.

"Oh shit," he says—I can imagine him smiling—the bastard. "I had it all ready and forgot to pick it up. I'll bring it next trip—maybe you'll have something to tell me by then."

"I'll bet you will," I think, and then say aloud, "I don't think you have any intentions of bringing me food."

Alex laughs through the door—I imagine his crooked, broken face grimacing and his body hunched in agony as it shakes with laughter. "William, why would I do that after you have been so good to me and my brothers? I'll leave you to your thoughts and discovery, and go get your food—hold your breath!" Then I hear him dragging his decrepit body away from the door and up the stairs, and he is gone.

I need to get back to the past to find some answers for Alex, that bastard. Sure, he'll get me some food. The chances of that are about as good as winning a game of pick up sticks using only your butt cheeks.

I am discouraged, but what choice do I have? And with this thought I delve back into my past, trying to find clues to who killed the boys.

Chapter 39

Dad said, in his usual uncaring style, almost yelling, "They's found a body without a head. They's a-thinking it probably belongs to Pat. Let's go see it."

The body lay in state at the mortuary, inside a casket. It was morbid and disgusting—they were treating it as a whole body. It lay headless, twisted, wounded, and distorted, showing the torture it had suffered during its demise. Kids cutting through a vacant Victory Garden field had happened to find it. It was all puffed up and black and not easy to recognize as a human body, but that's what it was, lying there without a head. If not for the gravity of the occasion, the whole thing might have been funny. Pat's skull had been given to the coroner and it couldn't be found—he had lost it. Lost a human head, for hell's sakes. What a sloppy coroner.

"Some morbid bastard or vampire probably took it for a witches' stew," I smiled to myself.

But, seriously, it was hard to believe that the crazy little guy who used to live across the street, the one who had suffered so much from the inhumanity of man to man, was now being subjected to this, even in his death. The poor little boy.

Rule had discovered an old bum passed out nearby. His footprints looked like he had staggered around where the body was. His were the only fresh prints that the town dick could find, so the drunk had been taken in on suspicion. He was so drunk that Rule and his deputy, Oscar, had to carry him to the holding pen.

Because Pat had been a member of the choir, Rule took everybody who was associated with the choir, including Oscar, to the station, and grilled them individually, trying to find any clue or evidence that might lead to the conviction of the fiend or fiends who had taken young Pat's life. Dad expressed his discontent that they were wasting their time with the members and elders of the church. He thought that because they "held the priesthood" they should be exempt from such suspicion. He thought the police should be looking in bars or questioning bums down at the rail yard.

He obviously did not include himself among the people to be questioned, now that he was trying to fight off his addiction to the Shame and booze. Mom thought it could be anybody, but Dad insisted that a child molester or other criminal could be identified by sight.

With no other suspects, the old bum was charged and jailed to await trial for killing little Pat's body. Rule even included the head in the indictment, even though the skull that had been identified by dental records as belonging to Pat had somehow been lost by the police. And now they couldn't really be sure this was Pat's body, mostly because the head had been misplaced, so the case would stay in the unsolved murder file until the head was found again, if ever.

The bum was locked in the cell two down from where Mr. Cook was being held—they were the only accused felons that had ever been in the jail. It all made me laugh. What a detective.

"Are they watching them, Dad?" I asked.

"What the hell, William, they's in jail––they can't get away."

"Maybe they'll kill themselves to get out of it."

"Hell, that will just save us taxpayers some money."

"Dad, you don't pay any taxes, anyway."

He slapped me on the back of my head and tried to push me into my room.

I fought back. "I'm going down to see if they're watching him," I said, as I struggled past Dad and headed for the jail to do vigil for Mr. Cook and the bum. Mr. Cook had probably suffered enough—he didn't need to give his life to protect someone else.

Chapter 40

Victoria and I were growing older now, and maybe even beginning to grow apart. With everything that had happened, it was little wonder. Maybe because of the murders, everything was more exciting now, but frightening at the same time. I had finally passed my 14th birthday and was very big and mature for my age. I could even grow a beard and had been shaving with Dad's old straight razor for a while, an extremely sharp instrument that had belonged to his dad. I kept it sharp by lacing it back and fourth on the old razor strap. It would cut through about anything, especially flesh if I wasn't careful, and sometimes even if I was careful.

Victoria and I were beginning to act a little bit like old married people; we even had an argument once in a while. We decided to try to get involved with others, to begin doing things like other young people do. We joined the neighborhood kids' production of stupid plays that we made up. Victoria and I were chosen to play the leads in certain productions and performed with delight under the imaginary lights of the imaginary stage. Her father, James H., discovered we were still seeing each other, and restricted her to Mrs. MacLean's, allowing her out only to do errands and such. I couldn't wait to be older, when we could do as we pleased.

One day, Victoria and I were together in Mrs. MacLean's

garden, and her father came to get her. I hid. James H. looked meek and mild, an extremely foreign look for him, and he stood silently for awhile, like he was trying to find the right words.

"V-Victoria, find someone w-with royal b-blood. Don't settle for a w-white-trash nobody," he said. It was apparent that he was trying to act like he was kidding, but it was also obvious that he wasn't kidding.

"But I like him, Daddy," she said. "I think I love him."

"He's no-good w-white trash. God, Victoria, they live in the basement of a w-washhouse."

"It's not his fault. He's smart; he'll do all right. And he doesn't live in the basement anymore. He lives in the house now."

"He's just a w-welfare w-waif like your other grandma was—— he's no good. He'll break your heart. I don't w-want my kids and grandkids living in a dungeon."

"I love him, Daddy."

James H.'s countenance became firm. "Get into the house until w-we leave!" he shouted.

But even though he tried to separate us, we still found ways to meet. We met in the garden behind her grandma's house, when she was sent to get corn or tomatoes for dinner. I hid when someone came to see why it was taking her so long.

I carved her initials into my leg right above my knee, where only she and I could see it. When it got infected, we bathed the red and swollen declaration of our love with Lysol that she had taken from her grandmother's medicine cabinet, until the self-inflicted wound healed. But the scar stayed there, VLM, a reminder to both of us, as if to ensure and cement our feelings of love. We were becoming close again, and it was delightful. We decided to pretend that her last name was Jones, like we were married. It was all right, because someday we would be. Our names would be Victoria and William Jones. It would be our secret; no one else would ever know until we were ready.

"I'll need to change that "M" on my knee to a "J," I said, smiling.

We went to the shed, our Castle I.

"Our first child will be named William Robert Jones IV," I said.

"If that doesn't sound like royalty, nothing does," she giggled. "What if it's a girl?"

"It won't be a girl, but if it is, we'll figure it out then. Diarrhea, maybe?" I paused. "It's not so funny when we're talking about our child," I admitted. "But it would be a classy name if you were able to disassociate it from loose bowels."

We pushed close together, enjoying the comfort of our nakedness. We were growing up; her hair was getting longer with a few dark curly ones. Her nipples were growing and being pushed forward to make room for breasts that were beginning to fill the flatness of her chest. My hair was getting dark and curly, and thicker, and my voice was beginning to crack. It sounded gruff and deep. I was having trouble in the choir and was just moving my lips again, like when I started. More kids were now competing to get in.

We lay holding each other. Sunlight streamed into our castle through the cracks and knotholes. Floating dust turned the sunlight into strands of gold. It was as if God were sending us a vision, a message.

"Isn't it beautiful?" she said.

"Yes, but not as beautiful as you are."

"Oh, William."

I had things to tell her. I wanted her to know everything. I wanted her to know all about me––well, not everything. But I couldn't find the words. I had to find a way to be what I knew I should be …

Chapter 41

Dad sat facing me and he was sober, which was unusual. He looked older than I had ever seen him. He was shaking; he obviously needed a drink—but it was more than that.

"William, I need to talk to you. I'm sorry that I've been so neglectful, and it's probably my fault that you've taken up with Victoria and want to be with her. But it's better if you just leave her alone. Her family and us are just too different. They're rich and we're poor. If I can't find a job, then we'll be moving back into the dungeon as soon as Aunt Helen gets back. I need to find a job, a way to make a living."

He had really given up now; he was calling it the dungeon, too.

He looked like he was going to cry. "I'm sorry," he said. It sounded like he really meant it. He sat with his head down for a long moment. "Victoria's father, James H., and I have decided it's best if he takes her away again, this time to Scotland. We both think it is better to separate you two, at least for a while. What would happen if you got her pregnant?"

I was stunned. I couldn't say anything. I wanted to run and see if I could find her.

Dad held me there and went on. "Her father has told her and me that they are a royal family that has roots in Scotland. He thinks she should find a prince when she decides to marry—a nobleman, not a poor untitled boy like you."

I had to do something. It seemed like Dad was on my side now; he was even talking like a nobleman. I guess the other voice––the rough side of him––had been trying to fit in with his cronies at the Shame. "But Dad," I cried, my heart about to break in two. "The patriarch said I am of royal blood, that I am from the loins of King David in the Bible!"

Dad sat shaking his head. Finally, he spoke softly in a way that made my appeal seem vain indeed. "That's only good in the church. It don't mean squat in the real world." He stood. We looked at each other. "I would do anything, if I knew it would make you happy, but I don't think you and Victoria can ever be a reality."

I watched through the door as he walked toward town, disappearing around the corner of 2nd Street and Elm. He was going to the Shame. But this time, instead of anger and shame for him, I felt strong pity and even a twinge of love. Those unfamiliar feelings, combined with the futility about Victoria, brought a flood of tears to my eyes. But in spite of Dad's advice, I thought about all those summers and short winter visits when she would slip away to join me. Our love had blossomed through those years, good and bad, until it had completely filled our lives. I imagined her face, the beauty of her face, and I could feel her with me, as a part of me—a comfortable, essential part of me.

She had promised that she would wait for me until she was old enough, and we would be married even without her father's consent, and I believed with all my heart that that was the truth. I had no doubt that she was telling me the truth, and I had pledged my heart to her, forever and ever and, if need be, I would take her from her father's grasp onto my white stallion, and ride off into the sunset, where we would live together in the castle of our choice in whatever way we could.

I went to my room, the tears steaming down my face. I didn't care——I was unashamed. I had no idea what to do, but I did know two things: we weren't moving back into the dungeon, and I wasn't going to let Victoria leave me. My room became my sanctuary. I wouldn't leave it at all! And I sure as hell wouldn't be helping Oscar with his choir anymore—to hell with Oscar. His problems were his problems and mine were mine. For one reason or another, I thought I needed to stay away from him, if I wanted to live.

I had to be alone——I had to think and plan. There had to be a way. I made a vow to go to Victoria and bring her back. I knew I would find a way. I was creative and imaginative enough to do it. I knew there would be a way, not only to find her, but also a way for us to survive. But I also knew that it might take a while to achieve it.

Chapter 42

It was obvious that my guitar punishment hadn't worked out, as I wasn't learning to play the damned thing, so now my parents decided to try something else. I was informed that the owner of a sheep ranch, Hyrum, would be dropping by to haul my sorry ass away. He was a good friend of Dad's and was looking for some help with hauling hay, tromping wool, and such. It was to be the double-edged sword thing again, getting me away from Victoria while Hyrum got some free labor.

"Dad," I said, "I'm not feeling very well, and I hate sheep. And I've got a broken arm." My arm had healed, but now I wore the cast taped together whenever I needed to get some well-deserved compassion and sympathy.

"Hell, when I was a kid, I worked with broken arms and even broken legs a lot, and yer complaining about bein' a little bit sick and only one broken arm," he said with a smart-ass smile.

"Yeah, and I'll bet you walked ten miles to school through the snow, and it was uphill both ways," I mumbled.

"What'd you say?"

"Nothin'," I submitted.

"We decided ta get you and Victoria apart for a while again. Things'll cool off. That's what her dad thinks, too. Hell, stop and think, William, they's Catholics. Ya gets mixed up with her, yer not going ta get in the highest glory."

"Duh," I whispered.

I met Victoria in the shed at the end of our lot to tell her about me leaving.

"How long?" she asked. Tears already were forming in her green eyes.

"All summer, I guess. Maybe two months. I'll try to sneak away. It's only fifteen miles. I can walk that far easily."

She promised to wait for me, and I had no doubt that she would. "We will always be together," she assured me. "You are a part of me."

I met Hyrum for the first time when he pulled up in front of our house in an old Chevrolet pickup. In the cab with him were his wife Debbie, and the delight of Hyrum's life, his son, Jon. They all got out and stood by the side of the truck, as if posing for a Kodak picture.

Hyrum was a tall, hearty, bear-like man with graying hair that was thinning on top. He had a beard that needed to be trimmed and was turning white, like his hair already had. His face and the skin that showed were covered in red surface veins like thin little spiders. He wore a well-worn, blue work shirt and blue bib overalls, also well-worn and incredibly patched—patches on top of patches. Atop his head he wore a business hat, so dirty and caked with grime around the sweatband that it resembled leather. There was always a smile behind the hand-rolled Bull Durham cigarette perpetually clinched between his tobacco-stained, chipped teeth. He could move the scrawny, unlit cigarette from one side of his mouth to the other with his tongue, without missing a word as he talked. It was like it belonged there, like it was a part of his mouth. He seemed agile for a man of his size and age and demanded immediate respect, but in a gentle and comfortable way.

I would often hear him say over the next several weeks, "If you have one boy, you get one day's work. Two boys, you get half a day's work, and three boys, you get nothing," and then laugh like it was really funny. He loved to repeat bad jokes and always seemed to think them funnier than they really were. He had the habit of telling them over and over again and to him they never seemed to lose any of their humor.

"Hell, them boys looks enough alike ta be brothers," Hyrum said of Jon and me.

"God, don't put yer son down like that," Dad said, and they laughed.

"Well, it's mostly their coloring," Hyrum went on.

Hell, we didn't look anything alike. How could anyone think we looked alike?

Jon climbed into the back of the pickup. Dad and Hyrum exchanged a few words and then I lifted my Me box in and climbed up into the back with Jon.

"I'll bring them in to the choir practice," Hyrum said. Jon was in the Halleluiah Choir, too. I had seen him there, but only once I think. We hadn't ever talked.

Debbie never spoke. She just nodded her head in time to Hyrum's constant chatter and smiled occasionally, but mostly she just looked out the window. Her pallid face showed the signs of hard work and sacrifice so common to people who had lived through the depression. Her graying hair held some evidence of its original, darker color but not enough for me to discern for sure what color it had been. It was straight and combed back in a way that looked like her small ears were holding it in place. Her eyes looked hollow, lonely, and a little foreboding, and the light gray color only accented the loneliness. In contrast, when she smiled, even with those crooked and stained teeth, her wrinkled face opened up to become warm and friendly.

Hyrum ground the gears and the pickup came to life. It jerked ahead a few times and then smoothed out, leaving Mom and Dad standing at the side of the road waving. I waved but Mom and Dad were already hugging and walking toward the house. They got all lovey-dovey sometimes when Dad was home and sober and they were alone.

Before we had even turned the corner that put home and them out of sight, I was already beginning to be homesick. It didn't make sense; I didn't even like them much, or that home, and then I sort of missed them. Maybe it was Victoria that I really missed. She had decided not to tell me goodbye. "Just too sad," she had said.

Jon's pallid face held a pair of pale blue eyes set deep within their sockets and separated by a thin, hawk-like nose. He had almost no eyebrows. His thin lips revealed somewhat crooked teeth, whenever they were exposed by Jon's naturally sinister smile. A thin leather thong held his long, fine, yellow hair in place and nicks showed in several places where he or someone else had tried to trim it. Jon never seemed to sit completely still or ever stop talking. It was as if he were thinking out loud. He didn't look at me or address me directly; he just went about his business as if I wasn't there.

"How the hell does he look like me?" I thought.

Hyrum stopped for a stop sign, and after noisily searching for the right gear again—and finding it only after soft curses and more grinding of gears—the old pickup lurched into a newly paved street and headed east, toward whatever lay ahead. It was a hot day—as summer days are in Utah during July—so hot that heat waves rose from the asphalt pavement. Without looking at me or saying anything, Jon picked up a metal bar from the floor of the pickup bed. The bar was flat at one end and ground to a sharp point at the other.

He pushed the sharp end down between the bumper and the tailgate and pushed down into the soft asphalt below. It cut into the road and left a sort of wake, like Uncle Arthur's old motorboat did—but this wake didn't go away. It remained a deep rut as far back as I could see.

The old pickup shook and vibrated from the extra strain, but Hyrum seemed oblivious of it, probably thinking that was the way the old pickup was supposed to run. He just kept talking to Debbie, who listened submissively, in her usual silence.

Jon tried to force the bar down even farther; it seemed that he needed to get the bar down to a certain depth in order to accomplish something—but what?

"Can I help?" I asked, and moved closer to this mysterious stranger.

He didn't answer or even look at me, but he kept up a constant, low chatter to himself. I reached over to give what help I could. He moved a little; he seemed to expect it. With both of our weights on the bar, we were leaving an impressive trench. It went completely through the asphalt and brought up pieces of gravel from below along both sides of the newly plowed trench. I had to admit, it was exciting and fun.

The old pickup groaned under the extra load, and Hyrum shifted into a lower gear, but he just kept looking ahead and talking to Debbie. The road turned to gravel and Jon pulled in the bar and threw it to the floor with a loud BANG. Hyrum looked back for just a moment and then back at the road, and Jon went to stand behind the cab. I followed, as if hypnotized by this strange creature. Jon let the wind turn his face into horrible and grotesque features. I wanted to laugh but something about him prohibited laughter to be directed toward him. So instead I just stood beside him and let the wind disfigure my face as well.

All the time my Me box was rolling back and forth and Jon and I had to dodge it as we goofed around in the back of the pickup. It wasn't long before Jon had tired of this face-altering play and bent to pick up a sack on the floor of the pickup bed. Hyrum turned his head toward the sound of Jon's rock hitting a sign, and then looked at his wife and shrugged, an unperceptive look on his face. John's target practice went on for a time and then we saw a boy and girl about our age walking along the roadside. They made me think of Victoria, and I felt a pang of loneliness; I wanted to be with her. The young couple was going the same direction as we were, and they were holding hands. They looked at each other from time to time and smiled. It looked like they were in love. I missed Victoria so much!

And then Jon took that all away. He dropped the sack of rocks and picked up a couple of small, rotting fish that were lying on the floor. They looked like carp, probably from Utah Lake. With precise timing, he let one fly and then the other. The first one hit the boy on the back of the head and the second hit the girl between her shoulders. The fish were small but splattered into fragments all over the walking lovers. They both looked stunned and stood in dismay, arms and legs spread, not really sure what had happened.

Jon drew his fingers under his nose, wrinkled it in disgust, and finally spoke to me for the first time. "Want to smell my new girl friend?" he said, without even a smile. And then he turned his attention back to the bag of rocks and began pelting signs and animals that had made the mistake of being too close to the road.

It seemed that only minutes had passed when the pickup began to slow and then turned into a driveway, stopping in front of a closed, barbed wire gate. The dust caught up and passed us, laying down a thick, tawny coat on us and everything in its path. Jon jumped out and opened the gate by half-carrying, half-dragging it out of the driveway. After Hyrum had driven through, Jon dragged the gatepost back and by bracing his shoulder against it and holding onto the post, he looped the wire back over the matching post. Then he climbed back in with me.

A little white house sat a short distance down the lane. We drove to the front and the old pickup lurched to a stop. The house and a small, weed-filled yard and garden were nestled inside a weathered picket fence. The garden in back of the house had weeds taller than any of the vegetables, and a few chickens and ducks scoured the area in search of bugs or anything else to eat. We all got out. I reached back for my Me box, and we went inside. It immediately felt like home. Debbie cooked just about anytime we got hungry. It was as if she were our servant and her only goal in life was to please us and make us all content. I liked it. I liked it a lot. She hardly talked; she just worked silently.

"William," she said, "just set your little box over there in the corner, and take it when you go home. You won't have time for it up here. You're going to be too busy." That's about the only thing she ever said to me.

Hyrum talked almost continually, about like Jon did, and when he and Jon were together, they both talked and neither listened to the other. Hyrum had an almost sacrilegious view of religion and at times talked to God directly, as if they were standing face to face. He had a way of dismissing his own weaknesses or shortcomings. He was able to convince himself, and sometimes others, that most anything was right, or wrong, whichever side of the fence he happened to be on at any given time.

Hyrums' best friend, Lon Cox, lived just up the creek and was a constant visitor. He was a single man, never married, and he joined us for many of our meals and outings. Lon was an older European man, with long hair that was in the process of turning from yellow to white, making it look dirty. Hyrum called him a "Honyok." He had deep-set, pale blue eyes and, like Jon, almost no eyebrows. A thin, hawk-like nose was set above the wry, thin lips that were usually in a talking mode, which revealed crooked, tobacco-stained teeth. He was short with a slight build but was unusually strong and agile, with lots of nervous energy. Like Hyrum and Jon, he almost never stopped talking, as if he were thinking out loud.

Hyrum had two other sons and two daughters besides Jon. They were all tall with dark hair and were pretty good-looking, judging by their pictures, and apparently they were all good workers, like Hyrum. They had all left home either by marriage or for other reasons. Even though Jon bore none of Hyrum's characteristics except talkativeness, there was no doubt that he was his father's favorite.

Hyrum played the piano and tap-danced and we often stood around the old player piano in the front room to sing Western songs in the light of the coal oil lamp. When the mood struck him, Hyrum moved to the center of the room to perform amateurish tap dance steps. I sometimes accompanied him but just with my right foot. We were usually a hit.

It was a sheep ranch, so we ate a lot of mutton and the house had the smell of years of cooking the vile stuff. I can still remember when I had my first taste. It was hot so I drank some cold milk to cool it off a little. The tallow of that rich meat caked and gelled onto my upper pallet, about like the sulfur does when I'm terrified. Everybody stood around laughing as I tried to dig it off with my tongue and fingers.

I stayed in Jon's room and even slept with him. My Me box was stored in a corner of the room. Often, I opened it and wrote in my notebooks.

Chapter 43

It was relaxing to sit in the pea field eating the green peas that were being grown as feed for the cattle and sheep. It was also pretty nice to swim nude in the pond with Jon and his sisters, Martha and Vera, and a distant relative of mine up the road a little further, Bernice. They taught Jon and I a lot of fun tricks while we swam nude in the water or on the banks. Not so relaxing was the job of stuffing rolled-up bales of wool into a large canvas bag by tromping them into place. Sheep ticks embedded themselves all over our bodies.

Hyrum and Lon cut off the long tails of the young sheep, then turned the ewes loose and flipped the young bucks onto their backs on a crude-looking wooden table. Taking turns, one of them would hold the scrotum with one hand, as if he were trying to strangle it, and with the other he would slice the skin with a sharp knife. Then either Hyrum or Lon would stick his face into that gooey, bloody mess and pinch the testicle between his teeth and pull it out and sever the spermatic cord with his knife. These disgusting surgeons always had a mixture of tobacco juice and blood running from the corners of their mouths. They held large chaws of tobacco in their mouths, maybe to offset the taste or just the thought of it, and then they would spit the blood and tobacco mixture into a bucket along with the testicles, for Debbie to separate and cook as the sheepherder's gourmet delight, "Rocky Mountain Oysters."

Jon and I, not having been through sheep docking pre-med or wanting to, were assigned to paint orange brands onto the sides of the sheep, because real branding with a hot iron would ruin a good portion of the wool. We poured creosol onto the bleeding tails and scrotums to keep the flies from planting their eggs. When the creosol procedure wasn't effective or was misapplied, we picked off the maggots with sticks and by hand. Tromping the hay for cattle or horse for winter feed was tolerable, because it was tempered with the long ride to and from the hay field in a horse-drawn wagon. Hyrum and any neighbor he could con into helping would throw on the hay while Jon and I positioned it and tramped it into place. We made our way up to the top of the piles as more hay was thrown on.

When Hyrum determined that we had a load, everyone climbed up onto the mobile haystack. Hyrum made a special sound by clicking his tongue and lower jaw and slapped the horses with the reins. As the wagon moved slowly and precariously across the bumpy field and through the large irrigation ditches toward the barn, it rocked from side to side. It was difficult to believe it wouldn't tip over and suffocate us as we lay helplessly beneath it.

In the evening before dinner and after we had washed, Jon and I used fingers and pliers to remove sheep tics from each other. We looked like monkeys picking off salt deposits.

One day Jon led me up to a hill just above a seldom-traveled gravel road. We laboriously rolled a large truck tire along with us. After we had gone quite a way, Jon stopped and pointed up the steep bank, which I interpreted to mean we would be taking the tire up there. After we had rolled and dragged the tire well above the road to a small flat spot, we stopped to catch our breath. After a few minutes Jon, spoke to me. It was unusual for him to speak to me directly.

"Hold the tire up," he said.

As I held it, he forced his small body inside the tire and then said, almost apologetically, "You can go next."

"Oh, yeah?" I returned.

"Okay," he shouted, "push me over the edge."

I hesitated for a moment and he said again, "Push me over the edge. Don't worry, you can go next!"

I didn't think it looked very safe and decided that no matter what Jon said about my turn, I wasn't going to take this ride. "If he's dumb enough to want to do it, then I'll give him a shove," I thought. I pushed him and the tire toward the edge and let go. Picking up speed quickly, he went bouncing down the steep incline. As the tire bumped toward the road, it flew into the air and I saw Jon's arm sticking straight out. He was screaming gleefully. The tire hit the bank at the near side and bounced completely over the road and out into the field. Jon rolled a long way before the tire finally fell onto its side.

"He's dead. He killed himself!" I yelled. I held my cast to my side and ran as fast as I could to find out the awful truth. When I reached the tire and peered inside, Jon's smiling face looked back at me. "It's your turn now," he said. "Help me get my head out."

His head had become lodged in between the sides of the tire, but I couldn't pull the rubber apart far enough with my weakened arm for him to get out.

"I'll have to get help," I said, and started toward the house.

"Don't tell my dad how it happened," Jon called after me. "He won't let me do it anymore."

"How the hell did you get your head in there?" Hyrum asked when he arrived.

"I don't know," was Jon's feeble reply.

I always used the excuse of being too large to get inside the tire to do the death-defying trick, and Jon finally quit asking me to try. But it was one of his favorite activities and with my help, he did it often.

By using a long, heavy stick, the sides of the tire could be moved just enough to remove his head from the rubber death-trap without enlisting the aid of his father.

After the hay had been cut, we walked barefoot in the stubble of the fields until our feet became so tough they didn't bleed anymore. We played cars on the banks of the river in the sand, using blocks of wood as model cars, or the guides from the hay mower bar. I had never felt so free, so completely liberated. Our only chores were getting kindling, tromping hay and wool, or starting Debbie's gas-powered washing machine, which was kept out of the weather on the screened-in back porch.

And then one day it was all over. I was delighted to be going home to Victoria, but I hadn't really made an effort to get home to see her. The farm had been a lot of fun. It was a summer I would never forget, but now I was ready for it to end.

One morning, after a special breakfast, Hyrum, Debbie, Jon, and I sat quietly as the rattletrap pickup carried me back to Mom and Dad and my real life with my wonderful Victoria. When we finally got home, I said goodbye to the others, lifted out my Me box and pulled it along behind me as I went inside to face the music.

Chapter 44

Victoria wasn't in Springtown when I got home, and I became afraid that because I hadn't tried to contact her, she had gone and wasn't coming back. I tossed and turned all night, unable to sleep. I was about to get up when my bedroom door opened and Mom sort of oozed in. Something was wrong—she clutched a crumpled tissue in her hand and looked very sad as she tried to wipe the tears and the tragedy from her mascara-stained eyes.

The lightning shot up to fill my mouth with the taste of sulfur. "What's wrong? Is something wrong with Victoria?"

She tried not to cry. "No—no, not Victoria. B-but W-William, I do have s-some bad n-news."

I sat up, fully awake; anxiously waiting.

"I haven't even told your dad yet. I didn't want to tell him because he would squander the money at the Shame. It's terrible news, but we're going to be better off now, at least where money is concerned."

"What the hell is it, Mom?"

"Don't cuss, William."

"Mom..."

"Aunt Helen and Uncle Archibald have been in a terrible accident."

The lightning hit my spine, shoulders, and skull. The sulfur filled my mouth again. "Are they all right?"

Mom's eyes filled with tears again ... she couldn't speak for a moment. "They were both killed." The words came out with difficulty, between the sobs.

"Aunt Helen, too?" I asked. Hell, Uncle Archibald wouldn't be a loss.

Mom's face puckered to cry, and then she caught herself, wiped her wet eyes and nose with the crumpled tissue, and went on. "Yes. She lived for a few days––they thought she might make it––but she got pneumonia and passed on in her sleep. We can stay in the house. I feel so guilty––I'm almost glad." Her face lost color. "I don't know if I could have moved back into the dungeon." She sort of squeezed the words out.

Her face began to take back some of the sallow-gray appearance that the years in the dungeon had indelibly etched there. "But I think Aunt Helen was going to allow us to take over part of the house, now that all her kids have left. At least she said she would."

Aunt Helen was a saint, and everybody loved her. The funeral was a large, standing-room-only service that went on and on. Her dear friends sang songs until I thought they would never end: "When the Role Is Called Up Yonder," "Mother McRae," "Waiting at the Edge of Heaven," and many others. I became so sad, I was ready to kill myself. One by one, old men and women stood up, their eyes and faces filled with tears, to say what a good person she was, and then they groped for something good to say about Uncle Archibald. That was followed by the bearing of testimony, and then the Bishop tried to talk us all into being saved and getting into the highest glory by doing good and great works for the church here on earth.

Tears and red eyes were everywhere. I cried, too, a little bit for Aunt Helen, but mostly for Victoria. The sadness that filled the funeral only made my loneliness for her more acute. I wondered what she was doing and thinking about. I wondered if she still thought about me—if she still loved me. And then I wondered if I would be going to hell for some of things we had done—and I felt a soft surge of lightning, as the mild taste of sulfur coated the roof of my mouth. "If she was there with me, hell would be OK," I thought. And then, "Maybe with all this new money and the house, James H. will reconsider and accept me as royalty."

Aunt Helen's kids weren't very happy that Mom and Dad were included in the will and would get some of the money, as well as the use of the house. During the funeral, they shot vindictive glances in our direction. Or maybe we felt guilty about taking their money, and only imagined they were angry with us. Anyway, after what seemed to be forever, a long procession of cars slowly moved, headlights blazing, from the long, boring funeral at the church to the long, boring ritual at the gravesite.

We got to ride in a limousine: Dad, Mom, Ellen, Martha, and me, probably because we didn't have a car. The gravesite service was long and tearful, too, but finally the two caskets were slowly lowered into the ground, their heads pointing west, so when the deceased sat up on resurrection day, they would encounter the Lord with their resurrected eyes, as if He, She or It was the rising sun. I had to laugh as I imagined those bony bodies rising up, their little pioneer bonnets on their fleshless heads.

Two men, dressed in blue workman's uniforms, stood at the edge of the mourners, waiting for us to leave, so they could cover the ornate caskets with the concrete vault lid and begin slowly and carefully shoveling sandy dirt over our relatives. After we were out of sight, they would most assuredly use a Fresno Scraper or other equipment to cover it all up by more expeditious methods.

Chapter 45

Alex Stanze sits in the dim, near-empty bar, thinking about what has brought him here. He stares almost lovingly at his half-empty mug of yellow elixir as the blue neon lights of the Bel Aire Club blink monotonously from the other side of the window. He has learned to like this "devil rum" too much. He isn't a mean man, but the trials of his life should have made him mean, and they are at least partially responsible for his drinking more than he should. He feels that his homosexuality has caused almost everyone to hate him, even though he has no control over it. This situation alone could have made him mean, but the more extreme events concerning William have driven him to the point where he is now considering murder.

He considers going to the furnace room and allowing William to escape, or to at least bring him some food, but somehow, even given his gentle nature, he can't do that. William killed Alex's brothers and almost killed him, too—and disfigurement is a very hard thing to forgive. And who else has he killed? Alex wonders if it is only his imagination—maybe William is innocent. Maybe he should give him a final chance to convince him of his innocence. Maybe William has discovered some new information, and Alex will be able to forgive and forget. He stands, lifts his glass to his lips and drains it. Then he drops a few coins on the worn surface of the bar and nods a farewell to the oblivious barkeep.

It is raining and the few cars moving along the street lift a light spray behind their wheels as they pass. Alex smells the pleasant, clean odor of wetness that rain brings. He times his crossing of the street and as quickly as his crumpled body will allow, he limps to the dark, vacant building with "The Camelot-Avalon Apartments" in bold lettering on the front. Another sign is also displayed conspicuously on the front of the Avalon side in large letters, "THIS SIDE OF BUILDING CONDEMNED. DANGER, DO NOT ENTER."

He smiles as he reads it. "Appropriate for that creep," he whispers.

He stands for a moment trying to read the small, indistinguishable words below the sign's warning, and then fumbles for his flashlight and limps down the alley to the rear of the building, to the incline that leads to the heavy, wooden, ironclad door. It has been nailed shut. He smiles as he recalls driving in those nails only a few days earlier. He stands for a moment, listening for any sound from William, and then directs the light through a crack between the eroded boards of the heavy door and asks in a soft voice, "William, are you there?"

There is no response.

"Maybe he's dead," Alex thinks, but he is strangely disappointed. He wants William to suffer at least for a while longer, especially if he's guilty, and he's almost sure he is. "William?" he asks again and is startled by an answer.

"What do you want, Alex? Are you here to let me out?"

In a strange way, Alex is relieved. "I need to ask you some questions." There is no answer, so he goes on, "Are you hungry? Can I bring you something to eat?"

"I am a little hungry––what about some prime rib with caviar and red wine?"

Alex is amazed that William is so bold and imaginative. "I'll bring you something if you will answer a few questions. Maybe not prime rib with caviar and red wine, but something."

There is no answer. Alex places his ear against the crack in the heavy door. He can hear heavy breathing but can only imagine what is going on in that dark, damp hold. "Okay then, just suffer for a while. I'll be back when you feel more like talking." He turns and walks away as quickly as he can. He decides to come back when William is hungrier, and maybe more talkative.

It is dark inside the furnace room; I can barely see. There is only a hint of light from the street and from the blinking red Firestone sign next door to the Avalon side that filters through the dirty iron bars and screen-clad windows. If that ass Alex thinks he can patronize me and then have me tell him anything, he has another think coming. I wouldn't turn a hand to help him. I'll just stay here and wait for Victoria. She'll find me, I'm sure. I really need to tell her about the bastard's quest to ruin us. All Alex's intrusion did was take me away from the excursions, which are my only chance to find out what the hell he's talking about.

Chapter 46

Three days later, Aunt Helen's will was read in the lawyer's office. Ellen and I were allowed to attend, with the promise that we would keep our mouths shut and speak only when spoken to. Mrs. MacLean tended Martha at home. The bulk of the money had been left to Aunt Helen's kids but ten per cent went to the church. That could very well be the amount needed to nudge their souls into heaven, probably with Aunt Helen pulling Uncle Archibald's pitiful, despicable soul behind her. The almighty money should clinch it, I silently mused as that part of the will was read. Mom and Dad got an undisclosed amount of money as well as the use of the house––until and if they ever left it for good––and then it would go to Aunt Helen's kids.

"Bunch 'a ungrateful bustards," Dad whispered about the kids. "They ain't even human beins."

When I asked how much money he got, he said, "None a' yer damn' business!"

The house had a different feeling now that it was ours to stay in permanently. But Mom acted differently, too; she was beginning to take back the dungeon look. There was something on her mind. She wouldn't even go close to the washhouse. Finally she told me, "Dad's decided we're going to Montana. He wants to own a farm like his father did. He found a brochure about Montana and the cheap land up there."

"There must be a reason it's cheap," I said. "There's something wrong with it."

"Well, he's the man, and we are supposed to do what the man wants. That's what God wants us to do. That's what the church says, that's what the Bible says, and that's what God says, too. And Dad says we don't even own this house. We won't even be able to sell it if we ever have trouble."

"Mom, what the hell? Now we have everything, and maybe someday Victoria will come back––she won't know where to find me in Montana. And God didn't say the man is boss, for hell's sake––people did. Men said and say that."

"You know how he is. He'll probably just forget the whole thing," she said with a defeated smile. "He'll probably just stay here and spend all the money at the Shame. But I'd rather live in Montana, or anywhere else, than go back to the dungeon."

Dad decided to spend a little bit of the money on a car. We had never had a car, and he always said it was a waste of money to have a good one. He came home one day with an old, beat-up, oil-burning relic: a 1939 Dodge Sedan. He said, "I got us a truck too, in case we decide to move anywhere. It's bein' worked on and we just need ta pick it up." And he smiled anxiously.

I knew Dad, and my bet was that they would be moving to Montana soon. I had decided not to go; I was planning to stay and wait for Victoria. I could mow lawns and live in the dungeon if I had to. But wait for her, I would.

Chapter 47

Oscar and Alex Stanze sat in silence, staring at the off-white colored walls of the large room. It appeared to be a doctor's office of some sort because of the medical diplomas that lined the walls, boasting of long years of study to become psychologist. The room was antiseptically clean, but without the usual odor that such offices often have. There were no large bottles of white condoms or wooden tongue depressors sitting obviously in view. No pictures on the walls—no skeletons or people with their skin peeled off to show the muscles, veins, and essential body parts. There were books and magazines stacked neatly on the end tables and in bookcases; they all told about technical, scientific, and medical stuff.

The brothers were there for Oscar. The years of therapy had helped him, but it seemed that Oscar's frustrations were caused by more than just the guilt about his brother's death.

The door opened, and a tall, thin man with gray, receding hair and a thin, dark mustache sauntered in. The nameplate pinned to his lapel read, "Dr. Wainscot, PhD."

He looked and acted like a therapist or doctor should look and act. The thick, green-tinted, wire-rimmed glasses pinched his nose and made his washed-out green eyes even more sedate and lifeless. This fit very nicely with the light gray pants and clean but well-worn laboratory smock.

He had a feminine way about him, but in contrast, his secondary physical attributes were distinctly masculine: a five o'clock shadow, even though he was closely shaven, darkened the lower portion of his face. The long, dark hair of his chest was bushy and pushed out over the "V" of his closed smock. Below that, a sharp line where the thick hair had been shaved appeared to be quite out of place. His hands were large with protruding veins; he appeared to be well-toned and in excellent physical condition. He introduced himself and smiled, as both the brothers rose to accept his hand in an anxious, but friendly way.

"I'm Oscar––this is my brother Alex," Oscar announced nervously.

The three exchanged small talk for a few moments and then Oscar said, somewhat sheepishly, "I've just been released from rehab and scheduled here for a follow-up."

With his eyes and a sage nod, the doctor encouraged Oscar to continue.

"My brother was good enough to come with me. I usually try to keep an eye on him––to keep him out of trouble." Oscar said it like he was kidding. Alex nodded submissively.

The doctor held up a manila folder. "Yes, I know. It's all in here. The clinic sent it. And you were just released." He smiled at Oscar. "Well, the part about your brother isn't here," he continued. "Will you be coming with him from now on?" he asked of Alex.

"I'm sure I won't be, doc," Alex said. "And if you're going to take him inside, I'll just wait out here."

Oscar looked at his brother. "You stay here, Alex. I mean it."

Alex rolled his eyes, picked up a magazine, and began flipping the pages in his usual feminine fashion, obviously uninterested in what he saw.

After the door closed, the doctor motioned Oscar to a couch and took for himself an overstuffed, leather-covered recliner, the only other seating. The room was conservatively decorated, with obviously expensive wall coverings, pictures, and unobtrusive paraphernalia. The two chatted for a while, and Dr. Wainscot demonstrated that he knew when to listen, when to talk, when to look sad, and also when to snicker a little at forced humor from either of them.

"How's your brother doing?"

"You just met him. What do you think?"

"No, I mean Craig. How's he getting along?"

Oscar seemed troubled. "Haven't heard much from Craig."

"I just like to try to keep tabs on my old patients," the doctor said.

Oscar looked concerned. "I didn't know Craig had been a patient of yours."

"Yes, he was," Wainscot said. "I shouldn't have said anything, but I thought you knew."

"What was his problem?"

Wainscot gave a shallow smile. "Sorry, patient confidentiality." He went back to Oscar. "Do you feel like you're getting better?" He pushed back the recliner into a more comfortable position. "Do you think the therapy has helped at all?"

Oscar thought for a moment. "Yeah, I think it has," he said, and then followed the doctor's cue, squirming to find a more comfortable position on the couch.

The doctor stroked the stubble of his chin and asked, "Is there something else we need to discuss?"

There was an uncomfortable silence.

"Hell, yeah, I think things are getting better–but you're right, there *is* another problem."

Wainscot sat up straight. "What other problem are you having?"

After a moment, Oscar stuttered, "I-I-It's…" He paused before he went on.

Wainscot listened patiently.

"It's that I-I … I like boys. I have never been attracted to girls. I like boys. I'm trying to find a cure for that."

The doctor steepled his fingers under his chin. "It's not really a disease," he said, "it's just the way some people are born. People don't choose to be that way. I don't think anyone would wish that on themselves, especially the way our society treats them. It isn't a very pleasant life. But strangely enough, the discomfort about it isn't anything to do with them being that way. It's mostly because society, primarily religion, makes the life of a homosexual almost unbearable. Homosexuality is a mindset and probably a genetic misalignment. It is most certainly not a choice."

Tears filled Oscar's eyes. He lowered his head as his large body shook with sobs. Wainscot reached forward to cover Oscar's trembling hand with his own and then went on, "People say that God doesn't like gays. Some people enjoy putting words in God's mouth. Every person is different, Oscar, no two of us are the same. God throws away the mold. And people use certain words that make things worse. Sometimes we just don't think. Everybody needs to be more compassionate, more understanding."

"That's a strange thing about religion––I thought Jesus taught to forgive, not judge. Wasn't he about understanding and love?" Oscar fit the words in between soft sobs.

The doctor pulled his hand back, settled into his chair, and shrugged his shoulders. "You might need to ask that question of someone in a different field than mine."

Oscar had a lot to think about as he and Alex stepped into the cool night air.

"Do you feel better?" Alex asked.

"God, you sound like the doctor. Yeah, I think I do. I feel like God will forgive me for my transgressions. It's not all my fault that I'm like I am and have done what I have."

"We all have things to be forgiven for," Alex said, his face solemn and dispassionate. "I know I have."

The brothers strolled into the dim of late evening, along the side streets of Springtown, and then turned to walk along the trail at the banks of Hell Fire Creek, as they so often did. Then they turned toward the west side of town and the duplex that sat in front of that fateful pond.

Chapter 48

Oscar pulled his car to the curb and called to me, "Where ya goin', William?"

I tried to ignore him, the big dumb bastard.

"William, look at me!"

"Jesus, Oscar. I'm going to Boyer's to get some stuff fer Mom." I kept walking.

"Hey, can ya spare a minute fer an old friend?"

Hell, I didn't know what else to say. "Yeah." I walked over to the open window, but not close enough to get his fine spray of halitosis; just close enough to hear. "What's up?"

He looked sad, and asked me to get into the car, so I did. He told me about his meeting with Dr. Wainscot. He told me everything, even about being homosexual. I was shocked and frightened. I had heard about "homos," and was afraid he wanted to molest me, but he didn't do anything. He didn't even touch me. He just looked like he was going to cry.

Hell, I didn't even know homosexuals had feelings. Oscar said he had asked Dr. Wainscot if he could bring me to the next meeting. He said he had made an appointment, but could change it if that day wasn't good for me.

I didn't say much, just, "Okay," and then climbed out and went to Boyer's. Maybe a better description would be I fled, with him calling after me. I didn't even listen to what he was saying. I had heard about all the hugging and trying to touch you in private places and "corn-holing" those homos were supposed to do, and I just wanted to get away. I wondered if Mr. Tasker was a homo, even though he was married and had kids.

I avoided Oscar after that, and he seemed to avoid me as well. Maybe it was because now I knew his secret. But I felt a loss, and neglected.

I had become accustomed to the attention from him, the loss of which made my life seem more drab and boring. I liked him, and I liked being in the choir. I just didn't want to hang around with him because of all that awful stuff such people do. But without Victoria I was lonely, so I decided to go to the doctor with him, mostly to stay in good standing in the choir and to keep doing all that exciting stuff, even though I knew the choir couldn't last for long, because I had been mouthing the words for quite a while, and my voice change would probably soon be discovered. I missed Victoria so much. I needed to find something to fill the void. Maybe if Oscar promised not to get too close or touch me, I could still be his friend.

Dr. Wainscot looked at me for a long time as I sat on the leather couch in the inner office. I was getting pretty nervous before he spoke. I was thinking of getting the hell out of there. Oscar was waiting in the outer lobby. Finally Wainscot broke the silence. "Oscar has told me how you remind me of his little brother. He feels responsible for his death."

"Yeah, he's told me about all that, too."

"He really feels an attachment to you, William. He seems to be trying to resurrect an image of his brother in you."

I sat silently for a moment. "To tell the truth, I'm a little uncomfortable around a homo."

"Homosexuals aren't any more apt to seduce you than heterosexuals would be," the doctor said.

"I thought they would try to sneak up behind you and try to stick it in."

Now Wainscot laughed. "I know you're just kidding, William. You certainly couldn't mean something so absurd."

"Yeah, I was just kidding, but I do think they would all try to make it with any other man."

"No, they have feelings and morals, just like anyone else does."

I was silent.

"Oscar asked me to explain basically about his condition."

I had the feeling that I should say something. "What kind of disease is it, doc?"

"I can't say much, because of patient confidentiality, but I can tell you that homosexuality isn't a disease. It's just the way some people are born."

"Maybe like a DNA defect?" I asked.

"How do you know about DNA?"

"My dad and his friend talk to me about it," I said.

"Oh."

"And I have some books about Einstein and other scientists."

"Albert Einstein, the scientist, the nuclear physicist?"

I smiled. It felt good to feel so important. I was becoming more relaxed.

The doctor went on, "Oscar said he has feelings for men, and sometimes he has urges and feelings toward younger men, even boys. He also said he knows they are not right, so he dismisses them."

"Can't he control himself?"

"The mind is a complex set of mechanisms, William."

"If Oscar is a homosexual, is that the same as being a pedophile?"

"No, of course not," the doctor said. He seemed to be more like a doctor now as he began stating facts like he was reading them from a book. "In fact, heterosexuals are just as likely to be pedophiles as homosexuals are. Only a few homosexuals are pedophiles––about the same ratio as heterosexuals."

My eyes widened. "Fascinating," I said.

Dr. Wainscot studied me for a few moments, and then went on. "Being homosexual says nothing about a person, other than maybe whom they might want to sleep with. They can be good or bad, just like people who aren't homosexual can be. It's not like being psychotic or certain classifications of schizophrenia. "

"What are those, doctor?" I asked.

He regarded me again, as if thinking.

"Hell," I thought, "this is probably the way they told him to act at his doctor school, or wherever he learned to be a psychologist."

Finally, he went on. "Schizophrenia is quite a broad category that doesn't really describe much by itself. Generally speaking, the main categories under that heading are Positive and Negative, and other subcategories are under them. There are some pretty tame conditions within those classifications, but some pretty harsh and frightening ones as well. At its worst, schizophrenia is a type of psychosis."

And then he stopped and thought again, probably like his school had taught him to do. "Very confusing, doc," I said.

"Well, maybe I can simplify it all. Positive symptoms of schizophrenia are characterized by delusions, hallucinations, thought disorders and involuntary movements, and these things may come and go in a short span of time. Negative symptoms are characterized by reduction in the normal behavior of a person. Facial expressions are gone, and there is an inability to execute plans the person makes. Poor hygiene and infrequent speech are other negative symptoms. In some cases, schizophrenia occurs continuously while in other cases it doesn't last as long, which is sometimes called schizophreniform disorder."

He looked to see if I was still awake, and then continued. "There are basically five different types of schizophrenia, and the symptoms of these types vary accordingly. There's paranoid schizophrenia, catatonic schizophrenia, disorganized schizophrenia, undifferentiated schizophrenia, and residual.

These types have their respective symptoms and sub-categories as well. To make it even more obscure and confusing, schizophrenia includes some categories that are psychotic in nature, and some experts think schizophrenic conditions could be psychosomatic, which means there's no psychological problem. Instead, the condition derives from emotional stress or conflict."

Then he stopped again, but this time he looked more like he was confused than he was using a tactic taught in school. "Anyway, I hope you can sort of comprehend this."

I held back a grin. It was becoming a little humorous, but I forced myself to be serious. "Do you think Oscar is any of these? Do you think he might be involved in the murders that have been happening in town?" I asked.

"Oh, even if I have thoughts about that, I would be prohibited by patient confidentiality from saying anything. All I can is whoever is committing the murders is very clever, although a little amateurish. When people who do these sorts of things are psychotic—and I'm not saying that's necessarily the case here—they sometimes don't even realize that another of their own personalities is doing these things."

Dr. Wainscot looked at me again, probably to see if I was still paying attention. "Multiple personality is a rare condition. In order to understand it, you first have to eliminate a popular misconception. Many people confuse multiple personality with schizophrenia and bipolar disorder, but they're not related. One characteristic of schizophrenia is a "split" between thinking and affect, or feelings, which results in an inappropriate expression of affect. Some people incorrectly believe that schizophrenia is a "split personality" manifested by different, or multiple personalities. Bipolar disorder involves extreme and crippling swings in mood that go far beyond the 'ups and downs' that many people experience.

"The basic theoretical dynamic in multiple personality is that the person deals with conflicting feelings and thoughts by repressing them and compartmentalizing them so that certain kinds of feelings and thoughts are expressed in one personality or state of consciousness, and other conflicting feelings and thoughts are expressed in another personality, making it unnecessary to reconcile the different thoughts and feelings."

"What causes this condition, doctor?" I asked.

"Well," Dr. Wainscot replied, "sometimes a single incident can do it, like being responsible for hurting or killing someone you love. Sometimes, a series of incidents with tragic consequences can do it. As I said, the mind is a complicated organism. Every person and every incident is different."

"Maybe Oscar's worse than I thought," I said.

The doctor shook his head and smiled knowingly, then went on, "To get back to things we do know for sure, the percentage of people who are pedophiles or psychotic is probably about the same among heterosexuals as among homosexuals. Most homosexuals keep their sexuality concealed, and it's only the ones who commit crimes or become involved in aberrant behavior, getting their names into newspapers, who anyone ever hears about. That's probably why some people think all homosexuals are pedophiles and all homosexuals are bad."

He sat for a moment, thinking again. "It's a little bit like the popular opinion that atheists are immoral or wicked. Much evidence supports the contention that atheists are every bit as moral as the religious, and even that morality and virtue are historically attributable more to the non-religious than to the religious. People who want to hold up China or Russia as examples of atheists had better include Einstein, Paine, and Buddha, too."

God, was I getting confused. What if the person who was doing the murders didn't even remember doing it? "How many homosexual people are there?" I asked, trying to get back to our original topic.

As was his routine, the doctor was silent for a moment. This time, it looked again like the schooled kind of silence. "Well," he said, "there's no easy answer for that question. There seem to be degrees of homosexuality versus heterosexuality in both women and men. On top of that, some people are bisexual, which means they're attracted to both sexes at different times or even at the same time. It would be quite difficult to count all the people with different degrees of homosexuality.

"If it helps you, some experts think there might be as few as six categories of sexuality. For example, if we're talking about men, you have: one, being a man who only likes women; two, liking women but liking men just a little bit; three, liking both about the same, which is bisexuality, and so forth, up to six, who only likes men. So, in order to count homosexual people, I guess we would need to classify all of the degrees and categories. It would be an impossible undertaking. And there are some people who are homosexual and masquerade as heterosexual and are never found out." He stopped talking and looked at me, then went on, "Sorry I can't answer more precisely."

"Mind-boggling," I mused.

"If you think that's mind-boggling," Wainscot said, "think about this: most people have had some sort of homosexual experience during their life. It's unlikely that they will admit it, but most have, nonetheless."

"Have you?" I asked, as was my nature.

He sat silently, and then said, "Remember, I said most people won't admit it, but I will tell you this—a lot of people go into a field of study to find out the answer to a personal problem they might be trying to hide."

"Oh."

His expression turned sadder.

"A lot of young people commit suicide because of the scorn society shows them and for being and doing something that most of society has personally done, at least in one way or another. It's such a waste of children's lives. The men have it the toughest. People seem to be more sympathetic toward lesbians."

"Why is that?"

"I don't know. Lots of people say God doesn't like gay men—— but some people enjoy putting words in God's mouth. Funny," Wainscot went on, "religion, in its ignorance, is mostly to blame for driving these misconceptions. As good as some religious people are, they refuse to think for themselves."

"Do you believe in God?" I asked.

Dr. Wainscot sat looking at his feet for a moment, and then began rattling off, like it was an oath, "If you are talking about the God that longs for gold and power and is indiscriminate about getting it—the God that will trample and contaminate cultures and individuals with tricks and gimmicks to get control over the minds and wallets of the multitudes—then I can say unequivocally, no, I don't. But if you are talking about the God that is blind to color, sexuality, or race, one who will comfort any distraught child for any reason, will selflessly and honestly help anyone forlorn and lost without thought for His or Her own popularity or wealth and without tricks or gimmicks, then I have to say without reserve, yes, I do."

I was amazed. I had never thought about it in this way before.

Wainscot smiled and went on, "Keep this in mind, William. The human mind tends to protect its owner at all cost. Just because people have acted certain ways in the past doesn't mean they're not hiding something, or that they won't change. I'm just warning you, I'm not trying to frighten you, but always be careful. I'd like you to come in to talk to me again. I feel it's very important that you do."

"Let me think about that. Why do you know so much about homosexuality, doc?"

Wainscot smiled sadly. "Well, William, psychology emphasizes things like this, and also, as I said, people usually learn more about things they are a part of."

What the hell did that mean? One thing I did know–I was going to watch Oscar very closely from now on.

Chapter 49

One morning at breakfast, Dad dragged his shaking, bedraggled self out of bed and with great effort tried, with questionable success, to separate the "now" and the "last night" at the Shame. He stood before us in his magical underwear; he wasn't supposed to be wearing them because of his iniquity, but he was.

The fly was open, exposing his privates, as if we were so unimportant and he was so awesome that his exposure was of no concern.

"W-we don't need ta w-worry 'bout that old b-bastard Cook a-anymore," he stammered.

We all stopped eating to hear the rest.

"He kilt his'sef; they found him a-hangin' from the ceiling. Tied his shoelace to the light chord and jus stepped off the stool. Lucky I was out lookin' fer work or we wouldn't a-heard 'bout it." Mom's face turned gray, the sulfur cruelly filled my mouth, and Ellen and Martha stopped eating their Lumpy Dick cereal. "That's wha' the ol' bastard deserved," he finished with a gagging dry-heave, his hand over his mouth, his privates lurching disgustingly.

"And that old drunk Rule arrested got the door open and left, I guess," Dad went on. "Rule put out a statewide APB, but hell, them old drunks all look pretty much alike, so he's probably long gone."

"I didn't think a light cord would be strong enough to hold a body," I said.

"Well, it is. The only difference 'tween him doin' it or the electric chair is that the lights don't blink when they pull that there switch, but either way's just as effective," Dad said. Then he laughed. "Looks like Sheriff Everett solved another case. Nobody don't kill the'seves if'n they ain't guilty."

He sat for a while, trying to stop gagging and get his empty stomach to stop retching. He realized he was exposing himself, covered his crotch with his hand, and went on. "The only thing Rule couldn't figure was the shoelace was the kind out of a boot, and Mr. Cook always wore the little skinny kind in his wingtips.

"But ... " and then a retch expelled a small amount of phlegm that ran down his stubbled chin as his body struggled to rid itself of the overindulgence in last night's spirits. With the phlegm hanging from his chin and his privates visible again, all of us had stopped eating for good. After he got control of his body, he went on, seemingly too sick to do the hillbilly talking anymore. "...Rule and the guys at the jail are sure that Mr. Cook must have been wearing those damned heavy shoelaces wrapped around his ankles or something."

I felt a little bit sorry for old Mr. Cook, but I felt better too; safer, now that he was dead.

Chapter 50

That night I had a lot of trouble trying to fall asleep. Things about the killings bothered me, maybe more than they should have. Victoria was gone, possibly never to return, although I couldn't be sure. Dad seemed bent on knocking out the windows with his snoring in the next room. I needed to get out of there, into the fresh air and away from the noise. I needed some rest.

On the bridge, I finally was able to find sleep, as its reassuring ambience engulfed me. Pleasant at first, my thoughts became more serious as I began to conjure up the vividness that dreams are sometimes made of ...

> *The recent murders and the images of war overflowed from Europe to cover our fields and parks with the dead, just as we had been told they did in those far-off places. I stood heroically and stoically, appearing as a hero to the entire world. I was a hero, although I had never made a public statement that would go down in history as mine and give me immortality, like Abraham Lincoln at Gettysburg, or Jackson at the end of the Civil War or maybe a distant relative, John Paul Jones, on liberty and death. I began working on my statement, devising a title for it,*

with my name attached to make it easier for historians.

"The Valiant Address," by William Robert Jones III

"The sounds of battle are gone. Now the fields lie meek and fallow--only the stench of death endures. A gentle gust of wind like the judging hand of God pushes the thin veil of fog from the silent symbols of combat to reveal the inhumanity of man. Arms, legs, and body parts lie strewn about like abandoned toys in a careless child's room, leaving only an eerie feeling of evil and doom. Among the other dead lie two boys, Pat and Harvey, their faces steeped in anxious sadness and longing over their short and futile lives. And then, as if an embarrassed deity had reconsidered and decided to conceal its folly, a curious darkness falls, as small delicate snowflakes begin to hide the wasteful carnage."

My valiant address was interrupted ... in the distance, the dim figure of a man hovered in the gray darkness above the fallen soldiers; it looked like Mr. Cook. He was sitting on the translucent outline of a coffin and crying. A shoelace around his neck was tied to an incongruous light cord above him. The light blinked on and off. He was looking at me, like I should help him.

A dark, shrouded figure moved stealthily in front of him and floated toward me. It held a duffel bag, and a grotesque twisted head, black from death, stuck out. The eyes bulged from the sockets and bloody phlegm flowed from its mouth. A headless body holding its severed head floated in thin air above it. I tried to run, but my arms and legs wouldn't move. A cold chill found me; I shivered. The menacing creature came close and wound the cord around my neck. It pulled tight. I gasped; I couldn't breathe.!

"I'M NOT DEAD YET!" I yelled as I sat up from the nightmare, gasping for breath. "It wasn't Mr. Cook!" I screamed. I tested my arms and legs; they worked. The air was freezing cold, but I was soaked with sweat. I settled myself and then huddled back down onto the bridge in the required, fetal-like position, and pulled the meager blanket around the damp clothing and myself. I found the Me box and held it as if to comfort me.

I had to get some sleep; I needed more sleep. But now I somehow knew that Mr. Cook hadn't committed the murders and, with the information that Dr. Wainscot had given me, I felt sure I knew who it was. But I also suspected that the murderer probably didn't even know he had done anything. I was sure he was a psychotic or schizophrenic or maybe both, as the doctor had said they are sometimes. I was sure it was Oscar or at least one of the Stanze boys. Still half-asleep and half-awake, I tried to think. I knew I had to do something; I had to tell somebody. But first, I needed to forget about everything—at least for a while.

Chapter 51

The dark, silent figure waited, dressed as a Droogen in Halloween attire, concealed behind a scrub, watching an energetic youth as he tried to tug and drag a large truck tire to the top of the ridge. The silent Droogen was tired; it had walked through the spooky gloom of this autumn holiday among the other creatures, and then miles along a deserted road to get here. It watched as the struggling youth below pushed and pulled the large truck tire up the hill and into position.

After a lengthy struggle, the youth finally got the tire to where it needed to be. He tipped it upright and tried to get inside, but the tire fell on its side, and only luck kept it from rolling away. After several failures to climb inside it, the youth sat on the tire in despair, his head in his hands, almost in tears. He longed for the excitement of bouncing down the steep hill, going over the gravel road below with one gigantic bounce into the field, where the tire would roll, seemingly forever, before falling at last onto its side. Jon needed someone to help him. He wished William were here––he had always held the tire for him when he was here. William would never take the ride, but Jon didn't care––that left more rides for him.

The leaves had turned to autumn colors and fell in thick

clusters to the ground. The days were getting shorter, and snow on the mountaintops was getting closer and closer to the valley floor with each passing day. Crispness was in the air. Images of imps and goblins filled his thoughts. It was dusk, time for only one more quick ride—maybe the last one of the year. If only there was someone to help. Jon was startled by a sound and looked up as the Droogen left its floral sanctuary and advanced.

"Hi," Jon smiled. "It's not hard to tell who you are, but what are you supposed to be dressed as?"

"I'm a Droogen. You weren't at practice last time; the choir missed you."

"Yeah, I had to help with the sheep. But I'll be there next time, and that's for sure."

"Here, let me help you," said the Droogen.

In a matter of minutes, the huge tire was erect, and Jon was sitting inside and ready for his final ride.

Sometime later that evening in Springtown, the moon shone at its fullest. Ghouls and witches lined the streets, begging and threatening from door to door. Cars stopped at one end of a street to let tiny monsters dressed in shrouded costumes join those threatening to trade tricks for treats, in order to fill their already-bulging sacks with ill-gotten bounty. The chauffeured autos went cautiously and sometimes carelessly to opposite ends of streets, where liberated goblins were retrieved from the night back into parental captivity, to then be deposited again onto some other unwary, but hopefully fertile street.

A more-than-usually-ghoulish Droogen with unusually realistic-looking dried blood covering its body sauntered unnoticed amid the throngs of marauders. It carried across its shoulders a motionless burden wrapped in a thin blanket, the arms hanging limp and swaying to and fro with the motion of walking; possibly a Halloween hunchback transporting its prey. The Droogen had little interest in the candy or treats that were being handed out so generously. It seemed to have a more urgent goal.

The Droogen struggled under the weight and then stopped to lean against a street lamp to rest and survey the surroundings. It staggered forward a short distance, then stopped again to lean against a fence. After a few moments, it stood and disappeared into the dark recesses at the edge of the street. It followed an irrigation ditch and then picked its way cautiously along the trash-laden banks of Hell Fire Creek, the sound of its footsteps shrouded by the rush of the blood-colored water. It still held over its shoulders the bundle, and now stopped more frequently to rest or ponder before trudging along again.

Suddenly, the water began to rise. Obscured by the darkness, its redness turned gold in the moonlight. Caught off-guard, the Droogen dropped the bundle, which splashed softly into the churning water. The frightened masquerader stepped quickly to the safety of the bank and watched as Hell Fire Creek swirled the bundle into the fury of the current and quickly out of sight toward the sewage outlet of Utah Lake.

"Shit, not again," the Droogen complained. It stood watching as the bundle disappeared into the night and then, seeming to have no other choice, it painstakingly found its way through the dark to the sidewalk amidst the other goblins. It looked this way and that and then, blending in with the other disguised urchins, picked its way through the darkness to a spot inside the covered entry of the closed library on Main Street, to rest and contemplate. It breathed deeply rested, and then walked toward the west side of town, toward the duplex that sat in front of that fateful pond—intending to wash off and dispose of its clothing there.

Chapter 52

Mom had begun taking an interest in church now that we were living like human beings. She went to church almost every Sunday, even in the summer.

Dad went too when the choir sang, or when he was threatened with death from Mom for going to the Shame. I also went most of the time, although it usually took the prodding of both Mom and the bishop to get me there. The stuff just didn't make any sense to me. I would need a lot more proof about God and religion before I became fanatic enough to attend without prodding, but I was concerned about the devil and hell, which didn't seem like a great place, what with burning to a cinder forever and getting stabbed with that pitchfork.

One day at church, Oscar came and sat beside me, "How've you been William?"

"All right," I answered. I was ready for some fun and excitement but didn't want to be killed or have my head cut off. I wasn't going to tell anybody of my suspicions about Oscar. Hell, they wouldn't believe me, and he didn't even know he was doing anything, anyway.

"Have you heard from Victoria?" he asked.

"No."

"That's too bad; I know you like her and miss her. Maybe she will come back."

We sat on the back row and talked for a while. He had always been likeable and he seemed nice now; maybe the doctor had cured him. Maybe he was cured from killing.

"You seem to be better. Are you feeling better?" I asked.

"Yes," he said, "the doctor says I'm almost over my brother. I don't feel as guilty as I did before. But I need a few more sessions." His face turned sad. "The doctor decided to move to Canada to help some people there. I'm going there for a final session. He thinks I need to see him again, and maybe a vacation might help me as well." He looked at me; his eyes looked kind/ He had changed.

"Want to go?" he asked.

Hell, yes, I wanted to go. I wanted to do about anything to break the boredom. "Gee, I don't know. I don't think Mom and Dad would let me."

But a vacation to a foreign country sounded like fun; almost too good to pass up. Still, I was worried about him not being cured yet. "Yeah, I would like to go," I admitted. It would get my mind off from Victoria.

Oscar talked to Mom and Dad and they agreed that it would be a great experience for me, especially with all expenses paid. But while we were making plans to leave, Victoria came to Springtown without warning.

"I'm not going now," I told her.

"It's a chance of a lifetime William," she said. "You should go."

"But I want to stay here now."

"William, Daddy is here. He's going to stay for a few days, maybe a week. It might be better if you went. How long will you be gone?"

"Three or four days, I think. Maybe a week."

"You go. When you get back, I'll still be here and Daddy will be gone. I need to talk to you when you get back. I can't stand being away from you."

Finally, I agreed. "Okay, but wait for me. Don't leave until I get back."

"Okay. And we still have a little time before you leave."

We spent the following days together, but our life wasn't as carefree now. Everything seemed more serious. Victoria was growing up, which only made me love her more. We walked to Boyer's Store and drank from the same bottle of cola and talked about the future. We held each other close in the old shed at the back of our property and whispered our plans and desires to each other. I didn't want to leave her; not ever. We roamed the neighborhood, playing in the irrigation ditch and the sheds in back of our house. It was delightful, just as it always had been when we were younger. I was only half a person when she wasn't with me; she made me whole. We renewed our vows to always be together, to always love each other.

She looked like she was gaining some weight and looked a little tired and maybe a little haggard, but I still loved her. Nothing would ever change that.

"How long will you be gone?" she asked.

"I already said, did you forget?" I said briskly. I looked at her gentle face framed in blond hair and accented by her green eyes and caring smile. Tears filled her eyes. I folded her little body into my arms. "I'm an ass. I didn't mean to be mean," I said.

The sunshine made its way onto her face again.

"A few days," I said. "Maybe a week, maybe not quite a week."

Her face was pale but she was still Victoria; it didn't matter to me.

"I'll wait for you. You should go. I'll always wait for you."

She made me melt. I would do anything for her. "I might be able to help Oscar. He says he's almost better. And your dad will be gone when I get back. Old James H. will be gone." I almost cheered.

"He's still my daddy, William," she said. "I'll be with you while you're gone and here when you get back."

I didn't have any nice clothes for the trip, but I did have a small bank account from an inheritance that came to me after Uncle Ben passed on. He didn't have any family and we all ended up with a couple of bucks. Mom and Dad had borrowed some of it, as they had from my sisters, with the intention of paying it back some day, but even after they got the money from Aunt Helen's inheritance, they hadn't repaid us. It reminded me of the banana promise. Dad had the attitude that he had given it and that he could damned well take it away too, if he so chose. He had given us life, and we should owe him for that, as if he was some sort of a god.

"He's a god, all right," I thought. "A god-dammed idiot."

I asked Victoria if she thought I should take my money out of the bank for clothes.

"It's yours, isn't it?" she said. "But save some of it. We might need it."

"Well, yes, it is mine and we will need some money when we get married."

I found the little bank book and we walked to Main Street together.

The bank teller had the same stoic look as Miss Phelps at the library.

"You have about sixteen dollars left in your account, Mr. Jones," she announced, about as precisely as Miss Phelps might have done.

"Please give me all of it," I replied.

"Save a little, William," Victoria reminded me.

"That will close the account," the teller cautioned, with a concerned look on her face.

"Okay," I returned, "just give me $14.50." I tried to show my best grown-up look.

The money bought some nice clothes. Victoria helped with the selections. My favorite was a Hawaiian shirt with white leaves on a blue background that was made from silk and fit really well. I had to admit it made me look older and really good.

As usual, it was difficult for me to get away with anything. The new clothes caught my parents' attention and I was forced to tell where the money came from. I was sentenced to solitary confinement in my room without food or water for an undisclosed period of time, and my trip to Canada was cancelled.

Victoria came to my bedroom window. "Your parents are pretty strange," she laughed.

"Yeah, Mom and Dad look at things from their own selfish viewpoint, for sure."

"They seem to be trying to keep you from having any fun or enjoying yourself. They're a lot like Daddy."

"Well, you're right about your dad, and right about my parents too, I guess."

"I'm sorry you're stuck here." She stood on tiptoes to kiss me through the screen. "Daddy's going to Scotland in three days," she said.

"Well, I can't go to Canada now, because of the money thing."

"Can you get away from your room for a while? I need to talk to you. I was going to wait until you got back but now that you're not going, we really need to talk."

"About what?"

"See if you can get away for a few minutes."

Oscar did a lot of talking to help me out with Mom and Dad. He convinced them that spending money on clothes was just something kids do and it wouldn't be fair to deprive me of the opportunity to go to Canada. He told them he would even let me do odd jobs for him when we returned until I had earned back the $14.50. With Oscar's assurance about the money, my punishment was deferred until my return from Canada, after which the confinement and torture was supposed to continue, but I was pretty sure they would forget.

Finally, the day came for me us go. Oscar and Alex waited outside in his Suburban to pick me up, Alex sitting in the back seat. I hung around the door beside my pile of stuff, gazing across the irrigation ditch, trying to see Victoria. She wasn't there, which made me think she must be angry. I couldn't blame her. She had come by to have that talk she had mentioned, but I was preoccupied with getting ready for the trip, and had sort of blown her off. And now I was leaving, although I reminded myself it really was with her blessing. We had decided this together.

I picked up my stuff and slowly walked to the Suburban, pulling my Me box, which I loaded into the back. I turned to look for Victoria, and saw her sitting on the bridge holding the cardboard back and smiling at me; I went to tell her goodbye.

"Hurry, William," Oscar said. "We need to be on our way."

"Have a good time," Victoria said. "I'm not very happy you're leaving—come back soon. We still need to talk."

She was beautiful. I loved her. "I will," I said.

I started to leave, and then stepped back to her. We stood close and pressed our bodies together. We didn't dare kiss with everyone watching, so we just stood for a moment, holding hands and looking into each other's eyes.

"See you when I get back," I whispered. "What do you want to tell me?"

"I'll tell you when you get back. Remember, I'll wait for you forever. I'll always be with you."

"I know," I answered. "You are a part of me."

"I know you're coming back, but if you weren't, I would come find you. I'd never give up." She said this like she really meant it.

I looked at her for a moment longer, and then turned and walked to the Suburban. Victoria stood watching as the vehicle pulled away. We waved to each other until the Suburban turned the corner and we were out of sight.

"You're making a fool of yourself, William," Oscar said.

"What do you mean?"

"You're too young to get that serious about a girl. You should wait until you're older."

"I don't think so. God, I'm old enough. I can grow a beard; and I'm in love with her."

"That's silly." He frowned, and we dropped the subject.

Chapter 53

Dr. Wainscot's new office, in Canada, was about 65 miles from the border, in the little town of Crenshaw, which wasn't so much a town as a wide spot in the road with a few houses and buildings dotting the landscape. We pulled up in front of a small, run-down motel with a faded sign that told us it was the Dew Drop Inn. Below the name was written in smaller, even more faded letters, "The best place to stay in Canada."

"This is it," Oscar said, as he got out to go into the office.

"Let's take a walk into the woods, William," Alex said. "Oscar won't mind."

"Hell, no. I'm too tired, and besides, I don't want to go right now."

"Oscar's got you trained. Are you afraid?"

Oscar came running to the car and said excitedly, "With the exchange rate, the rooms are cheap, so I got two of them."

We had planned to only stay a few days, and had packed accordingly, so we were able to carry all of our belongings inside in one trip. I helped Oscar take our stuff into one of the rooms. I placed my Me box by the side of one of the beds and Oscar dumped his stuff onto the other one. Alex carried his stuff into the other room.

The trip turned out to be not as fun as I had imagined. All Oscar and Alex did was fight and argue. I wanted to be home with Victoria. The first night, Alex said a cool goodnight and went to his room, and Oscar and I went to ours. That's when it hit me that Oscar could be a pedophile. He was going to hurt me, like he had Pat and Harvey. I became afraid. My head began to spin––nothing seemed real.

"I know you are the killer, Oscar," I blurted. "Dr. Wainscot told me you probably don't even know."

He looked bewildered. "I don't know what you mean."

"I shouldn't have said that," I thought. "What the hell is wrong with me? Now he will kill me." I was frightened to death, and it was the longest night of my life. I thought again about leaving. I thought about calling Mom, but she wouldn't believe me, and besides, there were no phones. So I just lay there and worried, afraid to go to sleep.

Oscar said, "Everything will seem better in the morning. It always does."

"Like that bastard even cares. Like I will even live to see morning," I thought.

But as the night grew older and the sandman sprinkled sleep seeds into my eyes, the horrible events of the recent past began to slowly dissolve in my mind, becoming only a dim memory that seemed to be more illusory than real. Finally, far into the night, slumber overtook me, bringing wonderful dreams of Victoria.

I woke as the morning sun began to draw the darkness from the room. Oscar was right; morning did make me feel a little better, but I still didn't know what to do. Why did I have to say I knew he had committed the murders? Maybe I could say I was angry and afraid and the words had just come out. I could say I didn't really think he had done them ... but I knew he wouldn't believe that either, because he probably did know that he really was the killer.

He was already up and dressed, sitting in a chair watching me.

"Are you feeling better?" he asked.

I didn't say anything. I just scowled at him.

"William, talk to me. I'm going to the doctor's now. Will you come with me?"

"No. You're not serious about changing, and I don't want to go anywhere with you."

He looked angry. "Why the hell do I need you, anyway? You're no friend of mine anymore. You hurt me last night. You had no reason to think I would harm you."

In my mind's eye, I pictured myself found dead, like the others boys had been. His face was red and filled with rage. He stood in the doorway for a moment. "You better be here when I get back. If you're not, I'll hunt you down," he said. He looked at me for a moment longer, maybe to make it clear that he really meant what he said, and then slammed the door.

Now I was really frightened. I wanted to go home. I wanted to be with Victoria but there seemed to be no way to do that, at least not now or even any time soon, and maybe never.

Oscar wasn't gone long. When the door opened and he came into the room, he looked really mad. He said he had told the doctor about bringing me along on the trip, but the doctor had refused to see him.

Oscar mimicked the doctor: "'There are so many people here that need my help, I just can't fit you in. You should have called.' I can't believe he would allow me to travel all the way up here and then not see me."

I almost felt sorry for him.

"I'm sorry, William. I'm not angry with you anymore. It's just that everything is going wrong. The damned doctor said he was disgusted at me for bringing you here and subjecting you to this danger—whatever the hell that means."

I just looked at him; I didn't say anything. Hell, I didn't know what to say.

"We're leaving. Get the stuff packed," he said, and then left.

He came back in a few minutes with Alex. "You don't look well,

William," Alex said. "Are you all right?"

"Just had a rough night."

"I know. I've had a couple of those myself. Will you come to my room for a minute? I want to talk to you."

"Sure," I said. I would have gone about anywhere to get away from Oscar.

When we got to his room, he said, "Oscar told me that you think he wanted to hurt you. He asked if I would talk to you."

"He frightens me." I feigned a shudder to make my point.

"He wants you to go for a drive with him. He wants to explain everything to you." Alex smiled and I smiled back, thinking it was nice to have a friend.

As he looked at me, he nervously twisted a black shoelace around his fingers. "He thinks you will understand if you know everything. Be careful."

"Where did you get that shoelace?" I asked.

"Just changing my shoelaces. I broke one this morning."

"Oh, they do break at the worst time, huh? Murphy's Law."

"Oscar said that you would understand if you knew everything. Go with him and listen, but then try to come back here. I think we need to talk."

"What do you think, Alex?" I asked.

"I think you should at least give him a chance to explain."

The door burst open, and Oscar rushed in. "What are you doing here?" he screamed at Alex.

Alex cowered in a corner of the room, not speaking.

"I TOLD YOU TO LEAVE HIM ALONE!" Oscar screamed. "I've told you to stay away from young boys."

He turned to me. "Will you go with me, William?" he pleaded.

I was frightened, to be sure, but Oscar seemed sincere––and besides that, I was almost afraid not to do as he said. He became hostile when he was angry.

It looked like Oscar and I were going for a drive.

Chapter 54

"I thought we could drive out here where there is a beautiful view–somewhere where it will be as beautiful as our friendship might have been."

I looked ahead. I just wanted to get this over with and go home, back to Victoria.

"You look afraid. Don't be afraid, I'm not going to hurt you. I'm trying to protect you. I need to explain."

"I hope you won't hurt me."

"Did Alex say anything?"

"No," I lied.

"That asshole always tries to blame others. He's dangerous. He needs help more than I do. My whole family is screwed up."

Oscar looked out the side window. It looked like he was going to cry.

"Alex didn't say anything," I lied again.

"I'll deal with him when we get back," he said, and then his face immediately softened, like he was thinking about something good, like people do in church when they try to make the other members think they're holy. "I need to find a way to tell you. It's something that will be very difficult for you to believe. You probably don't even realize you are doing it."

Then he stopped talking and looked ahead, like he was thinking.

We drove to a wooded area. Many trees, close and thick, made it dark and foreboding. He stopped the big car in a wide cul-de-sac and put his arm up on the back of the seat behind me. He looked at me with that phony, holy smile. I could see his dingy teeth and the obviously false ones held in place by braces. I smelled his sour breath and moved away as far as possible.

"William," he said, "sometimes things aren't exactly as they seem."

"What are you going to do?" I asked, frightened.

"I need to protect myself. Just remember: whatever happens, I don't hate you. I know they suspect Alex and me of those murders. I'm just trying to protect myself, but you also. I'm trying to protect all of us."

"Jesus, my God. Protect me?" I was shocked.

"You l-look like y-you don't b-believe me," he stammered.

"You're absolutely crazy. You're a crazy bastard," I said.

"Don't you have any feelings for me?" Oscar asked. "I love you like Andrew, my little brother."

I didn't know what to say. Hell no, I didn't love him. I used to like him, but now I hated him. "I hate you." I pushed the words out, and held out my arms for emphasis.

Oscar's face turned red. The knuckles of his hands were white where he gripped the steering wheel, and his face looked mean and evil. I wanted to run. I wanted to go back to Alex. I reached for the door handle, but I was afraid to open the door. He opened the glove box and took out a long, leather shoelace, which looked like the one that had been around Harvey's neck—the one that had been used to bind Pat's hands behind his back. He just sat with his head bowed, his lips moving as if in silent prayer. He sat for a long time, during which I just looked out the side window. I could taste the sulfur. I felt lightning softly shooting up my spine and bouncing around in my skull.

"You're in danger," Oscar said. "I wish you would have come

with me to Wainscot's office. I told him I thought you were doing things that you didn't realize you were doing. That's why he was mad. I thought he would let you talk to him, because you wouldn't need your parents' consent up here." Oscar looked at the floor. "When he finally said he would try to find time to see you, I thought about tying you up and taking you in. But he said he wouldn't do it that way—you would need to come by your own consent. But I'm going to tie you up anyway, just to protect you from yourself. I told your Mom and Dad I would protect you, and I will. We need to go back and try to see Wainscot—he has the knowledge and skill to make you understand."

"Sure, you're going to protect me. You are going to cut my head off, like you did those other boys." I placed my hand on the door handle again. I wanted to jump out and run.

Oscar placed his hand on my leg. "Don't … don't try anything," he said.

My head was spinning. I felt like I was going to pass out; I knew I was going to pass out.

"I really like you, William, and I wouldn't ever do anything to hurt you. I would give my life to protect you."

I was terrified. I couldn't speak, and didn't know what to do. I was sure Oscar was going to kill me. He had killed those boys and now he was going to kill me. His face was filled with resolve and evil.

"Let's take a walk," he said. He slid over to my side, held my arm, opened the door, and forced me out. I tried to break free and run into the woods, but he held me tightly.

"I have to keep you safe. Maybe if I explain," he said.

"Please don't hurt me."

"I won't hurt you. I just need to tie you up while I explain, so you won't run away and get lost or hurt. It will all be for the best in the long run." His breath was coming in short puffs. His face was flushed. The sulfur was in my mouth; I wanted Victoria.

He pushed me along the path toward the deep overgrowth. I

felt the leather shoelace around my shoulders and his hands on my neck and him close behind me. The sky was overcast and the dreary day only added to my terror. Then the path ended. There was a hard-surfaced area with a few benches, a very steep drop-off over the side, and a railroad track some distance below. Tall weeds and bushes grew out of the gravel and rocky dirt that made up the steep hillside, with scrawny trees and underbrush here and there.

"Sit down, William," he whispered, "we need to talk."

Sulfur was in my mouth. Lightning shot up my spine and inside my skull. I knew what he was going to do.

Oscar nudged my back. "Sit down," he repeated.

"No," I said. "I'll stand."

"All right."

It was as if it were a dream. I wanted to wake up. It was like I had passed through the window, but I knew I hadn't. I tried to make the window effect come, but it wouldn't come. This was really happening.

Oscar said, "I feel like an ogre. I don't want to make you frightened. I'm going to take the shoelace off. I didn't have it tied, anyway. I just wanted to get your attention." He dropped the shoelace to the ground.

This was my chance. I decided to run. As I turned, his hands closed around my neck and choked me, momentarily. His hands were big and strong, and I couldn't break free. Everything began growing dim, black.

"Stop it," he screamed. "I'm not going to hurt you, I'm trying to help. We can get counseling, if you'll only let me help you."

I kept trying to escape, kicking and screaming, hoping someone would hear, someone would come.

"Sorry," he said softly. "I didn't mean to hurt you. I was just trying to control you."

He stood behind me. I pushed myself back, stepped on his foot and brought my elbow around swiftly to his face. His grip tightened even more, but it felt like he was staggering. Finally, he released his grip and fell to the ground. I stood as if hypnotized, looking at him lying there, holding his bleeding face. He was hurt, He tried to get up. His eyes looked glassy. Blood gushed from his swollen nose.

"To hell with you," I yelled as I ran to the steep bank and jumped over the edge. I fell several times as I half-slid, half-ran down the steep incline. "I hope the son of a bitch dies," I sputtered, but I was sure he wouldn't. By the time I reached the tracks, my shoes were full of rocks and dirt, but I ran as fast as I could. "I have to get away from him," I kept repeating to myself.

I ran until I thought my lungs would burst, and then turned to look back. There was no one in sight. I stopped to dump the rocks and dirt out of my shoes. My feet were cut and bleeding. After I shook out the dirt, I put my socks and shoes back on and began walking aimlessly along the tracks. My feet hurt terribly, but I walked on anyway. After a while, I saw cars far ahead, driving across the tracks. "It's a crossing––maybe I'll be able to get a ride," I thought.

As I got closer I could see a Suburban. Someone inside was looking toward me, and I recognized Oscar. He got out of the car, stopped for a moment, and then began walking along the tracks toward me. He motioned as if he wanted me to come to him.

"How dumb does he think I am?" I mumbled. I turned and began running. The railroad ties weren't equally spaced and my feet hurt, making it hard to run. I turned to see if Oscar was still following, and saw that he was running, too. I thought about trying to hide in the woods, and looked this way and that, frantically trying to decide what to do––and then I heard a train whistle.

Ahead of me, a steam engine pulling a long line of boxcars moved toward me. It looked like it had been stopped and was now building up speed as it chugged and puffed. White steam shot out from its lower bowels and puffs of black smoke billowed from the stack on top of the huge, dark engine. Waves of heat from the stoker and the hot tracks became one and enveloped the ominous monster to make it appear unreal, like a mirage. As it approached, it rocked gently back and forth, like a giant animal trying to escape from its prison of vapor.

I looked behind me. Oscar was getting closer and still waving for me to come to him. As the train drew beside me, I saw an open boxcar and ran toward it. It was high, but I jumped, grabbed an edge and tried to pull my body inside. I tried to get my feet up high enough but they just bounced off the side under the edge of the car. I was getting tired––I couldn't last much longer. I had to do something. I reached in as far as I could, and my fingers found a crack in the floorboards. I grasped tight, pulled myself in, and turned to look.

Oscar was running right alongside the car. He was puffing, and white thick foam had mixed with the blood that had congealed around his nose and mouth. The pink mixture dripped from his chin. The train picked up speed. Oscar jumped and hung on, his body bounced up and down slightly as his feet dragged over the ties. He pulled himself up onto his elbows and looked at me.

"You're going to get lost," he panted. "Let me help you."

I stood paralyzed with fear as he grabbed my ankle. I fell to the side of the car and held onto a brace. He used my leg to keep himself from falling off. The sharp edges of the boards cut into my fingers.

I felt something wet running down my arms, and saw that it was blood. It didn't matter–I had to hold on. His face was red as he puffed and struggled to hang on. The blood, now running more profusely from his nose and mouth, was a darker pink. He was obviously trying to pull me off with him. He was going to kill me. I held on tighter.

Finally, he let go of my ankle, grabbed the brace that I had used, and began pulling himself inside.

"I've got to do something," I thought, panicking. "If he falls and goes under the wheels he might be killed, and it might look like I killed him. Well, to hell with it. If I go to hell, then I go to hell. If I go to jail then I go to jail." I stomped on his hand. He didn't let go. I jumped on it again, and he fell back a little bit.

"Don't do that. You don't understand. I want to help you," he yelled.

I jumped on his hand again, and he slipped more, but he still didn't fall. I stepped forward and kicked his face as hard as I could. His eyes rolled back in his head so only the whites showed. A large gash immediately appeared under his left eye. It looked sickening. I could see the bone. Then bright blood came rushing in and streamed down his face to mix with the other frothy blood. He hung for a moment as if suspended in space, and then fell from sight.

I watched as he tumbled and slid along in the gravel and rocks and then rolled to a stop among weeds at the edge of the tracks. He staggered to his feet and stood, and then raised his hand in a desperate gesture as his mouth formed indistinguishable words. He held his three-fingered left hand over his bleeding eye while the blood flowed ran down his torn, creosote-stained shirt.

While we were struggling, the train had moved to the crossing where Oscar had parked his Suburban. I leaned out of the door and saw him stagger to his car and crawl inside. He sat motionless in the driver's seat for a moment, and then turned the big vehicle around and drove away.

"Serves him right. I hope he bleeds to death," I whispered, but I knew he wouldn't.

The incident had made me ill. I sat in the open doorway with my legs folded under me, watching for Oscar. I expected to see him at every turn and at every crossing, and didn't know what I was going to do. I wanted Victoria; she would make everything all right. I watched blankly out of the doorway of the empty boxcar as the train clicked along the tracks.

I watched and prayed that Victoria would be able to find me and that Oscar wouldn't. It was as if I were in a trance, almost like I had passed through the window, but it was different. I knew I was here and not inside the window. I wanted Victoria. I wanted to be home.

"I should try to use some of my magical power to get out of this pickle," I thought. I began chanting like the witchcraft books said to do, and then I prayed. I made a little doll from my emergency shoestring and pieces of wood and used Voodoo. Even if I had pins, I wouldn't have been sure where to stick them, but this meager effort seemed to help a little bit. When the train stopped, I slipped off and found water. I wasn't hungry. I didn't think I ever would be hungry again. I climbed back into the boxcar and sat in the open doorway. When the train began to move, I stared vacantly out the large doorway at the passing scenery. I tried again to pass completely inside the window, to make this whole thing less real, but the trick eluded me. I kept trying.

Then it occurred to me: "My Me box," I shouted.

I felt in the back of my pants for the notebook I had been writing in, and found it with the pencil still taped inside. Hell, it was always there, almost as if it was a part of me. I began writing. I would put this new information in the box as soon as I got home— because I knew that some way, somehow, I would find my Me box.

Chapter 55

I have no account of how long I traveled, but one day the train stopped on the outskirts of a small town. I saw an old Spanish building in the distance that seemed familiar. I knew where I was— Castle II. From the doorway of the train I saw that the windows in the hacienda were all broken out, the walls were black in evidence of a long-ago fire, and the tiled roof was tattered and broken from time and abuse.

"It's our castle," I laughed. I climbed out of the car and ran toward it.

It seemed there were hundreds of tracks. I stepped across them one at a time and made my way to the old building. A urine smell mixed with dust lingered in the air. The memories came rushing in. The closer I came, the stronger the smells became, and the sharper the memories. I pushed the door open and went inside. The dust and urine smell was stronger but so were memories of Victoria and the time we had shared here. There was also the smell of Victoria; I could almost feel her. This was our castle. I sat in the dismal semi-darkness trying to imagine Victoria with me. I missed her so much. I could almost feel her here with me. I needed to rest, and then tomorrow I would go to Springtown to be with her.

"Whatchadoin', William?"

I looked up. I couldn't believe it. It was Victoria, here! I guess I *had* smelled her. She seemed to float across the cluttered floor, like she had done when we first discovered this place, our castle. She looked like an angel. Her father was right; she was a princess.

"What were you doing sitting in the dark?" I asked as I hugged her.

"Waiting for you, silly. When you didn't come home, I got worried."

"How the hell did you know how to find me?"

"Where else would you go? This is our castle. I knew you'd come here. You weren't in Castle I, so I knew you'd be here."

"Did your dad bring you?"

"Are you kidding? Gramma did."

"There must be a God," I mumbled, and I found myself forgiving Him again.

We sat in the gloom with our arms around each other. It was wonderful to be together; I loved her. I wished I had stayed with her and hadn't gone to Canada, but now everything was all right. We were together again. I told her about Canada and Oscar. She understood. I told her I was sure now that it was Oscar who murdered the boys. She looked dismayed, as if she didn't believe me, or that she was astounded that Oscar had done such dastardly things. Then we stopped talking and just sat hugging and looking through the water-stained, dusty window at the trains as they arrived and left the yard.

"I promise I will always stay with you, William, no matter what. We will always be together. I love you now, and I will love you always." She kissed me.

The old lace curtains and velvet drapes we had used as bedding were still there. We shook out the dust and made a bed. We were tired; we would sleep until morning and then worry about getting home. I was used to the luxury and the royal feeling of the velvet drapes and lace curtains, and it made us feel like a king and queen. We lay awake in each other's arms well into the night, enjoying the luxury of it all and being together–and then finally sleep overtook us, and we dreamed of riches and kingdoms.

With morning came thin streams of dust-filled sunlight that burst through the cracks and dirty windows. I couldn't believe it—she was really here. We were hungry and dusty and our eyes were filled with sleep-seeds, or as Dad called them, mouse turds, but breakfast and washing would have to wait. We walked to the Orem Station, where we had waited so many times during guitar-lessons. A train was taking on passengers, so we got on.

"Ticket," the conductor said after the train had pulled away from the depot.

"We lost our money," I told him and motioned toward Victoria.

"You'll have to get off at the next stop. We don't carry deadwood, sorry. Does your friend have any money?" he said, shaking his head, as if he already knew that she didn't, and walked away down the aisle.

"No," I called after him. "She'll get off with me."

He turned for just a moment and rolled his eyes so only the whites showed, just like Mom always did.

"Damned freeloader. And this one is psychotic," he mumbled as he walked along the aisle, punching other passenger's tickets.

"Hell, he's the one who's crazy. The next town is where we want to get off anyway," I said.

Chapter 56

Mom was sitting and sewing when I walked in. Her eyes were red. It was obvious she had been crying. When she saw me she jumped up and ran to me. Tears streamed down her face as she hugged me and tried to talk.

"I-I've been so worried. W-where have you been? A-are you all right?"

"Yes, I'm all right," I said. "Of course I'm all right." I didn't want her to worry.

"Oscar dropped off your Me box and stuff. He said you ran away. Why did you do that? We even reported you missing to Sheriff Everett. I'll have to go tell them you're home. I'm so glad you're home!"

"Well, I wasn't really trying to run away, Mom. I was trying to save my life."

"Oscar said you can work at his place until you can pay back the money for the trip."

"Fat chance of that," I answered. "I don't want to be around that bastard."

"William, watch your language. Do you want some soap?" Mom said, but in a kidding way.

"No, I don't want soap."

"What happened to your arms, and your neck? They're all scratched and red."

"Oscar tried to kill me," I answered.

"Oh, is that all?" she said and laughed a sad sort of laugh, like she was relieved.

"I think he's the one who killed all those kids," I said.

"Why would you say such a thing? Looks like you got the best of him in the fight," she said, and smiled.

"It's not funny, Mom––he almost killed me."

"He looked horrible. He said he fell."

Mom didn't believe me. I shrugged.

"That's a nasty cut under his eye," she continued.

"He was trying to pull me off the train and kill me, so I kicked him in the face, and he fell off into the gravel along the tracks," I told her.

She looked at me and said, "What were you doing on a train? Where did you ever get such an imagination?"

"It's not imagination, Mom, it's the truth. Why don't you ever believe me?"

"Well, you do tell some fish stories. Oscar said he fell and cut himself, and the doctor put stitches in the big cut under his eye, and told him it would heal better if it wasn't bandaged," Mom said.

"What the hell's the use?" I fumed.

"William, you're not too old for soap. Now go wash your hands, and I'll fix some tomato soup. I just baked bread," she said, and turned to begin making the family's cure and comfort for just about everything—tomato soup and fresh bread.

I decided not to say anything else. "Hell, she wouldn't believe me anyway," I grumbled to myself. I wasn't hungry, so I just went to my room to lie on my bed.

"Victoria's been looking for you," Mom yelled at me through the door.

"I was just with her," I yelled back. "I'll go see her tomorrow." I just needed to be by myself for a while and think. I needed to try to figure it all out. The following morning, I wanted to see Victoria and find out what she wanted to tell me that was so important, because she had forgotten to tell me about it when we were in Castle II, but Oscar came to our house early. I was sitting at the table playing with what remained of my bowl of Lumpy Dick cereal when Mom invited him in.

"I just came to see about William. Did he get home?" he asked.

The bastard's voice made me sick.

"Yes, he did," Mom said. "He's in the kitchen eating. William, come in here," she yelled.

Oscar smiled when he saw me. I glared at him. He was silent for a few moments and then his lips drew back into a smile that revealed his stained teeth and braces. I could imagine his sour breath belching out.

"Glad you're all right."

I yelled at him, "I'LL BET YOU'RE GLAD, YOU BASTARD. YOU SHOULD BE IN JAIL!"

"William!" Mom screeched. "Go to your room."

Chapter 57

When Dad got home, both my parents came to talk to me. Mom talked first. "William, Oscar said he understands you're upset but he still wants you to get back into the choir. Dad and I think it would be good for you." Dad stood silently, his face red.

The large veins in his neck looked like they would burst. Mom continued, "It's a chance of a lifetime. You shouldn't give up so easily."

Dad finally found his voice. "William, you're a horse's ass and shouldeth be cast into hell for not doing God's work in the choir. I wish I had thine voice. You are most certainly blessed of God." He sounded like he was entering a spiritual plane.

"Oscar's evil. He wants to kill me!" I yelled at them.

Because of my rebellious attitude and to drive their point home, I was forced to stay in my room without food or water until I got some sense and learned how to behave, as they put it. Victoria came to my window, and we talked through the screen. It seemed like "déjà vú all over again."

She said, "William, when are you getting out? I miss you. You've been gone for so long. I need to tell you some things."

She looked sad. She also looked like she was gaining some

weight, but hell, I didn't care. I wouldn't care if she was as fat as Harvey—I would still love her.

She tried to smile. "When are you getting out? You spend most of your life behind this screen." She made a feeble attempt at a chuckle and then tears streamed down her face.

I tried to cheer her up. "Better than behind bars or being dead. I'll be getting out when things cool off, I guess."

"I can't wait. Hurry!"

"I can't wait, either," I told her. "What's the big secret? Tell me."

She kissed me through the screen like she had so many times before. She looked cute with those little dust squares from the screen on her nose and chin.

"I need to tell you when we're together."

"I hope you've learned your lesson. Well, have you?" Mom finally asked.

"Yeah, Mom, I have," I lied. I wanted to be with Victoria.

"All right, then, get cleaned up, and I'll fix you something to eat. Victoria's been waiting."

"Got tired of putting up with me, huh?" I said. She smiled.

"Are you really telling me the truth about Oscar?" Victoria asked when I told her again what had happened in Canada.

"I swear to God."

"It's hard to believe. I can understand why your parents don't believe it."

"You don't believe me either, do you? How do you think I got all scratched up and bruised?"

"Looks like the truth, William."

"If it's not the truth, what do you think happened to Oscar?"

"Don't get mad. I do believe you, but I don't know what to do," she sobbed.

I held her until she stopped crying. I couldn't stand to see her cry. It broke my heart. "I don't think Oscar will do anything to me now."

"Why not?"

"Well, Mom and Dad would have to believe it was Oscar who did it."

"Sorry I didn't believe you," she said and kissed me. I think she felt better; I know I did.

It wasn't long before we were back to our normal activities in the shed and along the ditch banks. The close encounter with death was becoming a distant recollection for me. As the red marks from my neck and shoulders faded, the horrible memories about them did as well. But there was always a veneer of what had happened that covered me, and us, or anything we did. It was always there.

"William, as soon as you feel a little better, we really need to talk. I've got something incredibly important to tell you."

"Well, what the hell is it?"

She couldn't seem to get it out. "I'll tell you next time I visit."

Chapter 58

Mr. And Mrs. Condie, Pat's parents from across the street, were having a very difficult time getting over their son's death, especially the part about his head being removed. Hell, who wasn't having trouble with that? They needed to get away for a while. They had relatives in a small town in Montana. The name of the town was Jordan, like the river in the Bible. They had decided to go there for a sabbatical, and asked Mom and Dad to help them drive. Of course, because it sounded like a free trip, Dad said yes––he wanted to save Aunt Helen's inheritance money for something more important, I guess. And he was really excited about the cheap land up there.

"It's like a miracle," he said.

As usual, Aunt Trudy would be our mainstay. Ellen would be staying with her and Mrs. MacLean would watch out for me. I guess they thought I would spend all my time there with Victoria anyway, so why not? Martha would be going with them. Dad acted out of character in volunteering to take his Dodge if the Condies would buy the gas, oil, and supplies. They all piled into Dad's car and set off down the road. Since it was the Condies who wanted to go, Dad thought it only fair that they pay for everything.

Mom and Dad were going to Montana, their first vacation

alone. Well, alone if you didn't count Martha and the Condies. Dad had made progress with his attempts to stop drinking, and they made a lovely couple, all dolled up in clean and ironed, store-bought clothes. His only remaining vices that we knew about were occasionally sneaking a smoke and "the naughty language," as Mom called it.

They seemed like newlyweds, all cooey and fawny after one another. Martha was a little put out by this immature adult activity. We waved goodbye as they drove away in that old 1939 Dodge, its blue trail of burning oil following closely behind and remaining suspended as pollution long after they had gone.

As soon as they were out of sight, Victoria and I set up housekeeping in Aunt Helen's house. It was delightful to live as if we were married. She could stay all night, if she wanted to—and also if Mrs. MacLean didn't catch us. We pretended that she worked in the all-night café, Buck and Edna's Place, with Aunt Mazy.

I was able to get quite a few mowing lawns jobs. It seemed like everybody had jobs and plenty of money because of the explosion in the economy following the end of the war. I always met Victoria after I had finished mowing lawns or whatever I was doing. It was another wonderful and exciting summer. We spent every moment we could together.

We pretended we were going to get married and planned to make meals of corn flakes and milk. Mom had even left me a little money for necessities.

We found a place to swim at Hell Fire Creek where we could be alone. It was a place covered by the low-hanging branches of a volunteer weeping willow tree right next to the abandoned power plant. The water swirled through and over the old dikes and turbine houses and made swift and interesting pools and riffles. It was fun to float and drift. No one else knew about it except us, so we could skinny dip there if we wanted. We felt free together, and I had no doubt that we were married. "All except the ceremony," I told her.

"You're so silly," she smiled. "Someday, we really will be married."

We lay naked on the sand at the edge of Hell Fire Creek next to the vacant, red brick Utah Power building, shrouded only by the shadows of the trees, casually enjoying our closeness. Without a doubt, this was the best summer yet. I loved to sit and write about our lives in one of my notebooks and then place it safe and sound in my Me box or in the back of my pants to read later.

Even so, I was worried. Victoria always seemed to be in deep thought, and she cried a lot, for no apparent reason. I was afraid to press her about what was going on. And I had never seen her eat so much or such a variety of different things. But Mom and Dad would soon be home, and then our delightful interlude would end—or at least be altered.

Chapter 59

"William, do you have anything to tell me?" Alex asks in his croaking whisper.

"It's that bastard Alex," I say under my breath. "Not yet. How about getting me something to eat?" It's the same question I always ask, and again, I imagine him smiling gleefully on the other side of the heavy iron clad door. I don't believe he has any intention of letting me out—he just wants me to suffer—but for what? He doesn't know who killed those boys, and even the one who did it probably doesn't know, either—at least that's what Wainscot seems to think. The bastard just wants me to suffer, I think once again.

"Oh, shit," Alex says. "I had the food all ready and forgot to pick it up. I'll bring it next trip. Maybe you'll have something to tell me by then."

I've heard this before, I think, and then say aloud, "You're full of shit."

He laughs through the door. "I'll leave you to your thoughts and discovery and go get your food ... Don't hold your breath."

I hear him dragging his decrepit body away from the door and up the stairs. But I need to get back to the past to find some answers for Alex, the bastard. Sure, he'll get me some food. There's about as much chance of that as a one-legged man winning an ass-kicking contest. I'm discouraged but what else can I do than go back into my past ...

Chapter 60

William Robert Jones II was determined to get a ranch. After he and his wife dropped the Condies at their relatives' place, they stopped at every real estate office or For Sale sign they saw. "It's not like we're being cruelly driven from our home, like the poor folks who had to leave the dust-bowl farms of Kansas. This was without cause. It's just your whim," she scolded.

It seemed to her that they had looked at hundreds of homes and farms, but finally, one suited her husband, both in price and in arrangement. By this time, she was so tired that anything would be welcomed, as long as it wasn't in the depths of the dungeon of Aunt Helen's washhouse. The closest town to the ranch he chose was named Eden.

The deal was quickly consummated with a cash down payment and paperwork. As the two new ranch owners climbed back into their old Dodge, William Robert Jones II hugged his frail, but now somewhat relieved wife.

"I love you," he said. "It will be all right. We will make a go of it."

Dark smoke poured out of the old car as William II shoved it into gear. The wheels spun just a little, as if in glee for the now the uncharacteristically happy man. He rolled a cigarette and lit it. "This is it. This is the finale for this damned tobacco habit," he smiled. He was determined to become holy in the eyes of his wife and the church. There was excitement in his voice.

She was encouraged because, after all, he had stopped his drinking and carousing and was now planning to work long hours of every day on the ranch. It was a farm, she knew it was a farm, but if he wanted to call it a ranch, that was all right, as long as he worked and stayed home and stop his drinking, like he had promised.

"We got a hell of a bargain on it, we did!" he shouted. "It's got a house and a huge barn with a cable system that takes the hay up and drops it down safe and sound from the bleachin' sun of summer, the pourin' rain of spring and fall, and the spoilin' snow of winter; and a house. Lot's better'n Helen's washhouse basement by a damned sight. And they's sheds fer everything and water everywhere. It's God's country, and it's beautiful."

The barn and sheds were nice and there was water everywhere, but the house was just a square, dim-lit, decrepit log building with unpainted, hand-split cedar shakes covering the roof, which were so weather-worn, they appeared translucent. There was a dividing wall right down the middle, more to support the roof than with any thought to design or convenience.

She thought as she sat beside her delighted husband, "I can fix it up. We can take some of the money and fix it up to make it livable. It will be all right." But she wasn't sure at all about how good a deal it had been.

"We's some lucky Danishmen," William II decreed. "We don't need ta answer ta nobody no more!"

His wife thought, "You are a Welshman, not a Danishman." She smiled, because it didn't matter, as long as he didn't carouse. The Condies decided to stay in Montana with their relatives for awhile. The town of Jordan suited them to a "T," and if they came back to Springtown at all, it would be later. As the new ranchers rambled along the road back toward Utah, they began making plans to move to their new spread, as William II called the farm. As the bedraggled woman watched her husband pour used crankcase oil into the smoking engine, or walk to the side of the road with his back toward her to relieve himself, she thought, "We could have lived for free in Aunt Helen and Uncle Archibald's beautiful brick house forever. My man was finally back full-time at the steel plant and was making really good money. The move here doesn't make any kind of sense. It's about like moving back into the basement of the washhouse––well, a little nicer, but not much. But maybe, at least, he's kicked the drinking bug." She crossed her fingers and thought, "Well, he does appear to be happy, anyway." She smiled at her husband, the former lazy drunkard who was now the Montana rancher. He looked straight ahead, staring empty-eyed at the windshield, seemingly unaware of her presence.

    She was finally as happy as a subjugated American woman could be.

Chapter 61

My whole life had changed, in a way that was wonderful beyond words. I felt like an adult. I was sure now that I would find a way to get James H. to like and accept me. Victoria and I were already married, if only in illusion. Now that she was here in Springtown, and we were living together in Aunt Helen's house, I tried to tell myself nothing would ever change, but I knew in my heart that soon we would need to face some difficult decisions.

One day, when Victoria had been at Mrs. MacLean's place late the previous night, I watched out the window as the new black Cadillac pulled in with James H. in the driver's seat and Sophia sitting beside him. I watched as they went inside, and kept watch until early into the morning when the lights in the house flickered off.

I had stood and watched all night, hoping Victoria would come out. Finally, James H. and Sophia had emerged, arguing violently. Then they got in the Cadillac and drove away. Almost immediately, I saw Victoria come out of Mrs. MacLean's back door and walk over my bridge toward me. My heart fluttered. I opened the door, but when I saw her, my heart almost stopped. I knew that something was really wrong: her eyes were red, and she seemed on the verge of crying. The lightning shot up my spine and sulfur filled my mouth. She didn't even hug me. She just looked at me pleadingly.

"William, I've got to tell you," she said. "I can't keep it to myself any longer." She was sobbing now.

"What is it?" I asked.

"I need to go with them for a few days."

"When will you be home?"

Between sobs she said, "In a few days. I need to work some things out with Momma."

"Please just stay, Victoria!"

"I begged Momma to let me stay for a few days. Daddy didn't like it but she insisted and he finally agreed. But just for a few days, then they will be back."

I couldn't figure out what was going on. I was afraid. Victoria stood silently for a moment and then went on, "I have something to tell you––it's important."

I moved close to hold her. She softly pushed me away.

"William, it's hard enough. Just let me tell you."

I didn't want to know. I was frightened. I knew it was something bad. "What the hell is it?"

Finally, she found the words to go on.

"Well, I really have two things to tell you. One of them is nice; the other is horrible. I can't keep it bottled up any longer." She was crying hard now, the tears rolling down her cheeks, her little body shaking violently.

I stood in silence as the lightning made its way up my spine, and the sulfur filled my mouth. She tried to talk, but the words still wouldn't come out. I grabbed her arms and shook her. "Victoria, tell me."

"W-We're going to have a b-baby." She looked down at her feet and then our eyes met, and she tried to smile through the tears. She tried to be brave. I was shocked … I didn't know what to say. I was happy but terrified at the same time.

"That's great," I said.

She smiled as she tried to wipe away the tears and the fear with a wadded-up tissue. "Is it all right? What will we do?"

"Of course it's all right. I'll think of something. I can mow more lawns and get a job somewhere. We'll be all right," I promised. But I wasn't too sure. I was worried.

"That's not all," she said. The tears continued to flood her eyes.

"What else is there?" Again, she couldn't seem to get the words out. "Tell me what it is, Victoria."

Her words came tumbling out. "W-We're going to move to Scotland."

"Scotland!" I yelled.

Her shoulders shook as she cried and tried to find the words to go on. "Daddy inherited a lot of money and a castle. It's on the island of Mull, off the coast of Scotland. I guess he really was some kind of royalty. We all thought he was kidding."

I couldn't believe it. I was so shaken, it was difficult to stand. I seemed to pass through a window; I was watching Victoria and William.

"When are you leaving?" William asked as he gently held her in his arms. His voice was soft, but it was also coarse. It rattled in his throat as he forced the words out, trying to control himself.

Finally, between sobs, she said, "I-in about a week. Daddy wants to separate you and me as soon as possible. Momma knows about the baby. I think she wants me to have an abortion before Daddy finds out." She shook with uncontrollable sobs.

William was furious. The lighting and sulfur filled his body completely. "I won't let you go. You said you would stay with me forever." He was nearly in tears now, too. "You can't go. What about the baby? I won't let them kill it."

"I want to stay here. I want to stay with you. Let's run away. Let's go where nobody can find us."

"I'll need to get a better job," William said. "We can't live with our parents. Our dads would kill me."

"I don't know," she said. "We have to think of something."

The window effect faded, and I thought about the sheep ranch of Hyrum and Debbie. "We can go to the sheep ranch, Victoria. You know, where I went that summer. We can work for our board and room until I can get a job."

"They will just call your Mom and Gramma," she said.

"Hell, they don't have phones up there."

"It won't work."

"I'll tell them we got married with our parents' consent. Lots of people get married young. Their daughter got married when she was young and ran off with an evangelist preacher. You're as old as she was."

Victoria was silent for a moment. "William, I'm afraid. I'm afraid we won't be able to do it."

"I'm not going to let you go to Scotland," I said.

"I don't want to lose you, either." She tried to smile through her tears. She was so brave. "Let's do it," she said.

We would need a little time to plan, but we had to leave before her dad came to get her. "Tomorrow," I said.

We planned what to take and how to tell Hyrum and Debbie when we got there.

I didn't sleep that night; I had too many things to think about. "Why is it always so hard for me?" I wondered.

"Maybe God is trying to make me strong by giving me tribulations, like Dad said. But what the hell is going to happen now?"

Next morning Victoria and I began packing. We took as much as we could carry from Mom's cupboard then went into Mrs. MacLean's garden and dug potatoes and carrots from the soft, rich soil. We picked some raspberries and strawberries and put them in bags. Victoria even put in some asparagus.

"You shouldn't pick it all," I told her. "The old maids like to play squat tag there."

"Oh, William," Victoria giggled. "You're so silly."

I felt strangely lonely now that I was actually going to leave. I had never liked living with my family, but I guess I did get some comfort knowing that at least I had a place to sleep and something to eat when I was hungry. But now I was going to be on my own, and not only would need to take care of myself but of Victoria and soon, a baby as well.

"Are you going to tell your Gramma goodbye?" I asked.

"I'm just going to leave a note."

"Ask her to go tell Mom and Dad when they get home. Don't tell her where where're going; just tell her goodbye and love and that stuff. And that we will be in touch soon."

The sun was high in the morning sky when we finally set out across Mrs. MacLean's back yard. We left through the shed that faced the alley at the side of her place. I couldn't leave my Me box; it was such a big part of me and my life. I tied a rope through one of the cut-out holding places so I could pull it behind us. I carried my Boy Scout cooking kit and canteen filled with water around my shoulder and one of Mom's pillowcases with our food in it, which I tied to the top of my Me box. Victoria carried a blanket to sleep on, in case we weren't able to make it there before dark. I had some matches and planned to build a fire, so we could cook Mulligan stew, like the Boy Scouts do.

We trudged on, talking about what we would do and how wonderful it was going to be now that we were together and how much we loved each other and that we would never part. We wondered what we would name the baby and if he might be president someday, or maybe a football player.

"You know, Lincoln was just a poor boy. Lots of presidents were poor," she said.

But I wasn't listening anymore. I was worried––so worried that the words wouldn't come out. The lightning shooting up my spine and the sulfur on the roof of my mouth were constant companions. After a while, Victoria fell silent too, and we walked along as if in a trance, just watching our feet and thinking to ourselves. It was dusk, soon to be dark, and we needed to think about finding a place to spend the night. I looked inside the pillowcase. The food had mixed with the berries and other things into a mass of gook and garbage.

"There's a car coming," Victoria said.

In the evening gloom, raising a large cloud of dust, an old car chugged toward us.

"Maybe they'll give us a ride."

Through the dusty, streaked windshield, we could see an old man driving and an old woman sitting in the passenger's side. I stood close to the road, sticking out my thumb as I'd seen the hitchhikers do. The car went right by and then skidded to a stop as the dust settled around us.

"They're going to give us a ride," I said.

"I'm glad. I'm getting tired."

The car backed up. "Where you kids a-goin'?" the old woman asked.

"The Anderson place; the old sheep ranch."

"We's goin' right past it. Guess ya kin ride if'n ya wants ta git in back."

"Thanks." I opened the back door and looked inside. It was an old Ford, in great shape. "Maybe I'll have one like it some day some day," I thought.

"Well, don't just stand there a-gawkin'," the old man said. "Get in, or you kin jus' keep a-walkin'."

My God, I laughed to myself, the old fart's a poet. And then I said aloud, "Sure."

I untied the pillow case filled with mush and let it fall to the ground. Then I lifted the Me box inside, and Victoria and I stepped in, too. The car smelled like some sort of fruit, maybe apples, but it smelled more like dust. There was dust everywhere. It was difficult to tell what color the seats were. When we sat down, more dust filled the air.

"Ain't youse guys a mite young to be out so late?" the old woman asked.

"We're going to live at the Andersons' for a while. Our folks sent us. We're going to help them out for a while," I lied as best as I could.

"They's always sumpin' ta do on a farm, that's fer sure," the old woman went on.

"I'm scared," Victoria whispered. "Maybe they're witches. Maybe we should just go back home. She does look like the wicked witch."

"Hell, I'm not going home," I whispered back. "I'd rather burn in hell than go back. Let's at least give it a try."

She laid her head on my shoulder. We were too tense to sit back. We leaned forward and looked ahead through the streaked and dirty windshield in silence. The dusty old car followed its headlights and rattled along the desolate country road, carrying us forward to meet our unknown destiny.

Suddenly, the car slid to a stop in front of an old barbed wire gate. Victoria and I lurched even farther ahead.

"Damned brakes," the old man said. "I've got ta get 'em fixed."

Startled out of my daydream, I looked at Victoria. She had been asleep resting on my shoulder. Her eyes were swollen, with sleep-seeds at the corners.

"This here's it," the old man said. "This here's where the Andersons live."

Victoria rubbed her eyes. "Those are mouse turds," I smiled. "While you're asleep, mice climb up and poop in your eyes."

"No, they don't," she pouted.

"We're here," the old man reminded us. "You want ta get out, er just go home with us?"

"No, thanks," I said, and opened the door to help Victoria out.

"Thanks. Thanks a lot," I said to the old couple. The old man ground the gears and finally found the one he was looking for. The wheels threw up loose gravel and more dust as the old couple left Victoria, me, and the Me box standing bewildered in the darkness. We watched them go, with only the red glowing taillights as evidence that they had been there at all, and then even they were gone, and we were all alone.

"This is it, Victoria," I said. "It's just down this lane a little way."

"Yes. I'll go anywhere with you––you are a part of me."

I opened the barbwire gate, like Jon had done before he vanished, and then closed it after Victoria and I had passed through. The night was eerily dark. "A night for killing," I thought. But there was still enough illumination from the moon and stars to allow us to see as we walked hand in hand, pulling the Me box together along the lane.

A dog barked a lonely sound ahead and a house loomed in the distance, a dark sinister shadow riddled with lights from a few windows.

The dog, still barking, began cautiously walking toward us. I saw it was old Spatcher, and wondered if he would remember me. We walked slower, anxiously waiting to see how he would react. Suddenly, as if by silent signal, he jumped ahead and ran toward us. He jumped up on me and tried to lick my face. My memory went back to an earlier time when Spatcher had accompanied Jon and me just about everywhere on our foolish, and sometimes dangerous, escapades. This brought a tinge of guilt that I hadn't done something to prevent poor Jon's disappearance.

"I wish Jon were here," I thought. Then, to get away from everything, I seemed compelled to go to my secret place, and I passed through the window and began watching William and Victoria.

> *A small white house with a weed-filled, unkempt yard and garden nestled inside a gated fence. Even in the dusk, the garden had weeds taller than the vegetables. A*

few ducks scoured the area in search of something to eat. Everywhere around the perimeter was discarded farm machinery in various degrees of disrepair. A menagerie of abandoned cars and trucks filled spots in between the other junk.

As the window effect faded, the faint illumination from the window lights gave an almost imaginary view of the house's cluttered surroundings.

"Not very neat," Victoria said, "but the house looks friendly."

"It is friendly. I hadn't even noticed the junk before," I said.

I knocked at the door—nothing. I knocked again. The door finally opened, and Debbie stood in the doorway, framed in the soft lantern-light. She appeared old and haggard, like the wicked witch in the fairy story of Hansel and Gretel.

After a startled pause, I said, "Hi?" It came out more a question than a greeting.

"Kin I hep ya?" she asked, after a moment, seemingly analyzing the situation.

I realized she didn't recognize me. "I'm William, Debbie. I came here to stay last year. I played with Jon. Don't you remember?"

"Oh, fer sure," she gushed. "It's so dark. I remember you. You and Jon had such a time, and I had such a time keepin' you away from the girls."

"What girls?" Victoria whispered.

"I'll tell you later, Victoria."

"What ya guy's doin out so late?" Debbie asked.

"We just decided to get married and get away from home for a while. Our folks want us to get some experience anyway," I lied.

"What about school?"

"We got caught up and don't need to go for a while––about a month. And hell, now we got a baby on the way, maybe school's out for us."

"Well, I declare," she said. "Who'd a-s'pected you'd be so good at schoolin' ta get ahed like that? And so young ta be a-gettin' hitched."

"Vera got married young," I reminded her.

"Yeah, but you seem so young. Guess it's 'cause now I'm so old. And Vera's marriage only lasted fer a time. Remember, she was home here, when you was here?"

"Where are the girls now?" I asked.

"Well, since Jon disappeared, they decided to go to Cal, to try to make some money. I guess I don't know fer sure—they's jus gone."

I produced my most pitying look. "Sorry about your problems." She gave a forlorn smile.

"Can we help out around the farm for food and a bed?"

"Have ta ask Hyrum, but I think it will be all right, yer Dad bein' his friend and all."

"We'll work really hard. Maybe you will give us a couple of bucks to go to the movie on Saturday and get a burger."

"We'll see," she said. "Have ta ask Hyrum––he's a-milkin' right now. He'll be in soon. We'll have supper an' you kin ask him then. Well, just don't stand there––come on in, and wash some of that dust off 'fore we eats."

There was a washbasin right next to the wood-burning stove. Well, it was just a large porcelain pan. We dipped water out of the reservoir on the stove and mixed it with cold, from the drinking bucket that was perched at the opposite side. I remembered the Saturday night baths, when Jon and I took turns in the large, galvanized washtub next to the gasoline washing machine on the back porch. Jon had been small and could get completely inside, but I sat with my long legs hanging out like a huge spider. Those were wonderful memories.

It felt good to get that dust off, even if it was just our arms and faces. We would have plenty of time to bathe later, if Hyrum allowed us to stay. The table was heavy with food and had a distinct odor of mutton––sort of a sour smell. A white but soiled tablecloth lay underneath the mismatched plates, bowls, and silverware, which all looked clean and neatly arranged. It looked as if some hillbilly Emily Post had arranged it all.

"It smells funny," Victoria whispered.

"Don't smell it, just eat it. It's really good. Just don't drink cold milk while you're eating," I cautioned, also in a whisper, as I remembered how mutton tallow sticks to the roof of your mouth when anything cold touches it.

"Hell, yes," Hyrum exploded when Debbie asked him if we could stay. "We'll get it all straightened out after we git ta town and see yer folks."

We all found a place at the table. Hyrum bowed his head and clenched his hands in front and surveyed the table and then spoke softly, with the authority of someone in charge. He clasped his hands in the classic prayer pose and sat for a moment, maybe for effect. Four small white scares appeared on the back of his right hand. Jon had put them there with a fork in reprisal for a vigorous flip to his head from Hyrum's middle finger for misbehaving, which was where I had gotten the idea for how to get even with when Dad flipped me. Both Hyrum and Dad now wore the four-little-scars brand.

"God, for what we is about to enjoy," Hyrum's voice boomed out, "we give thee thanks. But if we hadn't busted our damned asses ta get it, we wouldn't have nothin' at all. Amen."

Victoria and I smiled at each other. It was indeed an unusual prayer. "I'm sorry about Jon," I said. The room went silent for a moment, as every eye watched me. Then Hyrum began talking, his voice filled with anguish. "We miss him too much. I guess we don't even like to even think about it. We just wish we knew where he was—if he is suffering."

My mouth filled with sulfur, my head with lightning. Why did I say that? I felt horrible. I didn't know what to say—why did I do something so torturous to them? "I'm sorry. I shouldn't have brought that up."

"Hell, forget it," Hyrum said. "We had to stop looking. It was driving us crazy. We try ta hope that he'll be home someday, but we don't know. The longer it goes, the less likely it is ta happen." He stopped like he was thinking and then went on again. "That might be why the girls left. We probably drove them away. Let's just eat."

He began passing around the mutton, potatoes, dressing, gravy, and homemade bread. As the food found its way around the table, the tension eased, and a low drone of voices gradually replaced the awkwardness of the moment, and finally grew into boisterous chatter.

"If we had phones here and if your folks had a phone, I'd call ta let 'em know you made it all right," Hyrum announced. "But we don't and they don't, so I'll just wait 'til I gets ta town."

"We're going to help clean up and wash the dishes," Victoria said.

After everything was washed and put away, Hyrum sat down at the piano, and as he played, we all sang. It was great, my new life with Victoria––even better than I had imagined.

"William," Debbie said, "you an' Victoria kin sleep in Jon's old room. They's only one bed, but one of ya kin sleep on the floor if'n it's too small." She tried to wink, but both eyes closed.

"Hell, they couldn't hurt each other at their age even if they sleeps ta-gather," Hyrum laughed. We all blushed; Hyrum had even embarrassed himself.

"She's already with child, Hyrum," Debbie said.

Hyrum blushed a deeper red.

For some reason, I thought of Lon Cox, their frequent visitor who lived about a mile down the canyon road. The last time I was at the ranch, I had noticed that Jon looked a lot like old Lon Cox.

Chapter 62

The bed was great, and I felt like my life was turning into a wonderful miracle, as if it were a dream, but it wasn't a dream. I pinched myself for reassurance that it was real. Victoria's breasts were getting larger and her tummy was beginning to push out. It didn't show yet, and was only noticeable to the touch, but she was getting sick in the morning. We had an old coffee can for that, which we sometimes used for a pot as well. She wanted all sorts of strange food that we didn't have and couldn't get but most of all, she wanted to be close. She didn't want sex all the time like before, but that was all right––I just liked being close to her.

Hyrum and Debbie didn't expect us to do very much, and we spent lots of time alone together. We ran in the sand along the creek and played in the pea fields and hiked in the wooded areas around the farm, like Jon and I had done during that wonderful summer. Victoria and I pumped water by hand from the well, which needed to be primed with a small can with some water in it. We then refilled the can, to have water for the next priming. We washed our clothes in the old gasoline washing machine. Jon had taught me how to start it and how to make sure the flexible exhaust pipe was far enough outdoors so we wouldn't get asphyxiated. Sometimes I had to take out the spark plug and put a little gas on the electrode to get it to start. We hung the clothes on the line in front of the house. When they were dry, Victoria ironed them. I got in the kindling and wood for the fires for cooking.

We mowed the grass around the house and dumped the clippings into the pen for the sheep to eat, or at least to turn their noses green as they pushed it around. We gathered eggs from the chicken coop and played hide and seek in the buildings around the farm.

"Hope they don't find out about me chopping up Dad's tool handles," I laughed and told Victoria what I'd done when I was a kid. I explained about the girls, too.

Victoria said, "That's the way little children are able to explore their feelings and to grow up. I'm glad you got it out of your system while you were young," and she hugged me. "I guess I got it all out by being with you," and she dropped her eyes meekly.

It was as if I had died and gone to heaven. There was nothing else that I could ever ask from God. He had surely forgiven me for my transgressions, and I had forgiven Him completely for his cruelty, as well. "I'll sure as hell never curse you or do anything bad again," I exclaimed to God and held my arm out and looked up into the sky to reinforce the promise.

Just when I thought things couldn't get any better, they did. Hyrum came home pulling a small trailer house. "Got it in a trade," he said. "Traded the old Chev pickup fer it––hell, it didn't even run. I had to drag it into town." He showed his stained and rotting teeth in a sly smile as he moved his nearly permanent, handmade cigarette expertly from one side of his mouth to the other.

"What are you going to do with it, Hyrum?" I asked.

He looked at me. "Hell, never thought about that––jus park it and see, I reckon."

I looked at Victoria, who knew what I was thinking. "Can we live in it?" I asked.

"Don't know why not. I'll park it over by the orchard on the lane, and you kin move in. It will be a little farther away from the outhouse and the water, but yer young, and it won't be no big thing, I'm sure."

It was now even more like heaven; like I always imagined heaven would be. "This isn't the middle kingdom," I told Victoria. "It's the top one—the very top one."

The trailer was dirty and in disrepair, but with some hard work, hammer and nails, a drill, nuts and bolts, and soap, we cleaned it up and were ready to set up housekeeping. There was a good bed in it. Debbie gave us some old lace curtains and velvet drapes to use as bedding, and dishes, towels, that kind of stuff. I installed fence posts around the perimeter and tacked on field fence to keep the animals from invading us. And then we planted a little garden.

Debbie said it was too late for a garden, but we wanted to do it anyway. "Practice for next year and the rest of our lives," we told her. We faithfully watered and weeded and soon, tiny green plants struggled to make their way out into the world. "Too bad they won't be able to mature," I said.

"Just like we are already having kids," Victoria said.

"Yes it is, but the best one is yet to come," and I patted her stomach.

"I hope it does better than our garden."

"It will."

I was sure that things couldn't get any better than they were now.

Chapter 63

One day, after we had finished our work, we were sitting on the picnic table on the lawn in front of Hyrum and Debbie's house, playing with a tap-dancing doll that Hyrum had whittled out of a block of wood. He had made the body and all the parts separately, and then fastened them together loosely with wire pins. He had placed a long heavy wire in the body. I held the wire and with my knuckles I tapped a long, thin shingle on which the doll was standing, which brought it to life as a delightful dancer. Depending on how vigorously I tapped the shingle, the little doll followed with more or less activity. It was comical to see it make difficult steps and jumps. It was harder than it looked to operate, and I tried to show off for Victoria that I was really getting the hang of it. She laughed and yelled encouragement, clasping her hands under her chin in glee.

Then she looked up. "There's a car at the front gate."

A long black car stopped, a man got out, opened the gate, and threw it on the ground.

"Looks like Hyrum has some company," I said.

"They aren't very polite, just leaving the gate open like that," Victoria said.

The car looked new. It was a shiny black Cadillac limousine.

"My hell, somebody's rich," I said. It drove up right in front of us and stopped. Two very large men dressed in black suits and ties got out and walked over to Victoria and me.

"Hi," I said. "Lookin' for Hyrum?"

The men didn't even acknowledge me. One of them turned toward the car. "It's them," he yelled, and another man got out of the car.

It's Daddy!" Victoria screamed and ran to me. We stood, terrified, holding each other.

Very quickly, like they were some sort of karate experts, the men took Victoria from me. One man held me to the ground as James H. picked Victoria up.

She screamed and flailed her arms and feet. Another man came to help him as they forced her inside the car. Another man slammed the door shut.

"William, do something," she screamed from the window.

I tried to wriggle free. I hit the man in the face with my fist. He just smiled and took a leather shoelace from his pocket. I was afraid he was going to strangle me, but he didn't––he wrapped it around my legs and tied it with an exotic knot. Then he walked to the car, got in and slammed the door. I ripped at the shoelace, but before I could free myself, the car had turned around and was speeding toward the main road. I jumped up and ran after it.

I heard Victoria's muffled screams. "I love you, William––I'll find a way to come back!"

The car turned onto the road and disappeared in a cloud of dust. Victoria was gone. "I'll find you!" I shouted. "I'll never give up until I do!" I couldn't stand it. I passed through a window, and followed and watched the heartbroken William.

He didn't go back to Hyrum and Debbie's. He ran after the car. When he couldn't run anymore, he walked for a while and then ran again. The car was out of sight, but it had been headed toward Springtown. He would just have to keep going. They would probably stop to get Sophia, and he could catch them there, at Mrs. MacLean's.

The window effect faded.

I was out of breath and completely worn out when I finally got home. Mom and Dad were standing beside their old Dodge talking.

"Where've you been, William? We were about to have Rule send out an APB," Mom laughed. "Dad bought a ranch in Montana," she added. "We were gone longer than we expected, but Dad was trying to learn to do ranching better. He only knew what his father had taught him."

"I don't care, Mom. I need to find Victoria," I panted.

"It's a big ranch with a few cattle," she said.

"Have you seen Victoria?" I screamed. "They took her!" The tears flooded my eyes and ran down my face.

"Take it easy. What's going on?"

"Mom, have you seen Victoria?"

"Heavens to Betsy, don't have a fit. Mrs. MacLean told us her son-in-law inherited a castle in Scotland, and he's moving there. They all left a while ago."

"Did you talk to Victoria?"

"No, but I saw her in that big car. She was kneeling in the back seat watching out the back window as it drove away."

I ran next door to Mrs. MacLean's.

"I don't think her father liked you very much," she said.

"Yeah, I know. Where is she? What did she say?" I pleaded.

"Victoria told me she would send a message to you," Mrs. MacLean smiled. "She even wrote a note for you." Mrs. MacLean looked thoughtful. "It isn't very much; she only had a moment before they rushed her away." She handed me an old cardboard quarantine notice. It was the red kind that told of the worst diseases. On the back in pencil––and very difficult to read––she had scribbled a message.

"William, I couldn't get away. I guess we're going to Scotland. I'll get back some day, somehow. Wait for me. If you go to Montana with your parents, I'll come to you. Don't ever give up. I love you so much. You are a part of me. All of my love forever, Victoria."

I was speechless. It was so confusing, "Thanks, Mrs. MacLean. Did she say anything else?"

"Yes, she did. She said she would never forget you. She wished that you were some kind of royalty, too. She thought that her parents would approve if you were. She said she would find a way to find you."

"The patriarch of the church said I was royalty," I said. "Out of the very loins of King David."

"I don't think they count that, William." She put her hand on my shoulder, trying to comfort me.

Reality rushed in. I jumped across the small ditch, but what was the use? I'd already talked to Mrs. MacLean. Then I turned back. I'd talk to her again. I noticed the bridge, which had been my lifeline and fortress, but now it meant nothing. I stopped and looked at it, a feeble symbol of what? It reminded me of Victoria. Everything reminded me of Victoria. I picked up one end of the now-hated fortress and dumped it into the rushing, strawberry-colored water. I watched it in contempt for a moment, as the red water rushed around it, and then went to my room, fell onto my bed and cried like a baby.

"God, I will do anything if Victoria will come back, I promise." I sobbed until there were no more tears. Finally, exhausted and with tears and slobber running down my cheek and desperate for escape, I fell asleep and dreamed fitfully of Victoria being with me.

Chapter 64

The mood of the MacLean family was testy. Everyone was on edge. The worst thing in the world had happened to Victoria: she wanted to be with William, and she wanted to have her baby, whom she already loved almost as much as she loved William, but now she was hundreds of miles away from him. Confined to the car's backseat, she could see in the distance the thin stream of smoke coming from the stacks at the Wrigley Chewing Gum factory. The city bustled with happy, excited people, but she wasn't one of them—her heart was broken. Searching for some solace and comfort, she looked toward the ocean, where people who seemed as small as ants swam and frolicked on the boardwalk at the ocean's sandy edge, and raised their arms and screamed in mock terror as they rode the giant roller coaster. A few gulls flew overhead, the waves beat against the sandy beaches, and she inhaled the fishy ocean smells. It seemed everyone and everything she could see was happy, but in her heart was only doom.

Her father's voice penetrated her thoughts. "What the hell's wrong with you, Princess? Why did you run away with that skunk?"

James H. wasn't too sure now that he had done the right thing, but he wasn't about to change; that wasn't in his nature. Sophia turned her head to glare at him. She would have liked to be involved in making the decision about kidnapping their daughter. The flight had been a little bumpy, and Victoria was intensely feeling her morning sickness, but they were almost home, and then she would be able to lie down and try to cope with this ordeal, or more accurately, her ordeals: the kidnapping, the pregnancy, and not being with William.

"Daddy," she said, "why couldn't you just leave us alone?"

"Because we love you, Princess. We just want you to be happy."

"I will never be happy without William," she sobbed, holding her face in her hands.

"You will look back at this someday and laugh. You'll realize that it was all a mistake and that you're just too young. It's just puppy love," James H. said, trying in his inept way to comfort her.

"Daddy, it's not puppy love. I'm going to have a baby."

James H.'s face went white. He slammed on the brakes and the car screeched to a stop. He moved his upper body toward Victoria, but Sophia quickly forced herself between James H. and his threatening advance toward their daughter. All three faces were white as chalk. Sophia had a look of vengeance toward her husband, while James H. wore a look of utter shock, and Victoria's face was twisted into loathing of her father.

"What did you say?" James H. asked, hoping beyond hope she hadn't said what he thought he heard.

"I should have told you, dear," Sophia interrupted.

Victoria began to cry. "I'm pregnant," she sobbed.

James H. scowled at Sophia. "Y-you k-knew?" he managed to stutter.

Sophia's face was ashen. "I'm so sorry, James. I just didn't know what to say. I was trying to find a way to tell you. You are so damned bullheaded—you always think you're right."

They all sat silently, as if dissolving in their own grief, tears, and depression. They sat for a long time. Finally, James H. said softly and with conviction, "Well, that settles it. Now we *are* going to Scotland, for sure. But before we do, we will need to do something about the baby."

Chapter 65

Dad was anxious to get back to Montana, but a few things needed to be cleared up before they left. There was the final probate of Aunt Helen's will, and then Mom and Dad needed to sign the house back to the estate, because they had decided to leave. It was all legal sorts of stuff that I didn't understand, and I don't think Mom or Dad understood it very well, either. They were planning to make a quick trip back to Eden to finalize the deal on the ranch. They wanted to get some other things done, too, like getting a few animals and fixing the house up a little, to at least make it livable.

Mom always had a way of making me feel better and saying things to help me understand. When I had trouble at school she felt horrible, but she knew I felt bad too, and she forgot about her own feeling and tried to ease my suffering. "William," she gently nagged, "you need to eat. You're nothing but skin and bones."

But I couldn't eat. I couldn't do anything.

She wiped her red eyes with her lacy white hanky. "William, I'm sorry that Victoria is gone, but maybe it's all for the best. You are too young to raise a child anyway."

"I'm old enough. You and Dad got married young."

"Yeah, and we're doing so great."

"I would be happy to be poor, if only I could have her."

"We usually forget the bad things."

"Why?"

"It's God's way of protecting us."

"God is punishing me, Mom," I cried. "I hate Him."

"No, William, it's all in His plan. I'll bet He'll find a way to get her back to you."

"Do you really think so, Mom? The baby is your grandson, don't you know?"

"I know. I feel bad, too, but God knew you weren't ready for a baby yet. He is wiser than any of us. But I think Victoria will come back, if there is any way she can."

"I think you're right." And I really felt that she would if she could. I wiped my eyes on Mom's lacy hanky with the fancy embroidered "J," then blew my nose in it, opened it and looked at the bloody, green, and yellow glob—and put on a brave smile.

Mom looked inside her nice, lacy hanky and assumed a look of disgust, folded it and put it back inside her purse. Then she tried to change the subject. "Do you think they'll ever find out what happened to Jon?"

I was stunned. I guess I'd almost forgotten about that, or maybe pushed it way back into my psyche. "Hell, it was Oscar. I'm sure it was Oscar who murdered Pat and Harvey, and I'll bet it was him who did something to Jon, too. But I guess it could have been Alex or Craig ..."

"Why can't you get over that, William?"

"It's pretty hard to get over a murder."

She just looked at me for a moment. "I think we might be gone for a week or maybe two before Dad gets everything ready there and we get back. Can you stay out of trouble until then?"

"Okay." I almost cried. I wasn't going to go to Montana, and I knew I would miss them, but nothing could hurt worse than not being with Victoria. I didn't seem to have any feelings left except sadness. I knew Victoria would come home if she could. She had promised, and we would have the baby together. She was a part of me, and a part of me was inside her now. They were both a part of me.

Mom and Dad made arrangements with Aunt Trudy and Uncle Arthur to look in on me. I was too old to be tended, and I got permission to stay in Aunt Helen's house when I wasn't mowing lawns or waiting for Victoria.

"You're not as old as you think," Mom said. "Ask Aunt Trudy for help if you need it."

"I need to stay. What if Victoria comes home?"

Her eyes clouded like she was going to cry. "Find a new girl, William."

"She's the only girl for me," I said, and tears filled my eyes.

"If Aunt Helen's kids want to move in, you'll need to find another place," she said.

I sat in the rocker on Aunt Helen's wide concrete porch and watched them load into the old Dodge and drive away. Someone had lifted my bridge out, and it was lying on its side, broken, alongside the irrigation ditch.

"Some bastard," I yelled, and then remembered it had been me. I smiled, even though my heart was in shreds.

Mom and Dad waved. Mom blew me a kiss and then the Dodge stopped and she yelled to me, "Hyrum and Debbie brought your Me box and I put it our room behind the bed."

They were going to drop Ellen off at Aunt Trudy's on the way. I waved back. Soon, even the blue vapor from the oil-burning Dodge was gone, and I was alone.

It wasn't easy to mow the lawns and pretend to be happy. At night, instead of sleeping, I thought about Victoria and imagined and relived the things we had done and places we had been: the swimming hole, her kisses, our baby, our "honeymoon" at the sheep ranch. Nothing I did could fill the emptiness. That painful loneliness was now a part of me. The part that used to belong to Victoria and the baby had been torn away and now only loneliness filled the space. The painful loneliness hung on me, dripping like blood from my broken body and soul. The sheds in back only reminded me of her. I couldn't bear to even be there—— our hacienda, our Castle II, felt that way, too. Sprinkling salt on suckers reminded me of our first meeting. No matter how much fun it was, I just couldn't do it anymore.

The only relief was the movies. I could sit and watch as the actors jerked across the screen, cowboys chasing cowboys and loud music made me forget for a moment, until it hit me again, and the reality came rushing back that Victoria was gone. The sulfur coated my mouth and lightning shot up my spine, pelting my shoulders and skull. I had never felt so alone. I knew I couldn't live without her. I began thinking of ways to kill myself.

Chapter 66

It didn't seem like two weeks. It didn't even seem like a week, but one day the door flew open and Mom and Dad rushed inside, both talking at the same time, bringing electricity and excitement with them. They both liked Montana. It was the ranch Dad had always wanted. Even though they had told me about the place before leaving for their second visit, they began telling me about it again.

"It has a house, a barn, and acres of trees and pasture with water and Forest Service land on two sides. Nobody'll bother us there. We'll make a fortune," Dad grinned. "Got a bargain on it, I did."

I was now more determined than ever not to go to Montana. I was going to save enough money to go to Scotland and find Victoria. All the money I got for mowing lawns, running errands, or other things went into a pickle jar, but it was filling up too slowly. I had to have more money.

I noticed large bundles of newspapers waiting to be picked up by newsboys, and I began taking a few from each bundle and selling them on the street or in restaurants. They sold well for half price. I took empty pop bottles from the back of grocery stores and sold them at the check stand in front for the few pennies deposit. I dressed in my oldest clothes, rubbed dirt onto my face, and begged for coins from passers-by on Main Street in Springtown.

Everybody had a Victory Garden. I "borrowed" vegetables, and after cleaning and tying them into neat bundles with a piece of string, I sold them, sometimes back to the people who were good enough to raise them for me. The pickle jar was filling faster; it wouldn't be long.

The ticket agent laughed when I set the jar filled with coins on the counter and asked for a ticket to Scotland. "Hell," he said. "That might get ya ta New York. Then what ya gonna do, swim across the ocean?"

"How much for a ticket on an ocean liner?" I asked.

"I only know the bus fare to New York. I don't know the cost of the ocean liners or flights to Scotland, but I'll bet it's plenty. You might be able to stow away on a freighter, but you could end up in jail for that. It's too big to swim across, and even if ya get there, Scotland is a big place. Where in Scotland are you going?"

He's an ass, worse than Dad, I thought. "To the island of Mull."

"Never even heard of it. Where is it from Glasgow?"

"It's right where the Sound of Mull and the Firth of Lorn meet."

The agent rolled his eyes and hunched his shoulders. "What the hell are sounds and firths?"

"They're names for inlets and other bodies of water from the ocean. These are from the Atlantic Ocean."

The agent scratched his head. "I'm too busy for this. You need to go to an airline or ocean liner to find out about fares and schedules."

I walked out into the street and stood looking at nothing. On the other side of the street and down a few blocks was some sort of a medical building, and on the sidewalk on that side was a transient girl in a white gown, limping along the sidewalk. She stopped for a moment and looked at me. She reminded me a little bit of Victoria—but everything reminded me of Victoria. I thought about going across to help the poor thing, but before I could move, a black Cadillac limousine pulled up and a man in a chauffer uniform got out and helped her in. She lay down in back and they drove away. It looked like the black Cadillac that had taken Victoria away from me.

I went to Buck and Edna's at the other side of the Shame, ordered a cup of coffee, and waited in the booth way in back for Aunt Mazy to bring it, hopefully with a piece of apple pie steaming and smothered with vanilla ice cream.

When she finally saw me and brought my treat, I doctored the steaming coffee with sugar like I always did, and then I spooned it into my mouth between bites of the pie and melting ice cream. I had to drown my sorrow, and wished I were old enough to join Lou Crandall and his friends on the other side to drown my pain with stronger medication. I bummed 35 cents from my aunt, and went to see a movie and ate popcorn, a candy bar, and drank a Coke. It was George Raft playing a gangster in *They Drive by Night*. The film didn't help: I was still miserable–and I still wanted to die. Shit, I guess I might as well go to Montana and try to figure something out there, I thought.

When Dad finally brought the new truck home, I saw it was a Chevrolet, about like the one the Johnsons had when we thinned beets. "The damned thing will be paid for in two years. Credit is easy now. Get in, William," Dad said. "Yer goin to Montana, too."

I knew I was going. I had already decided on it. He always had to throw his weight around.

The truck was like new. There were no holes in the leather seats, and it had windshield wipers and a rubber mat on the floor. "Ain't this something, William?" Dad said.

"It really is something," I acknowledged.

Before getting too serious about the move, Mom and Dad went to say goodbye to all the neighbors. I went to Mrs. MacLean's. She was sitting in a chair with a blanket around her legs. She looked young, and reminded me of Victoria. We talked about me moving to Montana, and I asked her to say hi to Victoria.

"I will be happy to tell her." She paused. "Is that all you want to say to her?"

"What do you mean, Mrs. MacLean?"

"Well, I read her letter to you. It wasn't covered up or anything, and I couldn't resist. It was pretty nice. I just thought you might want to tell her something like that."

"Well," I stammered, "please tell her that I love her." I felt my face turning red.

"That's nice." She waited for more.

"Say I have a feeling that since the patriarch said I have royal blood, her parents might reconsider and like me." The sweat beaded on my forehead.

"I don't think they will count what the patriarch said, William."

"Tell her that I will wait for her forever. I will watch for her in Montana. I know that she will be there someday." The world was spinning. I felt as if I was going to pass out.

Mrs. MacLean said, "I'll tell her, and I'll send her letters to you. Your parents gave me your new address, and they have mine—and my phone number."

"Okay," I said.

"Are you all right? You look like you're going to faint."

"I'm okay," I said half-heartedly. "Thanks a lot, Mrs. MacLean—goodbye." I turned and walked slowly away.

She called softly to me, "I'm going to go to Scotland, too. They want me to be there to help with Victoria. I'm going to have my mail forwarded there, so it will take a while if you write. It will just be for a while. I will come back. I'm too old to change my address now. Come see me or call me on the phone once in a while."

The tears streamed down my face. I didn't care if I was a sissy. "I'll write. Tell Victoria I'll write."

"Goodbye, William. I'll tell her. And good luck in Montana."

Chapter 67

The room was white and antiseptically clean. Victoria lay drugged and semi-conscious. James H. and Sophia waited just outside the room in soft comfortable chairs, trying to read from an assortment of magazines and newspapers scattered on the tables, but they were just turning the pages. On the walls were documents proclaiming the competence and qualification of the doctor within.

James H. had a friend in Utah who would do about anything if the price was right. It was unheard of to have an abortion and it was, in fact, illegal, but there were choices, nevertheless: have it performed in an unsanitary alley or backroom using coat hangers or homemade gadgets or pay through the nose to have it done by someone competent like this, in a sanitary setting. They had decided a hurried trip back to Utah was the answer. It had taken a while to get everything set up, but they were here now. They needed to be discreet, not only because of the illegality, but also because they didn't want anyone to know--especially William--that they were back in Utah.

James H. stood and paced nervously while Sophia, with several magazines piled on her lap, sat on the edge of her chair wringing her hands, her eyes red and wet. They hadn't given Victoria a say in the decision. She was too young to be able to decide, they thought. The door opened and an older gentleman dressed in white walked into the room, followed by a nurse.

"Everything went great. She's resting peacefully. She should be ready to travel by tomorrow. She's sedated heavily and should sleep through the night," he said as he wiped his soft, clean-looking hands with a white towel and then threw it into a trash receptacle.

"I'll stay the night to monitor her recovery," the nurse said, and then turned and walked back into Victoria's room without waiting for a response.

"You can get your daughter tomorrow," the doctor said.

"Thank you so much, doctor," James H. said and shook his hand. "We are so grateful."

Sophia looked she was in a trance, like she had experienced a horrible accident of some sort––or a death in the family.

"You look like you could use a sedative yourself," the doctor said to Sophia.

"Yes, maybe I'll take you up on that. Can we just look in on her for a moment?" she asked.

"I think it will be all right, but don't stay too long. She really needs her rest. Oh, by the way, it was a boy."

The early morning light crept into the room through the drawn Venetian blinds, and Victoria lifted her head. She felt her stomach. "It's gone," she said in a semi-controlled whisper of near-horror, as tears flowed down her face. "They killed our baby. Oh, William."

The nurse had fallen asleep in an overstuffed chair with her head tilted to the side, snoring softly and evenly. A thin line of drool ran from the corner of her mouth and hung as a string to her shoulder. Victoria quietly sat up. She let her legs fall over the side of the bed and then didn't move, trying to recover from the wave of nausea that engulfed her. With more than a little pain, she dropped softly to the floor. She took a white office coat from the rack, put it on, and slipped her feet into the flimsy paper hospital slippers. She carefully opened the door and made her way toward the elevator and then outside, where she began walking along the early morning sidewalk.

She had no idea where she was going. She knew she was in Springtown by the name on the clinic glass door. She wanted to be with William, and hoped he would be able to understand and forgive her.

The sun bathed the sidewalk and the nearly vacant early-morning streets in light, but she barely noticed. The darkness and isolation were slowly being diluted by morning sounds. Cars and people were becoming more prevalent, and birds were busy with their daily ritual of looking for seeds and fat, tasty worms. A few squirrels sat in trees and the lush grass, barking at Victoria as she trudged past.

"Robins eat worms and the other birds eat seeds and tender shoots," William's soft and confident voice seemed to be telling her. He had taught her so much. She missed him and needed him so much. But could he ever forgive her for the baby? She was exhausted and felt faint, but walked on. She was afraid she wouldn't know how to find her grandmother. She was getting weaker, and her head began to swim. Her steps were uneven and unsure. She staggered more with each step.

She looked across the street. She couldn't believe it. There was William, right across the street in front of a travel agency, looking at her. She tried to wave, but her arms were too weak. He was looking this way and that, waiting for the sudden rush of cars to stop so he could cross the street. But a black Cadillac limousine slowed and pulled to the curb. A tall man dressed as a chauffeur jumped out and ran to her.

"Victoria, your Mom and Dad are frightened to death. Are you all right?"

She tried to speak but the words caught in her throat as she whispered, "I don't want to go with them. I want to stay with William." She fought to remain standing. The sidewalk was rocking back and forth beneath her.

The man locked his arm in hers to help her balance. "Can I help you?" he asked as he led her to the car.

"Would you take me across the street? I want to talk to William." She finally found the strength to speak.

"Yes, of course," the man said.

"I want to see William."

The man smiled. "That's right ... go to see William."

The wide back seat in the car was soft and cozy. There were blankets piled high and a fluffy pillow. She lay in her pitifully thin hospital robe, and the pitifully thin slippers dropped from her feet to the floor as she fell into a deep sleep.

> *William watched as the man looked across the street at him and then helped the bedraggled woman into the car and drove off. "I'm glad he helped her. She seemed to be really sick," he thought.*

Victoria dreamed that she and William were riding a white horse, entering a white and beautiful castle. The horse had no trouble flying, and the castle was soft and beautiful. This was all she wanted, all she had ever wanted. Just to be with William in their castle. And then the comfort and security of the castle was engulfed by darkness so thick that it took her breath away. She swirled down and down, until there was only softness as William held her in the gloom, stroking her hair. She saw Ellen standing on the other side of the ditch, smiling and stroking her finger. She had to smile.

Suddenly, William was wrenched away again, and she knew that it was all over–that it could never be. "I won't let it end!" she screamed and sat up.

She was back in the hospital. She had tubes in her arm. The nurse and Sophie jumped from their chairs and rushed to her side.

"It's okay, child," the nurse soothed. "You just need to rest."

"What's happening?" she thought, and then with a crash, it all came rushing in. "The baby was gone. They've killed it. William will hate me now." She didn't know what to do.

"Victoria," Sophia whispered, "you were tired. You've slept for two days. Are you feeling any better?" Her voice sounded guilty.

Victoria buried her face in her pillow. She didn't want to talk to anyone except William. She especially didn't want to talk to her mother. She hated her mother and her daddy. The nurse stood over Victoria's body and gently rubbed her shoulders. "Don't worry about anything; I've got some chicken soup heating. That will cure anything," she said with a knowing chuckle.

Victoria could remember William telling her tomato soup with homemade bread were what would do that. "These people are all traitors," she whispered, but when the soup arrived and was finally in her stomach, it did make her feel better. She hadn't realized how hungry she had been, but now she knew that she needed to get up and get going.

William's family would be going to Montana, and maybe he would be going as well. She didn't feel like getting out of bed but knew she had to. She felt as if anywhere William was, was where she wanted to be. She would go to her Gramma's place and sort it out from there.

"Will you take me to Gramma's now, Momma?" she asked.

Sophia was delighted that Victoria was talking to her. "First things first, dearie," she whispered.

They sat for a long time, Victoria staring at the ceiling and Sophia holding her daughter's limp and seemingly lifeless hand, neither of them knowing what to say. "Gramma is waiting out in the lobby with your father. Do you feel well enough to go there?"

"Yes, let's go to Gramma's. Maybe William hasn't left yet."

James H. and Mrs. MacLean were waiting when Sophia pushed Victoria's wheelchair into the lobby. After some scolding, hugging, and a lot of tears, everyone settled down.

"Let's get in the car and go," James H. said.

As they rode along the streets of Springtown, the car didn't turn toward Mrs. MacLean's house. Rather, it turned out onto the highway that led to the airport.

"Why aren't we going home?" Victoria cried out.

James H. looked stern and determined. "We're all going to Scotland."

"What about William?" Victoria shouted. "I want to at least see him one more time."

After a long pause, Sophia said, "It will be all right. I'll talk to Daddy, and we can come back to visit and see if we can find William in Montana. Or maybe we can have him come to Scotland. Gramma will be coming over in a few weeks. When she goes home, in a few months, maybe we can come back with her."

James H. rolled his eyes up into his head so only the whites showed and hunched his shoulders. "That's about as likely as keeping a bear from shitting in the woods."

Victoria looked even more betrayed now, and tears gushed from her eyes. "I want to write William a letter," she said.

Sophia dug in her purse and drew out a white piece of paper and a pen and handed them to Victoria.

Without pausing, she began to write …

Chapter 68

We drove Dad's new Chevrolet truck to the steel plant to notify them he was leaving and they could remove his name from the probation list. He wanted to make sure he didn't have any money coming.

"Good news, Jones," the comptroller announced when we got to the steel plant. "Yer probation is done. Ya kin come back full-time. Ya even got a promotion."

Dad had already made up his mind. "Shove yer god-damned job," he said sarcastically. "I bought me a ranch. I'm goin ta Montana."

"We sent out yer recall two days ago, so I guess you got show-up time a-comin'. That's four hours fer just showin' up today." He quickly made out a check and handed it to Dad. It was for $6.70.

"That'll come in handy," Dad said with a grin.

I thought again about staying in Utah to mow lawns and get by as best as I could and wait for Victoria. Dad said, "They's lot's a work on a ranch and rabbit huntin' and fishin' fer fun." It all sounded good to me but I knew Dad very often promised things that didn't materialize. Before we left, he sent me to a service station to get some "clean used crank case oil."

"That god-damned truck runs good, but the Dodge drinks oil

like a drunk drinks whiskey," Dad said. He was in a jovial mood.

The can for the oil was one of those square ones Dad always brought our yearly supply of honey home in. It had a screw-on lid and had been cleaned out pretty well. Once a year, in the fall, he would bring home a bushel of wormy apples from his cousin's place in Mapleton and one of these square cans filled with crystallized honey. Mom made applesauce by peeling the apples, cutting the worms out of them, and boiling them in with sugar and cinnamon. While she did this, we sat impatiently around the table, waiting for her to give us a slice of the delightful fruit.

The crystallized honey took the place of candy for us, and we all got long spoons or sticks to dig it out. When we couldn't reach any more of it, Dad put the can into a large kettle of water on the stove to melt the crystallized honey. It took hours and hours to melt and after it had cooled, he poured it into glass bottles and Mom wiped off the sticky sides. She put lids on the jars and stored them away for use through the coming year. We weren't allowed to eat any more honey after that, except during regular meals, to sweeten certain foods. The only exception was when we got to it without their knowledge.

I loaded the empty honey can into my wagon and headed for Holley's Garage. I don't think Dad had intended to embarrass me this time about the oil, as he had with the "striped paint" and "left-handed monkey wrenches." But when I asked for clean used crank case oil, it had the same embarrassing effect. It turned out that while old engine oil drained out of a car's engine during an oil change is always dirty, some oil is less dirty than other oil, and I guess that was what Dad meant. It must have sounded pretty funny when I asked for it, because all the guys at the station had a good laugh. But they gave me the cleanest used oil they could find, or at least that's what they said. I was mad at the guys at the service station, but I was madder at Dad.

Mom and Dad had bought a few things since they got the money and we began packing it all onto the truck. The piano that they had bought from Mrs. Richards was first to be loaded. We needed to get help from all the neighbors to get it in place right behind the truck cab. Everything else was easy, just loaded on helter-skelter. Dad didn't like to waste anything—food, energy, or space—so about everything was loaded on.

"That wagon's wore out, William. We're not taking it. It'll cost more in gas fer the extra weight than it's worth." I decided my wagon was not that important. It had outlived its usefulness. For one thing, I was too old for it, and for another thing, nothing mattered much now since Victoria had gone. But I was taking my Me box. There was no way I would go without that.

Before we were ready to leave town, the dreary shades of evening were upon us.

"We should wait for morning," Mom said.

"Ta hell with morning. We're goin' now. Strike while the iron's hot," Dad said. "We'll stay with Elmo and Maxine––that'll cut three hours off the trip ta'morrow. An they'll feed us a couple meals."

Dad and Ellen got into the cab of the truck. Dad yelled out the window, "Is everybody happy?" It was obvious he was, as he noisily ground the truck into gear and it lurched onto the road. He was a new man in about every way.

I got behind the wheel of the old Dodge. I wasn't old enough to drive legally, but after a crash course in the finer arts of the craft, Dad was convinced I was ready. Mom and Martha piled in amongst the essentials inside the Dodge that wouldn't fit onto the truck, and as I prepared to follow Dad, I had to laugh. It looked like part of my job would be to pollute the air with the clean, used crank case oil smoke. More important, I would need to stop frequently to pour in more clean-dirty-oil before it ran dry and burned out the bearings.

> Before we could leave, Mrs. MacLean ran toward us, yelling, "You have a letter from Victoria."

"Hell, William, that kin wait," Dad yelled from the truck window. "She's not coming back anyway. Her Dad is rich now in Scotland. They'd be fools ta give that up."

"Leave me if you want to," I said. "I'm going to stop long enough to read it."

I love you, William," the letter said.

Daddy is watching me really close. But I will find a way to get to you. Tell Gramma and she will tell me. She is on our side, I think. I don't think I'll like Scotland and I know I don't like being away from you. I'll always remember the summers we spent together and the time on the sheep ranch. It was all so wonderful; it was like our honeymoon. Don't give up. I will find a way to get back and I will find you. Daddy took me to a place and we don't have the baby anymore. I'm so sorry, I couldn't help it. I cried for days. It was a part of me, a part of you. We can have another one someday. It's so different now without you. If I had a choice, I wouldn't go to Scotland. I would wait here for you or find a way to Montana. I think the place we're going on Mull Island is named Castle Duart. Don't give up, William. I will find a way to get back, and I will find you. There is nothing I love as much as you; you are a part of me. I'll be there when you need me, I promise. I will always be with you. Leave Gramma your address and I'll come there.

All my love forever, Victoria.

I couldn't stop crying; the tears flowed from me like I was a baby. My heart was breaking.

"Have they left yet?" I asked Mrs. MacLean.

"Yes, but Sophia promised that she and Victoria would try to come back and come to Montana."

Then Mrs. MacLean told me I should write something back. She had a paper and a pencil. Hell, I didn't know what to write. I felt so helpless, but she was nice enough to write it for me. Hell, I couldn't spell that well. "Victoria, darling," I told her to write, "I hate your Dad. He's an ass. Did you tell your parents that I'm of royal blood like the patriarch said? Maybe that will make a difference. We're going to Montana. Mom and Dad bought a place there, it's a ranch. The name of the town is Eden, like the Garden of Eden in the Bible. Maybe God made it happen; maybe he wanted us to live there together like Adam and Eve. I have tried to think of a way to come to Scotland but it's not very likely that I can; it costs too much. See if you can come to Montana. I promise I will find a place for you to stay. I love you so much. I always will. I think about you all the time. All my love, William."

"You know," Mrs. MacLean said, "Victoria might not be allowed to read your letters. They are pretty upset about you and the baby and all."

"I'm going to find a way to bring her back!" I said as I tried unsuccessfully to hold back the tears.

Chapter 69

Aunt Maxine was Dad's other sister. She and Uncle Elmo lived about a hundred miles away and along our route to Montana. Their house was filled with things from novelty shops that Uncle Elmo had picked up during his travels. There was a little bird that rocked back and forth, sticking its beak into a glass of water before it stopped at the top of its pendulum-type motion. As if by magic, it then would slowly tip down to the water like it was thirsty and begin the cycle all over again. I loved it.

They always had bottles of wine and whiskey in plain view and usually kept their glasses filled with the urine-colored liquid. When Mom and Dad weren't looking, they let me sip. I guess I was their only niece or nephew who had an interest in experimenting.

Uncle Elmo was a chronic tease. He liked to undo my bib overalls straps and tie them in a knot behind my back, or tie my shoelaces together. Dad found it funny and laughed, maybe louder and longer than my Uncle Elmo did.

Someday when I'm bigger, Uncle Elmo, I'll get even, I silently promised, and knew I would.

Uncle Elmo was the classic salesman, fat and jolly like you'd expect a traveling salesman to be. His oddly shaped head and sandy hair had given way to baldness with just a sprig of shaggy growth around the sides. It was about like Dad's, except in color. Brown age splotches and red scratches and scabs randomly spotted the otherwise rosy, gleaming cranium. He had tried covering it with a "rug," but that had proven to be too much trouble and now the old shaggy toupee hung with the hats and coats, like a dead cat, on the rack by the front door.

"Hell," Uncle Elmo said, "I'm too ugly fer a little hair piece ta cure." He looked around like he was waiting for someone to disagree, but no one ever did. That's about the only thing Uncle Elmo ever said that was the truth. He had overcome some of the natural unattractiveness of his wide, humped nose and stained and crooked teeth with his playful nature and perpetual, mischievous smile. The deep wrinkles, which should have made him more unattractive, rather gave him a surprisingly distinguished and rugged appearance. He spent a lot of time in the Northwest on sales calls and because of his extensive travel considered himself an expert on the prime routes to travel anywhere in the region. He told Dad that the White Bird Pass in Idaho would be by far the best, safest, and quickest way to get to Eden, Montana.

"It's all paved and the scenery is beautiful," he said.

Dad liked Uncle Elmo and they sat well into the night laughing and talking and sampling Uncle Elmo's supply of wines and whiskey and his expensive smoking tobacco.

"Wish I was a goin with ya. Them White Bird Mountains is a sight ta see," Uncle Elmo continued to encourage. He frequently managed to get me away from Mom and Dad to let me sample certain exotic drinks. I was never sure just what they were, but some were pretty sweet and tasty and some burned as they went down my throat. Then he went about teaching me some pretty nasty poetry too, when we were alone. "When the bleeding piles annoy and the corns are on your feet and the crabs they crawl upon your balls and they begin to eat; when you're old and decrepit and are a syphilitic wreck, may you fall down through you're a-hole and break your fuckin' neck."

Another one was: "Before I'd lie between your thighs or suck your slimy tits, I'd drink a barrel of buzzard puke and die of the drizzlin' shits." He was a perverted bastard, for sure—but just the same he was exciting and I liked him a lot.

Dad thought it would be better and quicker if we all stayed "clad" for a quick getaway in the morning. "Clad" was what he called sleeping in our clothes. When it got late, I snuggled in the pallet of blankets on the floor with my clothes still on and tried not to hear Uncle Elmo and Dad as they sampled Uncle Elmo's intoxicants and discussed the things that inebriated men talk about. I lay trying to imagine what the trip would be like, and what it would be like in Montana. I thought about Victoria and wondered what she was doing. I wondered if she would be able to come to Montana or if I would ever get enough money to be able to find her. There was so much to worry about, it made my head swim.

Dad woke early. He was in a hurry to get to Montana and his ranch. We all stumbled into the kitchen without washing our faces or brushing our teeth. He did allow us to relieve ourselves in the commode, however, which was nice of him.

"Hurry," he prodded continually. "Times a-wastin.'"

Aunt Maxine dragged her large body about the kitchen trying her best to make it appear that she was in no hurry for us to leave. She lacked the jolly quality that her sister Aunt Trudy and her husband Uncle Elmo had so much of. "There's no water," she said. "Elmo didn't pay the water bill."

Uncle Elmo hadn't made an appearance yet. He was probably passed out from the drinking the previous night. Aunt Maxine set spoons and a stack of cereal bowls on the table, and then brought a bottle of milk and a box of cornflakes. We had acquired the habit of sugar now that the war allowed it in more abundance and we had the money to buy it, but apparently they hadn't gotten out of the habit of hoarding theirs. Aunt Maxine made some whole wheat toast and served it with margarine not mixed very well. It looked like white lard with dark orange streaks running through it.

Dad said in a whisper when Aunt Maxine had left the room, "I'd just a soon eat Vaseline as that margarine stuff." Then he ate his breakfast quickly, even the Vaseline-tasting margarine, trying to be an example for us and get us going.

Aunt Maxine said she was on a diet and would eat later. She said she wouldn't hear of anyone doing anything in her kitchen; that was her domain and her territory. She guided us all to the door and then out onto the front porch. We turned to wave our good-byes to her, but the door had already closed.

"They's sure as hell good relatives. A lot of people don't want their relations ta stay over. God bless them two," Dad said.

Mom said to him, "If you ever drink again after I've supported you by leaving Aunt Helen's house, William Robert, I swear to God I will go back and live in that dungeon. I'll just say to hell with you and go—I swear I will."

Along the way, we ate Mom's hurriedly made sandwiches and treats. Our suppers were eaten in the late evening, in some city park or farmer's field, where she created concoctions on a Coleman stove. We had green beans in warm milk with salt and butter, topped off with stale, whole wheat bread. She fixed fresh peas and little red potatoes with the skins left on cooked in tasty white gravy, pretending it was better for us to eat the skins of the potatoes, although I'm sure it was really because that was easier. Our whole wheat bread had lots of real butter on it, because Dad insisted on real butter. There was always plenty of Kool-Aid from the large cooler to go around. Kool-Aid was cheap and it contained your daily allowance of Vitamin C. It said so on the package. Dad was determined to save the inheritance money for the ranch.

Every night after dinner, he would lay down a large tarp and Mom would make our bed with the lace sheets and velvet blanket, and we would all crowd in. Then Dad would fold the other side of the tarp over us and crawl in next to Mom. In a few minutes he would be up, afraid there might be a snake or scorpion, so we would pack everything back on the truck and go a little farther to find a safer location. Dad's "in and out of bed" routine often lasted for the rest of the night. Sometimes, when we packed back up and continued out trip, he would become confused and go back the way we had come. I had to drive the smoking old Dodge fast to head him off. He would get mad and curse and call me a horse's ass, and then would turn and get going the right way. Shit, it was all pretty silly and demeaning.

But Mom and Dad were beginning to talk now and Mom was coming around. It looked like she was forgiving him for the drinking with Uncle Elmo.

The trip took days, the worst part being the White Bird Mountain Pass in Idaho that Uncle Elmo had told us was such a great route. Dad fumed, "That horse's ass, that son-a-bitch, I'll get even with him when I see's him. He's prob'ly sittin' on his coach having a good time a-laughin."

"Just about like getting your overall straps tied behind your back and having your Dad laugh at you," I whispered.

During all this, Victoria was on my mind. She had become a part of me, as real and essential as life itself. I knew I would never be able to forget her.

Chapter 70

The furnace room is now extremely cold. "I wish someone would start the fire, "I whisper to myself. "If they did, I could yell at them through the vents, and they would see me and I'd be able to get out." I have no idea when or if Alex will be back, but I intend to have some answers for him if he does return.

I try to ignore the cold and my hunger as I wait for the moment that will take away most of my pain. Finally, I begin to dissolve into its wonder and beauty, and make my way back to Montana and Dad's farm.

Chapter 71

Our closest neighbors in Montana were Mr. And Mrs. Helms, about two miles away. He was a thin, nervous man who was interested in inventing new things but she was so uninteresting and oblivious—as women were made to be at that time in history—as to be near invisible. He had made a hitch that allowed the driver of a tractor to simply back up to a piece of equipment and hitch it up to the tractor without getting off, and then drop it off in the same way. Mrs. Helms cooked and cleaned. He had more than his share of energy and was always intent on burning it all up as he hurried from place to place, almost at a run.

A friend stole his idea about the hitch and made a great deal of money after he patented it in his own name, but Mr. Helms, who claimed to be a Christian, said that learning from the philosophy of Jesus had helped him to forgive the man. He held no bad feelings, while the thief, who clamed to be a Christian as well, apparently had been able to construct his own rationalization for his actions.

Mr. Helms was the town's explosives expert; he did most of the blasting, which included blowing stumps out of fields for neighboring farmers and ranchers. His taut body showed no signs of his seventy-some years. His hair had turned completely white but was still thick and long. He said his father and mother had come from Scotland and he had always wanted to go there to examine his roots. He told me a lot about that country: where it was, how to get there, how much money it would cost and how long it would take to get there. He was planning to take the train to New York and then some ocean liner to Scotland, and then trains or busses from there.

"'Twas a small island named Mull," he smiled. "My father was a caretaker there at the Castle Duart. He worked in the beautiful gardens thereabouts." Mr. Helms stopped and smiled as he remembered his father telling about it. "Just a small bus ride from Glasgow to the Ferry Pier at Craignore, then across the Sound of Mull to the Ferry House at Obam. Then a short ride on the narrow gauge railroad or bus to the bridge near South Craignore." He smiled again, and went on. "Then a short walk or hitch a ride a mile or so east to Duart Castle. You can't miss it. It's right on the coast."

Although Mr. Helms said he had never been there, his father had indelibly impressed onto his mind all the details, until now it seemed that he had been there. He told about the beauty of the eagles and other birds and the far-off Mount Ben More that loomed like a vision through the almost-constant light rain and thin fog.

I was astounded at the coincidence of Mr. Helms's father working so many years ago at the same castle to which Victoria had gone. Maybe he was a relative of James H., or maybe his father knew some of those relatives. Maybe he can help me to get there, I thought.

"It all sounds nice," I said, trying to get Mr. Helms to come back to me from his short expedition. "I would like to talk to you about it."

"Let's talk later," he said. "Right now, I'm getting too old for dynamite. I need someone to learn the trade. I'm going to retire and go to Scotland, at least for a while."

My heart began to race. "If I train in explosives with you and get enough money, can I go with you?" I begged. "It would be nice to have your company."

It looked like I still had a chance to be with Victoria. "Hell, I like explosives," I said.

So Mr. Helms began my training on dad's land because dad wanted the land cleared to make a place to raise feed for his animals. Mr. Helms carried with him a wooden box, a little smaller than my Me box, but instead of wheels it had a leather strap, and was filled with all kinds of special tools. There was a tool to make a hole through the dynamite stick, so a cap with a length of fuse could be inserted. He actually made two holes in the dynamite stick and after he pushed it through one hole he bent the fuse and pushed it into the second hole to keep it from coming out. He had a special tool for crimping the cap onto the fuse and sharp knives to cut the fuse and the dynamite sticks, a gunny bag filled with loose dynamite powder, a long-handled auger to drill holes under the stumps, and a long stick that looked like a long rake handle for carefully tamping it all down.

"William," he said, "us guys who works with dynamite is called powder monkeys," and he smiled. Two teeth on top, the incisors, were missing; I always wanted to laugh when he smiled, but I didn't. He was slow and meticulous with dynamite, never in a hurry as he was when he raced around doing other things. He walked around the condemned stump, slowly deciding where to place the dynamite. After he decided, he drilled holes in strategic places with the auger and carefully removed all the dirt by repeatedly sliding the auger in and out. The holes he drilled were no less than perfect. He would cut a stick of dynamite in two and make two holes in one of the halves with his "hole-making" tool. Then he inserted one end of the role of black fuse into a blasting cap and crimped that into place. He then pushed the cap through the hole in the dynamite, doubled it back, and pushed it into the other hole to secure it. Then he carefully scooped in loose dynamite with his special scoop, until his conservative mental calculations told him it was enough, after which he tamped it all carefully with the long pole, which was rounded on the end that came in contact with the explosives. He continued to carefully tamp as he filled in dirt, until the hole had been filled. He cut the fuse to the proper length, and then we gathered all the tools and dynamite and carried them behind a tree a safe distance away.

He had a certain glow about his face as he struck a match and held it to the end of the fuse. As it caught and begin to spit out flame making its way to the dynamite, we hurried to a tree away from the reserve of dynamite and his tools.

"Don't stand by the dynamite. You could get sympathetic detonation," he said.

Whatever the hell that is, I thought. Maybe it's feeling some sort of pity—you know, 'sympathetic'? I laughed to myself.

He sat with his back against the tree with his hands on either side of his head. I poked my head out to get a view. There was a muffled explosion, barely audible, and the ground shook a little. The stump had been split and the ground around it looked a little loose. What a letdown. I wasn't impressed.

Mr. Helms loosened up a few more stumps and after I had assured him that I knew how to blow a stump, he had me do it under his supervision. Then he left me to deal with the stump-filled land by myself. He left his tools until I could get some of my own. I promised that I would get some the next day.

"Well, I'm not dead yet," I said to myself. "I'm a friggin' powder monkey. But first of all, the stumps needed to be taken out of the ground. That requires more dynamite; about three times as much. And instead of loading only one stump, I should load ten or so before setting them off."

The gloom of evening and then the dark of night dark fell upon me before I was able to finish. I took Mr. Helm's tools to him with the assurance that I was doing well and then went home for supper.

I didn't have enough dynamite so I had to buy more, which I just put on Dad's bill at the hardware store. Hell, he was charging everything anyway. An old wheelbarrow replaced the gunny bag and wooden box Mr. Helms used. I had been able to duplicate most of the tools except a crimper for the blasting caps and thought I could just very carefully and very dangerously, crimp them with my teeth. The first fuse would need to be a little longer and then each following one progressively shorter to give me time to get them all lit and get to a safe place to watch as the stumps jumped out of the ground, ready to be stacked and burned. I computed the lengths with a complicated mathematical formula that I made up. Well, actually, it was just a SWAG.

After the stumps had all been set with explosives, I quickly ran from stump to stump to get the fuses going. When the fuses were all spitting out sparks, I ran to a safe place and sat with my back against a tree to watch and enjoy. I took makings out of my pocket and rolled a cigarette, like Dad did when he was relaxing. The first stump blew and the others followed in rapid succession. I had made several miscalculations, one of which concerned being "a safe distance away." I ran, dodging dirt clods and large chunks of stumps.

Later that day, Dad and I stood at the edge of one of the gigantic holes. "I'd rather have the stumps than them god-damned holes," he frowned, shaking his head. "It'll take a couple truckloads of dirt to fill just one of them."

Dad had become intent on enlarging his chicken coop. Hell, it was better by far than our house, but as he reasoned, that was how we made our livelihood, and if it was good this big, it would be great if it was even bigger. But there was an obstacle in the form of a large cottonwood tree right at the end of the coop. It would have to be removed before doubling the size of the building could begin. Dad had been talking about chopping the tree down, sawing it up for stove wood, and then trying to dig out the stump. But, I thought, why go to all that work when I had dynamite? And besides that, I was an expert powder monkey—just ask Mr. Helms.

I assembled my blasting paraphernalia and began sizing up the job. I wanted the tree to fall away from the coop, so I reasoned that the charge should be set between that and the tree. Also the charge should be large enough to cause the tree to fall away from the coop, and it was one hell of a lot bigger than those minuscule stumps. It would take a lot of dynamite to do the job. I began drilling the hole to place the charge. Dad would be damned surprised and pleased as well, I thought. I decided to drill three hoes and fill them with a good portion of dynamite sticks as well as a good portion of loose dynamite with my tiny scoop. That would do the trick.

As I sat in the shade of a distant tree, smoking a roll-yer-own stogy, watching the fire race along the long fuse toward the charge, I was pleased. I imagined Dad being thrilled at my unprompted willingness to help. I expected to see just a little puff from underground, and then the big tree lifting and slowly falling to the ground, making a soft thud as it hit. I imagined Dad complementing me, not only on my expertise but also on my motivation to see a job that needed to be done and then doing it. I saw us standing right across the big tree from each other, smiling in a friendly way as we sawed the tree into blocks with the old Swedish fiddle, a hand operated cross-cut saw.

But none of these things happened. Instead, the earth seemed to open up and dirt flew everywhere. The tree was ripped into splinters and wood flew all over. There was a gigantic hole in the end of the coop and a gigantic hole in the ground as well. The young pullet chicks had been hurled against the far end of the coop with such force that their white bodies were broken open and hung pasted like pictures on the wall, glued in place with their own blood and guts. Uncharacteristically for Dad, he kept my initial ineptitude at handling dynamite to himself, and when the word got around about me being quite versatile using it, I got a lot of work. There were a lot of stumps in Montana. I cut back on the dynamite and usually blew a pretty good stump and began earning a few shekels, as Dad called money. Once again, I began saving money to go to Scotland. This time it was a realistic goal, with the support and promise from Mr. Helms that I could go with him.

Chapter 72

The barn and sheds on Dad's new ranch were nice and there was water everywhere. But the house had no running water or electricity. It was a shack that looked uninhabitable. Dad set an old galvanized bucket filled with water on the new-looking porcelain sink, and then he dropped a long-handled water dipper in it for everyone to drink from, which then was submersed back in the bucket with any backwash for the next drinker. There were a couple of old coal-oil lamps. The only thing a little bit nice was the new porcelain sink cabinet that the galvanized drinking bucket sat on. Mom had fallen in love with it the first time she visited the place, and now she began working on Dad, as women do, to some day have it fitted with water pipes to bring forth water, hot and cold, like Aunt Helen's did.

    I couldn't help thinking that our move to Montana had been without cause and at Dad's whim. We could have lived for free in Aunt Helen and Uncle Archibald's beautiful brick house, and Dad would've finally been fulltime at the steel plant and would have made really good money. And I could have been there when Victoria came back. The move here didn't make any kind of sense. It was almost like moving back into the basement of the washhouse; well, a little nicer—but not much. But it did seem like Mom was happier. Maybe some of that was due to Dad's not drinking anymore—at least, not out in the open. I really think Mom would have left him, as she had promised, if he did start again.

Mom and Dad quickly fell in love with Montana and they desperately wanted to share it with others. Dad wrote a long letter to Aunt Trudy and invited her and Uncle Arthur to come. He even offered to share his ranch with them. They would have to pay their share, of course, the amount acre-for-acre that Dad had paid. But it was beautiful country, and all the people were nice. Aunt Trudy and Uncle Arthur were excited, and it seemed that soon they would be coming to Montana.

The upstairs room in the house was mine. I had to go out onto the front porch and climb the covered, creaky stairs at the side of the house, which warned everyone of my comings and goings. For lights, we used candles or the coal-oil lamps. Our food was cooked on the antiquated kitchen stove. We ate without cooking during midday meals in the hot summers. Water had to be hauled from town, or from a spring, in a large barrel and then dipped out to fill the water bucket. If we had visitors, they would merge with the family and assume this same routine. We all became used to this exchange of saliva, except for Ellen, who always kept a "clean" bottle of water, and guarded it like a miser.

Every Saturday night, the copper boiler was set on the top of the stove and heated. After it was warm, some of the water was dipped into the "Number 2" washtub we all bathed in. Mom still made her killer root beer in this tub and still washed it out, always carefully, before she did. Ellen was first to bathe, because she refused to bathe in used or dirty water. Martha was next, and then me. The water was so dirty and frothy by then that I wouldn't wash my face with it. I washed my face later, if at all, with cold water poured into the washbasin from the drinking bucket. I'm not sure when, or if, Mom and Dad ever bathed. At least, I never saw them.

Everything was similar to what it had been like when we were living in the dungeon.

Chapter 73

There was a small store in Eden, but the prices were high, and mostly for this reason, we went for supplies and food to go to the nearest big town, Piedmont, about 50 miles away. Everybody went there one day, except for me. When they got home, I heard the truck pull in. They always took the truck in case Dad saw an animal or piece of equipment he wanted to buy.

There was a small post office in Eden run by an old spinster named Mrs. Larsen. Mom got to know her pretty well because they were in some sort of a woman's club together. They always stopped to pick up the mail and to gather any gossip going around.

"William, there's a letter for you. It's from Mrs. MacLean," Mom said.

I ran as fast as I could to grab it. "William Robert," Mom scolded. "Be civil––that's no way to act." And then she smiled. "I hope it's from Victoria."

I ran upstairs to my room and tore open the letter. It said:

I love you, William. Don't hate me for the baby. I didn't have a choice in that ... Daddy decided it was the best thing to do.

I couldn't stand it. I hated James H., that bastard. And I hated God for letting him do that to us and to the baby.

> *Mom and I are coming back. We'll be in Springtown soon. Daddy told us we could go. Mom says she will come to Montana with me.*

Everything was fuzzy. I read on, but it wasn't sinking in. It was bittersweet: the baby was gone, but she was coming back. Victoria was coming to Montana. Tears filled my eyes, making it hard to read. I couldn't let go of the letter. I held it to my nose and inhaled the sweet fragrance of Victoria. I would need to go to Utah before they left in case they couldn't find a way to get here. I would write a letter and tell her to stay with Mrs. MacLean until I got there. I could steal the Dodge and borrow money from Mrs. Larsen and maybe steal some of the inheritance money from Dad's wallet. But first I needed to write to her. I found paper and a pencil in Mom's junk drawer and began.

> *Dear Victoria, if you make it to Mrs. MacLean's, run away and go to Buck and Edna's Diner on Main Street. Tell Aunt Mazy to let you stay with her until I get there, and wait for me. I'm going to borrow the Dodge and come to get you and bring you up here. I can get a job in The Bucket of Blood—that's a bar—and you can live in Mrs. Larsen's apartment and work in her store. I'll ask her. Just stay there until I come. I love you so much. I feel bad about the baby, but we can have another one when we get on our feet a little bit.*
>
> *I didn't think I could go to Scotland even if I had the money; it just seemed too damned complicated, although our neighbor here is from*

Scotland, or his dad was from Scotland, and he's going there soon. He said I could go with him. He knows where the Island of Mull is, because his father used to work there. But now, you're coming to Utah so I'll try to go there. It sounds like one way or the other, we will be together soon. I know one thing for sure: I'm going to take school more seriously now and maybe I'll be a doctor. I have to go now to get ready. I want to be there soon. Stay there and wait. I love you more than anything. You are a part of me. Love, William.

Now I had something to look forward to. I had a lot of planning and scheming to do. I walked to the post office and mailed the letter to Mrs. MacLean and then went to talk to Dad.

"Can I take the Dodge for a while? I want to take a trip to Piedmont to see about a job. I need to stay overnight. And I need about a hundert bucks for expenses until I get my first check."

Just like he didn't even hear me he said, "Got ta strike while the iron's hot. God wants us ta eat wheat. Oats and barley is fer animals."

What the hell had that to do with anything? As he raved about our good fortune, Mom just smiled––she always tried to understand my problems, but Dad was a selfish, stupid son of a bitch. I intended to steal the money and take the damned Dodge anyway. Maybe in a week or maybe less I would be in Utah with Victoria. And if Utah didn't work out, I would go with Mr. Helms to Scotland.

Chapter 74

I was being given another chance with my scholastic career. The slate would be wiped clean. The schools in Montana had lower expectations from its students, and I was going to give it my best shot. I decided not to take my Me box to school. I would take only a notebook and when it was full, store it with the others.

Warren was my first friend in Montana. I met him on my first day, when he got on the school bus. His was the next stop, after Ellen and I got on at the end of our long driveway. I didn't sit with her—that would be so un-cool, to sit with your sister. Warren stood nonchalantly in the headlights of the bus, smoking a cigarette. He made us wait while he took a couple of quick puffs and dropped the snipe on the ground and twisted his new-looking engineer boots on it. Smoking wasn't allowed on the bus, but in Montana just about everybody smoked and actually almost everybody drank, too; anything to fight off the persistent boredom.

Warren took his time getting on, like he was a big shot. He smiled at Mr. Jensen, the driver, but didn't speak, and then came right to my seat and sat down without asking permission. We started talking and immediately became best friends.

"Any neat girls in Utah?" he asked. "Do they put out?"

I told him a little about the flirtations I had had and he told me about some of his. I told him about Victoria and that she was going to come up as soon as she could. He nodded his acceptance, but he thought I should wait until I had sampled the girls up here first. He said, "There is no problem getting laid up here in Montana," but I wasn't interested. I wanted to wait for Victoria. I admired Warren for his openness, and wished I had the courage to smoke in front of my parents like he did. But in contrast to his outward toughness, he had a gentle nature and liked to play his guitar and sing. Sometimes I would get Dad's old mandolin, which Warren called a "Potato Bug," and the two of us would sit around drinking beer or wine he had stolen from his step-dad, Ike, as we banged out some pretty nice-sounding songs. The drunker we got, the better we played and the better the music sounded.

He was tall, almost as tall as I was, but he looked taller because he was so thin. He wore tight Levis and thick glasses that made his hazel eyes, which had only wisps of lashes, look larger than they really were. He wore an expensive black leather motorcycle jacket in the colder weather, a western shirt open down the front when it was warmer, and the same kind of hat that motorcycle riders wear. He let his long blond hair hang out around the sides and back. He was about a year my senior in age but had been held back, so we were in the same grade in school.

When I should have been learning to tie knots and cooking Mulligan stew in a scout troop, he was showing me instead how to steal wine from the passed-out winos in the park, how to smoke, how to shoot a rifle, and how to clean a deer. One afternoon, he talked me into helping him rob the whiskey and cigarettes from Mrs. La'fey's cathouse. He always set me up as the fall guy at school. He was really like a big brother to me, although maybe not the best of big brothers.

Mr. Hentzman, the principle at school, tried to set an example by kicking me out of English the third time Warren tricked me into ringing the fire alarm. "What does English have to do with the fire bell?" I asked Hentzman.

"Nothing. It's that and all the other things you do or don't do that has gotten you kicked out." He shook his head. "Maybe you can try English again next quarter."

Mr. Madison escorted me out of typing class when he caught me throwing the carriage on the typewriter back so hard that it lifted one end of the typewriter up off the table. He walked in just as whatever holds the carriage on broke, and the carriage shot off and embedded itself in the plaster wall.

His weak excuse was, "I've had it with you. I've warned you since the first day of school."

"Yeah, well, then no specific reason, I guess?" I yelled at him. "Warren was doing it, too. He showed me how."

"I just know what I saw," Mr. Madison growled as he dragged me kicking and screaming to the study hall. Warren smiled as we went by, with Madison holding the back of my neck.

Mrs. Hentzman, the principle's wife, had received some sort of national award for helping gifted students, but it looked to me like she just wanted to capitalize on her husband's position as headmaster. She had no tact; that was obvious.

"William," she yelled at me in class, "You are the worst student I've ever had." Her face was red, and the veins in her neck bulged like they would burst, the way Dad's did. "I have always been able to recognize a gifted child, and I thought you were one. Your I.Q. is in the high-to- exceptional range, but you don't even try."

She stood waiting for an answer. Warren whispered, "Chicken shit, you going to let her talk to you like that?"

Well, no, I wasn't. I stood, turned, bent over, and farted toward her as the class roared with laughter. I was a hit! But it was the office for me, and Warren was in the clear again.

The shop teacher, Mr. Smyth, had no sense of humor, which was another reason for me to be discharged from a class. "You little shit," he yelled, and threw a small ball peen hammer at me. It missed by a mile, going through the front window and sending broken glass everywhere. What a jerk. I had done my assignment with probably more enthusiasm and studiousness than anyone else. After days of sanding, sawing, routing, and whittling, I had reduced a large piece of wood that I had meticulously sanded and glued together to a fancy toothpick. The toothpick was pretty long and quite impressive. At least I thought it was, with its square sides so your fingers wouldn't slip and the long pointed end to dig out particles of food or debris that had become lodged in between your teeth.

Even so, I found myself in the principal's office again, with Mr. Smyth trying to heap blame on me. He didn't mention the ball peen hammer and the broken window, so I did. "You're a liar, William. A piece of wood broke off the lathe and crashed through the window," the old fart said.

"You're the damned liar," I screeched, but to no avail.

Warren brought his mother's jewelry box from home and said he'd built it. He got an "A."

"If the school would let us give "A+s," Warren, I'd give you an 'A+," Mr. Smyth said.

"Brownnoser," I yelled. Mr. Smyth sent me to the office again and patted Warren on the head.

Mrs. McDonald tried to teach us English Literature. It fit in with my plans to be a writer, so I tried to listen and learn, but there was just too much temptation. I had to bring some life to this class. When she turned her back to illustrate a lesson on the board, I lit a cigarette and started passing it around the room. Everyone took a drag and passed it along. Mrs. McDonald chased after the telltale smoke, trying to find the cigarette. You had to hold your breath until she ran past. I laughed at the wrong time and let the smoke out. Warren had the cigarette and got caught, too.

"About time he had to 'fess up," was my conclusion.

Mrs. McDonald got a funny look on her face, like she was mad. She left the room and returned with Mr. Hentzman. "You two come with me," he said in a low, firm voice. That was the only class Warren was kicked out of, unless you want to count the assembly thing. One day a distinguished visitor came to demonstrate how to make a good first impression. He loosened us up with a few old jokes and then asked for a volunteer, and selected Eric, who was sitting in the front row. He held Eric by the back his neck until he presumed he had been sufficiently embarrassed, and then he began. "When you meet someone, Eric, you should smile, step slightly forward with your right foot and say something like, 'I've always wanted to meet someone like you,' and then shake hands firmly twice. Grip firmly, don't use the Dead Fish Handshake," he tried to joke.

He thanked Eric and dismissed him. Eric walked red-faced back to his seat.

"Are there any two people who would like to demonstrate what you've learned?" the visitor asked.

Warren and I headed for the stage. We faced each other and went through the handshake procedure, moving and talking as if we were robots. For our finale, we stepped forward, clasped hands, shook two times and chanted, robot-like, "One and two, I've always wanted to meet someone like you."

We were a hit with the student body but the faculty decided Warren and I wouldn't need to bother coming to assemblies any more.

I was finally and unfairly removed from all my classes except gym, or physical education, if you want to call it that, so I just sat in the study hall reading classic funny books, *King Arthur, Moby Dick, Robinson Crusoe, Huckleberry Finn*, a book about Albert Einstein, and others. Reading about Albert Einstein was like seeing an old friend again. I need to write him, I decided, as soon as my new theory of how the galaxy might relate to the atom had time to jell in my mind. I found some magazines with pictures and articles of current events and even practiced writing a few of my own opinionated articles. I wrote them in my mind and remembered them; I have an excellent memory. After a while, I got bored and began erasing the eyes off the people on the pictures in the periodicals, magazines, and textbooks and dubbed in crossed eyes and then added whiskers and glasses. I taught Warren and the other kids how to do it, too.

The teachers and Mr. Hentzman didn't think it was as funny as we did. "My God, William, what are we going to do with you? Do you have any interests? Is there anything you want to do?"

"I've always loved art," I lied. "Maybe commercial art." I had a cousin in Utah who was a commercial artist and he made a lot of money.

Mr. Hentzman said, "I'll send for a correspondence course in commercial art tomorrow and have it shipped express. Do you think you can stay out of trouble until it gets here?"

Of course, I thought I could, but just to make sure, I was taken out of study hall and placed in a small room; well, a large closet. A long electric cord with a light bulb hung down from the ceiling, but it was still too high to reach and there was a beaded brass chain hanging down from that to turn it off and on. There were no windows, just the door. It reminded me of the dungeon in the basement of Aunt Helen's washhouse, except the floor was wood instead of dirt.

Mr. Hentzman brought me an old book about commercial art, some pens, and paper. I was supposed to start practicing by reading it and doing the assignments, but I decided to wait until the real stuff got there and instead used my time to practice daydreaming and altering the eyes and faces in books and magazines. My new school curriculum was great—not too many classes, not too much pressure—but I still thought almost continually about Victoria. Thinking again of going to Scotland, I decided that I would really get serious about saving my money and would find out more about getting there. It didn't look like the Utah thing was not going to work out, I would pack a bag and go to Scotland with Mr. Helms.

Mr. Hentzman informed Warren and me that we would have to go into town and use the bathroom at Marion's Tavern, because someone had placed so many empty beer bottles in the overhead water tank that the school's toilet became plugged. The basement had been flooded like a swimming pool and needed to be pumped out. There wasn't too much damage and after it had dried out and some of the electrical stuff had been replaced, it would be as good as new.

What was the big deal? Accidents do happen. Of course, Warren and I were blamed. We now had to walk the two blocks to town once at mid-morning, at noon, and then once in the mid-afternoon for bathroom necessities.

While we were at Marion's, we usually had a glass or two of draft beer. Warren hadn't had his allowance confiscated like I had, so he usually had a few dimes. The nice thing was there was no age restriction about drinking in taverns in Montana, as there was in Utah.

Nobody except Warren and I seemed impressed that we had made it this far in school without learning how to multiply, divide, do fractions, or spell and punctuate. Ellen brought unflattering notes from school to Mom and Dad about my ineptitude with scholastic challenges. Finally, and unfairly, I was removed from my remaining class, gym.

The homecoming basket ball game had to be cancelled and the game forfeited, because someone had climbed into the rafters and urinated on one of the large, double-barrelled, wood-burning stoves that were used to heat the building. The difference in temperature between the heater's surface and the pee had caused the heater to crack, and resulted in the most disgusting stench that I had ever been witness to, as well as eliminating the building's heat source. Of course, I was blamed for this, and shortly after the incident, Warren and I were both expelled from school permanently. Hell, I didn't have any classes anyway, and Warren was already working on a job at a new dam being built nearby.

Mom cried, and I got the sulfur-lighting thing. I hated it when she cried, especially when I was the cause of it. I would have preferred that she strangled me while my dad tried to hold her back, and maybe not even have my dad hold her back. Her crying always broke my heart.

"I'm not dead yet," I tried to assure myself. "Someday, Mom," I thought, "I will go back to school and make you proud of me." I felt sure about that.

Now alone and completely without direction or incentive, I sat at home trying to ward off the boredom. My thoughts were of going someday soon to be with Victoria in Scotland or to bring her over here. I just needed to save my money and wait for Mr. Helms.

Chapter 75

Mull Island, Scotland, was usually overcast and cool. The sun seldom shone and the wind almost always blew. For the weather more than for any other reason, Victoria and her mother were usually confined inside the gorgeous Duart Castle, which had been in James H.'s family for hundreds of years.

Majestic birds, including eagles and all sorts of water birds, flew about, but after a while, even all of this got boring for Victoria and her mother. James H. was usually either off to England or elsewhere for business, or was entertaining guests on one of the historic golf links around his extravagant holdings. The weather is never bad on the golf course, so the saying goes, and James H. seemed to believe it.

The family was now indeed rich, and Sophia and James H. were happy about that, but Victoria still harbored an empty place in her heart for William, a void that couldn't be filled, no matter how much money or how many distractions were thrown at her. To the delight of Victoria, Sophia wanted to visit Mrs. MacLean in Springtown, as well as visiting her own mother's grave. For Sophia, to whom the money itself was pleasant but meant little, it would be nice to have a little more freedom. What's more, Victoria was beginning to show symptoms of depression and fatigue, which worried her mother. She talked to Victoria, and they devised a plan.

They would confront James H. that very night, and would try to turn the tables on him, making it appear that their trip to America was his decision. They would either be allowed to return to America on their terms, or it might mean a court battle that could very well divide their lucrative holdings in Scotland. It would be up to James H. to decide. Victoria told her mother that she would rather be dead than live without William, and if she couldn't at least see him one more time, she would find another way to leave Scotland. And Sophia was sure she knew what Victoria meant—feet first in a box.

James H. knew that there was something wrong when he entered the house; he could feel the tension. As was his custom, he poured his Scottish ale and sat to sip it while waiting for the news. He smiled his content as his family entered the room. "Hi, family." he greeted them.

"Hi, James" and "Hi, Daddy" returned the two poised litigators.

"What's up?" A deep silence fell on the room. "I know something is up," James H. said.

Sophia spoke first. "Yes, James––Victoria and I aren't completely happy. We need to go to America from time to time to rekindle old acquaintances."

James H. looked at Sophia and then at Victoria. "There won't be any rekindling of that bastard William, is that clear?"

"He's moved away. He moved to Montana," Sophia said. "But I do miss your mother. It would be nice to see her again—and to visit my mother's grave."

James H. pondered his wife's request. "Let's bring her over here—we can exhume your mother and bring her here, too."

"You know your mother won't travel, James, not again––she almost had a breakdown the last time. And that's not funny about my mother. I'm not going to disturb her grave."

"And you ...?" James looked at Victoria.

"Daddy, I will always love William," she said, "but now he probably hates me because of the baby and all. But it would be nice to go back and see the old house and visit all the old places."

James H. frowned, but after a great deal of pleading, bargaining, tears, and anger, he finally consented, and the girls began planning. "I will be sending some men with you to make sure you find your way back here," he smiled.

The two knew that having the men accompany them would make it more difficult for them to accomplish their plans, but they didn't think it was impossible.

After a long, laborious trip, Victoria and Sophia finally arrived in Utah. During the voyage on the ocean liner, both had been stricken with seasickness.

Their dizziness and nausea were subsiding, and they were finally were feeling a little better. "We've had a close relationship with those two—you know, the dizziness and nausea," Sophia laughed. They both thought this was funny.

They enjoyed seeing Mrs. MacLean again and after the hugging and a little crying, Victoria asked, "What's the name of the town in Montana where William lives?"

"Can't we visit for a little while first?" her mother replied.

"Hello," Victoria said, losing her patience, "what is the name of the town?"

"Eden," Mrs. MacLean said.

"I'm going to Eden."

"Who are the men out in the car?" Mrs. MacLean asked.

"Daddy sent bodyguards," Victoria said in disgust.

"I don't understand that boy. Even if he is my son, I don't understand him." Mrs. MacLean shook her head.

"Can we take your car, Gramma?" Victoria asked.

"Let's wait until tonight when it's dark, and I'll help you get it out. We can take the car out of the rear entrance down by the sheds in back. It leads to the alley. They won't see you leave from there."

Victoria remembered when William and she had gone out that way during their escape to the sheep ranch for their "honeymoon."

It was quite late before they felt comfortable enough to try their getaway. The moon was a sliver high in the night sky. Everything was illuminated with a soft, dim luster. Sophia was sure she could see well enough to drive without the lights, at least for a while–– long enough to get away from the watchful eyes of the bodyguards. She backed carefully out of the garage and followed the not-very-well-traveled road to the alley. They looked up and down the alley, and Sophia stopped. She shifted into low and then realized that when she applied the brakes, the taillights turned on.

It took only minutes for the bodyguards to rush down the lane and block their escape.

"I'll keep trying until I make it," Victoria moaned.

Sophia held her and tried to comfort her. "Dear, don't despair. I've checked it out, and the trains go right to Eden. I'll buy you a ticket."

Victoria stopped crying. "Oh, Mother, thanks so much. When can I go?"

"We will need to wait for a few days or maybe weeks. Maybe we'll need to wait until we come to Springtown the next time. But I've decided that we, or at least you, need to do it."

"I'll wait forever if I have to," Victoria said.

"The Rio Grand goes to Butte, and then you'll need to change and take the Northern Pacific to Eden. It makes a few stops, but will get you there in a couple of days. You can ask around to find William and then see if that's what you really want to do."

"Oh, Mom, I love you so much," Victoria smiled. It was a relief to know that some day she would be going to William, even if she more than likely would be going back to Scotland first, at least for a little while.

Chapter 76

Warren and I had worked for the Forest Service for a good part of the summer, clearing trails, maintaining phone lines, and had even spent some time in lookout towers. We decided to try our hand at "riding the rails;" well, a modified version of it. The way most bums did this was to either hop onto a flatcar, into a boxcar, or climb underneath one of the railroad cars and lie on the bars and structure that hold the car together. I think that's where the term "riding the rails" came from. "Yeah, a real hobo trip," we said, getting excited.

We told the ranger we were quitting and wanted to get our checks that evening. "Well, it would be nice to have some notice so I could have time to hire and train somebody else," he said.

"We all have our problems," I said, and we left.

After picking up our checks, we decided we would go a good portion of the way by train and then hitchhike, sleeping in barns and on the ground.

"We won't need very much," Warren advised. "We can eat with the other hobos in the hobo jungles."

"It's still pretty warm, so sleeping on the ground won't be a problem," I said. "Going to tell your mom?"

"Hell no," was the reply. "She wouldn't let me go."

So that was that—our parents wouldn't know. "Hell, mine wouldn't care anyway," I thought, but I didn't want to take the chance that they might.

The following morning, as Warren and I walked toward the train depot to begin the first leg of our hobo trip, Flash came riding by on his bicycle.

"Where you guy's goin'?"

"Hobo trip to California."

"Can I go?"

"Hell, no."

"I'll tell yer mom, Bill."

"Go ahead."

"I'll put itching powder in your beds."

I knew Flash would tell, and would probably put itching powder in our beds, too.

"What if we let you go?"

"I have some money and I have a little bag like those," he said, pointing at the ones Warren and I had.

"Okay, but you need to do what we tell you and give us each ten bucks."

Flash always had money. He rat-holed it away everywhere, and would never spend it without good incentive. "That will work," he said.

We waited for him to get his things together, and it wasn't long before the three of us were on the Northern Pacific train chugging away from Eden. We planned to get a job in California and not come back to this one-horse town. The first leg of the trip was by train. We ended up in Piedmont, about 35 miles away, and after trying unsuccessfully to get a ride for several hours, we got a cheap motel room for the night. At breakfast in a restaurant the next morning, Flash ate his own meal and then finished our leftovers, and even ate anything left on nearby tables. After he threw up and rested for a while, he tried to find something else to eat.

"Why did we bring him?" Warren asked.

"He's probably got some money hidden and if we're smart, we can probably get some of it," I replied.

"I don't know if it's worth it," Warren countered.

"Just act like you don't know him."

"That's a good idea."

After hours of trying to get a ride, we finally bought train tickets to Endicott, Washington, and had dinner on the train. None of us had ever eaten on a train before, so we considered it a worthwhile expense. Flash ate too much and went to the restroom, which set the theme for the rest of the hobo trip. We did get a few rides, cooked weenies over a fire, and even slept out a few times, but for the most part we just rode the train, ate in restaurants, stayed in hotels, and Flash threw up.

Our boots began to stink so we began putting them out on the motel front porch, unable to cope with a smell that resembled rotting flesh and decaying cow dung.

One morning our boots were scattered all over the front yard. It looked like a dog had chewed them up. The top of one of Flash's had nearly been torn off.

We took the last leg of the trip by Greyhound bus and by the time we stepped into the San Francisco depot, we were almost broke. We counted our remaining few coins.

"I don't have anything," Flash told us.

Well, we weren't entirely broke. Warren had seven cents and I had eight.

"What are we going to do?" Flash wanted to know.

Before long, the three of were sitting on the depot benches enjoying the nickel ice cream cones our fifteen cents had paid for. Flash watched to see if we were going to leave any ice cream and when we didn't he said, "Hey, I'm going to the restroom. I'll be right back."

"What the hell are we going to do?" I asked.

"Maybe I'll try to get Mom to send some money," Warren said.

"That's a good idea. We can call Mrs. Larsen collect and have her tell somebody to send some," I said, and we started to look for a phone.

As we passed the coffee shop, we saw Flash sitting at the counter eating a burger and drinking a cup of coffee.

"Where did you get the money, Flash?"

"I found a dollar on the floor. I was going to just eat half of this and then bring the rest to you guys," he sputtered.

The operator couldn't find Eden for a long time and once she did, the line was busy, and then Mrs. Larsen wouldn't accept a collect long-distance call.

"To hell with it," Warren said.

"Let's just get jobs and see what happens," was my opinion.

We hung out in the Greyhound Bus Depot and walked to a few places to ask about employment. It wasn't long before we realized that to get any job at all good, we would need high school diplomas. We could be garbage men and work five hours a day for really good pay, but we would be garbage men. We kept looking. We were getting pretty dirty and started to smell pretty bad, too. Whenever Flash came back from anywhere, he smelled like a burger and fries. We looked for work for a few days and slept on the benches inside the depot at night. It was a little hard to sleep, because the guys who roamed the depot kept waking us up to talk. They were really nice and even invited us to come home with them. We had been told about the dangers of strangers in the big cities and decided to stay at the depot, but occasionally, some of the nicer ones even brought us drinks and sandwiches. Finally, as it seemed there was nothing else to do, we started thinking about giving up and going home. We were closer to Salt Lake than to Eden, and Flash and I had relatives there.

"Let's try to get to Salt Lake and then decide what to do," I said. "My grandma lives there. I haven't seen her since I was young but she would be good for a few bucks and a bed."

"I can stay with Aunt Ardith," Flash said.

"Hell, maybe we should have just stayed in Eden," Warren said.

"It's a little late to be thinking about that now," I responded.

The sun wasn't even up when we walked onto the entry of the Oakland Bay Bridge the following morning. A sign on the bridge read, "No Hitchhiking."

We took the sign down. After that, it only took only about five minutes to catch a ride from a man in a new Lincoln, who said his car could go 100 miles an hour. He was drunk. He said he was going to Reno and would like to have the company and if he got tired he wanted one of us to drive. He stopped whenever there was a bar or tavern and we sat in the car and waited for him to come back out. He was a great guy, who brought us something to eat and drink and paid for everything. In Reno, after he bought us a burger for the road and gave us a five-dollar bill, he said goodbye and we began hitchhiking again.

"We better just save this for a while," I said, putting the five dollars in my wallet. "We can get some bread and some baloney when we get to a store."

We started trying to flag down a ride.

"I've got to pee," Flash said. "I'm going to see if there's a bathroom in that café over there." He walked toward a dilapidated building with a sign that said, "Top Of The Hill Café, Best Burgers In The World."

Warren and I were still trying to get a ride when he returned.

"You smell like a burger and fries." Warren said.

"Yeah, they're cooking a lot of them in there."

Flash seemed to be trying to get something out of his teeth with his tongue and then he burped. "Excuse me," he said. Now there was a stronger odor of fresh burger and fries.

"Where did you get the money for the food?" Warren asked him.

"Somebody left part of a burger and I just picked it up on the way to the john and finished it," Flash said.

Finally, two old guys in an old Plymouth coupe stopped. "You're welcome to a ride but you will have to sit in the rumble seat in the back. It will be hot going across the desert but we have water and some beer in the cooler and we should be OK," the driver said. "We can take you as far as Winnemucca."

They were right about almost everything. It was hot and the hot wind blew in our faces for hours. They had water and beer in the cooler, but we wondered about being OK. We could see the guys in the front talking and drinking beer. After a while, Warren knocked on the window and motioned like he was drinking and pointed to the beer. The guy on the passenger side picked up four bottles of the cold beers and passed them back to us. That was the best-tasting drink I ever had.

Warren and I drank about half of our beer and then lay back and fell asleep. We were awakened by Flash throwing up over the back of the rumble seat onto the highway. He had finished off both of our beers and then the other two full ones. Hours later, we arrived in Winnemucca, red with sunburn and completely exhausted. My eyes were so swollen I could only partially open them. We got some bread and baloney from the grocery store and spent the rest of that day trying to hitch a ride out of that God-forsaken town.

Flash had recovered from his beer poisoning and now, strengthened by the sandwich, he looked none the worse for wear. "Hey, how about another sandwich?"

"We got to save them. It might be a while before we get any more money."

Well after dark and long after we had given up getting a ride that night, we had decided to retire on the grass in front of one of the houses in a residential area that we had walked through earlier.

"We'll just have to see what tomorrow brings," I said. I dreamed of flowing rivers and streams. There were trees with fresh fruit and food on a huge table. It looked like Thanksgiving and the whole family had gathered. Uncle Arthur was there. He had had a feeling of patriotism and had enlisted in the Navy, even though he didn't need to go because of being married and with children, and he worked in a plant that gave him essential worker status. I had to smile; in my opinion, he had done it to get away from Aunt Trudy and her relentless nagging. He loved her immensely, but he probably had needed to get away for a while, and the Navy did that for him.

Uncle Arthur was called on to bless the food. After he had prayed and said amen, in character with his Navy mores, he blurted out, "Pass the fuckin' turkey." It was breathlessly quiet for a moment and then, almost immediately, we started fighting for the food and the wishbone and trying to put olives on our fingers to eat. I wondered if olives that hadn't had a finger in them were really the ones eventually made into extra virgin olive oil. I reached for a turkey leg and was beginning to eat the wonderful dark meat when I woke up. Warren was still asleep, but Flash was gone. The empty bread wrapper and the plastic container that the baloney had been in was on the grass.

"You son of a bitch," I yelled.

"What's going on?" Warren said as he sat up.

"Flash ate all the food," I told him.

We sat for a minute.

"Where do you think he is?" Warren asked.

"Don't know, but I hope he's gone for good. It would be a lot better if he wasn't around."

In a little while, Flash came walking toward us chewing and wiping his mouth with the back of his hands like he was trying to get something off, like a guy did after he had kissed a girl and was getting ready to go back into the dance.

"Where the hell have you been?"

"I couldn't sleep, so I just went for a little walk. I had to use the bathroom anyway."

I smelled onions and hamburger on his breath and figured he had rat-holed money away and after we had fallen asleep he had gone to get a cheeseburger and a cup of coffee. I knew Flash was bad but this was the worst thing that he ever had done.

I wished I had my boxing gloves with us so I could teach him a lesson.

"Let's find his money," Warren said.

I held him while Warren searched. He looked in his shoes and socks, his underwear, all of his pockets, and then he looked again. We dumped everything out of his bag and looked through that.

"Where the hell do you hide it?" I yelled.

"I don't have nothing," he yelled back.

We sat for a while, imagining how wonderful the cheeseburger must have tasted, and then fell asleep, only to be awakened by drops of rain beginning to fall.

Flash was gone again.

"Hey, Warren," I said, "it's raining. We need to find some sort of shelter. Flash is gone again."

"Good." Warren sat up.

We picked up all three bags, and then saw Flash walking toward us. He was chewing and wiping his mouth.

"Where the hell do you hide your money?" Warren yelled as we ran toward the train overpass that allowed the traffic to go under.

"I don't know what you're talking about," Flash yelled back, exhaling burger and fries fumes.

The rain was coming down in sheets as we entered the protection of the overpass. It took a long time to finally get back to sleep and when I finally did I dreamed of Flash's burger and the beer we had enjoyed in the back of the rumble seat, and it made me feel warm and cozy inside. We got very little sleep, because we were at the mercy of the truck drivers, who never missed the chance to scare hell out of us by blowing their air horns as they passed thorough our bedroom. The early daylight revealed squashed Gila monsters and rattlesnakes that had also been looking for shelter. We decided that we would not spend another day here, no matter what. Flash was still asleep, his back against the concrete wall of the underpass. He had stained the front of his shirt with the remains of probably several cheeseburgers.

"God, it would be great to be rid of that jerk," Warren said, and I agreed.

We still had a little money from the five dollars.

"It's worth it to be rid of him," I said, as Warren walked over and pushed the change from the five-dollar bill into Flash's shirt pocket. We waved goodbye, walked to the end of the overpass and began motioning for a ride. In a few minutes, a red-headed man in a pretty new car picked us up. He said he was going to Salt Lake and we were welcome to go if we were willing to help drive.

We said OK, and got in.

He handed us a dry towel.

"Been on the road long?" he wanted to know.

It was obvious that he was a little fruity and he kept directing subtle glances at us that we carefully dodged.

"Not too long. About two weeks," I said.

We didn't want him to think we were so disinterested that he would put us out in this God-forsaken desert and yet we didn't want to be forced into anything, either. We were walking a tight rope of sorts. Just like the man in Oakland, this man now bought us food when we stopped for gas or to refresh ourselves.

When we got to Salt Lake, he pulled into a motel and went in to get a room.

"You guys wait here, I'll be right back."

He gave us a look, somewhat like a cat might give a mouse just before it devoured him, and then disappeared through the office door. Warren opened the car door and we got out of there fast.

"I wonder if Flash is all right," I said to Warren.

"Hell, Bill, he always puts himself first. I'm sure he is."

I knew where my grandma lived and it didn't take us long to get to her place.

As we greeted her and were telling her of our plans to move in until we could get a job and enough money to go on with our trip, she hit me with a rolled-up newspaper she had been holding, and then ran out the door.

Well, she didn't run like an Olympic runner might, but it was pretty impressive for a woman in her 60s.

We waited a few hours for her to return, and then we finally took the hint and left. I pulled out my watch. "Well, Uncle Elmo should be home by now," I said.

I knew he lived here somewhere near and after some searching, we located his house on a little-traveled side street in a rundown corner of the city. Instead of running out the door like Grandma had done, he gave us $20 and said Maxine had diphtheria and they needed to be alone. We talked for a while and then decided to be on our way, but the $20 would come in handy.

"Wonder if Aunt Ardith would give us some money to get rid of us?" I said.

Her door was answered to our knock. "Well, I'll be damned," I said.

Flash stood there as Aunt Ardith walked toward us. "Who is it, Gordon?" she asked.

"It's Bill," Flash answered.

"You should be in jail," Aunt Ardith yelled at me. "You know Gordon could have been killed. You've gotten him so upset he throws up all the time." She glared, while Flash gave me his sinister smile. "I'm going to call the police," she said. "It's a good thing I saw him under that bridge as I drove through Winnemucca or he might very well be dead now." She walked away.

"Probably going to call the police," I said as we ran.

Resolving to get by on the twenty dollars from Uncle Elmo, we headed for Eden. Going back to our modified hobo-type travel, we made it to Twin Falls, Idaho, before the money ran out. Then we decided, mostly because we had no choice, to go back to the hobo plan in earnest. With a mixture of hitchhiking, riding freight trains, and walking, we finally made it back to Eden. It had been a trip that neither of us would ever forget, but would never want to do again. We had been gone about three weeks, but it seemed a lot longer. We were thin and worn from the ordeal.

Flash was already home when we got there, and we found out the whole story. Aunt Ardith had noticed him under the overpass when she was returning from California. Well, it would have been hard for her to miss a one-eyebrowed elf with sharp ears and a receding hairline. After we left her place, she fed him for a few days and took him to the train depot with a homemade lunch, and sent him home to Eden.

Chapter 77

After the down payment on the place in Montana and the remodeling, Dad used most of the remainder of the inheritance to buy a new Super C International Formal tractor and equipment, such as a hammer mill to grind his wheat into feed for the chicken and other animals, and he bought about a billion baby chicks from Sears. The chicks came to the post office in cardboard boxes with little air holes in them. He also bought eleven pure-bred Guernsey milk cows, a milking machine, two workhorses, Maude and Ned, and one for riding, Penny. He made down payments on about everything.

"Might need some money ta live on fer a while. The damned chickens will bring in a fortune and when they're too old ta lay, we'll sell them ta the dam workers for Sunday stew," Dad boasted. "It'll be a piece of cake. Won't be no problem makin' the payments."

The "dam workers" were the people who worked on the new dam that was being built. I didn't care about any of this, because in a few days, I was going to Utah to get Victoria.

Dad was right, the eggs sold like hotcakes at fifty cents a dozen, and we were all busy sanding off stains to make them chalky white and holding them up close to a candle, a technique aptly called candling, to look for baby chickens or imperfections inside. The roosters and the chicks that got too old or didn't lay were caught with a long wire with a hook on one end and sold "on the hoof" to the dam workers, which meant we didn't even have to clean and pluck them.

The cows produced milk, lots of milk, to sell to neighbors for household use. And after separating the cream from the surplus, the skim milk was fed to the chickens to take the place of laying mash and to feed the fat, sassy calves that frolicked about in the lush fields of clover. The cream from the separator was put into large cans and shipped to Piedmont to be used for ice cream and cheese. Mom and Dad got a nice check each month for this.

I spilled the cream cans off the truck once, when I was taking it to the train for shipping, and Dad threatened to kill me. Mom's eyes filled with tears, and I felt that I would have rather been killed than suffer that look. The rotting cream smelled so bad for weeks that the locals named the bend Sour Cream Corner.

The golden sea of grain was harvested and ground into mash on Dad's new hammer mill and fed to the chickens to increase egg production and to help other animals to be healthy and keep shiny coats. It looked like Dad had made a good decision for once. We were doing great.

For entertainment I was supposed to hunt rabbits with Dad's old beat-up .22 rifle but when I tried it, it didn't shoot right, and the exploding gun powder burned my eyes and face.

The gun was worn out, but when I tried to fix it, it worked well enough to shoot a bullet into Mom's porcelain sink and ricochet around inside, knocking off big patches of porcelain. She threatened to kill me but, again, the look she gave me was worse than killing.

"Soon's we get things a goin', we'll get a new gun," Dad said. "A new Model 94 30.30 Winchester lever action. I always wanted one." He gave the hollow, insincere smile that I had become so accustomed to. "It don't get no better'n this," he continued. "God meant man to be on a ranch and make his own way. He was just a-testin' us in the basement o' Helen's washhouse. Well, son, we passed the test."

"Yeah, Dad," I said, but I had heard all this before.

Things changed when others found out about the big money in the egg business and how easy it was to get started. Just have Sears send a bunch of chicks in a box with air holes, keep them warm, fed, and watered for a few weeks and presto, a new gaggle of egg producers. Just about everybody did it and the market become jammed with eggs at about the same time that the dam was completed and the workers moved away. Soon, you couldn't give a chicken or egg away, let alone sell one.

Almost all our meals began to include poultry in one form or another and Mom preserved the eggs we couldn't eat in large crocks in a thick, Jell-O like substance called Water Glass. She read about the magical liquid in a magazine at the dentist's office over in Piedmont. The ad claimed that eggs could be stored almost indefinably this way. The catch was that once they had been "water glassed," the inside became hard and could only be used for deviled egg, potato salad, or hardboiled. The good thing was that eventually the shell became rubbery and could be used in place of a baseball, when Mom wasn't around.

Dad had finally spent all the inheritance money and the dams had been completed, so there was no work to make payments. He began cutting trees off the place and hauling them to the mill on our small, ton-and-a-half truck to support his new and expensive hobby, the farm, or as he called it, the ranch. This left no money for the new rifle or anything else. So, instead of hunting rabbits, my "recreation" became the ranch work and cutting trees and loading them on the truck for the mill.   The cows had to be milked by hand, because the new milking machine Dad bought wouldn't work without electricity. He was afraid I might submerge his precious, new tractor in the beaver pond again, so he kept it chained with a combination lock and I had to use the workhorses to skid the logs. After some work and worry, I finally figured out how to get the harness and bridle on the horses and get the mower going so I could cut the hay, but after a few hours it became very tedious. To create some excitement, I whipped the huge beasts into a trot, which made the cutting bar move so fast it became a blur, and then broke. While the horses lounged and grazed in the pasture next to the house, I drank a bottle of Mom's homemade root beer and fashioned a replacement part in the shade of the old shop, and tried to make up stories about one thing or another.

When the hay was finally cut, I raked it up into neat, long rows. After it was partially dry, Dad used a hayfork to bunch it up and toss it onto the hay wagon. I had to use the embarrassing manure fork to help, because, as Dad put it, "Ya ain't growed up yet. Ya needs ta be a man ta use these big real forks."

When Mom wasn't cooking, she and Ellen would climb up on top and tromp the hay into place with their feet until Dad decided the wagon was loaded. This haying went on for a long time, and it, too got tiresome. I needed a break. Mom had told me once that God sometimes warns us with a feeling that something bad is going to happen and we should heed this warning. This gave me an idea, and I thought, it's worth a try.

"Yer a horse's ass, William," Dad said when I told him something bad would happen.

"I feel it, Dad."

"That's an old wives' tale," he scowled.

"I really feel it," I repeated. "Something bad's going to happen."

"Yer just lazy. Grab yer manure fork," he said in his sarcastic way, "and let's get ta loading." He walked ahead of me to the wagon with his real fork slung proudly over his shoulder and me trudging behind, dragging my embarrassing tool in the grass, trying to hide it. Mom and Ellen trailed along behind, playing and laughing, oblivious to my cruel and unusual treatment.

"Why doesn't Ellen have to work hard like I do?" I asked.

"Well, ya horse's ass," Dad said, "she's havin' womanly problems," and he blushed. He had finally embarrassed himself. I smiled.

One morning, we loaded four wagons and had placed the hay neatly inside the barn. Now, we all rode atop the final load as Dad clicked his jaw and slapped the workhorses across their rumps with the slack of the reins, urging them to pull the top-heavy wagon across the bumpy field. He slowed and coaxed them nervously and carefully through the irrigation ditches. The wagon rocked dangerously back and forth, threatening to tip over and smother us all beneath a mountain of hay, but miraculously, we ended up in front of the barn. I stayed on the load as the others scrambled off.

A hayfork attached to a pulley dangling from a cable made its way down. I pushed it deep into the hay and locked it into place. Then I yelled, "Take it away!" and a horse on the other end of the barn and a rider, probably Ellen, pulled the cable and lifted a large bundle of hay up to the top of the barn. I stood below watching and holding the release rope. When the huge bundle of hay reached the top, it magically lurched and went inside. Fragments of hay broke off and floated down, but most of it raced along the track inside and at Dad's signal, I tugged sharply on the rope and the hay fell into the storage area inside the barn.

Then the horse was backed up to be ready for the next lift, and I caught the fork-pulley assembly and repeated the process. Dad stood in the shade across from the hay wagon, smoking a cigarette and supervising, I guess. As the last forkful began going up, I noticed that the pulley had slipped to one side and I reached to straighten it. The frayed wire of the cable caught my glove and pulled my thumb into the pulley. I pulled as hard as I could but it wouldn't come out.

"STOP! STOP!" I yelled at the top of my lungs, as my gloved thumb was pulled in between the pulley and the frayed cable. I could see it going in. It didn't hurt; it all happened too fast. My mouth filled with sulfur. A lightning bolt shot up my spine and tried to make its way out of the top of my head. I pulled as hard as I could and my hand came out, but without the thumb. Blood shot out in spurts almost to the end of the wagon. The cut wasn't even and clean—it not only had taken the thumb, but also had pulled off a thick strip of skin on the inside of my left arm all the way to the elbow. Blood squirted and gushed everywhere.

"GOOD HELL!" Dad exclaimed when he saw it. He always said "good hell" when there was a crisis.

"I told you something was going to happen!" I yelled, trying to create some sarcasm in my voice, to pay him back for his ignorance.

He didn't answer. His face turned pale and his eyes went back in his head. I was sure he was going to pass out. I helped him back to his supervisor spot in the shade and propped up his feet like you're supposed to do to get the blood to go to a person's head. Martha rather than Ellen had been the one riding the horse that pulled the hay into the barn, and she blamed herself, and ran into the woods. Mom went to look for her. Martha was pretty young, but in school.

After Dad recovered a little, we wrapped a piece of chicken feed sack around where my thumb used to be and up to my elbow, and the bleeding slowed down a lot.

No turpentine was poured on to kill the germs, because Dad just wasn't up to it. Maybe he thought I had already suffered enough. He finally recovered enough to help me to the old Dodge and we headed for the doctor in Piedmont.

"I got ta get gas," he said. "The old Dodge won't run on air."

"Okay, Daddy," I answered. I don't know why I said "Daddy." Hell, I sounded like a little kid.

We stopped at a station on the way. I held my severed thumb and injured arm tight with the feed sack around it, trying to keep it from bleeding, like it says to do in the *Boy Scout Handbook*.

"Here," he said when he came out from paying. He held a newly opened package of Camel cigarettes out to me with one sticking out. I took it with my mouth and he shook another one out for himself and we leaned forward together to the burning match that he held in his fingers, just like grown men do,

"That might calm yer nerves," he said after we were puffing and filling the car with smoke.

"Yeah," I said. "I didn't know you knew I smoked."

"Maybe I know more than you know I know."

I tried some jocularity, although it was unheard of to joke with him. "You know, Dad, you might not know as much as you think you know. I smoke Lucky Strikes when I can afford them." I smiled and his return smile was unguarded and unforced; it just came of its own accord. He placed his arm over my shoulder. "I know, I know," he said.

As we sped along the road, smoking, with the gravel pelting the underside of the car, tears filled my eyes. I leaned against him and for about the only time in my life, I felt close to him. We enjoyed the camaraderie for about an hour, smoking and pretending we were friends, but it all ended when we got to the doctor's office and sat waiting with the other patients for about an hour. I guess Dad didn't want the other people there to think he was soft or that his son was a sissy, so he got all stoic and tough like his usual self. He acted like he didn't know me and sat away from me, pretending to read a magazine. I knew he was acting because he was holding it upside down, and it was *Woman's World.*

The blood had caked the flour-cloth bandage by now and the bleeding had nearly stopped.

"This is nothing," the pale, thin, creepy doctor said when he finally came in. "A guy came in two days ago that had his entire thumb pulled off and it ripped the skin off all the way up, not to his elbow but to his shoulder."

The nurse bathed the wound with peroxide to get the piece of blood-soaked feed sack off and then she placed a large Johnson and Johnson Band Aid over the end where the thumb had been and wrapped another one around to hold it in place. Then the doctor came in and gleefully sewed the dangling piece of skin that had been ripped off up to my elbow. He used a curved needle and string that he referred to as catgut.

"If you had that thumb, I could try to sew that back on too. Sometimes they take. That's about all I can do. Try to keep it clean." He showed his teeth, which were brown and stained from the wad of tobacco he held between his lower lip and gum. "It will heal better if we don't wrap a bandage around it, and besides, it would just stick."

"What a jerk," I thought.

"Come back in about a week," he said. "We'll need to take the stitches out."

"How about a cigarette, Dad?" I asked on the way home.

"God don't like ya ta smoke, William. I'm tryin' ta quit. You should, too." The window for enjoying Dad as a smoking companion and buddy had closed.

The wound developed a lot of "proud flesh," as the doctor called it, and kept me away from most physical activities. Much of the time it was because nobody wanted to be too close to the odor and sight of my terrible-looking arm and thumb. I tried to keep it covered with clean rags and gauze, whenever I could find them, but it was a horrible task to get the bandages off—I had to soak them off with hot water and Lysol. It was better to just leave the wound uncovered.

But some good did come from this ordeal. I learned to roll an almost perfect cigarette with my good right hand, which I considered to be an extraordinary gain in my personal and professional skills.

Chapter 78

Ned, Dad's big workhorse, had broken out of the barn and Dad wanted me to go find him.

"Hell, I have plans today," I said, "and besides, what about my arm?"

Ya horse's ass, go get the damned horse. We got ta get the work done. Take Martha. She can be yer arm."

Well, anyway, I could drive the old Dodge with one hand, and after some coaxing, Martha agreed to go with me. As we drove along the lane towards Mr. Helms's place, he came walking out of the driveway. His reaction was his classic quick, jerky motion, like he was a little bit surprised, and then he waved me to stop. "Goin ta town?" he said.

"Yeah, we're going to look for Dad's workhorse. The damned thing got out and ran away."

"Maybe I'll ride along as far as town then," Mr. Helms said.

"Okay, but first let me talk to you." I opened the door, got out, and guided him a little way away from the car.

" Mr. Helms, I'm going to go to Utah as soon as we catch the horse. When are you going to Scotland?"

He looked at me in a serious way, like old people sometimes do. "I can't go for about two weeks. I've just got too much to do."

"Okay, if I can't find my girl in Utah, then is it okay if I go to Scotland with you?"

"Sure, I'd like the company. I'll even pay your way and you can stay with me until you find her."

That was all I wanted to know. I put Martha in the back seat, Mr. Helms got in the passenger side, and we went looking for the damned horse. About halfway to town, we saw Ned at the side of the road, eating at a large clump of grass. I braked to a stop, and Mr. Helms took the lariat from the back seat and walked toward the horse, making a loop as he went. Mr. Helms fancied himself a cowboy and, sometimes, I had to agree with him. He shook a loop out to reasonable size and without swinging it around his head, like you'd expect a real cowboy to do, he swung it this way and that in a certain rhythm, and then all at once it shot out like magic, to nestle softly around the big horse's neck.

"I'll help ya get him back to your place, if you'll promise ta take me back down to town," he said.

"Hell, yes," I said—he didn't care if I cussed. I figured giving him a lift into town would work out perfectly. I could drop Martha off, try to find some money and then take off to Utah. I could stop at the post office and get a loan from Mrs. Larsen, too. She knew me now, and everybody borrowed money from her

Mr. Helms walked back to the car, opened the passenger door, handed the coiled up end of the rope through the open window to his other hand, and then he got in himself. He slammed the door and let the coil fall down to the floor at his feet.

"I'll just hold the rope and lead him along as you drive," he said. "Go slow."

It was a nice day, and it inspired me to think of Victoria—well, hell, about everything inspired me to think of Victoria. The thought that I would be seeing her soon enough made my heart jump. The clouds hung heavy from the sky and hinted at a storm ahead. The old Dodge usually ran pretty well, even if it did smoke a lot. But if you lugged it down, it sometimes backfired.

BAM! It backfired. Ned jumped, and then reared up. He turned and ran as fast as his huge legs would carry his huge body, his nostrils flaring from fright. His eyes looked red and evil—he was out of control. The rope zinged across the bottom part of the open window; it was smoking and wearing the paint off. Mr. Helms held on, trying to stop the big horse. The blood streamed down from where his hands held the hard-twisted rope. I slammed on the brakes and reached across in front of Mr. Helms with my good hand. The rope burned into my hand, too, and I saw blood running out. Suddenly, the coiled rope on the floor caught Mr. Helms' leg and lifted him up. He was crossways and wouldn't go through the window. It was horrible; I couldn't believe it was real, but it was. I passed through a window, and watched as Mr. Helms and William struggled with the big workhorse.

William struggled with the rope. He knew he had to hold it or his friend would be injured, maybe even torn apart and killed. At the very least, he wouldn't be able to go to Scotland. Martha was crying hysterically, and the look on Mr. Helms's face was mixture of disbelief and pain, from the rope burning the skin off his hand and now tightening and holding him up against the window.

He cried, "God, help me," and then his leg broke with a loud snap. It broke between the knee and his hip, bending as if it had developed another joint. At the same time, the hip joint was dislocated and ripped through the skin. For some reason, the big horse changed directions and ran toward the Dodge. The rope fell slack and Mr. Helms and his broken and bleeding leg fell limply to the floorboards. William fell to the floor and tried to loosen the rope from Mr. Helms's leg. As if in a dream, the horse stopped like it was confused, reared and then turned and galloped away from the Dodge. William struggled to undo the rope, but the galloping horse pulled the rope taut and Mr. Helms's leg lurched upward, pulling his body with it. His body was caught in the window, and the leg tore away completely from his body where the compound fracture had torn through the flesh near his hip.

Blood and Mr. Helms's insides flew everywhere. The horse ran free, dragging the amputated leg on the long rope, with grotesque strings of multi-colored body parts covered in dust, bouncing along behind it.

The window effect faded. I sat in shock. This couldn't have been real—but I knew I had to do something. Martha was chalk-white and covered in blood, along with everything else in the car. She already blamed herself for my arm and thumb because she was riding Ned, and now this. Poor little girl.

I regained my senses enough to turn the car and drive to town. Harlow, the owner of the Bucket of Blood tavern, was sitting on the front steps. As soon as we arrived, a window opened in my mind, and thankfully I was engulfed by a dark, deep pool of black. I sank into it, deeper and deeper.

When I woke up, I was in my bed in the upstairs of our house. Then I remembered the horrible event with Mr. Helms. I threw back the covers and ran downstairs. Mom was sitting in her rocker.

"Is Mr. Helms all right?" I asked.

Mom began to cry. "No, no he's not," she said softly. "He's dead."

I couldn't speak.

"We buried him yesterday. You've been asleep for three days now. We were just getting ready to take you to the doctor. We put Ned down. We thought it was the right thing to do."

"Hell, I don't think it was his fault." And then, "How's Martha?"

"She's fine. We got her cleaned up. She's in shock, but fine. It will take some time for her to get over it all."

"It isn't very funny that a little girl like her has to be exposed to so much violence."

She just shook her head.

"I'm going to Utah, Mom. I'm going to go get Victoria—she's there now. I want to take the Dodge, but if I have too, I'll walk."

"Sit down a minute and listen," she said. "You've got a bunged up hand and arm, Mr. Helms has been killed, and you may be in shock. You should go to Utah, but just wait for a few days. Now you need to stay home and rest."

"I'm going. I told Victoria I was coming down."

She sat in silence for a moment, and then said, as tears flooded her eyes, "Mrs. MacLean called Mrs. Larson and left a message. Victoria got your letter, but they have taken her back to Scotland. She's gone. She said she would watch for you and Mr. Helms."

I couldn't help it; I cried like a baby. I ran to my room and threw myself on my bed. I wanted to die. I wished I were Mr. Helms.

Chapter 79

In Eden, the Korean War was pretty much forgotten. Nobody had television sets and radios didn't work very well, so it was somewhat of a shocker when I got my "Greetings" from the draft board. Like with all wars and drafts, there were gimmicks to get able-bodied recruits, just like there were to keep people out. One incentive was that a young man could wait to be drafted and serve three years, or volunteer for the draft and serve only two, with a promise of being kept stateside, away from the fighting and midnight patrols in no-man's land, but like a lot of other promises, it proved to be an illusion.

There was a third option, although I wasn't aware of it: a petition could be circulated through the community, and with sufficient signatures, the community could sacrifice one of its own, usually someone considered to be a "troublemaker." It was by this method that I received my draft notice. The town of Eden gave me a short, insincere farewell that had the same flavor my school experiences always had—they were just trying to be rid of me.

This war certainly hadn't generated the same patriotism that World War II had. Well, it wasn't really a war, just a "police action." We all supported it, mainly because that's what was expected of us. Not that anyone really wanted to join up. The patriotism of supporting the war was a carryover from the big war, and besides, we were all brainwashed into thinking we had to do whatever our parents, the police, or the government told us to do. I decided to think on the bright side. Maybe this would be a way to get to Scotland and to Victoria. I was pretty sure I could find her now that I knew she lived on the Island of Mull in a castle named Duart, where the Firth of Lorn meets the Sound of Mull.

On the night of my farewell party before I would be going to the induction center in Butte, Mom and Dad had an important church meeting and couldn't make it. Hell, Aunt Trudy and Uncle Arthur even showed up, but Mom and Dad couldn't make it. There were quite a few girls there too, but I owed my allegiance to Victoria. I did sit out in the cars with some of them, but we just talked, mostly.

As the music played, I got an idea and went over to talk to Warren. "Why don't you go with me?" I asked.

"'Cause I'm not a stupid bastard, I guess," he replied.

"We could go everywhere together. You'll have to go soon, anyway. Why not get it over with? I'll tell them to keep us together."

He took a long pull on his bottle of Highlander beer. "Well, maybe it wouldn't be too bad."

We shook on it.

Very early the following morning, Warren and I sat at the Eden Depot, waiting for the train that would set us off on our soldiering experience. Warren's mom had driven us there and after hugging Warren she cried and said, "I just can't bear to sit here and see you go. Good luck, and make sure you write." She hugged him again and then she went through the old rough depot door. Only the faint odor of her cheap perfume lingered.

"The old depot certainly hasn't changed much," I said.

"Not much," Warren said, but he seemed distant.

"I think that's the same fly on the ceiling checking out the same spot black there," I said, trying to lift the mood.

"I've noticed that, too." He laughed, and then looked at me as if he was trying to say something. Hell, I knew what it was. He was having second thoughts about the army.

But before either of us could say anything, we heard the train in the distance, and then in a few minutes it pulled in, with its usual screeching and letting off of stream. I grabbed Warren by the arm and pulled him toward the train, which hadn't stopped yet. There was a car for inductees.

"Makes us feel sort of special, huh?"

Warren didn't say anything. He was pale, and looked ill.

When the train finally stopped, the conductor stood by the step stool. He wore a smile that was condescending, or maybe it was like he was going to tell a funny story, although I knew he wouldn't, because no conductor ever had.

One at a time, he whisked us past him up the stairs, me first, pulling a reluctant Warren behind me. We took the nearest seats available.

"Just like that first day at school," I smiled.

"Yeah. Just like school," Warren stammered.

Other young men in the car greeted us with guarded but friendly nods. Warren was poised to speak, when a young man came into the car from the other end. He probably had been to the bathroom, or the "head" as soldiers call it. He was obviously more mature than the rest of us. He stood out. I was sure that he would end up being a general, or at least a corporal.

His name was Clinton. He wore a dark suite that was very wrinkled. His shirttail hung out and his tie was loosened. He and his clothing looked quite used. We soon learned that his brothers had gotten him drunk the night before, and he was suffering from a hangover, but he was also trying not to let that ruin his good time. He told us that after an all-night drunk, his family had taken him to meet the train. He told us that his Dad had taken him to a local cathouse and got him laid, and had given him an entire box of fine cigars and a magnum of Wild Turkey whiskey.

I felt a little jealous, not so much about the drunk, the

cathouse, the cigars, or the whiskey, but I had gone to the depot with Warren's mom.

"Hi," he yelled to Warren and me. The other inductees took Clinton's cue, and greeted us. Everyone introduced themselves and then we sat and talked about being warriors, while hiding the fear I'm sure we all felt. We talked as grown men and not as the sixteen, seventeen, and eighteen year-old kids that we were. I guess that was because we were almost real soldiers now, who apparently were willing to risk our lives for our country. We would never be kids again. We would forgo that part of normal life and instead be trained to kill or be killed, all for someone else's opinion or profit. But we couldn't vote or legally drink beer or whiskey for years.

Well, these bad feelings didn't last for long. How could they with Clinton there? He soon had us all laughing and joking. He took a flask from his inside pocket, and produced a paper cup with a pointed end that he had found in the head, and was busy trying to empty it, encouraging us to drink. When that booze was all gone, he took another fifth out of his suitcase and passed it around. Then he made sure we all enjoyed a cigar along with our drinks. Soon, the car was filled with smoke and happy faces drinking from paper cups with pointed ends.

There was a short bus ride from the Butte Depot to the induction center, which was right in the heart of Butte. It looked a lot like a big storefront, but when you got inside it was just a large room like a gymnasium.

Expressionless doctors and nurses were situated at strategic stations, examining the new centurions. The induction process was already well underway. Nameless humans moved from station to station, as machinery might do on a production line. They were pinched, poked, and pushed farther along the assembly line. As the new batch, we were told to wait at the first station, where we would apparently begin our travel along the mass-production line. I noticed that the nude, mostly white bodies being poked and prodded by the white-clad doctor/nurse assembly personnel had black bags hanging around their necks.

There was a solid line of lockers against one wall of the hall. "Hey Warren," I said kiddingly, "watch for that square needle they were telling us about on the train."

The square needle was a joke everybody talked about to try to scare the new recruits—at least I hoped it was a joke.

"There's a guy," I said. "I'll ask if we can stay together."

I the question of a large man in a tight uniform who stood nearby and looked friendly. "What?" he said. "Are you guys queers?"

"No, we're just good friends."

"You look like queers. Get your stupid ass in that line," he yelled at me, and then pointed to a different line for Warren and said, "And you get yer ass in that one." And we were swiftly and unceremoniously separated.

"Well, can I at least go to Scotland?"

"Get yer fuckin' ass in that line."

The main honcho, who looked like a general—a large muscular soldier in a khaki uniform—yelled in a booming voice, "Take off all your clothes and put them in a locker. I don't mean, take off SOME of your clothing--I mean take off ALL of your clothing. Don't make me repeat this or answer any questions about underwear or socks. Take it ALL off, and put it in a locker."

He scowled. I didn't think he could look any meaner, but with the scowl, he did. "You will find a black bag in a vacant locker. Put all your valuable shit in it. The key IS valuable—put it in the black bag, too. Lock the locker so your clothes will be there when you want them, if you want them." He said this last part in such a way as to be insulting, like we were dumb bastards.

"Should we remember the number of the locker?" a nerdy kid said. I couldn't tell if he was just kidding, or if he really was just screwing around.

"Give me 29 pushups, shithead," the general yelled.

While the nerd was pushing himself up and down, the general

went on with his orders to the rest of us. "Hang the black bag with your valuables around your neck, and then get in line." He pointed to the line we had been assigned.

After I had put all my stuff in the locker, put my valuables in the black bag, locked my locker, and put the black bag around my neck, I headed for my line. I could see Clinton in the distance. Rather than going with us, he was talking to what looked like a sergeant or general. They laughed and slapped each other on the back in a good-natured way.

"That son-of a-bitch will make general, I'm sure," I said under my breath.

We stood in long lines for quite a while, and then, wearing only our black bags containing our valuables, we were herded here and there like cattle, punched and poked with needles and fingers as we progressed along the production line, working our way toward our final induction—or now, I hoped, my rejection. After being humiliated in about every way possible, we were given a paper form and were coerced into signing it before we read it.

We were herded into a room for what looked like a written test. I guess it was to measure our intelligence or something, although why a soldier needed to be smart to lie in a foxhole and get shot at, I didn't understand. We sat in chairs made of yellow wood, with a desk top that flipped up to write on. The chair felt cold to my bare butt, but not as cold as it felt when I leaned back against its surface. It was difficult to concentrate, because my butt kept sticking to the chair and squeaked like a fart when I moved. Other inductees were having the same problem. The room was filled with squeaking as bare flesh was forced along varnished wood—and it was obvious that not all the farts were fake, as the smell of methane gas attested. The body odors in the room were overpowering.

The guy sitting to my right seemed like a good guy, although maybe a little slow. We began a quiet conversation. He was from Bozeman, Montana, and lived with his parents on a large cattle ranch. He said his dad hadn't been very happy about his induction and him being taken away from the ranch. He had tried a number of different things to keep from being drafted but he was here just the same. His name was Norman. He was either very smart or very dumb, and as events would have it, he was one of the few to be excluded from this particular draft.

It was easy to see the papers on either side of me, and even though we had been sternly warned about looking at our neighbor's paper, I couldn't help it. As Norman awkwardly held his left thumb against the questions, to apparently help him keep track of them—or to make himself look dull—he began to write in the spaces.

The instructions said, "Last name first, first name, middle name last, enter suffix, (i. e. Jr., Sr., I, II, etc.)"

Norman wrote precisely as asked. (His name was Norman Dee Ambrose Jr.)

Norman wrote, "*Ambrose Norman Norman Dee Ambrose enter suffix (i. e. Jr., Sr., I, II, etc.)*" He wrote small and was successful in getting it all on the line.

I had to smile at him being so dumb—or so smart—I hadn't decided which yet. He looked at me as he finished, smiled and winked. Norman went through the entire paper with about the same degree of either dumbness or smartness and then handed it in. Shortly after that, a couple of M.P.'s came and took him into a room with a bunch of men in white coats. Out of the approximately 300 inductees, Norman was one of only three who were rejected.

A little latter, Norman, Billy, and I sat in an old bar on the southern outskirts of Butte, examining the events of the day. We drank draught beer and tried to knock pool balls into the pockets while waiting to use our vouchers at the Butte Northern Pacific Depot to get home. I hadn't passed muster because of my damaged arm and missing thumb. Billy had only one leg, and Norman, the crafty little bastard, was mentally deficient—sure he was. He was a flamin' genius!

The thing that was astounding was there had been an extensive examination of Billy and me, despite our obvious handicaps.

In my mind's eye, I saw Warren standing at attention, being sworn in. He stopped and looked at me and to the chagrin of the swearing-in officer, Warren held up his hand with the middle finger extended and his mouth carving out the words, "Fuck you, Bill." I couldn't help but smile.

And now I was going home to the community that had disowned and exiled me, but nonetheless I was going home—I guess I was happy about that. But I did miss Warren. I wondered where he was going to end up and how he had gotten himself into such a predicament, conveniently forgetting it was me who had gotten him into it. Now I was more confident than ever that God had me destined to be with Victoria. Now I knew in my heart she was coming to Eden.

Chapter 80

I'm not one to wallow in self-pity. I have always faced my problems. I know I'm not perfect but I do try, for hell's sake, just like I'm doing now, going back in time to try to resolve a serious problem with Alex, the ass. Shit, I've wasted all this time with the induction thing, which certainly won't yield anything useful to tell Alex. I need to be more selective. I only have a certain amount of time. I can only last so long without food. Water isn't a problem. I can get it from the old sink and the tin cup. I've got to write in that notebook in the Me box before I forget; things go by and are forgotten so quickly.

I glance at the old ironclad wooden door, hoping Alex is watching me. It would be nice to have some real company. I guess I'm not only hungry but also lonely. I long for Victoria and wonder why she hasn't found me yet. She does know where the furnace room is. Hell, we lived here for years. But to hell with it, I'm going to stop feeling sorry for myself and continue my quest for ammunition to deal with Alex.

I try to remember where I left off. I don't need to go to that precise time, but maybe close. I had failed my induction into the army and was back in Eden and the ranch in Montana, waiting for Victoria and trying to plot a plan to get to Island Mull, and the Duart Castle in Scotland, where she was being held prisoner.

Chapter 81

Something quite unusual happened about this time. Uncle Arthur and Aunt Trudy decided to come up to Montana for a visit. They had a tent and thought it would be fun and it would allow them to find their real religious selves—you know, to suffer a little. They also wanted to see about taking Dad up on his offer to give them land, for a price. But they hung around as days turned to weeks, and then to months, until it looked like they might not be going back to Utah. It would really test their religious mettle to live in their tent with Dale and Flash, even though it was a gigantic tent.

One thing Dad and Uncle Arthur did right away after his brother-in-law got to Eden was set up their own church, which was a mirror image of their mother church in Utah in an old schoolhouse on Main Street. They did this without the knowledge or sanction of the mother church. It took some work to get the chairs and stage set up in some sort of traditional fashion. There had to be sacramental glasses filled with water and bread broken into small pieces, as well as white sacred cloths to cover everything. I tolerated it all for weeks, all of the eating the little pieces of bread that had been through who knows whose fingers and hands, the little glasses of water that had never even been washed out, and then I listened to all the stories about how lucky and blessed we sinners were.

Jesus! Most of those stories weren't true—how could they be? People filled with the Devil, who made them fly up to the ceiling and only the power of the priesthood could get them down? Uncle Arthur even told a story about a head-on collision he had had while in a car in the company of five other holders of High Priesthood. The cars had passed right through each other without doing any damage, simply because of the high amount of priesthood in their car. Newton, Einstein, and Galileo would scoff at this paradox, and I agreed. What a bunch of shit.

Dad presented me with all sorts of chores, but I began to catch on that they were lying to gain members and their money, and then days passed before I got these ridiculous things done. In fact, they never got done at all. Because of my lack of faith, I was unceremoniously relieved of duties and responsibilities and was shunned. Uncle Arthur and Dad, staying within the attitude of Christian forgiveness, didn't say much. They just left early to get the work done but made it obvious that I was being ignored. Even though the town was very small, I could never seem to find my way to the makeshift church on time, either—if at all.

They formed a church choir of sorts. Uncle Arthur was the choirmaster and Dad was first seat. Dale, Flash, and I pretty much made up the rest of the singers. As I was never there, Mom or Aunt Trudy filled in as best as they could. A small community church in Eden happened to be located a few houses down from the schoolhouse where Dad and Uncle Arthur's meetings were held. The Eden Community Church had been First Methodist, but over time had taken on an all-community, non-denominational character. If there happened to be a Baptist preacher available or passing through, he would take charge and the meeting would be Baptist in nature. If there was no clergy available, one of the members, no matter his religious preference, would preside as best as he could. It was unspecific, yet decidedly Christian in nature.

Dad and Uncle Arthur saw an opportunity. After some negotiating and skullduggery, they found a way to combine their Sunday services with those of the Eden Community Church. After several meetings, the Community Church took on the flavor of their church. The Methodists partook of the water and broken bread sacrament and bore testimony. Many began to pay tithes to Uncle Arthur's and Dad's church, which guaranteed they would get into the highest portion of heaven. This was described as a more sure way of obtaining salvation than simply accepting Jesus as the savior.

What delighted Dad most about all this was he now had a broad base of male voices to draw from, and some pretty good ones, at that. He made plans to increase the attendance and the membership of their new and growing church. He invited the residents of Eden and outlying areas, regardless of their religions, in an effort to sway and recruit them. These efforts included helping people who were down on their luck, and the old and poor, to recruit them as well. The church grew by leaps and bounds and the already not-too-prosperous ranch that Dad owned and where Uncle Arthur and Aunt Trudy lived in their tent was increasingly neglected.

One day, all these plans were derailed, when the First Methodist Regional Bishop showed up. His name was Mersman. To say he was shocked by what had happened to his church would be an understatement. All the traditional crucifixes, pictures of Jesus, and other Methodist paraphernalia had been taken down and replaced with more dull accoutrements from Dad's and Uncle Arthur's church. But most disconcerting of all to the bishop was that the traditional Methodist dogma had been replaced with that of the upstart church.

Mersman was pissed—although of course he wouldn't say "pissed," even if he had a mouthful. He was about as effective as Jesus supposedly had been at driving the blasphemers out of the temple for misbehaving, even though he didn't use the jawbone of an ass. Soon Dad and Uncle Arthur and their gentle, shanghaied bunch were dispatched to their original church and faith, which came under the control of Mersman.

Dad brought in the "jawbone of an ass" thing often after that, but he shortened and amended it somewhat, by repeatedly calling Mersman a horse's ass. The rest of the family and other members were more charitable, calling him Billy Goat Mersman, because of his goatee. They all thought it despicable that he had been so un-Christian like. Now that the Methodist and other community flock had been reclaimed by Mersman, they went back to Methodist religious grazing, or at least to community religious fodder. Nothing really changed that much. The church-goers seemed just as content as they had been both before and during the intervention by Dad and Uncle Arthur, whose beliefs were just as strange and baffling as the ones they had temporarily replaced. They were a gentle and charitable bunch, a nice group in every respect, but Jesus Christ, were they a gullible lot—even though to say any religious people are not gullible would be stretching it.

Dad and Uncle Arthur decided to travel to an established church that also was new, which happened to be in a town about 50 miles away. They spent a lot of time there, trying to gain a place in the elusive highest glory of God, and both continued to neglect Dad's farm and their families. It was about like what Dad did when he had a close relationship with the Dirty Shame in Utah. Dad and Uncle Arthur hated Mersman for years afterward, for being so inattentive to the real teachings and philosophy of Jesus, the supposed leader and founder of their church, which they were sure was the only true church, placed on Earth personally by Jesus. But, of course, Jesus plays this same role in all Christian churches, which all seem to have a monopoly where deities are concerned.

If the truth were known, Uncle Arthur was and always had been the sole leader of this little church secluded in the wild woods. It was no secret that both he and Dad believed this. Uncle Arthur professed to know more about their strange cult, because he said he did, and Dad went along with that because he felt inadequate. I guess you could say Uncle Arthur was the biggest bullshitter—he was obviously smaller and weaker then Dad and he was not as smart, either, but was decidedly more crafty.

Everything changed one day when Dad got word that the mother church was planning to organize a branch in the Eden area. They had chosen Dad to be the representative of the very isolated, weird organization in the woods. It seemed that Dad and Uncle Arthur had been found out as imposters, but the mother church wanted to take advantage of the willing pigeons if they could. But now Dad would be in charge of doing the mother church's bidding. Uncle Arthur was pissed, to say the least, but because of his faith, and because he did not want to diminish his chances of attaining the highest glory, he buckled under and begrudgingly became Dad's right hand man, instead of the other way around. He tried to be amenable, but it was obvious that he was having a lot of difficulty acting like a worthy disciple of Dad.

After that, especially in church meetings, Uncle Arthur always wore a forced smile. And away from that holy environment, especially when he thought no one could hear him, he said derogatory things about Dad. But, hell, derogatory things about Dad were pretty easy to find, because he was still having trouble stopping smoking and drinking, two cardinal sins in the mother church. He often could be seen behind the barn, at a neighbor's place, or in the Bucket of Blood indulging in one of his (and the church's) prohibited vices. Even then, I'm sure Mom would have left him if she found him drinking, but she grudgingly accepted his sneaking around smoking and drinking coffee.

On the surface, everything went on as usual and the church and choir grew, in quality and size, for about a 150-mile radius around Eden. Dad was as busy as a one legged man in an ass-kicking contest, and Uncle Arthur went through the motions of helping him while covertly demeaning his lack of willpower.

I wrote all this down in my notebooks, and when one notebook was full, I stored it in my Me box and began another one. One thing I wrote was that I was sure now that Uncle Arthur would be going back to Utah. Suddenly, my prediction came true, as I watched him and Aunt Trudy pack up with Dale and Flash and leave town.

Chapter 82

On Mull Island, James H. had introduced Victoria to Fredric De'Plore II, an entitled French gentleman. About like James H., Fredric was polite and very proper in every sense. He and Victoria had gone out on occasion, but mostly because they had been almost forced to spend time together, and because it was isolated, and she was bored. Fredric had money as well as his title, and seemed to truly love Victoria, but she was still in love with William.

After Fredric and Victoria had gone to a number of occasions together, and were beginning to become a little friendlier, he asked her to marry him, but she knew she wanted to be with William. The memory of William wouldn't let any other in—she struggled daily with this reality, and yet, it had all been so long ago, a different world, a different time. Would he still love her? She was going out with another man. Had William had other girls in his life? Maybe he was even married. Was she brave enough to find out? She was now old enough to make her own decisions, and she had some money, too. She knew what she had to do—she had no choice. She smiled bravely to herself; she would do it.

Victoria stood barefoot in the sand at the edge of raging water. It had taken a while to walk there from Duart Castle. She shivered against the cold, wet wind, as it blew against her face. It was too cold to be barefoot and without a coat, but she didn't care. She held a bottle of pills in one hand and letters from William in the other. Her parents had finally let her have the letters. She could scarcely read in the fading light. She was more determined now than ever to go to him, even though she was still forbidden by her father to ever see him again. "Either go or this," she whispered, and held the pills toward the heavens, partly to show resolve, and partly as a vow to heaven and to God. In spite of everything, she still loved her parents, and wanted them to accept her decision. She stood for a long while—and then turned, as if having a change of heart.

"I'll ask Daddy one more time and then …" She sighed. "Oh William," she sobbed, as if he could hear her, "I can't live without you. I'll find a way to come to you."

A few days later, James H.'s face was red and scrunched up like he was being tortured. "I can't believe that you would do that," he said. "If I hadn't found you in time, you would be dead."

"Daddy, if I can't be with William, then I'm going to kill myself. I'll try again. I tried it before this, and Mom found me and had my stomach pumped."

James H. looked at Sophia. "Is this true?"

"Y-Yes, it's true," his wife admitted.

"Why didn't you tell me?"

"You are always so busy."

James H. looked through his image in the large cut-glass window. He didn't see the raging Firth of Lorn crashing against the Sound of Mull as they met in the distance; he was too deep in thought. The massive waves from the Atlantic seemed only an illusion behind his reflection. He began speaking, softly at first, but his voice quickly built in volume. "I'm going to make sure things work out all right. You will be happy, princess. I promise that you will be happy."

Victoria looked at her father. "I'm going to find a way to go to William," she repeated.

James H. knew she meant it. He still loved his daughter in spite of everything and he would do about anything for her happiness. It looked to Victoria and her mother as if James H. was about to make concessions.

Chapter 83

I had pretty much resolved that my life would just go on as it had; just getting through the day as best as I could and thinking about Victoria. I got out of bed when I was called, I did my chores and afterwards, walked aimlessly through the woods, vaguely hoping some wild creature would eat me, to put me out of my misery. My only other release was the tavern, the Bucket of Blood, where I could forget some of my pain with those wonderful and welcome spirits.

One morning, I had just finished milking and was sitting in the corner of the barn thinking about Victoria. "God, my life is a shambles," I reflected. I had no friends left in Eden. They were all either in the army or married. "I wish Victoria was here," I whispered, almost like a prayer. "I miss her so much." I looked up toward the heavens; well, at the boards in the loft of the barn. "God, I haven't bothered you very much lately, or ever, for that matter, but this is something really, really important. Please let Victoria come here. I will do anything—I promise."

I was sure that this prayer would be like all the rest; none of them garnered results. In fact, I had pretty much reached the conclusion that I had a better chance getting something if I didn't pray. A rope hung down from the loft; maybe it was a sign from

God. I stepped up the stairs to the loft and reached to take the rope in my hand. It was tied firmly. I pulled the slack out and made a noose in the end. I had read there are supposed to be 13 loops in a hangman's noose. I began to count, 1-2-3, up to 13. I slipped the noose around my neck and pulled it tight. I looked one more time at the ceiling and at God and moved to the edge of the stair to step off and end my suffering. Then I heard a noise in the corner, in the dimness. Maybe a mouse or a rat; I didn't like rats. Shit, it was nothing, just the shadows—that wasn't fair. I could have sworn there was something there. "Even a rat or mouse would be a welcome change to my dull and dreadful life." I inched forward to step off.

"Whatchadoin'?"

Victoria always said, "Whatchadoin."

"What?"

Maybe I did see something, yes, a dim image ... it looked like her. I couldn't believe it. I rubbed my eyes and looked again. It WAS Victoria. She stood in the shadows, smiling. She was there, I couldn't believe it. At first, it was as if she was only a translucent image and then, as I rubbed my eyes again, she materialized. She was there and real, every bit as much as I was there and real.

"You look surprised," she said softly. "I told you I would come. What are you doing?"

"If I couldn't be with you, I was going to end it all."

"Well, I'm here. Take the rope off, silly."

She had finally come to Eden to be with me. Finally, she had kept her promise.

"You're here," I cried. I looked up at the boards in the loft. "Thanks, God, you're a bitchin' gentleman," I yelled. And I meant it with all my heart.

Victoria seemed to float across the rough barn floor, like she had at the Mexican hacienda, when I had escaped from Oscar in Canada.

I rushed to her and held her in my arms. Her fragrance was

sublime. She hadn't changed; she was still beautiful and inviting. The tears gushed from my eyes.

"Victoria, I was saving money to come to Scotland."

"I told Daddy that I couldn't live without you," she said. "I didn't want to, and I was going to kill myself if I had to stay in Scotland."

"I was just thinking about you. I always think about you. How did you get here?"

"On a big boat and then a train to Gamma's, she told me where you were. I took the train to the Eden depot. I had to change trains in Butte."

"Why didn't you tell me you were coming?"

"I wanted to surprise you, and besides, my letters didn't have a great history of getting through."

"How did you find me?"

"Harlow at the Bucket of Blood said where you'd be."

"Stay out of that place," I kidded, "it's wicked." My eyes and face were wet from tears. "I didn't think I was ever going to see you again."

"Me, too."

I pushed her back to arm's length. "Just let me look at you."

"I love you," she said.

I felt a pang of guilt. "I need to tell you some things." I was going to tell about other affairs.

"Don't tell me anything," she smiled. "We're together, and that's enough. You're the only one I'll ever love."

"I know. Me too. Our happiness will be complete when we can get more money and then prove that I am of royal blood. I still have the papers from the patriarch folded and taped together. They're water-stained, a little the worse for wear, but safe and sound in the Me box."

The paper with my séance on it WAS a little worse for wear—I had fished it out of the Victory Garden and taped it back together. But it was still sort of official.

Arrangements were made for Victoria to stay in Mrs. Larsen's rental behind the post office. Victoria did all the work getting everything set up. She was so efficient; Mrs. Larsen loved her, but also loved the money her father sent every month for the rent, and maybe even loved it more. Mrs. Larsen let her work in the store and keep her own tips.

Victoria helped me to save for a car and then to get a place to live, so we could get married. She said she would wait for my arm and thumb to heal—forever, if it took that long. She blamed herself for me being hurt. "If you hadn't been thinking about me, that wouldn't have happened."

But I told her it wasn't her fault. The doctor said I should have an operation. Cosmetic surgery, he called it. The damned thing wouldn't heal. It just kept building up "proud flesh" and all this watery, yellow pussy stuff ran out of it.

"If anybody's to blame, it's Dad. He never listens. But sometimes things just happen and maybe there's a good side. Now I can sit with you and write stories." She remembered well that I've always loved to write stories. She knew how I would write them in my mind and remember them until I could jot them down and store them in my Me box.

"I can roll an almost perfect cigarette with one hand now," I bragged to Victoria, "Here, let me show you." I took the makings out of my pocket, held the paper in the fingers of my injured hand and poured in the tobacco. Then I rolled it up with my good hand and licked it, using the spit as glue. "Something good has come out of it. God works in mysterious ways his wonders to perform."

"That's neat. Do it again," she squealed. "I don't care about your arm and thumb. We'll save money and have them fixed."

"All right, I'll roll another one," I said, and rolled another one and gave her one of my know-it-all smiles as I lit up. "I'm glad you don't smoke, Victoria. Dad says it's not ladylike for girls to smoke."

"Tell me a story," she begged.

"What the hell kind of story could I tell?" I wanted to appear humble.

"I don't care," she said. "Tell me the rest of that fairy story—yeah, the fairy story."

"Okay," I said, "the fairy story it is. But I'm not using Vomit and Diarrhea. I'm going to use us, Victoria and William." I took a long drag on my cigarette and casually blew out the smoke as I began.

> The passengers from the coach were walking toward the enchanted castle, and because he didn't know what else to do, William followed the others. The comfort and knowledge that he was at least temporarily safe excited the young boy. He delighted in the walk to the large and somewhat unwelcoming building. He knew that the evil presences of the unholy beings were difficult to discern and he cautiously made the decision to advance. The hunger that gnawed at his stomach prodded him toward a family that was cooking some sort of meat over an open fire. The delightful smell beckoned to him and he followed it to their camp. As was his nature, he stopped to help a poor peasant of a different culture before taking care of his own needs.
>
> He was welcomed warmly by the strangers and was fed, and they became his friends. The man William had helped decided to accompany him on his quest for the magic carriage. Together they searched the Enchanted Castle, but to no avail. They found out soon enough that it had been stolen by a selfish oaf and taken to an even more desolate castle some distance away, a domicile that was not occupied by good people, as this one was, but rather by pure evil—the foreboding Castle of Duart. William's new friend knew of a coach that was leaving for the evil castle and he took him to it. As William ran to catch the departing coach, he stopped for a moment to wave a thank you to his new friend. He called out, asking him to please visit him in the future.

The handsome young man was sad that the magic coach had been taken to the city of Duart, guarded by many evil spirits in crafty disguise, but as was his nature, he bravely resolved to release the coach from evil and be its custodian, for the good of the people and for the land.

One of the passengers told William a story about himself being kidnapped and taken away and never finding his way home. This interested William and he vowed to remember this man, so that after he had retrieved the magical coach he would see what could be done about this man's plight. In fact he decided to write to the king, the father of his secret lover, Victoria, and try to have him send couriers to return the poor man to his rightful family.

After a long and dusty ride William arrived at Duart Castle and by the use of clever tricks and disguises, he gained control of the magic coach and without delay set out for his rightful home. There were urchins along the road and they tried to detain him, but he outwitted them. He used a gift in a very unusual way, to get the better of the most evil of them—one who called himself Oscar, the black prince. However, Oscar recovered from the clever trick and pursued poor William with two knights, Alex and Craig, and sought to slay him. But before they could, the king's sheriffs intervened, and this timely interruption allowed William to continue his journey, as the sheriffs bound and took Oscar and his wicked knights to lock them in the dungeon.

William knew it was only a temporary freedom that he had and planned for a future meeting with the evil prince. He knew that the magic carriage would make his mother's life more content. It was a treasure that would most certainly be worth the dangerous quest. He had great difficulty in concealing his delight and vowed that this gift would be for the benefit of his entire family. He was proud of how unselfish and brave he had become.

William, I'm proud of you. You are indeed a great writer. And I like it a lot better with you and me and not Vomit and Diarrhea."

"It's easy to write about things that you love," I said. "But it's not as exciting after you're used to hearing the bad words, is it?" She smiled, and I was finally content. "We need to get going, Victoria. We've wasted a lot of time. In fact, years. And now that we are together again, we need to begin living our lives as one."

Chapter 84

With my arm and thumb injured, the hay all in, no school, and my car money all spent on frivolous things, I began saving everything I earned—doing odd jobs or blasting stumps—for a car. But with Victoria working so many hours for Mrs. Larsen, I still had loads of free time to kill. She liked to stay busy because she wanted to have a good car, just like I did. While I was killing time, I decided to go fishing. I found Dad's old fishing pole. It was a fly rod and the old automatic reel held a tapered line that I had cut many years ago to mend my worn-out shoes.

This was the line I had received so much hell for cutting, I remembered. I hadn't known that it was tapered; who the hell would ever know that? Every kid wants to have nice new clothes for the first day of school, and some even had all new clothes—some even had tailored shirts. Grudgingly, Dad had bought me a pair of tan corduroy pants, because they were cheap, and a tee shirt because it was on sale. I needed shoes, too. The pair I had was coming apart, but he said, "Hell, ya can't have everything. I went ta school with bib-overalls and barefoot." He told me this as I stood before him barefoot, in my bib-overalls without a shirt.

Using some of his tapered fishing line and a large needle, I sewed the old shoes back together.

"What the hell ya thinkin', boy?" Dad had asked. "That's tapered fly line. It's god-damned expensive. Now it's ruined."

I didn't know what to say.

"Why ya such a horse's ass?" he said. I looked at my feet, trying to show the proper shame and reverence like I always did to cut the demeaning lectures short. "You'll never amount to a hill a beans," he yelled and slapped me on the back of my head.

Dad had changed since we came to Montana. He was nicer now. Unfortunately, it was too late. I think we had already grown to hate each other so much that we now just naturally sort of kept all those old feelings alive.

I borrowed a few flies and a small white bait box from Dad's overstocked larger one. I also stocked it with a few of his fishing supplies, including a small chrome fingernail clipper for cutting the line and leader. I found the old straw hat Dad had given me after he decided it was worn out, to make himself feel better after he beat me up one day. I looped a piece of orange bailing twine over my belt. "That's where the fish will hang," I smiled as I trudged along the road toward the river.

As I passed by an old log house on the way, a voice challenged, "Where the hell ya think yer goin'?"

I was speechless for a moment. "We just moved here from Utah. We bought the place down the road, the Jay Albano place. I'm just goin' to the river to fish," I finally got the words out.

When I was younger, Gene Autry and Roy Rodgers had been my heroes. I never missed a matinee episode of them or any other cowboy, and now, I stood face-to-face with what looked like a real cowboy. He was standing beside a large, dark gelding. The animal threw its head and stomped its front hooves on the hard, dusty ground. Its eyes were filled with fire. The cowboy held the reins in his gloved hands, fighting to keep the spirited animal in check.

The cowboy wore a large-brimmed, red-colored hat that didn't fit down far enough onto his head by my standards, but still far enough to shade most of the mysterious stranger's face from sight.

But he looked good; like a real cowboy should look. When he moved, his spurs jingled and his chaps moved just enough to reveal worn Levis underneath. The checkered, red flannel shirt showed beneath the black leather vest and even at this distance, I could smell the strong odor of days of hard work and infrequent bathing, combined with a scent of pine essence. The difference between this and the movies was the smell; the horse noisily emitted methane gas that mixed with the odor of the cowboy. The excitement of this encounter immediately made me want to smell like that. I wanted to stink like a real cowboy.

"You're welcome to fish in the river. Just close the gates and don't mess up the place with litter and shit," he said, and then swung up onto the impatient steed. He rode a short distance, and then turned in his saddle, his face still shadowed by his hat. "Hey, I like company. Come on up in the evenings and spend some time. Help me drink some coffee."

"Sure will," I said.

I fished along the bank up the river for a while and then stepped into the stream and carefully made my way downstream. As I rounded a bend, I heard a distant roar. I walked faster. The water was beginning to run faster. As it crashed over huge rocks and fallen trees, it became a torrent.

The sun was setting low in the sky; the dimness of the evening, mixed with the turbulence and the current pushing hard against the backs of my legs, threatened to engulf me. It was as if I suddenly passed through a window into a different dimension, and was outside my body watching myself.

> *William struggled to maintain his footing. Ahead, water forced its way over rocks and logs, frothing and splashing as it went. The scene was hypnotic. The water swirled and circled, seeming to resist going within the confines of the narrow passage. The sheer turbulence and violence and brutal beauty almost took William's breath*

away. He stood for a moment more to allow the ferocious beauty to become a part of him.

Rocky sides of the canyon rose high above to form ledges and pinnacles, like a gigantic castle.

"Maybe our castle in the sky," William excitedly exclaimed. "A castle in the sky for Victoria and me. Another castle!"

Lightning flashed in the distance and thunder rumbled. The swift water pushed against his legs, seemingly intent on taking him into the black abyss between the ledges and the crushing, white, frothing, cascading tumult there. Finally, he sought refuge and struggled to the shore, sitting for a moment on the rocks, trying to regain his breath. Then he began making his way toward the top, but finally realized it was impossible, and retreated to find an easier way.

An old animal trail of some kind made for a better ascent and he followed it to the top. He sat and looked as if hypnotized at the black and frothing water churning far below. He had a chilling feeling, as if a giant monster were intent on devouring him. Fright told him to leave, but more powerful senses of delight and intrigue wouldn't allow him to go.

"This is my purpose," he whispered. "This is what God wants me to do. He has bestowed on me the power to rule Eden from this castle, this kingdom—the Kingdom of Eden. The highest kingdom," he yelled against the roaring stream.

His eyes watered from emotion and from the wind blowing in his face. His hair was ruffled and mussed, but his smile was broad and natural. "A great, kind king stands not above but with his subjects," he shouted, trying to overcome the noise of the crashing stream. "But he as king is held above them all—and he can do no wrong."

He felt like royalty. "*Victoria and I will indeed rule this wonderful kingdom of Eden,*" *he shouted to the heavens as he stood on the very edge of the abyss, looking down with his arms outstretched and his heart pounding in his chest.*

"*I'M GOING TO CALL IT JONES'S CASTLE!*" *he yelled.* "*No,*" *he reconsidered.* "*Dad will try to claim it, then. William's Castle is better. But that's his name, too. I'll call it Castle III, after the III in William Robert III.*" *He smiled.* "*Dad is just a junior. Castle III,*" *he yelled into the roaring abyss.* "*Castle III.*"

He pictured Victoria sitting by his side as queen while he made wise decisions about right and wrong, who would live and who would die. "*I will be a wise and just king,*" *he whispered.* "*This is our new castle. I can't wait to tell her.*"

The window effect faded and I found myself looking down at the turbulence surging through the canyon below me. It all made sense now. God had kept Victoria and me apart for a reason. We had come to Montana for a reason. It all made so much sense now. I wasn't crazy; I was being guided as Moses was guided. I felt that my life was wonderful now.

"Where've you been William?" Mom asked when I got home.

"Fishing."

"You've been gone all day."

I handed her the orange twine, from which tattered pieces of fish hung.

"They look pretty beat up," she said. "Don't know if I can find enough to cook."

"I found a castle."

"How many can you eat?"

"Mom, didn't you hear me?"

"How many fish?"

"I'm not hungry anymore."

I went to tell Victoria about our new castle. She would listen and I knew she would be as delighted about our good fortune as I was. She certainly understood me a lot better than Mom or Dad did.

Chapter 85

Next morning, I went back to the cowboy's place. The door opened to my knock and the cowboy of yesterday stood framed in the rough doorway, looking rugged, even though he was clad in one-piece underwear buttoned clear to the top. In contrast to his tough nature, he was just a little too pretty to be a guy. The dark-black hair and sideburns and blue eyes with long, dark lashes accented his light olive complexion and made the even white teeth behind his thin lips seem to be even whiter. The friendly smile overflowed his lips, covering his entire face.

"My name is Colt," he said. Instead of a handshake, he placed his hand on my shoulder and waited.

"I'm William. Everybody calls me Bill," I said.

"Bill," Colt said. "Wild Bill. That'll be yer name."

An expensive but worn and dirty cowboy hat had replaced the red one from yesterday. It looked like the sweatband had been soaked in dirty crankcase oil and filth. As we talked, he began putting on a freshly ironed, expensive-looking western shirt, all the while looking at me. He thrust his feet, quickly and with great authority, into faded, dirty, and worn Levis. Then he struggled to stand, hopping to keep his balance. He pulled on scuffed-up, lace-up boots that had cowboy-type, medium-high heels.

I immediately liked him. I decided that if I had a big brother, I would want him to be Colt.

"Have you already eat?" he asked.

"No I haven't," I lied. His English sucked. Even I knew it was, "Have you already eaten?"

I *had* eaten a bowl of Lumpy Dick cereal at home, but he didn't need to know everything.

"Come on in, I's jus cookin' some taters and bull fuck to put on em, and some elk neck meat," he said, as he got hold of my shirtsleeve and pulled me inside.

"What's that?" I asked.

"What's what?"

"Bull fuck." The words had just flowed from his mouth, but I had to force them out.

He laughed. "It's just lard mixed with flour and then some milk poured in. It's white gravy," he said. "All the rodeo crowd calls it bull fuck."

"Oh."

After a surprisingly good meal, even the elk neck, we sat at the table talking and finishing our coffee. He told me about adventures in Colorado and herding cattle and the rough winters and almost freezing to death there.

I told him about things that I had done … sort of. But I placed myself in Gene or Roy's boots, things that I had seen them do at the matinee movies.

"Hell," he finally said, "I could use some hep taken the cows up over the divide for summer pasture. We don't have many outlaws here like you're used to, but we gots lots a dust and flies and stuff like that. Come on outside and we'll saddle up a bronc and see what you kin do."

I had never ridden a horse. I looked for a way out. "I don't know how to use spurs. We never used them in Utah," I stammered.

"Heck, ya jus stab em in and hang on," he said.

It wasn't long before I was sitting on top of old Jubilee, a tall paint mare. Colt had strapped an old pair of spurs onto my feet around my penny loafers.

"You looks like a real cowpoke, Wild Bill. I think you'll do as a hand," Colt said.

That pleased me. "A real cowboy," I thought as I put my foot in the stirrup and swung up into the saddle. I pictured Gene, Roy, and me riding with Colt over the Great Divide to take the cows to summer pasture around Coeur d'Alene River and shooting outlaws as they tried in vain to rustle our cattle.

The old horse didn't move.

I gave up any pretense of knowing what I was doing. "What do I do now?" I asked.

"Just stab the spurs in when you want the ringtail to go, then say whoa, and pull on the reins to stop her," he told me with his friendly, mischievous smile.

I lifted my legs, stabbed the spurs into the horse's belly, and held them there. The horse didn't take off quickly as Colt had promised; she started to buck. I stayed on for a few kicks and then flew over her head, taking the bridle with me. My head hit the ground first, and as the birds tweeted and flew around my head, trying to avoid the stars there, Colt fell to his knees laughing.

"Ya should see ya'self, Wild Bill," he laughed. "Ya looks redicolous."

The brim of my straw hat had broken off and was pushed down around my neck. The crown had remained on my head, but it was pushed down about as far as it could go.

"Hey, when ya stabs the spurs in, don't just hold em in, stab em and then take em away," Colt said through his laughter. He laughed some more and then went on, "Heck, ya can't blame him fer buckin'. Heck, I'd buck too if some dumb-ass held spurs in my ribs."

I laughed, too.

"I'm fer shur gonna call you Wild Bill! You look like a Wild Bill, fer shur."

My left foot and loafer had gone through the stirrup and now held up my leg as I lay on my back. It was uncomfortable, and I leaned forward and reached up to release my foot but it was too awkward. I appealed to Colt, "I need some help."

He got off Old Dan, still laughing, and walked over to help me, but he tripped on a clump of grass and stumbled. The quick movement startled the already frightened horse and she started across the field, pulling me along behind her. She wasn't moving very fast and she was turned sideways, as if she were trying to keep from stepping on me. She sauntered along, as if not knowing exactly what to do, her eyes reflecting the same terror I felt, and she began moving faster. As I bounced along the hard ground, I grabbed at clumps of grass and weeds and tried to remain on my back, kicking to get free of the stirrup, but all that did was frighten the horse even more. I imagined my leg being torn off and the horse dragging my bloody limb through the woods, like the accident Mr. Helms had.

Then I saw the flash of Colt racing Old Dan alongside. Rather than looking at me, he watched my horse as he leaned low from the saddle while holding onto the saddle horn. His free hand dangled so low, it almost touched the ground. The horse's hooves thundered alongside. I could have reached out and touched those flashing hooves. Colt reached and grabbed my belt, then as big as I was, and as small as he was, he lifted me just enough that I was able to kick off my shoe and free my foot. He let go and I rolled along the ground in the dry stubble between the horses and then, in a cloud of dust, Colt and the two horses were gone.

I stood, in a daze, with one shoe on. As the blood from the scratches and cuts mixed with the dust and ran down my face and body, a feeling of overwhelming gratitude welled up inside me. I was alive and in one piece. I was thankful to Old Dan and Colt, and I had to admit that, in spite of the danger, God, it was fun being a cowboy. I didn't mind risking my life; it was too damned much fun to worry about. If the truth were known, I would have paid Colt for letting me wallow in the mud and cow manure on the hill in back of his log house, wrestling calves to the ground and cutting off their horns with a carpenter's saw, or heating the "Rockin' R" branding irons in the bonfire until they were red hot, and burning the brand into the critter's right hip, like an artist might dab paint onto a canvas. It made me feel powerful, like a god, to bulldog and hog-tie a young calf and castrate it as Colt had taught me to do. It was a wonderful and fulfilling feeling, much better and more exciting than salting suckers or stomping on potato or pill bugs.

Because I liked it, well, probably because I became addicted to it, I became free labor for Colt from then on. For years, we rode up to the summer pasture, Colt on Old Dan and me on whatever was available. Once, we rode out double on my old paint mare after Old Dan had slipped off the trail and started sliding down the hillside. Colt had to jump off on the uphill side to avoid being crushed and then Dan had decided to go on home. Another time, the gray mare I was riding cut an artery in her leg crossing a raging creek and bled all day. We wrapped torn-up saddle blankets coated with flour around the wound, to keep her from bleeding to death.

And there was the time we took a bunch of young kids on a roundup, and I ended up leading and tending the packhorses instead of herding, because Colt thought I should. I was mad but I did it just the same, because he said to. I was better at getting the cows back into the herd, but the kids "needed to feel useful," as Colt put it, so that's the way it was. When a storm threatened, Colt had everyone lie down with our heads against a log on the ground and threw a tarp over us, something like Dad did when we moved up here, and then we just lay there listening to the rain pelt the tarp and waiting for the morning, when Colt cooked elk neck, taters, and bull fuck—or bull muck, as he called it for the young wranglers. No matter what it was called, it was a great meal to start the day with. Colt kidded me about the cooking I had learned as a boy scout, like wrapping biscuit dough around a stick and holding it over a fire, which he called "twisted bread."

All of us cowboys that Colt conned into helping took leftovers from breakfast—eggs, bacon, elk neck, and whatever—and rolled it up inside hot cakes or fried bread and put in our pockets. Later in the day, we took it out and after picking off the flies and lint, it made a hell of a meal to a hungry cowhand.

On one ride, Colt's boots got wet and he prepared to cut them down the front to get them on. I stopped him. "Why not cut down the stitching on the sides, then the cobbler can just stitch them back up? No one would even know they were cut."

"Good idea, Wild Bill," he said. Later, when we got into town, the cobbler said, "If you had just cut them down the side I could fix them but now it's impossible to repair." He was a little mad but it was funny to me. "I should get at least some humor out of all the free work," I told Colt, who just smiled.

Flash, Dale, and I were all welcomed at Colt's place, and one by one, we all moved in. We took turns cooking. Colt furnished the groceries and we were his helpers with the horses, the cows and about anything else he wanted done. I liked to cook hash browns and eggs with toast fried in butter on the griddle. Flash fixed biscuits and gravy. Dale wasn't very old and hadn't learned to cook like the rest of us. He usually made toast and oatmeal, and when Colt occasionally cooked, he made hot cakes with syrup, and we always had plenty of coffee. But he finally gave up cooking. He just stayed outside until the food was ready, and came in when we called him.

We all slept upstairs in a big room that had three beds. It was two to a bed and Colt slept by himself. About this time a young fellow Eric, the one who had been so embarrassed at the assembly in school, and who had a yellow Model A joined our cowboy troupe. The cars were parked out front under the small trees. Eric's's mother had bought him the Model A, a beautiful classic in "like new" condition. He was proud of it and treated it like a baby.

Once, while Eric was finishing breakfast, Flash removed the front bumper and pushed the car close to a tree, and then replaced the bumper so the tree was between the radiator and the inside of the bumper, hooking the vehicle to the tree. Then he walked to the porch, rolled a cigarette and sat waiting. Eric finally came out and got in his car. After spinning the wheels for a while, he figured out what was wrong and took the bumper off and made it right.

"God damn you, Flash," he said.

The following day, Eric left to drive his mother to Piedmont in her car and left the beautiful yellow car as fair game. Like Pavlov's dogs, we began to salivate. As soon as Eric's mother's car had disappeared in a cloud of dust, we were busy with chisels, hammers, hacksaws, and screwdrivers, removing the top of the automobile. After a few hours, the top was ready to come off. The upholstery was torn a little, because the edges of the metal body were sharp, and we all received impressive wounds, but they were a small price to pay.

When Eric got back he was mad for a while, but we pointed out the advantages of a convertible and he came around. He and Dale got in and began driving up and down the road at breakneck speed. We were having so much fun, I thought, why not have some more? Flash and I dragged a log out into the road. It was large, and we thought it would be a hoot to see the look on the others' faces when they saw the log and skidded to a stop. But they didn't skid to a halt. The Model A had no brakes. The look on their faces told it all.

There was a thick stand of trees on one side and a high drop-off on the other, far above the river. The car hit the log and flew through the air. The jolt lifted both passengers out of their seats. Eric was sitting up on the back of the front seat, hanging onto the steering wheel. Dale sat in the back seat peering over the passenger's seat, where the jolt had sent him. The ensemble sailed through the air, looking like cartoon characters, but the vehicle stopped before it went over the cliff edge. At the time it was terrifying, as we imagined the horrible things that could have happened. There were angry words from Eric, but after we all caught our breaths, the whole thing was quickly forgotten. Even Eric thought it was funny.

Cutting the top off Eric's car spawned a rash of other cars getting converted by younger kids in the area. It was as if we all had a death wish, or as if the freedom had made us go crazy. It was a real joy to live like this. As we drank beer one evening, someone placed a picture of a black man on the inside wall of the living room and we all took turn shooting Colt's .357 Magnum revolver at it. The room filled with smoke. We drank more beer, and felt damned grown-up. But then, suddenly, our life of bachelorhood was over. Colt broke the news that he was going to get married soon. We would all have to leave the place. One by one, we went.

I went home to Mom and Dad, and everything went back to how it had been. Victoria was a little angry but when I told her how much I'd learned and that I now thought I could get a job as a wrangler on a ranch, she came around.

Chapter 86

I think Victoria was happy about the breakup of the cowboys at the Rockin' R. She and I had sort of drifted apart since her return and now we began to be close again. And we finally had saved up enough for a car, which we really needed. I was going to ask her to marry me and we would move into the old John Lockwood place, just one ranch upriver from Colt and Sally, and try to make a living farming. It was a decrepit farm, to be sure, but with a lot of work, it could be nice, and the price of only $12,000 for 200 acres was about right.

I decided that Victoria and I would be going to Spokane very soon to see what we could find in the way of a car. Victoria slept over so we could get an early start in the morning. We slept under the edge of the woodshed, at the side of the house. It was partially sheltered there and kept the dew and rain off. And more important, it was out of the view of Mom and Dad. Before we went to bed, Victoria and I wanted to celebrate at the Bucket of Blood while we talked about the Spokane trip.

Those plans were thwarted, though, because Victoria was sick. I hoped it wasn't morning sickness. We weren't ready to have another baby yet. As she didn't feel like going out, I got her some medicine. She said I should go to the Bucket of Blood, and she would be okay. She didn't want me to miss out on the fun, and said she would call Mrs. Larsen if she needed anything. Mrs. Larsen lived right in front of her apartment.

I set out for Piedmont with Colt, and his new wife, Sally, to have a few drinks and maybe see a movie. I wouldn't have a very good time without Victoria, but it was better for her to sleep, and I would check on her when we got back. Colt had stopped at the Eden store to pick up a case of beer and we were trying to get rid of it before we got to Piedmont. I was driving and drinking, as I always did, trying to stay between the river and the mountains, and thought I was doing a pretty good job.

All of a sudden Sally screamed, "Watch out!"

I had crossed over into the opposite lane. When I realized what was happening, I went back into my lane, but another car already had crossed the centerline in an attempt to avoid me. We hit head-on. There was a horrible crunch, and the back end of our car lifted off the road as dust and glass flew everywhere.

I saw Colt hit the windshield with his head and his body followed after it. I felt my body push against the steering wheel and my forehead bounce off the windshield, and then everything went black. When I came to, people were rushing everywhere. Red lights were blazing and flashing. I could feel the steering wheel pushing into my gut, and blood was running down my face, into my mouth. Colt lay on the ground in front of the car.

A man was trying to pump life into him with some sort of cylinder contraption. Miraculously, beyond a bump on my forehead, a little dirt on my face, and some blood running out of my nose and mouth, I was unharmed. Colt's scalp had been ripped off, and was hanging onto the back of his head. Someone lifted his scalp back to its original place, and wrapped and taped a long piece of gauze around it. Then the man turned his attention to another guy who was working on Colt's leg.

"Hell," one of them said, "it's broken in so many places, we would do him a favor if we just cut it off. They'll have to do it anyway when we get him in."

"Look," the other man said as he held up Colt's leg at the knee. "It doesn't have a bone left in it." He wiggled Colt's leg, The pant leg of his Levis had been cut away.

"You bastards shouldn't treat a human that way," I yelled.

But Colt's leg did look like a bloody rope hanging without resistance from any bone. It made me sick. The ground was spinning; everything went black again.

"Hey," someone yelled, awakening me, "there's somebody over here. It's a woman. She looks bad. Bring the kit and the stretcher."

I saw a flashlight moving in the distance and people moving here and there.

"She's dead," someone said. "Look at her neck. It's got to be broken."

I tried to get out of the car, but I was wedged behind the wheel. I smelled gas.

"Hey," someone yelled. "Come help us get this woman to the ambulance." The flashlight provided a path of light for two figures clad in white coats as they made their way up the incline to where Sally lay.

I tried to get out of the car again; the steering wheel was pushed into my stomach so far that I was having trouble breathing. "Jesus, somebody help me," I yelled.

"Get that guy out of the car before he burns up," someone yelled.

I could smell gas now, and fire. "Hurry," I yelled.

I felt a hand on my shoulder. "Can you move?" a voice asked.

"I could if this god-damned steering wheel was out of the way."

"I'll adjust the seat back," the voice said, and he fiddled with the handle. I felt the seat go back, allowing me to breathe.

I heard a loud puff, like the time Mr. Richards and Flash were burned, and then flames were all around me. Two strong hands grabbed my jacket and I was pulled out of the inferno and dragged across the rocks and gravel to safety.

"You're lucky as hell," a man said. He helped me into his pickup, explaining, "All the ambulances are in use."

"How the hell can you call this lucky?" I asked him.

"You should see your friends." He shook his head. "It looks like all you have are a few burns and a bloody face. The guy in the other car is dead."

"How are my friends?" I asked.

"The guy's going to live, but it looks like Indians got hold of him."

'What do you mean?" I asked, my mind not working clearly enough to make the connection between what I'd seen and what the man was saying.

"His scalp was pulled off. But I think they will be able to put it back on."

"That's weird," I said.

"Your friend's leg was shattered. I don't think they will able to save it. The girl is hurt really bad; broken neck and all smashed to hell."

"Where are they?"

"Last time I saw 'em, they were in the ambulance headin' for the hospital."

"Is that where we're going?"

"Yeah," he said. He rolled down the pickup window and spat brown tobacco juice onto the side of the truck, but most of it stayed on his chin and hung there, like gooey phlegm. I held back a gag.

Chapter 87

"You can go home," the doctor said after he checked me over.

"Where are my friends?"

"You'll have to ask at the front desk."

"They're going to be here for a while," the lady at the front desk said after she checked with someone on the phone. "They're in pretty bad shape, especially Sally."

Colt's leg had been broken so badly and in so many places that the only way it could be saved was to cut it open and thread the broken pieces onto a silver pin.

They left in the pin to help the leg heal, after which the pin would be removed. He lay on the bed with a white bandage on his head. His leg was supported by a large contraption with a lot of belts and pulleys on it. A large plaster cast covered his hip and all of his leg. The ends of his toes were all that showed; the toenails were painted red.

My god, I said to myself, is Colt gay? Not that that was a bad thing ... but still. I can't wait to ask him, I thought.

Sally was in the operating room for most of the night. Finally, she was wheeled out and left on the gurney. She had a large bandage on her head and only a small part of her face was visible. What I could see of it looked black and her eyes bulged out of their sockets. It reminded me of Wendell, when Victoria and I found him in Cook's old barn.

"How's she doing?" I asked the orderly.

"Not so good. The bones in her head are smashed. Even if she makes it, she'll never function normally again," he said.

Over time, Sally had several operations, a metal plate was placed in her head, and she received extensive therapy. But because of the head trauma, she couldn't walk or talk and was only able to move her arms enough to eat and to signal to Colt. It was a miracle, but she was ready to leave the hospital before Colt was, and was sent to stay in a rest home.

A few weeks later, Colt had recovered enough to drag around his healing body with the help of crutches. The hospital lent him an electric wheelchair for Sally, and he drove to the rest home to pick her up. After that she usually sat where Colt had situated her and watched the birds and fish around their house. No one knew what she was thinking, but she wasn't a pain in the ass like some women would have been. The doctor said she had been locked into a pleasant frame of mind that made her happy; well, pretty happy. She just sat and watched as Colt plowed the garden and fed the exotic birds and animals that he had procured for her amusement. Colt hobbled around and spent his entire day taking care of Sally's needs, as well as his own. He was sure she was going to improve, and saw a day not too far away when she would be helping haul the hay and cooking wonderful meals again.

"What the hell are the painted toenails?"

"It's too embarrassing to say," he smiled.

"Tell me, Colt."

"Well, if you need to know, Sally and I were laying in bed one night. She was painting her toenails and asked if I wanted mine done. Of course, at the moment, I said yes—so she did it."

I laughed. "I won't tell anybody," I said, but I knew I was lying.

Colt and Sally were able to get some financial help from government agencies, but as he was unable to work, their money began to run out. I spent a lot of time at their place helping out, but they seemed to resent it. If I helped Sally get to the bathroom and empty her urine bag, Colt got mad. If I helped Colt and then wanted to take him to Piedmont to get drunk, Sally got mad. I couldn't win, and I think they blamed me for the accident and resented the fact that I wasn't hurt. Hell yes, I felt bad. I don't know how I could have felt any worse. But I didn't try to do it. I had done everything I could to avoid the accident. I just couldn't win.

I went there nonetheless. I cooked food and shoveled snow, and didn't mind because they were my friends. But it was getting a little tedious; they seemed to resent everything. They got mad at me for just about anything, and I started showing up less and less, and when I did, I didn't even go inside to see them. I just walked around and did things with Colt's horses and cows. Then I usually went to and the Bucket of Blood to play pool and drink beer before going to get Victoria.

Chapter 88

I opened my eyes with a start. The rooster had awakened me. It seemed morning had come quickly, but that was okay, I was anxious for it to be here. Victoria and I were going to Spokane today for our car. A noisy bird, perched proudly on a decrepit fence, stretched tall on his tiptoes to blow out strands of mist into the frosty air. He slowly flapped his wings as he strained to reach that all-important, highest note, then settled into place, cocked his head this way and that and strutted up and down, as if to boast his self-proclaimed ownership of the farm, and then readied his entire body to re-perform the noisy ritual.

"I'm not dead yet," I said, trying to find some confidence to begin the day. And then to the bird, "You noisy bastard, *you* might be dead soon. Maybe we'll have you for Sunday dinner."

The morning sun shot frosty streaks of light through the aspen trees, whose leaves fluttered about me like a heavenly vision. "What does God want now?" I mused with a sarcastic grin, and pushed my body close to Victoria to share a moment of warmth.

"I'm glad you're finally with me," I whispered. "Are you awake?"

"Humff," she answered and turned onto her stomach.

"Want to do it?" I asked softly, trying to be romantic.

"Let's wait until later," she whispered.

"Your sleep is so god-damned important. You promised."

"Let's talk later. Let me sleep now."

"Well, to hell with it then. What am I supposed to do?" But I needed to get up, anyway. I had to get the car and besides, I was mostly just kidding.

"Big baby," she said.

"You're the big baby," I grumbled as another cock-a-doodle-doo chased away what little was left of my romantic notions.

We were getting used to each other again. I sat up slowly and then stood and bent over with my hands on my knees to let the blood find its way out of my aching head as painlessly as possible. The excess of devil rum at the Blood had taken its toll. I was sick.

"We've got to stop going there so often."

"I'm not dead yet," I repeated, still trying to give myself some sort of encouragement.

Victoria had already gone back to sleep. The velvet blankets moved slightly as she breathed. "You can sleep for a while, my princess," I whispered. "It will take me a while to get ready anyway." I had already forgiven her for being so unfeeling.

Outside the woodshed, a light cover of frost crackled under my feet as I struggled to keep my balance. I stomped on the frozen ground to get some blood flowing. I shivered and blew a billow of steam into my hands, which I then placed under my armpits for some warmth. I walked warily to the backdoor, holding my throbbing head with one hand and trying to get the mouse turds out of my eyes with the other.

The odor of cooking struck me as I stepped inside. I held back a gag. Mom was standing by the stove stirring something. She looked up. "What happened to your face?" she asked.

"Whatchamakin', Mom?" I said, avoiding her question as I backed up to the stove beside her. The heat from the kitchen stove felt good, but the smell of the cooking food didn't sit well on my stomach.

"Lumpy Dick and toast," she said. "Want some?"

"No, too early. Not hungry."

"Where've you been?"

"Nowhere."

"Bucket of Blood?" Her face scrunched up in disapproval.

"No," I lied.

"Looks like you been in a fight."

She was right. "You should see the other guy," I said, trying through my misery to laugh.

"You didn't get the kindling last night," she said. "Dad was pretty mad. Go get it now so you don't forget."

"I'll do it later."

"William, go get the kindling."

She was getting mad again, but at least she was off the Blood. "You lied about the bananas," I said, just to make sure her mind was off my nearly all-night absence.

"You should be going to church and trying to get into the highest glory," she retorted.

"That's a bunch of bull."

"Go get the kindling."

"Okay. I don't even want the damned bananas anyway."

"Be careful, William. People are accountable for what they say."

"Okay, I'll get the damned kindling," I yelled, and stormed out the door, taking my counterfeit anger with me.

"Why the hell didn't Dad get the kindling in? I have to do everything," I grumbled as I began the task of looking for anything that would burn. But instead of searching, I cowered under cover of the porch, trying to gain some courage for getting the kindling in. I blew out steam, trying to make a smoke ring, but my breath dissolved into the frigid air. I hated these types of chores; I felt overcome by the unpleasantness of this menial task.

Almost magically, an eagle floated high in the crisp morning sky. Three white-tail deer at the edge of the woods tried to glean a mouthful of anything the brutal weather of late fall hadn't killed. A soft, cool northern breeze moved the tops of the trees slowly back and forth in time to the empty mood and the almost deafening silence. The air tasted brand new, as if it had never been used before. It always tasted that way here in the early morning. I breathed a deep breath and coughed as the cold, sharp air entered my lungs. It held just a hint of a flavor, something like a lime float at Ben's Malt Shop in Piedmont mixed with the smell of a working sawmill.

Thick frost covered the roofs of the outbuildings to conceal their torn and tattered condition, making them appear new. A heavy slush curled over the edge of the more modern metal roof of our house, as if trying to make its way to the ground before being devoured by the heat from the cook stove and the morning sun that peeked through a wisp of clouds. There was a shallow ridge of ice stalagmites on the ground under the eaves from the repeated dripping and as the new water froze in place, more water splattered from the stalactites above, creating a hypnotic rhythm as the freezing wetness was momentarily replenished.

A lot of stuff was stored under the overhang to protect it from the weather. That's where the old galvanized tub we used for bathing on Saturday and for Mom to make root beer was hung, along with the boiler for heating the water for dishes and baths. There were also sleds, and skis to take the edge off the long, boring winters, and a collection of junk that was never used at all.

I was pleased to discover that gathering the wood to make into kindling had become a lot easier. It turned out that Dad had brought some old slabs from the mill, cut them into kindling-length pieces with his chainsaw, and had stacked them neatly on the edge of the porch. "Guess he got tired of me chopping up the house and his tool handles," I muttered through a smile.

I picked up a piece of wood and began chopping it into little pieces. "This is something else I can do better than Ellen," I muttered as the scent of freshly chopped wood filled my nostrils. I reflected that Mom always said when she watched me, "William, you're going to chop off your hand." Warren had showed me the way to chop kindling when we first got to Montana. "Just hold the wood on the chopping block with one hand and chop with the other." If done right, the wood splitters came flying off. Maybe it was a little dangerous, but it was the way woodsmen did it. After I had chopped a sizable pile, I stuck the axe up in the chopping block, kicked open the door and dumped the splintered wood in the kindling box next to the stove. Then, in the most contemptuous tone I could muster, I said, "There's your kindling."

"What did you chop up this time?" she asked in a mischievous way, and winked.

I had to smile, too. "Just wood, Mom."

"Sure," she kidded.

"Well, you lied about the bananas."

"I'm not dead yet," she laughed. "And besides, I do some nice things, too."

"I know. I'll give you a ride in my new car when I get back."

"Back from where? What new car? I hope it has brakes."

"Didn't I tell you? Spokane. Yes, it'll have brakes. I'm going to get ready to go."

"You have to milk before you can go anywhere."

"Didn't Dad milk?" I complained.

"No, he got up late and expected you to do it. He said he will come home if he can get enough timber ready to take to the mill."

"Hell, I have to do everything," I yelled.

"Want some soap in your mouth?" she said, threatening to punish me for saying the H-word.

"I guess not," I said, and picked up the bucket and headed for the barn to milk before I left.

Joe, my mentally slow uncle, had tired of whittling and wanted to come with me. "C-c-can I h-h-help, W-William?" he asked.

"Yeah, ya sure as hell can, Uncle Joe," I said. "You can help me anytime. You're good at it."

"Yep," he said. "Yep, I-I guess I'm pretty good at it, all r-r-right. I done it a lot at t-t-the institution. Yep, I g-g-guess I am good at it."

Uncle Joe had been shanghaied to a training school with the sanction of Gramma, who thought him incapable of taking care of himself and wrongly thought the school would take care of him. There he was abused and exploited, because he was strong and able. He worked long hours in the kitchen, the laundry, and the dairy.

Large portions of his face had faded white from bleaching steam in the laundry, his body was bent from abuse, and his spirit was nearly broken from neglect and ignorance. He was a gallant and gentle soul, meek and mellow, whose only fault had been not standing up for himself.

As we stepped off the porch onto the gravel driveway, Dad was coming home from the woods. He had the old chainsaw across his shoulder, and was puffing and blowing out steam from the effort of carrying it. Why the hell he didn't just leave that old saw in the woods I'll never know, but he didn't want someone to steal it, I guess.

"What the hell happened to your face?" he questioned in that authoritative tone of his.

"Oh, I just got in a fight."

"Who with?"

"Hell, I don't know his name," I said, thinking it would be sort of grown up to say, "hell."

He looked at me for a minute and then said, "Why the hell are you fighting with somebody that you don't even know?"

I tried to appear as grown up as I could. "Hell, I usually fight with people I don't know. The ones I know are usually my friends."

"That's dumb, Will."

"What the hell does that mean?" I asked.

"You're a horse's ass." That's how he solved all his problems; either that or, "Get to your room."

"I could use some help cutting timber," he said, trying to fill me with guilt. "Hell, I couldn't even get Joe out of bed. He said he was sick. You sick, Joe?"

Joe stuttered, "No, no guess I'm n-n-not too sick now. No, g-g-guess I'm not too sick n-n-now."

I got in front of Joe to protect him, as I usually did. "Hell, Dad, we can always find something to do around here. If it was up to you, we'd just work from daylight 'til dark every day. At least you get money. What about me and Joe getting some of it?"

"You eat, don't you, and have a place to sleep?"

Joe smiled. Still standing in front of him, I declared, "Well, I'll be damned if I'm going to get up before light and milk cows and then go to work cutting timber for the rest of the day, and then milk cows when I get home like you do, and then not get paid anything for it."

"I wouldn't need to do so much if you would help a little."

"Try paying me for some of the work." I spat the words out.

He turned to Uncle Joe. "Joe, you can come out in the woods with me after we milk. You need to earn your keep."

"Y-y-yep," Joe said. "Yep, need to earn m-m-my keep, all r-r-right."

Dad turned to me. "I work hard, Will. It's a lot harder than when we lived in Utah." He looked like he was about to cry.

I felt bad. I didn't want him to feel bad or to cry. I knew he worked hard, but he spent all the money he made cutting timber or working on the farm on what I thought to be frivolous things, like the cows, new fences, tractors, food, clothing, and he gave a large portion to his church as sort of a penance and to get himself into the highest glory of God's Kingdom, and besides that, he had gotten himself and us into this mess. We could still be living in Aunt Helen's house in Utah and living like the MacLean's or Condie's

A baseball cap covered his head, which had a pitifully meager growth of hair that went along the side of his head and then was longer in back. His hair had been curly—well, kinky—before it mostly disappeared. His shirt was unbuttoned in front and the sleeves rolled up to reveal the upper portion of his muscular arms and chest covered in thick, kinky hair. His thick lips, which usually hid his ill-fitting false teeth, were slightly parted and his face bore a serious and stern demeanor. His large feet seemed to anchor him to the spot where he stood, making him appear almost immovable.

I handed him the milk bucket. "I'm not going to help with the cows," I told him. It felt good to be free. Dad's face turned even more serious now and his olive-colored skin took on a redder hue, almost black. He stood with the milk bucket hanging from the fingers of his large hand as he waited for me to fall in behind and follow him to the barn to begin the tortuous ritual.

"I'm not going to milk," I said again. "I'm going to Spokane." He stood looking up into my eyes, and I could tell he was mad. "Well," I thought, "I'm not dead yet. If this is the way it is, then this is the way it is."

I remembered the bully at the bar had been a lot bigger than Dad and I had done pretty well against him. In fact, I had beaten him up quite badly. I had always been big and strong for my age. I could lift more and hit harder than any other kid around, even with my bum arm.

Dad sat the bucket on the ground and stood there with his arms hanging to his sides and began slowly turning, so as to always face me. I sort of danced around him, ready to make my move. I saw an opening and swung a wide haymaker at his chin. I didn't swing hard.

Hell, I didn't want to hurt him; I just wanted to teach him a lesson. And then I was lying on the ground looking at the clouds floating past. Stars were floating around my head. I didn't know how I had gotten into this prone position but there I was, and I wasn't sore anywhere, except from the night before, and there were no new wounds. For some reason, I started to cry. With the tears running down my face and Uncle Joe at my side, smiling his perpetual smile, we followed Dad to the barn to engage in the grim task of milking the cows.

After the milking, Uncle Joe went to the woods with Dad and I pretended to be sick and retreated to my room to lick my wounds and tell Victoria what had happened.

She said, "It was nice of you not to hurt your Dad," which made me feel a little better.

I told her what Dad was always saying about sex before marriage.

"I think if two people really love each other and are going to spend their life together, then it's all right," she said. "We do have the same last name, Mr. Jones!"

We agreed it was all right and even if it wasn't, we would take the consequences for our actions, even going to hell, if that's what was in store for us.

Suddenly, we heard footstep on the stairs. The door burst open and Dad stepped in. Victoria made her way under the bed before Dad saw her. "Will, I'm sorry fer hurtin' you."

I didn't say anything. I let my hand drop down, and Victoria found it.

"I just want ya ta get yer shot at the highest kingdom," he went on.

I buried my face in the blankets, a little embarrassed that I had been so humiliated by such a dumb little guy.

"When I was about yer age, Will, my Dad gave me this gold watch."

I looked up; he was holding a gold watch and chain.

My God, I thought, he's giving me the watch.

"Yer great-grampa bought it when he was a young man," Dad smiled.

"It looks expensive."

"It's been passed down from father ta the oldest son and now, it's yers. I want ya ta have it."

My mouth dropped open; I couldn't speak. I just looked at the beautiful golden watch. "His name was William Robert Jones. That's why yer name is William Robert Jones III."

As was his nature, he then had to taunt me a little bit more, in the form of advice, and I knew what he was up to by the way he began. But instead of turning to his usual topics of religion or his ridiculous ways of making money, he said something that might actually come in handy for me some day. He started telling me again about the building blocks of life. My gawd, how many times is he going to tell me this? But, it was nice for him to make the effort.

"Dad, you already told me about all this stuff and Lou did, too. Don't you remember, at the Dirty Shame?"

"The atom," Dad went on, as if he hadn't heard me, "is not encapsulated and is held intact about the same way as our own solar system is, and the relative distance between the atoms and the elements that make up the atom is greater that the distance between the planets of our own solar system."

Just like the last time he told me all this, I was struck by how Dad sounded like a teacher, like Mr. Madison at school. But I didn't say anything.

He went on with a smile, "They's more space in matter than they is anything else. If you removed all the space from the atoms in the Statue Of Liberty, it would become so small, ya couldn't even see it without a microscope." Then he handed me the gold watch and chain.

"Joe and I need some help in the woods," he said before he left.

"Dad, I'm going to Spokane."

"You can go later. I need your help now."

I was angry and disappointed, but I knew I was going to go to Spokane no matter what he said or did. He looked at me for a moment, to make sure I understood he was serious about the help, and then rubbed my head like I was a puppy and left the room. I heard his muffled footsteps going down the stairs.

It was nice to finally be alone with Victoria as we admired my, or, I guess, our new watch. I daydreamed about the new golden watch and chain and being with Victoria as we presented it to our own oldest son. And then I was rudely drawn from these wonderful thoughts into a world that had to be physically dealt with. Dad was calling me, or I should say he was bitching at me. It was such an effort to drag this body around while awake, especially in contrast to how effortless it was when I was in a dream.

Chapter 89

"How are you doing, William? Are you having fun yet, you bastard?"

The words from Alex are strained and harsh, even thought they are husky whispers. They stab like needles into my psyche, which seems naturally drugged because of the lack of food. As my body begins to shut down, it is medicating itself against pain and reality.

"How are you doing William? Are you having fun yet, you bastard?" The same words come again. Maybe it's a hallucinogenic echo; I don't know. For a moment, I don't understand where I am. I know only that I am lying on royal blankets, those sheets of velvet drapes and lace curtains, on a hard surface somewhere. Slowly, it begins coming back. I am on the floor of the old furnace room at the Camelot-Avalon—and then, vividly, the harsh reality comes crashing in.

Alex Stanze is taunting me, and seems to be enjoying it too much to suit me. I still haven't been able to discover the reason for his anger. I need to keep looking. If only he would leave me in peace to pursue my discovery attempts. I force my body into a sitting position, resting most of my weight on my elbows. I see his eyes looking through a wide crack in the heavy, metal clad door and can imagine the cruel smirk on his face.

"I thought you might be dead by now." Alex spits the words at me, as he tries, not very successfully, to go against his inherently gentle nature. I don't know how to answer his rhetorical statement.

"I'm in no hurry," he goes on. "To be honest, I'm sort of enjoying it all."

I lie back down on the decrepit pallet and turn my back toward the door and to him. I need to go back, to find the reason for his hatred.

"Sleep well, William. I'll be back soon to see you die," Alex says in a hoarse whisper, and then I hear the sound of his crippled footsteps fading slowly into silence.

So far, everything I have re-lived in my vivid excursion has only reinforced my opinion that it was Alex and his brother, or brothers, who had murdered the little boys. Why does he feel so strongly that I had done something to do with it? I need to go onward, to learn more about my past. I must keep in mind Dr. Wainscot's opinion that the murderers probably don't even know they did it. I remember Wainscot explaining how the human mind protects its owner.

Again, I summon and await the moment, and when it arrives, I catch it as I have learned to do, and begin dissolving again into that familiar, comfortable, virtual past. When I finally am entirely enclosed within that comfort, which through the years has become an important part of me, I continue where I had left off with my wonderful life in Montana with Victoria.

Chapter 90

The sun awakened me. Its beams streamed through the windows and mixed with a thin cloud of dust, a haze that apparently was always there, but was visible only with the help of the prism of sunlight now making its way through cracks and knotholes.

"Hell," I thought, remembering something I had read during my early years in the library, "it's not really a prism. A prism is actually a polyhedron with two congruent and parallel faces, whose lateral faces are parallelograms."

Victoria was still sleeping, her face turned away from this barrage of dust-filled sunlight. We were in my room upstairs in the Montana house. She was snoring, but only slightly, and instead of being an annoying sound, it was pleasant and soothing. I would let her sleep for a while.

I quietly dressed and tiptoed downstairs, as quietly as the creaky steps would allow. After the welcome relief of expelling liquid from my bladder, I rolled a cigarette and sat inside the shelter of the woodshed to enjoy the wicked pleasure.

In the distance, coming pretty fast, was some sort of a vehicle kicking up as much dust as the partially frozen road would allow. I watched as it neared. The old truck came to a stop, sort of haphazardly, and parked in the driveway. A man opened the door and stepped out. He stretched and looked around.

Jesus, it was Uncle Arthur. And inside the cab, barking out instructions, sat Aunt Trudy. Then, like a stream of clowns pouring out of a little car at a circus, my cousins Flash and Dale emerged with Aunt Trudy. Not only in actions but also in appearance, they resembled clowns, dressed in wrinkled, unmatched, and miscellaneous garb. The truck was piled high with almost everything imaginable, and fastened behind was a very large, two-wheeled trailer, similarly piled high with junk. I quickly ground out my snip under my shoe, so as not to give Uncle Arthur ammunition to bitch at me about smoking, and stepped into view.

"Hi, William," Uncle Arthur said when he saw me.

"Hi, yourself," I smiled.

His family, dirty, haggard, and lean, looked like the refugees in Steinbeck's *The Grapes of Wrath*. That was one of the books in my "Me box," which by now had become almost a part of me. All of the commotion and activity had awakened Dad, who came onto the front porch. He had just rolled a cigarette and was touching a match to it when he recognized Uncle Arthur and dropped it on the porch, twisting it out with his boot. He seemed embarrassed to be caught smoking, but also delighted that they had finally arrived.

Mom came out as well, and the two of them groveled and made their salutations and such. Dad didn't kiss anybody as part of the welcome; he only did that with the young and pretty girls. Trudy, his sister, didn't qualify as being either young or pretty.

"Park the truck inside the barn, Arthur," Dad invited. "Ya kin move in with us; they's room. The boys'll sleep out in the barn 'til we gits yer house done."

Mom nodded her head in pleasant agreement. It was decided to clean out the front part of the barn and bring the truck and trailer in there, out of the weather, and then move the furnishings into Uncle Arthur's house when it was done. Mom and Dad were sure that the beds and the furniture inside our house would be ample for Uncle Arthur and Aunt Trudy, if they could somehow crowd into my small bed upstairs. In my mind's eye, I saw Uncle Arthur lying beside the bed on a made-up pallet while Aunt Trudy loudly snored with the blinders on her eyes, which would be put to better use over her gaping mouth. She was probably dreaming about a large aluminum bowl filled with kill-for fudge.

After the excitement of the new arrivals had died down, I sat with Victoria in my room, which was soon to be confiscated from us, while we would be thrown into exile, not by fate but by guided and designed circumstance.

"Dad is an ass. He is so damned generous with other people's stuff. Sorry about the room, or I should say our room."

"It's all right." Victoria said. "It will work out, and I'm at Mrs. Larson's most of the time, anyway."

We sat looking at the gold watch and chain. It's mine, I thought. I couldn't believe it. "The watch is really mine," I said aloud. "He really gave met the gold watch and chain."

"It's beautiful," she squealed.

"I wonder if our son will be this excited when I give it to him?"

"I'm sure he will."

I was silent for a moment and then said, "If we have only girls, then I'll have to think of something." I fell back onto bed and lay talking softly to Victoria as we marveled at the good fortune of the golden watch and chain and the good fortune that had culminated over these past days.

Chapter 91

Sleeping in the barn wasn't so bad. It was the way I had been routed out without ceremony or feeling that bothered me. It was as if the room was theirs and I was only a troublesome obstacle in the way.

It was like I was a fly or a cockroach and they were being generous to merely remove me instead of squashing me. But after we were resettled, it was sort of fun, and we had all sorts of freedom. I was undisputed boss over Flash and Dale and anyone else who happened to visit, and it was a lot easier to get Victoria into the barn than into the house. Flash and Dale never even seemed to notice her, concerned as they usually were with their own selfish stuff. And today, finally, Victoria and I were going to Spokane to get our car. We had slept out in the woodshed, as we had become accustomed to doing when we wanted to be alone. We wanted to get an early start.

I had been thinking about a car now for some time and had an idea what I wanted. I knew I didn't want a car like Dad's long, monstrous four-door Dodge. It did have some good features, though, such as I could get it going about 95 along the gravel on Eden's Upper Road. But it had a couple of drawbacks. It looked like an old man's car, and if you went around a corner too fast, the front wheel tipped out at an angle. You had to stop, jack it up, and kick it back into place.

I wanted something that would really turn heads; something a girl would fight to ride in, not that I wanted any girl aside from Victoria, but you know what I mean. A wheel tipping out wasn't too serious, but my car would have to look good. I looked in the mirror one more time, straightened my hair once more, and then took out my gold watch to check the time. "Right on schedule," I mumbled.

Mom was bending over the table, sewing a blanket or quilt or something, as I walked in the room. "Is Dad working in the woods?"

"You know he is. Why?"

"I need a ride to the depot."

"You'll have to walk. He's cutting logs with Uncle Joe to take to the mill."

"Jeez, I'm the son of a poor woodcutter," I smiled. "Mom, can I have the banana?"

"No, it's for Dad's lunch."

I opened the breadbox. "Can I have the crust of bread?"

"Yeah, I'm baking today." As an afterthought, she said, "Grandmother Andersen wrote today."

I stopped to see what she had to say. She was getting old and flipped in and out of reality. I was interested to hear what she might come up with now. I reminded Mom of Gramma's last letter when she told us that Grandpa had figured out how to take things with him before he died. "He is just going to stick what he wants to take with him up his ass," she wrote, which made me laugh.

"She's just old," Mom said.

"Hell," I replied, "I wish all old people were that much fun." Then I thought about being there in Utah with Warren. "Well, she can be a pain sometimes. What did she say this time?"

"Just the usual. You know, hope this letter finds you all well and healthy, and she closed with loves and kisses."

"Is that all?" I coaxed.

"Well, she did say that they had caught the maniac who killed the little boy, the one Mr. Cook was arrested for. You remember those little boys who were molested and strangled? And they found the other boy who was missing, the one named Jon. Do you remember all that?"

"Yeah, I remember all that. Hell, I found Pat's head, and me and Victoria found Wendell in Cook's old barn. Hell, yes, I remember."

"Don't use language like that."

"Who the hell was it, Mom?" I didn't need to ask; I already knew.

"William Robert! You'll get some soap."

"Okay, but who was it?"

Gramma said they found Jon's body down by the lake. There was such a stench, and when people went to see what it was, they found him. He was in the Hallelujah Choir like you were, remember?"

The sulfur filled my mouth and the lightning shot up my spine. I don't know why I was so bothered—I already knew he was dead. "My God, Mom, not little harmless Jon. That's really too bad. Who killed him? Jesus, just tell me."

Mom was crying, "It was such a shock. It wasn't Mr. Cook or the bum. We all thought he was such nice young man, and he did so much for the church."

"Who was it?"

"It was that nice man, your friend, Oscar. You're lucky he didn't do something to you, dear."

"Real lucky. They got the right guy. It was Oscar, I'm sure of that. I've been trying to tell you."

"All I know is what I read. Why were you so sure it was Oscar?"

"Well, remember when he came home from Canada all beat up and I told you he tried to kill me?"

"No, I guess I don't remember that, dear."

"You and Dad don't even listen to me!" I yelled. She turned her head and went back to her work. "I told you he tried to kill me!" I shouted.

She looked thoughtful for a moment and then, as she and Dad always did, she just went on like I hadn't said anything at all. "Well, you were lucky, son."

"Yeah, real lucky. Maybe your God was watching over me. If it hadn't been for Victoria, I don't know what I would have done."

"Whatever happened to Victoria, anyway?" she asked. "You and her acted like you were joined at the hip and then she was gone."

"You know she went to Scotland."

"I hope you learned something from the baby and all," she went on.

"I think we're going to have another one."

"What did you say? What about Victoria?"

"She went to Scotland."

"Don't be too late," Mom told me and then went on with her sewing.

"Victoria came back, Mom. I asked her to come back and she did. I see her when she can get away from her work." I went to the window to see if she was still sleeping.

"That's nice, son, but you should get a girl that's more down to earth. A girl more like we are."

Victoria was gone, but her side of the bed had been straightened out. "She's so neat. She never leaves anything out of order."

"What did you say, dear?"

"Nothing, I was just checking to see if my blankets were all right."

"That's nice. Too bad about Mr. Cook. It wasn't him. He didn't kill those little boys, but we all thought he did. I guess we all should have been more understanding."

"Well, just about everybody thought the same thing, Mom. And he did sort of bring it on himself, exposing himself and all."

"Yes, I hope we can all learn something from this. You can

learn from your mistakes, too. I guess the bum didn't kill that little boy Pat, either. So the bum was innocent, too."

"Who killed Pat, then?"

"Gramma said that was Oscar, too."

"Did they put him in prison?"

"Who?"

"For hell's sake—Oscar."

"Well, no. I guess after he was arrested he admitted that he knew a little about it, but that he wasn't the one who killed him or anyone else. He said it was someone else but wouldn't say who. Everybody thought it might have been Alex because he was so weird, because he was gay, so they arrested him and Oscar, too—but they both got away. When they found your little friend Jon in the bay at the lake, he was so decomposed that it wasn't easy to know who it had been. They had to use his teeth and dental records to identify him."

"My hell, I'm so glad we got out of there. How did Oscar and Alex get away?"

Mom looked thoughtful again. "Oscar went to the bank and drew out all his money and then he and Alex just disappeared in Oscar's Suburban. Nobody knows where they are. I guess because of his position in the church and his priesthood, they didn't put him in jail."

"Things aren't fair," I said.

"They probably just came to Montana," Mom said sarcastically. "That's where all the weirdos go."

"That's not funny," I said, and walked toward the back door.

"No, it's not funny." Her voice followed me toward the door, although it was obvious she wasn't really interested in the topic anymore.

"Oscar is an ass," I said. "I'll bet that son of a bitch killed all three of them. In fact, I'm sure he did."

"Don't talk like that," Mom said, but now she was just saying it.

"The jerk should be in prison," I shouted.

"Oscar said he is innocent and is going to prove it," Mom called as I walked past the side window.

I rolled my eyes. "Oscar's an asshole." I was too far from the soap and felt comfortable about "asshole." Then in a gentler tone I yelled, "Bye, Mom. See ya when I get back."

"Don't believe everything those salesmen tell you," she shouted. "You should believe nothing you hear and only about half of what you see."

"Yeah, yeah."

"Did you put on clean underwear in case you have to go to the hospital?" She laughed at her attempt to be motherly.

I didn't answer.

"Be careful, William," she called again. "Wear your jacket. You never know about the weather, and keep an eye out for Oscar and tell Victoria hello."

"God," I mumbled, "she just doesn't get it."

I stepped down the dilapidated wooded steps of the porch and began my trek toward Eden. "I'll walk with you, William," Victoria said after I'd taken a few steps.

"Glad you could make it. Glad you could spare the time," I said sarcastically.

She just smiled. "Sounds like you mother isn't too fond of me."

"It will be better after my aunt and uncle get into their own house. Then we'll get together and get some things straightened out."

I took out my gold watch again and held it to my ear to make sure that it was still running.

"Are we late?"

"No, plenty of time."

"It was nice of your Dad to give you the watch."

"Yeah, but what has he done for me lately?" I kidded.

She held my arm to pick up my stride.

"Hey, they found out about Oscar," I said.

"Did they put him in prison?"

"No, he got away. Mom says he might have come up here to Montana, but I think she was just kidding."

"That wouldn't be good, would it?"

"No it wouldn't. I'll have to keep an eye out."

"I'll help you watch," she said.

"You be careful, too."

"I can take care of myself."

"I know you can. They pretty much cleared Mr. Cook and that bum."

"Old Mr. Cook was just crazy. He wasn't a killer. We weren't fair to accuse him without proof. I'm sorry he killed himself, but maybe Oscar was responsible for that, too," Victoria said. "Maybe all of us were at fault for Mr. Cook's death, all of his friends losing trust in him, and him being accused and feeling guilty about his son, what was his name—Gayland? Everything rolled up together made him just act crazy and guilty, and he just simply couldn't deal with it."

I nodded. "And they also found Jon's body down at the lake by Springtown. Did you know that he was in the Hallelujah Choir, too? I'll bet Oscar was behind all the killings."

"He almost killed you, didn't he?" Victoria asked.

"Yeah, in Canada."

"That scares me. Let's talk about something else. What kind of car do you want, William?"

"I'll tell you when we get to the depot."

Chapter 92

The gravel crunched louder under my loafers as I began walking faster. I kicked rocks to try to keep my mind off the long walk and the almost unbearable excitement of getting a new car. Laughing softly, I kicked a rock and watched it tumble down the road, stirring up puffs of dust as it went.

"What's your big hurry?" Victoria asked, "You can't leave until the train gets there."

"I can't help it, I'm so excited. I can't wait to see what my new car will look like."

"Think of something else. I'm getting tired of you talking about your car and then not telling me what it will be, or saying 'Wait until we get to the depot.'"

"You're getting bitchy."

"You've never talked to me like that before."

"Bitchy," I whispered.

I stopped to kick a rock, which bounced along and then became lost in the tangle of grass and bushes that covered almost everything. The mountains loomed in the distance and a few ravens or crows floated in the sky, slowly flapping their wings with a noisy whoosh, but so effortlessly; some near, some far away, as they searched for something dead or small to feast on. I couldn't help but think, "Quoth the raven, nevermore." An osprey teased an eagle on the other side of the sky. Both floated, circling, the osprey always at just the right distance from the eagle to be safe. "Probably been trying to steal the eggs or baby eagles," I mused.

"Let's not fight," Victoria said.

"Okay, but I can't help thinking about the car. I'm sorry."

"Then think about it," she said, and walked ahead, stirring up soft tufts of dust with her dainty little feet.

I resumed thinking about my car, and then thought, Victoria is right. I've got to think about something else. It's going to drive me crazy. My mind began to look elsewhere. I shouldn't kick rocks anymore, I thought. One might hit her, and I don't want her pissed off again. Although I liked living in Montana, there wasn't a lot to do, not like the big cities. I had a lot of good friends and had had more than my share of fun when they were around, and I especially liked it now that Victoria was finally here. I'm not dead yet, I reminded myself, and thought again of my new car, which made my smile grow wider. God, I'm thinking about it again. I've got to stop. I looked for another subject. It seemed that I could walk forever and never get tired. I remembered a lesson from Sunday school that went, "Walk and not tire, run and not faint." I tried to walk faster, I wanted to be there. I wanted to have my car.

"Why are you walking so fast?"

"Can't help it. I'm excited."

"We could go into the woods and do it right now," she said, teasing me.

"That would be nice, but I need to get to the depot."

"Okay, then," she said. "I guess I'm not important."

"My hell, Victoria, you are more important than anything. But we do need a car, a dependable car, especially when we have the baby."

She placed hands on her stomach and smiled contentedly and she walked beside me.   Maybe, just maybe, I thought, she finally understands.

Chapter 93

The Eden area is a temperate rain forest. The encyclopedia says it gets more rainfall than any other place in Montana. It doesn't get hot in the summer, but it feels like it does. Eighty degrees in the sun can feel like Yuma in the summer, but in the shade, it's cool and comfortable. There's a lot of snow in the winter and some cold weather, too, but for the most part the temperature stays pretty mild. I guess it's the large amount of rainfall that makes all the trees and vegetation grow so abundantly. It's like a huge, manicured park that has ferns, wildflowers, and beautiful green ground-covering growing wild among the mushrooms and numerous wild and edible berries. A canopy of trees, of many varieties and sizes, creates a spectacular scene. If not periodically cut back, the overgrowth makes going out into the forest difficult, if not impossible, as the forest quickly reseeds and propagates. When roads are cut throughout the forest, it takes on the look of a huge canyon, with trees as the sides of its steep walls.

In a few places, the trees had been removed to make fields, where grass hay and a bit of grain could be grown. But if these fields were to lay fallow for a few years, the rapacious forest would soon reclaim them. We were so accustomed to this glorious scenery as we walked through it that we were oblivious to its magnificence.

Just ahead, I saw Mr. Johnson plowing his hay field. He had the look of someone who had resigned himself to his life's work. His dirty straw hat, which had probably once been white or at least light-colored, now was stained with sweat and caked with grime and oil. Even in the heat, he wore a faded, cotton-lined denim jacket over his red flannel shirt and bib overalls. Looming in the distance, the skin of his hands and face were the scarlet of his shirt. I imagined dirty, gray, long underwear underneath his clothing, buttoned to the top button, because that was typical of ranchers and cowboys hereabouts.

Mr. Johnson's three-bottomed plow was turning the rich clay soil over like the surface of an unsettled ocean but rather than the odor of the ocean, it was the odor of dirt and burnt deisel. As if it were an ocean, gulls hovered close above, while others searched the freshly plowed ground, picking up worms and other delicacies that had been uncovered. Dark smoke puffed in a ring from the exhaust pipe with each occasional misfire of the engine. As I watched, Mr. Johnson stopped the tractor and leaned over to look into the engine. He fiddled with something and then reached farther, using the steering wheel for balance. After a minute, he straightened up, threw his hat to the ground and then stepped down, cussing. He began fiddling with something inside the engine.

He looked up and saw me. "Hi, Bill. Goin' ta town?"

"Yeah, I'm getting a new car."

"Oh," he said in an unconcerned way. "Spokane?"

"Yeah."

"Hey, can ya hep me fer a minute?"

"Glad to, Mr. Johnson. Wh'da'ya want me ta do?"

"Just hold onto this bar while I put this dammed chain back on." He spat tobacco juice onto his boot and then looked up, embarrassed that he had missed the ground.

"Missed, huh?"

He ignored me. "The damned thing has never worked right. Maybe I should just get a new machine."

I moved into position and pulled on the bar while Mr. Johnson worked with the chain. The newly plowed soil had an inviting, clean smell. The gulls filled the ground behind the tractor as they screeched and fought. The tractor looked like it had been built from junked parts. When Mr. Johnson drove it, he sat sideways and the steering wheel and all the controls were in front of him and on the side. The hulking machine looked like it was going down the field sideways.

Well, I thought, it makes some sense, I guess. It's easier to see what's going on behind if you don't need to turn all the way around.

"Okay, that's got her. The chain is on. Thanks, Bill. Have fun in town. Hope you enjoy the movie." He climbed back on the tractor, ground the gears into place, and started down the row.

"Hell," I yelled, "I said I was going to get a car," but the tractor was already revved up, and he couldn't hear me. Just like everybody else, I thought, he doesn't listen.

Victoria was waiting when I got back to the road. "That was nice of you."

"He's an ornery old fart. He only worries about himself; doesn't even listen to me."

"He looks like he really loves driving his tractor," she said.

"Well, I like driving Dad's tractor, too, if I don't have to do it all the time. He doesn't think I ever need a break; even Mr. Johnson gets a break. My problem is that Dad's tractor is new, so it never breaks down, which means I have to keep going all the time. Mr. Johnson's lucky; his tractor breaks down once in a while, so he gets a break."

I reflected that whenever I was forced to work beyond my endurance, my only recourse was to drive to the corner of the north forty, as close as I could get to town and the Bucket of Blood, park the tractor and walk to town. I had gotten more than an angry glare from Dad when I parked it in a more inconspicuous place, over by Beaver Creek. That day, the beaver completed their dam while I was away and the water backed up. When I returned, only the exhaust pipe was sticking out of the new beaver pond. After we got the tractor out, all we had to do was change the gas and oil and it was almost as good as new. Dad, the jerk, chained it up, so I couldn't use it anymore. Hell, it was just like new after we got the water all out and changed the oil and stuff, I thought resentfully, but I have to use the work horses now.

Chapter 94

All of that stuff about the boys and Mr. Cook had been sad, but it had been such a long time ago—why did it hang with me, why did it plague me so? I had more important things to think about, such as the car, Victoria, our new baby, getting enough money, and being declared royalty, so Victoria's father finally would accept me. Even though I wanted a car that a guy could be proud to drive, Victoria had to like it, too. We had gone so far together. I thought of the time Ellen caught us on the ditch bank and told Dad, which made me laugh out loud.

"What are you laughing at?" she asked.

"I was just thinking about the time Ellen caught us naked by the ditch and we got separated."

"Was it that funny?"

"Not funny, but you know how sometimes something cute happens and it makes you laugh," I tried to defend myself.

"Oh, now it's cute?"

"For hell's sake, Victoria, get a grip."

She laughed. "I'm just kidding. I think it's cute, too." She held my hand.

The road became steep, turned right, leveled off at the bottom, and then took a sharp turn back to the left. My thoughts were broken by a loud putt, putt. I turned to see dust rising as a yellow jeep raced toward us. When it skidded to a stop, the dust caught up, covering everything.

"What the hell's wrong with you?" I yelled.

"Settle down, Bill. Just wanted to see if you want to work," Harlow said through dust that caked his face, especially under his nose. He looked like he had a dirt mustache. I stifled a laugh.

"What the hell happened to your jeep, Harlow?"

"Muffler fell off."

"Sounds loud. You won't be able to take that trip to Short Creek when you and Chuck join that group of Mormon polygamists." We both laughed.

"Hey, Bill, where ya goin'?"

"Goin' to get a car."

"Want to work today?"

"No."

"Chuck is sick and can't work. At least he told me he was sick, and I can't find him." Chuck's name was really Chester but he'd changed it to Chuck. Who could blame him? It would have been more correct to nickname him Chet, but what the hell.

"Hell, I'm too young to tend bar."

"Its okay, nobody cares in Eden."

We didn't say anything for a while, just looking blankly at the beauty surrounding us. To break the awkward silence, I told him again, "I'm going to Spokane to get a car. I can't work today."

"Will you if I can't get anybody else?"

"No."

"Okay, but I'll see if I can get somebody else first."

"Harlow, I said no."

"Get in. I'll drop you at the tavern. You can just wait there while I look for somebody else."

I gave up. I figured he could find somebody else to work, but it looked like he wouldn't do it until I went with him to the tavern, so I got into the Jeep, and turned to Victoria.

"You can go along with Harlow until he finds someone else to work," she said. "I'll just keep walking."

"That's what I was thinking," I said. "I'll see you at the depot."

"What did you say?" Harlow asked.

"Nothing. I wasn't talking to you."

"Oh?" He raised his eyebrows.

"Hey," I asked, "are you and Chuck still going to Short Creek?"

"Not if I kill the son of a bitch first," he said.

Harlow was about the only man I knew who was smaller than Dad. His friendly face and attitude made him a favorite not only of his family but also of everyone who knew him. His round face was topped with thick hair that had been cut short and flat on top. Thick-rimmed glasses sat low on his nose and he was always looking over them. Wrinkles covered his face, which was burned by the sun and wind and had no stubble. He wore a small-brimmed Stetson cowboy hat and a smile, even when he was angry.

"Harlow, I can't work today. Get Fred Cram. He's always in the bar anyway," I said.

"He's mad. Chuck and me's been kiddin' him about Short Creek and his red nose, from drinking too much booze, I guess."

The Jeep slid around the corner of the gravel road toward town, and in a moment it stopped in front of the tavern.

"You drive like a teenager," I said.

"See ya in a minute. Emma's inside. Have a beer and I'll be right back."

"I had enough last night."

"Beer never hurt nobody."

"I'm going to Spokane."

Dust flew as the jeep's wheels dug in.

"He must be deaf," I said, as I watched him race down the road and around the corner to Upper Road.

"I hope Victoria and the train get here before he gets back," I mumbled.

The main street was just a gravel road about two football fields long that turned right to disappear around a corner, where Harlow had gone. Eden wasn't incorporated, and the main street didn't even have a formal name. The general store, which sat on one side of the street, wasn't as big as most stores in big towns, but you could get just about anything there: engine oil, hats, a coat, a pickle, a wooden half-barrel, conversation in any weather, and in winter, a free cup of coffee to sip as you soaked up heat from the blazing, pot-bellied stove. Outside was a single pump from which gas was available for 18 cents a gallon, after old man Sunbloom turned it on and pumped fuel into the glass reservoir on top.

A small grove of Lombardy Poplars grew right in front of the store. On either side of it were hitching rails, in case farmers or cowboys rode their horses into town to shop or for the Saturday night dance. Three small children were playing in the trees in front of the store. The girl was up in a tree and two boys were teasing her and acting like they were going to pull her down, but it was the kind of play intended more to win her heart than to do any physical harm. I figured they were with whoever had driven the old Ford pickup parked in front at a haphazard angle. "Must be a mother," I mused. "Women don't understand cars and driving."

In front of the post office, an old paint mare was nipping at the lush grass that grew along the sides of the gravel road. "Looks like Sid rode his horse to work this morning," I thought, picturing Sid Sunbloom, owner of the general store. Several cars and a pickup driving down the dirt road added to the dust already in the air. One of the cars pulled into the bar and the driver went inside. "A beer for breakfast," I thought with a chuckle.

The Bucket of Blood Saloon stood to the side of the general store. Harlow and Edna were both recovering from recent divorces when they found each other and were married. Everybody said it wouldn't last, that they were just on the rebound, and I agreed, because neither of their original marriages had lasted. They bought the Bucket of Blood from old man Singbeil. Harlow helped at the bar when he wasn't working construction, but it was Emma, so short and frail that she had to step up on a box to pass a drink or a pickled egg over the bar to a customer, who really ran it. Chuck answered to her, although sometimes he left Emma alone to deal with the tough construction workers by herself.

They thought that just the presence of a man, or male, would tend to keep the patrons in line and keep them from using bad language or tearing up the place. I wasn't old enough to even be in a bar but I looked like I could carry two buckets of water and I got the job. Rather than age, the ability to carry two buckets full of water at the same time seemed to be the gauge that most bars in this area used for a patron to be allowed to drink alcohol or visit Madam Judy's cathouse. It was a lot of fun. I played pool for free and even played for the house. It made me feel important, and I made a little money as well.

I thought about Mr. Lady, who I first met in this place. He had come in holding a large bottle of Old Crow whiskey clumsily around the neck, more like it was a mallet than an expensive spirit. He wore a menacing grin and his dark, piercing eyes looked about impatiently, inviting trouble. He had on a white undershirt and faded, tight Levis on his narrow hips, with brown loafers and no socks. The muscles of his upper body rippled as he moved about. His dark crew-cut hair, bushy eyebrows, and sideburns added to his foreboding appearance. A long handlebar mustache below a Roman nose mostly concealed the ivory-white teeth that were only occasionally revealed by a smile. He reeked of evil; a bully, to be sure.

"Want to shoot some eight ball?" he asked me. It wasn't a question. It was a demand that left few options. I picked a cue stick from the rack and he ordered a beer from Emma. He drank about half of it, and then refilled the glass with whiskey from his bottle, stirred it with his fingers, gulped down the mixture, and fixed another one. He found a fairly straight stick in the rack and as we nursed our drinks, my beer and his boilermakers, we began knocking balls into the pockets.

"My name's Ford," he said without looking at me. "Ford Lady," he continued, observing my reaction.

I thought about making a crack about the name, but I didn't.

"You can call me Mr. Lady."

"I'm Bill," I said. "Just call me Bill." My voice trembled.

"I'll call ya anything I want ta call ya," he said, and shot in a ball.

We played and drank for a while and then he said, "This sure as hell is a dead town. I'm usually in a fight by this time." Without a doubt, it was an invitation.

"Well, Mr. Lady," I said, "this is a sort of peace-loving community, and I'm a peace-loving guy."

With a sharp crack, Mr. Lady dropped his cue stick to the floor. A string of words that I was sure I'd been hired to keep out of the Bucket of Blood and away from Emma flowed from his mouth. I turned to see how Emma had taken the offensive language, and also to look for a clue about how I was expected to subdue this rascal. Emma hadn't taken it very well. She had taken the triangle rack from its place on the wall behind the bar, where it hung to maintain some control over the pool play. Rage had turned her normally pale face a bright red and she screamed, and, much to my liking, she charged Mr. Lady. He brought his hands up to protect his face and head and then, using the same language that had offended her just a few moments before, Emma delivered savage blows with the three-sided weapon to all portions of Mr. Lady's upper body. Mr. Lady retreated to the front door and then cowered out into the street as Emma stood defiantly on the porch of the Bucket of Blood, daring the ruffian to advance.

He stood for a moment, bewildered, and then, looking like a whipped dog, he walked to his pickup, got in, and drove away. Mr. Lady was never seen in Eden again.

Emma didn't make a big thing out of protecting me from the bully. In fact, she gave me the credit for discharging Mr. Lady, and my cushy job remained secure. I certainly wasn't going to question my value as a deterrent of bad language and rowdiness in the

Bucket of Blood Saloon, but even so, I spent the rest of the day passing on the story of Emma and Mr. Lady to other patrons, and drinking a lot of free beer. Emma said I deserved it for being there to protect her as I had.

Saturday night dances were held in a hall next to the Bucket of Blood. The entry fee was twenty-five cents, and when there wasn't a town doin' at the school house, the dance hall filled up. Everybody who played any musical instrument came to show off their talent, and they got in free.

Behind the dance hall, Madam Judy's brothel sat in the tall weeds. A large, professional- looking sign proclaimed it as the Cherry Way Inn. Weeds worn down by foot traffic showed trails from all angles. Most of the male residents of Eden frequented it summer and winter. They slipped away from summer dances under the guise of drunkenness, but in the deep snow of winter, they left telltale footprints. Madam Judy had a few working girls who were fairly well-respected residents in town, just earning a few bucks for Christmas or a nice vacation. Madam Judy didn't recognize anybody. Even if you had seen her the night before, it was good for business not to. She gave money to the Community Center, the Ladies Talk and Do Things Club, and the local churches. They all competed for her membership and dollars.

As I walked past, she stood on the front porch, the soft wind fluttering her white hair and the formal, flowered dress. The tops of her black shoes were hidden under the loose skin of her ankles, and the deep dust made her feet appear to be hooves. Although definitely not beautiful, she had a classic countenance, and had achieved a kind of grudging stature in the community that came only from enough money being dispensed to the proper people and institutions. She looked left and right, cautiously waved to me and winked. I could feel the blood rise up into my neck; I turned my head. I always thought she knew that long ago Warren and I had robbed her. I wanted to give back the whiskey and cigarettes, but then she would know without a doubt it had been me.

An alarm clock dangled from a piece of orange twine around her neck. "An impressive timepiece," I mumbled, trying to divert attention from my embarrassment. I nervously took out my own golden timepiece, looked at it without noticing the time, slid it back into my pocket, and walked on. I turned for one last look. There was a discerning, soft smile on her lips. Her hands were on her hips, and she moved her head slowly back and forth. Again, I felt sure she knew about Warren and me.

A little farther down the street was the post office, run by Mrs. Larsen. She had a small hobby store in the back, and the only phone in town. In the rear was a small apartment that she rented only to special people. It was usually empty, but Victoria lived there when she wasn't with me. As I approached the post office, I saw Victoria coming down the road, having walked the rest of the way into town after Harlow and I left her. She joined me, and when we reached the post office, we saw Mrs. Larsen watching us through the window. She waved and we waved back.

Next to Mrs. Larsen's was the town church that the Methodists had built, the same one Dad and Uncle Arthur had swooped down upon like a couple of vultures figuratively ravaging the carcasses of the meek Methodists. As we passed the church, I thought of how Dad and Uncle Arthur had been like the Christian missionaries who had "saved" the souls of the Indians in the early West, even against their will, but to their greater benefit and salvation.

Beyond the church was a two-story schoolhouse with a large bell on top, the same building that Flash, Kirk, and I had escaped from the day that we met old man Lockwood and enjoyed his hospitality, along with his barley and ham-hock soup, and Raisin Jack home brew. A few houses were scattered along the street, half on each side. The main street branched off just in front of old man Sunbloom's Mercantile and went around the grove of Lombardy Poplars and then across the railroad tracks. The depot was beside the road that crossed the tracks on the town side. The train depot had burned down some years ago, after which a temporary one was built from two railroad boxcars. The depot subsequently was modified but it was still obvious that it had once been two boxcars. A large, antique door had been installed into the original sliding one, and crude stairs led up to it. We stepped up and went inside. The old boxcar depot had acquired the same odor that all depots have, as if someone had tried to coat the floor and walls with oil so thick and pungent, it made the whole place seem fake, although the stench was certainly real.

Classic, back-to-back wooden benches sat in several rows along the middle of the room. They were well-maintained, although they bore cigarette burns and other minor damage marks and were obviously old. Against the wall at either side were several more rows of single-backed benches. A ticket cage was at one end of the depot, occupied by the stationmaster, who didn't seem to mind whether he sold tickets or exchanged gossip and news. Like most people around there, he seemed to have an unlimited amount of time and nothing in particular to do with any of it. I left Victoria waiting on a bench and approached the ticket window.

"One way to Spokane," I requested in a friendly manner.

"Not a round trip?"

"No need. I'll be driving my car back."

"Oh," he said, not really listening. He was reading a book by Zane Gray, *Riders of the Purple Sage*.

"I'd like to be a writer or a poet," I said, trying to start a conversation. Ticket agents were replaced often at the depot, and I hadn't seen this guy before.

"Well, good luck. It's not an easy life," he answered, not even looking up.

"How do you know?"

He looked up. "My dad tried it and finally just got a job on the railroad."

"To each his own."

"The difference between using almost the right word and exactly the right word is like the difference between a lightning bug and a lightning bolt," he said, smiling at his cleverness. "I read that somewhere." His arrogant grin widened.

"I've got some good ideas," I said.

"Well," he replied, "try to use the right words." He stamped the ticket automatically, almost without looking, handed it back, and then returned to his book. "I think Mark Twain said that," he said, without looking up.

"Said what?"

"You know, about using the right words."

"I think I heard about Mark Twain. He was Samuel Clemens, wasn't he?" I asked, trying to show off my intellect.

He looked at me for a moment and then said, "Wonder if he changed his name before he burned down the whole god-damned forest at Lake Tahoe, or after?" and then sat silently, as if we were verbally dueling and he had just won with a thrust.

"How do you know that?" I asked, trying to time my parry prior to a *coup de grace.*

He raised one eyebrow. "I know because he wrote about it. Hell, he carelessly set it ablaze and then wrote about the beauty of the ravaging fire, as if it were a wonderful thing instead of a careless act that kept the forest's natural beauty from others for years. He was an arrogant ass." He sat waiting for me to attempt a counter-thrust.

"Well," I said, searching my memory for a date, "*The Riders of the Purple Sage* was written in 1921."

He turned the book to the title page and said, "You're wrong—it was 1912. Why don't you check before you make a fool of yourself?"

"If you tried to name the date from memory, you wouldn't know within a hundred years," I mumbled. "Well, do you know that Charles Darwin discovered the theory of the survival of the fittest?" I smiled a smart-ass smile, as if I'd pinned him to the wall with my foil.

The agent smiled back, as if it were me and not him who was

pinned by a foil to the wall. "Well, yes, I do know a little bit about Darwin. My dad was an expert on the subject." And then like he was reading it from a paper he began to reel it off. "Survival of the fittest is a phrase that cannot be attributed to Charles Darwin, at least not in its original context. The term was coined by Herbert Spencer as an alternative to 'natural selection' in evolutionary theory. Today the phrase is commonly used in contexts that are incompatible with the original meaning as intended by its first two proponents: Spencer, a British polymath philosopher, and Darwin. The latter never used this phrase in the context for which he is credited nowadays. Darwin was only concerned with natural selection in and by Nature." The agent smiled condescendingly and bent again to his book, a gesture meant to dismiss me, like anyone would dismiss a beetle or a bug.

"Horse's ass." I glared at the top of his head as he read. "Well, Hitler used Darwin's theory as a model for his super race," I said.

But the tables had turned now. He was the one administering the intellectual *coup de grace* as he continued, "To connect Darwin with Hitler's attempts to create a super race is like saying non-Christians themselves were responsible for the torturing and killings of the Spanish Inquisition because they didn't lock their doors or they hadn't converted convincingly enough to Christianity."

I stood speechless. Talk about overkill, I thought as I slipped the voucher into my shirt pocket and he went back to *The Riders*. I stepped to the bench, which was out of his sight, and sat next to Victoria to deal silently with my intellectual thrashin'.

Not a very friendly guy," she said. "In fact, he's a jerk." She seldom argued with me, which was one reason why I loved her so much. "You just need to be more adult than he is," she advised.

"Yes'm." I smiled submissively in a kidding way. "Maybe I should have just submitted to him like I always do to you."

"William, I'm sorry I said that about your car."

"Said what?"

"Not to talk about it." She pushed her body close and placed her hand on my crotch.

"You can't do that here, Victoria."

"Nobody will see."

"Let's just wait," I said, but I didn't move her hand. "I forgive you for the car thing—but you'd better stop or we'll get arrested."

I took out the golden Waltham watch and chain again.

"Hey," I shouted at the ticket agent. "Train on time?"

"Yeah, I guess," came his uninterested reply.

"Sort of a railroad thing," I said to Victoria. "None of them really gives a damn."

"Tell me about your dad," she said, trying to change the subject. "I don't know him very well, but he really scares me."

"I don't know what to tell you … he doesn't like me. We are so different. I guess we'll never get along."

"I don't like him," she said. "He's mean to you."

I tried to tell her about him, talking in a whisper so the asshole ticket agent wouldn't hear.

"I try hard to make him like me but it seems that the harder I try, the more we dislike each other. Most of the time when bad things happen, they aren't really my fault. He's so bull-headed, and always thinks he's right, like the time at the dinner table when I farted and then laughed. Well, it was funny. He flipped my head with his middle finger. He really hit me hard. I think I was knocked out for a few moments. I had a fork in my hand, and I remember how Jon had handled a similar situation, and I jabbed the fork deep into the flesh on the back of Dad's right hand. He seemed stunned for a moment and then he grabbed me and half-carried, half-dragged me out to the back yard where I had to endure the 'bend over and grab your ankles' thing as he wailed me with his razor strap."

Victoria was laughing, and I smiled. "I can laugh now," I said, "but it wasn't funny then. It always amazed me that Dad could sort of drag and carry me and still be enough of a contortionist to strike me about the head and shoulders with his other hand, even while he kicked my butt with both of his feet at the same time."

Victoria was really laughing now. "That's so funny. You should try to write it down; maybe make it into a poem or short story."

I was pleased. "Maybe I will write it down, or maybe I'll tell you another story. I'll flower it up a little bit to make it more interesting. I know you haven't formally met my sister, Ellen," I said. "She's Dad's favorite. Mom said that's just the way dads and daughters are. Mom said she wishes she had a sister instead of six brothers. She says she wouldn't complain about anything if she did."

"But your Dad likes you, too, I'll bet," Victoria said, trying to make me feel better.

"Well, I don't know. Maybe it's because Ellen is a girl."

"Watch it. I'm a girl too, you know," she said.

"I guess I should know." I put my arm around her to show that I was just kidding, and then I cupped my hand over her breast.

"Let's wait," she said, pushing my hand away.

"I guess it's okay when you do it," I teased.

"Tell me about Ellen."

I pushed out a fart and said, "Whoops," and then looked at the ceiling.

"You're turning into your dad," she giggled.

"Hey, hold it down," the ticket agent said.

"Whatever," I replied. "Hell, there's nobody here anyway."

"I am."

"Who gives a damn about you?" I whispered.

"Your dad is much stranger than Daddy," Victoria said. We both laughed softly for a while and then settled down and sat quietly, our bodies touching as we observed the emptiness of the depot. The agent lowered his head into his book.

I smiled. The bastard is content, I thought. A fly lit on my forehead. I swished it off and watched it fly away. It landed upside down on the ceiling. "Wonder how they do that?" I said, but Victoria didn't answer. "Guess everything's easy if you know how."

She still didn't answer. Guess she's thinking about something else, I thought.

The fly rubbed its feet together and walked a short distance in its inverted way. It stopped to taste something, and then quickly rubbed its feet together again before flying off in search of some other disgusting treat.

Victoria looked like she was still in thought, but then she said, "I'm going to run over to my apartment behind Mrs. Larson's and get some girls stuff. I'll be right back."

"Okay," I said. I closed my eyes and fell into a soft, dreamless sleep. When I awoke, she still wasn't back.

Maybe she's in the can, I thought. I walked over and opened the door. I shouted her name, but nobody answered. I pushed the door open slowly. The stalls were all empty except for one—I pushed the door open, but found only graffiti.

"What the hell ya doin'?" the agent yelled behind me. "You can get in trouble looking in the woman's bathroom."

"I got mixed up," I said, and went into the men's room. After I finished and washed, I went back to the uncomfortable bench, "The damned seats aren't getting any softer," I complained to myself. "I'll never get to Spokane." And Victoria still wasn't back. I began to feel at a loss. Victoria needs to be with me to get our car, I thought.

My life just wasn't fair. Everyone remembered when I spilled the cream on "Sour Cream Bend," but no one seemed to remember when I saved my money and paid for bringing electric power to the barn, to make milking a little less painful, or all the times I milked the cows morning and night, except when I occasionally needed a break. They remembered when I chopped up the tool handles for firewood, but not all the times I had gotten in the firewood, with only minor incidents. They remembered the time I parked the tractor in the field and walked into town to have a little time away from work and the beaver finished their dam and the tractor was covered with water, but no one remembered when I worked the fields from daylight to dark with the team of horses. They remembered when I was trying to remove a tree that was growing too close to the granary and blew out the end of it with dynamite, and all the grain flowed into the snow and slush to be ruined, but no one remembered when I removed all the stumps with dynamite and cleared and fenced a 20-acre parcel of creek-bottom land that produced 50 bushels per acre of grain.

Mom always said, "People only remember the good, they always forget the bad. That's the way God protects us."

Well she was wrong—everybody remembered only the bad things about me and forgot all the good. The whole thing was so unjust; tears flooded my eyes as I slumped in my seat, impatiently waiting for Victoria and the train to come. Finally, she walked in and sat by my side.   "Well, did you get your girly stuff?"

"Yes," she said, and smiled.

Chapter 95

I sat up straight. The train was at Cline's crossing. I could hear the whistle. I waited a few moments and then got up and walked to the boarding platform. I stood and looked across the street to the Bucket of Blood. Harlow stood by his Jeep, waving and yelling something. I waved back. Hell, I had worked in the bar as a bouncer occasionally but I couldn't mix drinks and draw beer like a real bartender did, and for Christ sakes, I was too young to even be in there.

The Northern Pacific chugged and puffed to a stop. Black smoke billowed from the large stack on top and steam belched from its bowels, dissolving in the midmorning sunlight. The conductor stepped off, sat the boarding step on the ground, and called, "Allaboard!"

Conductors are always about the same size, and they all dress in a blue-and-gray uniform with a little French police hat, and they move about their duties like robots. They hold the arms of passengers as if they find the task distasteful, but believe that by performing this insincere act, their comfortable jobs will somehow be secured. This conductor forced a smile and cradled my arm as I stepped up into the waiting coach. I pulled Victoria up behind me. She excused herself and went to the train's bathroom.

There were only a few others passengers. I took a seat near the rear and scooted over next to the window to have a view. The smell of stale cigarette and cigar smoke overpowered less obvious odors, such as the oily smell that is always present around railroads and trains. An old man, older than Dad, sat across the aisle. He had a full white beard and a tattered cowboy hat that allowed a good portion of his dirty-white hair to flow out from beneath it. He was smoking a roll-yer-own cigarette and looking out the window. He didn't turn to look as I entered.

The other passengers sat silently, kind of like we did in Dad's church meetings, bored but still showing proper reverence, if only to impress the other members. I couldn't miss this opportunity. "God," I said in a low voice, but still loud enough for the other passengers to hear, "looks like we have a pretty weak turnout for church this morning. All we need now is a prayer." They all either smiled or looked disgusted, but none of them even cast a glance at me. I smiled at my own clever observation and at the fact that no one noticed how extremely funny it was. This made me laugh out loud.

The old man across the aisle wore faded bib overalls and a clean white shirt buttoned all the way to the collar, with just the edge showing of his long underwear. He had on a faded but clean denim jacket, open in the front, heavy white socks and "Grandpa" slippers. Red surface veins and brown spots accented the thick hide of his large hands and face, which were burned by the sun and wind, but that didn't conceal the telltale lines from years of worry and sorrow. In spite of this, he looked surprisingly strong, resilient, and ruggedly handsome. He sat quietly for a while, nervously looking about, and then quite obviously tried to force himself into a relaxed pose. He looked at me and winked. I smiled back and we both looked away.

"Maybe his first train ride," I thought.

Through the windows of the double doors between the cars, I could see black waiters dressed in white uniforms serving food to passengers in the coach just ahead. The faint smell of cooking food reminded me of my own hunger.

I looked out the window. Harlow was driving toward the depot. "I wonder what he wants?" I muttered. But I already knew—he wanted me to work.

Slowly, the train began pulling away from the station. The comfort of the seat pushed against my back and surrounded me as the train made its powerful, smooth forward thrust. The tracks clicked softly, and the car began its gentle swaying back and forth, like a baby being cuddled softly in its mother's arms.

The conductor's voice broke into my trance. "Ticket?"

I shoved the cancelled ticket into my shirt pocket and pushed back in the seat to return to my fragile luxury. It would be hours before I would be in Spokane and because of the cost of train food, I decided to wait. "Hell, I'm too excited to eat, anyway. I'll get a cheeseburger or something when I get there," I promised myself.

I saw Harlow standing by his Jeep at the crossing, where the red lights were flashing. He was watching the train, and as my window passed, he pointed at me, and with the other hand, shook his fist in contempt.

I shook my head in disbelief. "I told him I couldn't work today."

The trees flashing past the train's window turned the river far below into a moving panorama of enchantment and color. A large stream cascaded breathtakingly down the steep, narrow canyon, which frothed white and bounced violently out of control over rocks and fallen trees, to then quickly lose its fury, as it collected into unbelievably beautiful, still, crystal-blue pools. The captive water circled aimlessly, as if looking for a way out, but then after finding a release, it enjoyed only brief freedom before repeating the futile, brutal ritual of moving violently downstream to again be held captive in a similar pool. Gigantic, tree-covered mountains rose to cradle the river on either side, as if controlling its course. It was a scene of astonishing beauty, tender influence, ruggedness, and perpetual conflict. The sky and mountains were so vast that even in their passive influence, they rendered the massive, raging waters almost insignificant.

In contrast, the interior of the coach was without grandeur. It took on the mountain's gentler nature. The wall coverings were made of a plain gray metal with small dimples. Several fancy lamps hung from the ceiling, swaying slightly as if attempting to make the otherwise plain décor more appealing. Lights that were set deep in the ceiling turned on only when the train stopped at stations or when it was dark outside. The coal-black, antique potbellied stove, held securely to the floor by large bolts, appeared to be out of place in the more modern setting of the car's interior. Probably for heat in the winter, I guessed.

A handrail had replaced the seats on either side of the stove, Probably for passengers to hold onto as they pass the heater while the train is moving, I surmised again. The rain-streaked windows were partially covered with dusty, forest-green curtains that were held in place on both sides in a way that allowed passengers to raise or lower them. The light brown seats were well- worn but clean, and had the smell of material that had been washed and hadn't completely dried. Added to that odor were the faint smells you'd expect a train car to have. I put my hand on the seat. It feels dry, I thought.

Years of use and re-painting had given the appealing hardwood flooring of the cars an exquisite, antique quality, but this pleasant ambience had been sabotaged by random insertions of cheap plywood squares. Probably to replace worn-out flooring, I thought, and laughed at my ability to use so much logic on such a mundane topic.

I raised the blind a little and smiled as I sat looking out the window. I felt bad that I hadn't worked for Harlow. I smiled at the cowboy with the big green hat who was looking at me from his place behind the dusty, water-streaked window, and muttered, "I don't care if he is mad." The cowboy sat as stoically as before. "I told him I couldn't work," I said. The cowboy remained silent. "Harlow has always helped me out when I needed help," I continued to torture myself, and apparently the cowboy in the window felt that way as well. I shifted in my seat, and the cowboy moved in his seat, like an echo following a voice. Maybe he's trying to advise me, I thought. Maybe he's trying to tell me to put off my trip.

I looked at him again. He was silent and still. "You're no help," I said, and turned away.

"Who are you talking to?" Victoria laughed.

"Nobody," I smiled. "I thought you got lost," I said, embarrassed about talking to the window.

"No, I just came out of the bathroom."

"I'm glad you're here," I said, and stood to let her pass in front of me to the window seat. "It will be easier to get a car we both like if you're with me."

"Did you say something?" the old man with the bibs asked.

"No, I was just talking to Victoria," and I motioned to her with a nod.

He greeted her by raising his eyebrows. She returned his greeting with a smile. He looked back at me. "Takes a long time ta get anywhere on a train, don't it?" he said.

"Yeah, it really does," I answered.

"William, did you know that the toilet just dumps out onto the tracks?" Victoria contributed.

"Yeah, I did know that. I think I've told you that before."

I didn't feel like talking to the old man. I wanted to think about my car and talk to Victoria but he went on, "I come all the way from Butte. It's nice to have somebody new to talk to."

Jeez, this is all I need to make my trip complete, I thought. A crazy old man.

"The damned train stops at almost every town, no matter how small," the old man said with a guarded smile. His teeth were stained from years of tobacco and other vices, but nonetheless he had a friendly and unthreatening nature.

"Yeah, I noticed," I answered coolly, trying to be polite.

The old man fell silent, as if trying to think of some other topic to bore me with. Finally, he found one. "My wife and I lived over in Hope. That's our next stop," he went on his monotone.

"Oh?" I said. "Hell, I know Hope. It's only twenty miles from Eden."

"I made pretty good money and bought her a new Oldsmobile."

"Oh?" I said, more interested in the passing scenery than in what he was saying.

"She ran off with a school teacher." He stopped and his eyes clouded as he continued. "We had three kids, a boy and two girls. They all went to California."

What the hell? I thought.

"You know, young man," he began again, "life is funny." He stopped and looked out the window for a moment, and then back at me. "My wife and I had a good marriage. The sex was great; she was a wonderful lay."

"Hey, watch the language, there's a lady present," I said.

Victoria blushed and said, "It's all right. He's just upset about his wife."

The old man looked toward Victoria. "Sorry," he mumbled, "I didn't realize." He obviously regretted his outburst, because he blushed and looked befuddled, and then he shrugged his shoulders and went on. "My wife and I went to the shore of the lake with the kids a lot, and had picnics, and I always brought them gifts and cooked when I was home. We laughed and read stories and we had a good television and had favorite programs. I got free train tickets because I worked for the railroad and we went a lot of places, hell …" He stopped and looked at Victoria. "Sorry, about the hell," he said, and then went on, "We even went to Disneyland. We were happy." He turned his sad face toward me. A tear made its way down his cheek. I felt sad too, and Victoria was crying. I pulled her close to comfort her. The closeness made me feel better, as well.

"One day, I forgot her birthday," the old man continued. "Hell, she got mad and never forgave me." His face went pale. "My life became a living hell. She started to be mean. She began sleeping in the spare room and going out alone at night." He waited for me to say something, and when I didn't, he continued. "She brought home the clap, but put the blame on me. She didn't give me any for months, and then one night she came home and wanted it. She almost raped me. Three days later, I started to drip. Hell, it was obvious it was her, but she blamed me. It didn't matter much; it was all over by then anyway."

He sat for a moment, watching the telephone poles blur past the window. "Hell, it seemed funny that forgetting a birthday was a reason to break up a family. But I guess that's the way people are. I guess we learn all this unimportant shit from our parents. Well, I still can't figure it out." Then his face lit up like the morning sun on a summer day. "But she came back to Hope," he said. "She always loved me to read poetry to her. She liked really meaningful and sad stuff. I wrote poetry and often read it to her." He stopped to look out the window, but I sensed there was more. "I wrote a poem on the train coming over. It's a tear-jerker about Christmas. I know it's a while 'til Christmas—but would you please listen to it and see what you think?"

I thought maybe he would go to sleep if I did." Sure, lay it on me."

The old man had it memorized, which was obvious as he began, but he held out a piece of paper like he was reading:

An Old Cowboy's Christmas Gift

His hands were gnarled and calloused and uncomfortable to touch
But inside his heart was tender; he didn't show that side too much
His face was tough as leather from the cold wind and freezing rain
And sallow eyes set deep within to mask and hide the gnawing pain.

His eyes were clouded-over now as I waited Christmas on his knee;
Maybe a profound dark secret held back that he couldn't tell to me.
Several stingy gifts of not much worth hung randomly, I could see,
Old, patched socks, not the fancy kind, hung sparsely from the tree.
But the solemn single point concealed in this cowboy's stoic way
Screamed loudly above his reverie for gifts and a happy joyful day.
He tried to speak, to make it clear, but then just smiled down at me,
And that certain look and protected smile was his only gift, you see.
A veiled tear rolled down his beard to reside amidst the matted hair;
A sad and aching heart, a man-made Christmas feeling hard to bear.
He tried to sooth my aching wounds of how hardship builds the man
And how no amount of formal schooling can teach like suffering can.
But it didn't seem so nice back then, a useless gift that wouldn't last
A soft warm look of love and bare smile that haunts me from the past.
But when you think about it, Christmas assumes gifts are from above,
Set in tinseled heaps of solemn gestures but are feudal swaps for love.
That old cowboy in vivid memory with me, his son, sitting on his knee,

I sought for more substance; he smiled, "Some day my child, you'll see."
And now so many years later, I've assumed that cowboy's role in time.
I now regard the holidays; my own loving children are no less sublime.
The image of that chanced and tactless gift comes to me from the past,
And then, it strikes me soft and swiftly, Dad's involuntary gift did last.
There are many parts to modern Christmas and gifts with certain stance,
Some given from pressure and some driven by thoughtless chance.
Some presents will bring the instant smiles and feelings that won't last.
I sit now in awe and insecurity with my own child, thinking of the past.
What gift to get for Christmas will make him consider of me the most?
What empty treasure can I find, not for concern but brother, just to boast?
Suddenly, the value of that long and hated present came rushing in, you see;
That old cowboy's somber gift was reflected in my own child's love for me.

That's pretty damned good." I smiled and applauded softly. Victoria thought it was good as well.

The old man smiled.

He seemed to be waiting for a longer reply, but I just looked at Victoria. The old man finally just looked at his feet and closed his eyes.

"Thank God," I whispered. "Maybe I can think about my car now."

"Of course you can," Victoria said, "but the poem was pretty good."

The river, through the moving train windows, was closer now and less violent. There were no pools, just the enormous stream making its way over and between the protruding rocks, with a few people fishing along the jagged shoreline on either side. I saw red-flashing lights ahead and then the train whistled and there was a bridge.

The wheels clicked against the connections in the track on the bridge as its supports flashed past. We crossed and then the train turned and the fishers were lost from view.

If there were no passengers at a station, the engineer would be forewarned by telegraph and the train would whiz through, simply throwing out mail from the open door of the mail car and picking up outgoing mail with a hook device designed for that purpose. It was fun and exciting to watch the large canvas bag hit the wooden deck of the station and slide to a stop.

And it was amazing to see the hook device pluck the bag from where it had been hung. The conductor or brakemen would pull the hinged device close to the open door of the baggage car and retrieve it.

I could see cars moving along the highway in the near distance. The cars seemed to speed up as the train slowed down. "Optical illusion," I said, attempting to call attention to my intellect, but no one was listening. Just the same, it was impressive.

An old motorcycle passed, going the other direction. "I hadn't thought of that." My mind began to churn. "Maybe I should think about a motorcycle instead of a car." The train slowed and the conductor strode down the aisle toward the loading door. He picked up the boarding step and went to perform his insincere act of assistance.

"Hope," he announced softly and only once as he walked past.

"Not a very big town, not a very big announcement," I mused.

The old man stood and stretched. "Here's where I get off," he said. "It's funny, this is where I started and now I'm coming back." He had a thoughtful, sad look on his face.

We lurched ahead slightly as the train came to a stop.

"I hope Hope works out this time," I said.

"I have missed her and the kids." He showed me his stained, crooked teeth.

I should have listened more closely to him, I thought. Is your wife going to meet you here?

"Don't know, she didn't say. I just told her I was coming." He looked sad. "It took a long time to forgive her. Don't throw people away, young man, they's important." He bent to look out the window. "I don't see her."

"She's probably hiding in the shadows," I said for his support.

"Things are only yers for a time. When you die, you lose everything you have, family and friends, forever."

That made sense. He thought for a moment and then continued, "Love and forgiveness goes with you too, but hate doesn't. The more you love and forgive, the more you take with you. "So long, young man," he said, but he stood looking at me like he was afraid to go.

"Good luck sir," I said. "I'm sure it will be all right."

He shuffled down the aisle and disappeared through the double doors.

Now I was really sorry that I hadn't been friendlier. He's right, I thought. We all do things we are sorry for.

Chapter 96

The far-off sound of banging hitches traveled along the train toward me, and my head drew back slightly as the noise reached my coach. It was nice to be moving again. I was anxious to be in Spokane.

An old woman who had boarded in Hope walked by my seat. "Hello young man," she said, giving a false-toothed smile. She looked like Aunt Helen.

"Hi," I said, having decided now to be friendlier.

When she said, "Beautiful sunny day," I thought her teeth were going to fall out, but she moved her tongue quickly to secure them.

"It looks like it might get hot," I said, trying to be nice.

"Are you a cowboy?" she asked.

"Yes ma'am, I am." I produced my version of a cowboy's smile. She looked at my penny loafers.

"Just wear them when I ride the train." I tipped my hat.

She held the backs of the seats as she made her way to a seat a few steps down the aisle and on the other side.

I was glad she was sitting down and hadn't fallen as the train began to move faster. She had a scarf on her head, tied under her chin just like Mom did. It hid most of her pure white hair, and didn't flatter her.

"But hell," I thought, "when you're that old, you probably don't even care what you look like, anyway."

She bent slightly forward and clutched the light sweater around her as though the comfortably cool late morning were winter. Her small, fragile face was tanned and wrinkled and showed the signs of wind, sun, and worry.

"Probably has kids," I thought, remembering what Mom said about kids. "I wish I had brought some crackers or a piece of bread," I mumbled. "It will be a long time before we got to Spokane."

Walking behind the old woman was a younger lady; well, a young girl about my age. She was making her way along the aisle as best as she could, trying to keep control over her kids as they moved along looking for the right seat. She held an infant in her arms that had green snot running from its nose and was crying. A little girl held onto her mother's hand as best she could, and a little boy was trying to compete for attention against the urgent shrieks of the baby as they all walked in disharmony along the isle. Finally, they found a section of seats that suited them a short distance in front of the old lady. After only a few moments, they became situated and dissolved into a sort of artificial contentment of staring out the window.

The dusty window again returned the vision of the cowboy in the green hat. Looking beyond him, I saw an old bridge that spanned the wide and winding river. This bridge and others like it weren't the fancy kind. They had apparently been built more with economy in mind, probably because of the great number that were needed. The railroad and narrow, undivided highway followed the dominant river, and all were all etched into the landscape along the wooded valley in their serpentine fashion. But the railroad and highway formed a rhythm of their own, as if in defiance to the majestic river. All together, it seemed to me they made a congenial and poetic but complex and meandering network.

The train swayed gently back and forth, click-clicking us into the events of our day, and as the coach took and gave, straining and moaning to blend with all the other elements and sounds, a rhythm arose as if from a natural orchestra that needed no conductor. I thought of the Deist's view of God as a watchmaker, who made a universe so perfect that it needed no further intervention, but simply ran like clockwork.

The dominant river set the rhythm, while cars slipped along the road like flutes or triangles, subtly enhancing the effect, and the train swayed and rattled along the tracks to create a tempo, a rhapsody. And then the train rumbled across a bridge like a crescendo. The distant automobiles changed sides and went over or under the train as it crossed bridges and passed under viaducts through the narrow valley. I picked up the melody and tapped my foot.

"The highway just takes what's left," I sang quietly to the rhythm. "It crosses the river where the train does, but the train takes what it wants," I sang on. "The river is the boss, and then the train, and then the highway, the road, is like me." I tapped my foot to the beat, like I'd learned to do at guitar lessons. "I just get what's left over," I finished with self-pitying smile. I turned to look out the window again. The cowboy in the big green hat was watching me and I smiled; he smiled back. "Gawd, he's good-looking," I murmured. "Sure is taking a long time to get to Piedmont," I told him. He smiled again, which I thought was probably because he was so excited. The old lady was looking at me again. "What the hell does she want now?" I said to myself. "I thought she was nice." She smiled, and I thought, "Hell, now she's laughing at me."

"Sonny?"

"Yes ma'am," I answered cautiously.

"Do you smoke?" She looked at the string from my Bull Durham that was hanging out of my shirt pocket.

"Well, yes I do," I said and prepared for a lecture, like I always got from Dad.

"Would you let me have a cigarette?" she asked. My mouth dropped open. "My daughter won't let me smoke," she went on.

She looks too old to smoke, I thought. "I used to smoke a pipe," the old lady continued, "but she took it away … said it was bad for my health and it didn't look lady-like."

"She's just worried about your health."

"Hell, I guess she thinks I'll live forever if I don't smoke. If you don't have any bad habits, you don't live longer; it just seems like you do," she said and let out a muffled chuckle; well, more of a cackle.

"I don't have any cigarettes," I confessed, "just roll-yer-owns. I can roll them with one hand," I said. "Had to learn when I cut my thumb off," I held up my thumb stub and mangled arm.

"Thank you, yes," she replied, not even seeming to notice my injuries.

I had a hard time getting the papers to separate, but finally peeled one off. I guess I was a little nervous. I wanted her to be impressed. I rolled a nice fat one with one hand in my usual fashion, with just a little help from the bad appendage, and then licked the edge of the paper, pressed it together, and handed it across the aisle.

"Got any matches?"

I returned her smile, leaned over, and struck a match on the back of my Levis to sort of show off, and then leaned across the aisle and held it to her stogy. She drew the smoke into her lungs, and then I rolled one for myself. After lighting it, we began filling the car with tobacco-scented smoke. She went back to her thoughts and I went back to daydreaming about my car. I finished the smoke and dropped the butt into the ashtray. I had plenty of time, so I decided to make the best cigarette I had ever rolled. I took out my package of makings. The thin, frail paper came out easily. Just my luck, I thought. Now that I have plenty of time, the papers just separate. I'm going to use both hands—well, as much as that's possible—and I'm going to make a really good one.

I held the paper in my left hand, cradled between the stub of my thumb and middle finger with the index finger on the top to hold the paper in place. I poured in the tobacco flakes. I filled it up really full, and then rolled it between the thumb and forefinger of my good hand, up and down several times. I looked at it to make sure it was perfect, and then rolled it up and down a few more times for good measure. I licked it, like I would the flap of an envelope, and rolled it down and sealed it. "My perfect cigarette."

Victoria woke up. "Is everything all right?"

"Everything is just ducky," I said.

"Have you thought anymore about the car?"

"I have. My car is going to better than anybody else's in town."

"What if the other kids cut the top off?"

"I need to find a way to keep them from doing that."

"You could get a convertible," she said and smiled.

"A convertible would do it, but I'm sure I don't have enough money for a convertible."

"I'm going to the bathroom."

"Okay, don't fall in."

I looked to see how the old woman was doing.

"Will you make me another one, young man?" she asked.

"Another cigarette?"

"Yes, please."

I quickly rolled a nice fat one and handed it across the aisle to her. "Thanks," she said. "Got a light?"

I lit it, and she pulled the smoke deep into her lungs and let it out with a sigh.

"That was godly of you to do that for me," she said.

"What?"

"To help me out with a cigarette."

"Anybody would do it," I blushed.

"No they wouldn't. A religious nut wouldn't." "Maybe not, but I ain't no religious nut."

"There's a difference between religious and godly, you know," the old lady said.

"Never thought about it," I admitted.

"Even the founding fathers knew that."

"Who the hell are the founding fathers?"

"Hell, son, didn't you go to school?"

"Yeah, but I didn't listen very much."

"They are the ones who wrote up the Constitution; the patriots who were responsible for creating this country."

"Oh. Well, what did they think about religion?" I asked, trying to settle her down.

"Thomas Jefferson, or at least one of the fathers—maybe it was Adams—said he didn't find a single redeeming feature in the Christian religion. Their God was cruel, vindictive, capricious, and unjust." It was over my head. For once, I had no comeback. She seemed to sense this and went on, "George Washington said that in no sense was the United States founded on religion, and his vice president, John Adams—or maybe that was Jefferson—thought the best of all possible worlds would be if there were no religion at all."

"Dad would be pissed," I said.

She laughed, but she had me on the run. "James Madison, the fourth president, thought that religion brought superstition, bigotry, and persecution." She stopped talking and waited for an answer. I had none and silently turned back in my seat.

"I can make something up," I said to myself. "I can hold my own with her. She's probably just making the shit up like Dad does anyway. I'll go over and talk to her. She seems nice, sort of like Aunt Helen. I can tell her some of the stuff Dad says. It might make her laugh."

I stood, but the old lady had closed her eyes. She had finished her cigarette and was sitting with her head down, like she was looking at her feet—the snip was burning along the floor, leaving a brown, worm-like trail behind it. That's gratitude for you, I thought. Now that I want to talk all she can think of is sleep. I sat back down, rolled another stogy, lit it, and pulled the smoke deep into my lungs.

Chapter 97

Victoria hadn't come back from the bathroom yet. I wondered what was taking so long. Maybe she *did* fall in. I laughed to myself. I would go look in a minute.

The river was gone now, replaced by small lakes, small farms, and a few houses here and there. Worn-out farm machinery that had been left to rust red in the harsh, wet climate bordering the lush green fields and deep blue reservoirs. An occasional farmer worked a field with an old tractor or a team of draft horses. Some of the men waved as we passed. Children played along the roads or in their yards. The older boys signaled their mock loathing by raising a middle finger and the girls hid their faces in playful embarrassment, but they couldn't conceal the admiration they had of the boys for being so bold. A few cars and trucks drove along the dusty roads, raising a trail of dust as we passed.

"Lots more people than in Eden," I muttered.

The cowboy in the window had taken off his hat, just as I had, and was looking at me.

I shrugged my shoulders. "What do you think?" I asked. I couldn't understand him; he shrugged his shoulders and talked while I did. "You're rude," I said, and I looked beyond him to the lake. Several small islands had homes on them. "Wonder how the people get there?" I answered myself. "By boat I guess ... I wonder about the winter?"

The old woman was watching me again.

I thought about Flash without one eyebrow, which made me laugh out loud. I smiled at the old lady and then turned to look at the tal,l handsome cowboy in the window again, but he just looked back and said nothing, like always. "I need to make it to Spokane before the car lots close," I told him. He didn't say anything. "To hell with you." The old woman had fallen asleep again. "That's the way to travel. Just sleep and when you wake up, you're there." I was getting so excited, I needed to stop thinking about the car. "I'm not dead yet," I assured myself.

The lady with the two kids was moving about now. The baby had a dirty diaper and she was busy changing it. The kids were trying to help, and she was becoming flustered.

Finally, she finished, and then she folded the dirty diaper and put it into a shopping bag. She turned and looked at me. "Sir, we got a little dirty. Will you hold the baby while we go to the bathroom to clean up?"

I hadn't noticed her too much when she came aboard. She was slim and attractive, with blond hair and sad brown eyes set deep in a sallow, faded face.

Her hair had probably once been brown but was now bleached. She had brown roots, and a green polka-dot scarf hung down with the hair, becoming part of a long ponytail.

She wore a lightweight, green summer dress and brown loafers without socks. Her brown, painted-on eyebrows rose impatiently as she waited for my response.

"It just keeps getting better," I thought. "Sure, be happy to," I said sheepishly as she handed me the baby and a bottle.

Two rows of crooked and stained teeth were revealed in a smile of gratitude. A tooth in front was missing and other teeth on either side were obviously moving over, trying to fill the void. An off-white, doughy substance was caked between her teeth, where they met the gum. The smile faded quickly as she turned and walked with the kids to the bathroom.

"You are sort of cute," I said to the baby in baby talk.

There was a certain smell that wasn't really good but it wasn't repulsive; just a baby smell. "All that was wrong was you shit your pants, didn't you?" I smiled at the tiny face and shoved the bottle into its mouth. "You're so cute and innocent I could just strangle you," I kidded in baby talk. It began sucking the bottle and closed its eyes.

The train was click-click-clicking along now and beginning to pick up speed. It swayed back and forth gently. It was as if an orchestra of expert percussion professionals was at work, while another group busily rocked us back and forth.

The baby slept, and the old lady's head swayed gently back and forth in time with the rhythm of the swaying coach. The mother of the baby finally came back from the toilet. "Thanks," she said as she took it.

"That's okay, it was sort of fun."

"Do you mind if we sit with you?" the girl asked.

I didn't know what to say, but Victoria wasn't there.

"Did you see anyone in the can?" I asked.

"No," she said, "but there are a couple of stalls in there."

There are a couple of bathrooms on the train, I thought. She's probably in one of the other ones—hope she didn't get motion sickness.

"Okay if we sit here?" she asked again.

"Yeah, okay," I stammered. I could have her move when Victoria came back.

They all crowded in the aisle side of the seat and as she stroked her children's heads in a loving gesture to comfort them against the long and boring ride.

She pushed her body close against me—more than was really necessary. I knew Victoria would be coming back soon, and I was nervous. I didn't want to have to deal with the anger of her jealousy, with so much on my mind. I pulled away as much as I could and looked out the window.

Fishermen along the shore looked like they were being patrolled by a few airborne, inquisitive sea birds that hovered and circled above. It was nearing midmorning and some of the fishermen were beginning to leave. Being a fisherman myself, I knew that fishing falls off in the heat of the day and then picks up again in the cool of the late afternoon. They will probably return later, I thought. I was pleased that I had become so wise at such an early age. "Well, I'm not dead yet," I muttered as I drifted into the daze that the monotony of travel can bring on.

It seemed to me that I was getting close to knowing about life and its secrets. If not, I certainly had learned a lot about people. I knew there are men who like women, there are men who like men, there are women who like women, and perverted people who do bad things to other people and even to little kids, and evil isn't reserved to any one of those segments. People don't talk about such things openly, I thought. It's not acceptable to say "sex" or "homosexual" or "seduce" or "pregnant" or anything like that. Any of these are among the reasons to get a bar of Lifebuoy soap wedged into a young boy's mouth. But beyond this, and worse than any of it, are the people who do really bad things and then try to put the blame on others. People like Oscar and Alex.

"Alex is an ass," I mumbled to myself, and began thinking of all the ways that he was an ass. But there was more to this Alex thing than I would allow my mind to acknowledge. For some reason, I was afraid to go there. Thinking about Alex too much made me feel uncomfortable.

"Hey mister, how come you wear shoes and not cowboy boots?" the little boy asked.

"I don't know. What do you mean?"

"Most cowboys have boots."

"I had to leave mine with the horse, so he wouldn't be lonely."

"Oh," the boy said.

"Are you tired? Want to go to sleep?" I asked.

"No," he said and then to my pleasure, he stopped talking and looked across me and out the window.

"Good," I mumbled. Then, without giving it much thought, I asked, "Where's your Daddy?"

"He got kilt."

Now I looked out the window, "Hell, this is really great," I thought. "Why did I have to ask that?"

The mother turned to look at me. Her eyes were misty, like she was about to cry. "He was killed a few months ago in a logging accident." She delivered this more-than-sad message through her one-tooth-missing grin; it would have looked funny, if the whole thing hadn't been so damned sad. My mouth opened, but I couldn't speak. A tear came to her eye as she stroked the heads of her sleeping little girl and the boy, while he gazed across me, out the window. The baby started to fuss but then settled down, as the mother shifted it to a more comfortable position. The smells of baby, mother, and kids, all of whom lacked regimented hygiene, flooded my nostrils.

"We don't have much money anymore," she said. "We go see my mother in Piedmont about every other week for a few days. She feeds us and we take showers in her big nice shower, and then gives us money for the next train ride over."

I covered my nose and mouth, trying to ward off the nausea.

"I wish I could find a good man," she said, her smile revealing the missing tooth, a white- coated tongue, and that off-white doughy substance that seemingly held her teeth in place.

"They say there's not many left," I said. "Good ones, I mean."

"Mister, will you be my Daddy?" the little boy asked.

Well, that should get my mind off my car, I thought. I had to get away. "Will you excuse me?" I found the courage to say. "I have to go to the bathroom."

I looked at the tall cowboy in the bathroom mirror. "Looks like you got tired riding outside the train," I said. "Looks like you moved indoors." He just looked at me with a questioning attitude. "If she didn't have the kids, I might go over to Hope to see her." The cowboy kept giving me his vacant look. "She is pretty good-looking, except for the teeth, and she smells pretty bad, but she's nice." The cowboy just mimicked me. "Cowboys are supposed to be tough and stoic," I said, forgiving his silent thoughtlessness. "I know you're just being stoic, not rude." I smiled and he smiled back. He was beginning to come around. "I guess I could have her teeth fixed or just keep our house dark and pinch a clothespin onto my nose." Now the cowboy was laughing. "Finally getting it, are you?"

The bathroom door opened and Victoria came in. I seemed to pass through a window, and began watching William and Victoria.

> "Looks like you have a replacement for me," she kidded.
> "Don't worry, I'll never replace you. It's just that every once in a while I need to talk to someone," William said.
> "Who were you talking to in here?"
> He blushed. "Nobody."
> "That's all right, I'm just kidding. I shouldn't be in here, I know, but now I'm ready to finish what you tried to start this morning."
> "Do I have a choice?"
> "Well, no you don't." She stepped close, unbuttoned his Levis, and let them fall to the floor. She pulled her dress off over her head and sat on the toilet seat. "Come over here, you stud," she demanded...
> "We better get back to our seat before we get caught in here together. We might get kicked off the train—but it would be worth it," William smiled.

The window effect faded and we made our way back to our seats. "We'll just sit over here," I said to the girl with the kids, as we took the seat right across the aisle from them. "I need to get some sleep. I have a big day tomorrow." I leaned back, placed my head on

Victoria's shoulder, and pulled my hat down over my eyes.

"Okay, have a nice rest," the girl with the missing tooth said and turned her head to look out the window. She held the baby comfortably as it slept and the children leaned against her as if they had accepted their ordeal and were now at ease again.

Victoria put her hand on my leg, near my crotch—too near to be casual. "Sleep well my prince," she cooed.

Chapter 98

"Piedmont, five minutes," the conductor yelled as he walked toward me through the coach. "Fifteen minute stop," he continued and then went to the next coach to announce the same news. The train slowed and finally came to a stop with a sudden but surprisingly soft nudge and we all involuntarily leaned ahead slightly, as if to meet it. I stood up in front of my seat and tried to stretch out the kinks from the long ride. I put my arms over my head and reaching for the coach's ceiling, involuntarily let out a muffled cry of relief. The old woman raised her head in alarm. I was glad she hadn't died. Her face softened, and she looked away.

The lady with the three kids was moving about, getting her belongings together. She stood, and in about the same way the four had entered the coach they walked along the aisle, the baby crying, the little girl holding onto the mother's hand as best she could, and the little boy trying to compete with his sister and the shrieks of the baby.

"Thanks," she said as they passed. "I'm sure God will bless and keep you for the nice things you do."

"Yeah, probably a bale of hay for being such a horse's ass," I said with a smile.

"I'm not sure I understand," she said, "but come over to Hope and visit us if you get time." She handed me a piece of paper that had an address written on it.

"Okay, I will," I said. "I guess she hasn't given up," I mumbled to Victoria.

"Thanks, ma'am. Have a nice day," Victoria said with a wry smile.

We watched them walk toward the end of the coach and pass through the windowed door. Through the window, we could see her and the kids as they walked away from the train and across the bridge to dissolve into the distance among the other pedestrians. "God, I'm glad that's you and not me," I said to the now-absent woman. "Those kids would drive me crazy."

The fifteen-minute layover seemed like hours, but finally the train was ready to leave. A soft humming of voices became a jumble of gibberish as seats were filled with boarding passengers and luggage was lifted into compartments overhead and forced under seats. Mothers and fathers tried unsuccessfully to keep their energetic children under control, as the youngsters stood or knelt on the seats, irritating other children or passengers. Some children had schoolbooks and were beginning to study or write in notebooks, while others continued to look excitedly around.

The train bumped slightly and began moving. It swayed in a soft, gentle manner as it picked up speed and with it, the rhythm and the click-click-clicking of the wheels against the tracks sounded like an out-of-synch, second-rate high school matching band. It had a medicinal effect, though, and before long everyone had settled down, and a lot of people fell asleep

A boy and girl about my age were in the seat across the aisle. They sat so close that they appeared to envelop each other. She looked quickly from side to side, and then took his hand in hers and placed it on her bosom. He just sat motionless, like he was afraid to do anything.

"She wants you to feel it, you dumb bastard," I mumbled to myself.

If anyone approached, she quickly removed his hand and after they passed, she put it back. Finally, she gave up and they drew together in a long embrace, then pulled apart to look into the other's eyes and then, as if not knowing what to say, they entwined again.

"Ticket," the conductor yelled as he moved along the aisle, and after the new passenger's tickets were punched and handed back, he moved to the next passengers to humiliate them with his condescending manner. I pulled my ticket out of my shirt pocket and held it for him to see. He winked as he passed. Wonder what he has up his sleeve? I thought.

I struggled to be somewhere else. I became a river guide in charge of a raft full of frightened and screaming passengers on whitewater; maybe it was the river we passed earlier. My clients looked to me for comfort and safety as the raft drifted onto a sharp rock, punctured, and then capsized, throwing the terrified tourists into the swirling water, where they struggled against the rushing current. After I saved them all by swimming back and forth several times, we warmed ourselves by a fire I had built by rubbing two sticks together. Then I comforted them, explaining how I would find our way out to safety in the morning …

I saw the conductor walking toward me, holding the edges of the seats as the gentle swaying of the train tried to dislodge him. I winked at the cowboy with the large green hat in the window. He winked back. "That's a good omen," I told myself.

Thinking about how Samuel Clemens wrote his stories under the pen name, Mark Twain, and how it seemed to work for him, I decided it might work for me, too. Always trying to be original, I decided that William Q. Pencil would become my pen name when I got serious about writing.

Chapter 99

That jerk the conductor was cruising the aisles again. I could see him through the sliding doors that separated the cars, coming toward me. As he emerged into our car, his loud, crass voice described the size of town, tempering his volume and repetitions in accordance with each town's size and importance. "Coeur d'Alene—five minutes!" he said several times and fairly loudly while walking through our car.

"Must be bigger that Piedmont," I mused. "He said it pretty loud and twice." I placed my cheek against the window, trying to peer ahead to see the town. The houses were getting closer together now and I saw people walking along the sidewalks and mowing their lawns, and children riding bicycles, and dogs running here and there.

A crumpled old car lay on its side. It looked like it might have been hit by a train just recently. Spectators, policemen, and medical people were milling about, and red lights blinked on emergency vehicles.

Some of the people on the train left their seats and were heading for the exit before the train had completely stopped. The old woman, sitting up straight in her seat, waited for the last of the vacating passengers to pass, and then, clutching her shopping bag and with her scarf undisturbed on her head, she stood and walked to my seat.

"Thanks for the kindness," she said and handed me a five-dollar bill. "You are a nice young man. You will do just fine. Remember, you usually have to make an ass of yourself for a while, if you're going to ever be good at anything." She placed her hand on my shoulder for a moment—she had a firm grip.

"Dad would think her honest. She had a strong grip, and that's his only criterion," I chuckled to myself.

She shuffled to the end of the car and without looking back, took one step down and then brought the other foot down to meet it. In that fashion, watching her feet, she departed.

"I wish she had stayed put until the train stopped," I said to myself. "She probably has folks here in town and is in a hurry to see them, but she could get hurt."

Finally, the train came to a complete stop and she came into view, walking slowly away. That was nice of her to give me the money and the advice, I thought. Her scarf fell from her neck to the ground and I subconsciously grabbed for it; she stooped to pick it up. It's another good omen, I thought. I'm going to get the car.

A younger man and a woman rushed to meet her, like they had just arrived and were sorry for being late. They hugged and everyone talked at once. She turned and pointed to the train and waved. Without thinking, I waved back. The younger woman stepped back and seemed to be scolding the old woman and began shaking her finger. The old woman just smiled, and then the young man smiled, and they all locked arms and walked away.

I miss her. I'm lonely. I wish Victoria would wake up, I thought.

It seemed like a long time before the people began to get back onto the train. "God, I'll be glad to leave this town," I mumbled. "It's taking long enough."

A lot of time passed, during which many of the original passengers returned to their seats. The new ones came in unsurely, not wanting confrontation if they claimed a seat already taken. They sat down cautiously and looked around, and then settled down when it looked okay. Everyone began trying to find ways to deal with the discomfort of travel, each in their own way. Some used pillows, some had books or magazines, some lay blankets in their seats, intending to catch a few winks. The train continued to make strange noises from time to time, as it lurched forward or backward like a huge, untamed animal pulling against its restraints, anxious to be on its way. Finally, it bumped, lurched, and began to move. The soft, forward thrust pulled me gently and comfortably into the seatback.

Directly in front of me, kneeling on her seat and looking back, was a young girl. Her dishwater blond hair was braided and hanging down on either side of her face. The braids were tied at the end with a dirty-looking, thick white string. She had forced an insincere smile onto her freckled face, which exposed a row of crooked light yellow teeth that had food-paste packed into the spaces, something like that girl from Hope. Looks like a relative of the girl with the three kids. All she needs is to have one knocked out, I chuckled to myself. If she doesn't turn around, maybe I'll be the one to knock it out.

I frowned and motioned at her to sit down. Her tongue came out and her lips closed around it. Her face scrunched up in a transmission of total contempt that reminded me of the conductor's sinister glare. The little girl's mother and younger brother sat looking out the window, apparently unaware of her actions. I looked out the window as well, but something made me look back. She placed her thumbs in her ears with the fingers flared and wiggled them while keeping the scrunched-up look on her face.

The rumble of a train passing the opposite way momentarily captured my interest and I began thinking about my car, but the little girl quickly took my attention again. She went down the aisle and began irritating a little boy whose mother had fallen asleep.

The little boy held a toy that she tried to wrench from his desperate grasp. Silently, he struggled to maintain possession.

His mother probably told him not to bother her, I told myself. The little girl turned her head in my direction. I quickly shut my eyes, hoping I had acted quickly enough, and then slowly, I let my head fall to into a sleeping posture. I waited for a long moment and then carefully looked out of the tops of my eyes. She had been successful in getting the toy, and the little boy, sadness etched across his face, sat silently watching her walk farther along the aisle, where she took an interest in a sleeping lady. She began to examine the purse that was resting on the floor in front of the woman.

Suddenly, the girl looked at me, but I was ready; I quickly looked out the window.

Outside, many houses whizzed past. "Must be getting close to Spokane," I mumbled. I could see the conductor walking through the dining car ahead, and imagined him screaming the town's name and telling the passengers six times, because of Spokane's size, that it was five minutes ahead. As he came through the door, my prophecy became reality. "Spokane, five minutes," he yelled, repeating the phrase before he reached my seat. He then yelled the warning four more times, very loudly, before passing through the windowed door into the next car.

"Good riddance."

The little girl had returned to her seat and had aggressively taken her brother's place next to their mother, whose mock delight masked a faint look of conditioned terror in her eyes, which only someone who had experienced the wrath of little girls, as I had, would recognize. The mother welcomed her and examined the new toy and other items from the woman's purse. Then she turned her dejected, weary eyes to silently look out the window.

The train began to slow and the passengers moved about, some standing and lifting their suitcases and bags down from the racks above the seats, others putting their belongings into bags or wiping off their children's faces with hankies they had touched to their tongues. I moved to the aisle and stretched, ready to get off.

"Are we in Spokane?" Victoria asked.

"Yes."

I saw the little girl and her family, who had walked ahead while the train was still moving—the mother seemed anxious to go. "If is was me, I'd leave the little shit here and flee," I muttered.

"What did you say?" Victoria asked.

"Nothing. Just talking to myself."

The little was girl was holding her mother's hand as she moved strategically to keep her brother from enjoying any maternal intimacy. He watched her in submissive silence.

"I'd beat her ass with my belt," I muttered.

"What?"

"I wouldn't let her do that to me," I said, and tried to muster a determined look on my face.

"Oh," Victoria said as she noticed what I was watching.

The three of them stood, waiting in line to exit with a few other passengers, who also seemed to be in a hurry to get off. The little girl turned her body, still holding her mother's hand and still holding her brother away. She looked back at me. I returned her look for a moment and then turned to Victoria. We slumped, mostly hidden, waiting for them to leave.

Through the window, the workers moved quickly here amid the steam, getting the train refreshed, cleaned, and ready to depart again. The shifting weight of the vacating passengers caused the huge animal to tremble slightly as they hurriedly found their belongings, and then they surged toward the exit to join the line. I stood up and saw that the little girl was gone. Reaching for Victoria's hand, I pulled her to her feet and we forced our bodies out into the aisle between the other passengers, whose mass then pushed us along to the exit.

We squinted against the midmorning sunlight as we stepped off and were again driven like cattle by the milling crowd into the huge

Northern Pacific Train Depot. The streaked, dirty windows along the high rotunda ceiling let through dust-filled rays of sunlight, as if God were revealing some sacred message to a favored disciple. "God always teases me," I whispered to Victoria, who just smiled.

Several rows of exquisitely decorated ceramic lights hanging on long chains tried desperately to help the restrained sunlight to illuminate the gloomy space. Everything inside the depot except the windows appeared to be spotlessly clean, though. Several men in coveralls, their carts filled with brooms, buckets, and mops, moved about polishing and cleaning the tile floors, the richly paneled walls, the oak back-to-back benches in the center and the single-sided ones along the walls.

Travelers sitting and waiting, some in suits and best dresses, with suitcases at their feet or on the bench next to them and tickets in their hands or sticking out of pockets, didn't even notice as we walked by. Others in tattered clothing sprawled comfortably, like they had taken up residence there. The typical oily smell of depots was present, along with other smells, including body odor that someone had tried to extinguish with cheap cologne. The effect was like a mild mixture of our outdoor toilet, the manure pile behind our barn, and our pigpen, which someone had tried unsuccessfully to cover with some magical odor-remover.

A small stand-alone coffee shop had been built into a wall along our route, somewhat like my cubbyhole in the basement of Aunt Helen's washhouse, but much larger. It was like a room within a room. But unlike my cubbyhole, it had real walls and a dirty, cluttered tile floor. A grubby-looking short order cook clad in an undershirt was pressing grease out of sizzling burgers and flipping charred ones with a stained, wooden-handled spatula, as he wiped beads of perspiration from his whiskered face with the tail of his soiled apron. He tried fruitlessly to keep the sweat from rolling down to sizzle on the smoking grill.

Flies maneuvered in the air, and others crept strategically on the counter and ceiling, as if they were the cook's out-of-control pets. Customers who had been lucky enough, or unlucky enough, to have already been served, sat at the small tables in front of the serving bar and competed with the insects for possession of their food. They waved their arms, newspapers, or magazines, trying to eat as quickly as was possible without ingesting too many flies.

"Let's eat someplace else, Victoria."

She was holding her hand over her mouth and nose. "That would be nice."

We followed the flow of people through the beautiful but stomach-turning building out to the street. The gutters and storefronts were lined with garbage packed into bags and cans waiting to be picked up by collectors. The awful smells were here, too, but not as strong as inside. People didn't speak or smile like they did in Eden. It was exciting to be here, but uncomfortable as well. I looked for a café or some place to get a meal. A billboard with large, faded red letters beckoned, "Pug's Café" and, in small black lettering, also faded and barely readable, "Best Food in Town."

"We'll see how good it is," I said.

Chapter 100

In front of the eatery, a large Negro man sat on the curb, his feet in the gutter. His big red car was jacked up and one of the front wheels had been taken off and was lying on the sidewalk. He wore a small business hat that had been carefully woven into interesting designs; it looked new. He also wore a lightweight, brown tweed sport coat and a black shirt with a large collar that lay over the top of the coat's collar. His sharply pleated, dark slacks were marked with dust. "Probably from working on the tire," I guessed. His pants flowed down evenly, covering a good portion of his polished black shoes.

We didn't have Negroes in Eden, but Dad talked about them sometimes and I had noticed them before, during the family's infrequent trips to Spokane. Dad said, "Them niggers all look pretty much alike, and ya need ta stomp on their toe ta hurt 'em, 'cause their heads is so hard ya can't knock 'em out."

"Well, they do look a lot alike," I thought.

The black man held a cigarette between his fingers as he cradled his large face between his two large hands in a gesture of pure desperation. As we walked by, he raised his head. "Hey son, I gots ta acks' ya sumpin."

He looked completely worn out. "Sure, go ahead," I said.

"Know anything bout fixin' tires?" His brown eyes were pleading.

I had to smile, because if there was anyone in the world who knew how to fix tires, it was me. I once had a job that required a long commute every day. I drove an old Studebaker that a man named Mr. Overneck loaned me. It didn't have a steering wheel, so I steered it with a box-end wrench, but the real problem was the lack of good tires.

To reach the job site I had to repair a flat tire or two every day. One day I had five flats—I always left for work early. I had rounded up all the old tires and tubes I could find and put them into the trunk and backseat to use for repair parts. Every time a tire blew out or went flat I removed it and patched the tube.

The man in front of me was large enough to be a little scary. He had a wide nose and thick lips and dark, kinky hair, the kind of thing Dad had warned me about. I didn't notice the special smell that black people were said to have. I stepped closer and sniffed; still nothing. Maybe he just took a bath or something, I concluded.

Along with the other advice Dad had given me, he had told me how to tell good people from bad. "Ya kin tell a hell of a lot 'bout a person by the handshake. Not jis Jews, niggers, and Catholics, but ever'body. If they's got a firm grip and looks ya right in the eye, then you kin be pretty sure that they's a pretty good person."

One of Dad's friends who was high up in his church, a branch president, had stolen the church's building fund, lied about it, and then ran off with his friend's wife, leaving his own family destitute. But he did have a strong handshake and looked you straight in the eye.

"Yes," I finally said, "I can change a tire. In fact, I'm pretty good at it. I had to learn to do a lot of thing after I hurt my arm."

"I'll just for you over there," Victoria said, and she went to lean against the building in the shade and to begin waiting.

"Okay," I said.

The black man asked, "What?"

"Just talking to my girl," I told him. He looked at Victoria, nodded a greeting, raised his eyebrows, and smiled.

He had all the tools to repair a tire, but didn't know how to use them. "I always gets a guy from the garage ta do my tire fixin'," he said. I started on the tire while he stood watching. "You shur look like you done that before," and he smiled. I spun the last lug bolt into place, and said, "There ya go, sir."

"Thanks," he said. "Youse a good guy fer a white." His large hand engulfed my own, even the thumb. He looked directly into my eyes and had a very firm handshake, but still, I don't think Dad would have liked him. "Thanks for da hep." His thick lips parted in a smile that showed real gratitude.

"You're welcome," I said, and found myself sort of liking him.

"Kin I gives ya something fer doin it? A few bucks or sumpin'?"

"Hell, no. You just do something nice for the next guy you find in trouble."

He doesn't have the thick, rough, elephant-type skin either, I thought. I waved to Victoria. My new friend looked at her, then back at me, and shook his head as he released his vise-like grip.

I walked to Victoria. "Pug's looks like a pretty good place to eat," I said.

"That was nice of you to help that man."

"I didn't mind. I'll bet he would help me if I needed it."

"It looks like Pug's Café will be just fine," she said.

Chapter 101

As we stepped inside Pug's, we were nearly overwhelmed by the aroma of stale cigarette smoke, beer, and some sort of cleaning product that was trying ineffectively to help the aroma of cooking food to subdue the less pleasing odors. An empty counter ran along two sides of a small eating area and behind it, I saw a cooking surface and paraphernalia, with some inexpensive, mismatched, plastic dishes and glasses stacked haphazardly on a clean but well-used shelves covered in oilcloth. Farther down and protected from the customers by the end of the counter was a hodgepodge of coffee cups turned upside-down on a towel next to a large coffee maker.

A portion of the counter was taken up by a glass display case that showed off pies and other desserts. One of the pies—it looked like lemon meringue—had a long cigarette ash lying on top of it. Pieces were missing, exposing the tin pie plate. The filling had begun to darken, and it oozed out a thick, wet substance.

"Remind me not to have pie," I said.

Several tables and other equipment took up most of the remaining area, and two customers sat at different tables. An old, shabbily dressed white man smoked a roll-yer-own cigarette. He looked like I imagined a bum would look. And there was a black man, who looked a little like the guy outside with the flat tire—he nodded and smiled as we walked in. I had noticed him watching from the window as I worked on the flat tire. "Well, they do all sort of look alike," I laughed to myself, and nodded back, then quickly looked away.

"I'm going to wash up," I told Victoria.

"I'll just wait here at the counter and look at the menu," she answered.

There were no towels in the restroom, so I wiped my hands on my pants and returned to sit on one of the worn, high-cushioned stools.

"Anything look good?" I asked her.

"What can you tell from a menu?" she laughed.

"You are so right."

"Looks like you're enjoying the menu," the waitress said as she arrived. Her nametag said, "Louise."

"No, it's just something she said." I motioned with my head at Victoria.

Louise looked at her and shrugged her shoulders, "What'll it be, sonny?" she asked in a gruff voice. She looked at Victoria again, raised her eyebrows, and then looked back at me.

Louise wore a soiled white bonnet in the shape of a princess's crown, except it wasn't gold, but rather a heavy, stiff-looking cloth. A cigarette hanging from the corner of her mouth had a long ash on the end. "Probably a relative of the one on the lemon pie," I whispered to Victoria.

Louise continued to wait, her mouth partially open, showing off two rows of rotting teeth below her lightly mustached upper lip. To accent her impatience, she shifted onto the other foot and blew a whiff of stale, halitosis-scented breath toward us. A soiled white blouse flowed over black slacks that were too short. Her white scalp showed beneath thinning brown hair, some of which had fallen out and clung to her pants.

"I'll have the cheeseburger," I said.

"Want sumpin' ta drink?" she asked with about the same interest as a train conductor.

"Cup'a coffee," I answered.

"Fries?"

"Yeah."

"What are you going to have?" I asked Victoria.

"I'll just have some of your fries," she said.

"I guess that's all," I told Louise.

She watched Victoria as she yelled over her shoulder toward the order window, possibly to Pug, "Cheeseburger with!"

The sound of a sizzling burger was almost immediate and then came scratching, scraping, and flipping sounds, as thick blue smoke billowed from the order window, confirming someone's existence in there. Louise took a last look at Victoria, raised her thickly arched, painted-on eyebrows, and then walked to the end of the counter and the cup of coffee that had been waiting for her. She took a couple of quick, deep sips, wrinkled her nose in disgust and went to the coffee urn. After looking into and discarding a couple of the cups, she found one she liked, poured it, and wobbled back to deliver my forbidden drink. Her black shoes were turned in, and seemed to make her knees bump together as she walked.

"Does your friend want anything?" she asked, and then without waiting for an answer, she went back to her coffee.

"No, she'll just have some of mine," I said to Louise's back.

She looked over her shoulder and rolled her eyes.

"She's sort of rude," I said to Victoria.

"It's just the big city."

The guy whose tire I had fixed came in and joined the Negro setting at the table. They were both looking at me and saying something. They smiled and waved. I turned my head, but was unable to resist looking back.

"Wonder what they're saying?" I asked Victoria.

"They don't look mad; probably talking about how you helped."

They were both large man and when they weren't looking at me, they ate their gravy-covered food. They paused from time to time to take a sip of coffee, smile again at me, and then go back to their meal. Dad's warnings about Negroes stressed that it's especially not a good idea to marry one. That's one thing that will keep you out of the celestial kingdom. He had cautioned me to watch for Negro traits in any white girl that I might have an interest in, such as big lips, kinky hair, dark skin, and big feet. "One drop a blood will keep ya outa the highest glory," he said.

Mom said people are people and no matter the color or how poor they are. God loves them all and we should, too. Dad said, "That's bullshit, Caroline."

"I'm going over to talk to them," I told Victoria after I had finished my burger and coffee.

"Be nice," she said.

"Hi?" My greeting came out as a question.

"How ya doin', young fella?" the man with the flat tire said. "Sure good of you to help me."

"Glad to help," I said, trying to show some confidence.

They had finished their meal and were now just sitting and smoking cigarettes and drinking coffee.

The black man held out his hand. "My name's Trooper. This here is my brother Louis," and he pointed to the other guy.

"Trooper?" William repeated. "Unusual name."

"Well, my name wa' Cropper when I's young, but my little sister, Joanna, couldn't say it. She said 'Twoopo.' It was cute, so's everybody b'gun saying that and it turned to Trooper."

"Pretty neat story," I said as Louis and I shook hands. He had a "dead fish" handshake but he looked right into my eyes. I'll need to watch this guy, I chuckled to myself.

"Sit down," Trooper said as he pushed out a chair with his foot.

I laid my hat on the floor by my feet and sat. I took my Bull Durham makings out of my shirt pocket and rolled a cigarette with one hand, making sure that they could see the stub of my cut-off thumb and my crippled arm to let them know how tough

I was. Then I put the stogy between my lips at the corner of my mouth, struck a match on my canine tooth, like Dad did, and touched the flame to the stogy. I drew the smoke deeply into my lungs to confirm my toughness and then exhaled with a cough that revealed my pretense.

They laughed, and then we sat talking about our families and ourselves. I told them about my fights and how I got my thumb cut off and how I didn't even cry.

"Looks like you is tough," Trooper smiled.

"Yeah, that's what they say. By the way," I said, "My name is William, but some people just call me Bill." They didn't say anything, so I continued, "I rode the train over this morning to get a car," and then I waited again. They just sat and smoked and didn't seem to care much about my new car. "Do you have an idea where I could get a good deal on a good car around here?"

Trooper asked, "How much you got to spend?"

"After I pay for the cheeseburger and coffee, about a hundert," I told him.

Trooper raised his eyebrows.

"Well, I got another five from a nice old lady."

Trooper rubbed his chin with his large hand. "You probably needs twice that much to get anything good."

My heart dropped, and a soft feeling of lighting went up my spine and bounced around in my mouth and head. It carried with it a slight taste of sulfur, but the kind that comes from disappointment rather than terror. I'm not dead yet, I silently tried to encourage myself.

"Hey," Trooper volunteered, "let's run 'round to some a-them lots in my car and jis see." He went on, "I even knows some a the owners, I kin acks some a 'em."

"That's great Trooper," I said, and walked to the counter to tell Victoria.

"All right then," she said. "I want to do some shopping anyway. I need some girl things. I'll just meet you here later."

The doors to Trooper's big red Cadillac were unlocked. I opened the back door. The big car had red leather seats that were clean and polished. In fact, the entire car was polished and clean. "This is different than my family's cars, where it's usually hard to find room to get in because of the junk," I said.

"Ain't got much else. We lives over by the tracks; not too nice over there."

"It's so clean and nice." I looked at him and winked. "Want to sell it?"

"I'd rather sell one of my kids," he said and winked back.

After visiting some car lots, I could see there were no cars for sale that I could afford, not even old wrecks. One salesman said, "We just sends those kinds of old cars to the junk for whatever we kin get."

"Hell, Trooper," I said, "guess I'll just go back home."

"That's too bad."

We sat in silence for a while as I tried to talk myself into giving up and going back to Eden.

"When you're ready, I'll take you to the train depot," Trooper said.

I was so depressed, I felt almost as if my life was over. I knew I wouldn't ever get a car.

Chapter 102

"How are you doing, William? Are you having fun, you bastard?" The words come with their usual sharpness. Alex Stanze has returned to taunt me, and once again is enjoying it too much to suit me. I still haven't discovered the reason for his anger. I need to keep looking; if only he would leave me in peace. I force my body into a sitting position.

I look in his direction for a quick moment and then lie down on the decrepit pallet and turn my back toward the door.

"Sleep well, William, I'll be back soon to see you die," Alex shouts in his hoarse whisper and the sound of his crippled footsteps fades slowly into silence.

Everything I have witnessed in my vivid excursions has only reinforced my opinion that Alex and his brother or brothers are the ones who murdered the little boys.

Why does he feel so strongly I had something to do with it? I need to go on with my journey, but I also need to stop wondering so much. I need to concentrate—I need to recall more about my past.

Again I wait for the moment, and when it arrives I catch it, as I have learned to do, and begin dissolving once more into the familiar, virtual past.

Chapter 103

The three of us sat in Trooper's car for a long while, me struggling with my disappointment and Victoria and Trooper watching the people walk past on the sidewalk. We all sat in silence. Finally, I remembered what Mom had said about feeling sorry for oneself: "You can do it for a while—everyone is entitled to feel sorry for a while—but then get over it."

I pulled myself together and said, "I'm not dead yet. If I can't have a car, then I might as well have me some cowboy boots." We all laughed, relieved that I was coming out of my depressed state. I told them how I had always wanted to have a pair of real cowboy boots, like the ones my friend Colt had.

There was a glint of humor in Trooper's voice, as he asked, "What the hell is, 'I'm not dead yet?'"

I told him about the bananas and my mother. "I'll have to remember that," he laughed. "I know a place that sells used boots and shoes," he added. "Want to go look?"

"Sure."

To make a long story short, I couldn't find any red boots, but I did find a pair of slightly used and slightly small yellow boots, and bought them. The man placed my loafers in the boot-box and tied it with a piece of orange twine. It came to $3.52, including that shameful Washington tax. I peeled off four one-dollar bills, and put the change in my front pocket. When we stepped out onto the sidewalk, I had the yellow boots on my feet and the shoebox with my loafers under my arm.

"I can't wait to show Colt my boots, Trooper, but I really hate going home without a car."

"I knows." He frowned.

As we walked along, I couldn't help looking at the reflection of my boots in the storefront windows. The boots and I looked great—like a real cowboy. "Have any more ideas about a car?" I asked, still watching the yellow boots.

"A friend a mine got a good car and cheap over in Missoula."

"There's no way I can get to Missoula tonight."

"The Great Northern goes there." He craned his neck to see what I was watching in the windows, and then he smiled. "Them boots looks good. I would be proud ta take ya to the station."

"When does the train leave?" I asked.

He thought for a moment. "Tomorrow just after noon. Too late ta get it taday."

"Hell, Trooper, I'll spend all my money getting a hotel room and something to eat."

"Ya's welcome ta stay with me. I owes ya sumpin' anyway fer the tire and all."

"What would your family say? I'm white, ya know."

"Yeah, but yer a good white."

"Dad would be furious," I laughed.

"Wha'd ya'think?" he nagged.

"Dad would really be furious," I repeated. "Hell, yes, let's do it. And you'll bring us back here tomorrow for the train?"

"Yep, whenever youse ready. My house ain't much, but you'll be welcome."

Chapter 104

Trooper hadn't lied; his house wasn't much. It was a few miles from the city and just across the bumpy, shattered, creosote-soaked timbers that had been laid in between the tracks to make getting across the almost-abandoned crossing a little less treacherous. Trooper slowed and carefully drove across and then pulled the big red car into the dirt driveway of a decrepit shanty snuggled in between the railroad tracks and a large, cluttered salvage yard. An odor similar to that of the city proper was carried about in a dusty mist from the road and accented by the smoke from fires that burned constantly in the trash and debris surrounding the little shacks that dotted the landscape.

At the salvage yard next door, a gigantic, noisy machine inside a partially fenced yard was picking up entire cars and positioning them onto a conveyor next to a large concrete bin. As the machine puffed out billows of gray smoke, the conveyor carried the car to a position under a tremendously heavy-looking lid. With a loud bang and crunching sound, the lid would drop down and squash the car flat. Then the heavy lid would be raised and a multicolored square block of crushed metal that had previously been the car would be lifted by the noisy machine onto the flatbed of a large Lowboy truck.

The entire area was steeped in poverty: the storage buildings, long-ago failed businesses, and shacks were all in shambles. A few black children played around the shacks and among the trash and old abandoned cars, which were set up on blocks.

All sorts of discarded furniture and appliances lay about in disarray. Men and women, mostly old, sat on old chairs on the worn and weathered boards of covered porches or in the dirt of the grass-free yards, watching us with vacancy and dejection in their eyes.

Even the faces of the more excited youths were filled with the masked desperation of accepted poverty. They watched the three of us with apprehension, but also with suppressed excitement, maybe wondering what reason there could be for bringing a young white boy and girl into their area.

"Well, this is it," Trooper announced.

I said, more to Victoria than to him, "Sure ain't much."

"Sure ain't much is right," she said.

Trooper echoed, "Sure ain't much."

A nice-looking black woman stood on the dilapidated porch holding a small child on her hip, trying unsuccessfully to control two older children who vied for her attention. The boys, both of middle grade-school age, milled excitedly around her bare feet, watching us anxiously. They were all dressed in patched but clean clothing, The smallest child, on the mother's hip, had a column of light green phlegm running from its nose.

"My God, woman," Trooper exclaimed, "wipe off that kid's nose."

The woman looked down and then with a routine motion, took the caterpillar column between her thumb and forefinger of her free hand, pinched it off, and then flung it to the ground, as if she were trying to assassinate it. She wiped her fingers on the side of her dress.

Satisfied with his wife's obedience, Trooper said, "Well, William, it ain't so bad here after quitting time, when the noise all stops. I wants ya ta meet the family. Matilda, this here's William. He heped me get my tire fixed; he's a good white."

Matilda held out the same hand that had removed the green caterpillar. "Howdy, William," she offered.

Hell, I didn't want to touch her hand, but I did—guardedly. "Hi Matilda. This is Victoria." Matilda welcomed Victoria by raising her eyebrows.

"Come on in, dinner's bout ready. We's havin' grits, chitlins, and fried chicken."

"Sounds good, but what about watermelon?" I smiled.

Matilda smiled, and seemed to take this comment as rhetorical.

The two kids stayed wound around Matilda's legs. She walked, hobbled, and dragged them inside while holding the baby gingerly, and we followed. The less-than-modern kitchen was almost filled with a large homemade table and a collection of fragile-looking and mismatched chairs held together with string and bailing wire. The furnishings seemed to be in mortal conflict over the meager space. A fancy but ancient kitchen stove with a warming oven above and a reservoir to keep water hot tried its best to peek through the clutter. A piece of timber stuck out of the open front, its burning end seemingly safe enough within the confines of the stove, but it still looked a bit dangerous.

"Looks like that keeps Trooper from having to chop wood," I said. "Hell, just burn it off and then push it in for more heat. Ingenious."

"I'll bet the fire wards off the stubborn edges of winter that linger after the sun goes down, at least long enough to get them all into bed," Victoria said.

I was stunned. "My God, Victoria, you're beginning to talk like me."

"Well, I am a part of you."

Two stand-alone, homemade cabinets occupied one wall alongside shelves cluttered with food, pots, and pans. The sink was filled with dirty dishes and more pots and pans, but the room lacked the stench that usually accompanies this sort of disarray and clutter. It had little odor of its own, or maybe just a hint of the cleanliness that scrubbing and care creates, without the partial masking effect of a strong cleaning product.

"Sit over on the couch," Trooper said and pointed to the large piece of furniture that was covered with a clean patchwork quilt.

I obeyed, taking Victoria along. Trooper smiled as the two children cautiously approached, like new puppies might do, a mixture of caution and admiration fixed on their youthful, dirty faces.

Finally, their fear gave way to curiosity and the oldest came close, smiled, and then climbed up on my lap.

"He likes you," Trooper said. "His name is Amos, after my father."

"Hi, Amos," I said as he tried to hide his embarrassment by pushing his face against my side. I felt the tight curls of his kinky hair; they had an unusual feel. He had a clean, childlike smell.

"Kids and dogs kin tell good people." Trooper smiled as he lounged on a chair that leaned against the wall.

"Well, I have special feeling for kids," I said.

Amos didn't have the darkness of his father. He favored his mom with lighter, almost olive skin and much lighter hair. Almost as if starving for attention, he clung to me. The other boy, the younger one, finally was secure enough to come over and sit between Victoria and me. He leaned over against my side and we sat uncomfortably, as new acquaintants do.

Matilda, holding the infant with the runny nose, put the finishing touches on our dinner and tried unsuccessfully to get Trooper to emulate her interest in getting the meal done and on the table.

"The boys sure seem to favor men over women," I said.

"They's always been like that. It will all change when they's older," Trooper said. "His name is Andy."

"Hey, just like the radio program, Amos and Andy."

"Yeah, didn't ever intend it ta be that's way. Guess we jus never thought about it. But it's done now, and it'll be all right."

"Guess he doesn't like you," I said, kidding Victoria as I placed my arm around Andy's shoulders.

"Girls usually like me more than boys do," she said.

"Well, I don't know, I'm a boy," I replied, and she smiled.

Andy was darker than Amos and his hair was darker as well, like his father. And he was as cute as a spotted puppy and as cuddly, too—they both were. With the highchair pushed up to the small table and the five of us, there wasn't a place for Victoria, so I invited her to sit on my knee. Hell, I liked it that way. I liked being close to her.

"You don't look too comfortable that'a way, William." Trooper said, "with yer leg spread out like that."

"It's okay," I said, "I don't mind. she's like a part of me."

"Yeah, guess she is a part a you, all right. A knee's 'bout as much a part as anything."

"We'll just eat from the same plate," I said.

Trooper shook his head and smiled.

Dinner was good, maybe partly because I was so hungry, and before long with the two of us working on our plate, the food was gone, and we dipped out more and ate that, too. I was afraid of hurting Matilda's feelings by asking what chitlins were, so I didn't ask—we just ate.

After dinner, Trooper and I sat on the porch, while Victoria and Matilda put the kids to bed and worked on the dirty dishes. I was tired, but I wanted Trooper to give in first. I wanted to show him how tough I really was.

Finally Trooper gave in. "Well, Bill, let's get some sleep. I'll show ya yer room."

"Sounds good to me," I said with a yawn.

My room was the back bedroom, with a double bed for Victoria and me. It was small like the one at the sheep ranch, but I liked being close to my girl. I lay well into the night listening to her breathe as she slept, and planning for tomorrow—and well, really, for the rest of our lives. Finally, sleep came. I wasn't conscious of it, but all at once I was in a dream. It was one of those dreams that seem real, yet you still know it's a dream.

Chapter 105

Morning came with bright sunlight bursting through the tattered white blinds and the car-crushing machine shaking the fragile house as it smashed the variously sized cars into uniform shapes. With that, the events of the previous day came rushing in. I sat up, rubbed my eyes and shook Victoria awake.

"What time is it?" she asked.

"It's late. The sun is high. We need to get going," I said, trying to be patient.

We took turns in the bathroom. As we came into the kitchen, Trooper sat at the table toying with a cup of coffee. The room was a little less depressing and looked a lot richer with the sunlight flooding in.

"Sleep good?" he asked.

"Yeah, we slept good, nice bed. It's narrow but the springs are really good."

Matilda was still holding the baby like it was part of her hip. The kids, Amos and Andy, sat in their chairs with semi-controlled anticipation on their faces, waiting for Victoria and me to join them for breakfast. Trooper went to the stove and brought a large steaming pot filled with some sort of porridge and began dipping it into the bowls.

"Hope ya likes yer mush, William."

"We'll just eat out'a one bowl." I said.

'Yeah, I'm getting used to you," he said.

With milk from a pitcher and plenty of sugar, toast, and coffee, breakfast was pretty good. I didn't ask what it was, but it tasted like Mom's whole-wheat cereal. Victoria didn't drink coffee; maybe she had picked that up from Mom. After breakfast, I decided to sit on the porch and smoke a cigarette and wait for Trooper to get dressed while Matilda and Victoria cleaned up the breakfast dishes. Amos and Andy played in the front yard, each one trying to do more and more dangerous stunts to get my attention and approval.

Trooper decided to go get some gas for the car. "I'll be right back; keep a eye on those kids," he smiled out the window as he backed out of the driveway and vanished in the dust of the road.

I rolled a stogy, lifting my eyes occasionally to check on Amos and Andy. I lit it and leaned back. Like a comfortable old friend, the smoke bit into my lungs and made me aware that I was alive and that maybe today, I would find my new car. I wanted Victoria to be done with the dishes and Trooper to be back so we could get to the Great Northern Station. But I liked my new friends. I liked them a lot; they made me feel welcome and comfortable, more than most whites did.

The boys ran around between stacks of worn-out tires and cars set up on blocks, and every now and then they glanced at me to make sure I was still watching. I moved my gaze to the sky. The clouds were beginning to fill in. "Cumulous," I muttered. I guess I had learned at least a little bit at school, at least on the day they talked about cumulous clouds. "They's storm clouds," I told myself, trying to imitate Trooper or Dad, and also like I was trying to teach myself something that I already knew, maybe like a philosopher.

"Missa William!" Amos screeched. "Come hep me gets Andy outer that there fridge."

"Is he caught?"

"He's caught. I cain't get the door ta open. It usually opens."

After the third try the door came open, and Andy stood there smiling like we were playing a game. "Hell, Andy, you could have suffocated in there. Don't do that anymore, okay?"

But they had run off and were chasing each other around a pile of tires, not much interested in what I had to say.

"Damned kids," I cussed. I stood for a moment just watching them. They were having a great time; they really liked each other. "They're about like white kids. Dad's wrong. I think they do have feelings, just like we do, and maybe they're smart, too."

I walked around the junky yard, found some old electric wire and tied each upright fridge shut. Then I went back to the porch, sat, and rolled myself another nice fat cigarette, lit it, and went back to thinking about my car. It was a nice, sleek black Mercury, a '49. It was leaded-in, lowered, chopped and channeled, and had twin mufflers; it was beautiful. That was the car I wanted.

"Missa William," Andy said, "I can't find Amos anywhere. I can't look in the fridges. They's all tied shut, so he ain't there, and he ain't inside the tires nowheres neither. I don't know where he be."

"Go look in the house," I said.

Andy raced inside, smiling now that he thought he had Amos to rights. Before long, he was back out. "Ain't in there. We cain't find him nowheres." Matilda, almost in tears, still held the nameless baby on her hip as she came out on the porch.

Victoria was almost in tears as well. "We can't find him," they said as one voice.

"There he is," Andy screamed, and pointed at the sky.

The demolition machine held a car in its claws and was moving it over to the crusher. Amos was waving from the window and crying. I threw down my cigarette and ran as fast as I could toward the noisy machine, waving my arms frantically and screaming at the operator, but he couldn't hear me over the noise, and he was looking the other way.

The machine sat the car on the conveyor and straightened it. The car began moving toward the crusher. "Jump out, Amos," I yelled, but he couldn't hear me. I ran toward the moving conveyor, jumped up and looked inside the car. His left leg was stuck between the seat and the door. He was crying softly, trying to be brave. Even with both of us pulling on his leg, it wouldn't come free. I imagined him being smashed flat and becoming part of the car. I wanted to leave but couldn't just abandon Amos. He looked terrified. The car was nearly to the concrete crypt. We were both going to be smashed and it would probably cut me in half first.

I pulled myself through the window of the car—maybe I could get him free if I was closer. I pulled and pulled. Amos was crying harder now. "Hep me, please," he begged.

Finally, I found the trip-lever for the seat and pulled, moving it back a little. Amos's leg came free. I picked him up, threw him out the window, and then followed, almost as if we were one bundle. We rolled down the concrete side. I looked up to see the car vanish, as the huge device fell onto it with a loud crunch.

We lay scratched and bleeding from superficial wounds. I picked Amos up. He hugged my neck, his small body shaking as he sobbed and slobbered, his snot running onto my neck and shirt collar. Trying to comfort him, I began walking slowly toward the house. My head was spinning from the excitement and exertion.

Trooper, who had just returned from the gas station, ran with Matilda, Andy, and Victoria across the dusty lot toward us. "William," Trooper yelled, "you shore as hell done saved that boy's life. I owes you a debt that I won't never be able ta pay." There were tears in the big man's eyes. He took Amos and held him in one arm as he tried to hug me with the other. Matilda and Victoria crowded in and trying to hug us as well.

"You don't owe me nothing, Trooper. We're just friends. You'd do the same for me. I know you would."

We sat on the porch, unwinding and talking about the almost-fatal incident and now laughing about it. I knew I would miss them a lot when we left, but life goes on—a phrase that had extra meaning to me now when I thought about Amos. "Hell, I guess I'm not all bad," I thought. "Not if I can save the life of some little boy. I'm sure as hell not all bad."

Even so, my thoughts quickly returned to my real quest. "You know, it's getting late and I want to catch that train to Missoula," I said. "We need to get going."

We said our goodbyes to Matilda, and the kids, our newfound friends, and left with Trooper for the Great Northern Depot.

Chapter 106

Trooper drove right up to the depot. He and Victoria waited in the car while I ran to get our tickets.

"Be nice to have them talk for a minute, let them get better acquainted," I said to myself.

I held up two fingers. "One way to Missoula," I told the agent.

"Better hurry, Tex, the train is leaving. You got about three minutes," the ticket agent said as he began fiddling with stamps and tickets. "Not coming back?" he asked with obvious unconcern as he wrote something on the voucher and then stamped down hard with a large silver stamp. He passed the voucher through the window to me.

"I'm getting a car," I told him.

"Hey, that's great," he said. "I can remember my first car, it was a ..."

"Hey, I need to get my bag and my girl. I'll drive over in my new car and talk to you sometime," I told him.

"Could be the same thing, you know—your bag and your girl," he said, and laughed. As I ran toward Trooper's car, I thought, I shouldn't have told him it was a bag. It's a box. But there wasn't time. And he would probably have some crude remark about a box, as well.

"The train's leavin'," I yelled. "We need to run to make it." Then, for no reason I was aware of, I said, "I'm not dead yet."

"You shore as hell ain't dead yet and I ain't neither," Trooper replied, winking at me. We shook hands. "Good luck," he said.

"Come over and see me in Eden."

"Not a good idea, Bill. Them small towns don't specially cotton to us black folks."

"To hell with them. Ask for me in the Bucket of Blood. It's a bar, the only bar in town. They'll tell ya where I live." I reached my hand out again and caressed his arm. He felt like a friend; a real friend.

"Don't count on it, but maybe." He covered my hand with his huge one in a tender gesture.

I picked up the box with my loafers and pushed it up under my arm. With the other, I took Victoria's hand and pulled her along as I ran toward the train, all the while looking down to see my new boots as I ran. They looked great. The train began to move as we got to it. The conductor held the handrail, leaning out and yelling for us to hurry. He grabbed my hand and rushed us up the steps and into the coach. I pulled Victoria up the stairs behind me and onto the train.

There were only a few seats left and no window seats at all. I noticed the familiar smell that coaches always have. Not a bad smell, not like the depot in Spokane, but maybe a distant relative, although covered by a soft fragrance, like something cooking or just beginning to rot. We walked ahead to the first vacant seat. "You sit here," I told Victoria. "I guess we'll just have to sit alone 'til we get to Missoula."

"I'll miss you," she said.

"I'll miss you, too," I said, squeezing her hand. Then I walked ahead to find a seat for myself.

Finally, I saw an empty one. I would rather have had the window, but an old Mexican- looking fellow was sitting there. He looked at me and nodded. I returned his courtesy, dropped the shoebox onto the floor and sat down. He held a large black cowboy hat in his lap. I removed my own large hat and laid it on my lap. He was looking out the window and I took in what I could see on either side of his head, and then we both sat quietly, as if hypnotized by the motion of the train, the passing scenery, and the wheels clicking against the track. Outside the windows were tall, thin, pine trees and small, blue lakes and cars traveling along the road.

"Looks like everybody has a car except me," I mumbled, feeling a little sorry for myself.

The Mexican looked at me, smiled, and then turned back to look out the window.

He looked to be of medium size, with leathery, sun-and-wind-burned skin on his hands and the part of his face and neck that hadn't been protected by his long, graying hair. Brown eyes and dark brows complemented his clean-shaven, ruggedly handsome face.

The thin, perfectly sculpted lips rarely hid two rows of straight, white teeth from his frequent smile. He wore the clothes of a cowboy, which bore the strong influence of a Mexican Vaquero.

We rode silently for a time, and then he asked, "Do you ride the train a lot?"

His voice carried no sign of the Spanish or Mexican accent I had expected.

"Yes, every time I get the chance," I said, a little suspicious of his perfect English.

His legs were extended and I admired his round-toed, expensive-looking cowboy boots.

I pushed my own yellow boots out so they could be more easily seen, but as my bare legs were visible above the tops, because of my too-short Levis, I quickly pulled them back under the edge of the seat.

"What about you?" I returned, so as not to seem disinterested.

"I have had a lot of train rides ..." He paused. I tried my best to look interested and he went on. "But my first train ride was when I was very young."

"Is that right?"

"Oh," he said, "my name is Tom. Or, actually, Thomas Jose Ualdo Lopez James Andersen."

I couldn't hold back the grin as he rattled off his long name. As we shook hands, I told him my name, a little embarrassed that William Robert Jones III was so unimpressive in comparison. Tom began telling me the story of his first train ride, in a way that suggested he had told it many times before. He seemed to take comfort in telling someone—anyone.

"One day," he began, "my mother asked me to go to my sister's place and help her. My sister's name was Susan."

"Sounds pretty boring."

He stopped and looked out the window. After a while, he went on, his voice awakening me from thoughts of the car I hadn't yet gotten.

"My sister's new husband had gone to tend to the lambing of a sheep, and she, too, was going to have a baby soon."

"What the hell?"

"Of course, I told my mother that I would go," he continued. Almost as an afterthought, he said, "My mother was thin and had dark hair. Her name was Mary. Dad was big and strong, and he had blond hair. Everybody called him Thomas, but I called him Daddy." The last part came out as if he was dreaming about something he remembered from long ago.

"Oh?" I smiled. "Daddy? That's pretty special."

"Well, yeah, he was Daddy when I was young," he eyed me defiantly and went on.

"We lived on a little farm with animals of all kinds. Mom kept a garden and worked in it often. She cooked and sewed and helped Dad with the chores around the farm." He stopped and smiled, "Well, I guess all of us helped."

"Oh," I answered with little interest.

"I had three sisters, including Susan, and three brothers. They had light hair like Dad. Just me and Susan were dark."

"Oh," I said, and turned away in the seat to discourage his talking. It didn't work.

"We did a lot of things together," he said. "I miss them all." A tear was forming in his eye.

I better try to listen, I thought, just like I had decided to do for the old man in Hope.

"Mom tried to teach us all to read and write and to play some sort of music and to sing. We sang a lot. I didn't want to play the piano."

"I know what you mean. I didn't either. Hell, I didn't even want to play the guitar or dance either, but I did. Well, sort of."

He went on like he hadn't heard me; like I hadn't said anything. "Momma said because we lived in America, we should speak American. One week she would teach us a big English word and the next week, she worked on helping us understand what it meant, and then when we did, she taught us another one and its meaning."

"Just like my Mom," I said, but he didn't hear me again.

"Dad tried to get us to learn Spanish. He seemed to think that anything you learned was somehow good."

"Oh, that's nice," I said, and then thought, what the hell; he doesn't listen to me anyway. I looked at my new boots, which were beginning to hurt. I can't wait until they're broken in, I thought. I'll bet Colt will be surprised when he sees them.

"I wish I had learned Spanish," he said.

I was trying to listen to Thomas, to develop some kind of interest in his story, but I desperately wanted to think about what my new car might look like and the adventures it and I would share.

"Hey, Bill, do you understand what I'm saying?"

"I'm not dead yet," I said, because I didn't know what else to say.

"What the hell does that mean?"

Our conversation got a little more interesting as I related the incident about the bananas, but then when I finished he just said, "Oh," and went on with *his* story.

I'll teach you to be so damned rude, I thought. Not even interested in a *good* story. I slipped into one of my sublime adventures, to get away from his, and maybe to punish him a little for his thoughtlessness.

"Ticket?" the conductor asked, startling me out of my thoughts before I was able to finish feeling sorry for myself. I handed him the ticket. "These are for me and that blond back there." I motioned toward Victoria.

He turned and looked toward Victoria. "Whatever."

Tom was still talking. He hadn't stopped even while the conductor was there. I needed to get away, to think about something else. "Maybe I'll go to the john, Tom."

Before I could leave, he nudged me. "Want a cheroot?"

Before I could answer, he reached into his inside pocket and took out a couple of black, twisted cigars. I had never denied myself the opportunity to acquire a new bad habit and even though I didn't have the foggiest idea what they were, I said, "Sure. Haven't had one in a while."

I lit it and began dragging on my newfound vice, and he lit up, as well. The train had slowed to a crawl as it made its way up the steep grade, winding in and out of chiseled-out rock cliffs. The terrain leveled off, and there were thick groves of trees for a while, and then more steep tracks and rocky cliffs. We sat smoking our cheroots together for a time, just looking out the window, at the interesting and—to tell the truth—somewhat frightening scenery. After we became accustomed to the dramatic view, he went on with his story.

"My mother made a sack lunch and helped put the bridle on Sandy, the old workhorse. Then with me on that big horse and Spatcher following along behind, we began our trip along the dusty, little-used road to my sister's place." The story was getting more interesting now, and I was able to forget about the car and stay beside him in the coach. "After a while, we stopped to eat lunch in the shade of a tree, next to a small, cool stream. There wasn't enough food for me and my dog, so I just threw him the crumbs and as we were getting ready to leave, his eyes got wide and excitement illuminated his face. Then, I heard it, too: a strange sound in the distance, and when I stood and looked I saw, chugging along the tracks, a big black steam engine, pulling a few boxcars and a caboose. The train slowed down and then came to a stop, and a man from the caboose walked along opening the doors of the boxcars. Mexican people climbed out and began building fires and cooking. Soon, I could smell it."

I took another long drag on my cheroot and waited for more. The Mexican cigar was strong. I coughed and, holding back a gag, held it up and sagely nodded my approval.

Tom went on, "My dog broke loose and ran to the Mexicans. They were just finishing their meal and starting to get back into the boxcars. Spatcher ran from one to another, enjoying the human company in true Border Collie fashion."

He paused and took a long drag on his black cigar, drew the smoke into his lungs, held it for a moment, and then blew it out. The strong, ill-smelling, blue haze completely engulfed the head of the man sitting directly in front of Tom. The man turned, looking through the blue cloud, a scowl of disapproval on his face. I turned my hands out and shrugged my shoulders to show my own bewilderment at Thomas's thoughtlessness.

"Hey, sorry. I'll be more careful next time," Tom groveled.

The man said, "That's okay. Maybe you can get a job as a conductor, insulting and demeaning the passengers." He winked at me as if to say, "The dumb Mexican doesn't even get it."

Tom just said, "Okay, thanks."

The dumb Mexican doesn't even get it, I thought.

Tom went on with his story. "A large black man picked up the dog and threw it into the moving boxcar and then climbed in himself." Now the man in front had turned in his seat and was listening, too.

Tom smiled and divided his attention between the two of us. He was a ham, for sure. "I ran to the train and ran alongside, yelling and trying to get the black man to throw Spatcher off. One of the train crew, the guy who rode in the caboose, had been in the woods and was now running toward the end of the train. He picked me up and tossed me through the open door and onto the train."

The story was beginning to be more interesting and I was able to be a more attentive audience for Tom, even though I now shared the role. My smoke had finally grown short enough that I was able, in good conscience, to grind it out in the ashtray. It had left such a horrible taste in my mouth that Tom's story would just have to wait.

I excused myself and walked forward through the sliding, windowed door to the restroom. I filled one of the pointed paper cups with water and tried to wash the taste of the cheroot from my mouth, which helped a little.

"It will be a while before I smoke another one of those things," I muttered.

I looked at the tall, handsome cowboy in the mirror and nodded. He nodded in return. The water splashed as I emptied my bladder and flushed. I noticed that when the little door opened in the bottom of the toilet, everything just dropped onto the ties underneath the train, which I could see whizzing past. "I'll be damned," I said. "It all does just go out onto the tracks. I thought Victoria was just making that up. I'll think twice about walking the rails next time, and I sure as hell won't eat anything I find along the tracks." I flushed a couple of more times, just to get the feel of it. A strange and wonderful feeling flooded over me, and, as so often had happened, a window opened and I entered through it.

"*I couldn't stay away from you any longer, William.*"
"*It's nice to have you here. I need you.*"
"*The old lady I'm sitting with never shuts up, and she smells funny.*"

William laughed. "You ought to see what I have to put up with: an old man who tells bad stories."

"I know. I can hear him."

They both smiled; it was nice to be together. She came closer and as they kissed, William's hands found her breast. They had done it so many times that it was now routine, but it was always exciting. Each time was almost like the first time on the ditch banks in Springtown.

"What were you thinking about?" she asked as she pulled her dress off over her head.

"Just about you."

A while later, she purred, "It's always over too soon, isn't it?"

"Yes, it is, and it's your fault," he kidded. "I have to do all the work."

"We better get back to our seats."

"You're right," he said.

She smiled and touched his arm.

"Hey, did you fall asleep in there?" Someone was banging on the door.

I stood and went to the sink, washed my hands, nodded to the cowboy in the mirror, threw the paper towel into the toilet and watched as it flushed onto the tracks below. "I still can't believe it just goes out onto the ties," I muttered to Victoria.

"Seems disgusting."

"Hi," I said, as we walked by the guy who had banged on the door. "Sorry we took so long." I winked at him.

He just shook his head and said, "Jerk," and then went inside.

Tom was napping when I got to my seat. I smiled a goodbye to Victoria and watched until she was in her seat. Then I carefully sat down.

I saw the conductor walking toward me holding the edges of the seats as the gentle swaying of the train tried to dislodge him. "It looks like he's punched all the new passengers," I thought. As he passed I asked, "Hey, sir, would you happen to have some writing paper, a pencil, and a dictionary?" He looked at me with what seemed to be complete disgust, the way Grandma Jones looked at me when she was alive. I always felt guilty about being glad she had died—but I was still glad.

"I'll bring some paper in a minute." His glare seemed to linger, to sustain the disgust I was sure he felt for me.

My school years had taught me something about dealing with anxiety and my feelings. I had always wanted to be a writer, although I have no idea why. Nobody else in my family was a writer, and I didn't know anybody who was. Maybe I had been impressed by a writer in a movie. God knows I saw enough of them, but if that was the case, I couldn't remember which movie it was. For a time, I had thought about people who write stories or poems. It seemed to me they were just writing down their daydreams or thoughts.

I could do that, too, I thought, if I just knew how to spell and punctuate. I had tried to use the dictionary to spell words but had difficulty in spelling them closely enough to find them in the volumes of words and secret, coded messages there. Maybe, I mused, I'll write a poem. I can use all little words in a poem, and I've heard it's not necessary to be too formal or grammatically correct with poetry. Or better yet, I'll just do it in my head and then write it down later, after I've gone back to school and learned how to spell and punctuate a little better.

"Here," the conductor said, and handed me a short pencil with an eraser, a ruled writing tablet, and a pocket dictionary.

"Thanks," I said.

He walked down the aisle.

"Now, what to write about?" I remembered sitting in the back of the classroom, playing solitaire with a small deck of cards with pictures of naked girls on the back. During literature class, I thought I heard my teacher say, "You can get away with murder with poetry. It's okay to misspell and to use words that don't rhyme." It was something like that, I thought. I had opened a book one day, possibly during that same year, and noticed that the poems were all sort of lined up, and then there would be a few rows of writing, and then a space, and then more writing.

Maybe I will make mine look something like that, I encouraged myself. Like with anything, it seemed that the hardest thing was just to get started. Maybe Dale, I thought. Maybe I'll write a poem about Dale.

When Dale was real young, we played tetherball and if he ever beat me, I would beat him up. There were a lot of interesting things concerning Dale to write about. He said he was going to get even someday for the beatings but, shit, he couldn't do nothin'—he was just my little cousin. And he was a fisherman and had very large ears and most important, he was afraid of me.

"Well, here goes," I said to myself and began to write.

A Fish's Tale

A Pome by William R. Jones III
"Down by the crick, in the shade of a pine
Stood a small boy, with his fish pole and line.
The fish were heeped hi, on the yellow clay bank,
The day was shore hot, for already they stank.
The boy had no shoes, of a shurt there's no sign
But he kept rite on holden, his fish pole and line.
His long yellow hair hang down his full lenth
I think he could fly, if his ears had the strenth.
His blue jeans were tatered and tore, I could see.
I thouht as I spied him, "whose boy can this be?"

And then as he turned, with the graise of a sale,
I knew who it was, twas that good hearted Dale.
He waved as he saw me, his lipes showed a grin
That seamed to streach from his ears to his chin.
As I walked on to meet him, I herd the boy jest,
"The one that got away, was by far the best."

    Well, that wasn't so hard, I thought, and it's pretty good, too. I read it out loud a couple of times. I can't wait to show that to Dale. I'll bet he likes that as much as I do. It doesn't quite rhyme, but then again poems don't need to, I reasoned. I looked up and winked at the cowboy with the large green hat in the window. He winked back. That's a good omen, I thought.

    The poem seemed to have a point and it flowed pretty well and it seemed to me to be a lot like Longfellow or Poe would do and I had written a lot of words in just a little while. I was pleased. I'll work on it more later, I promised myself. Maybe I'll become a poet. This whole poetry thing is pretty easy and fun, too, and I think I'm sort of getting the hang of it. Plus, poets are probably rich.

    The conductor came walking down the aisle, swaying in time with the train as it followed its seemingly uncertain but actually fixed course. "Better give me back the dictionary before you forget," he said. "Most people just try to take anything that's not tied down. I lose more stuff that way."

    I reached to get the tattered book and handed it to him. "Hey, want to read my new poem?" I asked.

    His look was about like it was when he held my arm helping me onto the train, but he said, "What the hell. I don't have much to do anyway until we get to Missoula."

    He took the paper with the poem scribbled on it, slumped into the seat next to me and began reading. "Jesus," he said, "I thought you were using the dictionary. It doesn't make much sense to me, and the spelling is so bad, it's almost impossible to read or understand." He sat for another minute, as if thinking of something else he could say to insult me a little more, just like Dad and Grandma Jones always did. "If I was you, I'd go back to school and get some more learnin," he said sarcastically, and then he laughed out loud, gave me the conductor look, and disappeared down the aisle.

"Well, he was sort of nice for a little while," I mumbled, but I was hurt. "If he's so god-damned smart, the son of a bitch should be more than just a conductor," I said louder. I had spoken too loudly and now almost everyone on the train turned to see to whom I was talking, and then after seeing I was talking to myself, they all turned back. "If I hadn't promised God I wouldn't do it anymore, I'd make a Voodoo doll of the bastard and stick some pins in his ass."

Chapter 107

My new boots were beginning to hurt my feet. In fact, my feet were numb. I slipped the boots off with a great deal of effort, sighing in relief as each was removed. Holes were worn in the heels and toes of my socks, my toes were sticking out, and there was a horrible stench.

I carefully peeled off what was left of my socks. "Shit, I'm going to have to wash," I laughed softly.

My instep, my heel, and where the boots pinched my toes all looked red and blistery and the skin in some places was peeling off. I carefully took my loafers out of the box, replaced what was left of my socks on my feet and slipped on the more comfortable footwear.

To my chagrin, Tom stirred in his seat and then sat up, and after a short and thorough stretch, he said, "Hi. Guess I fell asleep. Sorry about that."

"That's okay," I said, "I kept myself occupied." I shot him a knowing smile, hoping this wouldn't encourage him to go back to his story. I wanted to think more about my car.

"Did I miss anything?"

"No. Just a lot of trees."

"What's that wretched smell?"

I tried to avoid the question, but he kept looking at me and then at my boots. "It's my boots."

"That's bad!"

Then he unceremoniously began his story again, turning his head away from the stench of the boots. The man in front of us looked around, trying to discover the source of the odor.

"The black man on to the train sort of took care of me. He spoke English and Spanish and helped me get through the following days."

"Oh. The unintentional kidnapping," I said.

"Sorry, are you up to speed?"

"I guess. Whatever that means."

"Finally, I was brought to a farm with some of the immigrant Mexican farm workers and taken in by the farmer and his family. I grew up there, although I also traveled around, trying to find my real family."

Outside the window, a river had appeared, moving gracefully from one side of the wide valley to the other, in harmony with an occasional bridge. The river was wide and ran slowly, but occasionally it narrowed and ran in swift rapids over rocks and logs before becoming calm and graceful again. There were fewer bridges here, probably because the valley was wider and land more accessible. The river had a much different personality than the one near Eden. Calmly drifting, this one seemed wise and thoughtful as it went. It was seldom in a hurry or in conflict with its environment. Even the mountains and the sky appeared more friendly and relaxed.

"I have traveled these railroads so much now that I've lost track of everything. Plus, the landmarks have changed with time and reconstruction," Tom said.

"I've finally had to come to terms with the fact that my mother and father have long since died, and I've had to give up on ever seeing them again. But it makes me feel good to ride the trains and look anyway. I've searched up and down the tracks and even had detectives search, but with no luck." He looked sad, and then he lowered his head and sat silently.

I had lost interest in his story again. It was getting pretty dull and the self-pity thing didn't help either, but I thought, "It could just be the way he tells it. He certainly has no imagination."

I began making plans to re-do his story. "After the car business had been completed," I promise myself, "I will see what I can do for him, for two reasons: first, because it's very sad about Tom being taken away from his family, and second, because it's almost as sad that he tells his story without imagination. He really needs help."

I tried to get my yellow boots into the old shoebox, but they were too big. Tom handed the piece of twine that had held the shoebox together to me. "Tie this to the pull-on straps," he said, "and you'll be able to carry the boots around your neck."

"Thanks."

He wrinkled his nose and took a newspaper from the pocket of the seat in front of him. *The Missoulian,* it said on the front page. He peeled off full pages, one at a time, and stuffed them into my boots. "That should ward off the stench a little bit."

"Thanks, I guess," I said, and thought, the arrogant bastard.

Tom began telling his story again, and I began trying to put the pieces together, as if the story were a jigsaw puzzle. I imagined what his mother might have looked like. I turned her slim body fat, which made her look funny and brought a smile to my face. Then I turned her slim again, and with an imaginary eraser and colored pencil, I blanked out her brown eyes and put in blue ones that were quite crossed. This new look made me laugh out loud. Then I added a beard, moustache, and glasses. Then I added a friend, to give me a witness to this almost unbearably funny creature. I began laughing hysterically.

"What's so funny?" Tom asked.

I hadn't realized I had cut into his story. "I was thinking about something else," I said. "Go on."

He did, and even though I had not been giving him my full

attention, I had picked up little pieces here and there. He talked about how his new foster father had no wife, but there was a woman who cooked and cared for him and how he had bonded with her youngest son, who was about his age and was somewhat of a free spirit. In some detail, he told of events during his foster childhood, and as his voice began to fade in my ears, my mind began creating a more interesting version of his wistful tale. In between adding beards and crossed eyes to imaginary people, I began transforming Tom's boring story into one that might have more substance and appeal.

The Story of Thomas and the Unintentional Kidnapping

A Western by William Q. Pencil

Chapter 1

* * * * * * *

Mary and Thomas Anderson said they had settled in this God-forsaken, desolate place, away from everyone else, because they wanted to raise the kind of children who would see people for who they really were, for what was inside them, not for what they looked like. They wanted their children to be real people. But that was a lie—they had settled there because they had no other choice.

Mary, from a wealthy Mexican family, had met Thomas, a poor Danish immigrant, during one of her family's frequent pleasure trips to the United States. Much to the disappointment of their families, the two fell in love and tried to gain their parents' consent. Mary's family was outraged; they thought she should consider a suitor who had some status and wealth as well as sharing her ethnic heritage. The Andersons were against Mexican in-laws, no matter their status or wealth. When the lovers ran away and married anyway, with a justice of the peace and not even a Christian ceremony and with strangers as witnesses, Mary was disinherited, and Thomas disowned.

A baby was on the way, and as neither Mary nor Thomas had money nor means, they were forced to settle in a place so desolate and rundown that no else wanted it. They squatted, as homesteading was called in those days. Mary was not accustomed to hard work, but she learned fast, and was soon baking bread, canning, and sewing with the best of frontier women. She learned to cook and make decent meals from almost no ingredients. With hard work and long hours, they were able to eke out a humble living from the cruel desert, and year-by-year they managed to raise their family.

One morning, Mary noticed a large black man sitting on a stump some distance down the road. He had been there all morning, just looking at his feet. Finally, Mary could withstand her curiosity no longer, and went to ask if he was in some sort of trouble. In a friendly manner, she invited him to the house for water and something to eat. He told her he was Just Plain Sam, a descendent of freed slaves who hadn't been able to find work, so he roamed around, taking whatever was offered here and there. Sam got along well with the Andersons, so he decided to stay on for a while, to work mostly for board and room with a little money thrown in from time to time for tobacco or a jug of spirits. Eventually, he became almost one of the family.

The cash crop for the Andersons was sheep, the only trade Thomas knew anything about. "With sheep ya have three crops," Tom would say, whenever there was occasion to talk about his farming. "Lambs, when not needed to build the herd, can be sold at auction, and their wool is shorn off once a year and sold, and old ewes and bucks are sold for meat or butchered for the family."

They raised rabbits and pigeons for food when needed, although most of the animals were pets that roamed loose around the ranch buildings. Stepping in animal droppings was as routine as breathing. Thomas kept bees. The honey was used as sweetener and to eat as candy. The Andersons kept milk cows and most of the traditional farm animals. Two large workhorses were used for plowing, harvesting, and for pulling the old wagon into town.

On Sundays, the family loaded into the wagon and traveled to town for church and supplies. Mary always had good things to eat as they traveled. It was a community church, and whatever pastor, priest, or bishop happened to be available was the one who conducted the service. Peace and harmony were abundant in that spiritual place.

Chapter 2

* * * * * * *

The Andersons were humble, honest, and hardworking pioneers, but they were as poor as outhouse rats, which was obvious from the look of the house and outbuildings. The roofs of all the buildings sagged and the walls were propped up from the inside with poles cut to length and wedged against the sides, to keep them from falling over. They all showed signs of many years of use, unskilled repair, and the devastating effects of weather and time.

Thomas tried to keep up with repairs, but with tending the sheep and doing the other chores, as well as his total lack of ability pertaining to carpentry, he didn't do it proficiently. But the outbuildings, propped up as they were, managed to serve their purpose for the family's minimal needs.

Almost everything they ate was grown on the farm. The vegetables came from a small fenced-in garden, which received southern exposure. There were also fruit and nut trees. A building set aside for butchering and processing meat had large hooks hanging from strategic locations and a large, homemade cooler dug deep into the ground, *with a dirt ramp going down to the thick wooden door. Any extra meat was sold to neighbors or in town. With hard work and creativity, the Andersons survived rather nicely, especially in comparison to others in the area.*

Occasionally, they would go to town to purchase something they couldn't make or grow, such as cloth for shirts or dresses, or coffee when they had the money. More often, Mary sewed their clothing from the patterned cloth of feed sacks that the store-bought feed came in.

Chapter 3

* * * * * * *

Mary never tired of telling stories or teaching the children to sing. She delighted in playing games and was the heart and soul of the family. She had never been sorry that she had married a poor Danish immigrant, but she had always felt bad about being disowned by her family, and at times, longed to see and talk to them and to have them meet her family.

Thomas and Mary brought seven children into the world. Six were raised, married, and had left home when young Thomas, their unplanned but warmly welcomed latecomer, was born. They chose to name him in honor of Thomas's father and himself, while adding the names of Mary's father and grandfather, her mother's father, and big Thomas's only brother, who lived in America. The child's name became Thomas Jose Ualdo Lopez James Andersen.

No friends were nearby for Thomas to play with, and he only briefly met or saw other kids his age on occasional trips to town for supplies or to attend church on Sunday. He was well-accustomed to playing by himself, or with his mother, or his dog Spatcher. But even at his age, there was little time for idle play. When Thomas was six, he could have been mistaken for seven or eight or because of his height, but then again, because of his young, innocent face, he might have passed for younger. He was well-built and his ill-kept, long, black hair fell forward to cover most of his face, hanging down in back over his copper-brown shoulders. He had taken a good share of his genes from his Mexican mother, and only a few from his Danish father.

By this time, Thomas and Mary were wondering more than ever about their own parents and siblings. They longed to know what had happened to them. For all they knew, everyone could be dead.

Chapter 4

* * * * *

Fall arrived early. It was almost too cold to lounge outside, but the Andersons were enjoying the evening, wrapped in sweaters and light blankets. It might be the year's last day for this luxury, and they languished in its glory. Thomas sat next to Mary and held her hand in a fashion that told of their long years together as they rocked and talked of things that married people talk about. The large black man, Sam, their friend of many years, sat on the top step. His years in slavery had taken a toll. He was free now, but the years of bondage still held him in a semi-comfortable bondage of his own choosing that didn't involve locks and chains.

A slight, cool breeze rustled the few leaves that remained on the trees, an occasional one falling to flutter erratically to the ground to be with its kind. This assurance of the coming of winter and the deep snow would soon be whipped by the frigid winds into piles so high that even the horses could scarcely break through. Young Thomas sat at his father's feet as he pushed a small block of wood around in the dirt, pretending it was a car by making a humming sound. He looked up suddenly at a sound behind the row of trees that led to the house, where he saw dust. He dropped the block car, stepped to the edge of the gravel roadway and stood in the sharp gravel. His bare feet, toughened by the long summer's use, seemed not to notice the sharpness of the rocks. He stood as a statue, a magnificent, nearly perfect figure accented by the long black hair.

A fancy carriage pulled by two fine horses emerged from behind the trees. A man in fine clothing and formal attire urged the team toward the porch, and then reined them to a halt in front of the house. T

he driver wrapped the reins around the brake handle and climbed down to open the carriage door. A tall and thin man, aged by time and living, stepped out, bending forward onto his cane. His hair was so white that no evidence of its original color remained. He turned, balancing on his cane, and raised his hand to help a woman down. She was full-bodied and handsome, with graying hair and fair, olive-colored, wrinkled skin. She appeared to be of the same vintage as the man. They acted and reacted comfortably toward each other, as if they knew one another's thoughts. They had been together for a while.

A black-and-white Border Collie rose up from its place on the porch at Mary's feet and, as that breed of dog does, it went to meet the new arrivals. Thomas and Mary stood to welcome the strangers.

The old man from the coach touched young Thomas on the head as he limped past. "Yer a fine lookin' boy. You surely are."

Thomas smiled and felt his head where the gnarled hand had been.

"Good day to you. Come and sit a spell and rest your weary bones," Mary invited.

"Good day to you as well," the old man said. "Don't

mind if we do. We're kinda tired. We bin travelin' for a spell."

"Tie the horses to the rail and come up, too," Thomas directed the driver as he motioned them to the porch chairs.

"I'll get some hot drinks," Mary said.

The old man smiled. "That will be great, we're chilled and thirsty." He stood for a moment looking at Thomas. "My name is Thomas Andersen."

Thomas hadn't recognized his own father. After the usual salutations and crying and hugging to the delight of everyone, the couple was invited to stay and to meet Susan, their only grandchild, who lived close by. They did so, but all too soon it was time to leave, before winter made the journey impossible. They promised to visit often and, armed with the addresses of the other grandchildren, they climbed into the coach and vanished into the dust of the road as suddenly as they had arrived. As soon as the dust had settled, Thomas was struck by the crushing reality that his family was gone.

Chapter 5

* * * * * * *

The mood was more pleasant at the Anderson place now. Thomas felt less like an orphan and Mary was happy for him, but now she longed more than ever for her own family. Even so, she had other things to worry about. Her daughter, Susan, was pregnant and was having complications. Susan's husband, John, had driven the sheep to winter pasture and was having difficulty getting back to help her. Mary told young Thomas to ride one of the workhorses to Susan's place and sit with her. He could do the chores and help cook until John got home.

Thomas had been to Susan's place many times but had never gone there alone. It made him feel grown-up that his mother had that much confidence in him, and in his most mature voice, he told her he was sure he could do it. Thomas had trouble eating because of his excitement. He put the bridle on Sandy, the workhorse, and then, using the fence that surrounded the vegetable garden as a ladder, he climbed on top of the huge, gentle beast.

Mary had packed a scant lunch, which she handed to young Thomas. Lovingly, she laid her hand on her young son's dangling leg. "Just stay on the trail and Sandy will *take you straight to Susan's house. Stay there for several days, until John comes home, and then ride back home."*

Thomas assured his mother that he would be all right. He knew the way. A strange, lonely feeling came over Mary as she watched him ride away. He turned to wave, and she almost called him back, but brushed away the feeling as nonsense. She waved and watched as the horse carried her youngest son down the dusty road, with Spatcher trotting along behind. Mary stood watching for a long time, even after they had gone from sight, even after the dust had completely settled. Then she sighed, turned, and bent to her work in the garden.

Spatcher ran through the sparse weeds and sagebrush that dotted the red clay, but stayed generally behind the big horse. The dog left occasionally to chase a marmot or chipmunk, not really wanting to catch it, but simply enjoying the chase. Now and then he would run along behind Sandy, nipping at the tufts of dust kicked up by the horse's huge hooves. Sandy seemed not to notice. Thomas longed to be at the cool stream ahead, and dug his heels into Sandy's huge sides, trying to get him to move faster. Oblivious to Thomas's desires, the horse simply plodded on in workhorse fashion. Thomas finally surrendered to this impasse, and became content to sit and watch the antics of the dog as it raced here and there.

A warm wind blew in gusts that not only dried the sweat from Thomas's body, but also dried the insides of his nose and throat. Spatcher now ran far ahead, and Thomas was sure the stream was near. In his mind's eye, he saw Spatcher there, splashing and drinking the cool water. He tested Sandy again for speed, with the same results as before, and then sat back to bide his time. The stream was close—Thomas could smell the wetness. As they crested a small hill, he saw Spatcher playing and jumping in *the water. Sandy still showed no sign of urgency, simply plodding along.*

Thomas could stand it no longer. He slid off and ran toward the stream. The water tasted sweet and wonderful. He drank, and then sat in a deep hole, ducking his head under to wash the dust from his nose and throat. Sandy finally arrived and stepped in with both front feet, lowered her head and drank. She raised her head as if to look around, emptied her bladder and lower digestive tract of both substance and gas, and then drank again. This done, and filled with the cool water, she began eating the lush grass that grew along the stream bank.

Thomas moved upstream, for obvious reasons, and leaned back against the bank in the shade, soaking his bare, weathered feet in the sparkling water. He lay content for now, still clutching the food sack. He ate some of the biscuits and cheese and then threw the crumbs into the sand for Spatcher. The rhythmic sound of the stream cast its hypnotic spell over Thomas and soon he slept deeply, while Sandy grazed nonchalantly down the stream bank, filling her stomach with the lush, fresh grass.

Chapter 6

* * * * * * *

Thomas was suddenly startled awake by the distant sound of a train whistle. He and Spatcher rushed across the stream and scrambled up the far bank. A train! That would surely be something to tell his sister about. He saw the puffs of smoke as the train strained to climb the gradual grade. Thomas wanted a better look. He and Spatcher moved closer, crouching in the tall sagebrush. The train strained against the incline, black smoke billowing from its stack, and white steam from it bowels. The boy and dog watched in wide-eyed wonder. Thomas's heart raced and his eyes opened wide as the train puffed its way ever-closer, until it was almost upon them. He had never heard a sound so descriptive of pure power, and he wondered if his vantage point was too close. The ground shook, the train whistled—and then came another loud whistle. They were too close ... much too close!

Thomas held his hands over his ears and hid his face and tried to keep some control over Spatcher. He crossed himself and prayed that the train would pass quickly. Suddenly, a bang was followed by a loud pop-pop-pop, which then changed to a loud tick-tick-tick as the train *slowed and came to a stop. Thomas and Spatcher were so close to the train that either one of them could have read the small letters on the sides of the boxcars, if they had known how to read. Not daring to move, they just lay there, waiting to see what would happen next.*

Two men climbed down from the engine. Their talk was a jumble but finally, one of the men climbed up into the cab, pushed some levers and the engine slowed to an idle. He climbed down and walked to the spot between the engine and the coal car to make adjustments there. Two other men stepped down from the caboose and walked toward the first pair.

The shorter of the first two men was waving his arms and yelling, "Those god- damned company mechanics— they couldn't slap their ass with both hands without fallin' down. Couldn't they, just for once, do something right?"

All four men seemed to know exactly what was wrong, as they headed directly toward the center portion of the train. The two who had come from the caboose arrived first, and looked under the train at a piece of metal hanging down, mostly hidden by one of the train's wheels. As the other men arrived, much discussion began, everyone talking at once. They discussed whose fault it was, how it should be fixed, and how long it would take, all the while reaching in to feel the damaged area, as if to magically heal it.

"Might as well let the damn Mexicans out," said one of the men from the caboose.

"Looks like we'll be here for a while," said the other.

As the doors of the cars were opened, brown-skinned people streamed out and blinked against the daylight. Men jumped down first, turning to help the women and children. One large black man stood out among them. The men began gathering wood and building fires. The women prepared to cook, and soon the smell of coffee and cooking food spiced the air.

The railroad men had returned to the damage of the train, and were now surveying it in earnest. Two of them had crawled completely under the train while the others watched.

"Looks like everything's in pretty good shape," said one of the men under the train, but in a voice that seemed to be trying to convince himself as much as anyone else. "I think all we need to do is tie up those rods and hoses, to keep them from dragging until we get to civilization, where we can get it fixed right."

The other men thought for a moment and then agreed, although none of them appeared to be too sure. "Hell, it sure can't hurt to try, and I don't know what else we'd do anyways. I'll get some wire," one man said, and started toward the rear of the train.

It took the men about the same amount of time to make these temporary repairs as it did for Spatcher to finally work loose from Thomas's control and streak toward the train. There was a lot of excitement as the dog ran between the Mexicans, licking their hands as they petted him. It was obvious Spatcher was enjoying it immensely, as were the Mexicans.

Thomas lay watching, not sure what to do, and then he stood and raced after his dog. No one seemed to notice him. They were all quite amused by this dog that went from one to the other, seemingly in love with all, in the way of Border Collies. When Thomas reached the train, the engineer was already back in the engine and had begun getting up steam. The other men began kicking out the cook fires, pointing toward the train and yelling at the Mexicans to get back on. The large Negro man lifted the dog on board, and then quickly jumped in himself.

Thomas ran to the car and tried to coax Spatcher out. The men from the caboose, hurrying by on their way to the end of the train, stopped just long enough to pick Thomas up.

"Here, young fella. We'll give ya a hand." As the train picked up speed, straining against the grade, the men swung Thomas up and tossed him through the open door of the boxcar. Then they slid the door shut, locked it, and hurried to the caboose. The train chugged up the slope and into the twilight, as the frightened boy stood inside the dimly lit boxcar.

Chapter 7

The train continued to pick up speed. Thomas tried to open the heavy door, but even if it hadn't been locked, he wouldn't have been able to open it. Finally, he gave up and looked around. Evening's sunlight streamed through cracks in the battered walls and as his eyes became more accustomed to the dimness, he could see the Mexicans, their bodies crammed into the limited space. He smelled unwashed bodies and human waste. A bucket in one corner of the boxcar was running over, and a thin stream of muck made its way to the crack under the large sliding door. The smell made Thomas sick to his stomach; he felt like throwing up, and struggled to hold it back.

Spatcher lay on the floor next to the Negro man, looking at Thomas, his tail wagging and tongue hanging out, almost like he was smiling, but not willing to give up the scratching and petting that were being lavished on him by his new friend.

"This yer dog?" asked the Negro.

"Yah, I guess he is."

"Then how come he don't go to you?" the black man asked in a friendly, kidding way.

"It's the kind of dog he is." answered Thomas. "He just likes everybody. He just don't know no better, it seems."

"What's in the sack?"

Thomas hadn't realized he was still holding the food sack. "Just some food my mother sent for my trip."

"Yer Momma knowed you was a goin' on this here train?" the man asked in wonder.

"No. She thunk I was a-goin' to my sister's ta help her have a baby," was Thomas' weak reply.

"Le's see what ya'alls got in there." He reached over and took the sack. "Wow, they's lots a good stuff here! Lotsa cheese and biscuits. Wow."

The black man moved to sit next to Thomas, and without being asked, took some of the food and began eating. "They call's me Cropper, guess 'cause I gets so many crops in when I is a-workin'. What's yer name?"

"It's Thomas Jose Ualdo Lopez James Anderson, but you can jus' call me Thomas."

"Well I'll be go'damned," exclaimed Cropper. "I never in all my life heard a' such a name." He was silent for a moment, and then held out his hand and said, "Damned glad ta meet ya'all."

They shook hands, and over the following day, they shared Thomas's food as well as stories, and became friends.

Chapter 8

* * * * * * *

Cropper told Thomas how he had been a slave on a rich southern plantation. His parents had been slaves, and he was, too. He had been treated well and liked it there okay, but his parents decided to leave when the slaves were freed. And now that he finally "knew my place, and stayed there," he hadn't had many problems with Mexicans or whites. Cropper told him about the plantation and how the "niggers" had all been treated almost as well as the purebred horses and hunting dogs. He told Thomas how the slaves had always been given the "best leftovers" that weren't mixed together like the slop for the hogs, but were put in separate containers.

"We had our run of the garden for greens and such but weren't allowed to take the good stuff, but there was plenty of the other that just needed to be trimmed or cleaned, and it was good as anything. There was no takin' the berries or fruit or the cannin' stuff, but all the rest, we got all we wanted. Yeah, massa would sometimes give us a hog or sheep to butcher, and we made it last, we used it all. When times were short we would jus get the "leffovers," like the insides, you know, ta use however we could. Wasn't bad.

You kin make a pretty good meal of it if ya knows how. We had 'bout all the chick'n and watermelon we wanted."

Cropper was silent for a few moments. A tear came to his eye, and he went on. "I don't 'member much 'bout my mammy; seems soon's I's big 'nough, I's sold. All's I 'member is my mammy a-cryin' and a-tellin' me ta take care. Don't rightly knows who my Daddy is. Nobody never said ... well, no matter. Then I set out on my own later and finally made my way West and now travel with the Mexican farm workers. What 'bout you? Tell me 'bout you."

Thomas told Cropper about his mother, father, and his siblings, some of whom he had little or no memory of. He told him of his setting out to help one of them, Susan, the youngest. He told him about the way she had been unwillingly abandoned by her sheepherder husband in favor of sheep that had begun lambing early on the range. It seemed they needed his care more than Susan did and as young as he was, Thomas understood that without the sheep they would have no means at all. He talked about his father's escapades, about the fights and other things, that he had only heard about. Thomas told how he had heard the train and had wandered off the trail to get a better look, and how he had been thrown into the boxcar, and of course Cropper knew the rest.

"Somethin ta 'member," Cropper said. "Sure this don't make no sense, but 'member it anyhow—d'more things changes, d'more dey stays the same."

They stopped talking as each went to his own thoughts. Thomas hoped for a stop soon, because he was not anxious to add to the bucket of dung to the stench that filled the boxcar. But as time wore on, he had no other choice. Cropper had ridden this route many times before and thought they should stop sometime soon for water. Then they could build a fire and eat, but for now, he said they should try to get some sleep. With Thomas on one side and Spatcher on the other, both leaning against him, Cropper gently stroked the heads of his new friends.

"This sure as hell ain't no life fer a young boy alone," he mumbled.

The boxcar creaked in time with the rocking motion; the train chugged along the tracks and into the night, creating a melody of sorts—and soon they were overcome by sleep.

Chapter 9

When the ranchers in the area needed hired hands, they would sometimes wait at the water tower and "enlist" the migrant Mexicans. While the train was filling with water, the farmers had time to bargain. Usually, the promise of money and food was enough, but if not—with the help of the train crew—as many workers as were needed would be taken. After the work had been done, they would be taken back to the water tower and put back on the train. The workers were usually well-fed and well-paid for their labor, so they, as well as the ranchers, generally felt it was a good deal for everybody.

The two men sitting in the wagon next to the water tower drank in silence from a whiskey jug. They were trying to lessen the boredom as well as warm their bodies against the evening chill. The horses had been unhitched from the wagon, hobbled, and set to graze. They could be heard breaking tree limbs and making horse noises nearby. The longer the two men sat, and the more they pulled on the jug, the more they argued, about anything: who was the toughest, the biggest, the fastest, but they never made moves to prove any of it. As the night wore on, *they pulled the collars of their coats tighter around their necks, hunched down for warmth and continued to argue, neither of them really listening to the other.*

The men waiting and arguing were Big Joel and his rancher friend, Lenny Jensen. It wasn't clear if Big Joel had been given his name because of his size, or if it had been after his fourth son had been born and Big Joel's wife thought it was about time for one of their sons to be named after his father. Big Joel was a large man, with a bear-like body. He leaned forward when he walked and never seemed to be in a hurry. He was ruggedly handsome and well over six feet tall, with graying hair that was starting to thin on the top. It was said that he had done well with the women in days past. A short-cropped white beard, splotched with darker patches, surrounded full, well-shaped lips that were forever pulled back in a friendly grin to reveal even teeth that were slightly discolored and chipped.

He demanded immediate respect without asking for it, and only his closest friends challenged his wishes. He had an almost sacrilegious view of religion and at times talked to God as if they were standing face-to-face. He had a way of always dismissing his own weaknesses or shortcomings. His logic was strange but persuasive. He could sit and convince himself, as well others, that almost anything was true or, if it pleased him, that the same thing was false.

Big Joel was in a mood to tell a joke, but not wanting to waste it simply on one spectator, he put it away temporarily in the joke section of his brain until a bigger audience could be found, and instead continued his good-natured arguing with Lenny, an older Swedish man. He had long hair that was in the process of turning from yellow to white, which made it look dirty. He had deep-set, pale blue eyes and almost no eyebrows. A thin, hawk-like nose was set above the wry, thin lips that were usually in talking mode, which revealed crooked, tobacco-stained teeth. He was short with a slight build but was unusually strong and agile.

In the distance, the two heard a train whistle and then a chug, chug, chug. Big Joel got down from the wagon to fetch the horses. Lenny disliked physical activity, although he would work long and diligently to set up or carry out a practical joke or do something new or unusual. Big Joel had become used to Lenny's ways over the years and knew better than to expect any help from his friend, nor did any come. He rounded up the horses and hitched them to the wagon. He had just finished the job and was standing with one foot up on a front wagon wheel, engaged in arguing with Lenny again, when the lights from the train came around the corner.

Chapter 10

* * * * * * *

The train chugged and screeched to a stop and then let out what seemed to be its last breath, and sat idling, as if it were an animal in waiting. A man from the engine made his way to the water tower, and guided the spout to the fill hole on the train ... the water flowed in. Another man stepped down and walked toward the wagon where Big Joel and Lenny waited. The men grunted short greetings, and each drank from the jug. The other train workers showed up and drank their fill.

Big Joel saw his chance to tell his joke, which he had heard on one of his trips into town for supplies. "You guys hear about the new sheepherder that killed and cooked the camp's blue ribbon ewe?" Without waiting for a response, he went on. "The sheepherders were mad as hell at him, and he couldn't figure out why, so he asked them if he had fucked up the cookin."

Looking from face to face, he delivered the punch line. "'No,' they said, 'you cooked up the fuckin.'"

As always, when Big Joel told a joke, he laughed the hardest and longest. When he had finally finished laughing, he asked, "What ya got on the train this time?"

The smaller of the two men, the one who seemed to be the boss and probably was the engineer, took the jug from his lips, wiped his mouth with his sleeve, and said, "Got mostly just Mexican families this trip." He paused, took another pull from the jug, and handed it to his partner. "There's a couple of chinks and a wop and a big, headstrong nigger.

He paused again and looked toward the train. "He took up with a kid and a dog—hell, they'd be more trouble than they're worth. We picked up the stray kid a couple of days ago. He's 'bout five, maybe six, don't know exactly where he got on." He thought for an instant and then added, "He might be good for some chores or somethin' until he grows up. Oh yeah, it's a damned good-lookin' dog."

Then the trainmen turned to walk briskly to the first boxcar, where one of them pulled the wooden wedge from the hasp lock. With the help of the passengers inside, the door slid open and the Mexicans began streaming out, and then they opened the doors of all the cars. There was a hum of voices as the Mexicans slid down from the doorway onto the uneven ground to repeat their usual routine. The men went into the woods while the women hurried to gathered wood, start the fires, and begin cooking, before following the men into the woods themselves

Big Joel and Lenny walked among the Mexicans to select a few workers from the group. The Mexicans seemed oblivious. Men with families were never taken, and they didn't want women. They had Brenda, who was woman enough. "We sure as hell don't need kids," said Lenny, his face twisting into a look of disgust as he recalled what the engineer had said about the boy. Almost as if thinking out loud he went on, "Wouldn't mind haven another good dog on the place, though." He winked at Joel, who looked away.

Chapter 11

* * * * * * *

After examining the Mexicans for a while, Big Joel commented, "Hell, it doesn't look good."

The engineer and his men were helping to look too, because they were paid a fee for each suitable worker that the rancher hired or kidnapped. After finding few suitable hands other than the two "chinks," who had already been tied up and laid in the back of the wagon, Big Joel and Lenny climbed into the wagon to begin their long trek home. Lenny noticed a fire burning on the other side of the train, and jabbed an elbow into Big Joel's side, "Want to go have a look?" He pointed.

"What the hell—let's take a look," Big Joel said.

The railroad men began kicking out the fires as a signal for the Mexicans to get back on the train. The Mexicans knew the routine well enough by now, and slowly began to gather up their meager belongings and re-board the boxcars.

Big Joel and Lenny ducked down and passed under the train to the other side. Beside a small fire lay a large black man and a small Mexican boy with a purebred, black-and-white Border Collie. Joel's eyes lit up as he remembered the time he had watched a dog like this work with the sheep. The herder had sat in the shade and simply whistled and pointed his eager black-and-white partner here and there, almost as if he were another hand—well, better than another hand.

"Don't even need to pay him except a bone now and then," he mused under his breath. "What will you take for the dog?" he asked, trying not to seem too anxious.

The black man stood up, still holding the large knife he had used to fix supper. "Ain't fer sale. Belong to the boy," Cropper said, and then began to tell about the way the boy and his dog had been taken onto the train by mistake just days before. He was helping him out, at least for now. Then he motioned Big Joel to step with him closer to the train and away from Thomas. Spatcher had already made friends with Lenny, and would without a doubt have gone with him.

Joel followed the black man to the train and listened as he was told about Thomas—how he had cried and been so frightened. How the two of them and the dog had huddled together in the corner of the boxcar. Cropper still held the big knife between Big Joel and himself, being wise to the ways of the white farmers. He didn't want to have his journey interrupted. Joel eyed Cropper and began to plot a way to add him to the other workers who were waiting in the wagon. But as Big Joel looked at the knife and the muscles that bulged beneath the black man's skin, he remembered what the engineer had said about the big, headstrong nigger, and gave up the idea about taking him.

Cropper went on, "I'm a-liken that boy just fine, but it'll be no good, him a- stayin' with me and all. If'n you all will take him, you'll get that fine dog, too."

Joel needed to think about this. He knew that he wanted the dog, and then too, just maybe, the boy could *be of some use around the place. And it wouldn't cost anything, except a meal here and there. "Heck, he's just about the same age as Little Joel. Be a good mate for him. Hell, yes," he said. "I'm gonna do it."*

As Cropper was telling Thomas goodbye, Big Joel saw him wiping tears from his eyes. And then Cropper disappeared into the boxcar without looking back, and the train began to move. Thomas and Spatcher watched until the train disappeared into the night and then they walked to the wagon. Thomas was told to climb into the seat between the two strangers, while Spatcher jumped into the wagon and lay at their feet. After only a few miles, Thomas leaned against Big Joel and fell asleep. Joel smiled and braced himself against the added weight of his new ward. He wondered what Brenda and Little Joel might think of the family's new additions.

In one motion, he turned to check his tied-up and discontented cargo in the wagon and put his arm around Thomas's shoulder to keep him from falling off. With his free hand, Big Joel slapped the reins to prompt the horses into a faster gait toward the ranch that would be young Thomas's new home.

Chapter 108

My daydream story-writing ended with the slowing of my train and the distant calling of the conductor, "Missoula, five minutes," summoning me from my mental writing.

I saw the conductor through the glass door, walking toward me. As he got close, he slowed, like he was thinking, took a step, hesitated again, and turned to me—his face held an ingenuous smile. "Are you going to go into Missoula?"

"Yeah, as far as I know, I am."

"Would you do me a favor?"

"Shore will, if I can," I told him.

He looked a little perturbed, like he wanted to tell me what it was, but at the same time didn't want to say. "I have to work another shift. The regular guy can't make it, and they are expecting me to take it on for him."

"Well, how can I help?"

He seemed to struggle again and then, like he was forcing out the words, he went on. "Well, my wife and I haven't been getting along too well lately, and I was wondering if you might call her and tell her that I won't be home tonight? But I *will* be home tomorrow night."

"Shore I will. I'll have time, for sure."

He handed me a piece of paper with a phone number on it, and gave me a paper dollar.

"Her name is Ned. I really appreciate it."

"Ned? Strange name for a girl. We have a horse named Ned."

"Well, it's a nickname. Her name is Nadine, and she's not a horse. You can just keep the change from the dollar."

"That will be 95 cents," I grinned. "That will buy me and my girl a burger."

"Sorry about what I said about your poem—it was really pretty good," he said. "If you want to hear a classic, I'll tell you a classic." He began rattling off his poem, his face turning bright crimson as he recited. "There they lay, face-to-face, on a pillow trimmed in lace—a handful of tit, a mouthful of tongue, a cunt full of pecker and too drunk to come." His face turned even redder as he turned and strolled down the aisle, yelling that Missoula would soon come into view and would be our next stop, until he disappeared through the windowed door.

While I was talking to the conductor, Tom had gone on with his story, oblivious to my inattention. "Me and my Negro friend finally made it back to my sister's place," he said.

I must have missed some of the story, I thought, but I'll deal with it later.

"Well, I guess we're in Missoula," I said, and stood up as we stopped beside a large, magnificent brick building—the Great Northern Train Depot.

I placed the twine around my neck and the yellow boots banged against my chest, but it was less painful than they had been on my feet. I reached out with my hand in a farewell gesture to Tom, and he stood. Our hands clasped and for a moment it was almost as if we shared camaraderie—in a way, he had become a part of my life, a part of my psyche. As I stepped down to meet the Missoula dusk, I had the strange feeling that someday, in some way, we would meet again. In fact, I knew we would.

Chapter 109

"William!" Alex's voice cuts into the dark, dank chamber where I lie confined, not only in the enclosure of the furnace room but also in my royal bedding of velvet blankets and lace sheets. I can hear him, but I don't answer. "Let the bastard worry for a while."

"Are you there?" he nags.

"What the hell do you want?" I ask, but I already know the answer.

After a short pause, as if he is thinking, he says, "William, can you help me out?"

I pause, too. This pause is for effect, I think, and smile at my own effort to be humorous at such an un-humorous time. Then I say, "How can I help?"

"Is there any way that you can make me even a little bit sure that you are telling me the truth about not being involved in those murders?"

This is the opening I have been looking for. He's beginning to weaken. But I'm not ready yet. I need a little more time. I am on the verge of having an answer he can believe—I can feel it.

"Alex," I say, "I've been thinking, and it all fits together now. I know, almost with a certainty, that it was you and your brothers who did the dirty deeds. Dr. Wainscot suspected it was one of you, and he told me you might not even be aware of it. I think when you come again, I'll have it figured out and we can discuss it. If not then, it will be soon."

Alex seems strangely pleased, which makes me realize he doesn't want to be responsible for my death. He wants me to be free, if I really am innocent. But I'm sure another part of him wants me to suffer and die if I am guilty. His religion prescribes hell for murdering the innocent, or at least a form of hell. It's a milder hell than that of most Christian religions, but it's still hell. I wouldn't be surprised if he's thinking about getting a sword and stabbing me, to allow him to shed blood and be exalted, as is prescribed by his religion.

"Okay, that sounds fair." he returns. "I'll leave you to think and when I come back, maybe you'll be able to convince me—although I have to say, it's highly unlikely that you'll ever be able to make me believe my brothers or I killed people and can't even remember it."

That's all I need to spur me on, to continue my discovery.

"Do you have water, William?" he asks quietly. It really does sound like he's softening.

"Yes," I say. "There is a sink in here and a tin cup. I am hungry but I can live a long time on stored fat. I did it when I first came to Salt Lake, and I can do it again."

"Okay," he says through the crack of the door. He sounds almost sorry to leave me now, as he turns to make his way back to what I imagine is his one room, lonely flat, maybe one of those across the street from the Camelot-Avalon Apartments. But I think he's determined now to be fair, to give me every chance to convince him of my innocence. He's still an ass, though.

For me, it's becoming more difficult to go back in time, to catch a moment and retreat into it.

First, I need to remember where in time I was before that ass, Alex, disturbed me, and then go to that exact spot in time, or at least very close to it. I think back … I had just said goodbye to my Mexican friend, Thomas, on the train, and Victoria and I were getting ready to get off the Great Northern in Missoula, to search for our car.

"Yeah, that's the ticket," I exclaim. And with that, I begin dissolving into a moment of the past that will become, to me, the present.

Chapter 110

Victoria and I were first to get off the train, and as we stepped down into the late- afternoon sunshine of Missoula, the urgency of our purpose came rushing back.

We had little time to survey or enjoy the beautiful brick design of the depot, or the surroundings. I began surveying the area for any sign of a used car lot. To my delight, I saw one directly across the street to the south. We hurried over and began looking at the cars.

"Old man's cars and wrecks," I said aloud, after we had walked through the lot.

A salesman appeared. "Hey, we're about to close. The boss is getting married and we're closing early. We might as well be closed, anyway. He's just going around in a daze, selling cars cheap, real cheap. He's almost giving them away. I can help you if it's quick."

I told him of my plight and how I needed a car and, probably not with good judgment, how much money I had to spend.

"Pretty hard to get anything that runs for that much."

I stood silently, looking at the asphalt at my feet and not knowing what to do. A slight but accustomed combination of lightning and sulfur pelted my body.

He must have sensed my despair. "If you're looking for junk, we just got a clunker traded in. Haven't seen it myself yet, but I think it runs."

"Hell, I don't know."

"Go look at it if you want to. It's in the yard in back, right in front of the gate. It's an old convertible. We're getting ready to close, so you'll have to hurry."

"I don't know," I said again.

"We'll probably just haul it to the used parts lot tomorrow. They pay thirty or forty bucks for anything that runs."

"Hell, I don't know."

He gave me a look that suggested he had experienced such a dilemma himself and said, "Maybe it will run for a little while."

I didn't have much hope, but I walked around the building to the fenced rear lot, and went inside. My mouth dropped open. Before me sat a car, all right, but not a wreck as the salesman had promised.

It was the exact car I had imagined owning! I pinched my arm to see if I was dreaming, but I wasn't, so I walked around the car and did the classic kicking the tires and all that stuff you're supposed to do when buying a car. It was beautiful. "Well, I'm not dead yet," I muttered.

It was a 1939 Ford coupe convertible with a new-looking top and whitewall tires. The hood ornament and trunk handle had been removed and the holes had been filled in or, as we called it, "Leaded in." It had a new-looking, robin's egg blue paint job, almost scratch-free. Twin spotlights adorned the sides just in front of the driver and passenger doors. I opened the rumble seat at the rear. The brown leather seat looked new.

Well, I thought, I'll bet the inside is a mess, and I'm sure it runs like crap.

I opened the door and climbed inside. It looked like new. I pinched myself again. "I'm not dead yet!" I yelled.

I turned on the switch and pushed the starter with my foot. It started immediately. The engine ran so smoothly that I had to lean forward to make sure it was still running. I turned the engine off and tried to calm myself to face the salesman.

He had gone inside the office and as I approached he walked out. "Wha'da'ya think?"

"Well, maybe it will get me home," I said, trying to appear calm. "What do you think I can get it for?"

He rubbed his chin. "How much do you have?"

I'd already told him, but I thought his forgetfulness might be to my advantage, because I needed some money food and gas to get home. "Sixty-five dollars."

He raised his eyebrows. "Not very much," he said. "I'll have to ask the boss," and he walked to the old building and disappeared inside.

Hell, he sure changes his story, I thought. The wrecking yard gives them thirty or forty bucks, and he's trying to jack me up from sixty-five.

The ride from Eden to Spokane and then from Spokane to Missoula had seemed long, but now, the time it took for the salesman to return seemed decades longer. Why is it taking so long? I asked myself. Well, it was too good to be true anyway. Good things don't happen to me. It always seems to be harder for me than for anybody else.

I walked nervously about the yard. God, it's taking a long time. Well, it's too good to be true, anyway. I might as well just forget it. I turned to walk away.

"Hey, Bill," the salesman called. There was a sad look on his face. He stood on one foot and then the other, like he was trying to think how to tell me.

My heart dropped. Oh God, I want that car, I said to myself.

"Sorry, Bill," he said, and my mind raced to find a suitable counter-offer when he delivered the bad news.

"The boss said seventy bucks and no guarantees. You take it as is and get it off the lot now. Push it out in the street if you have to."

I was speechless. Only seventy bucks? I thought.

He looked at me for a minute and then said in a sad, apologetic voice, "Sorry, that's the best I could do."

Sorry, was he? I could have kissed him.

After signing a few papers, counting out the seventy dollars and getting a receipt, we shook hands and I went to get the car. I backed it out and drove onto the almost-vacant street, trying my best to hurry before anyone in the car lot saw the beauty of it and tried to get it back. I had rarely before known the joy of getting something I really wanted but never thought I would have. Well, I knew the feeling now. I couldn't believe it was true. My life had been filled with disappointment and despair, and now I couldn't believe that I had the car I had wanted all my life.

I looked at Victoria, who was obviously as happy as I was. "It's a beautiful car, William," she said.

Chapter 111

Getting the car had another meaning to me as well. "God has, in a special way, told me he has forgiven me for using Voodoo and witchcraft and for all the other stuff too. Thanks, God," I said.

I looked up into the sky, held my hands in a way to express my love, and winked.

"You can bet your ass I will only use my witchcraft and Voodoo for good from now on," I said like I was praying, and I was sure that I would keep my word, and that God knew this as well.

The gas gauge read almost empty, and at my first opportunity I pulled into a gas station. We hadn't eaten in a while, so I bought some food.

Our meal was a package of Twinkies, some chips, six bananas and a six-pack of Highlander beer. "This would make Mom proud," I smiled. "All the food groups."

As I drove, we ate in silence. We were both happy and hungry. I opened a beer and took a long, deep drag, which made me feel even better.

"Want a beer?" I asked.

"No, thank you. I'm a lady."

"Suit yourself," I said, but I was delighted she had turned it down. She *was* a lady, a real lady.

"I'm going to take the top down," I said, pulling off the road.

"Okay."

"Looks like you just undo these hooks at the top." I pulled the knob that said, "Top," and it slowly retracted into the opening at the rear. I got out and snapped the cover over it. The wind blew our hair. Victoria was in the seat beside me, I had a bottle of beer in my hand, and a full stomach. "Life is great," I yelled, as the air rushed past, muffling my voice and dulling my senses.

"Victoria," I said, "I met a man on the train who told me a story."

"I know. I was sitting right behind you."

"Oh, yeah. Maybe you can help me write up his story. It might be the western I've wanted to write."

My new car was like a miracle. I was starting to believe what Mom and Dad had told me about faith getting a person the things they wanted, and I now felt sure that God was real, because he wouldn't have forgiven me for the Voodoo thing and allowed me to have the car if he wasn't real.

It occurred to me that I was not really too bad. I had been in jail only once, if you didn't count the thing about fish-napping, and the time Warren and I were framed for stealing that logger's stuff, and the time I got caught fishing out of season down at the trestle and spent the weekend in jail. Dad was so mad that last time, he damned near killed me. But about a week later, he was arrested over in Idaho for about the same thing and spent the night in jail in Piedmont, like I had in Paradise. Of course, he had a better reason than I did for doing it. He always had a good excuse for being a horse's ass.

And now I've gotten the car, and I didn't need to cast a spell, use Voodoo, or pray for anything, I thought happily. God has really forgiven me. And wait until Dad sees this car. He'll want to drive it to work, I'll bet. I sat up a little taller in my seat. Mom will ride with me, I thought, and pressed the brakes, which made our bodies lurch ahead as the rubber screeched.

"What you doin', William?" Victoria screeched.

"Testing the brakes," I yelled with delight. "What can ever go wrong now?"

"Take it easy," she screeched again.

" Okay, I will." And then I yelled, "Hell, I forgot about the conductor's wife." I turned the car around.

"Use the payphone outside," the jerk of a storekeeper said. "This one's for customers."

"Hell, I just spent about three dollars in here."

"I never seen you around here until today. Use the payphone."

I dropped a nickel into the slot and dialed the number the conductor had given me. A woman answered and I told her what the conductor had said.

"That bastard," she yelled. "He always does that. We were supposed to go out tonight. If you see him, tell him I'm going barhopping."

She was silent for a moment and then, "Hey, why don't you go with me?"

"I have someone with me," I said. It came out as an apology.

"Drop them at a movie," she argued.

"Maybe I can do that," I said, thinking Victoria would consider it kind of me to keep the lady company, although she wouldn't want to come along to the bar.

"My name is Ned," the conductor's wife said, and told me how to get to her place.

"I'm Bill," I said. "I'll be right there." I hung up.

I explained things to Victoria. "She really needs me," I told her.

"Well, I guess I understand, although I don't think you would understand if I did the same thing," she said.

"I don't know, either," I said, "but it's just something I need to do, not just for her but for the conductor, too." I dropped her in front of the movie.

Victoria didn't kiss me goodbye. She just turned and walked to the ticket cage, got her ticket, and disappeared inside without even looking back.

I hope she forgives me, I thought as I drove to the conductor's house.

"I really appreciate this," Ned said when she answered the door.

"That's all right. I like going out," I said.

"Was your friend upset?"

"Not too much," I lied.

"I'm almost ready. Just sit on the couch for a minute. Get a drink out of the fridge."

I had finished my beer before she came out of the bedroom. "Man, you look great," I said.

"Well, thank you," she said with a smile.

"Your husband's a lot older."

"Yes. I was attracted to him because he was older, but now he's too old."

"Too old for what?"

"Too old to cut the mustard," she said, and laughed.

"Where do you want to go?" I asked. "To a movie?"

She raised her eyebrows. "Movie?"

"I'm too young to get into a nightclub in Missoula. If we were in Eden it would be all right, but not here. Besides, I don't have any money."

She looked up and down my body and her eyes stopped at my crotch for a little too long. "You won't need any money," she said. "Want another beer?"

"Sure, I love beer."

I began drinking my beer and she removed her coat, then her shoes, and then her blouse. I was getting warm. I took off my shoes. She moved to the couch, sat down beside me, and began unbuttoning my shirt. She took off all her clothes, her dress first, and then the rest. "A shame you got dressed for nothing," I smiled.

"Let's see if it was for nothing," she said and winked at me.

Her body didn't show the age that her face did. It was firm and shapely, with almost no fat. It was obvious she was proud of it. The breasts looked firm and well-formed. One was a little smaller than the other. The nipples looked like small, raised buttons with a large brown circle behind them.

I blushed as her hand went to my crotch, "Feels like there's nothing wasted here," she said.

"It can tell a good thing when it sees it," I said.

Her knees found the couch on both sides over me. "Let's take a look," she said as she undid my fly.

I sat waiting to see what would happen next. She carefully took it out and pulled it gently one way and then the other, like she was trying to make sure it was all there.

"That feels good," I said. "Your hands are soft and warm." I was getting hot, and was panting like a dog.

"You sound like my old dog," she said and laughed. "I'm going to treat you like a dog."

"Just don't make me pee on a water hydrant," I kidded.

She laughed and then stood. "Come with me, Rover," she ordered.

"Arf, arf," I said and walked behind her toward the bedroom, with her holding my aroused penis like a leash around a dog's neck.

We played dog tricks and games on the bed until I could play no more. "That's all I can do," I said.

"You're one hell of a dog, but you could have more stamina," she laughed.

It was wonderful; it was better than with Victoria. But I felt guilty, dirty and lonely, and was sorry it had happened. In shame and embarrassment, I hid my face in the pillow. "I love Victoria," I sobbed.

"Thanks, Bill," she said, not listening to me. "That was nice, but don't tell my husband." She laughed and then went to the bathroom, where I could hear water running.

I went to the kitchen sink and washed. I had to get rid of the scent, which made me feel more guilty. I dressed quickly. I didn't want to see her again. "She's awful," I thought.

She came out of the bathroom, still nude and wiping her crotch with a white towel. "Come over again, Bill," she said. "I know a lot of games."

I felt really bad about what I'd done, but it was the conductor and Ned's fault. If they hadn't set it up, if she hadn't tempted me, I wouldn't had done it. "We'll see," I said as I opened the door and stepped out into the night—then I reconsidered and went back inside to try somehow to make amends, or make myself feel better.

After wards, I opened the door again and then let it bang shut behind me. I felt a little better now.

It was a long drive to the movie theatre. Victoria was waiting for me, and when she got in, I saw she was mad. She just sat and watched me. I opened a beer and began drinking it, which made me feel a little better.

"Want a beer?" I asked.

"What do you think?" she snapped.

"My God, you're so perfect," I tried to kid her, but she turned her head and looked out the window. "I'll wait until she cools off," I mumbled. "I shouldn't have told her about the conductor's wife; I should have made up a story." I decided to think about something else and give her some time to cool off.

The wind rushed past and ruffled our hair as we glided along the narrow, deserted road between a thick grove of trees and undergrowth.

I imagined myself a fighter pilot tracking down and destroying menacing Messerschmitts of the German Luftwaffe in my own P-36 fighter. I had never had such a feeling of splendor; it was as though my entire life had changed because of this wonderful car. I now had everything.

Victoria didn't say anything. "Maybe it's all about the conductor's wife," I muttered to myself, but still loud enough for her to hear, although she just looked ahead. "It isn't like I have a new girlfriend," I went on. "Hell, I would never be untrue anymore than you would. But after all, I'm not dead. I can still have feelings for other things, even girls, as long as I don't love them. The conductor's wife thing just happened. That was something different; nobody could resist that," I said, and then waited.

"Well, it still makes me feel bad."

"Have you forgiven me?"

"Well, I have, sort of, but it will take a little time to completely forget."

"I feel bad too, Victoria. I felt bad right after. I won't ever do anything like that again, I promise." But she didn't look very happy. "Poor bastard," I said. "I feel sorry for that poor conductor."

"You didn't have to stay with her for that long," Victoria said.

"Well, we're not married yet, you know. We can both have a little fun until we are."

"What would you do if I did something like that?" she nagged.

I rolled my eyes. "I know you wouldn't, Victoria. You could, I know, but you wouldn't. You're just too damned nice," I reached over and stroked her head.

"You think so? Maybe I'll fool you. Maybe I'll go hustle Colt or Eric."

"Hell, it didn't mean anything. You're the only one I love," I pleaded, and pulled my arm back to wait for her answer. I didn't want her to go with any of my friends or anybody else either, for that matter.

She was silent for a minute and then said, "All right, I forgive you, but if that ever happens after we're married, I'll divorce you and then I'll kill you." Her laughter was sort of forced, and it frightened me. I think she really meant it.

"Don't worry, it won't ever happen after we're married," I said.

I guided my new car into the darkness with Victoria at my side, and I marveled at the unaccustomed good fortune of the day. I pushed the gas pedal to the floor and headed for Eden and home. A sign loomed ahead: "Rowdy, Population 137," and then another sign, "25—Strictly Enforced." And still another sign, this one on the front of an old building, "The Black Bear Inn."

"Hell," I muttered, "this is Oscar's brother Craig's place."

Well, I needed a break. I was hungry and it had been years since I'd seen Craig. Hell, I had barely known him even then. Anyway, I'd changed a lot. With this five o'clock shadow, no one would recognize me now. Cars and pickups were crowded into the limited space in front. I found a spot and squeezed in.

"Are you awake, Victoria?" I asked.

"Well, I am now," she said.

"There's a restaurant or something. Want to eat?"

"I'm not hungry, but I'll go in with you. Maybe I'll just have some of your fries or something."

I reached into the back and got my hat and yellow boots and put them on. Craig sure as hell won't recognize me in this outfit, I thought. We walked up the steps and across the wooden porch to the double swinging doors, and stepped inside. "Craig has probably sold it, or got himself killed by one of these tough Montana cowboys by now," I joked.

The place was filled with loggers and cowboys; it was easy to tell by their garb. They all sat drinking and talking noisily, but in a matter-of-fact way, trying to maintain the image of stoic toughness demanded in these parts. There was an unclean smell that disinfectant couldn't quite stifle; the same one that all triple-C-rated restaurants seem to have. Subtly interwoven was a hint of an odor like a gymnasium's shower room that had been improperly cleaned through the years, and above it, the mild fragrance of freshly sawed pine trees mixed with the stench of long- unwashed and hard-worked bodies.

Only the voices of the people closest to us could be distinguished above a loud buzzing of boisterous conversation that blended with drunken laughter. The marquee above the bar boasted a limited selection of sandwiches and burgers. Mismatched glasses hung upside down from the ceiling and bottles of liquor sat prominently under a large mirror at the far side of the bar. Rather than enhancing the bar, the mirror reflected the unrefined taste of the proprietor. Silver dollars had been inlaid in the bar and covered with thick glass, its scratches and chips providing evidence of years of abuse. Small buckets of peanuts had been set randomly along the bar, and shells covered the floor, along with sawdust and cigarette butts.

"Looks like they're trying to burn the place down," I mumbled to Victoria.

"Sure does," she said.

Only one high stool was unoccupied at the bar, "You sit," I said to Victoria." I'll just stand behind you."

"Thanks, you're such a gentleman," she smiled and took the stool. I leaned on the bar with my arms on either side of her. It made me feel masculine to be able to protect her from these hoodlums.

A thick haze of smoke hung in the air. Victoria coughed; she wasn't used to smoke. I was glad she didn't use tobacco. Dad said it wasn't ladylike for a woman to smoke, and that was about the only thing he and I agreed on. I stepped back from Victoria, although I was still touching her with my body. I took out my bag of Durham and papers and built a quick one-handed stogy, sort of showing off, and then lit it and leaned forward on the bar with the cigarette hanging from my mouth.

"Not a great place," I said.

"Not a great place is right."

I drew in the smoke and blew it out the corner of my mouth, away from her. The barkeep was down the bar. It looked like he was telling a story to patrons. He wore a soiled tee-shirt that had fresh sweat under the arms.

He had an even dirtier white apron folded to fit below the roll of fat at his midsection. He had become one of the patrons and was in no hurry to take orders. Finally, he got to the punch line: "I'll tell you one thing for sure. I didn't wish for a ten-inch pianist!" After a good laugh and without even taking a break, he began reciting a poem.

"*The Contest*," he announced the title, and went on:

Old Brynhild, a shield maiden, come out West.
She soon found she liked dirty screwing best.
And when she screwed, she screwed for keeps.
Just like in Denmark, her victims lay in heaps.
She made a challenge, the country round
For any man who could screw her down.
One amongst the contenders was Ragnar,
A Viking from old Norse legendary lore.
He was stout, and as he laid it on the bar,
I'd swear it stretched from here to thar.
The death duel between Ragnar and Brynhild
Would be near the cranny, and on top the hill.
People came from here and there to get a seat,
To see that all-too-confident urchin sink his meat.
Old Brynhild started off like a whispering breeze,
When it whispers through the green willow trees.
A twist and a twink, and a mighty grunt,
And strategy unknown to common cunt.
But unafraid Ragnar met her every trick,
And he just kept reeling off more prick.
They screwed, and screwed, and screwed for hours,
They tore down trees, plants, shrubs, and flowers.
The ground was tore for many miles around,
Where old Brynhild's ass had drug the ground.
And then—she gave up, with a sigh and cough,
And Ragnar, just smiled and began jackin' off!

The old drunks in the bar began to hoot and clap, and after a lot of attaboys and slaps on the back, the crowd finally settled down and faded back into being boring nobodies intent on getting as drunk as possible.

"That was disgusting," Victoria said.

"You can say that again."

"That was dis …"

"I was just kidding. It's a figure of speech, Victoria. You don't need to say it again."

"I was just kidding, too. I'm not stupid."

Finally, the bartender noticed us, and came to our end of the bar. "What'll it be, cowboy?" He was glowing with pride over his thespian talent.

He wore a long, dirty-looking, untrimmed beard and displayed a well-tanned, shaven head. Somehow, he balanced small, wire-rimmed and rose-tinted glasses on his nose, which had obviously been broken more than once. It lay flat on his face until it got almost to his nostrils, then exploded into a potato-like blob. He was large and boisterous, but at the same time, he had a gentle demeanor that was maybe a touch feminine. He leaned forward on the bar, sort of like I was doing, but in his case, the fingers of both hands were spread apart, as if for balance. He swayed slightly from side to side. His eyes were drunkenly vacant as he waited for our order.

"How much for a burger?" I queried.

"Thirty five cents. Forty with fries," he replied. "Headin' fer the rodeo?" he asked with a smile.

Asshole, I thought, and then aloud, "God, I get that a lot," and forced a smile.

"Hell, sit down. It don't cost no more."

"That's okay," I said. "I'll stand. I'm a gentleman."

He rolled his eyes. I pulled the change out of my pocket. I had twenty-one cents. "What can I get with a cup of coffee and fries for twenty-one cents?"

He flashed me a demeaning smile. "I can make you a toasted-cheese sandwich with chips." He added, "Didn't make all-round cowboy this year, huh?"

Jesus Christ, who wound you up? I thought, and then aloud, "The cheese sandwich will be good."

I looked back at him as I took a long drag on my cigarette, and tried to show the damning contempt I felt for him—but not so much that he wouldn't bring the cheese sandwich, coffee, and chips.

His beard had probably once been brown, but now it was nearly all white. There were very thin and straggly patches of thick hair and places where there was almost no hair at all, where the skin was bleached white, about like his bald head. He had virtually no eyebrows to shield his blue, bloodshot eyes. His body appeared to be supple and strong, even though he was extremely overweight.

"Sit down. It don't cost no more," he said again, good-naturedly.

"On her lap?" I questioned.

He laughed. "What the hell? Do what you want. What the hell do I care?"

"Dumb ass," I said to Victoria about him.

"Yeah."

He went a short distance down the counter and stopped to tell another joke about a cowboy or something. He pointed at me and everyone laughed. Taped to the mirror behind the counter facing me was a picture of a deluxe cheeseburger with a rat's tail hanging out of it. Below that was a sign showing a dingy-looking and stained cup of coffee that proclaimed, "Free refills." I'm sure it was intended as a joke, but it didn't make the fact that we were eating in this dirty establishment any easier to swallow.

"Okay if we share?" I asked Victoria.

"Sure. Can I have a couple of bites and a few chips?"

"Hell yes, you can have all you want. And we can have all the coffee we want, too, with the free refills."

The barkeep showed up with the sandwich and the coffee, and set them on the bar.

"Hey," someone yelled from down the bar. "I need a beer."

"Don't give me any shit, cowboy," the barkeep yelled back, trying to seem tough. He reached under the counter and turned to me. "This is what they get if they give me shit." He showed a 44-caliber Magnum revolver with a six-inch barrel.

I decided to end the conversation. "Hell, I didn't mean nothing.

It's just that you make your customers feel about as welcome as a dose of clap." I hadn't even said anything, but he was drunk and belligerent. He glared at me, which made the sulfur coat my mouth and lightning shoot up my spine.

"Hey," someone shouted from the other side of the room. "I said no gunplay, except for show. Put that thing away or you'll find yerself walkin' down the road kickin' horse turds."

"Okay, Craig," he yelled back. "Just havin' some fun!"

And then back to me, "Maybe I'll come and get you when Craig ain't around. I already killed one guy who gave me shit, and after the jury heard my side, they let me off."

"Hell, killing seems a little extravagant," I said, trying to find the proper big word to show off my intellect. Shit, I thought, I should have said "excessive." But he's so dumb, he probably won't even notice.

"What the hell are you, a scientist, with your big words? Just eat and get the hell out. You're not welcome here. I might decide to shoot you, anyways."

"That's real hospitality," I said to Victoria.

"Sure makes a person feel welcome," she said.

"Hey, Shorty, want yer ass kicked? Get over here!" someone yelled.

"Anything else?" Shorty asked, but it was more from habit than really wanting to know. Without waiting for an answer, he walked to the front door and stood looking out into the night.

"Blue convertible, huh?" he said. "I got the license number. Maybe I'll get your address from the sheriff and come visit." He went back behind the bar to get the beer for the drunk who had been nagging him. He seemed to forget about me and began mingling with the customers, not as a barkeep, but as one of them.

The sandwich was two slices of untoasted, thick, Texas bread open-faced on a grime- streaked saucer, with two slices of Velveeta cheese lying on one piece of bread. It was haphazardly garnished with a pickle slice and a few chips.

We rushed through our meal and coffee. Nobody returned with a refill.

Okay, I thought, there won't be a tip. I didn't have any money for a tip anyway, but it made me feel better to think that.

A man standing in the shadows at the end of the bar waved. I waved back, as sort of an involuntary reflex. He smiled and turned to vanish into a doorway. He looked familiar—he looked like Oscar, but that couldn't be him, so far away from Utah. It might have been Craig. The bartender had called the boss Craig. But whoever he was, I wasn't eager to meet him.

"Wonder who it was?" I asked Victoria.

"I'm sure I don't know."

"It really looked like Oscar. I wonder what he would be doing here? Maybe I should go talk to him."

"No, William. Let's just go."

"If Oscar's here, then Alex probably is, too. They're both wanted for those murders in Utah."

I left the twenty-one cents on the counter and we walked out. As we got in the car, I got a sort of Elvis Presley feeling, but my yellow boots were beginning to hurt again. I took them off and threw them with my hat into the back seat, and then leaned forward so Victoria could slide into the back seat and get some sleep. I jerked the car into gear and headed along the highway.

But I needed to do something to that idiot bartender. I turned the car around and headed back. I pulled up next to the big pickup, picked up napkins from the floor that I had used for lunch, and climbed up onto the hood of my car in my stocking feet. I gingerly stepped up onto the hood of the pickup, undid my belt, dropped my pants and shorts and squatted into position. Afterwards, I wiped on the napkin and dropped it onto the hood, being careful not to hide the surprise. I imagined Shorty coming out after the bar closed and seeing my surprise. It made me laugh. I had to take one more look before I got back into my car. It looked great!

"William," Victoria laughed, "I can't believe you did that."

Outside the bar, someone stood in the shadows on the porch. When he stepped into the light, I saw that he was stocky with sandy hair. He smiled; his dingy teeth had wire braces.

"My God," I shrieked. "It is Oscar!" The sulfur and lightning filled my body.

"I don't see anything," Victoria said.

"What am I going to do? The bartender knows my license number. He'll tell Oscar."

Oscar stepped down from the porch and walked toward us. I shifted into low gear, and the wheels threw gravel as my car fishtailed across the parking lot onto the highway.

"He's going to kill me," I shouted. When I looked back, he was running, waving his arms and yelling. "William, stop! I have to talk to you! You are in danger! Please stop, before you hurt yourself or someone else."

"No, it can't be him. I'm just tired," I said to Victoria. "It's just my imagination."

"It's just your imagination," she echoed.

"What if that wasn't Shorty's pickup?"

:My god, I hadn't thought about that. But I think it must be."

I found a western station on the radio and soon we were singing along, trying to forget about Oscar, Alex, and Shorty. But in the back of my mind, I kept thinking maybe she could forget, but I couldn't forget.

That was understandable—it was me who would be getting killed, not her.

"Maybe it would be better it the pickup belonged to someone who didn't know so much about me," I thought.

The road was getting narrow now, and there were more trees close to it. "I'll have to start watching for deer. They're harder to see when there are so many trees," I mumbled.

"Why are you driving so fast?" she asked.

"It might have been Oscar."

"Oh, I don't think so. He couldn't be up here."

"You're right," I said. "I'm just tired. Go back to sleep. I'll slow down."

"That was funny about the pickup, wasn't it?" she said.

"It was," I agreed, but I was still worried. "Maybe I shouldn't have done it …"

And then a window opened, and I saw William in the basement of the Camelot-Avalon.

Alex was waiting for William to give him a reason why he shouldn't die. And now, this was unmistakably the very evidence William had been looking for. Here was Oscar, and more than likely Alex and Craig.

As the window closed, I decided that William should come back over again, as soon as Victoria was safely in Eden, and check it out.

Chapter 112

My headlights flooded the road ahead, but rather than being drawn into an imaginary war or some other adventure, I began playing with the headlight dimmer. It was on the left side of the clutch pedal, tucked right up against the side of the car. Pressure from my foot would cause the headlights to dim or go bright. It was lots of fun to make it work.

There were more cars now. Maybe a basketball game had let out, or a large meeting of evangelists, or some other nutty religion, such as Dad's. I dimmed my lights as a car approached and then clicked them back on bright before the car had passed, but late enough that he couldn't retaliate with his own high beam. This took some critical timing, and I imagined the furious driver cursing, like Dad did, yelling, "Horse's ass," and shaking a fist in my direction or flipping me off. I laughed with glee.

In my rearview mirror, I saw a car turn onto a side road, back up, and then come after me. "I'm not dead yet," I said.

"What's the matter?" Victoria asked.

"I might have pissed someone off," I said. "Maybe I should stop doing the dim light trick."

The headlights quickly closed the distance between us. I pushed the gas pedal to the floor, but the lights kept coming. A new-looking, dark blue Mercury sedan with fender skirts and twin spotlights pulled up alongside, filled with angry faces.

"Hey, you jerk!" a guy yelled, his middle finger raised.

"Sorry, my dimmer switch isn't working right," I yelled back.

"Pull over," the guy commanded.

"William, were you playing with the dimmer switch?" Victoria asked.

"Not now! I'm in trouble. Lie down in the back seat and stay hidden. Let me handle this."

"Are you a mechanic?" I yelled.

"Hell, no," the angry face yelled.

"My dimmer switch is broken. Will you help me fix it?" I yelled above the roaring engines and rushing wind.

"Pull over."

The gravel pelted the underside of my car as I pulled well out onto the shoulder. The big Mercury pulled in beside me. Two guys got out and walked to my window. One of them, who had "Larry" written on a paper sticker on the lapel of his black leather jacket, said, "Get out. Let's take a look at the switch."

Looks like they've been to a class reunion or something, I thought.

Larry sat in the driver's seat, holding an almost empty bottle of beer, and the other guy, whose sticker on the lapel of his black leather coat read "Spike," stood in front of my car with his own nearly empty bottle of beer.

"Did it dim?" Larry called to Spike.

"Looks like it's working okay to me," Spike said. "Do it again."

"How's it doing now?" Larry asked, as he clicked it a few more times.

"There's nothing wrong with the switch," Spike said, and they both looked at me.

I'm not dead yet, I thought, my mind scrambling for a believable response. "It seems to have a real hair trigger sometimes," I pleaded. "I can hear it click sometimes when I don't even touch it."

It looked like they were beginning to soften. "Hell, I guess that could happen," Larry said.

I saw my opening. "Here, have a beer." I reached into the back seat, took out the remaining two beers and handed them over.

"How did you know we drink Highlander?"

"Lucky guess," I laughed.

As if Spike, Larry and I laughing and drinking beer was a signal, the other guys got out of the Mercury and we all stood drinking beer and relieving ourselves in the gravel.

"Hey, guys," I said. "Thanks for the help. I'm going to have Eldrin, the mechanic where I live, look at the switch as soon as I get home."

We were saying goodbye and getting back into our cars when a pickup raced up and screeched to a stop in the middle of the road. "You son of a bitch!" the driver yelled.

It was that asshole waiter, Shorty, from the Black Bear, my gift still sitting in all its glory like an ornament on his hood. Two people were with him, their heads tipped down like they were asleep.

"You're the asshole," I yelled back.

"I'm gonna whup your ass," Shorty yelled.

I felt comfortable with my new friends around me. "Better bring a lunch. It'll take you a while." I stepped forward and motioned him over.

"You god-damned chicken. Have ta have all your friends," he said. The other two in the car with him hadn't looked up yet.

"Poor baby," I said in baby talk. Spike, Larry, and their friends laughed.

"He shit on my hood." Shorty was almost in tears now.

My new friends laughed harder. "We could care less about the goddamned shit on your hood," they said in unison.

"See ya," Spike said, and signaled Shorty down the road, like he was shooing away a fly.

"You tell yer god-damned friend I've got his address and I'll make it over to Eden," he yelled.

"Thank you very much," Larry said sarcastically. "I will."

Shorty gunned the powerful pickup and smoke poured from the spinning wheels, causing two black marks to appear on the asphalt.

Now I was really worried. But this might give me material for Alex, I consoled myself.

Spike and his friends were getting ready to leave. "We'll be seeing you, Bill," they said. "We'll make it to Eden for a visit someday. Watch out for that idiot in the pickup. He really sounds mad."

"I'll be just fine," I said, but I wasn't too sure that I would be, especially now that he knew where I lived.

With a rooster-tail spray of gravel, the Mercury dug out in a semi-circle and as it hit the hardtop, it peeled rubber, almost completing a circle. In a moment, it had disappeared into the night, leaving me alone to worry about that asshole, Shorty, and his friends.

"Hey, Victoria," I said as I got back into my new car. "I think I'm in trouble. I think it was Oscar with the old fart barkeep at the Black Bear."

"I know. I'm not deaf. You guys *were* yelling, you know."

"I could only see Shorty, but there were two other guys in the cab with him. I think one of them was Oscar."

"Let's go. I'm afraid they might try to do something to us."

I turned the key and pushed the starter. The engine turned over and hummed. I wanted to get the hell out of there.

"A car's coming," Victoria whispered.

I saw headlights in the distance. It looked like a pickup. "Oh, shit," I said. "That has to be Shorty. Maybe I should try to outrun them."

"Might as well face him. He knows where you live. It's now or later."

She was right; she had a habit of being right. Maybe I can scare him off, I thought. The pickup pulled up in front of us. Its lights were bright and we couldn't see a thing. "Hey, you asshole," I yelled. "Shut off your goddamned lights."

With the headlights still blazing, two figures stepped out in front of the headlights. It was Shorty and Alex. The third one stayed back by the pickup, his face hidden in the shadows.

"You're the asshole," Shorty scowled.

My hands trembled. He looked angry enough to kill me. "I want to protect you, Victoria," I said. "Hell, killing is not new to them. Maybe I *should* try to outrun them."

"I can take care of myself," she said. "I'm not afraid."

I couldn't leave, anyway, without running over them.

"Get out," Shorty yelled.

I turned partway around in my seat. "Lie down, Victoria. It will be better if they don't see you."

The man who had been in the shadows at the bar stepped out and walked toward us. It was Oscar, all right. He pushed himself in front of the other two, sort of like he was shielding us from each other. He talked in a low, solid voice. "You are a friend, William. You tried to help me when nobody else would. You were a lot of help at Dr. Wainscot's office. I know you don't believe me, but I wouldn't hurt you. And I'll try to protect you, too."

I couldn't stand it anymore. I got out of the car and stood facing Oscar, with Alex and Shorty behind him. "Hell, Oscar, *some friend*. You tried to kill me in Canada," I yelled.

"I wasn't trying to kill you. I was trying to protect you. You were in danger." Oscar's voice was gentle, but I was frightened. He was so cunning. No wonder the boys had all been so easy to abduct, and according to Dr. Wainscot, he hadn't even known he was doing it. I turned to run, but Oscar grabbed my shirtfront and held me as I struggled. His face had changed. In the semidarkness, it seemed to be filled with hate and evil. The lightning shot up my spine and bounced around in my skull, and the sulfur coated my mouth. I knew these men were going to kill me.

I seemed to pass through a window ...

> "You are an arrogant asshole, Oscar," William screamed. The ground was spinning. He swung a looping haymaker at Oscar's chin, which connected with a sickening half-flap, half-pop. Oscar fell to the ground. Blood ran from his nose and mouth, and his eyes looked bleary.
>
> "He's knocked out," Alex said, stooping to pat his big brother on the cheek.
>
> "You son of a bitch, you wouldn't even listen to him," Shorty said, and rushed toward William. "I'll teach you a lesson." He swung at William's chin. It missed, but Shorty caught William's arm and pulled him to the ground.
>
> "A car's coming," Alex yelled, and they all stopped to face the oncoming headlights.

The window effect faded...

"What the hell's going on?" a green-uniformed "tree cop" asked as he stepped out of his forest-green pickup with the Forest Service insignia on its side. He walked authoritatively toward the pugilists.

"Just a friendly argument," Oscar said, as he stood cradling his injured jaw in his hand, with blood running from his mouth.

"Don't look too friendly," said the officer. Another officer appeared at the edge of the darkness, looking very proper and official, with his hand on the butt of his holstered weapon.

"What happened? Are you taking a piss?" asked the authoritative officer.

"That son of a bitch forced us off the road and tried to pick a fight. I was just doing what he wanted," Shorty lied.

"That's a bunch of shit," I said.

The taller tree cop, the authoritative one, laughed. "It looks like you guys were just having a little lovers' spat."

The silent officer laughed, looking at the talking officer as if he wanted his approval. Then he ventured an opinion, "Ya ought to go to yer trailer house to make love. Shouldn't do it along the highway." Then, even in the light of the headlights, he blushed bright red.

Horse's asses, I thought.

"Let's see your driver's license," the talking officer said to me.

"I haven't had time to get one yet," I said. "I just barely got my car."

"We left ours at the Black Bear Bar," Oscar answered.

"Whose pickup is that?" the officer asked.

"It was there when we got here," Oscar lied.

Both officers pushed back their caps and scratched their heads. The smaller one said with a smile, "Who shit on the hood?" Then he blushed again.

I was glad Victoria hadn't gotten out of the car.

That would just make things worse. Maybe her old man, James H., had an APB out.

That would be all I needed now: kidnapping, and with no driver's license.

"Guess we'll have to haul you in and let the constable sort this out," the officer said. "I'm going to charge you all with disturbing the peace and assault. The justice will probably just charge you with disturbing the peace and give you suspended sentences, unless you have priors or warrants."

Oscar, Alex, and Shorty looked at each other. Oscar whispered, so the officers couldn't hear, "Hell, yes, we've got priors. Remember, we left Utah during the investigation. I'm sure we can clear it all up, but the fact remains that we left. They will ship us back to Utah. Let's just go along and see what happens. We can deal with William later."

"Hell, I'm not going to just go along," Shorty whispered. "I ain't never been in Utah and I got priors. I got some dandies."

"We need ta handcuff ya—just procedure," the taller trooper said as both rangers approached.

"Let's take care of 'em and dump their bodies in the woods

for the coyotes and cougars, like I did with that other guy," Shorty whispered. "Nobody'll ever find 'em."

Oscar and Alex looked stunned. "We didn't know you did that."

"I'm sure I told you," Shorty said, and then he reached behind his body and pulled out a gun.

"Hey, you sons a bitches," he yelled at the officers, "put up your goddamned hands." The two officers were startled, but did as they were told. Now even the talking officer was silent for a moment. "You'll never get away with this," he finally said.

The lighting again shot up my spine and bounced around in my skull, and the sulfur coated my mouth as I realized I'd be discarded in the woods along with the rangers, and never be heard of again. What would Victoria do without me? I would never see our baby. I had to do something.

"I'll get him," I yelled, as I jumped forward and kicked Shorty in the groin. He bent over holding his crotch, and the gun fell to the road. The two officers acted quickly, subduing Shorty and spread-eagling him on the asphalt road.

After the three were securely cuffed, they were loaded into the back of the tree cops' pickup. Shorty sat in the middle, handcuffed to Alex and Oscar on either side, and the free hands of those two were cuffed to the sides of the pickup.

When the three had been secured, the tree cops came over to talk to me.

"You're pretty much out of trouble," the taller officer said, "but you'll need to come in next week to be a witness."

"Okay," I said. "I'll plan on it. I'll be looking for an excuse to drive my car, anyway."

The talking officer said, "Make sure you get a driver's license."

As the pickup carried the officers and the handcuffed desperados onto the road, I heard Oscar's loud voice, "Now ya got us into real trouble. I don't know how this is going to turn out now. I have to talk to William. I have to make him see what's going on—how much danger he's in."

Soon, only the taillights of the ranger's pickup were visible, and then even they dissolved into the darkness.

Chapter 113

The road was getting pretty straight now and I was able to pick up some speed. I was still glad I had given the barkeep the surprise on his hood. It gave me a warm and wonderful feeling, but I also had the chilling feeling that I hadn't seen the last of them. I really needed to stay alert, because the fog could hide and disguise the abundant animals along this desolate, dark portion of highway. The night was sublime as the fog rolled in to cover everything; an exquisite exercise in fantasy and delight, reminiscent of dancing fairies and imps. And then the fog would part, reminding me of a crescendo in a symphony, and the soft light from the stars and moon would turn the road and trees from eerie figures back into a road and trees. The stars provided an audience for the moon's spectacular command performance, but even that could not in the smallest way compete with the magnificence of my car as we sped along the desolate highway. And then everything would vanish again, as the fog quickly closed in, like a curtain coming down on the final act of a play, and the road and trees once more became eerie dancing fairies and imps.

Suddenly, a real figure loomed just ahead, along the edge of the road. "What the hell is that?" I pressed the brakes and slowed to get a better look. In the white darkness of the fog, it looked like a monster. As we came closer, I exclaimed, "It's the old man from Hope. How the hell did he get way over here?" I watched suspiciously. "Guess his wife decided not to take him." I felt a little pity.

He stood slightly bent at the waist, squinting into my headlights with his right thumb extended, his entire body begging for a ride. I slowed more and pulled to the edge of the road, the gravel flying up to pelt the undercarriage of the car as it left the hard surface. "Jeez, that's going to be good for my car," I complained. My headlights flooded the old man and the road ahead. He was wearing faded blue bib overalls and underneath, a white shirt buttoned up to his neck. His beard and what was visible of his hair, which flowed from under the tattered and sweat-stained cowboy hat, was dirty and matted. Scuffed western boots that were desperately turned over were well-suited to the sad ensemble. Even at this distance in the semi-darkness, I could see the weathered, wrinkled skin that covered his face and the exposed parts of his slender, skeletal body. Only an unlined denim jacket stood between him and the chill of the frigid Montana night.

The old man walked toward me and opened the passenger door. "Howdy, sir," he said in a soft, submissive voice.

I saw now that it wasn't the old man from Hope. It just looked a lot like him. "Hi yourself. Where 'ya goin?"

"Paradise. I works in a bar over there."

"Get in. They ain't no way to miss Paradise if you travel this here road," I said, trying to mimic his hillbilly lingo.

I ground the gears into low and continued along the road.

"Mind if I smoke?" he asked.

His hillbilly accent was gone. "Sure," I said.

He took out a bag of Durham. "Want me to roll you one?"

A smile broke across my face. "Let me roll you one with one hand," I said and took his makings. I quickly rolled a perfect cigarette with one hand as I held the steering wheel with my knees to show my competence. I handed him the perfect stogy and then rolled another one for me. He struck and held a match, and we both reached to the flame with scrunched-up lips and squinted eyes.

"I've never seen anybody do that before," he said. "Roll a stogy with one hand."

"Had to learn when I cut off my thumb." I held up the stub in such a way that it might have looked like I was bragging. "How come your accent went away after you got in?" I asked him.

"People seem to be less threatened when they think I'm just a dumb old man," he said.

"Oh."

We sat and smoked for a time, watching the headlights dance on the foggy road, and then he said, "I go to Missoula once a month or so, to see a movie and have a few drinks, to just change my routine a little."

"I like to go someplace once in a while myself," I said, trying to be a little friendlier than I had with the old man in Hope. "My name is Bill. What's yours?"

"Glen."

"You from around here?"

"No. Hamilton," he answered.

"What you doing over at Paradise?"

"I sort of got screwed out of my ranch, and didn't have any other place to settle."

"Screwed?" I asked, "How?"

"It's a long story," Glen said.

"I got time."

He sat for a moment, like he was finding a place to begin. "I had a big ranch over there. Raised cattle and horses and lots of hay and grain."

"How long ago was that?" I asked.

"Lost track; but a long time."

"How come you ended up over in Paradise?" I asked again.

"I'm a-gettin' to that," he snapped at me.

"Okay, I'll listen."

"Well, my wife and I had two kids, a boy and a girl, and we raised them on the ranch. We had a good life. A river ran through it, and it had Forest Service land on two sides as well." He paused, trying to stifle a sob, and then went on. "Our daughter was killed in a rafting accident on the river when she was young. It 'bout broke my wife's heart—and mine too, I guess."

"That's too bad," I volunteered.

"Well, life went on and the years passed and before long our boy was grown and he decided to marry a girl from Minnesota. She seemed like a nice girl and we took her in as our actual daughter."

"What was she like?"

"She was a lot like our daughter who got killed. We learned to love her just like she was family."

"Sounds like you sort of got your daughter back," I said.

"Not really. She turned out to be a real bitch," he snapped. "Mom and me had decided we wanted to retire and just travel and take it easy. Hell, we sure earned it for all the years we had worked, and the chances we took with the ranch and all."

"Well, what happened Glen?" I asked. And then, afraid he might scold me again, I said, "Sorry," and waited for him to continue.

This time the scolding was just a sour look, and he went on. "Mom and me, we signed the ranch over to our son and daughter-in-law, with a verbal agreement that we could just live there and share in the profits and do our travelin' and stuff. We all figured that would work out real good, but we didn't write nothin' down. We just trusted each other. Hell, we always had."

"Did she do something wrong?" I asked. The story was getting interesting.

The dirty look again—I directed a look of apology at him—and he went on. "Well it worked out good for a few years. We really enjoyed ourselves."

"What the hell happened?"

He rolled his eyes.

"Sorry," I said.

After another dirty look, he continued, "One day my wife went into Missoula with my son, to see the doctor. They had a head-on collision with some drunken bastard and were both killed. The drunk was killed, too, the bastard. It was sad buryin' them. I put them to rest right beside my daughter in the cemetery in Hamilton. I cried a lot and cursed God for being so cruel."

"Weren't you afraid of being struck by lightning?"

"Hell, I would have been glad if I had been."

"It takes a lot to get God to strike you with lightning," I said with a knowing grin.

He looked out the window as tears made their way down his cheeks. "Want another smoke?" he asked.

"Shur."

He rolled us each one, using both hands, licked the papers to keep them together, and handed me one. After we lit up, he took up his story again. "I sat around and felt sorry for myself for a few weeks, thinking that life couldn't get any worse, and then I found out that it could."

In the dim lights of the dash, I could see the anger in his face. His eyes were wet with tears. "The bitch called the police and had them throw me off my ranch for trespassing." He was sobbing now. "She threw me right off my own ranch. Said she was getting married to some guy, and that I would be in the way. I wanted to kill her and promised myself that someday I would go back and do it, but I never have yet."

"Didn't you tell the police what happened?"

"I did, but they said she was all legal. The cops took me into Missoula and dropped me off on the streets. I roamed around and slept wherever I could for weeks, and begged for food, and even ate out of the trash.

One day, I met a man who owned a bar in Paradise—The Paradise Bar and Grille. The bar owner was looking for somebody to clean up and take out the garbage, to take some of the work away from his wife and him, and I took the job. The pay was meager, a few bucks a week, but it came with a room over the bar and sandwiches from the grille. It was a lot better than I had."

He rolled down the window, threw his exhausted stogy onto the road, and spat after it.

"Hey, you're going to start a fire," I yelled at him.

"I always spit in my hand and put the hot end in it and crumble it up before I throw it away. It's called field stripping. I learned to do that in the Forest Service," he said.

"Oh. Sounds like a good way to put out your cigarette." I was embarrassed. I shouldn't have yelled at the poor old bastard.

"The job's not too bad, except for cleaning the johns. They get pretty rank."

"You could do better."

"Things can always get worse. That's a good thing to remember," he said, and then seemed to slip into a quiet mood, as his head sagged. After a while, his eyes closed.

God, he can use the rest, the poor old guy, I thought. The cloud cover suddenly lifted and the moon became the "star," as the lesser stars watched in silent awe. It was strikingly sublime, I thought, as my more gentle side surfaced.

Glen raised his head and mumbled something, and then fell back to sleep. The road made a sharp turn to cross a large bridge. "Paradise: Pop. 50," a sign said, and then another one, "25— Strictly Enforced."

"Hell, I'll bet they don't even have a cop in Paradise," I mumbled. The road straightened onto the deserted Main Street that had so few storefronts, it only hinted at more than proclaimed a town. There were lights on inside several houses, and a shirtless young man walked along the otherwise vacant street. He didn't even bother to look up as we drove past.

I stopped in front of the Paradise Bar and Grille and waited for Glen to wake up.

Right below the wording of the bar and grill there were two

dice, one showing a two and the other a five "Oh, I get it—"Par-a-dise"—a pair of dice, and a winner at that." I had to smile.

He didn't wake up, and I shook him. He still didn't wake up. "God, he's dead," I exclaimed. I shook him harder.

"What going on?" he said as he raised his head and looked around.

"We're here, Glen."

"Oh, good. I'm tired. I need to get to bed." He opened the door and stood for a moment, as if trying to orient himself.

"You okay?" I asked.

"Yeah. Just need to get my walking legs under me," and he showed his stained teeth. He gestured goodbye, slammed the door, and walked toward the side of the bar. I waited to make sure he got inside and then pulled onto the highway.

"What's going on?" Victoria asked from the backseat.

"Just let off a hitchhiker," I said. "Go back to sleep."

"You shouldn't pick up hitchhikers. You never know."

"I can tell," I said.

"Don't pick up any more hitchhikers. I'm glad I was asleep," she said.

"Okay. I'll wake you up and ask if I see anybody else," I laughed.

"You're so silly."

"Colt always calls Eden the Garden Of Eden," I said over the seat. "But I can't think of any reason the place should be called that."

"Who knows?"

"Just wait until I rule Eden with you at my side. We will make it a land of happiness and beauty, and our subjects will be pleased."

"We will indeed."

Finally, a road sign ahead said, "Eden." I turned onto the chuckhole-filled gravel road, dust flew, and I struggled to keep the car under control. I guided it across the bridge and along the road that led to Mom and Dad's house. We pulled up in front and stopped. The house was dark—the headlights illuminated the hovel and made it seem even smaller and more lonely than it actually was.

"What going on?" Victoria asked from the back seat.

"They're not home."

"Well, you should be used to that. They're never around much when you need them, are they?" She reached over the seat to push my hair back in a loving gesture, which felt good. Sometimes I just needed a little attention.

"I'll be all right," I said.

"I'm sure you will be. I'll stay over tonight."

Several times during the night, I went out to see the car, to make sure it wasn't just a dream, and to make sure the lights were off, so the battery wouldn't be dead in the morning. The night was unusually light, and the stars provided an impressive audience for the moon's spectacular command performance, but neither the stars nor the moon could compete with the magnificence of the car. There, in the dim light, it stood as if it were a creature with a soul and as if it were telling all who gazed upon it, "See my sublime supremacy."

Chapter 114

Finally, the long night came to an end. I had been so excited about the car that I hadn't taken my clothes off. I just got up from the chair where I'd sat all night, washed my face, pushed back my hair with my wet fingers, and went out to check on it. It looked even better in the full sunlight. I took the top down and walked around to look one more time, to make sure it was real. I opened the door and got in for a closer examination. "This is what a car should be." I had always had the feeling that God had destined me for something great, like being a king, just like the patriarch had said at my séance. Why else would He make my hands bleed when they touched dirt? That could only happen because I was King William III. Why did I feel faint when confronted with physical labor? This had to be the reason.

"But maybe God wants me to be a great scientist," I thought. "God's will be done."

I had ideas about a lot of things, including one about the galaxies. For a long time, I had intended to send my theories to Albert Einstein, the great scientist, to see what he thought, and now I decided to do it. I hoped he'd be able to understand. They were quite complicated. Dad had always discouraged me from bothering people, but he didn't need to know everything I did. I went into the house and found a piece of paper and an envelope in Mom's drawer and took the dictionary down from the shelf. Then I sat down at our dining room table. I was alone.

I thought for a moment and then began to write, looking up words as I went.

> *Dear Albert,*
> *My name is William Robert Jones III.*

I used my whole name. I wanted him to be impressed.

> *I've been thinking, and what if atoms are just small solar systems? And maybe our solar system is just one atom in a very, very large solar system. Please consider this theorem.*
> *Sincerely,*
> *William Robert Jones III.*

I placed the letter in the envelope and took it to Mrs. Larsen at the post office. I asked her to help me edit it. In fact, she rewrote it. And then she helped me find Einstein's address. She looked in a thick book. "I know he teaches in New York somewhere. Oh, here it is, in the Bronx. I'll write it on the envelope for you."

She placed my name and address in the upper left hand corner of the envelope, like you're supposed to do. What she had written on the envelope was: *Albert Einstein, Yeshiva University, Bronx, NY, 10461.* I handed the three cents to Mrs. Larsen. She licked a stamp, stuck it on the envelope, and then dropped it into the slot marked, "Out of Town."

I said thanks and goodbye to Mrs. Larsen. She stood on the front porch as I walked away.

After that, the time passed slowly as I imagined myself working with Einstein on my theory.

It was exciting, and I had trouble sleeping. Finally, I more or less forgot about it. But one day, some weeks later, Mom walked in all excited. "William," she called, "you have a letter—it's from

Albert Einstein! What's this all about?"

"Oh, nothing, Mom. We're just working on a new theory." I took the letter and went to my room to read it.

> Dear Sir or Madam,
> I was so pleased that you decided to write; it's always so interesting to get information from my friends. I was excited to read your letter and am now taking it under advisement. I will be in touch if I need more information. I am impressed with your knowledge.
> And just to mention an interesting item, James Watson and Francis Crick at the University of Cambridge are utilizing the process of X-ray crystallography to study the structure of protein molecules. They are near announcing a discovery about how a molecule of an atom could encode information to create static and reliable attributes. They are calling it DNA.
> Sincerely,
> Albert Einstein
> Signed for and on behalf of Albert Einstein by Margaret Manson, Director of Communications.

"He really thinks the theory is good. He will study it. He said he would!" I thought it a good idea to pursue this project. I passed through a window and watched myself with Albert Einstein.

> William had been summoned from his modest retreat in Montana to assist Albert Einstein. It had all come about because of a paper concerning the creation of human life and atomic theory that William had written, a copy of which had been forwarded to the famous scientist. Now William had been invited, well, coerced to the laboratory to assist the renowned scientist in his studies of living atomic memory. Albert had almost been successful at

duplicating the type of memory that exists in the human brain and now needed William's help to complete it.

The laboratory was more modern and larger than William could ever have imagined. Complicated-looking machinery and equipment were everywhere. The scientist had been impressed with the unusual knowledge exhibited by William in a letter, which had been followed by a very complicated hypothesis concerning the same subject. Then, of course, this was followed by documented research concerning the creation of life. This research was based on a theory that Einstein apparently had abandoned, but now seeing his folly, the scientist's interest had been revived and he had recruited William to be at his side to resume the research.

The good Dr. Einstein had waited until now so as not to waste William's talent on elementary research. Instead, he wished to tap his superior mind for more difficult and challenging discoveries. The atomic bomb had already been perfected and tested, but now something to benefit and not threaten mankind was on the horizon. The idea of a living, atomic memory had been Williams', and had been included in his original paper to Einstein explaining the basics of this astounding theory. Albert had been delighted and had understood the complicated theory almost immediately, and had even improved on it somewhat. But he also questioned what the hidden dangers might be. And now, as the research advanced, it seemed Einstein needed more guidance and assurance.

William was escorted to his luxurious room and, as it was late, he undressed and climbed between the sheets of the large, comfortable bed. He hadn't been too happy to leave his important work in Montana, but the iminence of a new, living atomic memory overshadowed his other work, causing it to pale in comparison. He slept a restful sleep, dreaming of times not so stressful, when he could just be a young man doing the things that boys do, and not have to carry the fate of nations or cultures on his shoulders.

A soft rap on the door and the gentle voice awakened him, and William arose to see the sun high in the morning sky.

"Breakfast is ready, doctor," a voice announced.

"Be right there," he responded.

The breakfast spared no expense and no breakfast item that he was aware of was held back from the table. He ate his fill.

"I've discovered," Albert said, eager to begin, "that if I collect certain living atoms in a certain way, I am able to communicate with them, with a device I call a 'track.'"

"What is a track made from, Albert?" William asked, so as not to seem uninterested. Of course, he already knew the answer, but he didn't want to alienate Albert.

"I have been successful in using a strand of microscopic carbon alloy. It seems to be by far the most stable material."

William considered this for a moment before he felt comfortable enough to reply to such an elementary concept. His main objective was politeness. "How is it possible to communicate with all the atoms in your collection?"

Albert's smile broadened. "I don't need to communicate with them all, William," the doctor said as he placed another forkful of egg and hash browns into his mouth and thoughtfully chewed. "Mostly, I let them talk to each other. I tell the ones that I talk to, to tell the others, and they tell them. And do so very quickly, I might add."

"That ingenious, Albert," William exclaimed. Under his breath he whispered, "Duh," and rolled his eyes to signal his boredom at this elementary concept. Catching himself before Albert became aware of his condescension, *he feigned a cough and held the napkin to his face.*

"Do you know what this means?" Albert asked.

"Not completely," William lied, trying to pamper the tired old man, "but I learn and catch on very quickly."

"This means we will have the memory not only thinking for itself but doing what we tell it to do." He smiled with delight.

"Duh," William thought again, but he said, "Have you considered coupling this memory of atoms with the new discovery of DNA?" *Unselfishly, he was trying to allow Albert to think it was his idea.*

Albert rubbed his stubble chin and returned, "No, William, I hadn't given it any thought, but it is a possibility. I'll study it some more. In fact, let's study it together some time."

A few weeks later, William smiled deviously as he thought, *it's time to take my thinking to a new level.* He said to Albert, "I can't accept the slow pace any longer. We can't continue to stall on this, and if you can't place urgency and priority on the DNA aspect of atomic memory, then I intend to go back to Eden and pursue other interests. Besides, I miss Victoria."

"I had no idea," Albert exclaimed.

"I'm sure you didn't," William said. "I'm sure you're struggling with these trivial data so much that you forgot about my tribulations."

"We will begin research right away." Albert put away his notes, suspended the experiments he was working on, and began setting up ones from the big wooden box labeled, "Atomic Memory by William."

"That's all I wanted, Albert," William exclaimed.

"Explain your hypothesis concerning the atoms being combined with DNA and having them train and develop other atomic/DNA memory," said Albert.

"Well, you will need to try to keep up with me. It's pretty advanced and I wouldn't want to lose you, so just stop me if you don't understand. Don't be embarrassed to ask questions."

"Very well," Albert said. "Please go on."

William tried to find a place to begin that was elementary enough that the old man could understand, and finally he did. "You already know about atoms doing the work. The big problem is being able to communicate with them. You have developed a device you call a track, with which you have achieved communication, but it's unreliable and very difficult to control."

He stopped to see if it was sinking in. Albert nodded, so he went on.

"I have postulated that if the atoms and DNA were combined in 'cakes' of some sort, allowing them to react and counter-react to each other at random, they might develop attributes that would be uniformly consistent, as well as reliable."

Albert looked confused. "Do you mean that the cakes, as you call them, might be able to do consistent things, if they were strictly and identically duplicated?" the old man asked.

"Yes, that's exactly what I mean," William said, and tried to further simplify, so the old man would really understand. "It will be a matter of testing and cataloging the attributes that appear when any given atoms and DNA are combined in any given ratios with any other array of the cakes."

Albert was silent and then, "That sounds monumental. It makes my formula concerning time and speed seem trivial."

"Don't despair, Albert. This is as much your doing as mine." William was pleased with his unselfish willingness to share his ideas and credit with the old man. "Now, we need to improve the tracks for communicating and devise some usable devices for holding and testing the atom/DNA cakes."

"It's your idea," Albert said. "I will assist you. What can I do to help?"

"Just stay out of the way and keep the laboratory cleaned up until we discover a little bit more."

"Very well, young and wise scientist," Albert said as if in jest, although it was mostly to cover his injured pride.

William thought he detected a vein of resentment in the old scientist's response, but decided it was probably just his imagination. "It is at least nice to have someone to talk to," he concluded. As an afterthought, he added, "The cakes will be analyzed and placed with the other selected cakes to create attributes as they interact. Then these will be tested and their attributes cataloged. They will be tested again at random as to how they perform given tasks. And then in a very careful and orderly manner, they will be assigned a value to identify them to a precise task or function. I thought about calling them 'chips' but that made me think of cow or buffalo chips, so I went with cakes. Do you understand?" he asked.

"Sort of. I'll just watch for a while and try to keep up," he said, and gave a defeated smile that he hadn't needed to use for a long time.

As William worked, he tried to comfort the aging scientist.

"I can see that someday the assembled atom/DNA cakes will actually attain the ability to think for themselves and will begin doing whatever we tell them but at a very rapid rate," Albert mumbled.

William could see that Albert was finally getting it, and he added excitedly, "They will even replicate themselves *and create a string of atoms in space where only ether exists now, and do it so rapidly that a trip to other planets will take virtually no time at all."* Now William let his imagination run wild: *"The intelligent cakes will be able to examine a person or item, catalog it, dismantle it, and then replicate it at another location—all of this done in small increments, but very rapidly."*

Albert again looked puzzled. *"Do you mean that it would look like the person or item was instantly transported, but it really wasn't?"* He stopped, deep in thought for a moment, and then went on, *"Do you mean it will really just be disassembled, cataloged, and assembled at an incredible rate of speed through space, and then this process, when it reaches its final destination, just assembles it in the exact detail as the original?"*

William interjected his support. *"The process will be so rapid that it will appear that it was transported from one location to another instantly. But as it rebuilds itself trillions and trillions of times through space, it will be a completely new and different object when it reaches its final destination."*

"But what about its make-up?" Albert questioned, wide-eyed. *"Do you mean it will possess the same attributes and character of the original, even though it is a completely different entity? In other words, it will be different, but as the original no longer exists, it will be unique, with all the original attributes and character of the original? So for all practical purposes, it will be the original, even though it actually isn't?"*

"That's exactly what I mean, Albert."

"Are there any limits as to size or distance?" he asked.

"None," William said solemnly. *"We could conceivably build atomic/DNA ladders into space that would be much faster than the speed of light and transmit people or things*

to distant planets in the twinkling of an eye over millions of light years."

"How the hell could that be done?" Albert asked.

William stopped for a minute again, to find a way to express his idea in terms that Albert would be able to understand. "It's probably difficult for you to imagine how fast this process would be." He went on, slowly and carefully, "As it proceeds, time would also become a factor, just as you point out in your famous equation concerning speed and time."

"Oh," Albert replied, "now I'm beginning to get it. Time would be further reduced based on the unimaginably great speed."

"Bingo. Now you're catching on."

"That's a revolutionary concept."

"The Master Blaster, as I call it, and not any God or Jesus, will be man's salvation."

Albert's laugh was not one of humor but of admiration at William's unfathomable, unscientific labeling of such an advanced scientific discovery. "Master Blaster," he cried, tears of glee flowing from his eyes. And then he said with more decorum, "But I guess the 'Big-Bang Theory' doesn't sound very scientific, either."

William remarked, "That was more of a random accident than anything to do with man or God."

"Are you sure?"

"What do you mean?"

Albert smiled wryly. "There might be a God who does intervene at rare times. Most certainly, there is something behind all this wonder, and we humans, with our dull and feeble minds, can only begin to scrape its surface."

"I thought you were an atheist."

"No. It's just that I have trouble believing in a God that has been created from the imaginations of fanatics."

William was amazed. His mother would be, as well. He couldn't wait to tell her.

"But you were talking about the Master Blaster. Please go on."

"Very well. The Master Blaster will construct the atom/DNA ladder just ahead of itself very rapidly—more rapidly than is humanly imaginable—and then will immediately disassemble it, as it moves into the ladder it has just constructed, and then, at the same unimaginable speed, it will build another one just in front of that, and so on. As it builds, it will learn, and it will begin to build faster and faster. It will have the capacity to encapsulate and transport items or people, either in whole or as replicas of those persons or objects, as I've already explained. The Master Blaster will have the capacity to reach and carry persons and objects almost instantaneously to the ends of the galaxy, or even beyond."

"But how can it exceed the speed of light? That's impossible."

"It isn't based on the speed of light," William said patiently. "It's based on the concept of time and space, which has no restriction of speed, as light does."

"My God, William, that is astounding!"

"There would be no need for any kind of enclosure for the person or the object, because the Master Blaster would be creating all necessary critical elements for survival, whether the person or thing was being re-created or transported." He could see that Albert was becoming confused again, so he waited a moment to let the new concept sink into the old scientist's brain. Finally, Albert nodded that he understood and William went on. "After the desired destination has been reached, the Master Blaster creates all the elements needed to survive there."

"It will work," Albert said. "It's complicated but simple

at the same time. The Master Blaster does everything."

After a moment, he said, "The only danger is that it will eventually become so intelligent, it will take over."

"We will need to install safeguards for this," William agreed. "Each journey will be mapped and stored, so that when the person or object wants to return there will be 'bread crumbs' to follow, so to speak." He couldn't resist adding, "And hopefully with no little birds to eat them."

They both chuckled. Even though William sometimes longed for solitude and for the carefree life he had before he began assisting the famous scientist, or before the famous scientist began assisting him to develop the atomic memory, it was too late to go back to now. An impasse was imminent, because Albert didn't know what to do, and this sapped William's interest and energy, because all the responsibility had been loaded onto his young, albeit strong, shoulders.

"Let's get away from science for a while," he said. "We need a break. Tell me more about your thoughts concerning God and religion."

The old scientist considered for a moment. "Science has much more to do with God than religion does."

William was surprised at his answer.

"My religion," Albert went on, "consists of a humble admiration for the illimitable, superior spirit that reveals itself in the slight details we are able to perceive with our frail and feeble minds. That deeply emotional conviction of the presence of a superior reasoning power, which is revealed in the incomprehensible universe, forms my idea of God."

He smiled at William. "I cannot imagine a God who rewards and punishes the objects of its creation, whose purposes are modeled after our own—a God who, in short, is but a reflection of human frailty.

It is enough for me to contemplate the mystery of conscious life perpetuating itself through eternity, to reflect upon the marvelous structure of the universe, which we can dimly perceive, and to try humbly to comprehend even an infinitesimal part of the intelligence manifested in Nature."

His smile had now almost completely filled his face, and then it became a mirthful chuckle and finally a laugh, as he saw the astonished look on William's young face.

"Dad would send you to your room," William blurted out.

Albert went on, "Obviously, no religion is complete, and some well-meaning re-organizer occasionally breaks away, attempting to understand something that is impossible for humans to understand, and only succeeds in adding to the confusion by creating yet another incomplete religious club that competes for its own glory and not for God's. In comparison, it is more conceivable that humans could someday comprehend the concept of our solar system as only one atom of an entire universe, or that a single atom could be a solar system—as you pointed out in your initial letter to me—than it is for us to understand the truth about God and eternity. We mortals are incapable of completely understanding a God who is above all the other gods, and the complexities surrounding that truth."

Now William was really astounded. He had no idea that Albert even thought about such things, and he hadn't considered that science and God could exist harmoniously.

Albert continued, "You will hardly find one among the most profound scientific minds without a peculiar religious feeling of his own. But it is different from the religion of the naive man. For the latter, God is a being from whose care one hopes to benefit, and whose punishment one fears. It's a sublimation of a feeling similar to that of a child for its father, a being to whom one stands to some extent in a personal relation, however deeply it may be tinged with awe. But the scientist is possessed by the sense of universal causation. The future, to him, is every whit as necessary and determined as the past. There is nothing divine about morality; it is a purely human affair. His religious feeling takes the form of a rapturous amazement at the harmony of natural law, which reveals an intelligence of such superiority that, compared with it, all the systematic thinking and acting of human beings is an utterly insignificant reflection. This feeling is the guiding principle of his life and work, in so far as he succeeds in keeping himself from the shackles of selfish desire. It is beyond question closely akin to that which has possessed the religious geniuses of all ages."

Albert stopped to fill his lungs with oxygen and then went on. *"Religious clubs, as I call religions, only in a very small way represent God. Rather, they represent the writings and dogma of an incomplete history riddled with the opinions of those who invented it. They go through the motions of searching scriptures and writings, not to finds truths, but to confirm their existing beliefs. When a new club is formed, the things that were so detested and that caused the reform quickly make their way back into the new club, as the leaders realize the power and wealth their new office holds. Then, very quickly, the new club becomes as non-spiritual and evil as the mother church was. Obviously, if parents belong to a certain religious club, or believe in a certain political party, then almost always their offspring will adhere to that notion as well. Nevertheless, any intelligent being can see the power of faith and the strength and comfort that religious clubs give to their members. All have similar requirements and similar penalties as well as rewards and punishment,* because they are creations of man's imagination that attempt to answer age-old questions about life and death, as well as being supposedly irrefutable engines to control their members."

He paused, and then went on. "Men wish to live well while at the same time maintaining a sarcastic spiritual viewpoint on worldly gratifications. I think I got that from Franklin."

William was embarrassed. He reflected that Albert knew more about religion as it related to science than he did. He changed the subject back to pure science, in which he was dominant. That night, after a long day's work, he slept well, and dreamed of the time when mankind would benefit from his unselfish and dedicated efforts. In the morning, he realized that Albert's description of religion and science had fueled a whole new way to consider his work. There were so many kinds of churches and so many kinds of gods, and in defiance of their teachings, they competed and fought with each other savagely and continually. Who knew? Maybe a God could speak through these organizations in different ways, and it was the responsibility of members to interpret and understand the message. Maybe the gods, or God, had little reason to be concerned, and really cared little what we did, and just let us try to figure it all out on our own. William had vivid memories of when he had cursed God, and then waited for the lightning, which never came. Maybe now he understood.

"God understands and isn't offended," he thought. "It's the self-righteous people who don't understand, and it's they who are offended. It's like they think they know what God is thinking and what he wants, as if they were doing God's talking and thinking for him and making him something that he isn't and doesn't even want to be. He *might have larger fish to fry. Maybe there is really a God over the other gods, a Super God who directs the others, all of whom answer to Him or Her. Maybe he is over the Christian gods, the Jewish god, the Buddhist god, (well, they don't profess to have gods), the Islamic god, and all the others, even Mother Nature, the sports god, and Santa Claus.*

"People can become more evil by hiding their actions behind religion than people who aren't religious at all. Jesus didn't do anything complicated. He just showed people how to live, by living an exemplary, unselfish life and forgiving and loving everybody. Maybe it's wrong to consciously try to get ourselves into heaven. Maybe what he was showing us was that we need to forget about ourselves and just unselfishly help, love, and forgive others, with no thought of rewards to ourselves, from either God or man."

Chapter 115

With my new car and so much to do, I had pretty much forgotten about everything else and was just having one hell of a great time. The days passed quickly, and soon, months had gone by. But while taking some of the neighborhood kids fishing and joyriding, my beautiful new car had suffered some serious injuries. One of the twin spotlights had been knocked off and damaged so badly that I had been forced to throw it away. The handle and the parts of the assembly other than the light were still fine and looked pretty good. The convertible top had been pulled out of shape. I had forgotten to fasten it down during an expedition along Anderson Lane and it billowed up, nearly causing me to lose control. It wasn't anything serious, but the top wouldn't go all the way down anymore and stuck up quite a bit. It was more a nuisance than anything else. The door on the driver's side had been bent back when I ran into a tree with it open, and now it wouldn't open—you had to climb over the top of the door. But that was sort of neat, like it was a real hotrod. While I was driving down a steep part of the riverbank to a good fishing hole, the car had lost traction and slid down sideways, hitting a big rock. This had damaged the right side a little and had knocked off one fender skirt, as well as one of the tailpipes.

I decided to drive over to Uncle Arthur's place and take him for a ride. He was a great uncle, who had always been there for me when I needed him, and I hadn't even let him see my new car.

"Hey, William," he said when I arrived, "I don't have time right now, but I would like to take a ride in it when I do."

"Okay, it's a deal."

"Hear about the jailbreak?" he asked.

"No I didn't."

"Three guys broke out by subduing one of the guards."

With my luck, it's probably Oscar, I thought, and then asked, "Know who they were?"

"It's in the newspaper," he said.

I rushed home, grabbed the paper and scanned through it, finding a picture of a woman in Missoula named Ned Johnson who had been strangled to death with a leather shoelace about the same time these criminals had been arrested. These three were suspected as the culprits.

In a right-hand column I saw an obituary for my friend Warren. There was no picture, but I imagined him in his army uniform, smiling with his middle finger extended to me. As I read all the stuff they put there, trying to find something, anything, to say that was somewhat complementary, I imagined that I saw the words, "Wild Bill, if you see this—this finger is for you. Suck it!" He had been killed while on patrol, and I was sure he blamed me. I didn't know how he knew he was going to get it, but he seemed to have known. It was uncanny as hell. If I had passed the physical, it could just as well have been me.

As I continued to scan the paper, I saw what I was looking for: a picture of the escapees. My heart sank, and sulfur coated the roof of my mouth as lightning shot up my spine. It *was* Oscar, Alex, and that asshole bartender, Shorty. The article said they were being extradited from Montana to Utah, to be tried for at least three unsolved murders there, when they had somehow overpowered the sheriff and locked him in the trunk of his car. Bystanders had witnessed the three of them jumping onto a passing train that was heading east.

At least that's what the paper said. I was glad they were heading east, but who the hell knew where they would go from there? They knew where I lived. I could bet on that, because they had seen my license plate when we stopped at the Black Bear Bar.

Victoria had given up so much to be with me that I worried about her.

Sometimes I wished she hadn't left the castle in Scotland, and was still safe at home instead of being subjected to the discomfort and dangers that always surrounded me. I might as well be a secret agent—it seemed I was always on the edge. I knew that as soon as she had convinced her father that I was indeed of royal blood, he would approve of us, and then we would at last be able to be married officially and live as we both wanted to.

"I'm really glad you waited for me, Victoria. I was wondering if you would. I wondered if I would ever see you again."

"Of course I would wait—forever, if I had to."

She was careful with my thumb and arm when we were close. She took care of things that I used to do, although I helped as much as I could with my good hand. It was nice having her to myself most of the time, but it wasn't the same as before the accident. We had lots of time to talk and we often revisited those times in Utah and our younger years, that wonderful time, which was the light of our lives.

"I wonder if it was as good as we remember?" she asked.

"I'm sure it was."

"Momma says we forget the bad things and just remember the good."

I laughed. "That's exactly what my mom says."

"I don't understand why I don't get pregnant, William."

"Maybe it did something when your dad took you for the abortion."

"Could be."

"Maybe if we did it like we did the first time it would help."

"That would be nice."

We went to the bank of the river where the weeds were tall. She lay down and pulled up her dress. "I'll show you mine if you'll show me yours," she said, and smiled.

I laughed. "We don't have to do everything exactly the same." Nonetheless, the blood rushed to my face. It was exciting. I was red and swollen, her face was flushed, we touched and caressed. I had a slightly sick feeling, like I was doing something wrong but the desire to do it was vital. I felt hot, and it was wonderful.

I passed through a window and began watching William and Victoria.

> She lay looking at William. The edges of her lips were raised in a mysterious, pleasant smile. She seemed to be waiting for him to do just as he pleased, which excited him. He drew close. There was a delightful fragrance, like nothing he had ever before experienced—well, not since they were young. A pleasant but very basic scent; it was soft and wet. The essence was excitingly foreboding. She held his head between her hands and arched her body to meet him.
>
> "Oh, William," she moaned.
>
> He moved to kneel before her. She screamed softly, and he smiled.
>
> "I love you, William."
>
> "I love you, too."
>
> He was on top of her. Their breath came in short, soft bursts as they lay expressing their love. "I want to always be with you." Her words came out as shallow, soft gasps. Her face was flushed.
>
> "We will always be together."
>
> "Yes, my prince."
>
> There was a sensation he had seldom, if ever,

experienced ... it seemed as if a covey of quail had been frightened and were now fluttering softly from between his legs. The feeling was exquisite; better than he had ever felt before. They lay far into the night, savoring what they had experienced. He knew she was pregnant, and that they would have a son to rule over Eden after they were gone.

"I feel that I'm with child," Victoria whispered. "That was just like old times."

William smiled. "I was expecting Ellen to ask, 'Whatchadoin', William?'"

Victoria laughed softly. "You are so funny."

And the window effect faded.

Chapter 116

The younger kids were grown now and no longer yearned for my companionship, and the older ones had other passions. It seemed that I was in a time warp. I needed to search elsewhere. Victoria was after me to seek better employment, and I had to agree. A person of my age should be working at some meaningful job and should be buying a house, especially now with the baby coming soon. Our ploy had worked; she *was* with child.

My car, which I loved so much, had been wrecked and wouldn't run. While trying to dig, or rev up the car to maximum speed in minimum time and then pop the clutch to spin the wheels and throw up gravel, I broke a tooth off the transmission gear. When I placed it in gear, revved the engine, and let out the clutch, it didn't move. I had tried to bring some excitement to the car's boring existence, and this was the thanks I got. It isn't fair, I thought. Everything bad happens to me. I sat for a while and contemplated my revenge toward God, but not coming up with a suitable consequence, I walked home. After talking to a couple of friends, I was sure it was a gear in the transmission and began planning to repair it. Colt said I could put the car in his garage. It was starting to get cold, so I needed a place where I could put the car inside, ideally with heat. Colt's garage filled both requirements. It had a good roof and inside there was a large, wood-burning stove. Uncle Arthur helped me tow the car up to Colt's place and get it inside the garage.

At the same time, I had another, seemingly insurmountable problem. My damaged thumb and arm made me almost an invalid; they just wouldn't heal. I fought off the infection with Lysol and peroxide and kept it bandaged, but it remained painful and red. Bloody puss continually drained from it. I had to do something. I don't know how Victoria tolerated it. Any other person would have sent me packing.

I looked at my options. I had no education and no trade. I had no car, at least not one that would run. I had very few clothes, and very few belongings. I did have some money coming from Chuck, the bartender at the Bucket of Blood, for cutting the trees, who had never paid me. I had some serious hospital bills from the quack who had placed the Band Aids on my ruined thumb and arm, including the follow-up visits, which hadn't done any good.

I was getting older; too old to be doing childish things. I needed to begin growing up. I had to get an education and a real job, so Victoria and I could be married and live like married people do. Or else I just needed to forget about it all and let her go back to Scotland and let her father take care of her and the baby. But I was afraid he might kill it, as he had the last one.

After thinking about it for a while, I decided the best thing for me to do was to go back to Utah. I could stay with relatives or friends there and get an easy job that I could handle with my injured arm. And then maybe go to night school, maybe trade school or something. The menial work would only be for a while—after all, I was of royal blood and would soon have my rightful inheritance. I could live for a time on the money from Chuck, if I could get him to pay me. But I owed Dale some of it for his work. I talked to Dale, who said he would like to go to Utah with me, which he said would be pay enough for him.

I caught Chuck just right. He had just received some money

for oil royalties in Oklahoma, and while he was still rich, he paid me, although he docked me for some of the logs lying too long and turning blue.

"Hell, Chuck, that was years ago. And besides, it was your job to get the logs out."

"Take it or leave it," he said.

I took it. I talked to Victoria about what I had decided to do. "I'm glad you didn't go back to Scotland, but maybe you should think about it now. Maybe you and the baby would be better off."

"William," she said, "you know I will support you no matter what."

"I thought you would. We need to spend some time together before I go," I said.

"That would be nice," she said, "but when you go, don't feel guilty. I'll be here when you come for me. You can just send for me if you want—I'll be waiting for your message."

"I know it will be a rough trip. I'll probably need to hitchhike or ride the rails, or else I would take you with me," I said, hoping to make her understand.

"It's all right. I'm tough; I can take care of myself."

"I know you can. I'll get a job and a place to live, and then send for you," I promised.

"Don't worry."

"I will worry. I'll leave some of the logging money for you and the baby. It won't be long, I promise. If you can't take it, you can go to Scotland, and I'll try to understand."

She squeezed my hand.

I told Mom what I planned to do and that I was going to leave Victoria here.

"William, you're never going to find a girl that you can marry in the church and raise good religious children with if you don't start going to places where those kinds of girls are."

"I know that makes sense to you, Mom, but Victoria will do what I want her to do." I felt a tear running down my cheek. "Mom,

I know I'm right. If I go to Utah by myself, will you watch out for Victoria and the baby?"

Mom rolled her eyes. "Of course I will. Just go and find your life. You know we all have things happen that we don't like, and we just have to get past them, don't you?"

"I know," I said. "I'll try."

She hugged me. "It will be all right."

I started to cry. As the tears came, my body shook. I was embarrassed. "A man, a cowboy, doesn't cry like this," I sobbed.

Dad was sitting on the front porch in the dark when I went to find Victoria to tell her what Mom had said. "Will," he said, "It's hard for me ta show emotion, but if ya ever want ta come back, well, yer welcome here."

I was glad it was dark, because I felt the tears streaming down my face. "Thanks, Dad," I sobbed.

Chapter 117

It was going to be difficult without Victoria, I knew. It was nice having her change my bandage and pour on the peroxide. I wanted to do something nice for her—for us—before I left. I made a bed high in the loft of the barn and covered the hay with a soft blanket.

Her breasts were growing larger and her stomach was getting solid. It didn't show, but I could feel it. She was getting morning sickness and didn't want to have sex all the time like she usually did, but that was all right. It was just nice to be close.

She had been carrying this baby for a long time. "Are you sure the baby is okay?" I asked.

"Of course, silly. God and babies know when the time is right. We don't need to worry."

"Someday, we will have lace sheets and velvet blankets for our bed," I promised.

"Someday we will," she said. "When we rule Eden."

I pulled her close. "Are you in the mood?"

"I'm really not, but I want to do it before you leave so I will be able to remember you."

It was more delightful than ever. The mild fragrance seemed to surround me. She was moaning, I was moaning, and it seemed like a fantasy too wonderful to be real. In the morning, she was still sleeping when I woke. I quietly got dressed and kissed her forehead. "Sleep well, my love. I'll send for you soon," I said, climbed down from the loft and walked to meet Dale.

We each carried a small athletic bag that contained our worldly possessions: an extra shirt, some food, a bottle of water, and quite a few bags of Bull Durham tobacco and papers. I also carried a bottle of hydrogen peroxide and a few bandages to dress my injuries.

According to the doctor, I was to clean it with the hydrogen peroxide and change the bandage every day.

Flash had a question about my wounds. "Why do you think it hurts more than just having a cut?"

"Well, it's a pretty bad injury," I said.

"You're such a baby. I didn't make that big a fuss when I was bucked off Penny on the railroad tracks." He showed me his sinister smile.

"Hell," I said, "you weren't bucked off. You fell off."

"Oh, yeah? Mom is still mad because you and Warren took me down and poured beer down my throat."

"You ass. You broke into the car and drank our beer."

"That's a lie."

"And then you threw up in Warren's car. I can't believe Aunt Trudy would fall for a story like that."

Flash tried to think of a comeback. "If it wasn't true, then why did she get so mad?"

"You dumb bastard. What the hell does that mean? It doesn't even make sense."

We glared at each other, and then he said, "Dale said you're taking him to Utah."

"I told him not to tell anybody. Yeah, we're going."

"I want to go, too."

"Got any money?"

"How much do you have?"

I had $300 from Chuck. "Three hundred," I said.

"I don't have any money, but if you don't take me, I'll tell Mom you're taking Dale."

I knew Aunt Trudy wouldn't let Dale go if she knew. I didn't want to take Flash, but who said I had to take him all the way to Utah? "Okay. Go get some clothes and stuff and we'll wait for you."

The depot was the same as always. The smells, the comfortable friendliness, and the worn interior all felt like an old friend. I got our tickets from the station master and sat with Dale and Flash. In the distance, I heard the train whistle and knew it was at Clines Crossing and would be there in a few moments. I could hear it belching out steam from its bowels. As it pulled in, it shot out black smoke and steam as if in a dying gesture, and then idled to a stop.

"This is our cue," I said to my fledglings. We stood, stretched, and then walked toward the train. The conductor was just stepping down, reaching ahead with his foot, as conductors do, even before the train came to a complete stop. He ran for a few steps to regain balance, holding the little stepping platform for passengers. After everyone had been helped off, he went through the usual routine of holding our elbows in his counterfeit way.

This Northern Pacific coach was just like all the others, even to the pot-bellied stove in the middle. The coaches always had the same dull and lifeless look, showing little thought for the interest or luxury of the passengers, but rather making it just bearable to sit and wait for a destination to arrive. The conductor had that same old "who the hell cares" attitude. All the smells were there. It was familiar to be riding the train, and in spite of everything, I liked it. Riding the train was always a great release for me.

Three of the four other passengers in the car seemed to be uneasy, like they had either just met, or maybe had known each other but hadn't been together for a while before this trip. There was a middle-aged woman and a man. He had a handlebar mustache that curled into an almost complete circle. They were dressed like

Mom and Dad when they went to church on Sunday—as flashy and fancy as they owned. The man wore a dark brown suit with a brown tie holding the collar of his white shirt together. He held an expensive-looking walking stick, which he passed nervously from one hand to the other. The woman was dressed in a long, silky, peach- colored gown with matching shoes and tight-fitting gloves. She wore a white hat that covered most of her auburn hair and held a small white parasol, which she raised and lowered and pointed to emphasize her boisterous remarks. She had none of the nervousness so obvious in the other three.

The other man had an expensive-looking, dark suit and the same color of tie holding the collar of his starched-stiff white shirt firmly around his neck. He held a dark business hat in his lap and seemed to be uncomfortable with it, as he constantly moved it here and there in a nervous fashion. His woman wore an off-white lace dress and a small lacy hat that was the same color as her dress. She had on ankle-high, black shoes whose laces were tied in a large bow. She held a white lacy parasol in much the same manner as her man held his hat. These two appeared to be stiff and uncomfortable, very much out of place.

The back of the seats in the coach could be turned either way, and they had been arranged so that one woman and man sat facing the other woman and man. I took the window seat across the aisle from them and Dale sat next to me on the aisle. Flash, who sat across the aisle just in front of the foursome, quickly fell asleep.

The train effortlessly pulled into motion, and floated smoothly along the tracks, picking up speed. Soon the scenery was blurring past the windows. The train swayed gently along the tracks, clicking softly as it carried us into the day and toward our destinations.

The people had stopped talking and were looking across the aisle at Dale and me, like they had just noticed we were there. They all spoke at once, greeting us as if we had suddenly materialized.

"Looks like you're going to church," I offered, trying to put on my best front.

They laughed. "Well no, it's not Sunday. We're on our way to Paradise to attend the wedding of a friend. He's an old man we knew in Hamilton some years ago. He lost his ranch and has been working over in Paradise for a time."

"That's funny," I said. "I met an old man in Paradise some time ago. I think his name was Glen. He lost his ranch in Hamilton, too, I think."

"Well, that's him."

"Who is he going to marry?" I asked.

"It's the lady who owned the Pair a Dice Bar and Grill. Her name is Priscilla," the lady in the peach dress said.

"I'll be damned," I returned. "I thought a guy owned that place."

"Well, Priscilla owned it with her husband, but after Glen began hanging around and cleaning up the place, it seems Glen and Pricilla were always together. Finally, they fell in love and kicked her husband out and took the place over. The displaced husband went to Missoula and is working in a café washing dishes. He got a one-room flat in the Stockman's Hotel. Says he's happier than he's ever been. He forgave them and is even planning on coming to the wedding."

"Life is funny," I said.

We all fell silent as the train made its way along the tracks. Before long, the conductor strode through the coach, warning us in the usual fashion, "Paradise, five minutes." The four of them stood to take their small suitcases down from the overhead storage and then began walking toward the exit.

"We'll tell Glen we saw you," said the lady in peach. "What's your name?"

"Just tell him you saw the guy who can roll a cigarette with one hand," I returned." They all waved a farewell, and then went to the end of the coach and waited to get off. I watched through the window as they walked toward town and then disappeared into the small hotel just a small distance from the Pair a Dice Bar and Grill. The train groaned, grunted, spat out steam, and began to move. It wasn't long before Dale laid his head on my shoulder, sleeping to the rhythmic sounds of the train as it clicked down the track. Maybe I can teach him something, I thought of Dale. Hell, I don't want him ending up like me.

The soft clicking of the wheels against the tracks and the swaying had a therapeutic, almost hypnotic effect. My mind began to wander. I wonder if atoms could be used something like electricity to run stuff? Dad said that they are full of energy. It might be dangerous to play around with them. But then electricity is dangerous and people play around with that. They even make it work for them.

I looked at the pale vision of the cowboy watching me from his place in the window. He looked worried. "I wonder what's going to happen to me and Dale?" I said softly. "I wonder how atoms can be so small? And I wonder what Victoria is doing now?" The cowboy just looked at me and said nothing. I pulled out my golden watch, more out of habit than anything else. Then without even looking at it, I put it away. "If the atoms could be held together and a person could get to them and make them understand and then somehow teach them to do things and then talk back to you, it would be amazing."

Impressed by my intelligence, I began to dissolve into the other side of that illusory window … Einstein would be surprised to see me.

Albert had finally cataloged all the possible attributes of the atom/DNA cakes and had found a way to reliably couple them together. He was on the verge of an exciting discovery. He would soon know the secrets of creating an organism that would become the Master Blaster. But best of all, he was well on his way to finding a reliable method of communication with the new discovery.

"I better call William," he said aloud. "He will know what to do next."

William packed for a long stay, because of the urgency of Albert's message. When he arrived, his room was ready, as it always had been. Because William was exhausted from his trip, there were no gala greetings or attempts at humor like there usually were. Albert was always excited when there was a new discovery on the horizon; well, William was always excited too. He remembered when they had first met and found that they had many things in common.

They both were advanced in concepts that involved time and speed, or time and matter, and other things most people found difficult to understand. They each had difficulty with simpler or lower disciplines. There were stories about Einstein having trouble spelling simple words, or understanding basic arithmetic, but William had never had occasion to witness things of this nature. Einstein seemed to be apt in every endeavor and on any subject.

William commented to Albert on their similarity. "I assume," Albert replied, "it's because we already know so much, and are confused only by the elementary methods teachers use to examine these basic concepts of our works and theories."

William responded, "In school, everything always seemed so simple that I took the questions as rhetorical, or thought them so basic that I refused to belittle myself by even voicing the obvious answers."

Einstein nodded. "You look tired. Get some sleep, and we will begin our research in the morning."

William was happy to heed this advice. Soon, he was asleep between the soft velvet blankets and lace sheets that adorned the master guest room. He arose early, and after a hot shower, he had a hearty breakfast with Albert, and the two scientists entered the laboratory to begin creating intelligence. They worked long hours and days, sometimes not even stopping to eat or sleep.

"You know," Albert finally said, "we are but one step from creating life. Think of it ... life!"

William thought for a moment. "What the hell," he said, "let's go for it."

The two scientists went back to work to begin creating life, as only God had done before them. Some days later, Albert said, "William, by golly we have it." A deep furrow in his forehead indicated his worry. "I need to ask you: do you think we're doing the right thing?"

"I've been thinking about that as well."

"We're not God. We need to consider what this will mean," Albert said, looking sad. "I've dreamed of this for years, and now that we are at the threshold of achieving it, I'm a little hesitant to continue."

"Tell me about your concern," William prodded.

"Maybe we're overstepping our bounds."

"To tell the truth, I've been concerned as well. Maybe we need to stay with things that are of this world. Maybe creating life should be God's work and not ours," William said.

They discussed their concerns well into the night, and finally was decided that they would stop the work on life and file away all of the papers and formulas and save them until they were sure it was the right thing to do.

"However, I think that by pursuing it. we have learned a lot about DNA and atoms," Albert said. "Our work hasn't been in vain."

"We have learned a lot."

Almost in one voice, they agreed, "We should take what we have learned and use it to improve living and travel. Maybe even to travel back and forth in time. We can and should pursue the atom/DNA/memory and the Master Blaster."

Now they were excited again. "No sleep tonight,"

William said, and they both laughed, but it was a nervous laugh to rationalize what might be the consequences of their monumental decision concerning life. Almost as frightening were the atom/DNA/memory and the awful Master Blaster.

I was rudely brought back to the train coach by Flash bitching, as he shook his head in disgust, "Dale sure is a baby, isn't he?"

"You're the baby, you dumb shit."

I thought about this new adventure and the added responsibility of my juvenile wards. I also plotted a way to be rid of Flash. But short of killing him, I was hard pressed to think of a strategy. "Dale should still be in school," I told myself. He had stirred from time to time and even sat up and looked around, but he finally fell into a deep sleep and soon afterward, I did as well.

I was awakened by a strange noise, and opened my eyes to see Flash hanging over the armrest of the seat, puking into the aisle. I walked over to hold his head, so he wouldn't get the vile liquid on any of our stuff. All of our bags were open and there was wax paper everywhere.

I couldn't believe it. "Jesus, Flash, you ate all the food."

"I was hungry."

I was embarrassed for him. "You have no heart or conscience."

"Hey, can't you see I'm sick?" he complained.

We all moved to a place a little farther down the car. I was happy we were the only ones in this car. "I'm not dead yet," I mumbled, but I wished Flash was. I helped him to a seat at the end of the car and helped him lie down. Soon, he was sleeping like a baby. Dale and I went to the other end of the car to get some sleep, too. Now all our food was gone—it was a good thing I had some money. Before long, Dale laid his head on my shoulder and the rhythmic sounds of the clicking of the train medicated him into deep sleep.

It was late when we arrived in Butte. I looked across the street, where the bus had picked up Warren and me for our induction.

It was sad to think of Warren now. I carefully and quietly shook Dale awake. I helped him with his jacket and handed him his bag. Carefully and quietly, I led him past his sleeping brother. I laid Flash's bag on the floor in front of his seat, waved him a silent goodbye, and then guided Dale through the large and almost vacant depot. After asking a couple of times for directions, we found the train that would take us to Salt Lake.

After the usual routine of boarding, we made our way down the aisle to find a suitable seat. There were only a few people in the dimly lit coach, and they all seemed to be asleep or engrossed in reading, with only their individual, overhead lights turned on. An elderly man was across the aisle from where we decided to sit. He looked up and nodded as we slumped into our places. It seemed like only seconds before the train began to move softly, almost secretly bumping and jerking us toward the uncertainty and the consequences of our decision to leave Eden.

"Windy night, huh?" the old man across the aisle said.

"Yeah, it sure is," I returned and then we both fell silent.

I began to think about Flash. He'll be okay, I told myself. I've been in worse predicaments myself and I always came out okay. Well, there's nothing I can do now. Flash is already heading toward someplace. Maybe I should have just killed him. I smiled to myself, like I was kidding, but the idea sounded more than reasonable. Well, if I know him, he's got some money stashed away. He'll be okay. And then I forgot about him in the present and thought instead about him in the past, about what a jerk he had always been, which helped to calm me. Anyway, I thought, he's gone now. But to where?

Chapter 118

"Where ya goin'?" It was the pest from across the aisle. I didn't feel like talking now. I was too engrossed in worry. "We're goin to Salt Lake," was my short reply.

"Hi. My name is Clark. I used to live in Salt Lake," he said, as he tried to add kindling to make a conversational fire.

"Oh."

"I had some apartments. I really made good money." He was dressed in a dark suit with a white shirt and a blue-and-red striped tie. He looked like he had stepped out of a shower and shaved, combed his hair and beard, and got dressed just a moment earlier.

I wonder if there is a shower on the train, I thought, and then said, in regard to his statement about money, "I wish I had some."

"Money?"

"Yeah." I could smell an odor from clear across the aisle that resembled mothballs.

The old man looked sad. He began to say something and then stopped. It looked like he was holding back a sob. His black hair and beard were accented with white in all of the right places. It looked like he had had it done in a beauty shop. His blue eyes seemed out of place next to the black hair and olive skin. He had even white teeth and a perfectly placed gold one that showed whenever he smiled. He was, I was sure, what a girl would consider to be handsome and desirable, even at his age. He wore a ruby ring on the ring finger of his left hand.

I thought about telling him a joke about mothballs, where you ask, "Have you ever smelled a moth's balls?" And when they say yes, you say, "How did you get him to spread his legs?" But I didn't.

He began to talk again. "One day I had a fire in one of the apartment buildings. One of the tenants had a girl over for the evening, and as they drank and did whatever young people do, she unknowingly dropped a cigarette on the couch, and then they left to see a movie."

He stopped talking. It looked like he was going to cry again.

"I'd like to own some apartments," I said, in an effort to make him feel better.

He composed himself, and went on, as if I hadn't said anything, "The fire wasn't discovered until it was too late, and by the time the fire department got there and put it out, there was a significant amount of damage."

"Didn't you have insurance?" I asked.

"Those damned insurance companies." He spat the words out. "You never know if you have insurance. They are the ones who decide whether you do or not. It's sort of like having each team in sports refereeing themselves. The bastards." His face turned red. "I had several buildings, which were all insured by the same company. When I notified them about the fire, they told me that the premiums hadn't been applied to the burned one, but to another one."

His eyes clouded over again, and he looked at me, maybe waiting for me to say something. Hell, I didn't know what to say.

"Do you know what insurance companies do, young man?" he asked.

"I guess I don't."

His face had turned even redder. "If a policy happens to lapse and the insured wants to have it reinstated, the insurance company checks to see if there has been a loss. If there hasn't been any loss, then they reinstate it as insured continuously. If there has been a loss, then it isn't reinstated. If there's no loss, the insured has to pay for the time that the insurance wasn't in force, just the same. If there has been a loss, then the insurance isn't reinstated but the insurance remains classified as lapsed. It's not fair."

He was almost in tears again, but he stifled them and began slamming the insurance companies again. "I called a week before the fire about the status of the insurance on that building. The agent assured me it was paid to date, but when we went to trial, that same agent denied that I had even called."

He was really getting wound up now. I decided I would try to think about something else besides his pain and suffering, but before I could find a more pleasant topic, he went on. "We went to court and I discovered that because of the loss of the building and the large mortgage on it, the bank could go after my other buildings, and my house as well. I went to court every day. I finally had to quit my job and ..."

I stopped listening. I had decided to do something else. Maybe I would go see Einstein, and work on our atomic/DNA/memory project, or something else for a while ...

"... I lost everything, just because of those unfair insurance companies." Clark was still going. He hadn't even noticed I wasn't listening. "What the hell do they care if they ruin anybody? It doesn't cost them anything to go to court. They have legal staff on retainer all the time. I had to pay for mine."

He had breached my barrier and was coming in loud and clear. I tried to appear as if I was listening.

"The insurance company had the entire two top floors of the Boston Building staffed with lawyers on permanent salary. And the damned banks are just as bad—oh, they joined the insurance company in the suit; they have about as many lawyers. They're corrupt, too—almost as bad as the insurance companies."

"Oh," I said.

Clark seemed pleased that I had now joined in the conversation. "Do you know that the insurance companies could pay off the whole national debt in a few years with the money they make on home owners' insurance alone?"

"No," I said, "I didn't know that."

His face was getting dangerously flushed. He looked like he was going to pass out.

"Are you all right?" I asked.

"Yeah, but I need to go to the bathroom. Do you know where it is?"

"It's at the end of the coach." I pointed.

"Thanks." As he stood to leave, for just a moment he seemed to have second thoughts. "I'll tell you the rest when I get back."

Dale was sleeping. I shook him and said, "Come on, we have to leave."

"Are we in Salt Lake?"

"No, but we're in mortal danger," I kidded. "My ears are almost worn off."

We picked up our baggage and went through the double doors into the coach ahead, and then hurried through several more coaches.

After we found seats, I didn't look left or right or talk to anybody. I didn't want to go through that torture again. Dale and I didn't talk very much during the remainder of the eight-hour ride. We just sat and thought. He asked me where Flash was. I told him he had gone on to Billings.

"Well, he always did like to travel," Dale said, and then fell silent. We looked blankly out the window at the bleary and vacant landscape. We ate some of the few goodies Flash had left. Because of the uneventful trip, we both looked forward to the routine of changing the dressing on my arm.

"Doesn't look like it's getting any better," Dale said.

"The color is better. Doesn't look like infection anymore," I told him—but it didn't really look much better.

"Hey, where is Flash?" he asked again.

"He decided to go on to Billings," I repeated.

And that was that. Dale went through the washing with peroxide and placing a new gauze bandage around the thumb and arm, and then he tore off a couple of pieces of adhesive tape and wrapped them into place, as he had done many times before. As he worked, I watched, but not idly. I rolled us each a cigarette with my free hand. After he finished, we lit up and talked as we smoked.

"You should see a doctor," he said.

"Hell, I'll be just fine," I assured him, but I was a little worried.

We kept our own thoughts and watched with vacant eyes as the early morning wasteland rolled past the window.

"How much longer, Bill?"

"Oh, we're almost there," I told him. My amateurish prophecy proved to be true as the conductor walked toward us yelling, "Salt Lake, fifteen minutes."

The trip had taken us through the night. As we stepped down from the train, we were greeted by wind and an overcast morning sky.

The man who hated insurance companies walked past. "What happened to you?"

"My young friend got motion sickness and I took him to the other bathroom and then we just stayed near it," I lied.

"Well, maybe we will meet again, and I'll tell you the rest of the story." He walked away with his fancy luggage, his expensive hat, and an expensive overcoat hung over his arm.

"That would be great," I said out loud, adding to myself, "I'd rather be dead."

"He doesn't look too poor. I wish I was poor like he is," Dale smiled.

The wind whipped dust and loose papers everywhere. Little dirt-devils played about here and there, and we tried to shield ourselves with our arms and small bags, but the wind and grime found our eyes, which watered and burned. We had no idea where to go or what to do. I hadn't expected to see so many people and cars hurrying in every direction. There was activity and noise everywhere. We began walking.

Dale had lived in Salt Lake before coming to Montana and he knew a few of our relatives, and where they lived. He was sort of a favorite, although I don't think I had many admirers among our relatives. They would go to great lengths to keep younger kids away from the "unsaintly" influence of me.

After walking aimlessly for a while, we stopped at a greasy spoon and while eating burgers with coffee for breakfast, we discussed our future. We sat long after the meal was over, nursing coffee and smoking cigarettes, but we finally had a plan. We would go stay with Uncle Elmo and Aunt Maxine for a while.

On the way to our new hospice, we passed a large tent. The sign on the front said, "Home Show." It looked like there were a lot of people inside. More people were going in, and a few were coming out to brave the winds and dust.

"Let's go in and get out of the weather for a while," I said.

A lot of venders were inside, doing their best to sell this and that to groups of people who were either just standing in the area or sitting in chairs listening to reasons why it was ridiculous to go through life without certain gadgets. Most of the devices had been designed to easily peel and then to reduce a variety of vegetables to a certain size and texture that would allow them to be used in a variety of different and delicious-looking dishes.

There were tempting samples everywhere, and after Dale and I had eaten our fill, we stood for a moment to enjoy the skillful showmanship of the vendors. One vendor immediately caught my attention. He was a short, stocky man with a bright red face, whose green coat and blue and white-striped pants made him even more conspicuous. He wore a flat-topped straw hat over sandy hair that poked out uncontrollably around the edges. As he talked, his blue eyes seemed to twinkle.

He talked about how the gadget could save a housewife many

hours of drudgery in the kitchen. His fat, nimble fingers seemed to fly around, picking up and peeling, and then slicing or chopping up all kinds and sizes of vegetables and fruits. Every now and then, maybe to make the audience more attentive or to keep them awake, he made a feeble attempt at wit. When the stoical audience didn't respond, the vendor, with the same indifference as the audience but with a smile on his face, gave them a pointed yet subtle insult about their ineptness at recognizing his humor. But it was clear that all this went right over the audience's heads. They sat stone-faced, probably just waiting here in this sanctuary until the winds died down outside, so they could travel more comfortably to their destinations.

The vendor's jokes were far from being funny. However, the lack of reaction from his audience, and their refusal to purchase any of his wares, and their resistance to even listening or to be aware that he was performing, combined with their willingness to stay and watch anyway, struck me as so funny that I began to laugh. He mistook my amusement, thinking it was spawned by his feeble jokes, and now he began directing his attention at me, as if I was his only audience. This made the whole thing even funnier; so funny that I laughed hysterically.

The entire, lackadaisical audience now began to laugh, probably thinking that what the vendor was saying was actually funny and they just weren't getting it. Now the vendor turned his attention back to the crowd. They seemed to have become very interested in what was going on. They began purchasing the gadget and after paying, they walked away with happiness almost dripping from their faces. It wasn't long before the man had sold all of his wares, and he began to put away his boxes and paraphernalia.

He walked over to Dale and me. "Hey, thanks," he blurted out. "I have to ask, you seemed to be the only one who thought my jokes were funny. Can you tell me why?"

I tried to explain, but I just couldn't find the words to make him understand and finally he just shook his head, "Well, anyways, thanks a lot. Want some fruit?" He picked up a sack filled with apples, oranges, and peaches from a table and handed it to us.

As Dale and I walked out of the tent, the man yelled, "Come back anytime."

The wind had nearly stopped and the sun had dropped low in the sky as we walked toward Uncle Elmo's place.

"I always thought Uncle Elmo owed us something anyway, for sending us on that shortcut through the White Bird Mountains in Idaho when we went to Montana," I told Dale.

"And for all of the pranks I had to endure … like when he tied the straps on my bib-overalls together behind my back," Dale added

"I know that feeling," I said. Maybe, I thought, we can find a way to get even.

Chapter 119

Aunt Maxine was quite friendly when she answered our knock, although she was also patronizing. She treated us as one might treat magazine salesmen, but when she found out who we were, and that we were planning on staying for a while, she yelled for Uncle Elmo for support against us. They stood together, blocking our entrance and reciting a long list of reasons why it was not a good idea for us to stay. Dale and I countered all of their objections with reasons why it was not just a good idea, but also a great idea.

Aunt Maxine was Aunt Trudy and Dad's sister. "We are family," we said. Finally, they agreed with reluctance to give it a try, for just a few days.

Like all houses built right after the war, their place was small. It had an unfinished basement where bottled fruit and a variety of items too good to throw away were stored. Shelves along the walls were filled with bottles of fruit and vegetables and empty bottles for canning next year.

The walls were unpainted concrete that had begun to crumble into little piles of powder and rubble on the unfinished concrete floor. There was a double bed and a couple of blankets. The room had a small window, high up, that opened, but it was too small to get out of, in case of fire. It bore a striking resemblance to Aunt Helen's dungeon.

The stairs led down from the kitchen to a small landing, where a door opened onto the backyard and Uncle Elmo's hobby shed. Several other small sheds looked as if they might have been built elsewhere and then moved to the property. If you turned ninety degrees, stairs went down to the basement where Dale and I were to be kept. There was no door and we could see whenever someone went by.

This arrangement worked out great for Dale and me, but after we had been there for about a week we were informed that we were welcome to stay only until we could find something else. It seemed to bother Aunt Maxine that we didn't ever go anywhere else. We just hung around reading the books that Uncle Elmo had stored in the basement, wrestling with each other, and waiting for the next meal. Her attitude was, "Please find somewhere else to live—the sooner the better."

This relationship deteriorated further when we were told that they had run out of food and only had enough for themselves. We had really enjoyed eating with them, but we agreed that this would still be an agreeable arrangement. We would find food for ourselves. Another condition to our continuing to abide there was that we were to go out and use the bathroom in Uncle Elmo's hobby room, so as not to disturb them during the night.

This too, seemed to be a pretty good arrangement, until it began to get colder or when it rained. Eventually, we got lazy and began using the empty fruit jars in the basement to relieve ourselves. The following day, we would empty them in the backyard. Then we got even lazier and only emptied them on occasion, and finally, not at all. We were pretty content with this arrangement, and began spending the late nights and early mornings with our uncle and aunt, and then going out on adventures during the day. We spent a large portion of our free time at double feature movies, eating theater treats, or in fast food cafes. We showed up quite late at night at our relatives' place, trying to be quiet, and then slept far into the following morning.

I was beginning to like my new lifestyle, and I think Dale was, too. But things began to break down the day Uncle Elmo ventured into the basement and discovered the jars filled with the yellow liquid. We were lying on the bed, reading and smoking. With a disgusted look, he said, "I've got some bad news. I've sold the bed. I need to deliver it tomorrow, so I guess this is the last night you will be able to stay here." As Uncle Elmo stood waiting for a response, his red and angry face was sort of silhouetted by the yellow liquid-filled fruit jars on the shelf behind him. It was kind of funny.

Next morning, Aunt Maxine called us for our "last meal." We ate slowly and then found other ways to delay our departure. Finally, we were unable to find a reason to stay longer, and she cheerfully escorted us to the door and bade us farewell. She was careful not to provide any encouragement for us to stay or to return.

It had taken so long for her to finally get us to leave that it was early afternoon. To ensure our departure, she prepared a light lunch for us. As we walked away I said, "I guess we did get even with Uncle Elmo—both for us and for Dad."

Chapter 120

We wandered around for quite a while. By the time we sat down on a bus stop bench to change the dressing on my arm, it was getting well into evening. We sat and ate Aunt Maxine's lunch and tried to make a plan, but after talking for a while, we still had no plan except to walk on, which is what we did. It was dusk as we walked toward the city.

We heard music and loud voices in the distance and began heading toward the sounds. The evening was summer-warm but with a hint of the coolness of autumn, which was accented by a slight change in color of some of the leaves. There was a certain smell and feeling, a mood; a lonely mood that can be felt in a city even when people are all around.

As always, Dale plodded along beside me, doing what I did or as I directed him to do. It was comfortable to have a companion, and I knew it would be hard to be alone. All the houses along the street seemed to be related. They all had been built of brick of one color or another, and all had dull asphalt shingles and a wood or metal fence enclosing a small front yard, with a gate in front. The landscaping was similar, as well. Small lawns were surrounded by beautiful gardens that boasted of tender care, but the full flowers and mature vegetables and the leaves were all turning autumn colors. The dirty sidewalk was old and cracked, and in places the tree roots had lifted it up, which made walking unsure.

"Step on a crack, break your mother's back," Dale chanted as he dodged here and there. "Step on a line, break your mother's spine." He added, "Hell, I wouldn't care if she broke her back," and smiled at me. "Maybe she wouldn't be so damned mean if she had it broken." Dale had good reason to feel that way. Aunt Trudy had always been unnecessarily mean to him.

It didn't take long to get to the park and the source of the music. We saw a large crowd on a grassy hillside, some on blankets, some in chairs, and some just standing. They were watching some sort of thespian performance. The performers appeared to be making asses of themselves, something like Mom, Dad, Uncle Arthur, and Aunt Trudy might do when they performed with the Eden Players. A marquee on a lamppost revealed what was going on: "The Liberty Park Theatre Guild presents William Shakespeare's Comedy of Errors. Donations are greatly appreciated."

Ignoring the plea for dollars, Dale and I found a place near the back of the crowd and sat on the cool grass. The actors were speaking loudly, almost yelling. It was so loud that it was hard to distinguish just what they were saying.

"What are they saying?" I asked Dale.

"I think someone's brother got mixed up and stayed overnight with someone else's wife," he said.

"I think they're twins and got separated in a shipwreck or something," I offered my interpretation.

I looked around the crowd. "Hell," I said, "there's drama's going on everywhere."

A man sat on a blanket surrounded by his family. He was intent on watching the players, but looked like he really wasn't really enjoying it. The knowing grin on his slightly open mouth seemed like an attempt to convey to others that he was knowledgeable about classical culture, and it was obvious he knew the play by heart. His wife echoed this performance, even while dealing with the three young children of varied ages. She seemed to be content that she had this diversion to release her from the drudgery of upholding the couple's façade.

The children were just children, and it mattered little that they were there or in a church or train station. They just did what children do. The smallest, who could barely walk, made her way to the small, tripod-supported marquee that had been placed there by the troupe and seemed intent on dismantling it, as if she were in direct conflict with its appeal for money. Her diaper had slipped and was hanging almost to the ground, obviously heavy with wetness or substance, but held in place with a pin. The other two children, a boy and a girl, sat eating sandwiches that the mother had taken out of a shoebox and handed to them. They were more interested in the play than the food, and attempted to stand to better see what was happening on stage. But their view of the colorfully clad and loud actors on the stage was blocked by the crowd in front of them. The mother used glaring looks and soft nudges to counter their attempts at refusing to consume their fare, and after awhile, they accepted things as they were and sat quietly nibbling their sandwiches and gazing at the crowd, like Dale and I were doing.

On my other side, an old man was lying on the grass with his head on the ground, bent in an uncomfortable-looking fashion. His eyes were partly closed, but the blue was still slightly visible. He cradled a large bottle of Seagram's Seven whiskey, like he was protecting it. A thin line of foamy saliva hung sickeningly from the corner of his mouth, with clear drops running down it to the grass.

A raindrop hit my face, and then another, and then it began to rain hard. I lifted the bottle from where the old man cradled it and we ran to find shelter under a tree. People ran here and there, trying to escape the downpour. The old man just lay there, drenched and oblivious to the storm.

The rain slowed to a soft, steady drizzle.

"Dale, let's find a place to sleep," I said, and we began walking deeper into the park. We came to a small shed, the door of which was unlocked. We went inside and sat down with our backs against the wall. "We'll find something to eat in the morning," I said.

"Yeah."

I took the cap off the bottle, pulled in a good swig of the liquid, and handed it to Dale

He took a drink, coughed and gagged, and said, "Hell, that's good," and we both laughed. Warmed by the gracious contribution of the old man, we slept.

"What the hell you kids doin' in here?" a man in a blue uniform yelled.

It was light. Sunlight streamed into the shed.

I stood. I think my size startled the man, and before he could say anything else, we ran through the door and across the lawn. We kept running and then slowed to a walk. My entire body ached. It was difficult to keep going. "Dale, we need to find something to eat and a place to stay."

"Yeah!"

"Man, a hot cup of coffee would be wonderful now."

"Yeah!"

Every shop and store seemed to be closed. "Guess they don't open up 'til later."

"What about Aunt Ardith?" Dale asked.

I told Dale I had forgotten about her, but I could remember my last encounter with her. "I hope she has forgotten about it."

"What happened?"

"I made fun of her cats."

"I think I was always her favorite," Dale said. "Well, me and Flash."

I couldn't think of anything better to do, so I said, "Hell, let's go see her."

Aunt Ardith was delighted to see us, but her attitude changed completely, just like that of Uncle Elmo and Aunt Maxine, when she found that neither of us had immediate plans to return to

Montana and that we were planning to grace her with our company indefinitely. She was more than a little concerned that Dale was under the charge of someone so unspiritual as I was. After Dale had told her she had always been his favorite aunt, she began to soften and said, "If it's just for a short while, it will be all right."

Aunt Ardith lived alone. She wasn't my blood aunt. She had married my mother's brother, Uncle Gordon, who had died several years earlier. Everybody said he had lots of insurance and left her extremely wealthy.

She was Dale's real aunt, his dad's sister. Dale's dad was my Uncle Arthur. My mother's brother, Uncle Gordon, had married Dale's dad's sister, Aunt Ardith, which maybe meant Dale and I were double cousins. I think Flash was named after Uncle Gordon. Mom used to go visit her when we lived in Aunt Helen's dungeon in Springtown. I had only been there once, usually because of some sort of a weird punishment.

Aunt Ardith's house was antiseptically clean, but even strong cleaning products couldn't completely erase the stench of her three cats. She didn't have a litter box. She had trained them to use the toilet in the bathroom. Each in turn, they would crouch on the lid and let it go. She found little humor in my advice, "You should try to teach them to wipe their asses." This is what she had been mad about from the last time I saw her, and she still couldn't seem to forgive me. Maybe her objection to my comment about asses was because of her religious background.

Aunt Ardith often stated that she was not happy about Dale being away from his parents and with me. I don't think she had forgiven me for my repeated attempts to annihilate Flash.

"Where is Gordon?" she asked.

"He got a job in Billings."

She insisted that we eat only at meal times and clean up every time we ate. We couldn't smoke in the house, we had to bathe every day, and we had to mow the lawn and pull weeds. She left me home to complete work assignments and took Dale various places, sometimes for long periods. Dale told me later that she was trying to encourage him to go back home to Montana.

I put off doing the troublesome chores, and usually just lay on the bed for a while. Wonder where she got this wallpaper? I thought. It looks like it belongs in a cathouse. Red velvet with flowers and red carpet. Maybe she's a madam and just sent her girls home until Dale and I leave.

Maybe I was getting onto something. I was having some interesting daydreams and was just beginning another when I heard Aunt Ardith and Dale open the front door. Aunt Ardith had a stern look on her face, and before she even had her coat off, she began telling me that Dale could stay but I would have to leave. There just wasn't enough room for both of us there. She said that I could stay tonight and then I would need to find another place tomorrow.

After I bathed my sore thumb and arm with peroxide and re-bandaged it, I went to bed. I lay trying to figure out what to do. I was more worried about Dale than about myself, even if he had a place to sleep. I was just dozing off when the door opened, I could see the dim outline of someone walking toward me.

"Who is it?" I whispered, and then I seemed to pass through a window.

"Be quiet," someone said.
"What's going on?" William whispered.
"Move over," came a hushed voice.
He moved over as a naked body slid in under the covers. A hand found his crotch and pulled down his shorts; he was getting hard. The body slowly moved on top and rubbed wetness against him; it went inside. William arched his body in response to the motion and began breathing hard. It seemed that with each motion he was going farther and farther inside; a wonderful sensation. Then it was over. She muffled a scream and William

moaned, and then they lay for a moment holding each other in a post-sexual, impersonal way. Then, as quickly as she had come, she was gone without a word.

The window effect faded.

I lay there well into the night, smoking a forbidden cigarette, and wondering what the hell had happened and what tomorrow might bring. Finally, sleep overtook me.

Chapter 121

In the morning, Aunt Ardith said she wanted to be alone with Dale for a few days. She asked me if I would just leave them alone for that amount of time, and then I could come back and we would talk some more. She was friendlier now and even smiled at me and touched me when we talked. Her face had a glow.

She said, "You both should be going to church and reading the Bible, in order to receive the blessings that are in store for you if you do."

We both agreed with her as we ate the bacon and eggs that she had prepared. I understood what she was talking about. I had studied the Bible, as well as other religions.

It seemed important in most of them to keep a history that could be altered, to support the way believers had become accustomed to thinking and believing.

The Bible seemed to be just a history of events that had happened a long time ago, written by forebears of the crazed religious zealots who were killing each other nowadays in the Middle East in the name of their inherent beliefs. I placed little value or meaning in most of it, with the exception of the wonderful and God-like things Jesus was supposed to have said. But there was very little in that book that described the right way to live or told in detail what God was or where we go when we die. It certainly didn't tell us which religion was right.

Everything written there seemed inconsistent and confusing. It was written in an appealing poetry that seemed maybe more for entertainment than as a guide to life or to inspire spirituality. It seemed to be a little like the cavemen might have written about the gods and demons of their era, like the Fire God and the Rain God and such. "Just like the cavemen, we have many gods," I thought. "The sports gods, power gods, and money gods." The only thing that seemed to have any credible religious tone was the life of Jesus. It was inspiring to me to read about the way he lived his life and about his attitude in general, but I knew there were other great philosophers, too.

Most people, it seemed, were indoctrinated into a certain religion while they were young and then sort of worshipped that religion, instead of any god or deity. Mostly, it was the same religion their parents believed in, and they clung obediently to it despite reason or logic. They often were willing to defend to the death their inherited beliefs and ideals, and aggressively refuted others. Of course, their ideals were construed or misconstrued by their families' interpretation of religion as it had been passed down through the generations, until it had probably lost all its original meaning and message. Individual beliefs are probably tailored by a need to support a person's own family's religion. Most people, but not necessarily religions, lack the forgiveness and love that are the very basis of the religion passed along by Jesus and other great teachers. But what the hell did I know? I was, after all, just a dumb kid.

"What do you think?" Aunt Ardith asked as she startled me out of my philosophical wanderings. "Will you leave us alone for a few days?"

I had little choice, so I said, "Okay. Happy to."

Dale was torn between going with me or staying with her, but finally, with her coaxing, he chose to stay.

My earlier misgivings about this were gone, and I was glad. He's better off, I told myself.

It didn't take long to get my few things ready to leave and to say farewell. As the two stood in the doorway of Aunt Ardith's house, waving goodbye to me, I walked slowly down the sidewalk and into the foreboding day. I turned to look back. Aunt Ardith was smiling. She pursed her lips, placed her right hand over her left breast and softly massaged it, and blew a kiss toward me.

Dale waved. I waved back, and then I turned and slowly walked away.

Chapter 122

I can't remember the names of the movies I watched that day. All I remember is that I watched three of them, all double features. After they were over, I stepped into the dark, empty night. The street was deserted. I stood looking this way and that, trying to decide where to go and what to do. A stench in the air that all cities have was accompanied by a loneliness that seemed to penetrate the skin, like cold or heat does. It isn't something you can feel; it just becomes a part of you. Once it's there, it never completely goes away and always brings back the same mood and feeling whenever it's encountered again. The stench wasn't as strong as it was in Spokane, but even a hint of it made the loneliness stronger.

Walking aimlessly, I passed a young blond girl sitting cockeyed in a wheelchair. I smiled and she returned a crippled sort of smile. A large apartment building loomed behind her. "The Camelot-Avalon Apartments," it said in large lettering on the front. Across the street were the colorful, flashing lights of a tavern called the Bel Aire Club. It was inviting and I almost went in to drown my sorrow, but rethinking this, I walked on, past street signs that said "Broadway" and "West North Cromwell." At Main Street, I turned and walked north for half a block, and saw a sign in a window that read, "Rooms, 25 cents."

"Wow," I said aloud, "this looks like my kind of place." I added, "I'm not dead yet."

"You're lucky," the landlord said when I asked for a bed. "Only one left—number 5."

I handed him my quarter and headed toward the door where he directed me. It was a large room in which beds were lined up almost touching each other. There was the strong smell of body odor and methane gas. Five rows of beds separated by narrow aisles allowed a person to walk sideways between them. I found my bed, number 5, lay down, and tried to think of something besides being there. A sound like a train chugging down the track was actually the combined snoring and the farts of the sleeping misfits.

There was a hook on a pipe attached to the head of the bed, which I thought might be for hanging one's clothing. As it was almost impossible for me to sleep with my clothes on, I undressed, hung them on the hooks, and crawled into bed. I always had had the habit of slipping my money into one of my shoes and pushing my socks on top of it, leaving only a dollar or two in my wallet, and this night was no exception. I lay well into the night, listening to the snoring of the other tenants, thinking of Dale and Aunt Ardith and wondering if I would have a welcome place there when I returned the day after tomorrow. Late at night, I finally fell asleep, and dreamed of becoming a doctor and living on a beautiful ranch in the country. It seemed that I returned to Montana after making a fortune, which made all my friends look at me in awe and marvel at my success.

I woke up, and proclaimed, "Maybe I will become a king," and then slept again. This was a deep sleep, during which my earlier dream continued, and seemed to be real. I was glad that I had turned out so well, because it seemed at times that I wouldn't. And then the glamour of my dream was over, as morning and the other sounds of people waking shook me awake, too. The sounds of the night were replaced by the sounds of people mumbling softly and moving about, but the smell of methane gas was still there, maybe even stronger now, and mixed with the odor of unclean bodies.

My wallet had been taken, but when I looked into my shoe, I found my money still there. I dressed and pushed the money down deep into the front pocket of my Levis.

I related the sad story of the theft to the landlord, but he just said, "We have a lot of that. It's best to slip your wallet down in the front of your shorts. It usually wakes a person if someone starts feeling around there." He went back to his paperwork.

I wasn't going to spend another night at that place; I was sure of that. I checked out a couple of hotels, and as it didn't cost anymore to stay all day than it did to stay for just the night, I paid the $3.50 for a room in the Main Street Hotel and moved in. It was nice to be alone, and kind of fun to see through the open window the tiny figures of people far below. I took a shower and then walked around the city to pass some time. I was glad that the hotel had an elevator and the operator would take passengers to any floor they chose without complaining.

I went to several movies and then ended up in a bar, the Bel Aire Club, on Broadway. I spent a few hours there, drinking beer and dancing with some of the barmaids and trying to get my bearings about my life, and more urgently the coming days, and how to deal with the possibility of being alone and homeless.

Chapter 123

When I returned to Aunt Ardith's the following day, she told me she had decided Dale could stay, but I would need to find another place. "You can stay the night, and then you will really need to go somewhere else. One more night," she said, and touched my shoulder.

That night, I waited for the mysterious stranger to join me again, but well into the morning she hadn't. Finally, I turned onto my side, intending to get some sleep. But as I was beginning to doze, the window effect caught me.

> *William heard the door creak, and then the covers were pulled back and a naked body slid in beside him.*
>
> *"It took Dale a long time to fall asleep," the voice said, as a hand found his crotch.*
>
> *He had hoped this would happen, and had gone to bed without his underwear. The mysterious stranger mounted him like a rider trying to break a stubborn bronc, so he assumed the role of the steed. He reached up and found her breasts. They were flat and hung like saddlebags from her chest. He rolled her onto her back and gravity molded them into little solid muffins for him to knead and fondle. It ended as before, with groans and grunts, and*

they lay again unconcerned and almost unaware of their surroundings, and then without a word, she stood and left the room, as the door quietly closed.

The window effect faded.

In the morning, Aunt Ardith called that breakfast was ready. She fed us a hearty breakfast and then stood by the door with a satisfied smile on her lips. She waved a fond farewell, her face flushed and radiant.

Dale was going with me to help me find a place to stay, but he had promised Aunt Ardith that he would return as soon as I was settled. After I got him to myself, I changed my mind about him being better off with her, and convinced him that I would be a lot more fun than Aunt Ardith and her cats. "Dale," I said, "you know you should be in school. Look at me. I didn't get my education when I was young, and now I have to go back and try to make something of myself." I said this because I was trying to fill in for his dad, who had taken the job of parenting about as seriously as mine had.

"That's a good one," he said.

"Don't you even listen to me?"

"Well, sometimes I do."

After this short "father-son" talk, we forgot about any good intentions and motivations concerning our futures and sat on one of the benches intended for bus patrons, rolling and smoking cigarettes and talking about what movies might be playing. It was nice to be able to smoke again without Aunt Ardith bitching at us when she caught wind of our tobacco breath or caught us standing in the bathtub, blowing smoke out the open window.

The days were still quite warm. We shielded our eyes against the bright sunshine. The nights, however, were getting cold, and it was clear that fall wasn't far away. I had forgotten to clean my wound that morning, so I opened my bag, took out the medical supplies, and we went through the boring ritual. Dale had become pretty good at doing the whole thing, because he had two hands available. With this distasteful job done, Dale wiped his hands on his Levis and we set out to discover a new day, and to put this one behind us. We walked toward downtown Salt Lake City, to see what circumstances might offer.

Chapter 124

Being the older and, in my opinion, the wiser of the two of us, I made the major decisions, like how the money should be spent, where and what we should eat, and what movies we should see. We had quite a lot of money left, so it seemed ridiculous to think about getting any kind of job yet. "Why the hell work when we have money?"

I knew I would need to get a job eventually, and I thought I could wash dishes in a café, although with my bad arm, that might be a problem. Maybe I could sweep the streets. I had observed a guy sweeping the streets. It was something that made sense to me and that I could probably handle. Not only would I have to be selective about what I did because of my injured arm, but also its failure to heal well didn't give me a lot of hope about doing much of anything. It had stopped bleeding, but looked like a wad of hamburger that had been fastened to my arm and where my thumb used to be. It constantly discharged a thick, yellow liquid. Whenever I bumped it or happened to lie on it, the pain was excruciating. I knew I needed to have something done with it, but I would just have to wait until I had some money.

I thought a dishwashing job would probably be more practical than street sweeping, because it would last through all the seasons.

I would just need rubber gloves to protect my arm and the dishes. I thought about driving a cab, but there was a test required for the Commercial License and I was sure I wouldn't be able to pass it. Even if I could, I wouldn't be able to do all the things a cabbie has to do, like finding addresses and such. I dismissed cab driving as unattainable, and went back to planning how to dispose of the money we had.

Over the following weeks, we stayed in cheap hotels, ate in cheap restaurants, or made our own meals from bread, lunch meat, cheese, and cornflakes. A good portion of our money was spent at the movies, seeing double features. Dale and I developed a routine for my injury. The doctor had told me that until it healed, the peroxide bath and bandaging would be necessary, and my arm should be tied up when I slept, so I wouldn't roll over on it. I usually didn't take the time and effort to tie it up, but it was better whenever I did. Among my medical supplies, I carried a gauze bandage that I had intended to use to tie my arm, but for one reason or another, I had yet to use it. Instead, I tried to be careful and anyway, the pain wouldn't allow me to lie on it.

"We ought to drop in on Ellen," Dale suggested one day.

"That's a hell of an idea," I said. "We might get some food and maybe some money as well. Let's go see her."

My sister Ellen had moved back to Utah and lived with a roommate, Uzanna, in a small two-bedroom apartment in a nice area of Salt Lake. I hadn't seen her for years. Uzanna wasn't home, but after a short visit during which we reacquainted ourselves, I saw that Ellen had changed. She seemed worldly and educated, having gone to some sort of a business school. I hardly knew her. But I liked what it had done to her, and it made me want to try to get some schooling.

Dale and I were able to achieve both our goals. The meal was scant, but lots better than nothing, and the twenty bucks she gave me would come in handy. I think the money was to reduce her guilt for not letting us stay for a few days. Ellen seemed concerned about my putrid injury, which she said was gross and sickening. "You better do something with it or you're going to lose your arm," she warned me. I told her I knew that, but I didn't have the money for the doctor or hospital. She told me that her roommate worked for a doctor and he was looking for an injury like this one to take pictures of and put in a new book he was publishing. She also said that this doctor sometimes did work for free when patients let him take pictures. Excited by the prospect of getting rid of the puss and soreness, I told her I'd do it. She said she would ask Uzanna, and see if she could get me an appointment. "I'll let you know what he says."

And then, in about the same way and with about the same attitude and ceremony that both Uncle Elmo and Aunt Maxine and Aunt Ardith had discharged us, we were dispatched. But I was still excited about possibly getting my arm fixed. We would just have to see, as Mom would say.

Chapter 125

In order to get to Ellen's apartment, we had to walk through a sort of ghetto. It probably wasn't as bad as Harlem, but it was still a borderline ghetto. As we walked by a large, rundown apartment building, we noticed that same blond, crippled girl sitting in a wheelchair I had seen a few days before. She was right in the middle of the sidewalk, as if she owned it. Once again, I noticed that the name on the building was the Camelot-Avalon Apartments. My island; maybe this is my island of Avalon, I mused with a smile. Maybe this was like King Arthur's island retreat, which seemed to be reaching toward heaven, possibly even his real heaven.

As we made our way around the girl, Dale spoke to her, and then stopped, and they entered into light conversation. Her name was Gloria Merlin and she had been stricken with cerebral palsy at birth. She sat cockeyed and twisted in her wheelchair. Her blond hair was rumpled and stringy from having been statically pressed against the chair all day.

She had trouble moving or talking, but if a listener was patient enough, she could eventually get her meaning across. It seemed that as she talked, she was trying to escape from her confinement, because she rocked, not violently, but softly and continuously back and forth, as if to add feeling and emphasis to her weak verbal exchange. But it was really because she had no control over her body's mild convulsions.

Dale was a patient fellow; more patient than I was. He accepted her slow response and stuttering and waited for her to complete her train of thought. I had heard somewhere that if a person does something that helps someone, and does it without expecting a reward, and then doesn't tell anyone about it, there would be a reward in heaven. On the other hand, if that person performs that same act and then allows it to be revealed to anyone at all, then the good feeling that accompanies it is the reward, and the debt has been paid. To take this premise to an extreme, if a reward in heaven is expected and desired, then that expectation is in fact the reward, and any reward in the afterlife, if there is one, would be cancelled.

This seems about as hard as getting a camel into heaven through the eye of a needle, I mused, or to make a seemingly religious person reasonable, able to discern, or truly charitable.

Dale did good stuff for people, simply because he thought it the right thing to do, and he didn't think it a big enough deal to even mention it. I thought he had stored up lots of rewards for later, unless I had taken them away from him by revealing his goodness. Dale and Gloria became great friends over the next few weeks, and we all spend hours talking and passing the time. We learned from Gloria that almost half of the large building's western portion, the Avalon side, had been condemned. She told us that several people lived there, even though they weren't supposed to. She said her parents managed the entire building but only the eastern half, which was in pretty good condition, had paying tenants. Her parents were supposed to keep people out of the condemned part but didn't have the heart to kick them out into the street. Gloria's Mom pretty much managed the place by herself, actually. Her name was Mary Katherine Merlin, but everybody called her "Aunt Mary." I soon discovered she was so nice to everyone, just like my own Aunt Helen in Springtown had been.

There was a small separate building out back of the complex, a washhouse that had a couple of washing machines and dryers. It was a separate building, but it was attached to the larger Camelot-Avalon building. There was also a small, dingy basement under the washroom. It was the furnace room. A huge, automatic stoker-type furnace was only operated in the winter months. And there was a bathroom; well, not a real bathroom, just a toilet and sink set against the wall, out in the open, with a small tin cup hanging on the wall. Both Dale and I knew without words that we had found our new abode.

After we picked a room in the upstairs of the condemned portion—the Avalon—that didn't look like it had been claimed, we prepared to set up housekeeping. All the furniture and fridges had been removed from most of the rooms, but some of the cupboards were still intact. There was soiled carpet on the floors, and dusty velvet drapes and lace curtains still hung at the windows. The view through the dirty windows to the west was the red brick side of the Firestone Building next door. The wallpaper looked dirty and some of it had either been pulled off or maybe just got tired of holding on and now hung down, trying to make its way to the floor. Our apartment was on the second floor and was one of the few that didn't have a toilet filled with dried human feces. There was no running water, heat, or electricity in the building.

"God, it's just like Eden," I told Dale.

"Yeah," he laughed.

After buying some cheese, cornflakes, milk, drinking water, and bread and storing it in the cupboard, we looked for ways to make our new place even nicer. By taking down the velvet drapes and lace curtains from window in some of the other apartments, we were able to fashion some pretty nice beds on the floor. I placed my bed near a nail that had been driven into the wall, so I would have a spot to tie up my arm at night if I decided to, and had the time. Dale made his bed nearby. We got a couple of candles to light the place after dark. And we bought a padlock and screwed a latch into place, so as to have some privacy and to keep vandals away from our bounty of food.

The only place we had to relieve ourselves was the toilet in the basement furnace room. Or we could, and very often did, use the yard at the back of our side—the Avalon side of the building. On dreary, rainy days or when we were lazy, we just used one of the overflowing commodes in one of the other condemned apartments, or peed out the window.

I had always said that I had been on my own since I was thirteen or so, and in a way I had been. But I had always been close enough that I could go home if the going got too tough. I couldn't go home now. Well, I guess I could if I wanted to, but I had decided that I wouldn't go home.

Our first night at the Avalon felt a lot like we were finally home. I lay in the dark, snug in my royal bed, waiting for Dale to go to sleep. I knew he was awake; I could feel it. After a while, his breathing became steady and deep, and I knew he was asleep. I lay awake into the late hours, listening to Dale's comfortable breathing and trying to plan. I was a little unsure of my future, and maybe a little bit afraid of what was going to happen to Dale, as well. I didn't really feel like trying to figure out the answers to life's questions anymore. At least for now, I just wanted to sleep and dream about Victoria at my side while we ruled, as we were intended to do, over Eden.

Chapter 126

Suddenly, it hits me. There is no one on earth who knows more about this furnace room than I do. Hell, I've spent years here. If anyone can escape from here, I'm the one. Becoming excited, I throw back the lace curtains and velvet drapes and struggle to sit. "To hell with you, Alex," I yell. "I'm throwing a wrench into the cogs of this plan—deal with that, you ass."

A little light filters through the dirty, screened windows, and I can see reasonably well. I look at the unfinished ceiling, where the decrepit beams are laden with spider webs, soot, and filth accumulated over the years. Maybe there will be a broken or damaged board I can use to my advantage, like the one I had in that boxcar in Canada when I was trying to escape from Oscar. I look around the room for something, anything, that I can use as a tool to escape. Why had I assumed that the door and windows were the only way out? Why hadn't I focused before now on the ladder leaning against the wall by the sink? It's so near to the rusty tin cup I have been drinking from, and it's right next to my Me box. Why hadn't I seen it? It isn't tall or in good repair, but it's nonetheless a ladder.

I scan the ceiling again, and try to position the ladder for best advantage. But even if I stand on it, I still can't see much—it is so dim and dank up here. I will need to feel my way along with my hands, to see if there could possibly be a way out. I know it's a long shot, but what do I have to lose? The ceiling is actually lower than it looks and I can easily reach it with my hand, although it's a balancing act, and I have to keep hold of the ladder with my free hand. I decide it will be better if I develop a strategy of discovery, blocking off the ceiling into sections and making sure I cover the entire area.

I feel in every direction, as far as I can reach, but find nothing. The only thing I accomplish is getting my hands filthy. I move the ladder and try again—and again, and again. Suddenly, my fingers find a depression of some sort. It's a small opening in the ceiling boards, not big enough to get my hand through, let alone my body, but maybe I can pass a note through it. If only I had paper and pencil ... or maybe someone will hear me if I yell through the hole.

I make my way down the ladder and scan the room for any paper I might have failed to see earlier. My Me box is filled with notebooks, including the notebook I had stuck in the back of my pants, but I'd like to maintain the integrity of these journals. If I have to, I'll defile them, but I will try to find something else first. I check my pockets, and feel something in my back pocket. I pull out the taped-together, fortune telling document from the patriarch.

I can use the back of it, I realize. I write on it, "I am being held captive in the basement below. Please call police."

I fold the message, climb the ladder, locate the slit in the ceiling, and push the message through. Now I will just need to wait to see if someone finds it, even one of the transients who sometimes occupy this condemned building. Finally, I hear a soft noise—it sounds like someone walking above me, very softly, perhaps in dancing slippers. I stop breathing and listen. There it is again. I see a movement at the hole, a flicker of light. I climb the ladder and reached up. My note is gone.

"Help, help!" I place my mouth close to the opening and yell. Time and again, I yell, "Help, help!"

I see slight movement at the hole. It is a small piece of paper being pushed through. I take it carefully, climb down and go to the window, where there is enough light to read. It's the paper that I had passed through the slit, and a note is written right below the one I had written: "I can hear you. Is there something I can do for you? I can't speak, but I am able to hear and read."

My heart almost stops, and then begins to race in my chest, so fast I'm afraid it will explode. I place the note in my back pocket. I don't know why, but it holds value to me and seems safe there. I climb the ladder and yell into the hole, "Yes, yes, please help me! There is a crazy man trying to kill me. Please come downstairs into the basement, and let me out."

In a moment, I see another piece of paper, which I grab and take to the window. It's a page from a lined school notebook. "Why is he trying to kill you? Did you do something to him?"

I climb the ladder and yell, "Let me out and I'll tell you all about it. If you don't want to let me out, go get a policeman and tell him I'm being murdered."

After a long silence, another piece of paper appears. I run to the window with it, and read, "Okay, I'll go try to open the door and then go get a policeman if I can't open it."

I run to the big, ironclad door.

Finally, I hear something, and see movement beyond the crack in the door. Then I see a piece of paper sticking through. I take it and run to the window. It's from the same notebook, and it says, "I can't open the door. It's nailed shut. I'm going to run to town and report this to the police. I'll be right back, wait for me. It shouldn't be long ... your old friend, Alex."

My heart drops, and I feel sick. That ass Alex thinks he's funny. I've got to find a way to get even with him.

"Do you have anything to tell me yet?" Alex asks from the other side of the door.

"Not yet, but soon—very soon. That was a disgusting thing you did, to give me hope, and then dash it cruelly."

"Something like you did to us? Bastard! It was a blast watching you getting the ladder and cleaning off that grungy ceiling. Do you think I'm dumb enough to let anyone in to that room above you? I read that séance you got at church. I guess you believe that, huh?"

Distraught, I think, he is evil. To hell with him. I don't have anything to tell him yet—but I know I will soon. I try to remember where I had left off ... I was about to go to Ellen's roommate's doctor's office to get my arm fixed.

I accept the illusion, allowing the window of the past to envelop me.

Chapter 127

The morning came with its usual authority, startling me awake. Dale was still asleep and he looked bedraggled and unkempt. I was discouraged.

I thought about giving up and going home to Eden. I knew Dale had become discontent, as well. Among other things, he had gotten tired of our diet, which now consisted of dry corn flakes and cheese. When Dale woke up, he was on the verge of tears and said he was homesick and wanted to go home. I told him we would find a way to get him there.

This life was not good for a young boy.

We were pretty broke and I didn't have enough money to get him home, or even enough to buy more food. I didn't have anything that I could sell to raise a little money, but Dale did. He had a calf at home that Uncle Arthur had given him. He said he would have his Mom and Dad sell it and send him the money. I agreed it was the thing to do, because I couldn't think of any alternative. Aunt Mary let us use her phone to call Mrs. Larsen in Eden, so we could ask her to contact Aunt Trudy and Uncle Arthur and ask them to sell Dale's calf and send the money here.

We gave her Aunt Mary's address and asked her to please hurry.

Before Dale hung up, I asked to talk to Mrs. Larsen. "Is Victoria there?" I said.

"I don't think so. At least, I haven't seen her."

"Okay, thanks. If you see her, please tell her I love her and will be coming for her as soon as I get a job."

"Okay, but I'm really busy and have to go now. I'll see you when you get here."

"Please tell Victoria."

"Okay, William. Goodbye."

While we were waiting for Dale's money I decided to see about getting into night school. I knew I need some sort of education or vocation. We walked to West High School and I talked to the lady in the office about the possibility of finishing my high school career there.

"Night school begins in two weeks," she told me.

I was a little excited. I could attend free of charge under a hardship program, because of my injured arm.

Over the next few days, Dale spent a lot of time talking to Gloria and doing things on his own and I spent a lot of time trying to figure out some of the answers to life's questions. I found that my retreat of choice was the furnace room. It was warm, although dirty, and was a place where I could be alone. This furnace room was becoming a part of me.

Religion and spirituality were always high on my list of interesting and challenging things to examine. For example, I considered that the only people Jesus ever criticized were the moneychangers in the temple or the people who were intent on stoning the adulteress to death, and I had no doubt that he forgave them as soon as he had dispensed his lessons. Maybe the moneychanger incident had just been a fable that the priests in the temple made up in order to squelch the competition with other moneychangers.

Maybe none of it ever really happened and someone just made it up for their own selfish advantage. Most things are written just to make a point, and to get others to think in the same or similar way.

"There certainly are moneychangers in all of the prominent religious places now, even in the churches," I thought. They had a choice concerning their status, whereas others, such as blacks, gays, ugly or fat people usually didn't have a choice. Well, maybe fat people did.

I rolled a cigarette and lit it. My lungs welcomed the soothing sensation of the smoke. I held it for a moment and then watched it stream out of my mouth and nose. It gave me a lot of comfort, as it always did. I was more than a little pleased with the way I had grown, and how I now understood things, even more than people who were much older than I was. This helped to make me sure I was special and had some sort of special mission. I was indeed of royal blood, I had no doubt.

History is written by biased people who often have a position to support, money to make, or an axe to grind from their point of view, which is based on their culture, beliefs, and indoctrination, I considered. There is little that is logical concerning theology and spirituality. It seems that anyone can support any belief, pro or con, simply by maintaining their point of view concerning these things held sacred by Christians or other spiritual sects.

"I'm not dead yet," I said, as I recovered from my philosophical meanderings and came back to what seemed to be the real word. I felt that I had exhausted the subject and looked for another. Maybe atoms, I thought. Maybe Dad knew more than he let on. The atom thing sounded pretty interesting. I would be able to say and think what I wanted, because nobody else knew any more about it than I did, and they would be hard-pressed to contest my findings, I was sure. I thought the atoms could be the key to knowing and doing some of the things that the Bible tells about, the magic and all. Maybe they make it possible for people to travel from distant planets or to send messages from long distances away, I thought. Maybe that's how God was able to cut the Ten Commandments into the stone for Moses on the top of Mount Sinai, or maybe Moses just took a chisel and hammer and a bottle of wine and made them himself. It is a mystery, to be sure.

These commandments struck me as mundane. What's more, I thought God might be a woman. Four of the Commandments try to compel all of mankind to kiss Her ass, and six others are simply things all humanity does and understands as the right things to do, even if not commanded. Well, Moses asked God for a vision and he got one: a burning bush. Worth a try, I thought. Maybe there will be a woman attached to my bush. I unscrewed the cap from a bottle of Thunderbird wine I had stored for such occasions, dropped to my knees, tipped the bottle back, and asked God to reveal the truth to me. I sipped away at the amber Night Train Express and repeated the request for knowledge. As the bottle began to empty, I seemed to pass through the window, and watched William besieging his God.

> The furnace room was suddenly filled with streaks of light and a glowing ball of brightness appeared before William. It floated, suspended in the air. He was unable to look directly at it. A gentle voice rumbled in his ears, "William, you have asked with a pure heart. You shall know the truth."
>
> William did not see a body.
>
> He only heard a voice that was soft and yet sought to break his eardrums. "The secret of life, the meaning of life is at hand."
>
> "Yes," William whispered. "Tell me. Please tell me."
>
> "It is the Holy Grail, William. You have asked with a pure heart."
>
> 'What is it?"
>
> "I am unable to tell you what it is," the voice boomed. "I am able, however, to tell you how it might be obtained."
>
> "I don't understand."

"The Holy Grail is built piece-by-piece, by a certain type of action."

William's jaw dropped open. "A certain type of action," echoed in his mind. "What the hell does that mean? Not a thing, not a person?" His voice quivered.

"Don't be impatient, young William. I'll tell you what it means," the voice whispered.

"What sort of action?"

"It can be any person. Maybe you could say that more than just being a person, it is an attitude, a way of life that leads to a certain destiny."

"Go on."

"Have you heard it told how a rich man may enter eternity?"

"Yes. More than once, when asked by rich men for eternal life, Jesus said, 'Give away all of your money.'"

"See how easy it is?" said the voice.

"That would be hard to do."

"Indeed, but Jesus meant more than that. He meant give and forget about it."

"But what about the Holy Grail?"

"The Holy Grail," said the voice, *"is the vessel that will carry a person into everlasting glory."*

"How do you get it?"

"It's almost impossible to get. The flesh is willing, but the spirit is weak."

"Tell me more," William couldn't help shouting.

There was only silence for a moment. *"Consider the warm and wonderful feeling you get when you do something good for someone. If you accept or seek reward of any kind for that good deed, including recognition, then that feeling is your reward. You will have no other reward in store."*

"But what about the Holy Grail?" William asked. "I don't understand."

"The Holy Grail is built piece by piece, as I said before. Each piece is put in place when you do a good or great thing unselfishly, without expecting any reward, and do not allow anyone to know about it. These things must be done solely because they are the right things to do, and not for any other reason or any other motive. This process is all-powerful and will carry a person to eternal glory, but only under the conditions that I have explained. Remember, no one must ever know, and the more you forget yourself, the greater the reward. Now, here's the hard part: you must do it even without looking for or expecting this reward. You must do it without trying to build the Holy Grail or thinking of its reward."

"Doesn't sound too hard," William said.

"Try it. You'll see how hard it is. Anyway, that's what the Holy Grail is. That's what eternal life really is. Good luck," the voice said.

As the streaks of light and glowing ball slowly faded, William fell to the floor, engulfed in a deep sleep. He dreamed of what was sure to become of him now. He was indeed special, he was indeed of royal blood, and it was now evident to him after this experience that he was also holy.

Chapter 128

"Dale, you have a letter," Aunt Mary called. "It's from Montana." She held it out to him.

Dale tore open the letter. It was the money from the sale of the calf, $40 dollars. Dale had had enough of city life and without even waiting for one more night, he and I walked the eight blocks to the Union Pacific Depot to get a ticket back to Eden for him. We passed a street sign that said West North Cromwell. "Hell, Dale, we're going in a circle. We're on North Cromwell."

Dale looked. "It's West North Cromwell," he said. "The one over by our apartment is East North Cromwell."

"That's confusing. If there are two streets named North Cromwell, I guess you need to know which one you're talking about."

We discovered that the train wouldn't arrive for a while, so to fill this time, we found a booth where we could make recordings of our voices. We looked at each other, and I think we both thought the same thing, "Maybe I could be the next Elvis Presley."

Dale and I often sang. Christmas songs were our specialty, but we could actually sing about anything, and very well, too, I might add. The cost of recording was twenty-five cents, so we crowded into the booth together and prepared to launch our new singing careers. As the needle cut into the record, we found the whole thing so funny that we began to laugh. We laughed through the entire session and only when the recording stopped did we stop laughing.   "It's a sad thing," I said. "We wasted the quarter and now the world will never enjoy this treat." And then we laughed about that.

It was sad that our voices and our song had been lost, to be sure, but not as sad as the fact that Dale was leaving. We had always been close, but had never shown our affections openly. Now we did. I hugged him. I didn't want him to go.

Dale got a one-way ticket to Butte, which turned out to be about nine dollars. Once there, he planned to get a ticket to Missoula. "Hell, I can walk home from Missoula if I have to," he smiled.

While we sat in the Union Pacific Depot waiting for the train, Dale opened his wallet and handed me $20 dollars. This was the only money either of us had. He thought he could make it home on his $8, but we were both a little worried. I had made up my mind that I was going to stay and try to get some kind of schooling. I hoped the $20 dollars would keep me going until I got some kind of job that I could do with my injured hand.

Even though I was far from anxious for him to leave, my wishes didn't stop him from walking to the waiting train, and I knew it was the best thing for him. After he climbed partway up the walkway, he turned and waved.

I yelled, "Tell Victoria I'm all right and I'll come for her soon."

He stepped up into the train and then turned and laughed in a strange way. "I will for sure, Bill." Then he stepped inside.

I stood watching as the train smoothly pulled away, picking up speed as it went. The lights got smaller and dimmer and soon disappeared. I was left with an acute feeling of abandonment. So alone. It was a deep, selfish pit of loneliness. I kept watching, hoping the train would come back down the tracks. The indelible loneliness that always surrounded the city was more apparent now, and it seemed almost unbearable. Only a few people walked around the boarding platform. Others stood or sat, reading papers or magazines, or amusing themselves by observing others, but I stood looking in the direction of the departed train. A small dust devil ruffled my hair and swirled bits of paper and debris aimlessly about, which only added to my loneliness and despair.

The $20 would buy a one-way ticket to Butte and then it would take a day of hitchhiking or riding a boxcar to enjoy the security of Mom running her fingers through my hair and telling me fables of kings and royalty, and lounging, and living with and loving Victoria. It would even be nice to see Dad, but if I'm to ever fulfill my destiny, I will need to be strong, I told myself. I drew in a deep breath. I'm not dead yet, I thought. The life of a prince is not is not an easy one. My life is not my own. I must do in the long run what is best for the kingdom of Eden and for my queen.

I turned away from the comfort of the tracks and of my alliance with Dale and walked toward the Avalon, my island of retreat, a condemned and dangerous building that was now a painfully lonely refuge, but my only refuge.

Chapter 129

Today was my appointment with Ellen's roommate's doctor. The dawn welcomed me with a gray sky that was beginning to give way to a blue morning. I could see just a sliver of it at the top rim of the eastern mountains. All about me hung an empty, almost reverent feeling; the secluded gap that lies between the peaceful night and early morning rush. I made my way, step after step, along the vacant sidewalk.

A noisy, dusty street-sweeper drudged along, pushing the grime and stench of the previous day out of the way and into the gutters, where two men in white coveralls and with vacancy behind their eyes patiently gathered it, using long-handled brooms and shovels, and then expertly lifted it into a truck as the pageant moved slowly ahead to unendingly repeat the monotonous ceremony.

I went around a corner to leave the distraction behind, and the solitude returned. Ellen's solemn warning echoed in my mind: "William, you'd better do something with that arm or you're going to lose it." She was more worried about it than I was.

A large building loomed ahead: "Doxey Layton Medical Building," it boasted on the front. This was it. I was glad, but not elated. I dodged the Rain Bird sprinklers and entered the large, cold, unwelcoming building that housed the doctor's office. The directory in the lobby told me Dr. Batchelor was on the third floor. The odor of alcohol and disinfectant was stronger as I stepped out of the elevator and stood directly in front of room 305.

"Sit there," the receptionist said, after I told her who I was. "The doctor is expecting you, and will be right here. She jammed a thermometer into my mouth, "Keep your mouth closed. Read a magazine if you want." She was an attractive girl. Her brown, auburn-tinted hair flowed down to partially cover the right side of her face like she was intent on hiding something, and then she softly brushed it back and looked at me to reveal there was nothing horrible to hide. She took out the thermometer and shook her head and then shook the glass instrument and went to her desk and dropped her head to work. She occasionally moved freely about while still sitting in her chair, jotting something into a ledger, and as she turned the pages of the ledger, her hair stubbornly fell back to hide what wasn't there.

There wasn't much to read in the magazines, most of which were about hunting and fishing. What the hell is there to read about that? I thought. If ya hunt, ya just shoot a damned elk or bear. If ya fish, ya just catch fish. I thumbed through a couple more magazines, although "thumbed" was more a figure of speech for me, because I had learned to turn the pages with my index and middle fingers. Maybe I should say "fingered" through the magazines. Then I slid the unread ones back onto the pile and sat looking at the walls and the attractive receptionist as I waited for the doctor. Finally, he stepped out. He was a large man with a full beard, dressed in green scrubs. He had little green eyes set deep in a pallid face, and a long, hawk-like nose that seemed to compete with the rest of his face for the title of "ugly." He wore a stethoscope around his neck and seemed nervous; like he was in such a hurry, with so many things to do, that he wasn't comfortable just passing the time of day.

He held out his hand for me to shake. "Hi," he said.

"Hi."

"You know, you have a fever, quite high actually. If it were to prove chronic you could experience hallucinations. Have you been hallucinating?"

I laughed, "It seem my life it a continual hallucination," I shrugged my shoulders.

He smiled a knowing smile, "Let's see that pesky injury."

I pulled off the bandage and held it under his nose. He turned my arm slowly back and forth, like he was reading it in small print. He had Uncle Arthur's halitosis, and like Uncle Arthur, he was eager to share it.

"It would have been lots easier to fix if it had been attended to immediately." He continued to look at it. "But I will do it without cost, if you will consent to pictures."

"That's great with me."

"It will be a simple operation. First, we will need to remove all the proud flesh that has grown on your arm and where your thumb used to be. Then we will take skin from your butt and use that to rebuild and repair the injury." He shook his head and repeated, "It would have been a lot easier to do when it was new."

"Whatever. It doesn't sound simple," I mumbled.

"We'll use a local, and numb only the portions of your hand, arm, and butt that we'll be cutting. You will need to stay awake and help me get your body parts in the proper position for me to take pictures and such," he said.

"I can do that." I smiled my tough, Montana-acquired cowboy smile.

"After the operation, you will need to take it easy and protect your arm it until it heals."

"That's not too much to ask," I answered with that same tough smile.

He tried to imitate my tough smile and dialog; it was contagious. "Just let Mom and Dad take care of you for a while."

That would be the day, I thought, but I said, "Okay."

"After I fix it, make sure to keep your arm tied up so you don't roll over on it," he said while drenching me one last time with his version of Uncle Arthur's halitosis.

My operation was to be in two days.

Chapter 130

I was about as anxious for the operation as I was to see Monday morning roll around when I was in school, and I did everything I could think of to keep that morning away, but eventually it was there, anyway.

I solemnly dressed and walked the several miles to the huge, red-brown brick hospital, which said "Saint Mark's Hospital" on the front in large, block lettering. I considered for a moment what I had gotten myself into. I looked up and down the street, trying to find a reason not to go inside.

To the north was a large sign, "The Wasatch Springs Plunge." I had heard of this swimming pool's healing effects from its natural, hot mineral water. To the south, all I saw were cars and people driving and walking along the streets. I imagined I could smell the chlorine from the pool and the body odor and farts of the people in cars and along the streets and walking; or maybe these smells were real.

A lady in a white dress, white stockings, and white shoes met me outside the main door of the hospital and tried to make me get into a wheelchair. She wore a little white princess hat, something like what the waitress, Louise, had worn at Pug's Café in Spokane, but this one was white and clean. Beneath the hat and framed by light ginger hair was a round, moon-like face with dark eyelashes that had been relocated from where God had intended and placed well above her brown eyes in a high arch, like she had been permanently startled. Her lips were full and painted red, and they looked sexy. She was old, maybe 30, and emitted a fragrance of flowers, maybe gardenias. Hell, I didn't even know what a gardenia was, but it was a pleasant scent, I was sure, just the same. Hell, what if she was 30? I was 21, or at least I had told Robert Merlin I was. So she wasn't really too old.

"Hell, I can walk," I told her.

"It's just hospital policy," she said and insisted that I sit down.

She wheeled me into a dressing room and handed me a well-worn, flowered gown. It looked like it had been made from old chicken mash sacks like Mom used to make my shirts from. "Take off all of your clothes, even your underwear, and put this on." She leaned forward held the flour sack garment toward me. The cleavage was so close I could have easily snuggled my nose into it. I leaned closer as well. She smiled and pulled away like she was teasing me, like she was daring me to do something.

"Push that button when you're ready and I'll come and get you." She winked and then turned and pulled the door shut behind her.

The gown, which was faded and obviously designed to tie in back, wasn't in good repair. Just for fun, I put it on backwards which allowed my privates to be exposed in front. "William," the nurse said after I had pressed the button, "it doesn't go that way," and she laughed." Put it on right, and then press the button when you're ready."

When she came back, she picked up my clothes and hung them in the small closet. "They'll be here when you need them," she said. Her teeth were white; too white to be real, and they were straight and even, too.

Must be false teeth, I said to myself, and then imagined what it might be like to have her take them out—what she might look like, what she might do.

"Do you have any valuables or money?" she asked, interrupting my short fantasy.

"Yeah, I've got some money in my wallet."

"You can trust me, " she smiled. "I'll keep it in this locker. It will be here when you're done."

"Okay," I said, looking at her too-pretty-to-be-real teeth.

I felt like an invalid as two orderlies lifted me into the wheelchair. They treated me like a piece of meat, like one of the sides of beef or pork that we hung on a hook in the cooling locker back in Montana to cure before we cut it up into ribs, chops, and roasts.

"Can you walk?" one of them said.

"Sure," I answered, and stepped out of the wheelchair and crawled onto the table.

A different man, also in green scrubs, held something that looked like an upside-down strainer over my nose and mouth and told me to count backwards from 100 and to breathe deeply… When I woke, I sat up slowly. I was lightheaded and the room was spinning. I had a vague memory of needles being stuck here and there, and of someone moving my arm, and of flashing as pictures were taken. I struggled out of bed. My arm was bandaged. My arm and butt were bandaged, too, and were numb, and it was difficult to walk. With the help of the nurse with the not-real teeth, I put on my clothes. The halls of the hospital were uncharacteristically vacant. No nurse or orderly was around to insist that I ride a wheelchair to the exit. No agent of the hospital tried to be the big shot and charge me for additional processes to take any money I might have. It looked like they had done their part and now I was on my own.

The unusually hot day made the walk home seem a lot longer than it was. I felt sick, as if I would pass out. The people on the sidewalk were mere ghosts floating past and the buildings were wisps of incandescent concrete and glass. The sidewalk tilted slowly from side to side as I slid past, one feeble step at a time.

Cars honked as I crossed the street and people yelled obscenities. Finally, I saw the red-and-white outline of the Firestone Building next door to the Camelot-Avalon Apartments. "At last, I'm home."

I made my way up the stairs to my room and took a couple of the pain pills the nurse had given me. I tied my hand in place and lay down on my royal bed of lace sheets and velvet blankets. The feeling of passing through a window overwhelmed me. I began watching William.

> *The room was a castle with beautiful white lace curtains and velvet drapes everywhere. William had the ability to move about the room without touching the floor. He was wise beyond his years; he was a king. He had been asked to decide a question about the Bible, but it was a trap, and he knew it. He could be liable for blasphemy. He had to be careful.*
>
> *He began to preach: "Scholars of the Bible know that giving away money will buy salvation. It is easier for a camel to pass through the eye of a needle than for a rich man to enter into the kingdom of heaven. People always seem to live by those things that are easy. Hardest of all, and that which will bring the most blessings, is to do righteous things and then never reveal them to anyone. If the deed is revealed, then the good feeling that accompanies the telling of it is the reward for doing it. It is still a good thing and the person who is so unselfish is indeed a good person, but the deed has been paid off with the good feeling, and there is no more reward in store."*
>
> *This is such a conundrum, William thought. It's impossible to do and to not do. Narrow is the way and wide is the way. Now that I'm revealing this information to others, I'm taking the risk of having someone think I'm doing good things and then revealing them, and this will diminish any blessings I would otherwise have in store.*

Even by talking to people in this manner, I could be taking away any future blessing. He muttered, "God, you expect too much. This is too difficult."

He stretched his arms and looked into the heavens for the answer.

"I am but a boy, God. However, your will be done."

White streaks of light appeared and a voice thundered in his ears. He clutched his lace sheets and velvet blankets. The ball of light appeared again, even more brilliant that before.

"You are troubled, William. You have no cause for concern. You have discovered the secret of salvation." The voice was a whisper, yet it thundered in his ears

"What do I call you?" William asked. "Do I simply call you Ball of Light?"

"I am what I am. Do not be concerned. I can be anything and anywhere. Do not be concerned with things of this world."

"I have tried to do the things concerning the Holy Grail," William told the Ball of Light.

"You have the power, which is in your pen. Your pen is mightier than a sword. It is your Excalibur. You must write, to make others understand and seek the sweet nectar of salvation. Make them understand that it is not for just a few, a select group, but for everyone who seeks it in earnest. Victoria is your Lady of the Lake and Queen Guinevere in one. Listen to her; she will help you in this quest. You will have her; you will rule Eden with her at your side. You will acquire the Holy Grail and it shall lift you into paradise. No one shall be excluded. I love all my children, and only in the selfish minds of men who distort my word with their own words and build churches in their own glory are any of them despised. Satan shrouds those unholy hypocrites and the ones misled by them. In altering *my words and harshly judging others, they do evil and are in danger of damnation. Many are they who will appear in sheep's clothing but within, they are ravening wolves. William, you must return to Eden and bring Victoria, your queen, to Avalon, your fortress."*

William got to his knees. He knew what he was going to do. He knew what he had to do. He was now compelled to seek the Holy Grail. He now knew it was his quest, commanded by God, and only he had the knowledge and courage to attain this goal.

Chapter 131

It was getting cold on the second floor of the Avalon; winter was just around the corner. The milk and other food were beginning to freeze. I knew I would need to get a warmer place soon. My arm was healing nicely and the doctor had given me an aluminum guard to place over it for protection from bumps and such.

The doctor had me go to Saint Marks Hospital rather than his office at the Doxy Layton Medical Building. He had finished with the pictures and it looked like I was doing just fine. The nurse with the perfect white teeth had moved to Oregon for a better job. I was sorry to see her go; she was nice and really cared about her patients, but now I would never know if those teeth were false or not. I had to smile at the thought.

The doctor promised that the feeling would come back to my arm and where flesh had been taken from my butt for patching, and that the hair growing in strange places on my arm and hand would soon just go away; there was no need for me to go back anymore.

"I'm not dead yet," I exclaimed. I tried to make up something funny about the old joke Dad used to say about playing with yourself and hair on your palm, but I couldn't think of anything that sounded funny. Things were finally starting to go my way, although

I had almost no money and was having some trouble keeping the cornflakes and cheese in stock. I had to do something...

I was grinding out my third stogy on the sidewalk and leaning against the storefront when in the distance I heard booming like thunder.

As it neared, the less boisterous sounds of tambourines and maybe flutes were audible. And then a group of stoical, robot-like people in the red-trimmed, blue uniforms of the Salvation Army came into view. Years ago I had head beating of their drums and tambourines were attempts to lure sinners to the chapel to be forgiven, spiritually saved, and then saved again physically with hot soup, pie, coffee, and a bed. It was for the latter that I hoped to be enlisted.

I held my bandaged arm high for sympathy, and rolled a fat cigarette with the other hand as I stood with a few other desperate sinners waiting for the well-meaning crusaders. As they passed, we sinners fell in behind and with eyes cast to the ground to show proper humility, we followed them toward the hall. The music was more suitable to summon rain than to attracting sinners for conversion and salvation.

We sinners were herded into seats at the rear of the chapel, like cattle awaiting slaughter. After an impressively boring meeting that rivaled the excruciating testimony meetings in Dad's church, we were urged to step forward, one by one, to confess our belief in Jesus as Christ by nodding and saying "amen" to key questions. After that, we were assembled, a shoddy, tattered mob now magically cleansed of sin. Thus aligned, we were instructed to echo in unison the Army captain's chant of willingness to love Jesus and walk in his light, followed by more "amens" and more preaching.

Finally, we reaped the fruits of our humiliation in the form of warm showers and clean towels and shirts, and then we were seated at long, clean tables for hot bread, soup, coffee, and apple pie—after which, we were silently escorted to soft, tall, clean beds. There was still a flophouse ambience, but the place was clean and didn't have a lot of methane gas. It reminded me of the luxury of the lace sheets and velvet blankets at the Camelot-Avalon.

The sinner in the bed next to me was an old man with a long white beard who seemed to have a glow about him, an aura. He was mumbling something; I moved to the edge of my bed to hear. "People are blind; they are sheep to follow blindly without thought. I have been driven to this, to take from these ungodly hands that hate me and that I hate, the ones that have sought to destroy me. You see I am homosexual, not the distorted form that churches have taught and coerced the people to believe in, but the pure form of loving one of my own gender. Oh, how I wish he were here with me now."

I thought, "He must be crazy." I decided to ignore him, but he went on. "Matthew 7:1-5, about hypocrites who judge others. 'Do not judge lest you be judged yourselves … Why do you look at the speck in your brother's eye, but do not notice the log that is in your own eye? … Oh, ye hypocrite!"

I recognized that from the Bible. He continued talking to the ceiling as he went on: "Mark 7:18-23, Jesus chided his disciples for their lack of spiritual understanding. The religious leaders had condemned Jesus and his disciples because they did not wash and eat according to the Law. Jesus said, "Are you too so uncomprehending? Don't you see that whatever goes into your mouth from the outside cannot defile you, because it does not go into your heart, but into your stomach, and is eliminated? That which proceeds from within you, out of your heart, defiles you; evil thoughts, abusive sex acts, thefts, murders, adulteries, deeds of coveting, wickedness, deceit, not caring, envy, slander, arrogance and foolishness: all of these evil things proceed from within and defile you."

I had little interest in his babbling. I tried to look away and shut him out but he went on. "Paul also rejected the absolute commands of Leviticus in Colossians 2:8-23. He said, 'If you have died with Christ to the elementary principles of the world, why, as if you were living in the world, do you submit yourself to decrees, such as, 'Do not handle, do not taste, do not touch' (all of which refer to things destined to perish with the using) in accordance with human commandments and teachings? These are matters which have, to be sure, the appearance of wisdom in self-made religion and self-abasement and severe treatment of the body, but are of no value against human indulgence."

"My God," I thought, "why don't you go to sleep?" but he went on mumbling idiotically. "Romans 2:1: "Therefore you are without excuse, every one of you who passes judgment, for in that you judge another, you condemn yourself; for you who judge practice the same things. Blessed are the poor in spirit, for theirs is the kingdom of heaven, Mathew, 5:3."

I sat up on the edge of the bed. He didn't even notice as he raved on, in a whisper. "Paul declared in Romans 2:14 that Jesus has 'canceled out the certificate of debt consisting of decrees against us which was hostile to us; and Jesus has taken it out of the way, having nailed it to the cross.' And then of course, the story of having he without sin cast the first stone."

I had no defense; I might be stoned myself or put in prison if I smothered him. I decided to wait and hope he might finally go to sleep, but he went on, and this time I listened more closely, because he was beginning to make some sense, and besides, I had no choice. "We wrestle with religious 'principalities and powers and the rulers of the darkness of this world.' Religion has been darkened by well-meaning but overzealous leaders, and the real God and Jesus have been blinded to the minds and eyes of millions of people. The real truth of God's love and acceptance of all people as having equal value before him has been replaced by abusive churches that have abandoned the true personality and purpose of Jesus of Nazareth. Slick portraits and statues of crucified, feeble Christs have obscured the real Jesus and filled the imagination of millions of people with false images that have no social or cultural impact beyond the teachings and demands of oppressive religious institutions. The traditional images of Jesus with a flock of sheep, or alone with face upturned to a blazing light, or on a cross, have created a remoteness that makes it almost impossible for the average person to identify with the real Jesus. These artistic pictures of Jesus are far more vivid in the minds of most people than a simple human portrait of Jesus sitting with outcasts, eating with the unclean people of his community. Jesus accepted and welcomed the people that everybody else, including religion, rejected and despised. The "pitiful Jesus" has been magnified in art beyond the evidence to induce emotional self-rejection and to arouse remorse instead of discipleship, sadness instead of joy. 'Man of sorrows and acquainted with grief' is an unfortunate misrepresentation of the true Jesus, who enjoyed life with his friends so much that his enemies accused him of being party boy and a heavy drinker. Jesus welcomed and 'ate with sinners' rather than condemning and rejecting them. Why is that so difficult to grasp? Is it because religion itself has taught us to reject our true nature and reason for being? Religion has betrayed you, and religion also has betrayed Jesus.

What kind of God would create us as gay or lesbian and then condemn us to eternal fires of hell because it? Whenever religion condemns and rejects people because of how God made them, it is obviously false and out of touch with reality. Leaving the comfortable fold of traditional abusive religion is often the hardest decision a person has to make. It is far more difficult than joining the religion in the first place. Leaving the fold invites rejection, condemnation, judgment and self-blame and guilt. It is not an easy path out of delusion into the truth. Yet health and wholeness as a person depends upon escape from abusive religion. No piece of ancient literature is more filled with violence, treachery, war and genocide than the "Holy Bible." Misled by the robots of religious abuse and oppression and the deadly power of regimented social/religious indoctrination, people reflect mindless decisions in their great emotional responses to old-fashioned country revivals. Jesus supposedly said in John 8:32, 'You will know the truth, and the truth will make you free.' John the divine was onto something."

He finally stopped and noticed me. He smiled, and then went on, but now more as human might do. You know—rational.

"I've thought about it a lot, and even if the organized religions are immensely evil and self-serving, they do play an important part in creating a decent world. I guess in order to make you understand, I need to go back to the Middle East about a half-century after Jesus died. That's when Paul, a crusader in his own right, began pushing for the words and philosophy of Jesus to become a part of the culture—a part of the whole world. Well, that area was really the whole world then.

"Paul traveled and preached, trying to attract the multitudes as Jesus had done, but he lacked the charisma that Jesus had. That was probably because the message from Jesus about pure selflessness was sincere and genuine, but from Paul it contained too much selfishness and greed. But to say that Paul didn't believe it would probably be a lie, because I think he did. But to echo Benjamin Franklin, who was born much later, but who had a great deal of charisma himself, 'Men wish to live religiously while at the same time maintaining a sarcastic spiritual viewpoint on worldly gratifications.'

"Paul could see that people should live like Jesus said and taught, but people were just too damned selfish and greedy to do that. Then it occurred to Paul that people could be frightened into doing the right thing. It would take some time and some effort, but it would be worth doing what he assumed to be the bidding of Jesus. And then would come the easier and more rewarding part: just turn the brainwashing over to the parents, and they would do the recruiting and indoctrination—and in the end, wouldn't this be what Jesus wanted, anyway?

"This didn't happen overnight. It took decades. Paul's first invention was taken from the concept of the Greek gods, but it was a lot more complicated than an array of gods fighting for dominance. Punishments and rewards and an afterlife were added, where people would go and dwell either in a good place or a bad place. Then Paul emphasized the good place as heaven and the bad place as hell. But he had to have a way to get them there, or at least their souls. To do this, he set the Devil against God as an adversary, and had Jesus be sacrificed as a martyr, making people believe in a ridiculous system through which God would 'save' them. Yeah, I know it sounds far-fetched, but if kids are given the choice to either burn in a horrible hell forever or adhere to some ludicrous set of laws, it's unlikely they will choose the former.

"Then he and his associates invented more horrible demons that were also based on ancient Greek mythology. One was named Pan, a god who was a goat-man with horns, cloven hooves, and a pointed tail, but there were others as well. Through the years, these were enhanced to cause even more fear until many people decided it would be better by far to attend some boring meeting and pay a tithe than to go to this horrifying hell. But then, to the delight of Paul and his cronies, the fact that these things were so frightening was cause for more people to begin to attend organized church meetings—just like contemporary people are drawn to vampire or zombie books and stories. This, along with the beautiful and garnished church building and décor, made it nearly impossible to resist.

"As Paul aged, he handed off what he had accomplished to Constantine, the Emperor of Rome, because Constantine saw it as a great way to control the people. And he was right, as it quickly took the place of the dungeons and torture chambers and became an engine to steal the minds of the people and to control them through fear, just as the old torture devices and methods had done before.

"It was easy to convert people to Paul's new religion, because most people at that time and in that area were Jewish or pagans, and after Paul had redesigned his Christian church, it was more pagan than anything to do with the philosophy and teachings of

Jesus. So when the people converted, they were converting only in name. And then when the city of Rome burned, it was this religion, foreign to the teachings of Jesus, that made its way out of the ashes to become, or at least to greatly influence, all the earth's religions today.

"There were fragments and stories about Jesus in these writings of Paul, and maybe even Constantine—if he even knew how to write. And these made their way into the New Testament when it was compiled, or canonized about a hundred years after Jesus died, but these were hidden under tons of garbage and trash. Thomas Jefferson called it dung. But he called the hidden words from Jesus diamonds. Then when the Bible was put together, and the New Testament was added, about a thousand years after Jesus died, there was even more 'dung' added and all of these 'diamonds' were hidden even more. Now the diamonds are nearly impossible to find.

"But I have to say, I think a lot of the world's morality comes from these little glimpses of Jesus and his philosophy and teaching in that bewildering book, the Bible. Little pieces and shreds somehow come through and cause people to be pretty good. And if it hadn't been for the Bible, this hideous book that tells of wicked kings and worthless people and atrocities, the book that Tomas Paine, a founding father, thought more likely to be from demons than from any decent god, then these little threads, or diamonds, from Jesus would probably have never made it to our century.

"But to say that there is any church on earth today that is Christian, that is, which contains the real philosophy and teaching of Jesus, has to be a lie. All churches on earth today are heavily influenced by the writings and work of Paul and almost nothing of the real Jesus is there.

"The giant, rich and powerful organized religions, not the misled and mindless members, are the Devil, if there even is a Devil. It's strange that the huge and rich organized religions are able to be so evil and the people, for the most part, are so moral, worthwhile, and good. If you think about it, most people, religious or not, are pretty good people."

He smiled and went on, but now more in a trance than before.

"Wouldn't it be a kick in the nuts, oh sorry, I mean a kick in the head, if the thing was true about Jesus visiting the Americas after they killed him in the Middle East?"

The old man looked at me. Tears of sincerity ran down his face.

"Well, I assumed you were a Mormon; we are in Utah. Are you familiar with this religion?"

"I was raised in it," I frowned.

"Okay, so you know the story. What if He did come over and taught the people, the Indians or Native Americans, how they should live? Then the early American Christian crusading settlers and the ones just looking for a better life took all of the Indians' land and unmercifully forced this tainted religion from Paul and Rome onto them. This would have actually wiped out all evidence of Jesus even being on earth at that time, except for those little, very well-concealed fragments in the New Testament of the Bible."

I thought the old man was on to something here. Maybe he wasn't so crazy. "That is a point well taken," I said.

The old man smiled a wry smile and went on, "I can imagine having a conversation with the real Jesus. It's hard to imagine what I would say." He smiled again, showing his toothless gums. "I might say, 'Do you think I'm going to hell, Jesus?'"

"What? What the hell is hell?" Jesus would reply.

"It's just the opposite of heaven."

"What in heaven's name is heaven?"

"You don't know? You said those things in your book."

"I can't remember saying that—what book?"

"You can't remember? The Bible!"

"This sort of talk makes me want to roll over in my tomb! That 'roll over' is just a figure of speech by the way," Jesus would say.

"Then what's it all about?"

Jesus would look a bit puzzled. "Can you remember anything

about, love, forgiveness, being passive, judging not, humility, compassion, selflessness, simplicity, and tolerance?"

"But how can we all be saved with something so simple?"

"Saved from what?"

"You know, when you died on the cross to save the souls of mankind."

Now Jesus looked really puzzled. "That's a new one to me."

"You know, when your father, God, sent you to earth as a sacrificial lamb for humanity?"

"That doesn't make sense. Who would believe that sort of nonsense? What decent father would do something like that?"

"What about a sweet little child? A sweet, innocent child would believe it."

"Yeah, I guess, but I do remember saying something about it being better that a millstone was tied around their neck and they were thrown into the sea than to cause one of my little ones to stumble."

"But what about paying tithes and being obedient, to live a great afterlife after we die?"

"Live, but you will be dead." Jesus would smile a wry, mischievous smile.

"Jesus Christ, Jesus, you know what I mean," I might impatiently say.

Jesus would smile softly. "I was just shitting you about 'being dead.' You should have seen the look on your face—being saved is much like a verb. It's not a place, it's more a state of being."

The old man paused a long moment, not sure what to say that wouldn't be too sacrilegious, but he seemed to be doing this mostly for my benefit, and then he went on. "I noticed you are sort of a potty mouth, Jesus."

Now it would be Jesus's turn to pause. "What's a potty mouth?"

"You know, using bad words."

"Words don't hurt anybody or do any harm. Only thoughtless people do that—and, by the way, money isn't bad either. It's the way words and money are used that can injure or harm. Humans are the only species that uses these tactics of vengeance and thoughtlessness to hurt or injure. Did you ever hear, 'Sticks and stones will break…'"

"Yeah, I head that. I think you said it."

"I get a lot of credit for stuff I didn't do. If people would just think and listen and open their eyes, the rich, wicked churches would cease to exist, at least as evil empires. But to say sticks and stones will not hurt is a big fat lie. They do hurt, and so does thoughtless name- calling."

"Boy, the old man and allusive Jesus really screwed that up," I thought—but even so I got the gist.

The old man asked the allusive Jesus, "What about that bitchin' great reward that I've taken all the shit for here on earth to get?"

Jesus would smile a more genuine gentle loving smile now. "Sorry, the reward is just in doing it selflessly. But that is one hell of a lot MORE than it sounds like it is!"

"I'll need to do some thinking, Jesus—it all seems so different from you."

"Well, it's not. Humans are so naïve and enterprising. Do you remember, 'Narrow is the way and few there be that find it?'"

I had to laugh at the old man's antics. "You make a great point."

The old man went on, this time without Jesus. "Everybody reads things differently—they all read the same writings and take different things away. It seems that people read only to reinforce what they already believe and not what's really there. Old Paul really set loose a hell of a system to enslave mankind and render a lot of them mindless. I don't think he would have ever done it if he'd know what it would eventually do to humanity."

Finally, the old man slept and I did as well, but mine was a fitful sleep in which religious fanatics tried to lure me to hell. My dreams probably were influenced by my own opinion about Paul the Apostle, or as Thomas Jefferson called him, the great corruptor. Jefferson and I had a difference of opinion about that. Jefferson thought Paul to be corrupt to the core, while I thought him to be honorable but unable to get the people to follow the teachings of Jesus without giving them good reason to do it. Instead, he compelled them to do so, using fear and money as his tools. But I agreed with Jefferson that religion is the most powerful engine ever invented to enslave mankind, even if Paul was a sincere man.

The morning brought with it hot water to wash my hands and face and another clean towel. The old man found me at the table, where I was trying to dig a gob of instant oatmeal covered with milk and sugar out of a small bowl, using a large wooden spoon. He sat next to me, closer than was comfortable. He bowed his head in silent prayer and then resumed his humdrum philosophizing from last night.

"Why are the well-meaning religious zealots concerned with things in the Bible that are written in parable, lost in interpretation, and carefully hidden so no one is able to find them? Why can't they read and understand the teachings that are obvious, that I recited to you last night?" He bent his head and spooned the rough cereal into his mouth and was silent.

I thought about the old man often after that, and wondered about the fanatically religious, and their unwillingness to see the real Jesus. For me, the following days and weeks were spent being saved at the hospice with regularity, until finally I was recognized as a heathen sinner whose only interest was the food and lodging, and I was turned away with out fare. Before I left, I asked about the old man and found that he had died the previous night. "It was his time to go," the captain said.

His body lay in state in the back room; this had been the only home he had known, with people who hated him. Even so, out of kindness these, people who had been taught by their religion to hate him for what he was, for what God had made him, still had the grace and charity to provide him a refuge. "It's a complicated world," I thought as I visited his body to pay my last respects.

A smile adorned his face, and even in death he retained a glow, an aura that overshadowed the ragged clothing in which he would be buried. I couldn't help myself—I bent to kiss his wrinkled forehead and say a silent prayer that God would forgive him, if forgiveness was even due to one who had suffered so much. I had somehow, in spite of everything—perhaps because of my strong character—retained some faith in prayer and even in God.

Chapter 132

Gloria's father, Robert Merlin, took most of the credit for managing The Camelot-Avalon Apartments, while his wife, Aunt Mary, actually really did all or at least most of the work. Robert Merlin had earned dual degrees in psychology and philosophy, with an emphasis on evolutionary anthropology. He never said where he worked, but he was gone for extended periods and left Aunt Mary to fend for herself and tend to the details of the apartment complex.

Robert and I frequently jousted with ideas. It was my meager knowledge, common sense, and imagination against his counterfeit, imitation learning. We were like David and Goliath, I with a slingshot (little education) and he with his vast knowledge. He had a fine array of mental weaponry and enormous strength (education mixed with illusion and dogma). He delighted in throwing around big words and phrases, like, "attribute," "DNA," the theory of relativity," and such. When it became obvious that nobody understood what he was talking about, he loved to explain the meanings of such words, in a condescending way that was obviously intended to embarrass and belittle the listener.

I would respond, "Oh, I see."

After one impressively boring evening with him, as I sat biting the end of my good thumb in silent defeat and humiliation again, he told me that a friend of his worked for Noel Brothers Lumber Company and that they were looking for a yardman as well as a truck driver. "It's better than nothing," he said. "You can't expect too much with no education or intelligence," and he smiled his condescending smile. "I wonder if you're old enough? You look old enough, but how old are you?"

This question took me by surprise. "Twenty-one," I answered. I wasn't 21, but he didn't need to know everything, I thought.

I intended to go to the lumberyard to apply for the job early the next morning, but Aunt Mary wouldn't let me go until I showered in their apartment. It was a good thing, because even though I had gotten used to my own stench, others probably hadn't. She also gave me a hot breakfast and a dollar to get some lunch. When I arrived, I learned that the yardman job had just been filled, but the delivery job was still vacant and was offered. I quickly accepted, because it seemed to be a job I could handle with my quickly healing limb.

It was Friday and I was to report for work Monday morning. It paid seventy-two cents an hour and there would probably be a little overtime occasionally. Gloria's parents told me that if I wanted to, I could clean up the furnace room and sleep there and eat with them. I would have to pay $35 a month and tend Gloria and their two other little girls one night a week, when their parents went to some sort of church meeting. They would trust me for the rent until I got my first paycheck.

The furnace room was good-sized, not as large as the apartment on the second floor but it had the distinct advantage of being warm. The huge furnace was nestled in one corner, next to the stoker. The single light that hung down from the ceiling reminded me of the light in the basement of Aunt Sara's washhouse. "God, I've graduated to my own dungeon," I laughed.

The covered stoker was used to store the coal outside the furnace room. Whenever the furnace needed more fuel, it would nosily and automatically bring more into the flame by some mechanical conveyor. For a while, every time the stoker worked, the noise would wake me up, and then it just became a part of my bedroom and I didn't notice it anymore. About twice a month during the colder months a large coal truck would back up to the chute, just outside, and dump its entire load of coal into the stoker. In the warm months of summer, the stoker sat empty, an appealing home for cats, mice, and rats.

The only other openings in the room were two windows and the large, heavy door that had been covered with sheet metal, maybe to keep mice or other rodents from chewing it and to keep them out, at least via that entry. Metal strap bars crisscrossed the windows outside the glass, and heavy screens had been placed on the inside. The window looked like they could have been opened years ago, but now they were painted shut with so many coats that they were permanently set in place, even if the bars and screen hadn't been there to prohibit anyone from coming or going through them. The glass had become so covered with coal dust that it let light through only grudgingly. Several panes in the window had been cracked into spider-web arrays, allowing streaks of sunlight to shine through in the morning, creating a sort of holy vision effect.

I decided to use the area right next to the door and as far away from the furnace as I could get for my sleeping abode. I borrowed a broom from Aunt Mary and cleaned that area, and then carried water and scrubbed the floor. It didn't come completely clean, but it was cleaner. Aunt Mary helped me clean the walls. "The ceiling will just need to take care of itself," she smiled.

I found an old mattress in the pile of trash that was being thrown away in front of the apartment building, laid it on the floor in my corner and placed pieces of cardboard over the stains. Then I placed a couple of cardboard boxes at the foot, as storage for the few clothes and personal items I had. If the door was left partially open, it created a cooling effect from the cool hallway, and the light in the hall helped the single dangling light inside to dimly illuminate the room. Compared to the darkness and cold of my second-floor apartment, the dim light and the too-warm furnace room were a welcome change.

It was a nice arrangement, but I missed Victoria. I wanted to go to Montana and bring her here to live with me, but that would have to wait, maybe until Christmas.

Aunt Mary said I could use their shower anytime I wanted and I did, every chance I got. I hadn't had the opportunity to do so through much of my life and most certainly not recently, and I loved the luxury of it. On my first day of work, I was excited, because now I could get some supplies and maybe think about a car. It wouldn't be long before I would be going to Montana to bring Victoria home, where she should be.

I didn't sleep much that night and was up early to take a hot shower at Aunt Mary's. I had dried off with a nice fluffy towel that she handed me, and then that gracious lady fixed me a hot breakfast. As I was wiping my mouth and saying goodbye to her, she handed me a sack lunch. God, that was nice of her—if there ever was a saint, it was Aunt Mary. With tears of gratitude welling up inside me, I stepped into the cold morning to begin my walk to the lumberyard, which was a little over a mile away. I had no coat, it was getting colder by the day, and I knew I would need to get one pretty soon. While I was cleaning the furnace room, I had found a pair of gloves and a stocking cap that were in pretty good shape, and I was wearing a couple of tee shirts and the western flannel shirt that I had brought from Montana. They would have to do for now.

Noel Brothers Lumber Company was on the south side of the street between West Temple and Second West on North Temple Street, and The Camelot-Avalon Apartments was on the south side of the street on Broadway between Second and Third East. It was about eight blocks to work. Salt Lake blocks are big—old Brigham planned them that way. I guess he was good for something, at least. It was uphill going and downhill coming home, which was nice. After a long day of work, I could just sort of coast back to the Avalon. Sometimes, I walked to work on East North Cromwell and sometimes I walked home on West North Cromwell, and sometimes vice-versa. It was sort of exciting, and made me wonder if an English person had developed this area and built the apartments—maybe a descendent of King Arthur—maybe Uncle Arthur was also a descendent of King Arthur. I had to smile as I imagined him as royalty.

I liked the work at Noel Brothers. I would pick up a loading slip from the office and then load the stuff on my truck or pickup and deliver it to the address, and either have the customer sign, or I would bring a check or cash back to the office and get another loading slip, and then repeat the process. The hills on the east side of Salt Lake, where the city's elite were building their homes, were quickly developing.

My life was becoming wonderful, to be sure. Now it was time to send for Victoria, I could feel it. I had saved a little bit from each paycheck and sent it to Mrs. Larsen to give to Victoria. With the most recent money I had attached a note telling Victoria to catch the train and come on down. About a week later she arrived, on the same train that Dale had left on, in the same depot where I had been so distraught when he left. It had a whole new feeling now that Victoria was here.

I felt smarter, and my life was getting better and better. I had about everything I could want. I had bought a few clothes from Good Will, and even had a coat. I was working at the lumberyard and Victoria was finally with me at the Avalon; life was grand. I was going to school three nights a week, and it was free. I had found that if I read the books, the classes were pretty easy. I didn't know why I hadn't thought of that before.

Anyway, I needed to get cleaned up. With Victoria here, I wanted to look as nice as I could. She was so patient, saying she knew it would all pay off in the long run, after I had a college degree and a good income and we had a better place to live. The water in the house had been turned off for repairs, so I decided to fill a five-gallon bucket with cold water in the washhouse, like I used to do in Montana. After I had cleaned myself from the bucket and wiped myself dry, I walked out and sat on the concrete steps in front of the Camelot-Avalon Apartments, on the side that wasn't condemned, and watched the people walk by. That had always been a form of entertainment I could afford, which also meant I could buy an occasional beer, and I loved it.

My life had taken a whole different feeling now that I had my new job. Aunt Mary had hired me to clean the Camelot side of the apartments and sort of watch the Avalon side in my spare time. Now I got to stay for free in the furnace room and she paid me a small fee for keeping the halls vacuumed and cleaning rooms when someone moved out—and little extra things, too. It wasn't as much as I made at Noel Brothers but if I was careful, it was enough.

Noel Brothers finally fired me for a small infraction. That asshole Benton, the boss, was pissed off because he said he had planned out how a large truck and trailer filled with lumber and such would be just the right amount of materials to build an entire house.

I was supposed to guide the truck and trailer to the construction site, where it would be unloaded. But I couldn't find the location, so I guided the truck and trailer loaded with the lumber back to the lumberyard and we unloaded it during lunchtime, when most everyone else was gone. Then they had to load all of the lumber back onto little trucks and take it to the site again, with many trips and at great expense, old man Benton said. The asshole fired me, but I was glad that now I didn't need to go to the damned Noel Brothers at all. I could do as I pleased and concentrate on school and the job for Aunt Mary, and that would see Victoria and I through.

I was sitting and enjoying the evening and a beer on the steps when Aunt Mary came out to tell me I was wanted on the phone.

It was Dale. "Colt and his wife Sally are both dead," he told me.

It was like I was having a dream, a nightmare; I didn't want to believe it. "What happened?" I asked, my voice trembling.

"It was unusual, they both died of heart attacks," Dale said.

I was shocked. "You've got to be kidding."

"Everybody thinks that, it's unusual but it's the truth. She passed on and then Colt followed her the next day."

It took a few moments to catch my breath, "When is the funeral?"

"Saturday at 11:30 at the Community Center," he told me. "Are you coming?"

"Of course," I said, "I'll be there."

"Oh, by the way, I got married."

"You got married? Why?"

"Well, I knocked up the girl I was going with. You know how that goes."

"Yeah, I guess I do. It happens. It happened with me and Victoria."

"Yeah, I remember that. See ya when ya get here, Bill."

"Okay."

Aunt Mary loaned me enough money for a one-way ticket. I spent the entire day with Victoria, and explained why I needed to go back to Eden for the funeral. "I don't have enough money for both of us and I really need to go. They were my best friends. I will be back in a few days." I begged her to understand.

"You just go, William, and don't worry, I'll be all right. I won't have the baby until you get back, I promise," she said and smiled.

"You're so neat."

"I've saved a little bit of money and will just be fine until you get home," she said.

It pleased me that she called it "home." That was nice.

"If you need to, you can go to Scotland and have your father take care of you and the baby. I'll understand."

"I will wait for you forever; I've always told you that, silly," she said.

"You are a part of me."

After hurriedly buying my ticket, I had to run to catch the departing train. It was almost filled with passengers. I held onto the back of a seat as the train smoothly pulled away, and then looked for a place to sit down. I seated myself in the first vacant seat I found. I would have preferred a window seat but a young Mexican-looking fellow was sitting there. He looked at me and nodded, and I returned his courtesy as I dropped my traveling bag on the floor in front of my seat and sat.

Chapter 133

The young Mexican man held a large black cowboy hat in his lap. Following suit, I removed my own cap and laid it on my lap. As he looked out the window, I took in what I could see of the passing scenery on either side of his head. We both seemed to fall into a daze, as if hypnotized by the motion of the train and the clicking of the wheels against the track.

I started to think about all the legal organizations that take advantage of the small people, places like banks and insurance companies. I considered becoming a politician and trying to make some changes, and then, because of my somewhat shady past and the fact that it might require some work, I went on to an easier topic. The reason I liked to think and talk about religion was that it was so subjective and nothing was possible to prove or disprove. I could ramble and not so easily be cornered with my lack of knowledge as with other, more exacting topics.

"What if God was just ourselves?" I thought. "What if, in some way, we were our own judges and would ultimately deposit our souls into heaven or hell by our own admission?"

My mother had once told me, "If you want to hide something really well, hide it in plain sight." She told of a workman who would hide a wheelbarrow in a unique way to steal it. Each night while leaving the workplace, the workman would fill a wheelbarrow with straw and as he wheeled it through the checkout station, he would wait patiently as the guard searched through the straw to make sure the man wasn't hiding anything. After a thorough search, he would allow the man to pass through with the wheelbarrow. The next day, the man would steal another wheelbarrow filled with straw.

She also told me of a wealthy woman who was being deported from her war-ravaged, occupied country, from which it was almost impossible to remove any wealth. She had used all her money to purchase a few very rare and expensive coins, and had placed them in her coin purse with the other coins. In this way, she had been able to take out the seemingly valueless tokens under the very noses of the guards.

It occurred to me that if words of truth were written and mixed in with vast volumes of other writings that had little or no meaning, then the valuable writings would be hidden from view. Maybe writings were like valuable coins—we should be pushing aside their companions of little or no value. The morality that we enjoy in this nation, in the world, to an extent, has been inspired by organized religion, I thought. New religions are pure and nearly true to their beliefs for a time, but that phase quickly passes and they fall away from basic beliefs and gradually become just the same as the things that they originally despised and taught against. Fanatical, mature, organized religion can be the root of selfish, evil actions that too often are disguised as godly intent by men and women who put words into the mouth of God to justify their wicked actions.

The written example of how to live is most certainly not complex or complicated, it seemed to me. As a matter of fact, it was quite simple: don't covet, don't kill, don't steal. These were some of the easy ones. Love everyone, forgive everyone, do good things and don't expect anything in return, just do it because it's the right thing to do. These are harder. In the end, being selfless, forgiving, tolerant, and loving is all Jesus really taught. That was his real philosophy and it has been craftily and carefully concealed in the dung that almost completely covers it.

I was deep in such philosophical wandering when the young man next to me stirred. Interrupted, I glared at him, irritated that he had not allowed me to complete my astounding observations. He looked blankly at me for a moment, and then just looked away.

We rode silently for a time and then he asked, "Do you ride the train a lot?"

His voice carried no sign of a Spanish or Mexican accent, as I had expected.

"Yes, in fact I do," I informed him, still a little suspicious of his perfect English.

His feet were extended in front and I admired his round-toed, expensive-looking cowboy boots.

"What about you?" I returned, so as not to seem disinterested, but he certainly seemed that way.

And then I seemed to pass through a window, but it was a little different his time. It seemed to have a strong element of déjà vu, and I wasn't really looking at the scene from outside myself.

"I have had a lot of train rides." He paused, and then went on. "I'm a writer; well, I want to be a writer. I travel a lot, trying to get some of my stuff published. I'm ashamed to say that I'm afraid of flying, so I ride the trains and write as I go. My name is Tom," he said. "Thomas Jose Ualdo Lopez James Andersen."

I couldn't believe it. His name was the same as the old man I had met on the trip to Missoula while looking for my car. A wide grin covered my face as I shook hands and began telling him about meeting the old man with the same name.

He was speechless for a moment. "That was my great-grandfather. My dad and granddad were both named Thomas, too, but they had different middle names."

With a look that seemed to be one of pride, he said, "They named me after my great- grandfather. My family tells the story of how he disappeared when he was young. Last year, we finally found him, and he got to know his brothers and sisters and my dad." His face saddened. "He got back just in time, because he passed on about a month ago. I had heard about him so often that I felt I knew him."

He wanted to know all about my chance meeting with his elusive relative. I filled him in as I tried to distinguish what the old man had said from what I had made up. It was a little hard to remember the real story after I had altered it with my rewriting, but I did my best.

Young Thomas sat and drank in all the information that I spewed out, nodding his head sleepily. I had always enjoyed an audience but had never found anyone very interested in my stories, so I really appreciated his attention, even though I could see he was getting tired. Maybe I wove more of what I imagined than what had really happened into old Thomas's story.

After young Thomas fell asleep, I decided to go on with the story. I picked it up where I had left off years ago.

Chapter 12

* * * * * * *

The Unintentional Kidnapping, Continued

 Brenda, the ranch cook, had been at the Twitchel Ranch, where young Thomas arrived, for eight years. She had come to work shortly after Big Joel's wife died while giving birth to their youngest son, Joel. Brenda had a way in the kitchen, and the treats she produced would melt in your mouth. Even though she never seemed to eat, she still managed to maintain a nice full shape. Her dark eyes sparkled beneath even darker eyebrows, and her long hair was pulled back into a bun but was still thick enough to frame a somewhat handsome, leathery face. Her thin lips, which contrasted with her wide flat nose, bore a perpetual, genuine smile. She moved her large body so quickly about the kitchen that she appeared to be only half-finished with one stride before she was half-finished with the next.

 Finishing preparations for the morning meal, she continued to survey the work while she yelled upstairs, where some of the favored cowhands slept. In the end, the intoxicating odor of the food was more responsible than was Brenda's coaxing for bringing the sleepy vaqueros down to breakfast. By the time Thomas awakened, the other cowhands had dressed and were already stumbling down the stairs to vie for places at Brenda's breakfast table. Thomas, who had slept in his clothes, simply got out of bed and descended to the kitchen. Timidly, he walked outside and relieved himself against a tree, as some of the cowboys were doing.

He went to the kitchen, took the dipper from the wall, fetched a few cupfuls from the cook stove's reservoir, poured them into the basin and then added cold water from the large drinking bucket. He drank deeply and poured the remainder into the basin before washing his hands. He sloshed a few handfuls onto his face and then combed back his hair with wet fingers, as his father always had done. Then he wiped his hands on an old towel that hung above the basin. He turned, wondering what would happen next.

The cowhands' attire was a jumble of old and new, soiled and clean, loose and tight, but they all wore bandanas around the necks. The colors differed, and the bandana might be old or new, but it nevertheless was there. All the men wore boots, in brown, black, or gray, old or new, but all with high tops and high heels, and everyone wore tight-fitting jeans that only were loose where they fit over the boot-tops. Shirts were user's choice; it seemed that most every color, style, and age was represented. Brenda didn't allow hats at the table except for Big Joel's. All the others hung on the far wall.

Brenda had found a shirt for Thomas to wear. It was too big, but it was better than nothing. Brenda promised she would see about finding some boots for him. He had never had real cowboy boots before. In the summer, he would go barefoot and in the winter, he had always worn hand-me-down rubber boots.

The large kitchen that doubled as the dinning room had been built many years before, but except for the stained glass windows from an old church, it lacked the ornate, stylish décor and craftsmanship prevalent in wealthy ranch buildings of the early West. The spaces between the logs of different species and sizes had been originally filled in or chinked with cow manure. After that eroded away, the spaces were filled in with a mixture of mud and straw. Dust danced in the streams of sunlight where repairs hadn't been kept up.

The large kitchen had, however, been kept modern. Store-bought cupboards, brought from the East by wagon train or by train, filled an entire wall. A sturdy wooden work area ran the length of the lower cupboards, which was where Brenda mixed dough, chopped vegetables, prepared meat, and washed dishes. A large, well-built, six-lidded, wood-burning stove sat against the other wall. It had warming ovens on top and a reservoir at the side. A huge box full of stove wood sat beside it, near a wooden table that held a white porcelain basin on one side and a bucket for cold drinking water on the other.

A weathered and repainted heavy door with the two stained-glass, former church windows on either side took up another wall and on the last wall, large nails had been driven into the logs on either side of a narrow door in the floor that led to the root cellar. Coats, hats, and cowboy paraphernalia hung on the nails. This wall showed bullets holes that had resulted from the boredom of long evenings and slow winter days. A few riddled targets still hung amidst the cowboys' stuff.

A long leather cord that dangled from one of the open beams was fastened to a coal oil lamp for late-night or early morning light. A large wooden table stretched almost the full length of the kitchen and a collection of mismatched, old wooden chairs, most of them wired together, lined the sides. The floor and table were worn, their cracks and chips filled with food and stains that had become embedded despite years of scrubbing. Everything looked meticulously clean.

The door burst open and Big Joel strode in, the morning sun silhouetting his bear-like figure. He wore a light denim jacket against the cold of the morning. His hair was wet and combed back and his face had the shine of a recent washing. He stood poised for a moment and then made his way to the head of the table, sitting with authority in a big-armed chair.

Close behind him came Little Joel, who looked to be about the same age as Thomas but actually was a few years older and much wiser to the ways of the world. His face held pale blue eyes set in deep sockets above a thin, hawk-like nose. He had almost no eyebrows, and his thin lips were pulled back in a sinister smile that revealed two rows of crooked teeth. A thin leather strand held his long, fine, yellow hair in place, and nicks showed in several places where he or someone else had tried to trim it. He strode to the chair at the immediate right of his father. Little Joel never seemed to sit completely still, nor did he ever seem to stop talking. Probably because he didn't talk loudly, no one seemed to be bothered by the insistent chatter.

Chapter 13

* * * * * * *

Brenda motioned to Thomas to take the empty chair next to little Joel and he shyly obeyed. Big Joel removed his large, weathered, buckskin hat and placed his large, calloused hands together in food-blessing fashion. When Little Joel was only four, his father had tried to settle him down with a stinging finger flip to the head and Little Joel had stabbed a dinner fork deep into the flesh of the offending hand. Now, as Big Joel's large hand was whitened by the "prayer clutch," four tiny red scars could be seen. But this and many other incidents had been forgotten and forgiven.

Big Joel surveyed the table and waited as the rowdy cowboys settled down and silence filled the room.

"Lord, for what we is about to receive make us grateful, but if'n we didn't work our damned asses off, we sure as hell would have none. Amen."

He placed his hat back on his head and reached for the food. As if on signal, everyone else reached and fought, and soon everyone was buttering, pouring syrup, sipping coffee and reaching for more while there was still some left. Brenda scurried about replacing empty plates and dishes with full ones, pouring new coffee, and wiping up spills, all the while smiling with contentment.

Little Joel was clearly the light of his father's life, and it seemed obvious that he would inherit the ranch over the more entitled two older brothers, who sat with the other hired hands. Those two cowboys bore identical features, temperament and personality to their father and openly challenged and disliked Little Joel. They only stayed on because there were few places to work. Occasionally, they would leave and look for other jobs, but they were always unsuccessful and came back. As bad as it was for them at the ranch, it was still better than nothing at all.

Brenda continued to rush about the kitchen to satisfy the needs and desires of the men, as they held out their cups for more coffee and forked more food onto their plates. Even in Brenda's presence, the conversation was not censored, but she seemed not to notice. Big Joel decided to tell a joke, stopped eating, and stood. Silence filled the room. Everyone stopped eating.

"It seems," he began, "that a patron came into a bar holding a small satchel. He ordered a drink and laid the bag on the bar. After a while the barkeep could stand it no longer and asked what he had in the small bag. 'Here,' said the patron, 'I'll show you.' At that, he opened the top of the bag and took out a small man, about a foot tall, and stood him on the bar. He then reached back into the satchel and lifted out a small piano. The small man walked to the piano and started to play."

Big Joel spoke with eloquence when he told a joke, but afterwards, he quickly returned to his Murder-the-King's English. He also picked up accents and slang quickly from anyone he happened to be around.

Big Joel continued, "The barkeep said in amazement, 'That's really something,' and he asked the man where he had found the small pianist. The patron began to tell the story."

It was unusual for Big Joel to retain an audience for his jokes. Only during certain occasions, such as meal, was he able to do it. "'One day,'" he went on in the patron's voice, "'as I was walking through the thick jungles of Africa, I came upon a witch doctor about to be devoured by a hungry lion, whereupon I shot and killed the lion. The witch doctor was so grateful that he offered to grant me one wish.'

"'What was your wish?' asked the bartender."

Big Joel paused and scanned his audience. With his tongue in his cheek and wearing a faint smile, he got ready to deliver the punch line. The cowboys tried to appear attentive, but their forks were poised for use as soon as the joke ended. Big Joel was close to breaking into laughter. "'Well,' said the patron, 'there must have been a language barrier but I can tell you one thing for sure: I didn't wish for a foot-long pianist.'"

As usual, Big Joel laughed harder and longer than anyone else, and then hurried to catch up with the breakfast he had neglected while he had been laughing. The men were finishing up now and with sighs of contentment and loud burps, they began reaching into their shirt pockets for makings to roll a smoke before putting on their coats and gloves to face the cruelness of the morning and their chores. Smoke filled the kitchen as all the cowboys joined this routine. Even Little Joel, barely nine years old, rolled one and lit up as Thomas watched in admiration.

As the men smoked, Brenda began cleaning up. She worked around the men, being careful not to interrupt their conversation, and even before the men were starting to get up and leave, she had the table cleaned off and was beginning to wash the dishes. She used two small *washtubs, one with suds and one with clean water to rinse. After dipping the washed dishes into the rinse water, she laid them out sort of piggyback, one on top of another on towels, to dry before putting them away in the cupboard.*

Water was either brought in with buckets from the pump just outside the back door or melted from snow in the winter, and Brenda was careful to make it stretch as far as she could. She cooked two meals a day, one in the morning and one in the evening, and if the hands wanted lunch or midnight snacks, they made them from one of these meals. Eggs and bacon were rolled up in a hot cake or fried bread and placed in pockets or a saddlebag. Others placed some of their leftovers in waxed paper and tied it with string. Each had his own way of packing it. Later in the day, it was dug out and, after picking off lint and flies or whatever else had accumulated on it during the day, it was enjoyed every bit as much as a fly enjoys a turd.

Chapter 14

* * * * * * * *

Brenda milked three cows, used some of the milk in her cooking and sold the excess to town folks for a little spending money. She chopped and brought in the wood for the cook stove and heater. She brought ice from the Long Shed, where it was stored under a thick layer of straw and used it in the cooler. She did all of the women's work and then helped with some of the men's work as well. During the long winter months, when work was slow, the men would saw large pieces of ice from the pond and bring it on the sled for summer use. On occasion, and to everyone's delight, Brenda would make ice cream.

She looked after the sick or injured with turpentine, antiseptic, Bag Balm, mustard poultice, and for deep-rooted chest colds or sore throats, bitterroot or catnip tea and steam vaporizers, or a dirty sock laced with Musterole tied around the neck. She bandaged injured cowhands, as well as performing many other tasks any mother might do. She ripped old sheets into bandages for cuts and abrasions, passed them over a candle to kill the germs, and then rolled them up into neat, even rolls and stored them with other medical supplies. On occasion, she even helped to mend a broken heart when some poor cowpoke's romantic affair hadn't worked out.

Most hands were young, still in their teens. A few were in their early twenties. Some had previously been employed by the now-failed Pony Express. Others had been more aggressively brought from the migrant train at the water tank, as Thomas had been, and some simply showed up.

Brenda cleaned and took care of the main house and slept in one of the spare bedrooms. Rumor had it that Big Joel would occasionally visit her bedroom during the night.

Chapter 15

It was finally spring at the Twitchel Ranch and the snow was starting to melt. The days were getting warm and sunny and the larger streams were accepting runoff from tributaries and were beginning to swell. Everybody was in good spirits. The ranch hadn't had any mail for a time and now with the good weather, someone would have to go into town to pick it up. This was one job that Little Joel could stomach. In fact, he cherished it.

Old Dan, the horse that had been given to Little Joel, was a strong and good mount. He seemed to never tire, although he also seemed to have a mind of his own. Even with hobbles on his front legs and a sideline that hooked his front to his rear leg, he was somehow capable of getting out of a four-foot-high, fenced field. Little Joel didn't like Old Dan very much. Maybe they had too much in common. He did like Big Joel's big red stallion, however, and delighted in using it whenever he could.

After much pleading and bargaining, Big Joel had agreed to allow his youngest son the use of Big Red for a quick trip into town through the deep mud and melting snow, but then he had to come straight home again.

"Watch out for flash flooding," Big Joel cautioned his son.

Big Red was a large roan stallion used exclusively by Big Joel, except for the few times he had been conned out of him, as on this day.

Big Red had sired most of the horses on the ranch and most of them, even though not as striking and gallant, bore an obvious resemblance to him.

Thomas was to go with Little Joel, to help hold Big Red and help keep Little Joel out of trouble. Before they were allowed to leave, however, Big Joel had a joke to tell. It had been inspired by the large number of hands on the ranch, who had finished breakfast and were getting ready to head out for the day's work. Big Joel squared off before his captive audience of employees and began.

"Once several years ago, we had an easterner come here to work, and even though he was a good worker, the other hands just didn't take up with him and he sort of became a loner. Having not had any sex for quite some time, one day he asked me what I did in a case like this. I looked at him and said, I just use one of the horses in the barn."

Big Joel was smiling now as he closed in on the punch line. "Several days later, I went into the barn to get some oats and was surprised to see him up on a box behind one of the mares. When I saw him, I started to laugh. The easterner looked around with a puzzled look on his face. 'Why the heck are you laughing?' he questioned. 'You told me that you use one of the horses in the barn when you got restless.' I told him, still laughing, 'Yes, I did, but what I meant was, I used one of the horses to ride into town!'"

Big Joel all but doubled over in laughter. Everyone had stayed to hear the joke, but it was for about the tenth time. Now they quickly dispersed before Big Joel could think of another repetitive joke. With tears still rolling down his cheeks and still trying to stifle the laughter as much as he could, Big Joel told the boys he would see them when they got back, and went to do his chores, or whatever he did on his frequent trips here and there.

Even though Big Red was twelve years old, he could easily keep up with or outdo any horse on the ranch in terms of work and temperament. He was easy to handle and would behave himself even around a filly when he had a rider or was at work. It seemed that when Big Joel wasn't earning money by racing or breeding the big horse, he was telling stories of his adventures while riding him. Little Joel and Thomas sat astride this wonderful horse and rode toward town and the post office. Thomas was glad that Little Joel had taken the saddle and had given him the cantle, where Little Joel's body would give him a little shelter from the icy cold, late winter winds. With his spurs, Little Joel urged the big horse into a gentle, ground-eating lope along the snow-covered road.

It usually took about two hours to get into town, including rests and pee stops. The miles seemed to melt away as the horse carried the two young equestrians along the road, kicking up giant snowballs and throwing them far behind with his gigantic hooves. As they rounded a sharp bend in the road, a bobcat darted across the road. Big Red lowered to his haunches in fright, and stumbled while trying to regain his footing, half-skidding and half-falling into tall clumps of oak brush that grew along the road. The brush wasn't big enough to stop them outright, but it was big enough to trip Big Red and send all three of them sprawling and sliding into the snow and mud on the river side of the road.

Red staggered to his feet, as did the boys. Thomas grabbed the reins to keep the frightened horse from running off. As he walked over to Little Joel, he joked, "That was *one heck of a ride."*

"Sure as heck."

"Are you hurt?" Thomas asked.

"Heck no, I ain't hurt. But I think Red might be. He's a-limpin."

The boys examined the horse, which was standing with his head hung low.

"Should we try ta get him back home?" asked Thomas.

Little Joel stood and looked at the injured horse for a few minutes and then thoughtfully said, "No, I think if we just go ahead and walk into town, he will be okay when we get back here. His leg is hurt, but it's not broke, I'll bet my butt on that. It's jus a bad sprain."

Thomas wasn't too sure, and he didn't think Little Joel was, either. But as usual, Little Joel got his way. They tied Red to a sturdy tree in a gully by the stream, so he wouldn't be seen by passersby. They took off the saddle and bridle and tied him with the "catch rope" that was coiled on the saddle.

"I'll tie him short," said Thomas. "Big Joel said they are less likely to get their foot over the rope and choke their fool selves if you do that. But I'll tie him long enough so's he'll be able to get a drink. Them beavers has got the dam nearly done and the water's right close."

The beaver were swimming around, dragging logs and brush with them, slapping their tails as they swam. After putting the saddle and bridle in a safe place high up on the bank, the two made their way over the trees that had been knocked down by beaver, which were building their dam a short distance away.

"Heck, we'll be right back. Town is right around that corner," said Little Joel, pointing in the direction they were beginning to walk.

They looked back once before they rounded the corner,

and were still in sight of the wounded horse. Red stood with his head low, like he was looking for something on the ground.

The town was small and had been built mostly on one side of the main street. Between the general store and the saloon stood the post office, a little wooden building. On its front were a couple of windows and a door with a window in it. There wasn't a sign, but it did look like a post office. The road was muddy from the recent rain and melting snow. Both boys' boots were generously caked with the glue-like substance, making walking somewhat difficult. Three boys stood under the shelter of the porch at the general store. They looked to be just a little older and maybe a little tougher than the two boys who innocently walked toward the post office

One of the toughest-looking boys, the biggest, called to Little Joel and Thomas in a mocking tone, "Hey, you gonna get webbed feet if'n you's not careful," and then all three boys laughed. "Better wipe that mud off if'n ya know what's good fer ya," mocked another of the three, getting courage from the bigger boy's remark, as well as from the greater number in his gang.

Little Joel and Thomas looked ahead and continued their trek. The three boys walked into the street and stopped at a place where Little Joel and Thomas would either have to walk right through them or go around. "How come you's pals with an Injun?" asked one of the boys after Little Joel and Thomas had stopped to assess the situation.

Little Joel looked into the kid's eyes and returned, "Cause it's better'n crawlin' and playin' with little girls like you do, ya wimpy skunk."

The three boys stood still, shocked by this remark, and then, as if they had rehearsed their next move, all three of them acted at once. Rushing forward, they knocked

Thomas flat onto his back and into deep mud. Little Joel sidestepped them and with his hands held up to prepare for the fight, he danced, as pugilists do, and turned in his tracks, ready to strike whoever challenged him first.

Thomas regained his footing and stood alongside Little Joel with hands up, trying to emulate Little Joel's pose. The bullies moved closer, looking for an opening. With a quick right cross, Little Joel caught the smallest of the three and sent him to the muddy ground, after which the boy ran bawling down the street. The remaining four paired off and jabbed and ducked in an awkward fashion that was mostly pushing and shoving.

"Gonna knock yer god dammed head off," the largest boy threatened, and unleashed a haymaker that narrowly missed Thomas's jaw. The swing was so powerful that when it missed its target, the force of it and the slick muddy road caused the boy to fall and strike his head on the wooden boardwalk in front of the general store. He sat dazed, holding his head in his hands as blood seeped through his shaking fingers and fell to mix with mud and water on the road.

The remaining boy lost his taste for fighting. Under the guise of helping his injured friend, he half-dragged, half-carried the boy down the street. From a safe distance away, he turned and yelled, "Next time we'll get you guys. You'll be sorry. Next time it'll be a fair fight."

Little Joel was intent on finishing the fight, but Thomas held him back, reasoning that they should get the mail and attend to Big Red. Even the hot-tempered Little Joel couldn't argue with this logic and in an effort to discharge some of his rage, he yelled after the retreating duo, "If you ever see me again, ya better get the heck out'a my way, cause next time I'll kill ya, ya god-damned wimps." This seemed to settle him, and the two turned and walked *toward the post office.*

The inside of the post office was old like the outside, but it was better kept. It was scrubbed clean and freshly painted. There was a place for letters and other mail to be handled and at the rear of the narrow long room was a shop of sorts where certain luxury items could be purchased, such as lace hankies and ladies' purses. A wooden table had several chairs where a person could write or stamp letters. Against one wall, boxes were neatly stacked, some with letters lying atop them. A gray-haired woman with a knitted shawl around her shoulders sat in a rocking chair, knitting and humming softly.

"What's all the frettin' and fightin' outside there?" she asked. She was still looking down at her knitting but had a slight, mischievous smile on her face. "Some sort of a game, was it?"

Little Joel, unwilling to pursue this topic, just nodded and asked for the mail for the Twitchel Ranch. As if looking for a place to stop knitting, the old lady kept at it, and then seemed to find a place to quit. Laying her yarn and needles on the floor beside the chair, she stood and walked behind the counter. She picked up a bundle of mail and sorted through it. She had a weathered face and a hint of a mustache, as old women sometimes have. She placed the handful of letters in a canvas pouch, and then handed the package to the boys.

As it was beneath Little Joel's status to do this kind of manual labor, Thomas accepted the bundle and with it under his arm, the two boys stepped back into the street and headed toward Big Red and home, to face the consequences of their actions. They were tired, cold and hungry. Their feet were not only cold, but also soaked to the skin. They could do something about the hunger and the cold—they could get a piece of jerky from the general store and a hot cup of coffee—but their feet would just have to be wet and cold until they could build a fire.

After the warm coffee and jerky dissolved in their stomachs, they felt a little better, and the walk back to Big Red went quickly. It was their intention to lead the horse back to the ranch and then have Brenda nurse him back to good health. They had hastily made up an excuse concerning how the horse got hurt, but it fell well short of being as believable or as justifiable as what had actually happened. They decided that they needed to keep working on it.

Chapter 16

The place where the horse had been tied looked different. Where there had been a grassy riverbank several hours earlier, now there was a deep pond where beaver still swam and pulled small logs and slapped their tails to warn of danger as they put the finishing touches on the dam.

"What the heck?" exclaimed Little Joel. "I'm sure this is the place we left Red."

Walking closer, the boys looked down into the pond and saw Big Red lying on his side, peacefully staring up at them from underneath the water, his large head held up slightly by the tightly stretched catch rope.

"Them damned beavers killed Big Red!" Little Joel yelled. "Them god-damned beavers dammed up the water and killed Big Red."

In his anger, Little Joel waded into the deep water and swung his arms savagely at the beaver, splashing water as he walked. He fell into a deep hole, which cooled him off, and he was quieter by the time he found his way back to the edge of the road and sat with Thomas. Together, they tried to rework their excuse about Big Red's injuries *and demise. Thomas, typically prepared, had matches encased in wax to keep them dry. Before long, the two had a roaring fire and were dry. But they still needed a believable story to tell Big Joel. They quickly discarded the idea to tell him what had really happened. They decided that a better way would be to say someone else had been involved and that it had been their fault. They began to work on that plan.*

"This's what we need ta do," said Little Joel, "is ta jus say that we was held up and that Big Red was took." He thought for a minute. "Then when Big Joel goes and discovers the horse, it'll seem that it jus had a heart attack and fell over the edge of the road and that will be that." With this, the plan was set. "The problem we still have," Little Joel went on, "is we got this pond. We got to get rid of it." Little Joel thought on, and finally came up with an idea. "You stay here, Thomas, and guard the mail and Big Red."

Little Joel started toward the farmhouse that they had passed a way down the road. Thomas was discouraged and a little amazed by his friend's actions, but he did as he had been told and sat obediently by the fire. Before long, Little Joel returned. He had a large gunny bag across his shoulders, and he struggled with the weight of it. He dropped the heavy parcel at Thomas's side close to the fire and then opened it. He removed a role of fuse, some blasting caps, and some old-looking dynamite.

"Let's go," he commanded.

Thomas reluctantly followed his master along the top of the newly installed small logs, and onto the beaver dam. After the dam had been extensively examined and Little Joel had determined the proper place to set the explosives, Thomas was sent back to retrieve the dynamite and its accessories. As was Little Joel's nature, all of the dynamite, as well as all of the caps and fuses, would be used. This probably wasn't exactly the way old man Elms, the powder monkey who worked for Big Joel, would have advised, but this was the way Little Joel was going to do it.

"No need ta save any," was Little Joel's conclusion. "Let's get rid o' the evidence."

After all of the explosives had been placed, the fuses were lit and the boys retreated to what appeared to be a safe distance to watch. Thomas's makings were still dry, so they each rolled a cigarette to enhance their enjoyment of the coming spectacle. The boys had had no idea of the magnitude of explosion an entire gunny bag full of dynamite can generate. When the fire of the fuse met the nitro of the blasting cap, the ground shook as if from an earthquake. Water, dirt, logs, and surprised beaver were lifted high into the air, in what resembled a volcano expelling magma—but of a watery consistency rather than molten rock.

As the debris began hitting the ground around them, the two boys scrambled for cover.

The explosion opened up a gaping hole in the dam, and as the water raced out, it carried with it most of the evidence of the blast except a few small, shattered logs, some dirt, and pieces of beaver.

The boys fared pretty well, receiving only a few scrapes and bruises, the most serious of which was an ugly gash on Little Joel's forehead where a small, jagged piece of log had struck him.

After most of the area had been cleaned up and Big Red had been examined again, with some hope that he would still somehow be alive, the boys gave up and began their long walk toward the ranch to deliver the mail and endure whatever might come.

They hoped to minimize their punishment not only

with a carefully thought-out story about Big Red's demise, but also with their convincing delivery of the details.

Old Mr. Larkin saw the weary boys as they trudged passed his place. He hitched up his team to the wagon, delivering them to Twitchel Ranch. The boys sat eating and drinking in front of the fireplace as the others patiently waited to hear what had gotten them so wet and so cold, and what had happened to Big Red. Little Joel and Thomas had agreed that they would say as little as possible, and let Big Joel draw his own conclusions

After the hot bath Brenda had prepared for them, when they sat in front of the fireplace with warm blankets and cigarettes Big Joel had rolled for them because of their plight, they got around to talking about the day's events. The story went off pretty well, and as Big Joel wouldn't have believed the real story anyway (who would believe it?), Little Joel and Thomas thought it had been wise to tell the story that they had made up.

After Big Joel visited the sight of Big Red's fatal journey, he returned to give his assessment of the situation. He seemed to always get some comfort from strumming his guitar and either whistling or singing, and as he entered the ranch house, he took the instrument down from where it hung on the wall and began a mournful ballad. The song was about a small child who was often left unattended by his mother and father and wished for their company while they frequented the bars. He finished up with "…and how I wish they would go there no more."

Some of the cowboys who had been interested in what Big Joel would say about the whole thing had not thought the pain of his droning voice was worth the torture, and had gone back to the bunkhouse. Now that Big Joel had finished his music, he put the guitar down and prepared to say his piece.

"Funny thing," he started, "that horse was kind of old, but he seemed strong as a mule." He fell silent again and looked at the floor and at his boots for a time, and then was ready to speak again. "Died of old age, I reckon. I guess I figured he never would die."

He walked over to where the two boys were enjoying their smoke. "Don't feel too bad. Death is just part of life. We all need to die some day."

Everyone, maybe even Big Joel himself, was a little surprised with the philosophy that had just been expounded and the room fell silent, almost in reverence. "A funny thing," Big Joel went on, "Red was covered with ice, like he'd been soaked with water just before he died." He looked at them and waited for their response.

The two passive scoundrels shrugged their shoulders in unison and looked away.

Chapter 17

* * * * * * * *

Six years went by since the day Thomas was brought from the water tower to live with the Twitchels. Even though still young, he had become one of the top hands. He seemed to be a natural at riding and breaking horses and doing other ranching jobs. He stayed outdoors long after the other hands came in for supper. Brenda would always make him something special when he finally came in, and over the years they became great friends. She made him think of his mother, or at least what he could remember of his mother, so many years ago. His mother was also a kindly woman, and his eyes clouded as he thought about her. He began to recall those long-ago times when he had listened in awe as his mother sang or told stories.

He remembered his father as a gentle and patient man. It seemed that he had been very tall and thin, with light brown hair and blue eyes. And though the family was poor, he somehow still provided the necessities and cared for his family well. Thomas remembered that he wasn't easy to talk to, as his mother was, or as understanding. When he said no, he meant no, and only Mary, his wife, was occasionally able to change his mind,

Thomas thought about the neighbor kids making fun of him because, unlike his seven sisters, he looked Mexican and was named Anderson. He remembered, and his eyes moistened even more. His dog Spatcher had had her day, and after helping with the sheep and cows for years, was now getting old. She spent most of her time either lying on the front porch of the bunkhouse or on a rug Brenda had given her, or in the kitchen curled up in the corner by the wood box. Once in a while, she would follow Little Joel and Thomas on one of their adventures, but then she would get tired and go home. The Twitchels had used the pick of one of Spatcher's litters for their housedog—they named her Spatcher, too. But even though the Twitchels had accepted Thomas and both Spatchers as family, he still had haunting memories of his childhood and of his real family, whom he had some difficulty remembering. He knew that he had to try to find them.

Big Joel had told the story many times of how he had found Thomas at the water tower with the black man named Cropper. After making several unsuccessful trips down the railroad tracks, trying to find the place where he had been picked up, Thomas was about ready to give up. He realized there hadn't been a water tower or any landmark where he had been picked up. The train had simply broken down and stopped. So he decided he would, at least for now, be content to stay on with the Twitchels.

He thought often of the train ride, of how frightened and tired he had been the night Big Joel and Lenny found him, and how he had wanted to stay with Cropper, although now he was glad he had gone. He remembered the train and the smells of unclean bodies crowded into the boxcars. He remembered the stops the train made, and how the people quickly got water and cooked what little food they had, not knowing how long they would be *there. He remembered how Cropper had told him to go with Big Joel, and how he'd told him he didn't want to be bothered with a youn'un; and he remembered the tears that welled in the big man's eyes. In his mind's eye, he could see the way Cropper looked at him for the last time, and then climbed into the boxcar without looking back, and he remembered the train leaving and how lonely he had felt.*

He had lots to think about, that was for sure, and etched into his memory were the last words Cropper had said: "The more things change, the more they stays the same." He still didn't understand what that meant. Thomas shrugged his shoulders, forced a small grin, dropped his roll-yer-own butt into the coal bucket, and went upstairs to the room he shared with other ranch hands. He crawled into bed and was soon fast asleep.

Chapter 18

Even though Thomas worked very hard and long, he still had found time through the years to get into some trouble and have some adventures. In addition to adventure and trouble, on occasion he even found time, as young men do, for that normal body function welling up inside. He would go the barn or outhouse, or maybe deep into the woods to sow his wild oats. Usually, any mischief he got into was brought on, one way or another, by Little Joe, who had an uncanny way of escaping work or responsibility. He also had an uncanny way of distorting circumstances with logic that not only let him escape blame or punishment for his antics, but made him appear to be the valiant hero rather than the villain.

On one such occasion, he took Thomas aside and told him of a friend he had met in town who could pour alcohol into a cupped hand and light it on fire without suffering any pain or burn. Thomas's eyes lit up as Little Joel said he had thought of trying that on Brenda's cat, Fluffy. He said inasmuch as she wouldn't be harmed, it would be "just to see what the heck the cat might do." Thomas usually did as Little Joel directed, and this day was no exception.

He was directed to get the alcohol from the medicine cabinet in the house while Little Joel went to look for Fluffy. When they met a few minutes later, Little Joel had Fluffy gripped tightly with a strange, evil smile on his face, and Thomas held a bronze-tinted bottle full of liquid. He said he hadn't been able to find the alcohol but he knew where Brenda kept the turpentine and had brought it instead.

Brenda used the turpentine as an antiseptic for minor scrapes and cuts, but everyone except newcomers hid their injuries to avoid the excruciating pain of the treatment. Another remedy she used for minor things was an ointment named Bag Balm. Big Joel used it for the milk cow's udders and teats when they became chapped and sore. It was stored in the barn, where the cows were milked. When one of the workers had chapped lips or minor scratches, Brenda would bring the tin of ointment from the barn, scrape off the flies, manure, or whatever else was on top, and apply a healthy gob to the injured or chapped area. Given that this was almost as unpleasant as the turpentine, medical complaints were rare.

"Whatchadoin'?" It was Mary, a little tomboy who was the youngest daughter of a neighboring rancher, Lenny Jensen. "Can I help?"

"Heck, no," said Little Joel.

"If you don't let me, then I'll tell yer dad." She waited.

"Okay, yeh," said Little Joel, and after a short hesitation, "Just stay out of the way. Yer such a pain in the butt." He spat the words at her and then went on about his work.

Little Joel thought the turpentine was an excellent substitute for the alcohol. As he stretched out Fluffy's tail, he told Thomas to pour it on. Thomas lit it, and Little Joel allowed Fluffy to leap to the ground. The boys expected to see her head across the plowed field or down the dusty road leading into town, or maybe just disappear into the winter-soaked woods, but she did none of these things. Instead, she headed straight for the horse barn, where not only the horses were sheltered and fed, but where the winter supply of hay oats was kept. Warm in the winter and cool in the summer, with a good supply of mice that were attracted by the grain and hay, this was home to Fluffy. As she ran, she spread fire with every terrified leap and then went into the hole she had burrowed for her home.

The boys stood with mouths open in wonder and regret, even as the fire spread so fast, they had no reasonable chance to douse it. They turned and ran into the woods, out of sight of the house, hoping to escape the wrath of Big Joel. They need not have worried, however, because Little Joel's charmed life continued.

That evening at supper, after the fire had burned itself out, Big Joel decided it was a good time for a joke. Fluffy, who had survived the ordeal, glared at the two boys with contempt in her green eyes. If a cat could look pissed off, Fluffy did, for sure. She lay at Brenda's feet with what was left of her tail stretched out behind her on the floor. It bore a striking resemblance to a rat's tail.

Big Joel began his joke: "Two cowboys were a talkin' and one told the other he could make animals talk. 'Yer a liar,' said the other. 'Oh, yah,' said the first, 'come on and I'll show you,' and they made a bet as they walked toward the barn. Now, earlier, the cowboy had covered up a friend in the cows' feed box and told him to answer for the cow when he talked to it. As the cowboys walked up, the first cowboy turned to the cow and said, 'Nice day, isn't it?'"

As usual, Big Joel was at the height of his glory when telling a joke, and with a contented grin, he continued. "The cow, as cows will do when someone walks up to them, raised its head and looked at them, still chewing its cud.

The friend in the feed box answered, 'Pretty good, but I'll sure as heck be glad when it's spring.' The cowboy looked stunned. His face turned pale and as he looked at the joking cowboy, he announced, 'Hey, if that jersey cow over in the north pasture says I screwed her, she's a damned liar!'"

They all laughed, but as usual, no one laughed as hard as Big Joel. When he settled down, he began to tell his theory about the house-barn fire. He explained they were lucky to have saved all of the horses. The way he figured it, the fire had been started by spontaneous combustion, a condition he had heard of some years before on one of his trips to the East. "It's caused by wet hay building up so much heat that it begins to burn."

Little Joel and Thomas stared into their plates as they ate. They didn't ask for seconds, and after they finished eating, they went straight to their beds. They both knew that Mary now would have the ammunition to make them do whatever she directed. They would now be her captives and slaves. They stayed awake long into the night, feeling a little guilty, but marveling that Fluffy had run into the barn at the very instant of the spontaneous combustion! And maybe they felt nervous about the control that little Mary now had over them.

Chapter 19

* * * * * * *

Every Christmas at the Twitchels' seemed better than the last. There was fruitcake, oranges, bottled peaches, and even an occasional gift from Santa. Thomas's favorite tradition was the stocking that everyone hung by the fireplace on Christmas Eve. In the morning it would be filled with all sorts of hard-to-find treats. On the top were oranges and under them, nuts and candy, and maybe a banana. "Don't eat it all at once," cautioned Brenda, imitating what she had heard when she was a child. "You don't want to get a stomachache, do you?" Then she would steal tasty morsels here and there, until it was she and not the children who became ill from over- indulgence. Christmas brought welcome relief from the monotony of the winter, because school was out from November until March—and then for about the same amount of time in the summer—and almost everyone was glad when it started up again. There were chores to do, but it was usually more trouble for Brenda to get the youngsters to do them than to do them herself. This left the children a great deal of time for getting into trouble and most took good advantage of the opportunity, especially Little Joel.

The one-room schoolhouse was in town, about 10 miles away. Class started at 10:00 am sharp, with a half-hour break at noon. School continued until about 2:30 pm, and students were expected to attend and stay awake at least three days a week in order to receive passing grades. It wasn't uncommon for the school to have a high absentee rate. Few students were dedicated enough to walk hours to get there, and if no ride was available, they simply wouldn't go.

Big Joel was relatively well-educated, having finished seven years of schooling, and he encouraged his family to emulate this achievement. He had designated horses for this purpose that could be ridden double, triple or quadruple, as was needed. They were turned loose hobbled in the school's pasture, to be caught and ridden home when school was over that afternoon. Some kids who lived closer to town completed eight or even nine years of education. Big Joel told a story about one boy in the next town who had gone back east to a college in Boston. He had gone to school for three years and had become a doctor. He was now rich and lived in a mansion. He had servants and a coach with a driver to take him here and there.

But now it was Christmas and school was out, and everything was cheery, because Santa would arrive soon. Thomas and Little Joel had become pretty good friends, and as long as Thomas did as Little Joel directed, their friendship continued. It became strained, however, whenever Thomas wanted things to be done a different way, or even if he had an idea of his own. Thomas had never been able to understand Little Joel. He just knew he was exciting to be with, and that he liked him. But trouble followed Little Joel like metal shavings follow a magnet. Thomas had noticed that without even trying, Little Joel was forever creating havoc and then escaping the slightest *blame for anything. Sometimes he was even praised, when circumstances changed the outcome of an event in his favor.*

Big Joel decided to take Little Joel and Thomas with him this year to get the Christmas tree. He had also taken a jug of whiskey to "ward off the cold." They walked a good distance from the house, discussing several possibilities for the perfect tree as Big Joel nipped at the jug. Finally, they decided that someone should climb up and take the top out of a giant blue spruce that stood before them.

Big Joel lectured the boys on how they should catch the tree so it wouldn't break after he cut it off and dropped it down to them. He screwed the whiskey jug into a snow bank to keep it cold, and then walked to the base of the tree. He looked up for a moment and then began to climb. A spruce has small limbs and sharp, prickly needles and the taller it grows, the smaller the limbs become. If a climber is not careful to step close to the trunk, the limbs will give way and a climber will lose his balance and fall down through the sharp needles to the ground.

About halfway up, Big Joel started to slip. He wrapped his large arms around the main trunk of the tree. The limbs, not strong enough to stop his descent, were at least flexible enough to slow him down. He reached the ground shaken but unhurt, except for many bleeding scratches on his hands, arms, and face. His hat still hung in the branches high above, and after looking at it for a moment, he picked up his jug for a swig, put it down, and chopped down a small pine, saying, "Here's a nice tree."

Without looking at the boys, he started toward the ranch house, dragging the tree behind him. The boys followed, their sides aching as they tried to hold back their laughter.

The ranch had two creeks, and a river ran through it

for the entire length. These streams fed several large ponds that provided water in the summer and winter ice for use in the hot weather. It was cut and taken to the Long Shed for storage. The men had been cutting and hauling ice from one of the ponds for several days and this day, Little Joel decided he and Thomas should go help them. Big Joel was still nursing wounds that he said he didn't have.

The men drilled a hole through the ice and then used what they called a "Swedish fiddle," which was a cross-cut saw also used for cutting timber and sawing logs. Swedish fiddles could be one-man or two-man saws, but for ice, the one-man saw was used. The men would saw the ice into blocks the right size to be handled easily.

Ice tongs were used to grasp the blocks, and then a horse gently pulled them up a ramp and onto a sled. After the sled was filled, the ice was taken to the Long Shed, so named because of its great length, and stored on wood with a deep straw coating over the top. Brenda used the ice to cool food, make ice cream, and such. One summer, everyone took a block of ice to the top of a hill, placed a piece of carpeting on it so their butts didn't freeze, and took turns sliding down the steep side.

This winter, after the first load of ice had been unloaded into the Long Shed and the men were starting back to the pond, Little Joel and Thomas ran and jumped on the sled. As they came to the pond, they saw men cutting the ice and getting it ready to load. They pitched in, and soon the wagon was filled and heading back. The boys stayed at the pond to help cut the ice.

"Ya get tired doin' this kin'a work?" Little Joel asked a sawyer; one of the men who sawed the ice.

"Nah," answered the man, "it's better'en sittin' there in the bunkhouse all day."

The man had no sooner gotten these words out when

he slipped and fell headfirst into the water. The force of the fall took him under the ice ledge. The boys could see him through the clear ice, his arm flailing as he fought for air.

"He's in a heap'a trouble," exclaimed Little Joel, and then, apparently without thinking, he jumped in and worked himself under the ice to where the man was drowning.

He grabbed an arm and guided him out to clear water, yelling at Thomas to get a pole or something. Thomas took off his coat and held it out to him, and Little Joel climbed up the coat to solid ice. Then the two turned their attention to the man still in the water. With both of them pulling, the man was soon standing with them on solid ice. As they sat around the roaring fire, drying out and waiting for the wagon to come back, they joked nervously about the close call and how they could have drowned. The man was grateful that they had been there.

He said he certainly would have perished if they hadn't helped him.

Later, after the wagon had brought them to the bunkhouse, they sat in front of the open oven of Brenda's cook stove and the man told the story of how the boys had saved him from certain drowning, and how Little Joel had risked his own life in doing it. Big Joel sat leaning his chair against the wall, smoking a roll-yer-own, nursing his wounds from the Christmas tree incident, and probably feeling a twinge of jealousy that they were putting on the show instead of him.

A few days later, Big Joel had just about healed up and was getting restless. He had promised Little Joel and Thomas he would take them to the hill to slide down, so he went looking for the two boys. As he walked toward the barn, he called to them.

As he opened the door and entered, he saw the two

boys walking toward him making some adjustments to their clothing and looking a little guilty.

"What you boy's been a-doin'?" *Big Joel asked in his kidding way. Both boys shook their heads and assured him—nothing.*

"Well," *Big Joel went on, to show his wisdom.* "They's two kinds of liars, those that say they don't, and those that say they's quit." *He smiled at them, and they returned weak, uncertain smiles.*

Big Joel asked if they were ready to go skiing. He had fashioned skis out of one of the boards from a wooden barrel. He had nailed a strap made from leather to one side of each ski, about in the middle, and then passed it over and nailed it to the other side. He had left just enough room to make loops big enough for the boys to slide their boots into. He hadn't made a set for himself, as the Christmas tree episode was still fresh in his mind, and he wasn't ready to risk his body again, at least not quite so soon.

After climbing a ways up the hill, the three stopped and turned around. Big Joel gave them instruction and advice, supposedly based on his experience, as they slid their boots into the leather straps and looked down the hill. It was steep, and they picked up speed quickly. Little Joel was in the lead with Thomas close behind him. Little Joel fell, diving headfirst into the snow. He laughed. "Heck that's fun." *Thomas, trying to keep from hitting Little Joel, leaned far to the left and while just missing him, he hit smack dab in the middle of a large tree that stood just ahead.*

Big Joel raced his horse, Old Dan, into town to fetch the doctor.

When the doctor arrived, he did some checking here and there, pinched and poked Thomas, and then said, "He *looks pretty good, 'cept fer those bruises and scratches."*

He looked at Brenda and Big Joel for a minute and then continued, "Left arm's broken, a compound break. That means we need to set it and put on a splint."

While Big Joel held Thomas's shoulder, the doctor pulled and worked the bone into place and then bandaged a splint to hold it. Thomas was to stay in bed for a week and then take extra good care of the arm afterwards for at least a month. The doctor said he would come by and check it, and to not take off the splint until he told them to.

Thomas was treated as royalty. He was fed in bed and Brenda read to him. It turned out to be not too bad a Christmas season after all.

Chapter 20

* * * * * * *

The years piled up, year upon year, until too many had passed. Big Joel had long since stopped visiting the water tower to get hired hands and just did the best he could by taking anyone he could find around town. Anyway, now men would simply show up at the ranch looking for work.

Big Joel traveled and told his jokes when an audience could be found. He acquired a fat belly and a balding head. He and Brenda had been married for some time now, and had a little girl. They had named her Brenda. Big Joel visited the bedroom of the new hired girl several times each week, just as he had done with Brenda before and after his first wife had died.

Little Joel had aged, too, but kept living his life in the usual haphazard way, dodging the blame for his antics. He had a love affair with a neighboring farmer's daughter, Tanya, and his charmed life came to an end when she became pregnant. Under the threat of the shotguns of her three brothers and her father, he married her, and the couple had been happy now for seven years or so. They named their son Joel. They had a place on the south side of the Twitchel Ranch, right next to Lenny Jensen's ranch house. Little Joel's oldest brother's wife had given birth to a son, her fourth, and darned if it didn't have much the same looks as Little Joel. The little feller had been given the name of his father, Daniel.

As Thomas aged, he stayed on for Big Joel and worked the ranch until he fell in love with Mary, Lenny Jensen's youngest daughter, the tomboy who had accompanied Little Joel and him on many of their wild escapades, including the Fluffy thing. After a long courtship, Thomas finally persuaded her to marry him. Lenny and his wife weren't very unhappy about this, even though Thomas was almost like a son. For a short time, they disowned Mary, but eventually, all was forgiven.

Thomas and Mary lived in a log house on the north side of the Twitchel Ranch, near the water tower along the railroad tracks where he had first arrived so long ago. They had three children: Thomas, who was six; James, four; and Brenda, two. They planned to have more. The entire family got together at least once a week for meal, picnics, or whatever. The second Spatcher had long since passed on, but Thomas had taken one of her puppies before she died, the pick of the litter, for their housedog. The pup grew up and became a true Border Collie. She was black-and-white in color, friendly by nature, and ready to go with anyone. They named her Spatcher, just as the Twitchels had done with their earlier pick of the litter from the original Spatcher.

Thomas's stay at the Twitchel Ranch had been good, but now his thoughts were increasingly of his family. One night, as he and Big Joel sat alone enjoying a good smoke, Thomas got the courage to speak about how he felt. Big Joel had been aware of Thomas's feelings even though they had never spoken of it before. Big Joel just knew, as older men sometimes do. They sat for some time, and then, in *his clumsy way, Big Joel began to advise his young ward of many years about what might be best for him.*

"Well, you kin jis stay here and ne'r know how they's a doin, or ya kin take the train down the line to where ya think might be it, and do some scoutin' round." Big Joel had just returned from a trip to the East in the company of Jeb Bracken, a friend originally from Arkansas. As was Big Joel's nature, he had adopted Jeb's Arky accent during the trip. He thought a minute and then went on, "It'd be a right smart thing you take a ho'se ta hep ya ta look round. I'll give ya some time ta do this."

Again they sat in silence and then, as much to cheer the moment as to break the silence, Big Joel began to tell a joke, in his most eloquent English, without his newly acquired accent. "It seems," he said, "a rabbi in the East made a satchel for his best friend from the foreskins of young men that he had circumcised." He looked at Thomas to see if he had shocked him. Seeing that he had, he smiled and went on with the story. "When he presented it to his friend, he told him that this was a very special satchel. 'If you need a small bag for just one night, you can use it as it is,' he said, 'but if you intend to stay longer and need to pack more, you simply give the satchel a few good strokes and stop when it reaches the proper size.'"

With an exchange of smiles and a knowing look, Big Joel's large hand comforted Thomas's back, and in that second, Thomas's trip was confirmed.

The following morning found Thomas and Brenda getting his things together for the trip. "You'll need lots of hardtack and jerky, and some coffee and bacon, some beans, and some flour," Brenda said.

"I'm only goin' for a coupla days," Thomas told her, and they decided on just coffee, jerky, and hardtack. That night, Thomas sat in the wagon beside Big Joel. Old Dan, the horse that loved to jump, was tied to the rear of the wagon. Little Joel had given Thomas his horse to use. Big Joel's plan was to ask the engineer for permission to have the horse jump into one of the cars and then after Thomas had traveled for about what he thought was the right distance, they would simply jump off the train and search for his family.

"If you don't have good luck, it'll be easy findin' this place. Just ride the tracks 'til ya come to the water tower yonder. Hell, you should know it by now. And then come on home." But Thomas was only half-listening. He was thinking of his family.

In the distance, they heard the train. Thomas climbed down to untie Old Dan and get him ready to go. As the train lights came into view, Big Joel climbed down, too, and started walking toward the water tower, to where the engine would most likely stop. Thomas watched big Joel shake hands with the engineer. They talked for a long time, and then they shook hands again and Big Joel came back to the wagon. He had a look that Thomas had never seen. In the dim light, Thomas thought he saw a tear roll down Big Joel's face and drop to the ground. Big Joel pushed back his hat and in the same motion, wiped the back of his hand across his eyes.

"They said it'll be okay. They got a empty car. You kin load Dan in there and they'll stop when you say. You'll need to ride in there with the horse and clean up his shit and stuff. Just kick it off with yer foot. And if they pick up payin' fare, you'll need to get off. Sounds pretty good to me. They won't pick up payin' fare goin' this a-way."

As Thomas led the horse toward the boxcar, Big Joel brought the wagon to the open door and tossed in a good measure of feed hay. Thomas took the saddlebags Brenda had packed for him, which included more food than they *had agreed on. Big Joel gave Thomas a leg-up into the car and then just had time to get out of the way before the big horse jumped up through the open door.*

Thomas tied Dan at the far end of the car and then jumped down to exchange some last words with the man who had been his father all these years.

The engineer said, "Just wave yer coat or somethin' out the door when you think yer there and we'll stop and let you out. If ya remember it bein' six days travel gettin here, it might be not so long goin' back. The train should make better time, it bein' downhill and all."

Big Joel and Thomas shook hands and looked deeply into each other's eyes, seemingly knowing each other's feelings. As the train began to move, Big Joel once again legged up Thomas into the boxcar, and then he stood and watched as the train disappeared into the night.

As Big Joel climbed back into the wagon, he had a strange, empty feeling. He shrugged it off, whipped the horses into a trot, and headed them toward the ranch.

Chapter 21

* * * * * * *

After five days, the train passed a spot that seemed familiar to Thomas, if anything around here could be familiar after all these years. Even so, in this part of the country, nothing ever changes much. Hell, he thought, why should it, and how could it? It's mostly dry dust and sagebrush and what can change about that? It doesn't grow much and remains about the same from year to year. Thomas didn't know exactly why but he felt like this was the place to begin his search.

He held his coat out the open door and flapped it. After a few minutes, the train began to slow. When it stopped, he slid to the ground and pulled the big horse behind him. He waved to the engineer and mounted Old Dan. Thomas was on his own, and he felt a little bit like he had when he had been kidnapped so many years ago. Moments later, he was cantering Old Dan alongside the tracks when seven riders came out of the trees that lined the track, heading in the other direction. The train was still stopped, and the crew had gotten out to stretch and relieve themselves. The riders looked like Indians, but they rode with saddles and bridles with metal bits and wore high-heeled boots.

They rode up to the train crew and without saying a word, pointed their guns, motioning the crew toward the train. As Thomas turned to wave a final goodbye to the engineer, he saw what was going on, and turned Old Dan to start back.

Each of the Indians led a string of three packhorses behind him. Two wagons pulled in behind the riders and stopped. The man who looked like the chief stepped forward and motioned the crew into one of the empty boxcars. They were securely tied with leather cords, and then gagged with their own bandanas. Still without speaking, the chief motioned his band toward boxcars where a number of Mexicans were being held.

Seeing Thomas and Old Dan in the distance, the chief held up a hand signal for the braves to wait, and then he walked to meet the young rider. Thomas had had some experience with Indians and knew them to be honest and loyal, once you understood their ways. He was not afraid as he held his hand in the traditional Indian greeting. He looked at the Indian's feet and said, "Never saw no Injun with boots on afore."

Hearing that the Mexican-looking boy spoke English, the chief now spoke in English as well, while he held his revolver on Thomas. "We need some help. You and the Mexicans are going to come with us to work for a time. You'll be well paid and you have nothing to worry about."

He took Old Dan's reins from Thomas's hands, led the horse and rider to the other waiting braves, and then dismounted.

This is just like it was when Big Joel used to force workers to his ranch, thought Thomas.

It wasn't long before all of the Mexicans had been unloaded. The Indians picked the best and strongest-looking men and women, and loaded them either onto the *packhorses or into one of their wagons. Because Thomas was used to this kind of recruiting, he wasn't too worried. He imagined that at worst he would be gone for a short time and after the job had been completed, he would be set free to continue his search. The young men were put on the horses, two to a horse, with their feet hobbled or tied together under the animal's belly. The selected women were placed in the back of the wagons.*

The chief sat on his horse and decided which Mexicans went to the wagons and which ones went back to the boxcars. The braves obeyed without question. Thomas had dismounted, and when the chief had completed filling the horses and the wagons, he motioned for Thomas to get back on Old Dan.

"You look Mexican," said the chief. "Can you speak Mexican as well as English?" He talked in a sort of sly way. "We could sure use an interpreter with this crew."

Thomas screamed at him, "You're nothing but damned outlaws. I wouldn't help no damned outlaws even if I could."

Even though he could speak a little Spanish and could understand it as well as any Mexican, he wasn't about to tell the chief. Laughing at Thomas's outburst, the chief stepped down and hobbled his feet under Dan, took the reins, and then remounted his own horse. He pushed his hat back and, still laughing, shrugged his shoulders. Leading Old Dan, he brought his horse around to the head of the group of outlaw braves. The Mexican men, hobbled and riding double, waited to see what would happen next.

After a good number of the prettier Mexican women had been loaded into the wagons, the chief signaled his men to mount. The outlaws got on their horses or climbed onto the driver's seats of the wagons. The chief, still leading Old Dan, rode slowly away from the track and into the trees, with the strange-looking caravan of Mexicans and Indians following. Soon they all disappeared into a thick stand of trees that grew a short distance from the tracks.

Chapter 22

The long, dusty days were broken with occasional water and food stops. The Mexicans were let off of their horses or out of the wagons to relieve themselves as they stood beside their horse or wagon. Late at night, the party would stop and all of the Mexicans would be forced to sit around a fire with several guards holding guns on them. In the morning, without being given food or coffee, they would once again continue the journey. Days later, they arrived at the bank of a wide river.

Thomas heard the chief tell his men, "This is where we will meet the other two groups, who should have other able bodies and nice-looking captives we can sell." At first, Thomas figured the other groups were bringing in workers, as well, but now he changed his mind. "They should be here in a few days," the chief said.

Shortly after kidnapping the Mexicans, the outlaws had taken off their costumes, at which Thomas realized they were white men who had been posing as Indians, as he had suspected. They stored the outfits in a large trunk in one of the wagons. The Mexicans, having become accustomed to being kidnapped to do farm work, didn't appear to be too concerned, but now that he had overheard the chief, Thomas became worried. From what he had heard and what he was able to piece together, he feared the worse. The Mexicans were not going on a work detail, as they thought, but to the coast, to be sold to slave traders, and then taken as slaves and concubines to some distant land. Not speaking the white man's language, the Mexicans were content to travel, do the work they expected to be assigned, get their pay, and then go to the next job.

The outlaws took the hostages to the river's edge, where they were allowed to briefly bathe in the refreshing water and then, too soon, were herded out, hands and feet tied, and were made to sit motionless between the outlaws and the shore. The wagons were then rolled into place just far enough away so a guard sitting inside could see them all. The outlaws took turns guarding the hostages and then sleeping or drinking whiskey. Some would eat or cool themselves in the river. As the evening wore on, the whiskey jugs became more plentiful, and the outlaws became louder. After some time, three of them approached the Mexicans and selected three of the women to cook, they told them, and then they led them behind the wagons.

Thomas hadn't been put with the others, because during the long trek, the chief had taken a liking to the young man and had him do camp chores, take care of the horses, and such. Thomas had tried to get close enough to the Mexicans to tell them in his broken Spanish about their plight. Every time he tried, the Mexicans would just tell him in Spanish that they needed the work and didn't mind having their trip home delayed for a time. Finally, he gave up in discouragement.

The group camped for two-and-a-half days before the first of the other parties showed up. It looked as though their efforts had also been rewarding, as their packhorses and wagons were filled with Mexicans. As the party drew closer, Thomas noticed a large black man on a horse behind one of the outlaws. "My hell," he drew in a breath, "it's Cropper!"

He was both glad and disturbed to see his old friend under these circumstances. As the group came closer, he wondered if Cropper would still remember him after all these years. His mother had told him often while he was growing up, "Older people don't change much, but you sometimes can't even pick out your own brood when you haven't seen them for years." Cropper's legs were not only hobbled underneath the horse but his hands were tied behind him, as well. A rope dangling from his thick neck dragged along the ground behind him.

Cropper's face told of injuries days old, and wet blood flowed in a small line from his swollen nose. His fingers and knuckles were scraped and swollen as well, but scabs were forming over the injured places. He was covered with scratches and dirt. As he passed Thomas, Cropper exclaimed, "Well, I'll surely be damned, it's Thomas, the little lost boy." And then catching himself, not knowing quite what to do, he went on, "It's my mistake. All you whites look alike. I's sorry, massa," and he resumed his forward, glassy-eyed stare as he followed the group to the water's edge.

Cropper was allowed to refresh and bathe his injuries in the cool water, but he remained tied and two outlaws aimed guns at him. Another outlaw held the rope that hung from his neck, ready to jerk it at the slightest hint of trouble. When the men thought Cropper had bathed enough, he was led to one of the wagons, the rope around his neck was pulled tight, and he was tied to the top of one of the wagon wheels. There he stayed, receiving food and water only once or twice a day.

Chapter 23

* * * * * * * *

Thomas had been watching his old friend, and as he lay in bed he plotted far into the night to free him, along with as many Mexicans as possible. He had heard the outlaws talking about the ferry a few miles downriver. He had pieced together that the three groups planned to take the entire group to the ferry a few miles farther downriver and cross to the other side. After crossing with all the goods, horses, and wagons, they would continue their trek to the sea, and meet with a ship that would carry the unwary Mexican passengers, as well as Cropper and him, to their new homes.

The Mexicans were fed enough to keep them healthy, because if they were sick or pale, they would bring small prices. The Mexicans were made to cook the food, clean the dishes, and do whatever else happened to be the outlaws' pleasure; they were, however, careful not to harm or mark them.

After four more days of waiting, the third party arrived. They had fared well also, as all their horses and wagons were full. In the camp, they followed the same routine of depositing their hostages with the others at the river's edge and then arranging their wagons in a half-circle, inside of which the Mexicans were kept. This being done, they bathed, ate, drank, and slept.

The plan was to rest horses and men here for two more days, and then take one more easy day to travel to the ferry. It would take another day to cross the river on the ferry, after which they would camp on the other side for the night, and begin their long trek to the sea the following morning. The chief intended to go to the ferry the next morning with a couple of his men to make arrangements for the crossing. He told Thomas to get some sleep, because he would be going, too.

Thomas had been awake for a while when the chief and his men began moving about. They all sat and talked for a while and then had a quick breakfast, a cup of coffee, and a smoke, and then saddled their horses. The chief, two of his men, and Thomas then set off toward the ferry. The men talked and joked for a while and then fell silent. Each was content to be with his thoughts as the horses picked the way along the little-used trail. The time went fast and soon, in the distance, they saw an old log building. A man stood out in front, waving a greeting.

Thomas and the other two men fed and watered the horses while the chief introduced himself to the ferry owner. "They call me Chief," he said. "I don't know why, they just do."

"I'm Ben," the old man returned, and they shook hands and made small talk, as polite folks do before getting down to business.

The ferry site had been carefully selected. It was a place wider than the rest of the river and very deep, and it ran somewhat slower, although it was still rather fast. Large trees lined both banks and some had been selected and used to anchor the cables that held the heavy vessel.

Even here, where the river ran slower, the ferry had difficulty crossing, especially with heavy loads. If not properly loaded, with the heavier items placed on the downriver side, the ferry could easily capsize when water came up over the front. This had happened several times in the past, although to prevent discouragement of paying customers, this feature of the ferry was not advertised.

Chief told Ben of his plan to bring horses, wagons, and people across the river. He wanted details about how many of each could be taken over at a time, as well as what the cost would be. Ben not only had operated this ferry for years, but he had also helped the engineer who built it. Together they had put the cables and ropes in place. It had been improved through the years and, in his opinion, he had the "best damned ferry in the country." It was a lot more complicated than any other ferry in the West, he said. Thomas didn't know if that meant it worked any better, or if maybe it was not as good as others, but Ben thought it was indeed the most complicated one.

Ben never missed a chance to tell people about it but, like Big Joel and his jokes, it wasn't always easy for him to find a willing audience. It was clear that the old man was not going to talk business until he had explained fully how the ferry worked, and maybe even a little about its history as well. So the others pushed back their hats, rolled cigarettes, and sat to listen to Ben's story of the ferry.

As if he had been holding it inside for too long, it now burst out. "It's a simple principle," he began, and then, sensing that only Thomas was listening, he spoke just to him. He wore a smug expression and obviously was basking in his ability to describe in great detail and eloquence the mechanics of the ferry, as he had repeatedly heard it described by the eastern engineer. "There are ropes at both the front and rear of the ferry and a pole that holds the ropes apart at the point where they fasten with a pulley to the main cable that spans the river."

He stopped to see if the others were listening yet, but as they weren't, Ben turned back to Thomas and continued. "There are two anchor trees at each side of the river and depending on which way the ferry is going, the anchors are either taken up or down the river, so the river power itself is used to push the ferry to the other side." Ben didn't say anything about the engineer, giving all credit for the design and construction of the craft to himself. "The only time the anchor ropes can be changed is when the ferry is in dock at either side of the river. A team of horses is used to bring the ferry back up the river in position for the return trip. After the cables are switched to the other anchors on the trees, the current of the river brings the ferry back across."

The old man was losing interest in telling his story with just the young man listening, so he wound up by saying, "See those big eye bolts hanging on the anchor trees and the big hooks on each end of the cable that goes across the river? Those hooks are put into the eye bolts to get the proper angle to send the ferry over or to bring it back across the river."

After losing the main cable in the river on several occasions and having great difficulty recovering it, the ferry owner had installed a safety feature. It was an eyebolt fastened to each end of the main cable about ten feet from the end. A cable was passed through these eyebolts and then was fastened between the two anchor trees that stood at each side of the river. With this assembly in place, the worst thing that could happen was that the main cable, if dropped, would simply return to the lower anchor tree. This had been his own design, but not having it explained to him by the engineer, he had trouble describing it.

"Well," the white-haired ferry owner said thoughtfully,

"put a lotta myself into this contraption, ya know. I got the idea from an easterner, an engineer or sumpin' like a-that." He added, *"If either side of the safety hooks was removed, the ferry would just go and float out of control down the river."*

He rubbed his chin, and eyed the three outlaws and the young man as he tried to figure them for top dollar, while not wanting them to go down the river about a day's ride, where another ferry could take them across. Without mentioning the other ferry, he said, "Tell ya what I'll do." *He stroked his chin again.* "Do it fer two cents each for people, five cents fer animals, and wagons fer, let's see, 'bout 10 cents each." *He waited for them to decide.*

Chief took out an old piece of paper and a stub of a pencil and started to write, talking while he tried to figure out the cost of the crossing. "That's a heap a' money," *he said,* "but we need ta get ta the other side."

Ben's eyes lit up. That is a heap of money, he thought. Chief wanted to know how many trips it would take to get everything across, and as the old man told him, the stubby pencil worked on the scrap of paper again. "The boat will carry quite a bit if it's loaded right, depending on how the river's actin'," *Ben said.* "Horses are hard because they're so tall and they shift the weight. Wagons is easy; ya kin put a few of em on if'n yer careful."

"How many trips?" *Chief asked again.*

The old man, now eager to help plan the crossing, said, "'Bout ten trips should do it."

"That makes sense."

Ben volunteered, "I'll take over a load of yer horses and men first so they'll be there to help unload the wagons when they come over. Then a load of horses, maybe the draft horses. They're big, but we can maybe take six and maybe nine of the riding ones, maybe more. Coupla loads, *then we'll take over the wagons. Some of ya kin ride with them if'n ya feels like it. You kin mix in the other folk as ya kin, where there's room."*

He thought for a minute and went on. "Then the rest of the horses in three or so trips and then the rest of the people. Ya know that som'a 'ya will needs to be there ta steady the horses and to make sure the brakes on the wagons hold. The ferry will come back okay empty." Ben again thought for a moment. "Pay for ten trips and if it's more, I'll just forget about that."

The old man smiled as he watched the three men and the boy mount and start back up the river. He had a promise that they would be back day after tomorrow, and to secure the deal, Chief had left a deposit with the ferry owner in return for a promise that they would be his only customers for that day. Chief was sort of proud, too, and he smiled as they rode silently along the river and back to their camp.

Chapter 24

An idea had been hatching in Thomas's brain, and he was now sure he could disrupt the outlaw's plans. He figured that he'd rather see everyone injured or killed than what was sure to happen if he did nothing. For the next two days, the outlaws sat around eating, smoking, and resting. The horses grazed on the grass that grew along the riverbank. They would need their strength, and nobody knew how far the coast was; only that it was a far piece. Each evening, some of the men would start drinking and after a time get quite loud and boisterous. Some would take women from the group to go behind the wagons to cook, as they called it.

Even during these times, Chief would have several armed guards watching, ready to shoot anyone trying to escape. The Mexican women were forced to keep large fires burning throughout the night, so any escape attempt could be spotted and stopped. They had all heard Chief threaten that if any Mexicans escaped, the guards would take their place, and they knew better than to believe that these were idle threats. Even though Thomas watched for a chance to get to Cropper or the other hostages, none came, and he *was forced to wait.*

He longed to hear one of Big Joel's jokes and he thought of Brenda and Little Joel, missing them now more than his family. He remembered the meals Brenda had prepared and her doctoring him with turpentine, Bag Balm, and her other home remedies. Those treatments didn't seem so bad now. That night, remembering his mother's bedtime ritual, he said a prayer. It couldn't hurt, he thought.

The morning after the second day finally came. Chief sent some men to gather the horses while others were assigned to get the Mexicans ready to travel. It would be an easy ride down the river to the ferry except for a few places where getting the wagons over rocks, fallen logs, or across deep sand would be a problem. The Mexicans were loaded into the wagons and onto their horses with their feet hobbled underneath. Cropper sat atop his mount, feet and hands tied and with the rope still around his neck.

The outlaws had a final cup of coffee and a smoke as they talked about what they planned to do with their share of the money. After a time, they climbed aboard the wagons and horses and the long caravan got slowly underway. It made much slower time than the four riders had made on their earlier trip, as the wagons had to be unloaded and lifted over logs and rocks, as well as having to be pushed through sand or sometimes pulled with lariats tied to the wagons and wrapped around saddle horns. The extra work wore on the outlaws, whose tempers became short. Outbursts were frequent, and the group stopped often to rest.

Thomas knew he had to talk to Cropper, but he also knew he couldn't be seen talking to his old friend. He continued to watch for his chance, which came without warning and couldn't have happened better if Thomas had planned it. One of the horses pulling a wagon became frightened and prodded its mate into flight. Together, they ran toward a stand of trees inland from the river a few hundred feet. The other outlaws stopped and waited for the driver to regain control of the frightened beasts, but control didn't come and they continued at breakneck speed toward the trees, with a wagon full of frightened women hanging on.

Chief called to several of his men to drop their ropes and follow him. As he started after the wagon, he turned in his saddle and yelled to Thomas, "You go hold that big nigger 'til we gets back," and then he and the other outlaws raced into the trees where the wagon had gone.

Thomas ran to Cropper, his words coming in short, choppy sentences as he panted, "We don't have much time, Cropper, so's you just listen. I got a plan to set the ferry loose when most of the men have crossed and they're sending the wagons over." He stopped long enough to take a quick breath. "I don't have time to tell ya everything, so you'll jus' need to play along." He paused to breathe again and then said, "I know how the ferry works. I think we can do it."

They talked about how this could be done, who should do what, and when it should be done, and then Thomas said to his old friend, "Sure as hell good to see you again." Cropper smiled through swollen and battered lips.

The men came back, leading the runaway wagon. Thomas stopped talking, walked back to his horse and climbed up. The going got easier now, and just at dusk they saw the ferry owner's cabin in the distance. The old man came out to meet them. "Hell, I'd about given up you a-cumin' at all, you bein' so late and all," he said with a shrewd smile.

"Wouldn't mind, though, a havin' that deposit without doin' no work," and he laughed out loud. "Got a big pot'a

stew on, and some coffee. For 10 cents each, you kin have it all."

Chief agreed to the deal and they all sat down to eat as best as they could. The outlaws ate their fill and then let the Mexican women eat and gave what was left to the Mexican men. The work of the day had tired them completely and everyone fell asleep, except the guards.

Chapter 25

* * * * * * *

Thomas lay awake and tried to remember just how the old man had described the ferry's workings and hoped he would be able to find the right time and be able to do the right thing to send the ferry downstream.

They rose early the following morning. The old man was already awake and began telling them how they should handle the crossing. "Ya aut'a put on a load of horses." And then more to himself, he added, "We need to sort of test the ferry."

Chief decided to trust the old man's advice, and he and the outlaws set about doing as he said. After 14 horses were led on board and tied securely to the sturdy railing that completely enclosed three sides of the ferry, the old man checked the load. "Looks okay," he said. "Better have about 10 or even 14 of your men ride over to keep them calm. I got a hired man over there who fetches the ferry up to the high anchor with his team of horses. They kin help him some ta bring her up."

The men climbed on board, looking a little pale and unsure that they wanted to be sailors. The old man pulled the lever that held the ferry in place and it started its way *quickly, very quickly, across the river. The horses fussed some, but the men were able to keep them controlled, and soon the ferry was on the other side, held in place by the river's current. The horses were unloaded, their saddles and bridles removed, and they were hobbled with buckskin hobbles and set to graze on the lush grass that grew on that side of the river.*

Ben's hired man on the far side removed the large hook from the eye at the lower anchor tree, hooked it into the ring on the double tree and then urged his two horses forward. They strained against the ferry and the swift current and then slowly moved upstream until the large hook could be fastened to the metal eye on the large tree there. Then some of the outlaws got back on the ferry for the trip back.

Ben changed his side from "high" to "low" with his own team of horses. Then the lever at the far side of the river was released and the ferry came back and was held in place again by the current, ready to be reloaded. It was exciting enough that the men now began vying to get a ride. The old man was pleased, and Chief looked pleased as well.

"Let's take another load of horses," Chief said, and the outlaws began loading more horses. Men then boarded to control them and the load was quickly taken across. After most of the horses had been taken over, Ben said, "Let's take the wagons now. Ya got men and animals over there to get them off with."

There was room for six wagons on the ferry, but it looked heavy and Chief was worried. He considered stopping and taking off two of the wagons, and then thought better of it and let them go. A man on the seat of each wagon held the brakes. The ferry tugged and pulled at the main cable and dipped dangerously low at the front side, threatening to take on water and swamp. After several successful trips, the ferry came back to take the wagons that contained the food supply and all the ammunition. By now, most of the outlaws had been taken across. All that remained to cross were several wagons, the Mexicans, who were tied and bound securely, four horses, the chief, three outlaws, Thomas, and Cropper, who was tied fast to a tree.

All eyes were on the ferry as the trip carrying the food and ammo began. Thomas saw his chance and ran to Cropper, untying the ropes that held his feet and hands. Cropper took the rope off his neck and together, they ran to the tree that held the high anchor. Chief and the outlaws, still engrossed in watching the ferry, showed no interest in the black man and Thomas. "We gots to find some way to get it loose afore the ferry gets across," said Thomas as he ran to the safety cable and removed the giant hook from the ring.

Cropper picked up a maul that was leaning against the tree and gave three mighty blows to the cable that was wrapped around the tree. These blows, combined with the force of the ferry pulling against the tree that held the cable, caused the cable to give way, and the ferry quickly went to the far side, crashing with such force that the wagons and their contents were nearly thrown off. Some men who were thrown off either floated slowly into the river, trying to swim to shore, or were stranded in the mud or against the side of the crippled ferry. Slowly, the ferry floated into the current and it soon was carried downstream, along with the essential goods. Chief looked on in disbelief, and then ran down the bank, yelling at his men on the other side to get their horses and ride after the floating cache of their survival bounty. Chief ran back, saddled his horse and he and the three men he had left on his side of the river started after the ferry. He stopped, turned in his saddle, aimed his revolver at Thomas, and then reconsidered, maybe thinking he might need him later. He yelled, "I'll take care of you when I get back, you little son of a bitch." And then they all disappeared in a cloud of dust as they raced downstream after their supplies.

Chapter 26

"Don't know what he'll do if he catches them big wagons," Ben said, "but he'll sure as hell run into that ferry downriver if he keeps a-goin'. That's a hell of a thing," he said, "losin' ten bucks and swampin' my ferry all at the same time."

"That's too bad," Thomas offered.

"Well, I'll just have to build another one," the old man concluded.

"You got horses and wagons?" Thomas asked the old man.

"I kin sell you some. I got about 12 head and the workhorses, and two wagons, and a buckboard. How much ya got?"

Thomas and Cropper knew there wasn't time to haggle, because one way or another, the outlaws would soon be back. They set all of the Mexicans free and told them what was going on.

Then went back to the old man. "Tell you what," Thomas said, "I'll get what I can from the Mexicans and we'll take your horses and wagons. As soon as we've put some distance between us and them outlaws, we'll cut 'em *loose. Some or all will come back, but one way or another, we're taken 'em."*

As the old man thought about this, Thomas added, "Probably a better deal than Chief would of given ya. He would most likely just cut your damned throat and let ya bleed ta death."

"Not a very good deal," Ben frowned.

"A hell of a lot better than nothing. If I was you, I'd get the hell out of here before Chief gets back. He is no good for sure."

Finally, Ben agreed and they sealed the deal with the small amount of money he gathered from the Mexicans. "Not enough," said the old man, but neither Thomas, Cropper, nor the Mexicans were listening.

They crowded into the wagons and buckboard. Some rode double on the horses and some were left to walk. They set out, not the way they had come, but into the woods, and then they turned to head back in the general direction they had traveled to get there. After going a short distance, they ran into an old trail that was heading about the same way they were, so they changed their course a bit and followed it. No matter what they did or said, they couldn't get the Mexicans to hurry. Thomas tried to tell them of the plan the Chief had had for them. They just smiled, not really understanding. They were so used to being kidnapped and taken to work for short periods of time that they thought this was another work detail. Finally, Thomas gave up and decided to just worry about Cropper and himself.

It was difficult to travel with so many people, and Chief would want to settle his score only with Thomas, not the Mexicans, so they decided to let the Mexicans take the wagons and horses, except Old Dan and a horse for Cropper, and they went on ahead. Chief and his men weren't likely to follow for quite some time, if at all. If they came, they would most likely just be seeking vengeance rather than continuing with their original plan, which seemed unlikely.

Thomas and Cropper waved goodbye as they parted from the Mexicans and then set their horses to a short lope. They intended to ride at this gait for a time and then use a fast walk to rest the horses. They wanted to place as much distance between themselves and the outlaws as possible, but they stopped to rest and drink whenever there was water. Thomas felt guilty about leaving the Mexicans, and about how he and the ranchers had taken advantage of them, and about the abuse that had made them so accustomed to this kind of treatment. The kidnapping of the Mexicans for ranch help hadn't seemed so bad at the time, but now, after being kidnapped himself, he thought differently about it.

Chapter 27

Thomas told Cropper his plans to find his family and home. He told Cropper he could come too if he wanted, and as he had nothing else planned, he decided he would tag along. Thomas didn't know how far they had been taken from the tracks, but he was pretty sure they were going in the right direction to get them back to the railroad.

"It seem like ya'all attracks lots a 'citment," Cropper said. "I kin'a like's it. Les get a-goin."

"You sure as hell been my guardian angel since we met," Thomas said. "I thought God used Indians for guardian angels."

"I ain't no Indian."

Having little food, they were forced to beg or work for food at farmhouses that they passed, or to eat snakes or small rodents they were able to catch. They ate berries, dug roots, and caught a few rabbits in snares, as neither of them had a gun.

One night, as they lay by the campfire, Cropper said, "Ya know, Thomas, I been a-thinkin'. It seems that the more things change, the more they stays the same." With this, he rolled over, closed his eyes, and fell asleep.

Thomas stayed awake well into the night thinking about this statement, the same one Cropper had made to him years ago. He hadn't been able to make sense of it then, and he still couldn't make sense of it. Eventually, he too fell asleep.

After days of traveling, they finally saw railroad tracks in the distance. Thomas let out a sharp yelp that made Old Dan kick up his heels and dump Thomas on his head into soft sand. He climbed back on, and without even stopping to rest, they started down the tracks toward home. The two men searched the tracks up and down for several days and were just thinking of giving up when Thomas noticed a row of trees growing over a rise in the land a short distance from the tracks.

"I'm gonna have a look," he told Cropper." You kin jus sit here a spell; I'll be back shortly." He and Old Dan set out toward the trees. As he crested the rise, he noticed that the landscape looked familiar, "There's the stream. There's the trail to my sister's place. Well, I'll be damned. I found it!" he shouted.

He rode to the top of the rise and motioned Cropper to join him.

Thomas had already left when Cropper finally got there, and was a long way along the trail heading toward his father's place. He watched him for a moment and then followed. Thomas could remember Spatcher running through the weeds and sage that spotted the sandy landscape, and he remembered the warm wind drying his nose and throat and how he had hurried to the cool stream so many years ago. He thought about what his mother and father would do when he rode up to the old place. Then he worried, maybe they won't remember me or maybe they'll be gone.

In the distance, he could just make out the outline of

the buildings. He set Old Dan to a full gallop, the wind blowing his hair. He was home; it was grand. The old place looked deserted. He pulled up just outside the house, got off the horse, and walked about. Nobody had lived there for a long time, maybe for years.

"Wonder where the hell everybody is?" *he asked himself.*

"Looks sorta like the poor farm we had in Georgia," *Cropper said as he rode up.* "All the old poor white folks that couldn't make it were put there to live. Blacks wasn't allowed."

Thomas didn't know what to say.

"They got better carin' for when they was there than when they was with their own, I reckon," *Cropper went on.*

"Im gonna ride over to my sis's place. Her name is Susan," *said Thomas.* "See if she knows what happened to everybody."

He climbed onto Old Dan's back and headed for Susan's place, not waiting for Cropper. Thomas prodded Old Dan into a gentle short-lope and Cropper followed at a slower gait.

Chapter 28

Thomas was worried now, not so much about finding his sister or if she would remember him as about what might have happened since he had last seen her. He set Dan into a steady, ground-eating short lope, and before long he reached the stream that marked the turn to Susan's place. It had been so easy to find that he thought something must be wrong. He stopped Old Dan for a moment and thought about going back to Big Joel and the place he knew as home, and forgetting about his family." I'm not dead yet," he muttered, trying to get enough courage to continue. And then he reined his horse upstream toward his sister's place.

Susan was outside, hanging clothes on a line. She turned, still holding a towel in her hand, to see who was coming. Three small boys and a girl came running out of the house. One of the boys had black hair and dark eyes. The other children were blond with lighter skin.

Thomas rode close and then swung down out of the saddle. "Hi, Susan," he smiled.

With tears running down her cheeks, she ran to Thomas and hugged his neck. They held each other, their *bodies shaking as they sobbed in this happy and enchanted moment.*

Thomas met his nieces and nephew and was ushered inside for a bowl of Lumpy Dick, which he was just finishing when Cropper rode up to the house on a sorrel mare. Thomas explained to Susan that he was a friend.

"Come get something ta eat," she told the Cropper and as he did, she began telling Thomas what had happened while he had been gone. Their mother and father had searched for him for several years, and then had decided to systematically comb the area. To do this, they sold the ranch to a rich easterner. Their mother said she would never give up until she knew what had happened to Thomas. Their parents had been gone now for several years.

Thomas told Susan of his adventure. She sat wide-eyed, thinking he must surely be making it up. After supper, when the kids had been put to bed, the three of them sat far into the night telling stories and catching up on news.

Susan's husband, John, was still a sheepherder and still away with the sheep, so Susan had the two men sleep in her bed and she made up a pallet for herself.

"Don't John never come home?" Thomas kidded. "Ya must not treat him good."

Thomas and Cropper talked a while after they were in bed, but finally sleep overcame them. They stayed with Susan and the kids for several weeks, helping her catch up on some of the past due work, until Thomas decided he would head back to the Twitchel Ranch, as he didn't know what else to do.

He had told Susan about how they had taken him in and almost became his family; but not quite, he assured her. Now he gave her a detailed description of the ranch's whereabouts. Taking what food he could carry, he set out the following morning along the tracks that led back to the water tower and the Twitchel Ranch. Hell, trains and tracks have sure been a big part of my life, he laughed to himself.

Chapter 29

* * * * * * *

The Twitchels were glad to see Thomas—"delighted" would better describe their feelings—and they accepted Cropper as well. In fact, Cropper was accepted as family, especially after they found out how he had helped Thomas. They all talked at once, until some of the excitement of his return wore off. He described finding his home with no one there and about his visit with his sister, and then the long ride back to this place that now seemed like his real home.

Seeing everyone together, Big Joel took control, and began a story. "You know, Thomas, while you were gone, I let Spatcher go with an easterner who trains dogs. He said he could teach her some things. You remember, don't you, how I would have her go to the sheep or cows and then just by giving her a hand signal and whistling have her take them here or there as I pleased? Well, I think he taught her a few things, because the next time I took her out to the herd, I sat on one side of the sheep and put her on the other side, and then motioned to send her here and there for a while. And then she stopped and stood up on her hind legs and whistled to me, and motioned with her front paw for me to go here or there."

Big Joel held his large stomach and laughed. Thomas was glad to be back. He spent a great deal of time talking with Brenda and Little Joel and catching up on what had happened since he had been gone.

It was now the fall of the year and almost too cold to be outside. The Andersons, however, were enjoying what was probably the last day of the year for this luxury. Thomas sat next to his wife, Mary, and held her hand as they rocked and talked of things that married people talk of. Young Thomas, age six, played at their feet. His own feet showed the signs of wear of doing without shoes during the long summer. His long black hair hung down over the dark shoulders and back that he had acquired from his Mexican ancestry. Cropper, Thomas's friend of many years, sat on the top step leading down from the porch. His years in slavery had made such a mark on him that even now he was, in effect, still somewhat in bondage, even though it was contrary to the wishes of Thomas and Mary.

A slight breeze rustled the few leaves that remained on the trees and told of the coming winter and the snow. The love within the family was their real wealth, and nothing else mattered.   From down the dusty road came a fancy buckboard pulled by two fine horses and driven by a man in a fancy outfit. They looked like people of some means. The driver whipped the team toward the porch, pulled up in front and then stopped as the Andersons watched. An old man and a woman sat inside. The driver wrapped the reins around the brake handle and climbed down to help the old people out of the carriage. They looked strangely familiar to Thomas.

The man was tall and thin and slightly bent forward, his graying hair so white that no evidence of its original color remained. He walked slowly around to the woman's side and raised his hand to help her get down. She was a *little on the heavy side, with graying hair, but a handsome woman just the same. It was obvious they had deep feelings for each other and that they had been together for a long time. They didn't seem to need to speak, but instinctively knew each other's thoughts.*

The black-and-white Border Collie got up from her spot by Mary's feet and, wagging her tail, went to meet and welcome the new arrivals. As they walked to the bottom of the porch stairs, Thomas and Mary approached them to bid them good day. The old man bent down now to touch young Thomas on the head and say, "Yer a fine lookin' boy, you surely are."

Mary said, "Good day to you. Come and sit a spell and rest your selves."

The old man said to Thomas and Mary, "Good day to you as well, young folks. Don't mind if we do; we're kinda tired, as we been a travelin' for quite a spell." He smiled and then continued, "My name is Thomas Anderson."

Thomas realized it was his mother and father from so long ago—he was finally home. In fact, in a way, they were now all home.

THE END of "The Unintentional Kidnapping."

Chapter 134

The window effect faded and I sat next to the Mexican-looking young man.

It had been a delightful journey. Really, two delightful journeys: the kidnapped Thomas's, and mine with the train Thomas. I related my experience with the original Thomas, the ancestor of this Thomas, and recited the things he had told me or that I had made up, and drank in the imagined glory of myself as a successful author and young Thomas as my admiring public.

Then strangely I passed through the window watching this new Thomas and William.

> He told me all he knew about the original Thomas, the things that had been passed down as fact or dogma, the way most things are recorded. And I had tried to end the story on a happy note and maybe make it a little unusual, too.

The window effect faded.

"Thanks for the nice story," I said to him.

He gave me a strange look and said, "I have no idea what you're talking about. I only know you are talking machine and you do ramble on." Then he got up, stepped down from the train car, and was gone. It all ended much too soon. It had been delightful to meet him. I had the same feeling of camaraderie after meeting him as I had had with his great-grandfather so long ago in Missoula. But he sure was an aloof sort of a guy, anxious to be gone. He must have lots to do as an author, I thought.

As I stepped off the train in Eden, Dale was there to meet me. "Took you long enough to get here," he kidded. He introduced me to his wife, Kitty, who I knew from when we were younger and I lived here. We said hi to each other, and then got in their car.

"It was a long ride, but I met an interesting character on the train."

After I told Dale about the young Thomas, he asked, "Where does he live?"

"Jeez, I didn't even ask. Maybe I'll ask the ticket agent who he was."

"They won't give out that kind of information," Dale said.

As it turned out, the funeral was the biggest gathering Eden had ever seen. Colt and Sally had made a lot of friends through the years and people came from far away to show their respects.

Through the years, Colt had cared for Sally and they had grown to love and understand each other and could communicate without speaking at all, just by a look or an action. It seemed that this was natures way of relieving Sally of her pain and embarrassment, her heart couldn't take anymore and it stopped beating. And Colt had pretty much worn his own heart out by caring for her through the years. The pains in his chest were becoming worse and knew he was nearing the end.

He wrote a few notes; one note ended something like, "... We want to be cremated and both put in to the same urn. I love you all, Colt."

Strangely, everybody thought he had written the note specifically to them. Thinking about what Colt's life as a cowboy and a caretaker and the end must have been like, my imagination took over; I just couldn't help it.

"The Last Cowboy"

The sun and wind had turned the face of the old cowboy to leather. His look was stern and determined but strangely soft and concerned as he limped across the unfinished wooden floor and began to sort through the pile of old bills and papers that were lying in disarray on the table. He placed a glycerin pill under his tongue and took a swig of water from a glass that sat near by. His heart responded, settling its pace. He carefully arranged the bills in one pile and the checks in another, and then proceeded to write. He wrote what was due to him, from whom, and to whom he owed money and why. After the note was completed, he put it aside, took another sheet, and began to detail the instructions of how to tend to his beloved animals. After writing for a moment, he crumpled the paper, dropped it to the floor, reached for a clean paper, and began writing again.

The glycerin pill worked until the writing was done and then as if synchronized to that moment, he fell lifelessly to the floor his heart finally worn completely out.

Now they were both gone and I missed them sorely.

Chapter 135

Everything is going as well as can be expected, although I don't have anything concrete to tell Alex to change his mind yet. Everything seems to blur into oblivion, with no clear-cut edges. I am now quite sure that Alex or Oscar was the killer. I had expected Alex to pay me a visit before this, to torment me, as is his nature. I am extremely hungry and cold here in the basement of the furnace room of the Avalon. I know the answer is near—I must keep looking. It shouldn't be long now. I will feel better when I have some information for Alex—that bastard. I have to keep looking.

Chapter 136

Now that I was here in Eden and the funeral of Colt and Sally was over, and I was feeling a little better, I decided as there was very little snow on the ground, I would ride Dad's horse, Penny, to Castle III for a while to reflect. I loved to sit on the high cliffs there and dream about someday actually owning all of it. After we built our castle, Victoria and I would lounge there in ecstasy, dreaming and planning. It was about an hour's ride from Dad's place to Castle III, and as I rode past the Bucket of Blood, I began to salivate. God, I thought, I've turned into one of Pavlov's dogs because of this good Highlander beer.

I tied the horse to the hitching post in front of the store.

"Gimme a beer, Chuck," I said. "A Highlander."

"Good ta have ya back, Bill," Chuck said as he fished a bottle out of the cooler.

"Good ta be here," I told him as he pulled the cap off the bottle and half-filled a glass with a healthy head.

"Don't seem like you get around to say hello to everybody like you used to," he said as he handed me the two half-filled vessels, the glass and the bottle.

I finished filling the glass myself and took a long drink. "Ya know, Chuck, they don't have beer like this in Utah," and we both laughed. It wasn't really very funny, but we wanted to relieve the tension that can come from old friends who haven't seen each other in a long while.

It was nice to be with Chuck. "Next time I come, I'm going to stay at your place," I told him.

"Well, maybe just come and see us," he said and laughed nervously. Then he said, "I've made up a poem about you. Want to hear it?"

"Sure, go ahead."

He took out a sheet of paper and began to read.

The Jones Boy

Where mountains rise to pierce the skies, the frozen lakes below

The pale moonbeams on yonder streams, while heavy lays the snow

The evergreen does make the scene, where gusty winds do speak

Where men grow bold in land so cold, and mountains bare and bleak

This land of mine, this tall white pine, a man comes breaking through

Where waters flow beneath the snow, this man we all well knew

This man was so bold in this land so cold, his voice was like the thunder

His guns swung low they drug the snow, his yellow boots went under

His broad green hat high up in the sky, his face was hard and set

His eyes were dim, his figure slim, his feet, they must be wet

Though Wild Bill was quick to draw, and Daniel Boone was so brave

They'd both give ground and look around, to watch the Jones boy rave

The maidens fair did gaze on him, with blond and wavy hair

He was their pride from far and wide, the answer to their prayer

I don't know why we want to cry, and why it's here or there

We all feel sad and kind of mad, I guess—the jealousy of men

I guess you saw he got my squaw, a man said feeling lonely

I guess you knew, he got mine too, she was my one and only

Did you see how he got my frau, I can't say much more

I'm feeling sick he got my chick spoke up number four

I guess we'll go and have a show; the crap is deep enough you see

He's had his fling, let's watch him swing, we'll hang him from a tree

The mob came out and looked about, their valiant eyes were pleadin',

They cornered him; his chance was slim, there in that town of Eden

His shoulders wide turned to the side, his gun hand tense and ready

The silence broke, the Jones boy spoke, his voice was calm and steady

Now don't get mad and think you're bad, because you have the blues

For even now, anyone can see how, you're a-shaking in your shoes

Just turn your backs and trace your tracks, for I'm not chicken-hearted

> *Don't feel rough and think you're tough; it won't be good ta get me started*
> *And when you see me on the street, just circle plenty wide*
> *Just take your ropes, you simple dopes, and play it suicide*
> *Where waters flow beneath the snow, we now sit here and wonder*
> *We sang our song, the tune was wrong; we know we made a blunder*
> *Where mountains rise to pierce the skies, and lakes are filled to brimmin'*
> *We hear a loud and happy crowd, it's the Jones boy with our women*

"Okay, I get it. I can come over, but leave the women alone, huh?"

"Yeah, something like that." And then as an afterthought he said, "There was a guy looking for you a while ago. I told him how to get to your dad's place."

"Jesus," I said, "Oscar's in Eden. What'd he look like?" I was afraid to hear the answer.

"He was big and looked mean."

"Chuck, what did he look like?"

"He was black, he had wide shoulders and wore really nice clothes. I think he said his name was Trooper or something like that."

My old friend Trooper from Spokane was keeping his promise to visit. "Where did he go?"

"Said his car wasn't running right and he was going over to Piedmont to have the mechanic look at it. He said he would stop in when he came back to make sure where you lived." Chuck gave me a look. "Most people don't have Negroes for friends."

"Trooper's a good guy," I said. "Maybe I'll take him to meet

Dad." I smiled. "Hey Chuck, before I go home, I'm going over to my castle. If Trooper gets back before I do, tell him how to get there. Tell him to drive up Lower Road and walk up that way; it's a lot shorter. And I'll be working on a poem to get even."

"What the hell, now I'm your message boy, huh?" Chuck laughed. "Yeah, do the poem."

I stepped onto the porch and sucked in a deep breath of cold air that bit into my lungs. I coughed out steam from my mouth and nose. "I could be mistaken for a train," I mumbled in a feeble attempt at humor, which was a waste, because no one was there to hear me.

A pickup was parked in front of Mrs. Larson's post office, the driver slumping down in the seat. "Probably some old drunk who didn't make it home yet," I mumbled. A soft wind had come up and was blowing skiffs of snow here and there, piling them against trees and buildings. The snow and the late afternoon haze made an eerie and lonely scene.

"Maybe the driver's Oscar. Maybe he didn't head east on the train," I joked, but the idea scared me. I considered it for a moment and then thought, the pickup doesn't have any shit on the hood, and laughed to myself. I decided to get something to eat.

I walked into the Eden Merc and said, "Hi, Sid. Got any bananas?"

"Just some old ones. Their turnin' brown."

"Hell, that's okay. I like 'em that way, especially if there's a lot of fruit flies," I said, trying to look tough like a Montana cowboy. "Mom would be proud," I said to myself as I left the store with a package of Twinkies, a six-pack of Highlander beer, and six over-ripe bananas. I put my lunch in the saddlebag and planned to enjoy it as I sat at my castle.

I mounted Penny and as I rode toward the pickup, it started up, slowly made its way down the road, and then stopped. "What the hell is he doing?"

I mumbled and pulled the horse to a stop. The pickup moved

again, and disappeared around the corner a corner of Upper Road. I nudged Penny into a walk and noticed the pickup idling a short distance up the road.

"Idiot," I hissed.

As I passed Mrs. Larsen's store, she came out onto the porch.

"Hi, William. You're finally back in Eden."

"Yeah, I'm trying to tie up some loose ends, and I went to the funeral."

"It's so sad," she said, as her eyes clouded up.

"Maybe she is better off, and maybe he is, too." I didn't know what else to say.

"I've got some money for you," she said, and handed me an envelope.

I put it into my back pocket. It would look seedy to open it in front of her. "I guess Victoria didn't spend it all," I smiled. I knew we could use it when I got back to the Avalon.

Mrs. Larsen smiled in an understanding way. "Take care of yourself, William."

The trail was well-traveled by deer and other wild animals, but after a while it narrowed and became so rough that it was easier for me to get off Penny and walk. I tied her to a tree, and then took out my lunch. The stillness was lonely, icy. It seemed that every shadow held danger, as if evil and peril were everywhere.

I began walking along an animal trail. Something moved just ahead. It had long hair and brown coloring. It looked like Bigfoot. I caught glimpses as it passed in and out of sight in the shadows of the trees. It stopped for a moment to look back at me, and then disappeared into the woods.

"It can't be Oscar," I whispered to myself. "It couldn't be him." I began to sweat, even though it was cold. "That son of a bitch has the nerve to come to my castle," I said aloud. I expected him to jump out from behind a tree at any second. I knew he could have Shorty's .44 Magnum that I'd seen it at the Black Bear. "God, maybe he'll torture me," I thought as my imagination took over.

Something moved in the brush ahead. I stopped and watched. The hair on the back of my neck stood on end as I waited. The brush moved again. I turned to run, and then stopped. A mother bear and her two last year cubs were grazing on the lush clover that grew amid the flowers and foliage. They interrupted their grazing occasionally to paw at rotting stumps and logs to uncover grubs and bugs. They stopped eating for a moment, looked at me, and then went back to their scavenging.

I stepped forward and the bear ran into a thicket. "This Oscar thing is really starting to get to me," I mumbled. "I need to get hold of myself. Oscar's gone east. The law is looking for him." I sat on a rock to work on my lunch, and thought a moment about writing Chuck's poem for him, but decided not to do that just yet.

It was dusk when I got to the upper portions of Castle III. It hadn't changed. The rock ledges still jutted high above the turbulent, rushing water far below. I walked along the rocks to watch the beautiful scene of the water rushing down the steep ledges of rocks and strangely, to enjoy the fear of being so high and so vulnerable as the noise below drowned my thoughts. I sat and watched in awe. The air was clean and wet. This could be heaven, I thought.

I placed my feet on a log and pushed. It took several tries, but finally it dislodged and rolled over the edge to tumble down the steep, rocky crag. In a moment it floated into view, now shattered and broken. As it floated out into the cove, it was caught by the current, which would carry it downstream toward the reservoir and then to the dam, to be captured by the watchman there, or ground to bits in the dam's giant turbines.

"Well, what better time could there be to do the poem than now?" I thought. I took out the envelope Mrs. Larsen had given me and began writing on the back of it. I would need to write small to get a poem the same size as Chuck's or longer. It seemed to flow out. Even if it wasn't as good as his, at least it would be fast, I chuckled. When it was done, I slipped it back in my pocket with the plan to read it to him later.

"I've waited a long time for this," a soft harsh voice echoed behind me. The words brought the taste of sulfur to my mouth. It was Oscar. He was here, breathing down the back of my neck. The strong smell of marijuana and some sort of alcohol, and maybe gasoline, mixed with stale food and an unclean body, drifted into my nostrils, "You little fool," he whispered.

I stood frozen in place by fear. I couldn't speak.

"I was never trying to do anything to you. You were my friend. I just wanted to help you with your singing and protect you from yourself."

Alex and Craig stood behind him. Craig had a gun tucked in his thick belt. It looked like the .44 Mag. He took it out. "I ought to just pull the trigger for the hell you've put us though," he hissed.

"You'll get caught if you do," I countered, which was the only thing I could think to say.

"Jesus Christ, do you think it will look like a murder after you land down there and go through the rapids?" Alex laughed. "Be lucky if you still look like a human."

I'm going to die. This is the way it happens. This is how I die, I thought.

"Hold Oscar," Alex said to Craig. "He won't let me hurt the little son of a bitch."

Craig grabbed Oscar's arm and twisted it up behind his back. Alex looped a rope around my neck. It was a rough, hard twist of some kind. The rope scratched my skin. "This time you won't get away." He spat the words at me. "Put yer god-damned hands behind your back, you son of a bitch." Alex formed the words carefully, with obvious hatred and contempt, like they had been rehearsed for this moment. "Give me the gun, Craig," he demanded.

Alex wrapped the rope around my hands and pulled my arms halfway up my back. It hurt, but I had to do it to keep the rope from choking me. My arms ached and my neck burned from the rope cutting in. I felt the barrel of the gun pressing into my back.

Daylight was fading as Alex half-dragged, half-pulled me

up the trail toward the highest part of the castle. Craig and the subdued Oscar followed along behind. Alex cussed me and kicked the back of my legs as we walked. I lost my balance often, and then he would jerk me to my feet with a vicious upward thrust. I thought my arms would break. I could scarcely breathe as we arrived at the rock cliffs high above the rushing river. My arms would no longer accept the pain, and I coughed and gasped for air.

"I don't want nobody thinking you wasn't just accidentally killed," Alex said.

"What do you mean?" I coughed the words out.

"You son of a bitch," he whispered. "We could have been enjoying each other every day instead of you going into the river. But now it's too late."

I wanted to puke, but I didn't say anything. He was a confused bastard.

Alex pushed me down onto the rocks, and then pulled me to my feet by lifting my arms with the rope again. The pain was excruciating. I cried out. He pushed me to the edge of the cliff and stood directly behind me. I heard the river crashing far below. Alex lifted my arms just enough to untie the rope. My arms felt numb. I felt the gun pushing into my back, and knew what he was going to do. He would take off the rope and push me into the gorge, so my death would look like an accident.

"Don't do it," Oscar shouted. "I can help him."

He will need to get the rope off my neck before he pushes me in, I thought. I imagined my body, broken after it hit the rock below, being swiftly rushed into the turbulent pools below the trestle, floating gently into the cove, and then going even slower into the reservoir, and finally finding its way down to the dam. Many days later, it would be discovered and my death would be declared an accidental fall into the gorge. Or if it wasn't discovered, it would simply drift down to where it would be ground into oblivion by the gigantic turbines inside the dam.

If I were going to do anything to upset their plans, I would have to do it as soon as the rope came off my neck. I decided Alex probably wouldn't shoot me, because it wouldn't look like an accident, and there would be an investigation. As the rope came off my wrists, I twisted around, caught Alex's arm in my hand, and then twisted him around. As he went past me, he tripped on my leg and fell over the edge of the cliff. The gun fell into the gorge. He still held the rope that was around my neck with one hand. With the other, he hung to the edge of the cliff by some sort of scrub.

I thought about giving up and going over with him, ending it all for the both of us, and then, as I gasped for air, I screamed at him, "You son of a bitch, you're the one who's going to die."

I had been able to reach the branch of a tree. As I held on, I kicked Alex in the face under his left eye. It was eerie; the same sickening opening appeared as it had on Oscar's face when I kicked him off the train years ago. It quickly filled with blood that ran down his face. He lost his footing and fell down against the side of the rock cliff, sliding out of sight.

"It's your turn to go down the cliff this time," I yelled at him.

As he fell, he grabbed a tree root that protruded a few feet from the cliff. He held on as he twisted around, trying to find anything to secure his precarious position. I held onto the rope with both hands, trying to keep from falling into the gorge, and also so I wouldn't be choked to death. A by-product of this effort was that I was saving Alex. Our eyes met; we both were trying to find a way to get free of the other and also make the other fall into the ravine. Behind me, Craig was struggling to hold Oscar.

"Alex," I yelled, "this is getting us nowhere."

"If you pull me up," he said, "I'll forget everything and we'll be friends."

"Okay," I said. "That sounds good to me." What choice did I have? "You will need to let the rope go. Then I will be able to get it off my neck and pull you up."

"How do I know you will pull me up?" he challenged.

"What choice do you have?" I asked.

"Not much," he said. "But I'll be damned if I'll let you take the rope off your neck. You can pull me up just as well with it on. I'll help you get the rope off when I get up there."

I was getting tired, and knew I couldn't argue much longer. "Okay, give me some slack and hold onto the root until I get a better hold on the rope."

"You better as hell pull me up, you little son of a bitch."

"Just hang onto the root until I get set," I said.

"You better, or you'll come down, too."

"Do it, William," Craig yelled from behind me as he continued to struggle with Oscar.

Alex gave the rope some slack, I took a better grip on the rope, and began pulling. It was as if I had a giant fish and was trying to land it.

It reminded me of little Pat when I had him under my bridge. Pat deserved it. When I had gone with him and his parents to the circus and we stopped at a restaurant for something to eat, they asked me to have a hamburger and I said no, because I didn't think I should be so brazen. But Pat was my friend. He could have insisted that I eat, the little bastard. I was glad he was dead.

Jon had deserved to die, too. He did something to me so bad that I'm embarrassed to even talk about it. It involved a circle jerk with his cousins out in the woods. That two-faced, lying bastard.

As Alex twisted and fought for footing, I had to find footing also, and fight for leverage. I stood looking down at him and just for an instant, I felt a pang of pity for the poor bastard. "He is, after all, a human," I said to myself as I wrestled with the question of what to do now.

"Hold on for a minute, Alex. I need to get more leverage—give me a little slack."

I was back far enough now that he couldn't see me.

"William, do you need more slack? I'll just hang on and help you get me out of here."

"Yes, I need just a little more slack to get a better hold." When the slack came, I quickly slipped the noose off my neck. I knew what I had to do. I had to do the right thing. It would be hard, but I had to do it. I couldn't see what Craig and Oscar were doing but I could hear them struggling behind me.

"You better pull him up," Craig screamed again.

"Okay, Alex, I'm ready. Come on up." I braced my feet against a large rock.

He swung out onto the rock ledge to begin his ascent. "This is easy. I'm almost out," he said.

I stopped pulling and said, "It's nice to be friends again, isn't it?"

"I've always liked you. It's just that we have had a few misunderstandings. In fact, William, I adore you," he said in a soft, warm way. "I always have."

I looked down at him and knew that if he got out, my troubles would be back. But it seemed wrong to let a human being die. "Alex," I said, "you're a lying, no good son of a bitch. Dying is too good for you. But I'm sure you'll go directly to hell."

I wanted to let him go, but couldn't do it. I held the rope as he climbed to safety. "You dumb son of a bitch," he said, and grabbed me. He pulled me to the cliff's edge and we struggled as he tried to push me over. I grasped for anything I could reach.

"I should have let you fall into the creek," I yelled.

"Too late now, you dumb shit."

A dark figure loomed behind Alex and rushed forward, grabbing him. For a moment, the moonlight caught his face. It was Oscar. He held Craig with one arm and Alex with the other, at the very edge of the ravine.

"Have a good life, William. You are the epitome of what was best in Andrew, my little brother." He stepped over the edge, taking the other two with him. The rope sawed into the edge of the cliff as they fell. I tried to jump clear, but I was too late. The rope looped around my ankle and pulled me to the edge of the cliff. I reached out and caught a sapling tree. There was a hard tug and then the weight lessened. I looked below. Alex was suspended like a puppet, hanging onto the rope, spinning around as Oscar and Craig fell like bags of grain. The roots of the small tree began to pull out, and I was losing my grip. "God," I yelled, "I'm going to die with this son of a bitch Alex after all."

Then someone was holding me, lifting me. I looked up. It was Trooper. "God, it's good to see you!" I yelled.

"Youse looks different than the las' time we was together, Bill." He lifted me up and fiddled with the rope around my leg. "Can't get it to let go. I'm gonna hafta pull him up some more." He pulled, and then set me down on the rocks and took out a straight razor. He held the rope with one hand and used the other to cut through it with a large, sharp blade. He held Alex suspended with one strong hand. "Want me to let him go?" he asked.

I didn't want Trooper mixed up in this, but decided, I didn't think I had a choice. "Let him go."

Trooper stood for a moment, like he was saying a prayer, and then asked, "Do ya means for me to let him go or does ya means fer me ta drop him?"

"Just let the rope go, Trooper," I said.

We watched as Alex fell and hit the other two dead bodies. All three of them drifted into the raging waters. Trooper began removing the ropes from my leg.

"You saved my life," I yelled at him.

"No way in hell I was gonna let you die," Trooper said. "Just a payin' ya back fer my little boy."

"How is Amos doing?"

Trooper looked like he was going to cry. "Hell, Bill. A while after you left, both Amos and Andy disappeared, and we ain't seen hide ner hair a' them sinct."

I felt bad for Trooper, but I also had an almost overwhelming feeling of guilt.

It was as if I should have saved them—should have saved them all from this sort of grief.

"Sure as hell we'll go to prison even for killing three pieces of trash like that," I said.

"Only if'n we gets caught."

"What will happen to the bodies?"

"They'll jus float out into the bay," he said. "Some' 'ne 'ill find 'em and think they's accidentally killed. I sure as hell won't say no different."

"Come to my place," I told Trooper.

"No," he said. "My kind ain't welcomed in these parts. But I'll stop at the bar ta have a beer with ya."

"Well," I said, "I'll never forget you for what you did."

I imagined the three bodies far below drifting slowly into the eddies of the river and then entering the mainstream and going into the lake. I stood for a few minutes, thinking about what I'd done, and about what might happen now. It is surely murder, I told myself, but also felt sure it was justified. All right by God but maybe not by the law. Laws are stupid, anyway, I thought.

Trooper left to get his car and I went to get my horse. We met at the Bucket of Blood for a couple of beers. I was anxious to do anything that would help to get the killings off my mind.

"Hey, Chuck, I got a poem for you. Maybe we should call this the dueling poets."

We both laughed, and Trooper laughed, too.

"Want to hear it?"

"Hell, yes, let's see what you got."

The Bucket of Blood

The wind was blowing fiercely that night in Eden town.
The snow was thick and heavy with six feet on the ground.
Inside a little tavern sat a man dressed all in black.

He cursed the town of Eden, for the business had been slack.

The lights were burning dimly; the shades all pulled down low.
The glasses and whiskey bottles shining, and all were in a row.
The man who wore the black clothes sat there again the wall,
But then the door swung open, wind and snow gust into the hall.

Chuck's eyes they lifted quickly, his hand flew to his gun,
Then his brown eyes softened, to his face come back the fun.
He knew the man who stood there, his partner in this deal.
It was Harlow Pennington, to Chuck this meant "big wheel."

His frame filled the doorway, his face looked mean and cold.
Lightning bolt went up Chuck's spine, to see a man so bold.
Chuck said to him as friendly as a stoic man's allowed to speak.
"Well, Harlow," he said with glee "Let's go to old Short Creek."

It was now a fact in Eden that the entire town was sick.
Of hearing Chuck and Harlow, talk of goin' to Short Creek.

The little tavern that they tended, if they didn't let it slip,
Was gonna grubstake them, and then pay for their trip.

Chuck threw a rope on Sandy, his big horse strong and fine.
Her muscles were hard as steel; Chuck feeds her on white pine.
  One warm day late next summer, the brave men finely came
    To old Short Creek Tavern; both men were strong and game.

Then Chuck he spied a maiden, her hair was black as coal.
And right there Chuck knew that this had been their goal.
He dug his heels in Sandy, and shyly rode up to her side;
His face was as red as fire, as he asked her if she'd ride.

Chuck hadn't seen the stranger with twin guns at his sides.
His eyes were hot branding irons, his face a smooth rawhide.
Chuck stared back at the stranger; and his fear it didn't show.
He told the stranger boldly, "I'll be gawd-damned if I will go."

The air seemed thick and heavy, as these two men faced death.

The only smell left in the air was Sandy's white pine breath.
The stranger's hands moved first; his draw was quick as light.
His guns kicked in his hands; Chuck's head was in their sights.

Chuck's eye had seen the killer move, then his brain come to
That he would be the gallant hero, if this killer he but slew.
Chuck's shot had hit the stranger right between the eyes,
And he watched in amazement at how a brave man dies.

Then Chuck knew with a tearful eye, the thing that he must do.
He must go back to Eden, because Short Creek had been a ruse.
The summer months were over, the snow fell thick and fast.
And Chuck was back in Eden, to think and talk the awful past.

His family took him back, I'm told, with wide and open arms.
I'm sure it was the fear of him, and not his artificial charms.
Chuck has told me since then, ten thousand times or more
About all his sleepless nights and how he walks the floor.

He thinks sometimes of maidens with hair of ebony sheen.
But he wouldn't trade one hair for the family love he's seen
Nothin's more important, when the push becomes a shove
Than havin' family around, that's there and filled with love.

"Okay," I said, "what do you think?"

"Not too bad, Bill, but not a winner."

I just smiled and went back to Trooper as some customers came in and Chuck got busy.

"Glad I came over," Trooper said. "Glad I was able to help."

I held my index finger to my lips as a signal for him to be quiet.

"Come see me in Spokane," he said.

"Maybe, but probably not," I said. "I've got to take care of Victoria now. She's in Utah and we're going to have a baby."

I told Trooper about how I had gone to Utah and gone back to school in an attempt to make something of myself. I told him about wanting to become a writer and that I had graduated a few years ago from night high school, excelling in English, creative writing, and grammar, and how now I could spell and write pretty good.

"Ya mean makin' all them little squiggles and funny looking marks make some sort a sense?"

"Yeah, and getting all those little letters in the right places and make some sort of sense, too." I told him how Victoria and I would be married soon and eventually would come back to rule Eden. "You remember Victoria, don't you?" I asked.

"Don't reckon as how I does."

"She was with me in Spokane. She stood by the buildings while I changed your tire. She was with me when we stayed with you and Matilda and Amos and Andy, and when we caught the Great Northern to Missoula."

"Don't member 'nothin bout no Victoria," he said.

This surprised me. It was hard to understand how he could forget her after we spent so much time together. "I'll bring her and our baby over to Spokane for a visit," I said.

We sat well into the night, talking and laughing and drinking beer, and then it was time for Chuck to close, so he kicked us out. Outside, I hugged the big black guy and promised to see him later, and then watched as the big red car carried him into the darkness and out of my life once more. I had the feeling, like you do sometimes, that we would never meet again.

I didn't mention the incident of Oscar and his brothers to anyone after that. I did my best to forget about it, and was simply glad I didn't need to worry about them anymore. It wasn't easy to live with killing anyone, not even Craig and Alex, but they didn't even know they had killed those little boys. At least that's what Wainscot said. But I felt really bad about Oscar, who had saved my life, about as much as Trooper had. I could see that now. He had been a good guy; he just happened to be different, and at the wrong place at the wrong time, or maybe the right place at the wrong time. Just because he was gay didn't make him bad—or good, for that matter. He was just trying to take care of his brothers, and of me, too. I had sort of become his little brother after Andrew died, but I had failed to realize it. He just couldn't save us all.

Chapter 137

The trip back to Utah went quickly. I hitchhiked most of the way, wanting to save as much money as I could for the baby and Victoria. Soon, I was back at the Avalon.

"This is a nice place," Victoria said. "I like living here."

"It's better with you here."

"My father wouldn't be impressed," she laughed.

"Yeah, James H. would shit a brick."

"I missed our closeness when you're away," she said.

That made me feel like the long trip, and the long wait, had been worthwhile. "I know, dear," I said. "Me, too."

It was easier to sleep when I had Victoria with me, as it always had been.

Things got better in the furnace room. I cleaned it up and painted it and found a couple of pieces of furniture, an old chest of drawers, a hot plate, a table and two chairs, and we cooked and ate there often. I wanted to make it as nice as I could for her. Victoria didn't mind that I began going out to the Bel Aire Club every Thursday night for a few drinks and to dance with some of the barmaids there. She liked to stay home and do housework, sew, and wait for me.

The scuffle with Alex on the cliff made me think some killing is justified. I gave myself examples, such as self-defense or during a war, or things like that, but I had a little trouble fitting all such killings into a single category that I could be comfortable with. Killing is killing, and as for as one human taking another human's life, I felt I might deserve to be punished. In our society and in our religious beliefs, murder is about as bad a sin as a person can commit. But what about what Dad had told me? He said sex before marriage was the same as murder. That didn't make sense to me.

During a war, men fight for something they usually don't even understand, or sometimes don't believe in, and they might very well kill someone with whom they have no argument. It might be someone who is very much like them, maybe even with the same religion and political beliefs, but because it is war, the soldiers have been made to believe it is okay, and they do it without conscience. They might even have a good feeling about killing the enemy, because he's "bad." It seemed to me that standards are twisted by a few, who design attitudes and shape events for their own benefit. Was my life in danger when Alex was hanging helplessly from the rocks over the river? It wouldn't seem so, but at the very moment that he had gotten back onto land, then my life was most certainly in jeopardy again. If it hadn't been for Oscar and Trooper, I would have been the one killed and ground into hamburger at the dam.

Well, I decided to take what I had coming. I felt a lot more comfortable waiting for my punishment from God than accepting my fate from a court that places more value on the lives of criminals and lowlifes than on the lives of victims and innocent people. They seemed bent on trying to rehabilitate even the scum of the earth. Values are subjective and are based on the opinion of whoever is in a position of power. It wouldn't be my choice to have a farmer lose his farm and be ruined because someone finds a few marijuana plants growing on it, or because a few fish die when the reservoir gets too low. It wouldn't be my choice to put thousands of loggers out of work to save a few turtles or spotted owls. The passing of time creates casualties, and maybe it wouldn't be a big deal if some animals became extinct. Hell, the dinosaurs and kiwis are extinct, and I hardly even miss them, I thought.

The ordeal at Castle III now seemed like a dream, like it hadn't really happened, but it was always on my mind, like those kids being killed in Utah was, and that lady in Missoula—the conductor's wife—Ned, was it? And now, Amos and Andy were missing. On the other hand, things had all been settled, and the punishments and resolutions seemed to be fitting and just. God would be satisfied, and I was, as well.

Chapter 138

It would soon be Christmas again—the streetlights and decorations screamed it—but this year would be different. For one thing, I wasn't going home. Hell, there wasn't anything left in Eden for me, anyway. Victoria and I would stay at the Avalon, celebrate together, and wait for the baby. But … she was gone. I had no idea where she was. She never left without telling me, and I worried that this had become okay, taking each other for granted. I felt something in my back pocket: Maybe a note from Victoria?

It was the envelope from Mrs. Larsen. Inside it was $321. God, she hadn't even charged Victoria for living there. What a lady, I thought. I hope I can be that charitable when I get old.

To conceal my real feelings about the holiday and feign respectfulness, I broke a limb from a walnut tree, sprayed some shaving cream on the branch, and hung a single red Christmas bulb and one icicle on it. Throughout my life, I had criticized the very existence of the popular holiday, because it had forgotten about Christ, the one it was supposed to be honoring. It was commercialized, to be sure, but that didn't necessarily make it bad. Even though it had almost completely removed itself from any references to the *real* Jesus, it still had the potential to carry his message of unselfishness and love.

We should love people and do what we can for them, I reflected. We're all children of God in a certain sense, no matter what religion or origin we were chosen to be, and no matter even whatever God might be. God, I exclaimed to myself, don't tell me I am beginning to understand and love Christmas.

I decided to do some Christmas stuff this year. Christmas certainly hadn't meant much to us in the dungeon in Springtown and maybe that's why I had mixed feeling about it now—I guess you could say it was the time of year when everybody else got stuff from Santa. It was always a time of year when everybody hurried around buying expensive gifts and Christmas trees that we couldn't afford. Then the day after Christmas, everything was so inexpensive—especially Christmas trees. I had to laugh. Maybe we should change Christmas to the 26th and then everybody could afford it.

I had been waiting for hours, and Victoria still hadn't shown up. This isn't like her, I thought. She'd better have a good reason for not being here. I was upset, but I needed to be mature and willing to forgive her. I haven't written her a poem for a while, I thought. That's what I'll do. She should be given the credit for what she's done. She will be delighted when she gets home.

> *I feel it's time the fact was known*
> *That what I've done was not alone*
> *But with a maiden true and strong,*
> *One who guides when I go wrong.*
> *How can I thank the one I've got?*
> *Who helps me do when I cannot?*
> *She wants no praise, it's not her call,*
> *Just content to have me take it all.*
> *Of course we have had ups and downs.*
> *At times I thought there'd be no crowns.*
> *Now I know, what I am and what I'll be...*

Shit what to make rhyme with "be?" It shouldn't be so hard, I thought, and then it occurred to me. James H. used to call Victoria "princess" or "Victoria Leigh." James H., the bastard—as bad as he was and as much as I hated him—he might still have just a little bit of good in him, just about like Dad. I smiled at the thought that "Victoria Leigh" rhymes with "be." I liked James H. now; in fact maybe I loved him. I finished the poem:

Has been because of Victoria Leigh.

She'll be delighted to get this, I thought. "Maybe she went back to Scotland," I whispered to myself. I wished I hadn't told her it was okay to go. I hope she didn't go, I thought, and then laughed at my nervousness. She's probably at her Gramma's place in Springtown. She wouldn't go anywhere else without telling me, I'm sure. I'll call Mrs. MacLean in the morning. Aunt Mary will let me use her phone, I'm sure she will.

But right now, I needed sleep. The velvet blankets and lace sheet I had learned to love through a lifetime of use felt good and relaxing. I thought about Mrs. Larsen's selflessness. She's what Jesus was talking about, I thought. I slept like a baby.

Chapter 139

"Well, I'll be," Mrs. MacLean said when she answered the phone. "It's almost like you knew."

"What do you mean, like I knew? Like I knew what?" I asked.

"About the wedding."

"Well, I didn't know. Have you seen Victoria?"

"Well, either her or someone who looks a lot like her. She's here right now." Mrs. MacLean's voice trembled and tailed off as she spoke.

"Tell her that I miss her," I said.

"Tell her yourself. Victoria come here, it's William!"

"Hello, William."

Hearing Victoria's voice, I said, "I'm so sorry. I'll do better."

"What do you mean?"

"When are you coming back?" I asked.

"I am back. We're having the wedding tomorrow, William. I want you to come," she said. Her voice sounded different.

"You know I could never say no to you. What time shall I be there? Who's getting married?"

"I am. Come as soon as you can. Be here early, so we can talk. We have a lot to talk about," she said.

"Aren't you coming home tonight?" I asked.

"What?"

"Coming home. Aren't you coming home tonight?" I repeated.

"What does that mean?"

"Never mind. I'll talk to you tomorrow," I said.

"I can't wait," she said.

"I'll be there, I promise."

"Okay then, see you tomorrow," she cooed.

"I love you Victoria," I said.

"I love you, too, William," she said. "I have such a special love for you. It was so much fun when we were young. You will always be a part of me."

I didn't sleep very well. I thought about Victoria and the wedding. I didn't want to embarrass her. I hadn't been to very many weddings. I wondered what was going on, and assumed she had finally convinced her father I was of royal blood, and he had decided it would be okay for us to get married. My heart raced. It felt as if it would beat right out of my chest. She must have mentioned the wedding to me earlier, although it wasn't like me to forget. Maybe I'd just had too much on my mind lately, with the night school and all. I decided to take a bath tomorrow, and wear my best clothes. "It's not every day a guy gets married," I smiled.

Chapter 140

The shower in Aunt Mary's place was plugged and the water heating system was being repaired. I found a five-gallon bucket, filled it with cold water, and washed like I had done so often in Montana.

A sponge bath like the old times, I chuckled to myself. I dried with the towel Aunt Mary kept in the washroom and pulled on clean underwear. After I buttoned my western shirt and pulled the tight-fitting Levis over the tail and buttoned them, I looked in the mirror.

Sure looks like I'll turn some heads today. Looks like a tall, handsome cowboy's going to wow his best girl, I kidded my reflection in the mirror. My thick white socks made the old penny loafers a little tight, but I knew after a while my feet would become numb and the pain would go away.

I was late getting to Mrs. MacLean's place; the Orem Tram had been late. I was very nervous. The old place looked hauntingly familiar. Aunt Helen's house had been painted. There was a cinderblock garage at the end of the drive, where I used to practice spitting. I didn't like what they'd done to it. The old washhouse had been torn down and a flower garden was there now. My bridge was gone, completely gone!

Why am I so nervous? I asked myself. I'm never nervous around Victoria.

There were lots of people at Mrs. MacLean's place. I stood for a while outside, trying to get the courage to go in. I almost turned away a couple of times, but at last I walked toward the house. People were standing on the lawn and sitting at tables, talking and laughing. Some were eating little sandwiches and drinking colored punch. I smiled and nodded as I walked past them, and they all returned my greeting. Welcoming the groom, I thought.

On the front porch, I wiped my teeth with my index finger, rubbed my loafers against the back of my Levis, pushed back my hair and combed it with my fingers, like I did when I wanted to look just right. I knocked. Nothing. I knocked again. The door opened. It was Mrs. MacLean. She looked old and thin. Her wrinkled face was pallid and her eyes were sunken. Her body shook uncontrollably.

"Are you all right, Mrs. MacLean?" I asked.

"Well, yes I am. And how are you?"

I could tell she didn't recognize me. "I'm William, Mrs. MacLean. William Robert Jones," I said. "We used to live next door. I'm here for our wedding."

"Well, for goodness sakes, William, I didn't even recognize you. You've really grown up. You've changed. Your hair is thinning and going gray."

She stood looking for a while, like she didn't know what to say next. "I'm getting old, too," she finally said. "Sometimes, I lose track of things. Victoria would like to see you, I'm sure. She's been talking about you all morning."

"Yes," I said, "I would like to see her, too. I'd like to talk a little bit before the wedding. I know I shouldn't see her before the wedding, but I'm not too into tradition."

"What's in the Grand Rapids box?"

"It's a gift for Victoria."

"A wedding present?"

"Well, sort of. It's just for Victoria, and maybe for me, too. It's sort of a story about our lives together."

Mrs. MacLean looked puzzled. "Come on in and get something to eat," she said.

A huge table was filled with food, just about everything I could imagine, and at the head of the table, on the other side of a multileveled, white cake that had a bride and groom on top, stood a man and Victoria. She was wearing a white lace gown and a little white lacy hat with a veil. The man was wearing a tuxedo. She held a knife, and the man had wrapped one hand around hers and had the other hand on her waist. People were flashing pictures. A photographer was going here and there, getting people to pose.

Lightning shot up my spine and sulfur filled my mouth. Mrs. MacLean walked to Victoria and whispered something and then pointed to me. Victoria smiled, waved, and then walked toward me. She put her arms around me and hugged. I hugged her back.

"I'm glad you came, William."

"You knew I would, Victoria. I could never tell you no," I smiled.

"I'm so excited," she said.

"You look different," I said. "You're thin. What happened to the baby?"

"Oh, William, didn't you get my letter? Daddy had it taken. I'm sorry. I thought you knew. It was probably for the best. We were so young."

"Not again," I said. I felt like crying.

"Don't cry, William. It was a long time ago."

"You look different," I said again.

"I am different. I'm older," she said.

She had a lot of make-up on her face. "I love you, Victoria," I said.

"It's so good to see you," Victoria squealed. "I've missed you so much."

"You haven't been gone that long," I said. "It's only been a couple of days."

She looked puzzled, and then said, "I feel that way sometimes, too. I was in a home for a long time."

"We can have another baby, Victoria," I said.

Her look of puzzlement deepened. "I would like to someday, but maybe I'm too old now."

"Hell, you're only as old as me, and as old as you feel."

"Let's go to the garden and talk," she said, and we walked out the back door.

We sat and talked about all the things we had done when we were young, and how silly we had been. We talked about playing in the garden and picking the vegetables to take to the sheep ranch. We laughed about her father not liking me, and how we had gone to live with Hyrum and Debbie.

"Did your father finally agree to us being married?" I asked.

Victoria looked bewildered. "What's in the box?" she asked.

I felt myself blushing. "It's sort of a record of my life; maybe of our lives together." I pulled it over a little bit and handed the rope to her. I opened the lid and pointed inside at the books and the notebooks. "Everything's there. I just wrote a new poem for you. It's in there, on top."

"Thank you. I'll read it all, for sure. I'll leave it here and have Daddy help me take it home. Oh, Daddy's here, William. I know he would like to see you. Wait here, I'll get him. Watch my box while I'm gone."

She wasn't the same. Her breath smelled funny. She had body odor, her face had wrinkles, and she had pimples. There were small scars on her fingers and hands. It wasn't Victoria. Something funny was going on.

"Well, I'll be. William—I wouldn't have recognized you."

"You look different, too," I said to Victoria's father, James H., as we shook hands. "You look older."

"Looks like you came to steal my little girl again," he laughed.

I thought I was the groom," I said. My head was spinning around. Sulfur and lightning invaded my body.

James H. asked, "William, would you like to meet the groom? His name is Fredric De'Plore."

"No, I guess not."

"Are you going to steal her away?"

"Oh, Daddy," the girl giggled. "You're so silly."

"No, sir," I said. "I've got a girl of my own."

"Is she here?" the girl asked.

"No," I said. "But when I want her, she's always there."

"What's she like?" the girl asked.

"A lot like you," I said to the girl. "But she's better-looking and nicer," and then I smiled and touched her arm to show I was kidding.

"I'd like to meet her someday," the girl said.

"She's shy, but she is so beautiful. We're having a baby. Someday, I'll let you see it. I promise."

The girl smiled. Everybody looked happy. "I just came down because you asked me," I finally said, "but I have to go. I'll come and see you again."

"Goodbye, William." The girl hugged me again. "I'm so glad you came. I think we're going to live in Utah, maybe Springtown."

Her breath smelled like cake and stale ice cream. An odor came from under her arms and she had a faint mustache. She wasn't Victoria. I made my way quickly to the door and then outside. "That's an imposter," I said. "She's not my Victoria. My Victoria will find me. I know she will."

I had a strange, sad feeling in my chest. It was extreme loneliness, which was a feeling like homesickness, like I had when I was young and spent the summer with Hyrum and Debbie, but worse. Lighting and the taste of sulfur filled my body and mouth. It was difficult to see, because tears were running down my face. Unable to see the sidewalk, I stopped and held my head in my hands. My body shook as I sobbed. I couldn't stop crying. I went through a window, and watched William.

Little Pat and Jon and the others surrounded him, clawing at William, trying to hurt him. He screamed and tried to escape. He needed Victoria. He had to get away.

"William, it's me. I couldn't stay there. I had to go with you."

It was Victoria. The images of the little boys vanished. It was better now.

"It's so good to see you, Victoria. I really need you." She cuddled close to William, so tight that he could feel her soft body. He felt her stomach, which was hard and full; the baby was all right. I'm sorry, William. I couldn't marry Fredric De'Plore. That would be deplorable." She was trying to cheer him up. She had forgotten about herself and her feelings, and was concerned only about him.

She didn't smell. She didn't have any wrinkles or scars, and she didn't have a mustache. It was Victoria.

"Everything is all right now," he smiled.

"Yes, it is, my prince."

"Let's go home," he whispered.

As the window effect faded, my real Victoria and I boarded the Orem Tram, heading for Salt Lake, the Avalon, and our home.

Chapter 141

Alex isn't sure he has been right to be so abusive to William. He can imagine William suffering as he lies alone in the Avalon's dingy furnace room. Yet it seems that William is not suffering alone; somehow, he appears to have gained a companion. A part of Alex wants him to suffer, but he seems not to be suffering as he imagined he would. Alex is amazed that he himself has become a captive of his little studio hotel room while he waits for William to die, as if that will set him free. He laughs to himself. "Jesus, the little shit has turned the tables on me," he thinks. "I'm as much his captive as he is mine."

He can hardly believe he's actually thinking of releasing William and forgetting all about everything. It seems to him that William at least thinks he is innocent; who knows, maybe he and Oscar really did imagine everything. Oscar had, after all, been in the nut house, and Alex knows he himself is prone to hallucinations and delusions of grandeur. In any event, he thinks it's time to go see how William is getting along. It has been quite awhile, and maybe circumstances will decide William's fate once and for all.

Actually, keeping William prisoner makes him no better than William, he thinks. He is murdering his captive, in a sense. Keeping food from him until he starves to death would be murder, wouldn't it? Alex, who has always been prone to argue with himself, finally decides, yes, this is what he will do. He'll cross the busy street, pull out the nails from the giant, ironclad door, and release William. Maybe he will try to get the case reopened, and let the law deal with William. But he has had enough—William has won.

As fast as his crooked body will allow, Alex takes a shower, brushes his teeth, dresses, and then looks in the mirror one last time. He is happy to have decided to release William, but he now thinks that rather than just releasing him, he will take him bound and gagged to the police station and tell the desk sergeant what William did. They might not believe him, but it's worth a try and it will serve as vengeance—not as well as starving him to death, but maybe it will be enough.

The street is unusually busy, and he thinks for a moment about struggling to the crosswalk, but it's too far for his crumpled body to travel. Anyway, he has crossed this road away from the intersection many times to look in on William, so he feels comfortable doing it again.

Occasionally, he went to the Avalon and then decided not to look in to see if William was dead yet. Now, he hopes he is still alive. He times his crossing and then, as fast as he can, he begins to make his way across the first half of the busy street. His plan is to cross halfway and then stand in the median before completing the crossing. Halfway across, he turns his attention to the other side. The sound of screeching brakes makes him look up. A car, out of control, is heading straight for him. With the sickening sound of heavy metal hitting flesh and bone, Alex is catapulted through the air. For a moment, his body seems to be suspended in space, until the sound of flesh and bone hitting metal repeats itself, and Alex's body wraps awkwardly around the front end of an oncoming car.

A few minutes later, red lights flash at the scene. Milling about are medics with resuscitation devices and blue clad officers measuring, taking pictures, writing in little books, or eating doughnuts and drinking coffee as they look on. Later, a convoy of vehicles is dispatched from the site, one of them the city coroner's van, carrying Alex's lifeless body.

Chapter 142

A thin, almost nonexistent veil appears before my eyes. It is as if I am emerging out of water, or some other liquid. And then I remember: I had delved back in time to find information that would help me to deal with Alex. But I'm now back in the present—or am I? The soft veil surrounds me again as I pass through the window, watching …

"Are you all right, William?" Victoria had found him.
"You're always here when I need you," he said.
"I love you." She held him. He could feel her breasts and her hard stomach with the baby inside.
"I love you, too," he said. "Is the baby all right?"
"Yes it is. Let's rest."
"Yes, I need to think," he said. "We will decide what to do in the morning."
"Tomorrow is another day."
"Yes, tomorrow is another day," he echoed, "and who knows what life has in store for me—for us? I only know I want to do better than my dad, and I want Mom to be proud of me." He speaks to Victoria softly, "I know when we have kids, I won't treat them like Mom and Dad treated

me. I'll give them about everything they want and I'll be nice to them. If I promise them bananas, I'll give them bananas. And if they have money in a bank account, they can keep it."

"You'll be such a good father."

He was glad she had finally come to live with him, even though they hadn't married yet. "All in good time," he told her.

"It's all right, you're worth waiting for. Besides, we have the same last name," she said, winking at him.

"We do, indeed." She always made him feel so good, so important. "We have a good arrangement. We get along a lot better than anybody else I know. We do everything together, make decisions, clean, cook, everything, just the way it should be."

She smiled. "You don't do anything, William. I wait on you hand and foot; but I love to. I wish you would let me do more."

Victoria loved cornflakes and cheese; at least, she said she did. And she loved living in the furnace room. She seemed to understand Mom and Dad better than William did, even though she hadn't seen them since she was young.

The window effect fades.

I reflect that I never understood Mom and Dad. With a shock that sends lighting up my spine and sulfur into my mouth, I remember they are both dead now. During my final moments with mom, I rubbed her feet. She loved that. And dad looked so pathetic and wasted, it broke my heart. I can't believe I did it, but I bent and kissed the old fart on his forehead. I miss them so. I thought I hated them, but now I miss them. They had wanted me to be in the choir, and I had had to get into it so they would love me. That's why it was necessary to get rid of those other boys in the choir—to please Mom and Dad, although also because of the deplorable things they had done to me.

"Victoria," I whisper. "Did I ever tell you about the time the patriarch told me I was of royal blood? He said I was out of the loins of King David, who was sold into slavery."

"I'm not surprised. I can't wait to tell my parents. They will be surprised and happy, and now there won't be any excuse for our not getting married."

"Here, let me show you. I have the evidence here in my pocket. It's a little worse for wear, but it's here just the same." I take out the taped-together, weathered document and hold it before her, but by mistake I show her the back of it, which reads, "I have been trapped against my will in the basement below. Please, call police!" And below that, "I can hear you. Is there something I can do for you? I can't speak, but I am able to hear and read."

"What's this, William?"

I blush. "Hell, it's nothing. Someday I'll tell you about it."

"Okay."

"My parents weren't who they seemed," I say. "An evil dredge caused me to be taken from my real parents, and they suffered through the years, as I did. They had no more choice in my being kidnapped than I did, but someday all will be made right. I am destined to be King of Eden. But all in good time," I whisper. "All in good time."

"I have no doubt you will," Victoria says," and then we will be married and I will be your queen and we will rule the land."

"Yes, but first I must prove myself. I must pose as a commoner for a time. Be patient, my love."

She smiles and nods in agreement.

Chapter 143

It's freezing cold in the furnace room. The furnace hasn't been started yet, even though it's been cold enough. I'm starving. I need something to eat; I could use some of the food in my two years supply, dad's church pushed for all members to have a food supply for famines. But this is no famine. But if I use my storage, what if there is a famine? I had always been frugal and had tried to keep food stored for such things. I need to save for a famine.

I had the feeling that Alex is softening, maybe he's unlocked the door. I quickly moved to see but it's still impossible to open. That jerk Alex never did bring any food. He probably won't, either, unless I confess. That's it—I'll confess and he will let me out! He's just toying with me, trying to make me confess. None of what happened was my fault. I just wanted everyone to be proud of me, to like me.

I become dizzy and seem to pass through that window.

William pulled back the velvet drapes and lace curtains that made up their bed and waited for Victoria to get in, and then he climbed in and sat beside her. He looked toward the heavens. "Someday, Mom, I'll make you proud of me," he said, which was maybe something like a prayer, or a hope that his mother might be able to hear him, because in spite of everything, he still regarded her as his real mother and had no doubt that someday he would make her proud.

He sat for a time and watched Victoria's shoulders rise and lower slightly as she breathed. "I'm so lucky," he thought, "to have you."

He was tired. He hadn't really done very much, but it had been a tiring day. He felt strangely lonely, even with Victoria there. He leaned to kiss the soft, rosy cheek and stroked her beautiful blond hair, and then lay down to cuddle close. That was all he needed; just to be close.

She turned her head and whispered, "Everything will be okay. You know it will be."

He pulled the lace sheets and velvet blankets over them and whispered, "I know, angel. I know it will be. I'm not dead yet."

The window effect fades and my head is spinning. I don't know what to do. I reach for Victoria. She isn't here. She's gone again. I stand. I have to do something, I can't let it all end like this.

"Einstein!" I scream. "The time machine. I'll have Einstein help me."

The window reopens slowly and I watch William and Einstein in the laboratory again.

It was good to be back with Albert. William felt needed, and it was obvious that Albert felt the same way about him. The laboratory had been further modernized, and William was anxious to get to work.

"Where are the papers from our last research?" he asked.

"Right where you left them," the old scientist said.

"You didn't disturb them?"

"Well, no. I didn't want to take the chance of slowing down your research. I can't wait to see what you will

conceive this time."

"Don't despair, you help a lot," William reassured him, sensing Albert's insecurity. "You help a lot."

They donned laboratory coats and soon were waist-deep in test tubes and Bunsen burners, jotting down theories and conclusions.

"I've been thinking of ways to make the Master Blaster even faster," William said.

"I have some new theories as well, young friend."

"I have improved the Master Blaster," William told him.

Albert looked at William in dismay. "How could it be improved?" He shook his head.

"It operates at many times the speed of light, thinks for itself, and creates food and water from nothing. How could it be improved?"

William laughed. "Well, you forgot about my old theory of Ten-Numbers-Ten, or TNT. I applied that to the Master Blaster and now it's one hundred times faster than it was before."

"But is it still reliable?"

"More reliable and more stable. I surrounded it with my old application of Smooth-As-Silk, or SAS."

"I can't wait to try it," the renowned scientist giggled.

There were no breaks or distractions for the following days, only short meals hurriedly swallowed. Every day seemed the same. The two scientists never even saw the light of day. One day piled upon the next, as a great deal of time passed.

"I think I have found the formula for our new theory of relativity," William finally announced.

"Let's see what you have," Albert said, his voice full of joy.

"Try this on for size: $SAS=TNT/2$."

"My God," Albert squealed after he had worked the formula on the board and gotten rid of unwanted, unnecessary, and troublesome exponents. "It fits!"

They danced about the room arm-in-arm. "I want to go first," William yelled.

"You discovered it," Albert said. "You should go first."

Before long, William stood on the outer deck of Albert's new laboratory, looking into the heavens. Albert stood behind him. "William, I wish it were I going, but you certainly deserve the honor." He handed William a thick note pad and a pencil.

"What's this for?"

"Try to document the trip and we will analyze it when you return."

"That's a great idea, but if you don't mind, I'll use my own notebook. I always carry one with me, to jot down important things."

But when William looked into his notebook, he realized it had been completely filled with essential formulas and data. He excused himself and walked to the "Me box," over by the sink, searching through the pile of notebooks there until he finally found one with at least a few empty pages at the back.

"Here's one I can use. I would assume there won't be much time for writing."

Albert couldn't help but snicker as he observed, "You may be younger when you get back, if my theory of time and velocity is correct."

"Let's do it," William said.

"All right. I'll set the Master Blaster to leave in 30 seconds." As Albert held the timer in place, William slipped his arms into the shoulder straps of a silver-colored pack and drew it taut as he snapped the snaps in place.

"See ya," William said.

"See ya."

William saw a bright flash, and then his life seemed to be speeding past. He was going back in time but also growing younger, and then he was driving his new convertible. He saw Alex, Oscar, and Craig falling into the raging water of the river, and he saw Victoria crying.

"I forgot about Victoria!" William screamed. "She will be old when I get back."

He was driving his father's old Dodge toward their new home in Montana. Aunt Trudy nagged from the back seat. A little girl beckoned him into a closet at Sunday school by showing him her unclad crotch. His mother scolded him for telling a lie. He was picking peaches with his sister and putting them into a small, battered wagon. And then he was in the basement of Aunt Helen's washhouse. His mother swept the dirt floor with a bristle broom until she got down to the hard-packed bottom, and then she picked up the dust with a piece of cardboard. The room was very dark. Two small windows were high up, almost to the ceiling, and a single light bulb dangled from a frayed electric cord. He saw a table, chairs, a bed, a hot plate, a few dishes, and the Grand Rapids box filled with notebooks, old magazines, and books under the card table. His sister was pretending she could read and showing William pictures in a book. She cautioned him about the wickedness in the world and the greatness of God, if a person will just believe.

Three decapitated little boys held their heads in their arms, looking at him. Their bodies were suspended in place by a long, leather shoestring. They had hints of smiles on their almost translucent faces and in their vacant, hollow eyes. Mr. Cook smiled at him.

They had all forgiven him.

A ball of light appeared. It was more brilliant than

anything he had ever seen. "You are troubled, William. You have no cause for concern, for you have discovered the secret of salvation."

"I have been troubled," he admitted. "But what do I call you? Do I call you simply 'ball of light?'"

"I am what I am. Don't be concerned. I can be anything, I can be anywhere. Don't be concerned with things of this world. But of course, I have told you such things before."

"I have tried to do the things concerning the Holy Grail," William told the ball of light.

Its voice was a whisper, but it was also loud and it echoed. "You have the power. The power is in your pen. Your pen is mightier than a sword. It is your Excalibur. You must write about salvation. You must make others understand and seek its sweet nectar. I have brought you to Avalon to rest and train for your destiny. Make them understand that salvation is not for just a few, a select group, but for everyone who seeks it in earnest. Victoria is your Lady of the Lake and Queen Guinevere in one. Listen to her; she will help you in this quest. You will have her. You will rule Eden with her at your side. You will acquire the Holy Grail and it shall lift you into paradise.

"No one shall be excluded. I love all my children, and only in the selfish minds of men who distort my word with their own words and build churches to their own glory are any of my children despised. Satan shrouds those selfish, unholy hypocrites and the ones misled by them. For altering my words and judging others harshly, they are evil and are in danger of damnation. Many are they who will appear in sheep's clothing but within, they are ravening wolves. Write about these things, young and valiant William," the ball of light said.

William got to his knees. He knew what he was going to do. He knew what he had to do. He was now compelled to *seek the Holy Grail. He had no choice. He knew it was his quest, commanded by God, and only he had the knowledge and courage to attain it. The more things change, the more they stay the same. He certainly knew now what Trooper, and Cropper, had meant when they said, "The end is sometimes the beginning. The more things change, the more they stays the same."*

The ball of light continued, "Write about it now, King William. You must write it."

The window effect seems to fade again. I take out the gold watch and chain Dad gave me and hold it to my heart. I know that now, not only has God forgiven me as I have forgiven Him, but moreover, I have forgiven my horse's ass of a father. But it's getting late. I take out the huge Daniel Boone knife and lay it in front of me on the worn, cold concrete floor of the furnace room. "If that asshole Alex comes in here, I'll cut his damned head off."

"Whatchadoin', William?"

It is Victoria, young and beautiful like she was when we played on the banks of the irrigation stream and walked to Boyer's Grocery Store, and lived at the sheep ranch.

"How did you get here?" I ask her. "I thought you would be old."

Her beautiful green eyes sparkle as they always do when she looks at me. "I'm always with you," she says softly. "No matter what, I'm always with you. You are a part of me."

I close my eyes. Finally, after all of this fuss and confusion, now and forever more, Victoria will be a part of me. As she sleeps, I take out the notebook and my pen from my Me box. I have to make them all believe, just like the ball of light told me to do. Its words echo in my psyche: "The end is really the beginning. The more things change, the more they stay the same."

I will be forgiven for everything, even for those three little boys in the Hallelujah Choir—hell, they were my friends, just like Amos and Andy, and even that bitch in Missoula.

I'm not even sure what happened there, unless it was because she made me be untrue to Victoria, but they all betrayed me in one way or another.

It all has become so clear, so easy to understand now. I write as best as I can remember the way everything began ...

A sudden breath of warm air moves the evening mist from the symbols of royalty, which, to the unbelieving eye, are simply refuse and stench. This tepid breeze carries with it the assurance that winter's relentless bluster is nearly exhausted. I sit amazed at this splendor, as I so often do, here at the rear of the Camelot-Avalon Apartments on the washhouse steps; it's my favorite place to ponder life and its difficult questions. The fleeting winter bluster has turned the concrete steps frigid—they feel bitterly cold against my butt. Nonetheless, it's a good and almost comfortable feeling. It makes me realize I am alive and I have Victoria by my side—maybe forever this time.

Well, Victoria, my queen-to-be, is not really here with me now, but she is "with" me nonetheless, in wish and intent—if you know what I mean. We will soon no longer need to use pretense or illusion. Our new abode, Castle III, will dwarf Castle I and Castle II. High above the rugged Elk River in Eden, Montana, Castle III will make the other castles appear to be hovels by contrast. There, we will rule side-by-side in our rightful kingdom, with little, if any, need for pretense!...

THE END ... OR THE BEGINNING?

Epilogue

When I, Dr. Gordon Lamont, or Flash, as Bill called me, decided to write this story, I went to Springtown to track down Victoria. She gave me all of William's notebooks, which she said he had given to her at her wedding. I went through them for almost a year before beginning to write this story. Then I gave them all to my brother, Dale, because he said he was looking for Bill and would return them to him. Dale told me he couldn't find Bill, but he did find his sister, Ellen, in a rest home, and gave the papers to her. She had gone blind, and when Alex came by to visit her, she gave the box of papers to him, because he asked if she knew where Bill was. She told him she thought William was in Salt Lake City at some apartment building, maybe the Avalon.

I never got to see Bill after I began writing this story, but I understand he was in pretty bad shape when they went inside to begin renovation of the crumbling building. He had a stash of food that could last for years and there was water, but it wasn't a very healthy diet and the stay there surely took its toll. I wish I could have known him at this part of his life—he really needed help from a professional. Nobody seems to know where he is, or if he survived.